Masterpieces of Modern Chinese Fiction

1919-1949

by Lu Xun and Others

Fredonia Books
Amsterdam, The Netherlands

Masterpieces of Modern Chinese Fiction 1919 - 1949

by
Lu Xun
and Others

ISBN: 1-4101-0675-6

Fredonia Books
Amsterdam, The Netherlands
http://www.fredoniabooks.com

CONTENTS

The True Story of Ah Q

Lu Xun

Chapter 1

Introduction

For several years now I have been meaning to write the true story of Ah Q. But while wanting to write I was in some trepidation too, which goes to show that I am not one of those who achieve glory by writing; for an immortal pen has always been required to record the deeds of an immortal man, the man becoming known to posterity through the writing and the writing known to posterity through the man — until finally it is not clear who is making whom known. But in the end, as though possessed by some fiend, I always came back to the idea of writing the story of Ah Q.

And yet no sooner had I taken up my pen than I became conscious of tremendous difficulties in writing this far-from-immortal work. The first was the question of what to call it. Confucius said, "If the name is not correct, the words will not ring true"; and this axiom should be most scrupulously observed. There are many types of biography: official biographies, autobiographies, unauthorized biographies, legends, supplementary biographies, family histories, sketches . . . but unfortunately none of these suited my purpose. "Official biography"? This

account will obviously not be included with those of many
eminent people in some authentic history. "Autobiography"?
But I am obviously not Ah Q. If I were to call this an "unauthorized biography," then where is his "authenticated biography"? The use of "legend" is impossible because Ah Q was
no legendary figure. "Supplementary biography"? But no president has ever ordered the National Historical Institute to write
a "standard life" of Ah Q. It is true that although there are
no "lives of gamblers" in authentic English history, the well-
known author Conan Doyle nevertheless wrote *Rodney Stone*;*
but while this is permissible for a well-known author it is not
permissible for such as I. Then there is "family history"; but
I do not know whether I belong to the same family as Ah Q or
not, nor have his children or grandchildren ever entrusted me
with such a task. If I were to use "sketch," it might be objected
that Ah Q has no "complete account." In short, this is really
a "life," but since I write in vulgar vein using the language of
hucksters and pedlars, I dare not presume to give it so high-
sounding a title. So I will take as my title the last two words
of a stock phrase of the novelists, who are not reckoned among
the Three Cults and Nine Schools.** "Enough of this digres-
sion, and back to the *true story*"; and if this is reminiscent of
the *True Story of Calligraphy**** of the ancients, it cannot be
helped.

The second difficulty confronting me was that a biography
of this type should start off something like this: "So-and-so,
whose other name was so-and-so, was a native of such-and-such
a place"; but I don't really know what Ah Q's surname was.

---

* In Chinese this title was translated as *Supplementary Biographies of
the Gamblers.*

** The Three Cults were Confucianism, Buddhism and Taoism. The
Nine Schools included the Confucian, Taoist, Legalist, Mohist and other
schools.

*** A book by Feng Wu of the Qing Dynasty (1644-1911).

ONCE, he seemed to be named Zhao, but the next day there was some confusion about the matter again. This was after Mr. Zhao's son had passed the county examination and, to the sound of gongs, his success was announced in the village. Ah Q, who had just drunk two bowls of yellow wine, began to prance about declaring that this reflected credit on him too, since he belonged to the same clan as Mr. Zhao and by an exact reckoning was three generations senior to the successful candidate. At the time several bystanders even began to stand slightly in awe of Ah Q. But the next day the bailiff summoned him to Mr. Zhao's house. When the old gentleman set eyes on him his face turned crimson with fury and he roared:

"Ah Q, you miserable wretch! Did you say I belonged to the same clan as you?"

Ah Q made no reply.

The more he looked at him the angrier Mr. Zhao became. Advancing menacingly a few steps he said, "How dare you talk such nonsense! How could I have such a relative as you? Is your surname Zhao?"

Ah Q made no reply and was planning a retreat, when Mr. Zhao darted forward and gave him a slap on the face.

"How could *you* be named Zhao? Are you worthy of the name Zhao?"

Ah Q made no attempt to defend his right to the name Zhao but rubbing his left cheek went out with the bailiff from whom, once outside, he had to listen to another torrent of abuse. He then by way of atonement paid him two hundred cash. All who heard this said Ah Q was a great fool to ask for a beating like that. Even if his surname *were* Zhao — which wasn't likely — he should have known better than to boast like that when there was a Mr. Zhao living in the village. After this no further mention was made of Ah Q's ancestry, thus I still have no idea what his surname really was.

The third difficulty I encountered in writing this work

was that I don't know how Ah Q's personal name should be
written either.   During his lifetime everybody called him Ah
Gui, but after his death not a soul mentioned Ah Gui again; for
he was obviously not one of those whose name is "preserved
on bamboo tablets and silk."*   If there is any question of preserving his name, this essay must be the first attempt at doing
so.   Hence I am confronted with this difficulty at the outset.
I have given the question careful thought.   Ah Gui — would
that be the "Gui" meaning fragrant osmanthus or the "Gui"
meaning nobility?   If his other name had been Moon Pavilion,
or if he had celebrated his birthday in the month of the Moon
Festival, then it would certainly be the "Gui" for fragrant
osmanthus.**   But since he had no other name — or if he had,
no one knew it — and since he never sent out invitations on his
birthday to secure complimentary verses, it would be arbitrary
to write Ah Gui (fragrant osmanthus).   Again, if he had had
an elder or younger brother called Ah Fu (prosperity), then he
would certainly be called Ah Gui (nobility).   But he was all
on his own; thus there is no justification for writing Ah Gui
(nobility).   All the other, unusual characters with the sound
gui are even less suitable.   I once put this question to Mr.
Zhao's son, the successful county candidate, but even such a
learned man as he was baffled by it.   According to him, however, the reason why this name could not be traced was that
Chen Duxiu*** had brought out the magazine New Youth ad-
vocating the use of the Western alphabet, hence the national
culture was going to the dogs.   As a last resort, I asked some-

* A phrase used before paper was invented when bamboo and silk
served as writing material in China.

** The fragrant osmanthus blooms in the month of the Moon Festival.
And according to Chinese folklore, the shadow on the moon is an osmanthus
tree.

*** Chen Duxiu (1880-1942) was then chief editor of New Youth, the
magazine which gave the lead in the movement for a new culture.

one from my district to go and look up the legal documents re-
cording Ah Q's case, but after eight months he sent me a letter
saying that there was no name anything like Ah Gui in those
records.   Although uncertain whether this was the truth or
whether my friend had simply done nothing, after failing to trace
the name this way I could think of no other means of finding it.
Since I am afraid the new system of phonetics has not yet come
into common use, there is nothing for it but to use the Western
alphabet, writing the name according to the English spelling as
Ah Gui and abbreviating it to Ah Q.   This approximates to
blindly following *New Youth*, and I am thoroughly ashamed of
myself; but since even such a learned man as Mr. Zhao's son
could not solve my problem, what else can I do?

My fourth difficulty was with Ah Q's place of origin.   If
his surname were Zhao, then according to the old custom which
still prevails of classifying people by their district, one might
look up the commentary in *The Hundred Surnames** and find
"Native of Tianshui in Gansu."   But unfortunately this surname
is open to question, with the result that Ah Q's place of origin
must also remain uncertain.   Although he lived for the most part
in Weizhuang, he often stayed in other places, so that it would
be wrong to call him a native of Weizhuang.   It would, in fact,
amount to a distortion of history.

The only thing that consoles me is the fact that the
character "Ah" is absolutely correct.   This is definitely not the
result of false analogy, and is well able to stand the test
of scholarly criticism.   As for the other problems, it is not for
such unlearned people as myself to solve them, and I can only
hope that disciples of Dr. Hu Shi, who have such "a passion for
history and research," may be able in future to throw new light
on them.   I am afraid, however, that by that time my "True
Story of Ah Q" will have long since passed into oblivion.

The foregoing may be considered as an introduction.

---

* A school primer in which surnames were written into verse.

Chapter 2

A Brief Account of Ah Q's Victories

In addition to the uncertainty regarding Ah Q's surname, personal name, and place of origin, there is even some uncertainty regarding his "background." This is because the people of Weizhuang only made use of his services or treated him as a laughing-stock, without ever paying the slightest attention to his "background." Ah Q himself remained silent on this subject, except that when quarrelling with someone he might glare at him and say, "We used to be much better off than you! Who do you think you are?"

Ah Q had no family but lived in the Tutelary God's Temple at Weizhuang. He had no regular work either, being simply an odd-job man for others: when there was wheat to be cut he would cut it, when there was rice to be hulled he would hull it, when there was a boat to be punted he would punt it. If the work lasted for any length of time he might stay in the house of his temporary employer, but as soon as it was finished he would leave. Thus whenever people had work to be done they would remember Ah Q, but what they remembered was his service and not his "background." By the time the job was done even Ah Q himself was forgotten, to say nothing of his "background." Once indeed an old man remarked, "What a worker Ah Q is!" Ah Q, bare-backed scrawny sluggard, was standing before him at the time, and others could not tell whether the remark was serious or derisive, but Ah Q was overjoyed.

Ah Q, again, had a very high opinion of himself. He looked down on all the inhabitants of Weizhuang, thinking even the two young "scholars" not worth a smile, though most young scholars were likely to pass the official examinations. Mr. Zhao and Mr. Qian were held in great respect by the villagers, for in addition to being rich they were both the fathers of young

scholars. Ah Q alone showed them no exceptional deference, thinking to himself, "My sons may be much greater."

Moreover, after Ah Q had been to town several times he naturally became even more conceited, although at the same time he had the greatest contempt for townspeople. For instance, a bench made of a wooden plank three feet by three inches the Weizhuang villagers called a "long bench." Ah Q called it a "long bench" too; but the townspeople called it a "straight bench," and he thought, "This is wrong. Ridiculous!" Again, when they fried large-headed fish in oil the Weizhuang villagers all added shallots sliced half an inch thick, whereas the townspeople added finely shredded shallots, and he thought, "This is wrong too. Ridiculous!" But the Weizhuang villagers were really ignorant rustics who had never seen fish fried in town.

Ah Q who "used to be much better off," who was a man of the world and a "worker," would have been almost the perfect man had it not been for a few unfortunate physical blemishes. The most annoying were some patches on his scalp where at some uncertain date shiny ringworm scars had appeared. Although these were on his own head, apparently Ah Q did not consider them as altogether honourable, for he refrained from using the word "ringworm" or any words that sounded anything like it. Later he improved on this, making "bright" and "light" forbidden words, while later still even "lamp" and "candle" were taboo. Whenever this taboo was disregarded, whether intentionally or not, Ah Q would fly into a rage, his ringworm scars turning scarlet. He would look over the offender, and if it were someone weak in repartee he would curse him, while if it were a poor fighter he would hit him. Yet, curiously enough, it was usually Ah Q who was worsted in these encounters, until finally he adopted new tactics, contenting himself in general with a furious glare.

It so happened, however, that after Ah Q had taken to using this furious glare, the idlers in Weizhuang grew even more fond of making jokes at his expense. As soon as they saw him they would pretend to give a start and say:

"Look! It's lighting up."

Ah Q rising to the bait as usual would glare in fury.

"So there is a paraffin lamp here," they would continue, unafraid.

Ah Q could do nothing but rack his brains for some retort. "You don't even deserve...." At this juncture it seemed as if the bald patches on his scalp were noble and honourable, not just ordinary ringworm scars. However, as we said above, Ah Q was a man of the world: he knew at once that he had nearly broken the "taboo" and refrained from saying any more.

If the idlers were still not satisfied but continued to pester him, they would in the end come to blows. Then only after Ah Q had to all appearances been defeated, had his brownish queue pulled and his head bumped against the wall four or five times, would the idlers walk away, satisfied at having won. And Ah Q would stand there for a second thinking to himself, "It's as if I were beaten by my son. What the world is coming to nowadays!..." Thereupon he too would walk away, satisfied at having won.

Whatever Ah Q thought he was sure to tell people later; thus almost all who made fun of Ah Q knew that he had this means of winning a psychological victory. So after this anyone who pulled or twisted his brown queue would forestall him by saying, "Ah Q, this is not a son beating his father, it is a man beating a beast. Let's hear you say it: A man beating a beast!"

Then Ah Q, clutching at the root of his queue, his head on one side, would say, "Beating an insect — how about that? I am an insect — now will you let me go?"

But although he was an insect the idlers would not let him go until they had knocked his head five or six times against something nearby, according to their custom, after which they would walk away satisfied that they had won, confident that this time Ah Q was done for. In less than ten seconds, however,

Ah Q would walk away also satisfied that he had won, thinking that he was the "Number One self-belittler," and that after subtracting "self-belittler" what remained was "Number One." Was not the highest successful candidate in the official examination also "Number One"? "And who do you think *you* are?"

After employing such cunning devices to get even with his enemies, Ah Q would make his way cheerfully to the tavern to drink a few bowls of wine, joke with the others again, quarrel with them again, come off victorious again, and return cheerfully to the Tutelary God's Temple, there to fall asleep as soon as his head touched the pillow. If he had money he would gamble. A group of men would squat on the ground, Ah Q sandwiched in their midst, his face streaming with sweat; and his voice would shout the loudest: "Four hundred on the Green Dragon!"

"Hey — open there!"

The stake-holder, his face streaming with sweat too, would open the box and chant: "Heavenly Gate! — Nothing for the Corner! . . . No stakes on Popularity Passage! Pass over Ah Q's coppers!"

"The Passage — one hundred — one hundred and fifty."

To the tune of this chanting, Ah Q's money would gradually vanish into the pockets of other sweating players. Finally he would be forced to squeeze his way out of the crowd and watch from the back, taking a vicarious interest in the game until it broke up, when he would return reluctantly to the Tutelary God's Temple. The next day he would go to work with swollen eyes.

However, the truth of the proverb "Misfortune may prove a blessing in disguise" was shown when Ah Q was unfortunate enough to win and almost suffered defeat in the end.

This was the evening of the Festival of the Gods in Wei-zhuang. According to custom there was an opera; and close to the stage, also according to custom, were numerous gambling tables. The drums and gongs of the opera sounded miles away to Ah Q who had ears only for the stake-holder's chant. He staked successfully again and again, his coppers turning into silver coins, his silver coins into dollars, and his dollars mounting up. In his excitement he cried out, "Two dollars on Heavenly Gate!"

He never knew who started the fight, nor for what reason. Curses, blows and footsteps formed a confused medley of sound in his head, and by the time he clambered to his feet the gambling tables had vanished and so had the gamblers. Several parts of his body seemed to be aching as if he had been kicked and knocked about, while a number of people were looking at him in astonishment. Feeling as if something were amiss he walked back to the Tutelary God's Temple, and by the time he had calmed down again he realized that his pile of dollars had gone. Since most of the people who ran gambling tables at the Festival were not natives of Weizhuang, where could he look for the culprits?

So white and glittering a pile of silver! All of it his . . . but now it had disappeared. Even to consider this tantamount to being robbed by his son did not comfort him. To consider himself as an insect did not comfort him either. This time he really tasted something of the bitterness of defeat.

But presently he changed defeat into victory. Raising his right hand he slapped his own face hard, twice, so that it tingled with pain. After this slapping his heart felt lighter, for it seemed as if the one who had given the slap was himself, the one slapped some other self, and soon it was just as if he had beaten someone else — in spite of the fact that his face was still tingling. He lay down satisfied that he had gained the victory.

Soon he was asleep.

Chapter 3

A Further Account of Ah Q's Victories

Although Ah Q was always gaining victories, it was only

after he was favoured with a slap in the face by Mr. Zhao that he became famous.

After paying the bailiff two hundred cash he lay down angrily. Then he said to himself, "What is the world coming to nowadays, with sons beating their fathers!" And then the thought of the prestige of Mr. Zhao, who was now his son, gradually raised his spirits. He scrambled up and made his way to the tavern singing *The Young Widow at Her Husband's Grave*.* At that time he did feel that Mr. Zhao was a cut above most people.

After this incident, strange to relate, it was true that everybody seemed to pay him unusual respect. He probably attributed this to the fact that he was Mr. Zhao's father, but actually such was not the case. In Weizhuang, as a rule, if the seventh child hit the eighth child or Li So-and-so hit Zhang So-and-so, it was not taken seriously. A beating had to be connected with some important personage like Mr. Zhao before the villagers thought it worth talking about. But once they thought it worth talking about, since the beater was famous the one beaten enjoyed some of his reflected fame. As for the fault being Ah Q's, that was naturally taken for granted, the reason being that Mr. Zhao could do no wrong. But if Ah Q were wrong, why did everybody seem to treat him with unusual respect? This is difficult to explain. We may put forward the hypothesis that it was because Ah Q had said he belonged to the same family as Mr. Zhao; thus, although he had been beaten, people were still afraid there might be some truth in his assertion and therefore thought it safer to treat him more respectfully. Or, alternatively, it may have been like the case of the sacrificial beef in the Confucian temple: although the beef was in the same category as the pork and mutton, being of animal origin just as they were, later Confucians did not dare touch it since the sage had enjoyed it.

After this Ah Q prospered for several years.

---

* A local opera popular in Shaoxing.

One spring, when he was walking along in a state of happy intoxication, he saw Whiskers Wang sitting stripped to the waist in the sunlight at the foot of a wall, catching lice; and at this sight his own body began to itch. Since Whiskers Wang was scabby and bewhiskered, everybody called him "Ringworm Whiskers Wang." Although Ah Q omitted the word "Ringworm," he had the greatest contempt for the man. To Ah Q, while scabs were nothing to take exception to, such hairy cheeks were really too outlandish and could excite nothing but scorn. So Ah Q sat down by his side. Had it been any other idler, Ah Q would never have dared sit down so casually; but what had he to fear by the side of Whiskers Wang? In fact, his willingness to sit down was doing the fellow an honour.

Ah Q took off his tattered lined jacket and turned it inside out; but either because he had washed it recently or because he was too clumsy, a long search yielded only three or four lice. He saw that Whiskers Wang, on the other hand, was catching first one and then another in swift succession, cracking them between his teeth with a popping sound.

Ah Q felt first disappointed, then resentful: the despicable Whiskers Wang had so many, he himself so few — what a great loss of face! He longed to find one or two big ones, but there were none, and when at last he managed to catch a middle-sized one, stuffed it fiercely between his thick lips and bit hard, the resultant pop was again inferior to the noise made by Whiskers Wang.

All Ah Q's ringworm patches turned scarlet. He flung his jacket on the ground, spat, and swore, "Hairy worm!"

"Mangy dog, who are you calling names?" Whiskers Wang looked up contemptuously.

Although the relative respect accorded him in recent years had increased Ah Q's pride, he was still rather timid when confronted by those loafers accustomed to fighting. But today he was feeling exceptionally pugnacious. How dare a hairy-cheeked creature like this insult him?

"If the cap fits wear it," he retorted, standing up and putting his hands on his hips.

"Are your bones itching?" demanded Whiskers Wang, standing up too and draping his jacket over his shoulders.

Thinking that the fellow meant to run away, Ah Q lunged forward to punch him. But before his fist reached the target, his opponent seized him and gave him a tug which sent him staggering. Then Whiskers Wang seized his queue and started dragging him towards the wall to knock his head in the time-honoured manner.

" 'A gentleman uses his tongue but not his hands!' " protested Ah Q, his head on one side.

Apparently Whiskers Wang was no gentleman, for without paying the slightest attention to what Ah Q said he knocked his head against the wall five times in succession, then with a great push shoved him two yards away, after which he walked off in triumph.

As far as Ah Q could remember, this was the first humiliation of his life, because he had always scoffed at Whiskers Wang on account of his ugly bewhiskered cheeks, but had never been scoffed at, much less beaten by him. And now, contrary to all expectations, Whiskers Wang had beaten him. Could it really be true, as they said in the market-place: "The Emperor has abolished the official examinations, so that scholars who have passed them are no longer in demand"? This must have undermined the Zhao family's prestige. Was this why people were treating him contemptuously too?

Ah Q stood there irresolutely.

From the distance approached another of Ah Q's enemies. This was Mr. Qian's eldest son whom Ah Q thoroughly despised. After studying in a foreign-style school in the city, it seemed he had gone to Japan. When he came home half a year later his legs were straight* and his queue had disappeared. His mother

---

* The stiff-legged stride of many foreigners led some Chinese to believe that their knees had no joints.

wept bitterly a dozen times, and his wife tried three times to jump into the well. Later his mother told everyone, "His queue was cut off by some scoundrel when he was drunk. By rights he ought to be a big official, but now he'll have to wait till it's grown again." Ah Q, however, did not believe this, and insisted on calling him a "Bogus Foreign Devil" or "Traitor in Foreign Pay." At sight of him he would start cursing under his breath.

What Ah Q despised and detested most in him was his false queue. When it came to having a false queue, a man could scarcely be considered human; and the fact that his wife had not attempted to jump into the well a fourth time showed that she was not a good woman either.

Now this "Bogus Foreign Devil" was approaching.

"Baldhead! Ass...." In the past Ah Q had just cursed under his breath, inaudibly; but today, because he was in a rage and itching for revenge, the words slipped out involuntarily.

Unfortunately this Baldhead was carrying a shiny brown cane which looked to Ah Q like the "staff carried by a mourner." With great strides he bore down on Ah Q who, guessing at once that a beating was in the offing, hastily flexed his muscles and hunched his shoulders in anticipation. Sure enough, *Thwack!* something struck him on the head.

"I meant him!" explained Ah Q, pointing to a nearby child.
Thwack! Thwack! Thwack!

As far as Ah Q could remember, this was the second humiliation of his life. Fortunately after the thwacking stopped it seemed to him that the matter was closed, and he even felt somewhat relieved. Moreover, the precious "ability to forget" handed down by his ancestors stood him in good stead. He walked slowly away and by the time he approached the tavern door he was quite cheerful again.

Just then, however, a little nun from the Convent of Quiet Self-Improvement came walking towards him. The sight of a nun always made Ah Q swear; how much more so, then, after these humiliations? When he recalled what had happened, his anger flared up again.

"I couldn't think what made my luck so bad today — so it's meeting you that did it!" he fumed to himself.

Going towards her he spat noisily. "Ugh! . . . Pah!"

The little nun paid not the least attention but walked on with lowered head. Ah Q stepped up to her and shot out a hand to rub her newly shaved scalp, then with a guffaw cried, "Baldhead! Go back quick, your monk's waiting for you. . . ."

"Who are you pawing? . . ." demanded the nun, flushing all over her face as she quickened her pace.

The men in the tavern roared with laughter. This appreciation of his feat added to Ah Q's elation.

"If the monk paws you, why can't I?" He pinched her cheek.

Again the men in the tavern roared with laughter. More bucked than ever, and eager to please his admirers, Ah Q pinched her hard again before letting her go.

This encounter had made him forget Whiskers Wang and the Bogus Foreign Devil, as if all the day's bad luck had been avenged. And strange to relate, even more completely relaxed than after the thwacking, he felt as light as if he were walking on air.

"Ah Q, may you die sonless!" wailed the little nun already some distance away.

Ah Q roared with delighted laughter.

The men in the tavern joined in, with only a shade less gusto in their laughter.

Chapter 4

The Tragedy of Love

There are said to be some victors who take no pleasure in a victory unless their opponents are as fierce as tigers or eagles:

in the case of foes as timid as sheep or chickens they find their triumph empty. There are other victors who, having carried all before them, with the enemy slain or surrendered, utterly cowed, realize that now no foe, no rival, no friend is left — none but themselves, supreme, lonely, lost, and forlorn. Then they find their triumph a tragedy. But not so our hero: he was always exultant. This may be a proof of the moral supremacy of China over the rest of the world.

Look at Ah Q, elated as if he were walking on air!

This victory was not without strange consequences, though. For after walking on air for quite a time he floated into the Tutelary God's Temple, where he would normally have started snoring as soon as he lay down. This evening, however, he found it very hard to close his eyes, being struck by something odd about his thumb and first finger, which seemed to be smoother than usual. It is impossible to say whether something soft and smooth on the little nun's face had stuck to his fingers, or whether his fingers had been rubbed smooth against her cheek.

"Ah Q, may you die sonless!"

These words sounded again in Ah Q's ears, and he thought, "Quite right, I should take a wife; for if a man dies sonless he has no one to sacrifice a bowl of rice to his spirit. . . . I ought to have a wife." As the saying goes, "There are three forms of unfilial conduct, of which the worst is to have no descendants,"* and it is one of the tragedies of life that "spirits without descendants go hungry."** Thus his view was absolutely in accordance with the teachings of the saints and sages, and it is indeed a pity that later he should have run amok.

"Woman, woman! . . ." he thought.

". . . The monk paws. . . . Woman, woman! . . . Woman!" he thought again.

We shall never know when Ah Q finally fell asleep that

---

* A quotation from Mencius (372-289 B.C.).
** A quotation from the old classic *Zuo Zhuan.*

evening.   After this, however, he probably always found his fingers rather soft and smooth, and always remained a little light-headed. "Woman . . ." he kept thinking.

From this we can see that woman is a menace to mankind.

The majority of Chinese men could become saints and sages, were it not for the unfortunate fact that they are ruined by women. The Shang Dynasty was destroyed by Da Ji, the Zhou Dynasty was undermined by Bao Si; as for the Qin Dynasty, although there is no historical evidence to that effect, if we assume that it fell on account of some woman we shall probably not be far wrong. And it is a fact that Dong Zhuo's death was caused by Diao Chan.*

Ah Q, too, was a man of strict morals to begin with. Although we do not know whether he was guided by some good teacher, he had always shown himself most scrupulous in observing "strict segregation of the sexes," and was righteous enough to denounce such heretics as the little nun and the Bogus Foreign Devil. His view was, "All nuns must carry on in secret with monks. If a woman walks alone on the street, she must want to seduce bad men. When a man and a woman talk together, it must be to arrange to meet." In order to correct such people, he would glare furiously, pass loud, cutting remarks, or, if the place were deserted, throw a small stone from behind.

Who could tell that close on thirty, when a man should "stand firm,"** he would lose his head like this over a little nun? Such light-headedness, according to the classical canons, is most reprehensible; thus women certainly are hateful creatures. For if the little nun's face had not been soft and smooth, Ah Q would not have been bewitched by her; nor would this have

---

* Da Ji, in the twelfth century B.C., was the concubine of the last king of the Shang Dynasty. Bao Si, in the eighth century B.C., was the concubine of the last king of the Western Zhou Dynasty. Diao Chan was the concubine of Dong Zhuo, a powerful warlord at the end of the Han Dynasty.

** Confucius said that at thirty he "stood firm." The phrase was later used to indicate that a man was thirty years old.

happened if the little nun's face had been covered by a cloth. Five or six years before, when watching an open-air opera, he had pinched the leg of a woman in the audience; but because it was separated from him by the cloth of her trousers he had not had this light-headed feeling afterwards. The little nun had not covered her face, however, and this is another proof of the odiousness of the heretic.

"Woman..." thought Ah Q.

He kept a close watch on those women who he believed must "want to seduce men," but they did not smile at him. He listened very carefully to those women who talked to him, but not one of them mentioned anything relevant to a secret rendezvous. Ah! This was simply another example of the odiousness of women: they all assumed a false modesty.

One day when Ah Q was grinding rice in Mr. Zhao's house, he sat down in the kitchen after supper to smoke a pipe. If it had been anyone else's house, he could have gone home after supper, but they dined early in the Zhao family. Although it was the rule that you must not light a lamp but go to bed after eating, there were occasional exceptions to the rule. Before Mr. Zhao's son passed the county examination he was allowed to light a lamp to study the examination essays, and when Ah Q went to do odd jobs he was allowed to light a lamp to grind rice. Because of this latter exception to the rule, Ah Q still sat in the kitchen smoking before going on with his work.

When Amah Wu, the only maidservant in the Zhao household, had finished washing the dishes, she sat down on the long bench too and started chatting to Ah Q:

"Our mistress hasn't eaten anything for two days, because the master wants to get a concubine...."

"Woman... Amah Wu... this little widow," thought Ah Q.

"Our young mistress is going to have a baby in the eighth moon...."

"Woman..." thought Ah Q.

He put down his pipe and stood up.

"Our young mistress —" Amah Wu chattered on.

"Sleep with me!" Ah Q suddenly rushed forward and threw himself at her feet.

There was a moment of absolute silence.

"*Aiya*!" Dumbfounded for an instant, Amah Wu suddenly began to tremble, then rushed out shrieking and could soon be heard sobbing.

Ah Q kneeling opposite the wall was dumbfounded too. He grasped the empty bench with both hands and stood up slowly, dimly aware that something was wrong. In fact, by this time he was in rather a nervous state himself. In a flurry, he stuck his pipe into his belt and decided to go back to grind rice. But — *Bang!* — a heavy blow landed on his head, and he spun round to see the successful county candidate standing before him brandishing a big bamboo pole.

"How dare you . . . you. . . ."

The big bamboo pole came down across Ah Q's shoulders. When he put up both hands to protect his head, the blow landed on his knuckles, causing him considerable pain. As he escaped through the kitchen door it seemed as if his back also received a blow.

"Turtle's egg!" shouted the successful candidate, cursing him in mandarin from behind.

Ah Q fled to the hulling-floor where he stood alone, his knuckles still aching and still remembering that "Turtle's egg!" because it was an expression never used by the Weizhuang villagers but only by the rich who had seen something of official life. This made it the more alarming, the more impressive. By now, however, all thought of "Woman . . ." had flown. After this cursing and beating it seemed as if something were done with, and quite light-heartedly he began to grind rice again. Soon this made him hot, and he stopped to take off his shirt.

While taking off his shirt he heard an uproar outside, and since Ah Q was all for excitement he went out in search of the sound. Step by step he traced it into Mr. Zhao's inner courtyard. Although it was dusk he could see many people there: all the Zhao family including the mistress who had not eaten for two days. In addition, their neighbour Mrs. Zou was there, as well as their relatives Zhao Baiyan and Zhao Sichen.

The young mistress was leading Amah Wu out of the servants' quarters, saying as she did so:

"Come outside . . . don't stay brooding in your own room."

"Everybody knows you are a good woman," put in Mrs. Zou from the side. "You mustn't think of committing suicide."

Amah Wu merely wailed, muttering something inaudible.

"This is interesting," thought Ah Q. "What mischief can this little widow be up to?" Wanting to find out, he was approaching Zhao Sichen when suddenly he caught sight of Mr. Zhao's eldest son rushing towards him with, what was worse, the big bamboo pole in his hand. The sight of this big bamboo pole reminded him that he had been beaten by it, and he realized that apparently he was connected in some way with all this excitement. He turned and ran, hoping to escape to the hulling-floor, not foreseeing that the bamboo pole would cut off his retreat. When it did, he turned and ran in the other direction, leaving without further ado by the back gate. Soon he was back in the Tutelary God's Temple.

After Ah Q had been sitting down for a time, he broke out in goose-flesh and felt cold, because although it was spring the nights were still chilly and not suited to bare backs. He remembered that he had left his shirt in the Zhaos' house but was afraid that if he went to fetch it he might get another taste of the successful candidate's bamboo pole.

Then the bailiff came in.

"Curse you, Ah Q!" said the bailiff. "So you can't even keep your hands off the Zhao family servants, you rebel! You've made me lose my sleep, damn it! . . ."

Under this torrent of abuse Ah Q naturally had nothing to say. Finally, since it was night-time, he had to pay the bailiff double: four hundred cash. Because he happened to have no ready money by him, he gave his felt hat as security, and agreed to the following five terms:

1. The next morning Ah Q must take a pair of red candles, weighing one pound each, and a bundle of incense sticks to the Zhao family to atone for his misdeeds.

2. Ah Q must pay for the Taoist priests whom the Zhao family had called to exorcize evil spirits.

3. Ah Q must never again set foot in the Zhao household.

4. If anything unfortunate should happen to Amah Wu, Ah Q must be held responsible.

5. Ah Q must not go back for his wages or shirt.

Ah Q naturally agreed to everything, but unfortunately he had no ready money. Luckily it was already spring, so it was possible to do without his padded quilt which he pawned for two thousand cash to comply with the terms stipulated. After kowtowing with bare back he still had a few cash left, but instead of using these to redeem his felt hat from the bailiff, he spent them all on drink.

Actually, the Zhao family burned neither the incense nor the candles, because these could be used when the mistress worshipped Buddha and were put aside for that purpose. Most of the ragged shirt was made into diapers for the baby which was born to the young mistress in the eighth moon, while the tattered remainder was used by Amah Wu to make shoe-soles.

Chapter 5

The Problem of Making a Living

After Ah Q had kowtowed and complied with the Zhao family's terms, he went back as usual to the Tutelary God's Temple. The sun had gone down, and he began to feel that something was wrong. Careful thought led him to the conclusion that this was probably because his back was bare. Remembering that he still had a ragged lined jacket, he put it on and lay down, and when he opened his eyes again the sun was already shining on the top of the west wall. He sat up, saying, "Curse it!"

After getting up he loafed about the streets as usual, until he began to feel that something else was wrong, though this was not to be compared to the physical discomfort of a bare back. Apparently, from that day onwards all the women in Weizhuang fought shy of Ah Q, whenever they saw him coming they took refuge indoors. In fact, even Mrs. Zou who was nearing fifty retreated in confusion with the rest, calling her eleven-year-old daughter to go inside. This struck Ah Q as very strange. "The bitches!" he thought. "All of a sudden they're behaving like young ladies. . . ."

A good many days later, however, he felt even more forcibly that something was wrong. First, the tavern refused him credit; secondly, the old man in charge of the Tutelary God's Temple made some uncalled-for remarks, as if he wanted Ah Q to leave; and thirdly, for many days — how many exactly he could not remember — not a soul had come to hire him. To be refused credit in the tavern he could put up with; if the old man kept urging him to leave, he could just ignore his complaints; but when no one came to hire him he had to go hungry, and this was really a "cursed" state to be in.

When Ah Q could stand it no longer he went to his former employers' homes to find out what was the matter — it was only Mr. Zhao's threshold that he was not allowed to cross. But he met with a strange reception. The one to appear was always a man looking thoroughly annoyed who waved him away as if he were a beggar, saying:

"There's nothing for you, get out!"

Ah Q found it more and more extraordinary. "These people always needed help in the past," he thought. "They can't suddenly have nothing to be done. This looks fishy." After making careful inquiries he found out that when they had any odd jobs they all called in Young D. Now this Young D was a thin and weakly pauper, even lower in Ah Q's eyes than Whiskers Wang. Who could have thought that this low fellow would steal his living from him? So this time Ah Q's indignation was greater than usual, and going on his way, fuming, he suddenly raised his arm and sang:

"*Steel mace in hand I shall trounce you....*"*

A few days later he did indeed meet Young D in front of Mr. Qian's house. "When two foes meet, there is no mistaking each other." As Ah Q advanced upon him, Young D stood his ground.

"Beast!" spluttered Ah Q, glaring.

"I'm an insect — will that do?" rejoined Young D.

Such modesty only enraged Ah Q even more, but since he had no steel mace in his hand all he could do was rush forward to grab at Young D's queue. Young D, protecting his own queue with one hand, grabbed at Ah Q's with the other, whereupon Ah Q also used his free hand to protect his own queue. In the past Ah Q had never considered Young D worth taking seriously, but owing to his recent privations he was now as thin and weak as his opponent, so that they presented a spectacle of evenly matched antagonists, four hands clutching at two heads, both men bending at the waist, casting a blue, rainbow-shaped shadow on the Qian family's white wall for over half an hour.

"All right! All right!" exclaimed some of the onlookers, probably by way of mediation.

"Good, good!" exclaimed others, but whether to mediate, applaud the fighters, or spur them on to further efforts, is not certain.

The two combatants turned deaf ears to them all, however. If Ah Q advanced three paces, Young D would recoil three paces, and there they would stand. If Young D advanced three paces, Ah Q would recoil three paces, and there they would

---

* A line from *The Battle of the Dragon and the Tiger*, an opera popular in Shaoxing.

stand again. After about half an hour — Weizhuang had few
clocks, so it is difficult to tell the time; it may have been twenty
minutes — when steam was rising from their heads and sweat
pouring down their cheeks. Ah Q let fall his hands, and in the
same second Young D's hands fell too. They straightened up
simultaneously and stepped back simultaneously, pushing their
way out through the crowd.

"Just you wait, curse you!" called Ah Q over his shoulder.

"Curse you! Just you wait . . ." echoed Young D, also over
his shoulder.

This epic struggle had apparently ended in neither victory
nor defeat, and it is not known whether the spectators were
satisfied or not, for none of them expressed any opinion. But
still not a soul came to hire Ah Q for odd jobs.

One warm day, when a balmy breeze seemed to give some
foretaste of summer, Ah Q actually felt cold; but he could put
up with this — his greatest worry was an empty stomach. His
cotton quilt, felt hat, and shirt had long since disappeared, and
after that he had sold his padded jacket. Now nothing was left
but his trousers, and these of course he could not take off. He
had a ragged lined jacket, it is true; but this was certainly worthless, unless he gave it away to be made into shoe-soles. He had
long been dreaming of finding some money on the road, but
hitherto he had not come across any; he had also been hoping he
might suddenly discover some money in his tumble-down room,
and had frantically ransacked it, but the room was quite, quite
empty. Then he made up his mind to go out in search of food.

As he walked along the road "in search of food" he saw
the familiar tavern and the familiar steamed bread, but he
passed them by without pausing for a second, without even
hankering after them. It was not these he was looking for,
although what exactly he was looking for he did not know
himself.

Since Weizhuang was not a big place, he soon left it behind. Most of the country outside the village consisted of

paddy fields, green as far as the eye could see with the tender shoots of young rice, dotted here and there with round black, moving objects — peasants cultivating their fields. But blind to the delights of country life, Ah Q simply went on his way, for he knew instinctively that this was far removed from his "search for food." Finally, however, he came to the walls of the Convent of Quiet Self-Improvement.

The convent too was surrounded by paddy fields, its white walls standing out sharply in the fresh green, and inside the low earthen wall at the back was a vegetable garden. Ah Q hesitated for a time, looking around him. Since there was no one in sight he scrambled on to the low wall, holding on to some milkwort. The mud wall started crumbling, and Ah Q shook with fear; however, by clutching at the branch of a mulberry tree he managed to jump over it. Within was a wild profusion of vegetation, but no sign of yellow wine, steamed bread, or anything edible. A clump of bamboos by the west wall had put forth many young shoots, but unfortunately these were not cooked. There was also rape which had long since gone to seed, mustard already about to flower, and some tough old cabbages.

Resentful as a scholar who has failed the examinations, Ah Q walked slowly towards the gate of the garden. Suddenly, however, he gave a start of joy, for what did he see there but a patch of turnips! He knelt down and had just begun pulling when a round head appeared from behind the gate, only to be promptly withdrawn. This was no other than the little nun. Now though Ah Q had always had the greatest contempt for such people as little nuns, there are times when "Discretion is the better part of valour." He hastily pulled up four turnips, tore off the leaves, and stuffed them under his jacket. By this time an old nun had already come out.

"May Buddha preserve us, Ah Q! How dare you climb into our garden to steal turnips! . . . Mercy on us, what a wicked thing to do! *Aiya*, Buddha preserve us!"

"When did I ever climb into your garden and steal turnips?" retorted Ah Q as he started off, keeping his eyes on her.

"Now — aren't you?" The old nun pointed at the bulge
in his jacket.

"Are these yours? Will they come when you call? You. . . ."

Leaving his sentence unfinished, Ah Q took to his heels as
fast as he could, followed by a huge fat black dog. Originally
this dog had been at the front gate, and how it reached the back
garden was a mystery. With a snarl the black dog gave chase
and was just about to bite Ah Q's leg when most opportunely
a turnip fell from his jacket, and the dog, taken by surprise,
stopped for a second. During this time Ah Q scrambled up
the mulberry tree, scaled the mud wall, and fell, turnips and
all, outside the convent. He left the black dog still barking by
the mulberry tree, and the old nun saying her prayers.

Fearing that the nun would let the black dog out again,
Ah Q gathered together his turnips and ran, picking up a few
small stones as he went. But the black dog did not reappear.
Ah Q threw away the stones and walked on, eating as he went,
thinking to himself, "There is nothing to be had here: better go
to town. . . ."

By the time the third turnip was finished he had made up
his mind to go to town.

Chapter 6

From Resurgence to Decline

Weizhuang did not see Ah Q again till just after the Moon
Festival that year. Everybody was surprised to hear of his return, and this made them think back and wonder where he had
been all that time. In the past Ah Q had usually taken great
pleasure in announcing his few visits to town; but since he had
not done so this time, his going had passed unnoticed. He may
have told the old man in charge of the Tutelary God's Temple,

but according to the custom of Weizhuang only a trip to town by Mr. Zhao, Mr. Qian, or the successful county candidate counted as important. Even the Bogus Foreign Devil's going was not talked about, much less Ah Q's. This would explain why the old man had not spread the news for him, with the result that the villagers remained in the dark.

Ah Q's return this time was very different from before, and in fact quite enough to occasion astonishment. The day was growing dark when he showed up, bleary-eyed, at the tavern door, walked up to the counter, and tossed down on it a handful of silver and coppers produced from his belt. "Cash!" he announced. "Bring the wine!" He was wearing a new lined jacket and at his waist hung a large purse, the great weight of which caused his belt to sag in a sharp curve.

It was the custom in Weizhuang that anyone in any way unusual should be treated with respect rather than disregarded, and now, although they knew quite well that this was Ah Q, still he was very different from the Ah Q of the ragged coat. The ancients say, "A scholar who has been away three days must be looked at with new eyes." So the waiter, tavern-keeper, customers and passers-by all quite naturally expressed a kind of suspicion mingled with respect. The tavern-keeper started off by nodding, following this up with the words:

"So you're back, Ah Q!"

"Yes, I'm back."

"Made a pretty packet, eh? . . . Where. . . ?"

"I've been in town."

By the next day this piece of news had spread through Weizhuang. And since everybody wanted to hear the success story of this Ah Q of the ready money and the new lined jacket, in the tavern, teahouse, and under the temple eaves, the villagers gradually ferreted out the news. The result was that they began to treat Ah Q with a new deference.

According to Ah Q, he had been a servant in the house of a successful provincial candidate. This part of the story filled all who heard it with awe. This successful provincial candidate was named Bai, but because he was the only successful provincial candidate in the whole town there was no need to use his surname: whenever anyone spoke of the successful provincial candidate, it meant him. And this was so not only in Weizhuang, for almost everyone within a radius of a hundred li imagined his name to be Mr. Successful Provincial Candidate. To have worked in the household of such a man naturally called for respect; but according to Ah Q's further statements, he was unwilling to go on working there because this successful candidate was really too much of a "turtle's egg." This part of the story made all who heard it sigh, but with a sense of pleasure, because it showed that Ah Q was unworthy to work in the household of such a man, yet not to work there was a pity.

According to Ah Q, his return was also due to his dissatisfaction with the townspeople because they called a long bench a straight bench, used shredded shallots to fry fish, and — a defect he had recently discovered — the women did not sway in a very satisfactory manner as they walked. However, the town had its good points too: for instance, in Weizhuang everyone played with thirty-two bamboo counters and only the Bogus Foreign Devil could play mahjong, but in town even the street urchins excelled at mahjong. You had only to place the Bogus Foreign Devil in the hands of these young rascals in their teens for him straightway to become like "a small devil before the King of Hell." This part of the story made all who heard it blush.

"Have you seen an execution?" asked Ah Q. "Ah, that's a fine sight.... When they execute the revolutionaries.... Ah, that's a fine sight, a fine sight...." He shook his head, sending his spittle flying on to the face of Zhao Sichen who was standing opposite him. This part of the story made all who heard it tremble. Then with a glance around, he suddenly raised his right hand and dropped it on the neck of Whiskers Wang who, craning forward, was listening with rapt attention.

"Off with his head!" shouted Ah Q.

Whiskers Wang gave a start, and jerked back his head as fast as lightning or a spark struck from a flint, while the bystanders shivered with pleasurable apprehension. After this, Whiskers Wang went about in a daze for many days and dared not go near Ah Q, nor did the others.

Although we cannot say that in the eyes of the inhabitants of Weizhuang Ah Q's status at this time was superior to that of Mr. Zhao, we can at least affirm without any danger of inaccuracy that it was approximately equivalent.

Not long after, Ah Q's fame suddenly spread into the women's apartments of Weizhuang too. Although the only two families of any pretensions in Weizhuang were those of Qian and Zhao, and nine-tenths of the rest were poor, still women's apartments are women's apartments, and the way Ah Q's fame spread into them was quite miraculous. When the womenfolk met they would say to each other, "Mrs. Zou bought a blue silk skirt from Ah Q. Although it was old, it only cost ninety cents. And Zhao Baiyan's mother (this has yet to be verified, because some say it was Zhao Sichen's mother) bought a child's costume of crimson foreign calico which was nearly new for only three hundred cash, less eight per cent discount."

Then those who had no silk skirt or needed foreign calico were most anxious to see Ah Q in order to buy from him. Far from avoiding him now, they sometimes followed him when he passed, calling to him to stop.

"Ah Q, have you any more silk skirts?" they would ask. "No? We want foreign calico too. Do you have any?"

This news later spread from the poor households to the rich ones, because Mrs. Zou was so pleased with her silk skirt that she took it to Mrs. Zhao for her approval, and Mrs. Zhao told Mr. Zhao, speaking very highly of it.

Mr. Zhao discussed the matter that evening at dinner with his son the successful county candidate, suggesting that there was certainly something strange about Ah Q and that they should be more careful about their doors and windows. They did not know, though, what if anything Ah Q had left — he might still have something good. Since Mrs. Zhao happened to want a good cheap fur jacket, after a family council it was decided to ask Mrs. Zou to find Ah Q for them at once. For this a third exception was made to the rule, special permission being given that evening for a lamp to be lit.

A considerable amount of oil had been burned, but still there was no sign of Ah Q. The whole Zhao household was yawning with impatience, some of them resenting Ah Q's casualness, others blaming Mrs. Zou for not making a greater effort. Mrs. Zhao was afraid that Ah Q dared not come because of the terms agreed upon that spring, but Mr. Zhao did not think this anything to worry about because, as he said, "This time *I* sent for him." Sure enough, Mr. Zhao proved himself a man of insight, for Ah Q finally arrived with Mrs. Zou.

"He keeps saying he has nothing left," panted Mrs. Zou as she came in. "When I told him to come and tell you so himself he kept talking back. I told him. . . ."

"Sir!" cried Ah Q with an attempt at a smile, coming to a halt under the eaves.

"I hear you did well for yourself in town, Ah Q," said Mr. Zhao, going up to him and looking him over carefully. "Very good. Now . . . they say you have some old things. . . . Bring them all here for us to look at. This is simply because I happen to want. . . ."

"I told Mrs. Zou — there's nothing left."

"Nothing left?" Mr. Zhao could not help sounding disappointed. "How could they go so quickly?"

"They belonged to a friend, and there wasn't much to begin with. People bought some. . . ."

"There must be something left."

"Only a door curtain."

"Then bring the door curtain for us to see," said Mrs. Zhao hurriedly.

"Well, tomorrow will do," said Mr. Zhao without much enthusiasm. "When you have anything in future, Ah Q, you must bring it to us first. . . ."

"We certainly won't pay less than other people!" said the successful county candidate. His wife shot a hasty glance at Ah Q to see his reaction.

"I need a fur jacket," said Mrs. Zhao.

Although Ah Q agreed, he slouched out so carelessly that they did not know whether he had taken their instructions to heart or not. This so disappointed, annoyed and worried Mr. Zhao that he even stopped yawning. The successful candidate was also far from satisfied with Ah Q's attitude. "People should be on their guard against such a turtle's egg," he said. "It might be best to order the bailiff to forbid him to live in Weizhuang."

Mr. Zhao did not agree, saying that then Ah Q might bear a grudge, and that in a business like this it was probably a case of "the eagle does not prey on its own nest": his own village need not worry so long as they were a little more watchful at night. The successful candidate, much impressed by this parental instruction, immediately withdrew his proposal for banishing Ah Q but cautioned Mrs. Zou on no account to repeat what had been said.

The next day, however, when Mrs. Zou took her blue skirt to be dyed black she repeated these insinuations about Ah Q, although not actually mentioning what the successful candidate had said about driving him away. Even so, it was most damaging to Ah Q. In the first place, the bailiff appeared at his door and took away the door curtain. Although Ah Q protested that Mrs. Zhao wanted to see it, the bailiff would not give it back and even demanded monthly hush money. In the second place, the villagers' respect for Ah Q suddenly changed. Although they still dared not take liberties, they avoided him as much as possible. While this differed from their previous fear of his "Off with his head!" it closely resembled the attitude of the ancients to spirits: they kept a respectful distance.

Some idlers who wanted to get to the bottom of the business went to question Ah Q carefully. And with no attempt at concealment Ah Q told them proudly of his experiences. They learned that he had merely been a petty thief, not only unable to climb walls but even unable to go through openings: he simply stood outside an opening to receive the stolen goods.

One night he had just received a package and his chief had gone in again, when he heard a great uproar inside and took to his heels as fast as he could. He fled from the town that same night, back to Weizhuang; and after this he dared not return to do any more thieving. This story, however, was even more damaging to Ah Q, since the villagers had been keeping a respectful distance because they did not want to incur his enmity; for who could have guessed that he was only a thief who dared not steal again? Now they knew he was really too low to inspire fear.

Chapter 7

The Revolution

On the fourteenth day of the ninth moon of the third year in the reign of Emperor Xuan Tong* — the day on which Ah Q sold his purse to Zhao Baiyan — at midnight, after the fourth stroke of the third watch, a large boat with a big black awning arrived at the Zhao family's landing-place. This boat floated up in the darkness while the villagers were sound asleep, so that they knew nothing about it; but it left again about dawn, when quite a number of people saw it. Investigation revealed that this boat actually belonged to the successful provincial candidate!

---

* November 4, 1911, the day on which Shaoxing was freed in the 1911 Revolution.

This incident caused great uneasiness in Weizhuang, and before midday the hearts of all the villagers were beating faster. The Zhao family kept very quiet about the errand of the boat, but according to gossip in the teahouse and tavern, the revolutionaries were going to enter the town and the successful provincial candidate had come to the country to take refuge. Mrs. Zou alone thought otherwise, maintaining that the successful candidate merely wanted to deposit a few battered cases in Weizhuang, but that Mr. Zhao had sent them back. Actually the successful provincial candidate and the successful county candidate in the Zhao family were not on good terms, so that it was scarcely logical to expect them to prove friends in adversity; moreover, since Mrs. Zou was a neighbour of the Zhao family and had a better idea of what was going on, she ought to have known.

Then a rumour spread to the effect that although the scholar had not come in person, he had sent a long letter tracing some distant relationship with the Zhao family; and since Mr. Zhao after thinking it over had decided it could after all do him no harm to keep the cases, they were now stowed under his wife's bed. As for the revolutionaries, some people said they had entered the town that night in white helmets and white armour — in mourning for Emperor Chong Zhen.*

Ah Q had long since known of revolutionaries and this year with his own eyes had seen revolutionaries decapitated. But since it had occurred to him that the revolutionaries were rebels and that a rebellion would make things difficult for him, he had always detested and kept away from them. Who could have guessed that they could strike such fear into a successful provincial candidate renowned for a hundred li around? In consequence, Ah Q could not help feeling rather fascinated, the terror of all the villagers only adding to his delight.

---

* Chong Zhen, the last emperor of the Ming Dynasty, reigned from 1628 to 1644. He hanged himself before the insurgent peasant army under Li Zicheng entered Beijing.

"Revolution is not a bad thing," thought Ah Q. "Finish off the whole lot of them ... curse them! ... I'd like to go over to the revolutionaries myself."

Ah Q had been hard up recently, which no doubt made him rather dissatisfied; moreover he had drunk two bowls of wine at noon on an empty stomach. Consequently he became drunk very quickly; and as he walked along thinking to himself, he seemed again to be treading on air. Suddenly, in some curious way, he felt as if he were a revolutionary and all the people in Weizhuang were his captives. Unable to contain himself for joy, he shouted at the top of his voice:

"Rebellion! Rebellion!"

All the villagers stared at him in consternation. Ah Q had never seen such pitiful looks before; they refreshed him as much as a drink of iced water in summer. So he walked on even more happily, shouting:

"Fine! ... I shall take what I want! I shall like whom I please!

"*Tra la tra la!*
Alas, in my cups I have slain my sworn brother Zheng.
Alas, ya-ya-ya ...
Tra la, tra la, tum ti tum tum!
Steel mace in hand I shall trounce you."

Mr. Zhao and his son were standing at their gate with two relatives discussing the revolution. Ah Q did not see them as he passed with his head thrown back, singing, "*Tra la la, tum ti tum!*"

"Q, old fellow!" called Mr. Zhao timidly in a low voice.

"*Tra la,*" sang Ah Q, unable to imagine that his name could be linked with those words "old fellow." Sure that he had heard wrongly and was in no way concerned, he simply went on singing, "*Tra la la, tum ti tum!*"

"Q, old fellow!"

"*Alas, in my cups....*"

"Ah Q!" The successful candidate had no choice but to name him outright.

Only then did Ah Q come to a stop. "Well?" he asked with his head on one side.

"Q, old fellow ... now...." But Mr. Zhao was at a loss for words again. "Are you well off now?"

"Well off? Of course. I get what I want...."

"Ah Q, old man, poor friends of yours like us are of no consequence..." faltered Zhao Baiyan, as if sounding out the revolutionaries' attitude.

"Poor friends? You're richer anyway than I am." With this Ah Q walked away.

This left them in speechless dismay. Back home that evening Mr. Zhao and his son discussed the question until it was time to light the lamps. And Zhao Baiyan once home took the purse from his waist and gave it to his wife to hide for him at the bottom of a chest.

For a while Ah Q walked upon air, but by the time he reached the Tutelary God's Temple he had come down to earth again. That evening the old man in charge of the temple was also unexpectedly friendly and offered him tea. Then Ah Q asked him for two flat cakes, and after eating these demanded a four-ounce candle that had been lighted once and a candlestick. He lit the candle and lay down alone in his little room feeling inexpressibly refreshed and happy, while the candlelight leaped and flickered as if this were the Lantern Festival and his imagination soared with it.

"Revolt? It would be fine.... A troop of revolutionaries would come, all in white helmets and white armour, with swords, steel maces, bombs, foreign guns, sharp-pointed double-edged knives, and spears with hooks. When they passed this temple they would call out, 'Ah Q! Come along with us!' And then I would go with them....

"Then the fun would start. All the villagers, the whole lousy lot, would kneel down and plead, 'Ah Q, spare us!' But

who would listen to them! The first to die would be Young D
and Mr. Zhao, then the successful county candidate and the
Bogus Foreign Devil. . . .   But perhaps I would spare a few. I
would once have spared Whiskers Wang, but now I don't even
want him. . . .

"Things . . . I would go straight in and open the cases:
silver ingots, foreign coins, foreign calico jackets. . . .   First I
would move the Ningbo bed of the successful county candidate's
wife to the temple, as well as the Qian family tables and chairs
— or else just use the Zhao family's. I wouldn't lift a finger
myself, but order Young D to move the things for me, and to
look smart about it if he didn't want his face slapped. . . .

"Zhao Sichen's younger sister is very ugly. In a few years
Mrs. Zou's daughter might be worth considering. The Bogus
Foreign Devil's wife is willing to sleep with a man without a
queue, hah! She can't be a good woman! The successful
county candidate's wife has scars on her eyelids. . . .   I haven't
seen Amah Wu for a long time and don't know where she is —
what a pity her feet are so big."

Before Ah Q had reached a satisfactory conclusion, there
was a sound of snoring. The four-ounce candle had burned
down only half an inch, and its flickering red light lit up his
open mouth.

"Ho, ho!" shouted Ah Q suddenly, raising his head and
looking wildly around. But at sight of the four-ounce candle,
he lay back and fell asleep again.

The next morning he got up very late, and when he went
out into the street everything was the same as usual. He was
still hungry, but though he racked his brains he did not seem
able to think of anything. All of a sudden, however, an idea
struck him and he walked slowly off until, either by design or
accident, he reached the Convent of Quiet Self-Improvement.

The convent was as peaceful as it had been that spring,
with its white wall and shining black gate. After a moment's
reflection he knocked at the gate, whereupon a dog on the other

side started barking. He hastily picked up some broken bricks, then went back again to knock more heavily, knocking until the black gate was pitted with pock-marks. At last he heard someone coming to open up.

Clutching a brick, Ah Q straddled there prepared to do battle with the black dog. The convent gate opened a crack, but no black dog rushed out. When he looked in all he could see was the old nun.

"What are you here for again?" she asked with a start.

"There's a revolution ... didn't you know?" said Ah Q vaguely.

"Revolution, revolution ... we've already had one." The old nun's eyes were red. "What more do you want to do to us?"

"What?" demanded Ah Q, dumbfounded.

"Didn't you know? The revolutionaries have already been here!"

"Who?" demanded Ah Q, still more dumbfounded.

"The successful county candidate and the Foreign Devil."

This completely took the wind out of Ah Q's sails. When the old nun saw there was no fight left in him she promptly shut the gate, so that when Ah Q pushed it again he could not budge it, and when he knocked again there was no answer.

It had happened that morning. The successful county candidate in the Zhao family was quick to learn the news. As soon as he heard that the revolutionaries had entered the town that night, he wound his queue up on his head and went out first thing to call on the Bogus Foreign Devil in the Qian family, with whom he had never been on very good terms. Because this was a time for all to work for reforms, they had a most satisfactory talk and on the spot became comrades who saw eye to eye and pledged themselves to make revolution.

After racking their brains for some time, they remembered that in the Convent of Quiet Self-Improvement there was an imperial tablet inscribed "Long live the Emperor" which ought to be done away with immediately. Thereupon they lost no time in going to the convent to carry out their revolutionary activities. Because the old nun tried to stop them and passed a few remarks, they considered her as the Qing government and gave her quite a few knocks on the head with a stick and with their knuckles. The nun, pulling herself together after they had gone, made an inspection. Naturally the imperial tablet had been smashed into fragments on the ground and the valuable Xuan De censer* before the shrine of Guanyin, the goddess of mercy, had also disappeared.

Ah Q only learned this later. He deeply regretted having been asleep at the time, and resented the fact that they had not come to call him. Then he said to himself. "Maybe they still don't know I have joined the revolutionaries."

Chapter 8

Barred from the Revolution

The people of Weizhuang felt easier in their minds with each passing day. From the news brought they knew that although the revolutionaries had entered the town their coming had not made a great deal of difference. The magistrate was still the highest official, it was only his title that had changed; and the successful provincial candidate also had some post — the Weizhuang villagers could not remember these names clearly — some kind of official post; while the head of the military was still the same old captain. The only cause for alarm was that, the day after their arrival, some bad revolutionaries made trouble by cutting off people's queues. It was said that the boatman Sevenpounder from the next village had fallen into their clutches, and that he no longer looked presentable. Still, the danger of this was not great, because the Weizhuang villagers seldom went to

_____

* Highly decorative bronze censers were made during the Xuan De period (1426-35) of the Ming Dynasty.

town to begin with, and those who had been considering a trip there at once changed their minds in order to avoid this risk. Ah Q had been thinking of going to town to look up his old friends, but as soon as he heard the news he gave up the idea.

It would be wrong, however, to say that there were no reforms in Weizhuang. During the next few days the number of people who coiled their queues on their heads gradually increased and, as has already been said, the first to do so was naturally the successful county candidate; the next were Zhao Sichen and Zhao Baiyan, and after them Ah Q. If it had been summer it would not have been considered strange if everybody had coiled their queues on their heads or tied them in knots; but this was late autumn, so that this autumn observance of a summer practice on the part of those who coiled their queues could be considered nothing short of a heroic decision, and as far as Weizhuang was concerned it could not be said to have had no connection with the reforms.

When Zhao Sichen approached with the nape of his neck bare, people who saw him remarked, "Ah! Here comes a revolutionary!"

When Ah Q heard this he was greatly impressed. Although he had long since heard how the successful county candidate had coiled his queue on his head, it had never occurred to him to do the same. Only now when he saw that Zhao Sichen had followed suit was he struck with the idea of doing the same himself. He made up his mind to copy them. He used a bamboo chopstick to twist his queue up on his head, and after some hesitation eventually summoned up the courage to go out.

As he walked along the street people looked at him, but without any comment. Ah Q, disgruntled at first, soon waxed indignant. Recently he had been losing his temper very easily. As a matter of fact he was no worse off than before the revolution, people treated him politely, and the shops no longer demanded payment in cash, yet Ah Q still felt dissatisfied. A revolution, he thought, should mean more than this. When he saw Young D, his anger boiled over.

Young D had also coiled his queue up on his head and, what was more, had actually used a bamboo chopstick to do so too. Ah Q had never imagined that Young D would also have the courage to do this; he certainly could not tolerate such a thing! Who was Young D anyway? He was greatly tempted to seize him then and there, break his bamboo chopstick, let down his queue and slap his face several times into the bargain to punish him for forgetting his place and for his presumption in becoming a revolutionary. But in the end he let him off, simply fixing him with a furious glare, spitting, and exclaiming, "Pah!"

These last few days the only one to go to town was the Bogus Foreign Devil. The successful county candidate in the Zhao family had thought of using the deposited cases as a pretext to call on the successful provincial candidate, but the danger that he might have his queue cut off had made him defer his visit. He had written an extremely formal letter, and asked the Bogus Foreign Devil to take it to town; he had also asked the latter to introduce him to the Freedom Party. When the Bogus Foreign Devil came back he collected four dollars from the successful county candidate, after which the latter wore a silver peach on his chest. All the Weizhuang villagers were overawed, and said that this was the badge of the Persimmon Oil Party,* equivalent to the rank of a Han Lin.** As a result, Mr. Zhao's prestige suddenly increased, far more so in fact than when his son first passed the official examination; consequently he started looking down on everyone else and when he saw Ah Q tended to ignore him a little.

Ah Q, disgruntled at finding himself cold-shouldered all the time, realized as soon as he heard of this silver peach why

---

* The Freedom Party was called Zi You Dang. The villagers, not understanding the word "freedom," turned Zi You into Shi You, which means persimmon oil.

** Member of the Imperial Academy in the Qing Dynasty.

he was left out in the cold. Simply to say that you had gone over was not enough to make anyone a revolutionary; nor was it enough merely to wind your queue up on your head; the most important thing was to get into touch with the revolutionary party. In all his life he had known only two revolutionaries, one of whom had already lost his head in town, leaving only the Bogus Foreign Devil. His only course was to go at once to talk things over with the Bogus Foreign Devil.

The front gate of the Qian house happened to be open, and Ah Q crept timidly in. Once inside he gave a start, for there was the Bogus Foreign Devil standing in the middle of the courtyard dressed entirely in black, no doubt in foreign dress, and also wearing a silver peach. In his hand he held the stick with which Ah Q was already acquainted to his cost, while the foot-long queue which he had grown again had been combed out to hang loosely over his shoulders, giving him a resemblance to the immortal Liu Hai.* Standing respectfully before him were Zhao Baiyan and three others, all of them listening with the utmost deference to what the Bogus Foreign Devil was saying.

Ah Q tiptoed inside and stood behind Zhao Baiyan, eager to pronounce some greeting, but not knowing what to say. Obviously he could not call the man "Bogus Foreign Devil," and neither "Foreigner" nor "Revolutionary" seemed quite the thing. Perhaps the best form of address would be "Mr. Foreigner."

But Mr. Foreigner had not seen him, because with eyes upraised he was holding forth with great gusto:

"I am so impetuous that when we met I kept urging, 'Old Hong, let's get down to business!' But he always answered 'Nein!' — that's a foreign word which you wouldn't understand. Otherwise we should have succeeded long ago. This just goes to show how cautious he is. Time and again he asked me to go

---

* A figure in Chinese folk legend, portrayed with flowing hair.

to Hubei, but I've not yet agreed. Who wants to work in a small district town?..."

"Er — well —" Ah Q waited for him to pause, then screwed up his courage to speak. But for some reason or other he still did not call him Mr. Foreigner.

The four men who had been listening gave a start and turned to stare at Ah Q. Mr. Foreigner too caught sight of him for the first time.

"What is it?"

"I...."

"Clear out!"

"I want to join...."

"Get out!" Mr. Foreigner raised the "mourner's stick."

Thereupon Zhao Baiyan and the others shouted, "Mr. Qian tells you to get out, don't you hear!"

Ah Q put up his hands to protect his head, and without knowing what he was doing fled through the gate; but this time Mr. Foreigner did not give chase. After running more than sixty steps Ah Q slowed down, and now his heart filled with dismay, because if Mr. Foreigner would not allow him to be a revolutionary, there was no other way open to him. In future he could never hope to have men in white helmets and white armour come to call him. All his ambitions, aims, hope and future had been blasted at one fell swoop. The fact that gossips might spread the news and make him a laughing-stock for the likes of Young D and Whiskers Wang was only a secondary consideration.

Never before had he felt so flat. Even coiling his queue on his head now struck him as pointless and ridiculous. As a form of revenge he was very tempted to let his queue down at once, but he did not do so. He wandered about till evening, when after drinking two bowls of wine on credit he began to feel in better spirits, and in his mind's eye saw fragmentary visions of white helmets and white armour once more.

One day he loafed about until late at night. Only when

the tavern was about to close did he start to stroll back to the
Tutelary God's Temple.

Crash-bang!

He suddenly heard an unusual sound, which could not have
been firecrackers. Ah Q, always fond of excitement and of poking his nose into other people's business, headed straight for the
noise in the darkness. He thought he heard footsteps ahead, and
was listening carefully when a man fled past from the opposite
direction. Ah Q instantly wheeled round to follow him. When
that man turned, Ah Q turned too, and when having turned a
corner that man stopped, Ah Q followed suit. He saw that there
was no one after them and that the man was Young D.

"What's up?" demanded Ah Q resentfully.

"The Zhao ... Zhao family has been robbed," panted
Young D.

Ah Q's heart went pit-a-pat. After saying this, Young D
went off. But Ah Q kept on running by fits and starts. However, having been in the business himself made him unusually
bold. Rounding the corner of a lane, he listened carefully and
thought he heard shouting; while by straining his eyes he thought
he could see a troop of men in white helmets and white armour
carrying off cases, carrying off furniture, even carrying off the
Ningbo bed of the successful county candidate's wife. He could
not, however, see them very clearly. He wanted to go nearer,
but his feet were rooted to the ground.

There was no moon that night, and Weizhuang was very
still in the pitch darkness, as quiet as in the peaceful days of Emperor Fu Xi.* Ah Q stood there until his patience ran out, yet
there seemed no end to the business, distant figures kept moving to and fro, carrying off cases, carrying off furniture, carrying
off the Ningbo bed of the successful county candidate's wife ...
carrying until he could hardly believe his own eyes. But he decided not to go any closer, and went back to the temple.

---

* One of the earliest legendary monarchs in China.

It was even darker in the Tutelary God's Temple. When he had closed the big gate he groped his way into his room, and only after he had been lying down for some time did he calm down sufficiently to begin thinking how this affected him. The men in white helmets and white armour had evidently arrived, but they had not come to call him; they had taken away fine things, but there was no share for him — this was all the fault of the Bogus Foreign Devil, who had barred him from the rebellion. Otherwise how could he have failed to have a share this time?

The more Ah Q thought of it the angrier he grew, until he was in a towering rage. "So no rebellion for me, only for you, eh?" he fumed, nodding furiously. "Curse you, you Bogus Foreign Devil — all right, be a rebel! That's a crime for which you get your head chopped off. I'll turn informer, then see you dragged off to town to have your head cut off — your whole family executed.... To hell with you!"

Chapter 9

The Grand Finale

After the Zhao family was robbed most of the people in Weizhuang felt pleased yet fearful, and Ah Q was no exception. But four days later Ah Q was suddenly dragged into town in the middle of the night. It happened to be a dark night. A squad of soldiers, a squad of militia, a squad of police, and five secret servicemen made their way quietly to Weizhuang and, after posting a machine-gun opposite the entrance, under cover of darkness surrounded the Tutelary God's Temple. But Ah Q did not bolt for it. For a long time nothing stirred till the captain, losing patience, offered a reward of twenty thousand cash. Only then did two militiamen summon up courage to jump over the wall and enter. With their co-operation, the others rushed in and dragged Ah Q out. But not until he had been carried out of the temple to somewhere near the machine-gun did he begin to wake up to what was happening.

It was already midday by the time they reached town, and Ah Q found himself carried to a dilapidated yamen where, after taking five or six turnings, he was pushed into a small room. No sooner had he stumbled inside than the door, in the form of a wooden grille, was slammed on his heels. The rest of the cell consisted of three blank walls, and when he looked carefully he saw two other men in a corner.

Although Ah Q was feeling rather uneasy, he was by no means depressed, because the room where he slept in the Tutelary God's Temple was in no way superior to this. The two other men also seemed to be villagers. They gradually fell into conversation with him, and one of them told him that the successful provincial candidate wanted to dun him for the rent owed by his grandfather; the other did not know why he was there. When they questioned Ah Q he answered quite frankly, "Because I wanted to revolt."

That afternoon he was dragged out through the grille and taken to a big hall, at the far end of which sat an old man with a cleanly shaven head. Ah Q took him for a monk at first, but when he saw soldiers standing guard and a dozen men in long coats on both sides, some with their heads clean-shaven like this old man and some with a foot or so of hair hanging over their shoulders like the Bogus Foreign Devil, all glaring furiously at him with grim faces, he knew that this man must be someone important. At once his knee-joints relaxed of their own accord, and he sank to his knees.

"Stand up to speak! Don't kneel!" shouted all the men in the long coats.

Although Ah Q understood, he felt quite incapable of standing up. He had involuntarily started squatting, improving on this finally to kneel down.

"Slave!" exclaimed the long-coated men contemptuously. They did not insist on his getting up, however.

"Tell the truth and you will receive a lighter sentence," said the old man with the shaven head in a low but clear voice, fixing his eyes on Ah Q. "We know everything already. When you have confessed, we will let you go."

"Confess!" repeated the long-coated men loudly.

"The fact is I wanted . . . to join . . ." muttered Ah Q disjointedly after a moment's confused thinking.

"In that case, why didn't you?" asked the old man gently.

"The Bogus Foreign Devil wouldn't let me."

"Nonsense. It's too late to talk now. Where are your accomplices?"

"What? . . ."

"The gang who robbed the Zhao family that night."

"They didn't come to call me. They moved the things away themselves." Mention of this made Ah Q indignant.

"Where are they now? When you have told me I will let you go," repeated the old man even more gently.

"I don't know. . . . They didn't come to call me. . . ."

Then, at a sign from the old man, Ah Q was dragged back through the grille. The following morning he was dragged out once more.

Everything was unchanged in the big hall. The old man with the clean-shaven head was still sitting there, and Ah Q knelt down again as before.

"Have you anything else to say?" asked the old man gently.

Ah Q thought, and decided there was nothing to say, so he answered, "Nothing."

Then a man in a long coat brought a sheet of paper and held a brush in front of Ah Q, which he wanted to thrust into his hand. Ah Q was now nearly frightened out of his wits, because this was the first time in his life that his hand had ever come into contact with a writing-brush. He was just wondering how to hold it when the man pointed out a place on the paper and told him to sign his name.

"I — I — can't write," said Ah Q, shamefaced, nervously holding the brush.

"In that case, to make it easy for you, draw a circle!"

Ah Q tried to draw a circle, but the hand with which he grasped the brush trembled, so the man spread the paper on the ground for him. Ah Q bent down and, as painstakingly as if his life depended on it, drew a circle. Afraid people would laugh at him, he determined to make the circle round; however, not only was that wretched brush very heavy, but it would not do his bidding. Instead it wobbled from side to side; and just as the line was about to close it swerved out again, making a shape like a melon-seed.

While Ah Q was still feeling mortified by his failure to draw a circle, the man took back the paper and brush without any comment. A number of people then dragged him back for the third time through the grille.

By now he felt not too upset. He supposed that in this world it was the fate of everybody at some time to be dragged in and out of prison and to have to draw circles on paper; it was only his circle not being round that he felt a blot on his escutcheon. Presently, however, he regained composure by thinking, "Only idiots can make perfect circles." And with this thought he fell asleep.

That night, however, the successful provincial candidate was unable to sleep, because he had quarrelled with the captain. The successful provincial candidate had insisted that the main thing was to recover the stolen goods, while the captain said the main thing was to make a public example. Recently the captain had come to treat the successful provincial candidate quite disdainfully. So banging his fist on the table he said, "Punish one to awe one hundred! See now, I have been a member of the revolutionary party for less than twenty days, but there have been a dozen cases of robbery, none of them yet solved; think how badly that reflects on me. Now this one has been solved, you come and haggle. It won't do. This is my affair."

The successful provincial candidate, most put out, insisted that if the stolen goods were not recovered he would resign immediately from his post as assistant civil administrator.

"As you please," said the captain.

In consequence the successful provincial candidate did not sleep that night; but happily he did not hand in his resignation the next day after all.

The third time that Ah Q was dragged out of the grille-door was the morning following the night on which the successful provincial candidate had been unable to sleep. When he reached the hall, the old man with the clean-shaven head was sitting there as usual. And Ah Q knelt down as usual.

Very gently the old man questioned him, "Have you anything more to say?"

Ah Q thought, and decided there was nothing to say, so he answered, "Nothing."

A number of men in long coats and short jackets put on him a white vest of foreign cloth with some black characters on it. Ah Q felt most disconcerted, because this was very like mourning dress and to wear mourning was unlucky. At the same time his hands were bound behind his back, and he was dragged out of the yamen.

Ah Q was lifted on to an uncovered cart, and several men in short jackets sat down beside him. The cart started off at once. In front were a number of soldiers and militiamen shouldering foreign rifles, and on both sides were crowds of gaping spectators, while what was behind Ah Q could not see. Suddenly it occurred to him — "Can I be going to have my head cut off?" Panic seized him and everything turned dark before his eyes, while there was a humming in his ears as if he had fainted. But he did not really faint. Although he felt frighten-ed some of the time, the rest of the time he was quite calm. It seemed to him that in this world probably it was the fate of everybody at some time to have his head cut off.

He still recognized the road and felt rather surprised: Why were they not going to the execution ground? He did not know that he was being paraded round the streets as a public example. But if he had known, it would have been the same: he would only have thought that in this world probably it was the fate of everybody at some time to be made a public example of.

Then he realized that they were making a detour to the execution ground, so after all he must be going to have his head cut off. He looked round him regretfully at the people swarming after him like ants, and unexpectedly in the crowd by the roadside he caught sight of Amah Wu. So that was why he had not seen her for so long: she was working in town.

Ah Q suddenly became ashamed of his lack of spirit, because he had not sung any lines from an opera. His thoughts revolved like a whirlwind: *The Young Widow at Her Husband's Grave* was not heroic enough. The passage "Alas, in my cups" in *The Battle of the Dragon and the Tiger* was too feeble. "Steel mace in hand I shall trounce you" was still the best. But when he wanted to raise his hands, he remembered that they were bound together; so he did not sing "Steel mace in hand" either.

"In twenty years I shall be another. . . ."* In his agitation Ah Q uttered half a saying which he had picked up for himself but never used before. "Good!!!" The roar of the crowd sounded like the growl of a wolf.

The cart moved steadily forward. During the snouting Ah Q's eyes turned in search of Amah Wu, but she did not seem

_____

* "In twenty years I shall be another stout young fellow" was a phrase often used by criminals before execution to show their scorn of death. Believing in transmigration, they thought that after death their souls would enter other living bodies.

to have seen him for she was looking intently at the foreign rifles carried by the soldiers.

So Ah Q took another look at the shouting crowd.

At that instant his thoughts revolved again like a whirl-wind. Four years before, at the foot of the mountain, he had met a hungry wolf which had followed him at a set distance, wanting to eat him. He had nearly died of fright, but luckily he happened to have a knife in his hand which gave him the courage to get back to Weizhuang. He had never forgotten that wolf's eyes, fierce yet cowardly, gleaming like two will-o'-the-wisps, as if boring into him from a distance. Now he saw eyes more terrible even than the wolf's: dull yet penetrating eyes that having devoured his words still seemed eager to devour something beyond his flesh and blood. And these eyes kept following him at a set distance.

These eyes seemed to have merged into one, biting into his soul.

"Help, help!"

But Ah Q never uttered these words. All had turned black before his eyes, there was a buzzing in his ears, and he felt as if his whole body were being scattered like so much light dust.

As for the after-effects of the robbery, the most affected was the successful provincial candidate, because the stolen goods were never recovered. All his family lamented bitterly. Next came the Zhao household; for when the successful county candidate went into town to report the robbery, not only did he have his queue cut off by bad revolutionaries, but he had to pay a reward of twenty thousand cash into the bargain; so all the Zhao family lamented bitterly too. From that day forward they gradually assumed the air of the survivors of a fallen dynasty.

As for any discussion of the event, no question was raised in Weizhuang. Naturally all agreed that Ah Q had been a bad man, the proof being that he had been shot; for if he had not been bad, how could he have been shot? But the consensus of opinion in town was unfavourable. Most people were dissatisfied, because a shooting was not such a fine spectacle as a decapitation; and what a ridiculous culprit he had been too, to pass through so many streets without singing a single line from an opera. They had followed him for nothing.

December 1921

Translated by Yang Xianyi and Gladys Yang

About the Author

LU XUN (1881-1936), father of contemporary Chinese literature whose real name was Zhou Shuren, was born in Shaoxing, Zhejiang Province. He was not only a great writer but also a great revolutionary and thinker. He went to Japan in 1902, to study medicine before becoming engaged in literary work. He taught middle school in Hangzhou and Shaoxing after he returned to China in 1909. After the Republican Revolution of 1911, he was appointed a member of the Ministry of Education of the Nanjing Provisional Revolutionary Government and the Beijing Government. At the same time he taught at Beijing University and Beijing Women's Normal College.

In May 1918, under the pen name Lu Xun he published "A Madman's Diary", the first short story written in the vernacular in the history of modern Chinese literature, which fiercely criticizes the man-eating feudal system. Around the time of the New Culture Movement of 1919, he helped edit a progressive magazine, *New Youth*. Standing in the forefront of the anti-imperialist and anti-feudalist New Culture Movement, Lu Xun strongly opposed the bourgeois intellectuals' tendency towards compromise and capitulation.

Between 1918 and 1926, he published *Call to Arms, The Grave, Hot Air, Wandering, Wild Grass, Dawn Blossoms Plucked at Dusk, Bad Luck (I), Bad Luck (II)* and other collections of short stories, in which he showed his patriotism and revolutionary spirit. Among them, the short novel "The True Story of Ah Q" is considered one of the masterpieces of modern Chinese literature. It was in this period that Lu Xun began to embrace Marxism. In 1926 he became wanted by the government of the reactionary warlords because of his support for the Beijing students' patriotic movement and was forced to leave Beijing for Fujian to teach at Xiamen University. In January 1927, he went to Guangzhou, then the centre of revolution, to teach at Sun Yat-sen University. In April of that year, when Chiang Kai-shek betrayed the revolution, he resigned from his post in sharp protest. He arrived at Shanghai in October 1927 where he studied Marxism. After 1930 he joined the China Freedom League, China League of Left-wing Writers, China League for Civil Rights and other progressive organizations. Despite threats and suppression by the Kuomintang reactionary government, he remained active in the revolutionary literary movement to which he introduced Marxist literary theory. Under the leadership of the Chinese Communist Party and together with other revolutionary writers, he waged persistent struggles against the hack writers of the Kuomintang. He joined the anti-Japanese united front of literature and art circles after the China League of Left-wing Writers was disbanded in early 1936.

Although suffering from tuberculosis, Lu Xun worked up to the day of his death in Shanghai, on October 19, 1936.

Lu Xun wrote many essays from 1927 to 1936. These essays are short but sharp "daggers" and "spears" against the reactionary rulers. Taking Marxism as their guide, these creative essays show Lu Xun's great political foresight and dogged fighting spirit while analysing various social problems.

Lu Xun made great contributions to Chinese culture. He organized and led the Unnamed Society, Dawn Blossom Society and other progressive literary groups, and supervised the publication of the *Vast Plain*, *The Torrent*, *Sprouts*, *Translations* and other literary magazines. He showed great concern in helping young writers with their work. He also translated foreign progressive literary works and introduced to the Chinese people paintings and woodcuts from overseas. To help pass on ancient Chinese culture, he collected and collated many works of classical literature and compiled *The Brief History of Chinese Fiction* and *An Outline of the Han Dynasty Literature*.

The *Collected Works of Lu Xun* (in twenty volumes) was first published in 1938. After the founding of the People's Republic, Lu Xun's works were published under the titles of the *Collected Works of Lu Xun* (in ten volumes), the *Collected Translations by Lu Xun* (in ten volumes), the *Diary of Lu Xun* (in two volumes) and the *Collections of Lu Xun's Correspondence*. Many of Lu Xun's works have also been published under single titles. A new edition of the *Collected Works of Lu Xun* (in twenty volumes) appeared in 1981. The English edition of the *Selected Works of Lu Xun* (in four volumes) and *The Brief History of Chinese Fiction* have been published by the Foreign Languages Press, Beijing, along with some of his other works.

"The True Story of Ah Q" is a representative work of Lu Xun. Written in 1921, the story is set in the China of 1911, during the old-democratic revolution. It tells the story of the tragedy of Ah Q, a farm labourer who — having suffered a lifetime of humiliation and persecution — dreams of revolution and ends up on the execution ground. The story colourfully reflects the rural conditions in semi-feudal and semi-colonial China in which there was a situation of sharp class contradictions and the peasant masses' demand for revolution. The story analyses the character of Ah Q, whose thinking is influenced and poisoned by the feudal ruling class which exploits and oppresses him. The feudal oppression affects Ah Q to the point of a neurosis from which he cannot really be awakened and in which he indulges in "moral victories" while putting up no resistance against the evils of society. But, while revealing Ah Q's weakness of will, the author shows deep sympathy for him. The author also criticizes the weak tendency to compromise by China's national bourgeoisie in the last three chapters of the story. He expresses his hope that the peasants, victims of feudal oppression and imperialist aggression, might be aroused to rise in resistance.

Crossroads

Guo Moruo

Remorse seized him. He went back to the hostel, dragging his feet — quite unlike his usual gait: the nearer he got to the gate, the weaker he felt. His fingers were already touching the door knocker, when he hesitated and run back out of the lane.

The trees flanking the Calm Monastery Road had long shed their leaves. The pale sickly sun shed a lustreless light over the flat surface of the road, and over the uneven silhouette of the buildings. Hat in hand, he walked hurriedly under the leafless trees, his dishevelled hair ruffled by the fierce north wind, and his bloodshot eyes staring straight ahead. However, he did not notice the crowded streets, or the red-bricked, white-washed buildings which he normally saw as blood-stained rivers, intensifying his distress. All he saw was the vision of a solitary ship tossing on the bloody waves of the Yellow Sea.

"They're probably still looking back at me through the portholes of the ship," he told himself, his tears flowing copiously.

The "they" on board the ship were his not quite thirty-year-old wife and three small sons. They had just left Shanghai that morning at 8:50.

His wife, the daughter of a Japanese clergyman, married him seven years ago when he was still a poor, medical student against her parents' wishes and was therefore disowned by her family. For seven years she had toiled by his side and given birth to three sons; waiting for the time when he would graduate from medical college. They only returned to Shanghai last April. She thought that once he left college and got a job they would leave behind them forever their poverty-stricken life. However, things did not turn out as she had expected. Once in Shanghai he seemed to have thrown his ten years of medical training into the Pacific, even the tubes of his stethoscope were blocked from the lack of use. When friends in Shanghai suggested opening a joint practice he excused himself by saying he didn't have the confidence. He was offered the job of superintendent in the Red-Cross Hospital of S County, in Sichuan, but he refused it by the simple expedient of not replying to the letter. Deeply interested in literature since his schooldays, he and a few like-minded friends on his return to Shanghai published a couple of literary magazines. While this helped to take his mind off things, he also hoped that the ideas promoted in them would reform society. As regards his material life; in a country like China where literature was not highly valued, it remained as barren as a seed fallen on stony soil, without any hope of germinating roots or healthy growth. When he was a student in Japan he and his family could just get by on the government scholarship of thirty to forty dollars, but now that he was out in the world even this means of support was cut off. He rented a room in a back alley with money borrowed from friends, but although he was unperturbed, his wife was as uneasy as sitting on a bed of nails. The children were growing up and needed to be clothed, fed and educated. This worried his wife so much that she couldn't sleep at nights. She frequently argued with him and wanted to know why he refused to practise medicine.

"Practise medicine? What for? I could have become a quack without going to college. Syphilis can be cured with shots of "606", malaria with quinine, diphtheria by injections of serum, amoebic dysentery with emetine and acute arthritis with salicylate and so forth. You can count these specializations on ten fingers. It won't make any difference whether I join the legion of quacks in Shanghai who practise these cures or not. One quack more or one less is of no importance."

"What's the use of medicine: If I cure a rich man, I increase the number of days he can exploit the poor. If a poor man is cured, his life of suffering is prolonged. What's the use of medicine? I would rather starve to death than scrape a living in this sordid way."

"Medicine can eliminate parasites and bacteria, but can it destroy the social system that breeds them? The enormous skill of a doctor is expended on prescribing indigestion tablets for the rich or cutting off a poor man's legs after he has been run over by a car. After people with guns has killed or wounded thousands of people, the doctor simply applies ointment to the wounds and bandages them up. What about fraternity and humanity! No, I won't practise under false pretences."

When he was irritable he would invariably reply to his wife in this way.

"You'll have to put up with things within the system," she would say.

"Then I prefer to be a thief — at least they only rob the rich."

Whenever his wife mentioned their sons' education he would harangue at length against the current educational system; in particular, education under a capitalist system. His wife had no alternative. After living with him in Shanghai for nearly a year she was forced to go back to Japan with the children. She said that she would practise midwifery there for a few months, and then come back to Shanghai and perhaps earn a living. It was impossible for her to leave the sons behind in Shanghai — she wanted to take them back with her. She was so determined that the most he could do was to persuade her to wait until a friend who was going back to Japan could accompany her and the children on the journey.

All the previous day was spent busy buying the tickets and borrowing money for travelling expenses, and the evening was spent packing up, so it was very late when they got to bed. At half past five in the morning they set off for the Huishan Wharf in two horse-drawn carriages. The street lights were still on and Shanghai was in a dreamy slumber. When they reached the Bund along the Huangpu River, the sky in the east was just touched with gold; the insensitive sun had started its day's journey, oblivious of the parting family's tears. His sons who were born in a seafaring country had an inherent love for water and steam-boats so they cheered up as soon as they saw the ships.

"Where are they going to?"

"Some up the Yangtze River, others to foreign countries."

"Oh, we've been to that park before, haven't we? But where's the ship that's going to Japan?"

"You can't see it from here. We have to get to the Huishan Wharf which is still some distance away."

This exchange was between him and his eldest son, while the second son who was standing between his father's knees declared:

"I'm not going to go to Japan. I'll stay here with Daddy."

"No, son. You go and collect lots of golden shells from the seaside for me. I'll come to fetch you soon."

"Hmm —, collecting shells. There must be lots and lots of them left."

While chatting with his sons, he kept imagining accidents that might happen to a young mother travelling with three children and a pile of luggage to Japan trying to get on and off the boat or the bus.

"Even the clerk at the ticket office was shocked when I asked for tickets for a woman and three kids. How can I, a husband and father, be so heartless as to let them travel all by themselves? I ought to accompany them. I must do that. Ten dollars would be enough for a third-class ticket to Nagasaki. I would need thirty to forty dollars at most for a return ticket, including the cost of staying there for a few days. Yes, I ought to go back with them. I'll buy a ticket on board. That's what I will do. . . ." Then he remembered the magazines he and his friends were publishing and the articles that had to be written for each issue. With him gone, his friends would find it hard to cope; also thirty or forty dollars could keep his wife and children for at least two weeks in Japan. There's no reason why there should be an accident on the trip, as it was easier travelling in Japan than in China.

"Anyway, there is Mr. T to take care of them. I can't go. No, I can't." He turned these thoughts over and over in his mind. One moment he decided not to escort them and the next moment he changed his mind when he thought of the difficulties on the way. This lasted all the way from Annam Road to the Huishan Wharf.

All this time his wife sat silently beside him holding the year-old baby who, bewildered at first by the jolting of the carriage, soon decided that it was like his cradle and fell soundly asleep in his mother's arms.

After driving for an hour they arrived at the wharf. Anchored alongside it, on the hazy Huangpu River, was an enormous ocean liner with the word *Nagasaki* painted on its stern. Apart from the waiting stevedores, there were no other passengers in sight — his friend wasn't there either — the wharf was quiet. When their berths had been located, he was still agonized by indecision.

The children were overjoyed, scrambling onto the bunks to look through a porthole at the river, they got their sweaters caught on the nails on the wall, so that their mother had to free them. As if saying good-bye to his father, the baby opened and closed his chubby hands, cooing, and stretched out his arms to him to be lifted up. As he held him on his knees, he grabbed hold of his father's neck and jumped up and down on him with his tiny feet.

"Japanese houses are very cold. As we can afford it, don't save on charcoal." He advised his wife.

Stroking her own hands, she said as if to herself, that once back in Japan she would have to carry water, do the washing, make the fire and do the cooking, and that her hands were bound to crack and bleed.

"You must hire a maid this time. Ten dollars a month would probably be enough for one."

"Probably." Her eyes were a little red. "I've heard that since the earthquake, maids in Tokyo only ask for board and lodging. But it's different in Fukuoka, where besides wages you have to provide them with their keep. So it probably adds up to over twenty dollars."

"I'll try and think of some way to earn more money . . ." as he said this he was doubtful of his abilities to earn more. How? By selling an article? Opening a private practice? Or joining the Shanghai Zigoma and be a gangster?"

"I have some friends in Fukuoka, and I can get by with their help. Anyway, I can find a job. I'm not going there on holiday."

"But there are the kids. You can't leave them."

"I'll carry the baby on my back and the bigger ones can play by themselves on the seashore. At least it's better there than in Shanghai."

When the first gong sounded, his wife leant forward and he gave her a lingering kiss, choking back his tears, then he kissed his sons and handed the baby back to his wife. Still, Mr. T hadn't shown up. Was he merely late or had he decided to postpone his journey? He blamed himself for not calling for him on his way to the wharf. He went on deck to look.

In his hand he was still holding the ticket he had bought for Mr. T yesterday; he half hoped that he would be here and half hoped he wouldn't appear so that he would have to accompany his family to Japan. There was a crowd on the wharf, some were waving their hats, others their handkerchiefs at their friends on board ship. In the distance a horse-drawn carriage had stopped at the entrance to the wharf — hopefully it was Mr. T — it

was him! He greeted him loudly and introduced him to his wife
and children. Just then, the gong sounded the second time.

"What am I to do?" he thought. "Buy a ticket on board or
go back on shore?" He heard his wife say:

"You'll feel less harassed when we're gone. You can concentrate on writing. It's better to write longer works. Don't
worry about us over there. We'll be back in a few months.
Come and look at the cherry blossoms when they bloom so that
you can relax a little."

These words fell suddenly on his ears like music from Heav-
en. This was the same sweet musical voice he had heard seven
years ago when they first fell in love. He was elated.

"Thank you, my sweetheart, my Beatrice. Longer works?
Yes, it's better to write longer works. Dante wrote *Divina* for
his love, and I'll write a long work for you so that you'll live
forever. Ava Maria, you are the eternal woman. . . ." He decided to stay in Shanghai. Shaking hands with Mr. T, he again
asked him to help his wife on the journey. Then he walked decisively out of the cabin, refusing to allow his wife to go on
deck so that the children would not see him leave and cry.

The siren blew and the Huangpu River stirred! The ship
was already slowly nosing it's way out to sea. He left the wharf
when he could no longer see Mr. T on the deck.

"Yes, a long work, I must work out something in the next
month or two. I know what the title should be: *The Divine
Light*. Wasn't there a divine light between her brows when I
first met her seven years ago? Ava Maria, the eternal woman,
my Beatrice, and the Divine Light." As he was boarding the
trolley bus, he blew a few surreptitious kisses towards the
Huangpu River.

The long ride on the trolley bus calmed him down and gave
him time to think. He thought of his insecure life and his literary achievements in recent years. "Ah, I've been too equivocal
in my life. My ideals can't be realized and what has been
realized are not my ideals. I've muddled along, frittering away

my best years. What have I achieved in the past ten years? It's obvious that I've given up medicine. I wrote some stories and poems when I was in the mood, but what do they amount to? What skill have I acquired that I can be proud of and which of the things I have written can I feel happy about? Oh, disgraceful, yet I compare myself with Dante. I'm a braggart, shame on me. Who am I?" It seemed as if he had fallen from the most radiant star into a dark abyss. His wife's encouragement became an onerous burden while his promise to her seemed impossible. His head felt heavy and his heart was burning. If the trolley bus had been empty he would have sobbed his heart out.

For years he had been overwhelmed by his own inadequacies. The more famous foreign works he read, the more he realized how hopelessly incompetent he was. His life was too ordinary and he couldn't express himself eloquently enough. Frustrated and humiliated, he seemed unable to write anything, and what he had written seemed to be worthless — half-baked literary criticisms and translations which were poor substitutes for the original.

"What do they amount to? Both my sympathizers and critics have called me a genius, but what kind of genius am I? Oh, I ought to be ashamed of myself, and I have brazenly pretended to be virtuous and superior. Now I can't even provide for my wife and sons, leaving them to fend for themselves. Why do I deceive myself and others? I'm no good to anyone."

He remembered one of John Davidson's poems about a destitute musician who, clasping the cold and wasted body of his loving wife, wailed:

> We drop into oblivion,
> And nourish some suburban sod.
> My work, this woman, this my son,
> And now no more: there is no God.

He recited this poem to the rattle of the trolley bus as if the words came from his own heart. But on reflection he realized

that he was not really like the musician whose compositions were
ignored and who was justified in complaining against the world
and against God. What right did he have? How could he
grumble against the world and against God for sending his wife
and sons away? The musician died mourning his wife, whereas
he and his wife have voluntarily gone their own way, she, crossing the troubled sea and he, dreaming of the unattainable. Again
he regretted not buying a ticket on the ship and accompanying
them to Japan.

"Why haven't I gone to share their life of hardship? I'm
selfish and irresponsible."

Remorse seized him. The clattering trolley bus took him
through the bright throbbing streets, while he remained silent
as the grove. He intended to go back to his hostel, but his room
was eerie, perhaps something more ominous than death lurked
there. He turned and run out of the lane and wandered under
the trees flanking the Calm Monastery Road, his bloodshot
eyes staring straight ahead. He was oblivious of the hooting and
spluttering cars. He stopped at the corner of the Cangzhou
Villa, and gazed at the red lights which his sons loved to watch
when they took a walk here; then he crossed Ximo Road and
walked south towards Fuxu Road until he was near the vicinity
of Shengzhi University. One evening late last summer, while he
and his sons were walking here they had seen a sparrow fall off
a plane tree, and the boys had chased and caught the bird. He
remembered he wrote a poem at the time:

> Lonely glimmers the golden sickle
> While we roam under the roadside trees.
> Breezes cool the lingering heat
> Of a burning evening sun.
> A sparrow falling off the boughs
> Sadly chirping, trying to flee
> From my pursuing sons' outstretched arms.
> A sad note echoes in my heart.

"Sons, we're like the nestless bird
Drifting to an alien gloomy world.
Where can we go
To escape catapults and stones?"
Strangers to life's bitterness
My smiling sons chase it with arms outstretched.
Forget my grief and be a child again.
But why do cicadas shrill "death — death—"
       incessantly?

Leaning on a tree he compared his former impecunious family
life with the present loneliness of separation, and couldn't hold
back his tears. He felt like a lonely soul in a hostile world when
he recalled all the abusive articles against him in the Nanjing
and Shanghai newspapers. Suddenly from under the wheels of
every car there seemed to lurk a weary smiling face, a dead body
on the street, its blood, intestines and brain splattered the dust,
the eyes fallen out of its sockets. "Yes, that would be a quick
end: let my enemies gloat over the sight, but I wouldn't wake up
or care. But how sad my wife and sons would feel and how disappointed my friends would be. She left with the children in
order to lighten my load, encouraging me to write longer works.
The magazines have to be supplied with articles every week like
fledglings waiting to be fed. Can I die now? No, I can't. I am
overwrought today. Ten years ago when I arrived at Japan I
was a living corpse until my wife instilled new life into me.
Besides, I haven't really frittered my life away these past few
years and it isn't the time yet for me to blow myself up. My
wife and sons must have crossed the Yellow Sea by now. So go
home and put the Divine Light into words within the next month
or so."

He walked home slowly and thought about how he had run
away to Japan from a marriage forced on him by his family,
how he didn't care about anything until he fell in love with his
present wife and regained his self-confidence through her. When

he reached the hostel, the clock in the hall pointed to just past one o'clock. The kitchen maid asked whether he wanted anything to eat. He shook his head and went upstairs to his room. When he opened the door, a cold blast hit him on the face and he winced. He stood in the middle of the room; the sight of the two beds, one of which was bare, the other still had on it the quilts he used, made his eyes fill with tears and he flopped into a wicker chair by the desk as if pushed into it. In the belief that only work could dispel his loneliness, he opened one of the drawers and found nothing but a few torn pages from his sons' *Children's Pictorial* and a doll minus its legs. These bits of rubbish suddenly became so precious that he wanted to keep them safe so he opened a wicker suitcase; in it he noticed a cotton-padded jacket his wife used to wear. He buried his face in it; the faint perfume from her body pained him physically. Closing the lid of the suitcase, he sat at the desk, spread a piece of paper out in front of him, soaked his brush with ink and wrote *The Divine Light* on it. There he stopped. How should he begin: starting from the very beginning like writing history or with a description of the setting like a play? Using flashback or straight narrative. From the point of view of one character or several? In the first or third person? Where should he begin in describing the last ten years of his life? With his mind in a turmoil, he bent his head and rested it in his right hand, deep in thought, but it was no use. There was no flash of inspiration from his tired, confused brain which seemed as dull as a stone lamp in a ruined monastery. His hearing, however, was extremely sharp, his neighbour's footsteps climbing the stairs sounded just like his wife's, and the crying of other people's babies sounded exactly the same as that of his own baby's. But where were his wife and sons? They must have crossed the Yellow Sea by now.

"Please, let them arrive safely at Fukuoka tomorrow," he prayed, throwing the brush aside. "My brain just won't function today!" He tore off his jacket and flopped onto the bed,

with the clattering of the horse's hoofs, the ship's siren, the squelching of a weighing anchor all sounding in his ears. And before his eyes flashed the images of the Virgin Mary holding the baby Jesus, a young woman carrying a broken water jar, the Yellow Sea, shells, a nestless sparrow, Beatrice, a cotton-padded jacket and the Divine Light.

A cold light seeped into the empty room and his exhausted brain slowly lost consciousness.

March 1924
Translated by Cheng Wen

About the Author

GUO MORUO (1892-1978), born in Sichuan, was a poet, historian, archaeologist, paleographer, political activist and fighter in the international peace movement. In his youth he studied in Japan. On his return in 1921 he began his literary career and founded the well-known literary group, "The Creation Society." The songs in his two collections of poems *The Goddess* and *Starry Sky* and his play *Three Women in Revolt* inspired many young people to take part in the revolutionary struggle.

During the Northern Expeditionary War of 1926-27, Guo Moruo was deputy director of the political department of the national revolutionary army. In 1927, when Chiang Kai-shek's betrayal of the Revolution became apparent, he openly exposed Chiang's crimes in the press. He participated in the Nanchang Uprising of August 1927, and after its failure fled to Japan, where he studied ancient Chinese history. His *Studies in Ancient Chinese Society* is the first historical study by a Chinese scholar from a Marxist view. He also made a great contribution to the study of ancient Chinese through his work on oracle bones and bronze inscriptions.

After the outbreak of the War of Resistance Against Japanese Aggression in 1937, he returned home to join in the war effort. During the war, he became an outstanding standard-bearer of progressive artists and writers while he worked in the Kuomintang-controlled area. The production of his play *Qu Yuan*, written in 1942, was an important historical event, giving forceful expression to the wrath of the people in the Kuomintang-controlled territory at that time.

Guo Moruo's many literary and political writings and the stirring speeches he made at various meetings during and after the war, won him the love of the people and the hate of the Kuomintang reactionaries. Finally in 1947, he was forced to take refuge in Hong Kong where he continued to write significant articles on the study of ancient Chinese society and the history of political thought. These essays were later published in two volumes, *Ten Critiques* and *The Bronze Age*.

After the founding of the People's Republic of China in 1949, he continued to engage in literary creative work and academic study and many of his historical plays and poems were published. *The Age of Slave System* was greatly esteemed among historians for his new idea of separating the society of the slave system and the feudal system in Chinese history.

"Crossroads" is one part of his early novel, *Wandering Trilogy*, which tells how a bourgeois intellectual recognizes step by step the dreadful face of the old society.

In 1949, he was elected Vice-Chairman of the National Committee of the Chinese People's Political Consultative Conference, Vice-Premier, Chairman of the Committee of Cultural and Educational Affairs of the Government, and President of Academia Sinica. He participated in the world peace congresses in 1949 and 1950. At the second congress he was elected a member of the World Peace Council and has since taken an active part in all the work of the World Peace Council. In 1952 he was honoured with an award of the International Stalin Prize for the Promotion of Peace Among Nations.

How Mr. Pan Weathered the Storm

Ye Shengtao

I

The station was crowded with people each of them pre-occupied with his own problems and looking not quite his usual self. The porters, hands thrust into the pockets of their numbered uniforms, stood motionless as if they had fallen asleep on their feet. They knew they still had a long wait ahead; it was not yet time for the tips they were hoping to get so there was no point in looking energetic at this moment. The oppressive atmosphere made breathing somewhat difficult. It looked like rain. The lights which had been turned on for some time were dimmer than usual and made everything appear as if in a fog.

A notice on the blackboard announced that the incoming express from the west was going to be four hours late. This notice had been read and reread several hours ago and now, like those old, torn theatre bills left to flutter in the wind, could no longer draw a single glance from anyone. Since such notices had been posted for practically every incoming train this week, they had become the thing to be expected.

This train which had been on the mind of so many people finally appeared. The sombre station became a hive of activity. We shall not go into the relief of the travellers who had reached their journey's end, the joy of those waiting for them, or the tips received by the porters. We are concerned only with a certain Mr. Pan who had come from a nearby small town, Rangli. Before the train chugged into the station, he had managed to arrange everything to his satisfaction: He was at the head of his small family, his right hand holding a black leather bag and his left leading his six-year-old son. The child's other hand held on to his eight-year-old brother who in turn held his mother's hand. Mr. Pan said he would not be able to take care of them all unless they held together like this. For with hands linked, they could wriggle through like a snake wherever they wanted to go. He told his family again and again to lock their hands tightly; they were not to let go whatever happened. Lest the others should forget, he kept swinging his left hand as a reminder to be passed down the line.

It was good of course to form a line, yet not without disadvantages too. As the train slowed to a stop all the passengers with their luggage surged towards the door. In this exigency, the line formed by Mr. Pan and his family suffered for its length. Using his black leather bag to clear the way, he had pushed on vigorously with his chest and stomach till he was only two windows away from the door. But his six-year-old son was still four windows away, wedged tightly in between other passengers and the wooden seats. Arms stretching out in two directions and pulled vigorously from both ends, the child felt that his limbs would soon be torn off. "Oh, my arms, my arms!" he wailed in desperation.

The other passengers were not aware that there was a child wedged in between their legs until his cries reached their ears. A closer look revealed that the family of four was linked in a long line with hands tightly locked.

"Let go at once," ordered one passenger. "Or else you'll be pulling the child apart."

"What's this! Why doesn't the man carry the child?" muttered another, his tone full of scorn, as he edged his own way towards the door.

"No," Mr. Pan disagreed with them. There were good reasons for holding on together. He realized, however, on second thought that not everyone was intelligent enough to see these reasons and it was a waste of breath to argue with them. But the six-year-old was still yelling, "My arms, my arms!" Since Mr. Pan could see no way either to advance or to turn back, he had to be the first to violate his own admonition and let go of the child's hand. "Keep your eyes on me, don't lose sight of me," he ordered, flustered and worried.

The train stopped with a clang and a jerk. A number of people shot out of the carriage door and Mr. Pan felt the pressure from the front suddenly relax but the pushing from behind gained in momentum so that his legs carried him forward without any effort on his part. He meant to turn to rally his small forces but finding that impossible merely shouted at the backs of the heads before him, "Follow close behind me! Follow me!"

Somehow or other he too shot out of the door. Turning round quickly, he saw that his wife and sons were not behind him; they were still squeezed in somewhere in the train. Waiting by the door seemed to him the best possible solution. Another hundred or so passengers alighted before the screwed up, tearful face of his younger son appeared under the lamplight. Mr. Pan hurried up and, after being swept back several times by alighting passengers, picked up his son in his left arm and set him down on the platform. Another short wait and Mrs. Pan and the eight-year-old emerged. Panting heavily and uttering groans of pain, she turned her mournful gaze to her husband's face, like a child seeking consolation.

Mr. Pan was after all a man with some presence of mind. Now that his forces had been reassembled he issued another order, "We must link hands again. See what a crowd there is on the platform and look at that bottle-neck at the exit. If we don't hold on together we're bound to lose each other."

The six-year-old had had enough. Hugging his father's legs, he said, "Carry me, daddy."

"You little nuisance!" Mr. Pan was exasperated, but he restrained himself and, stooping down, picked up the child. He told his older son to hold on to the tail of his long gown with one hand and on to Mrs. Pan with the other.

Never before had Mrs. Pan been through an ordeal like this. The prospect of an even greater crush was more than she could bear after the effort of getting off the train. "If I had known it was going to be like this," she grumbled, "I'd have stayed at home and waited for death rather than come out and be a refugee."

"What's the use of regretting?" Mr. Pan's annoyance was tinged with sympathy. "Now that we're here, why regret? Besides, at least we're safe here. Let's go now. Mind your steps!" And all four together, they staggered into the crowd.

A frantic rush and Mr. Pan emerged as if from a dream through the narrow exit guarded by the ticket collector. Like a drop of water in a torrent, he had no alternative but to be swept along by the multitude around him, his feet barely touching the ground. In a moment he had cleared the wire fence of the railway station, stepped across the tramway and arrived on the cement pavement of the street outside. Turning round hurriedly, he saw countless faces pale in the lamplight and numerous bags and bundles rolling in his direction. Suddenly he realized that the little hand that had been clutching the tail of his long gown was no longer there; he had no idea when it had let go. An indescribable sorrow filled his heart and he automatically turned his head round. But there was no sign of his wife and son. He felt he had lost his family. The lights and figures round him began to swim as tears filled his eyes.

Fortunately the child in his arm had sharp eyes. "Mama, there she is," he pointed. He had spied and recognized the fringe over his mother's brows.

Mr. Pan was overjoyed. He first rubbed his eyes on the

child's clothes before he looked in the direction pointed out for he hardly dared to believe the good news. After a slight search, he saw his wife darting left and right in the crowd, her hands held protectively round their older son. They were still on the other side of the tramway. "Ada!" he hailed and hurrying over brought them back to where he had been standing on the pavement. Putting down the six-year-old at last, he breathed a sigh of relief. "Now, all's well!" he said, mopping his face. Indeed all was well, for once they crossed that wire fencing* they were insured against war, fire and robbery. Besides, he had found his lost son and wife. It was as if from the jaws of disaster he had rescued four lives and one black bag. All was well, indeed. Authoritatively, Mr. Pan shouted, "Rickshaw!" Several rickshaw men pulled up clamouring to know where he wanted to go. He raised his head slightly as if to add dignity to his words and waved two fingers, "Only two, we want only two." Then, having given the matter some thought, he continued, "Ten coppers. Who'll go to Fourth Avenue for ten coppers?" This ought to show them he knew his way around in Shanghai.

After a fairly long argument they got two rickshaws for twelve coppers apiece. Mrs. Pan got into one with the older boy and Mr. Pan climbed into the other with the younger child and the black bag.

The outstretched arm of an Indian policeman shouldering a gun blocked the way just as the rickshaw man straightened up to go. This fearful apparition made the child on Mr. Pan's knee hide his head in fright.

"There's nothing to be afraid of," said his father. "That's only an Indian policeman. Look at his handsome red turban. We have to come here because we don't have policemen like him at home. He'll use his gun to protect us. His beard is interesting, look at it, like that of the arhats in the temples."

The child was too frightened to look even at a beard like

---

* Meaning that they have entered the foreign settlement.

that of an arhat. Only when the clanging of a tram caught his attention did he peep out and find that a very brightly lit room had swept past in a flash. On the other side of the road were also brightly lit houses full of dazzling objects. He finally raised his face from his father's chest.

When they reached Fourth Avenue they asked for a room at half a dozen hotels all of which had a big sign with the words "House Full". One glance was enough to assure them that it was no use trying to coax the manager into letting them have a room because temporary beds had been set up even in the lounge. Obviously the hotels were really full. At last, at one hotel they were met by a clerk who drawled lazily, "Want a room?"

"Yes, we want a room. Have you got one?" A ray of hope shot through Mr. Pan making him feel he had reached haven.

"We do have one. The last occupant vacated it only a moment ago. He has rented a house for himself. If you had come a few minutes later, it would have been snapped up."

"Let us have that room." Mr. Pan put his younger son down and turned back to help his wife and older son alight. "We are in luck after all," he told them. "We've finally got a room." When it came to paying off the rickshaws he generously offered one copper more than the agreed fee. It was his belief that if you treated others well when luck was with you, your luck would continue. But the rickshaw men turned out to be very ungrateful. They declared that they had spent a great deal of time taking them from one hotel to another so Mr. Pan must pay them five coppers extra each. In the end, the hotel attendant came out to mediate and Mr. Pan parted with four extra coppers.

The room was on the ground floor. Besides a bed, a lamp, a table and two chairs, it contained nothing but smoke. When Mr. Pan took his family inside, his nostrils were immediately assailed by the pungent odour of fried fish mixed with the stink of urine. "What a foul smell!" Mr. Pan muttered with annoyance. From next door came the sizzling of food frying in

hot oil, the kitchen was obviously only a wall away. However unpleasant the stench, it was better than getting shot at or sleeping without a roof, Mr. Pan decided, immediately feeling better. He settled himself comfortably in one of the chairs.

"Want some supper?" asked the hotel attendant putting down the black bag.

"I want ham soup with my rice," announced the younger child sucking his fingers.

His mother gave him a severe look. "Ham soup with rice indeed! We are refugees, lucky to have anything at all to eat. How can you ask for this or that!"

The older boy was no better than his brother. "Now that we're in Shanghai," he begged his father, "I want to try some European food."

Mrs. Pan was furious now. Rounding on her first-born, she said scathingly, "The idea! You deserve to have nothing to eat. You should simply starve. . . ."

Mr. Pan was embarrassed. "Children don't know what they're talking about," he said, trying to smooth things over. He told the attendant, "We had something on the train. Just bring us two orders of fried rice and eggs."

The waiter nodded in a non-committal way and left. He had no sooner got out of the door than Mr. Pan called him back. "Bring me a catty of Shaoxing wine and ten cents of smoked fish."

When the sound of the attendant's footsteps died away, Mr. Pan, looking relieved and uplifted, said to his wife, "Now we ought to relax a little and have a drink. Just think, we got away from a place fraught with danger to this haven where no harm can come to us. This is something to celebrate. Just now you two were lost and I had a hard time finding you. I was nearly frantic with worry. But A'er was sharp." Mr. Pan pulled his son closer and gently stroked his head. "He spied you at once and I was able to find you. That's another thing to celebrate. Everything's wonderful so let's relax and enjoy a few cups." Beaming with pleasure, he raised an imaginary cup to his lips.

His wife did not reply. She was thinking of home. True, they had packed their valuables away and deposited them for safe-keeping in a church, but there were still a number of things left in the house. She was not at all sure whether Wang, the maid, was reliable. She also wondered whether their poor neighbours knew that her whole family was away with only the maid to watch over the household. She wondered whether the maid would remember to close all the doors and windows at night. She also remembered her three fat hens in the backyard, the pair of trousers she was working on for her younger son, the bowl of braised duck in the kitchen. . . . These considerations, flashing through her mind, made her extremely uncomfortable. "I wonder what sort of mess they'll make of the place," she sighed.

A feeling of disappointment swept over the children. Vaguely they sensed that this Shanghai where they had just arrived was not as interesting and fascinating as that Shanghai they had heard so much about from their parents.

Raindrops drifted in through the window. "It's really raining. Lucky it didn't start any earlier," cried Mr. Pan standing up to close the window. Suddenly he caught sight of the hotel notice on the wall which had been half hidden by the opened window. Remembering a most important thing, he fixed his eyes unblinkingly on the piece of paper.

"My, my! Two dollars, no less," was his startled cry and he turned round to look significantly into his wife's eyes, gasping at what he had discovered.

2

When the next day dawned, the hotel attendants were still curled up in deep slumber on a few benches put together in the hallway. The narrow skylight did not let in much light. Dim yellow lamps were still burning in several hotel rooms. But Mr. and Mrs. Pan were already talking things over. The two boys, hoping that today's Shanghai would turn out better than the Shanghai of yesterday, had been awake for some time. Their parents asked them to sleep a little longer so they were still in bed tickling each other.

"I think you'd better not go back," said Mrs. Pan, very worried. "How can you be sure what they say in the papers is true? Since we went through so much difficulty to get away, there's hardly any sense in your going back right away."

"Actually, I had some idea that this might happen. Director Gu was never one to let things go. 'Since there's no fighting here, the schools must naturally start as usual.' Yes, that sounds like him all right. I know this correspondent too. He happens to work in the Bureau of Education. So, there's no question about the authenticity of his report. I'll simply have to go back."

"Don't you know it's dangerous going back?" Mrs. Pan's tone was quite tragic. "Maybe in two or three days they'll be fighting in our parts. Suppose you went back and got the school started, do you think the students will come to school? Besides, even if the fighting doesn't spread to our parts, you'll have a good answer for the director of education if he wants to know why you didn't start school. You have only to ask him: What's more important, the school or human lives? He is not immortal himself, he could hardly blame you for not going back."

"You don't understand," said Mr. Pan with some contempt. "This is the kind of argument that only silly women like you, safe at home or in bed, can use. You don't expect me to go and say something like that? Now, don't try to stop me." His tone had become quite conciliatory. "For back I must go. There won't be the least danger. I know how to keep out of harm's way. Besides," Mr. Pan smiled at his own diplomacy, "weren't you worried just now about the things we left at home? Once I'm home I'll be able to keep an eye on them so you can stay here without worrying. When things settle down a bit I'll come promptly to fetch you and the boys home."

Mrs. Pan knew now there was absolutely no way to prevent her husband from going back. It would be nice to have him at home and keeping an eye on things but, in these uncertain times, once he left he would be like a pearl cast into the sea, she might never get him back. The sorrows of parting and fear of death overwhelmed her. Tears stung her eyelids and came so near to trickling out that she dared not even glance at her husband. It struck her at once that tears at this moment were a bad omen, nothing tragic had happened and she should not be weeping. Holding back her tears with an effort, more to comfort herself than in real earnest she said, "Then, just go back and see how things are. If the Bureau of Education doesn't say anything about starting the school according to schedule you just come right back, catching the afternoon train if you can and if not the early train the next morning. You see," here she could no longer restrain herself and one tear dropped on the back of her hand, to be hastily brushed away — "I worry about you so!"

Mr. Pan was feeling very vexed himself. Since the director of education wanted the schools to start as usual, he himself had no reason whatever to insist that they should remain closed. It followed naturally that he should go back. But how could he not worry about his family here? He noticed the look of gentle sorrow on his wife's face. It seemed heartless to leave a woman with two young children, so weak and helpless, without anyone to rely on. How could he be sure nothing untoward would happen to them. All this made him angry and disturbed. He was angry at those sending troops out to fight this army or that, angry at the director of education who talked about starting school without delay, angry at himself for not having a grown-up son who might have helped him out.

Nevertheless, he was not a woman, he had to look ahead. He knew that going back was the right thing to do. Forgetting his anger and without showing a trace of his inner disturbance, he nodded to show that he agreed with her. "If I find that the director has no intention of starting the schools, I'll do as you say and come back by the afternoon train," he said soothingly.

The children had overheard this last remark. The younger boy, his head half buried in the pillow, lisped babyishly, "I wanna go back too."

"Mama and daddy and I are going back and we'll leave you here all by yourself," teased the older boy, making a face.

The younger boy started to wail at the top of his voice, rubbing his eyes vigorously although there was not a single tear in them.

"You will both stay here with mama," said Mr. Pan raising his voice. "No more nonsense now. Get dressed and ready for breakfast." After a few more words with his wife, Mr. Pan set out for the station.

On the way, he heard passers-by commenting on the fact that trains were no longer running. "If the trains have stopped that settles the question for me. Even if they decide to fire me for staying away, I can't help it." The news gave him a let-down feeling. But if his luck held, it might prove no more than a rumour. To find out the true situation he was anxious that the rickshaw man should go faster.

His luck turned out to be good. There was no sign posted at the station saying that trains were suspended. On the black-board a notice declared that the night train would be four hours late. It was still not in yet. The ticket window was far from crowded. From time to time one or two people stepped up to buy tickets. The crowd in the station was made up half of peo-ple awaiting travellers, half of spectators. Some carried cameras and were waiting to snap the bustle accompanying the arrival of the night train so that the pictures could be used in some future "History of Wars and Changes". The baggage room was filled with an assortment of bags and cases piled so high that they nearly touched the ceiling.

He felt both relieved and depressed. After a slight hesitation he bought himself a third-class ticket and boarded the train. The clear sunlight made the whole compartment bright but not hot. There were plenty of empty seats. Had he wanted to, he could have lain down. He thought, "This is unusual. If I were in a better mood this could have been a very pleasant trip."

The train was held up at various stops to give right of way to troop trains. By the time he got into Rangli, it was past three in the afternoon. Mr. Pan hurried home and found his gate tightly closed. The tension in his heart eased a little for this precaution was one thing he had tried very hard to impress on Wang, the maid, before he left.

He had to knock a number of times before the maid appeared. She exclaimed in surprise at sight of Mr. Pan, "Is that you back, sir? Is there no need to run away now?"

Mr. Pan muttered a vague answer as he rushed in and looked around. Then he unlocked the door to his room, strode in and examined it with care. No change. There was no change at all. Everything was as he had left it the day before. His heart which had been palpitating relaxed somewhat but he was not yet fully assured. He locked the room again and turned to go. "See that the gate's properly locked," he told the maid.

The maid was very puzzled. Having closed the gate, she went in and began to wonder. The master and mistress must still be somewhere in town. Perhaps they were afraid she might want to go with them and had only pretended to run away to Shanghai. "Otherwise, why is the master back so soon? The mistress and the boys are not with him. Where can they be hiding themselves? But why didn't they want me with them? Of course, it's because they didn't have room for so many. They are probably in that red building belonging to the foreigner. Those soldiers are all in the know; they will not touch that red building even when they are fighting. Actually they could have told me the truth for I wouldn't have been keen on going even if they had asked me. I'm not a bit frightened. Even if fighting breaks out here, my burial costume has been ready a long time." She saw in her mind's eye the beautiful embroidered burial shoes presented to her by her niece and felt sure these would make the King of Hell treat her with respect when she went to the nether world. This reflection gave her a subtle pleasure which kept her mind off the question of where her master and mistress were.

Mr. Pan went to see the correspondent who was a member of the Bureau of Education to ask whether the director really intended the schools to start as usual. "But certainly," the man answered. "He also said some teachers were so busy getting themselves out of harm's way they quite neglected their duty. It just showed they were unworthy to work in the field of education and this was a good chance to eliminate some of them." This announcement made Mr. Pan sit up to take notice. At once he congratulated himself on his wisdom in coming back from Shanghai. He made straight for the school, picked up a writing brush and drafted a circular to the parents of the students. War and fighting might be worrisome, he stated, but the education of young people was like food and clothing which could not be dispensed with for a single day. Now that the summer holidays were over, the school would start as usual. In the time of the great war in Europe, a net was spread in the air to prevent bombing so that teaching might continue uninterrupted. This kind of heroism, the notice went on, should not go unrivalled. It was to be hoped that the parents would understand, and in this spirit would send their children to school as if nothing had happened. All this was in the interest of both the school and the students and also for the honour of the town and the country.

After reading the draft three times, he was finally satisfied that there was nothing more he could add. When the director of education saw this circular the least he could expect was the remark, "He thinks like me." In a mood of complacency, Mr. Pan cut the stencil himself and mimeographed more than a hundred copies which he dispatched through the school janitor. Now that he had done his duty by his work he let his mind return to his private affairs. Since the school must start, he could hardly go to Shanghai again. But his wife and children would have a hard time all by themselves in the hotel. There was nothing he could do about that, he must just tell them to be careful and remain there without worrying. He used what ink there was left after drafting his circular to write a letter to his wife.

The next day in the tea-house he got authentic news that the railway was cut. His heart sank. Somehow, his beloved wife and two sons seemed to have drifted away on the wind to a distant land, out of his reach. In a sad state of mind, he strolled to the school where the janitor reported on his mission the day before. "When I took the circular around I found more than twenty households with doors tightly locked and no one round to answer my knocking. I had to slip the circular in through a slit in the door. About thirty households had only servants at home; the masters had run away to Shanghai taking their children with them, of course. No one knew when they'd be back for school. The rest all took the circular but a few said since they were not sure how long they'd be alive, the question of schooling had better wait for the time being."

"I see," said Mr. Pan, his mind not on these matters at all but troubled by gloomier thoughts. After a cigarette, he reached a decision. He went to the branch office of the Red Cross Society.

He proclaimed himself willing to become a member of the Red Cross and paid his fees. He said his school had fairly spacious premises and he wanted the Red Cross to use it as a home for women refugees in case of emergency. Such a charitable offer was of course warmly accepted. Besides, Mr. Pan was a well-known and respected figure in the town. The branch office gave him a Red Cross banner to be hoisted up at the school entrance and a Red Cross badge to show that he was a member of that organization.

Mr. Pan held the flag and badge in his hands as if they were a talisman, a guarantee of life and security. A mysterious sense of satisfaction stole into his heart. "Everything is safe now. But. . . ." He turned back to the man in the branch office with a smile. "Give me an extra banner and a few more badges, will you?" His reason was that the school had a back door and the badge was so small he might easily lose it so it was better to have a few to spare.

"This isn't something you can eat," said the Red Cross man jokingly, "and you can hardly use it as a plaything! Even if you take more than one badge, you're still only a member, so why ask for more than one?" But in the end he gave Mr. Pan a few spare ones to make him happy.

Both Red Cross banners were soon fluttering in the light breeze of early autumn but neither of them was near the school's back entrance. The second banner had been placed over Mr. Pan's own door. One Red Cross badge glittered with the solemn light of charity on Mr. Pan's lapel, giving its wearer a new kind of courage. As for the rest, these were kept with care, wrapped in paper, in the pocket of Mr. Pan's shirt. "One is for her," he thought, "one is for Ada and the other for the little one." Although they were still in distant Shanghai, out of his reach, the badges were a sort of double insurance for their safety which should give them a new courage too.

3

The two armies opened fire at Bizhuang.

Very few households in Rangli kept their doors open; the shops naturally all remained closed. Soldiers marched past in the streets frequently. They would soon be going to the front and felt that they were endowed with the highest authority; nothing was of any account in their eyes. They could trample whatever they liked underfoot. This was how the press-gang started. To prevent those forced into the army from running away, the conscripts were bound and marched along in a line with soldiers escorting them. Thus it came about that people were afraid of going out on the streets. When it was absolutely necessary to leave their houses, they went by small paths and byways. Even people, like Mr. Pan, who were armed with Red Cross badges, were rather wary and dared not strut about openly. The streets of Rangli seemed quiet and very desolate.

For several days now, the Shanghai papers had not come. The local army headquarters, however, sometimes posted battle news which usually said that the enemy had been routed and our troops had advanced several li. When a fresh bulletin appeared on the street corner, a small group would gather slowly to read it carefully. They were not altogether convinced by what they read for they felt there were many things unsaid. They would disperse with a feeling of foreboding, their brows still tightly knit.

Mr. Pan had been downcast for the last few days. He worried most about his absent wife and children of whom he had no news. It seemed he might never be able to get in touch with them again. And then there was the question of his own safety. "It's only a march of a hundred li or so from Bizhuang. Although the Red Cross badge may serve some purpose, nobody ever wrote me a guarantee, so who can I ask for compensation if it turns out to be useless after all? Bullets, shells, robbers and fire are no laughing matter. I'll have to make more inquiries and find some other means to ensure my safety." So he asked here and there for news about the front and was sure there was a grain of truth in whatever news he got that was different from the current rumour. He then calculated its effect on his own interest. The sight of anyone rushing along the street with a look of panic would startle him for he was sure the man had learned some reliable but fearful news. Only the fact the man was a complete stranger prevented Mr. Pan from accosting and questioning him.

The Red Cross sent people to the front to look after the wounded; some of them came back frequently in army transports. The Red Cross was naturally the most reliable source of news. Although Mr. Pan belonged to the Red Cross he did not often go there for news for he was ashamed to admit his fear in public. Nevertheless, the Red Cross was a source of reliable information and it would be foolish to ask for news elsewhere. The result was Mr. Pan went at dusk every day to the house of Wu, a man who worked in the Red Cross office. Wu would tell him there was no news or that this side was doing all right at the front, after which Mr. Pan would go home with a sigh of relief.

One evening Mr. Pan went again to Wu's house. He had to wait a long time before Wu came back.

"Nothing new, eh?" asked Mr. Pan eagerly. "According to the bulletin, we launched a general offensive yesterday."

"Bad," said Wu looking worried and toying with his moustache.

"What!" Mr. Pan's heart skipped a beat and he felt trapped.

As if afraid of being overheard, Wu answered in a low voice, "The reliable news is that Zhengan, a town eight li from Bizhuang, fell to the other side this morning."

Mr. Pan uttered one desperate cry, paused for a second or so and turned to leave, muttering as he went, "I'm going."

The street lamps seemed particularly dim that evening. Mr. Pan felt as if he were being chased from behind. Frightened and worried, he stumbled home as quickly as he could and told the maid, "You lock the doors and go to sleep. I'll be busy tonight and will not come back for the night." He saw there was an old padded silk gown in the wardrobe; they had forgotten to pack it in the suitcases which had been deposited for safe-keeping. It would be a pity to lose it. There were also a few of the boys' lined cotton tunics. A close scrutiny showed that they were still wearable. There was also an old silk skirt which his wife would probably be loath to part with. He tied them all together and went out with his bundle.

"Rickshaw! The red building in Fuxing Lane. Ten cents."

"Whoever heard of ten cents?" drawled the rickshaw man. "How many rickshaws are out these days! Who would be out here risking his life for a few cents unless he needed them to keep alive? Thirty cents. Take it or leave it."

"Thirty cents then." Mr. Pan hurried over and stepped into the rickshaw. "But you must also do as I ask, go faster."

"Hey, Mr. Pan, where are you going?" a colleague by the name of Huang saw him and called out.

"Uh, Mr. . . . over there. . . ." Mr. Pan in his panic was not quite sure who had spoken to him. Suddenly he realized it would be a waste of breath to answer for the rickshaw was going too fast to allow the other to chase after him to demand an answer. He swallowed the rest of his words.

The red building was full of people most of whom had moved in ten days ago. Children cried and people talked, lights were lit in many rooms so that there was even an atmosphere of cheer and bustle. "There is no vacant room here," his host told Mr. Pan. "But since all your things are here I can hardly turn you away. Just now, several others arrived unexpectedly too, and as I could not refuse them I've put them in a side room ordinarily used as a kitchen. I'll go and see if they couldn't take in one more."

"Oh, yes, surely they can take in one more." Mr. Pan felt comforted. "Besides, at a time like this, I don't intend to sleep through the night; a place to sit would be just fine."

When he stepped into the side room, his bundle on one arm, he thought at first that all this fear and panic were giving him hallucinations. He closed his eyes and opened them again but what he saw did not change. There, sitting by the window with a thick moustache twitching over his upper lip as he talked to someone opposite him, was no other than the director of the Bureau of Education.

Mr. Pan hesitated, the foot that had stepped over the threshold wavered; he meant to withdraw but thought better of it. The director had seen him too. "Ah, Mr. Pan, there you are," said he, smiling to cover his embarrassment. "Come in and sit down." When the host realized that they were acquainted he withdrew to attend to his own business.

"So you're here too, director. Can you accommodate one more in this room?"

"There's only the three of us here, of course we can. We brought along a mat so we could take turns lying down a bit. Good thing it's not too cold yet."

Mr. Pan felt that the director was extremely affable that night, not at all his usual stern and dignified self. Forgetting his restraint, he strode in. "Then allow me to come in and keep you three company for the night."

The room was far from spacious. A middle-aged man with glasses sat on a mat spread on the floor. There was a look of fatigue on his face but he showed no inclination for sleep. The stove and pots and pans were placed against one wall. Near the window stood three chairs in a row; the director occupied one, the director's cousin, a young man in his twenties with sleek hair, another, the third one was empty. In one corner were an osier suitcase and three bundles — probably the three men's luggage. The few things were enough to clutter up the room, there was hardly any vacant space left. The coat of dust on the electric bulb made everything in the room hazy.

Mr. Pan put his bundle down with those of the others. He took the vacant seat with an air of apology. After the director had introduced him to his companions, he asked, "Have you also heard the news about Zhengan?"

"Yes. With Zhengan lost, Bizhuang is in great danger."

"Our side must have been careless along the southern route, the loss of Zhengan is a sign of this. It's the easiest thing for the other side to steal up to Bizhuang from Zhengan. At this very moment they may have got in. If so, I dare not think what will happen here!"

"If so, chaos will reign."

"But Commander Du on this side isn't a fool you know, he's noted for strategy. He's probably foreseen all this and has plans to forestall the other side. Maybe he'll turn the tables at this juncture and take up the offensive, attacking the enemy in its lair."

"If that happens there'll be an end to hostilities and that'll be great. We, in the field of education, can then start school and carry on as usual."

The director promptly became conscious of his dignity at the mention of the word "education". Twisting his thick moustache, he said with a sigh, "This fighting has certainly caused a loss to students of different ages, to say nothing of other people." He forgot his cramped and uncomfortable position in the tiny room and felt as if he were back again in the dignified office of the Bureau of Education.

"Commander Zhu of the other side is really hateful," said the middle-aged man on the mat with some indignation. "Why must he resist when this side attacked? He's bound to be defeated. If he'd been smart and offered no resistance, all this fighting would not have occurred."

"He's a fool," the director's cousin agreed. "He won't give up till the end. And in the meanwhile we have to suffer cooped up in this small, dark room!" His tone was not serious.

Mr. Pan's thoughts went to his wife and children in Shanghai. He wondered if they were all right, if they had kept out of trouble. Were they asleep at this moment? Since he could not feel them near him and his imagination conjured up only a very hazy picture, he felt that the fighting had injured him more than any of the others. He let his eyes rest mournfully on the little courtyard outside the window and stayed silent.

But then his thoughts turned to the terrible news he had

heard from Wu and the threat of danger to follow. "I wonder what is really happening!" he exclaimed.

"Hard to say!" The director spoke knowingly. "In war, everything depends on making use of the right moment. The tide may turn any time and things may not happen as we thought. Perhaps at this very moment ... we. ..." He smiled at the middle-aged man.

All the others in the room, the man on the mat, the director's cousin and Mr. Pan caught the significance of his smile. Assured that they were safe enough where they were, they also smiled with satisfaction.

The little yard overgrown with weeds provided a comfortable haven for mosquitoes and small insects of all descriptions. The lamp in the room drew the insects in swarms and the four frightened men had a bad time of it. Midges attacked their faces; a sudden sting from a particularly venomous mosquito kept making one or the other jump. From time to time they stopped talking to listen with trepidation for the sound of shooting or the clamour of frightened people. Sleep was out of the question, of course. They merely took turns lying down a bit as the director had predicted.

Mr. Pan's eyes were bloodshot the next morning and he shivered with cold. Longing to know how things were outside he slipped out all alone. The streets looked the same as on ordinary mornings. A few stray dogs, tails up, sniffed cheerily here and there. A man with drowsy eyes walked past now and then. Mr. Pan turned a corner, still he neither saw nor heard anything unusual. He could hardly suppress a smile at the recollection of his own panic the night before, but on second thought he felt there was really nothing funny about it. Better, after all, to be overcautious rather than take unnecessary risks.

Three weeks or so later, the fighting came to an end. People wagged their heads and assured each other, "Now, things'll be all right. As long as there's no fighting, we'll be safe." Mr. Pan, though, was not quite happy for the trains were still not running and he could not fetch his wife and children back from Shanghai. There had been two letters, both very brief, which, instead of making him feel better, only made him miss them more. He was annoyed with himself for being such a poor prophet. He could very well have saved all that extra expense of taking his family away to Shanghai, and then he need not have led this lonely bachelor's life for several weeks.

Realizing that the Bureau of Education would soon be considering the question of starting school, he went there for news. As soon as he stepped into the reception room he noticed several clerks busy cutting up large strips of paper and grinding fresh ink. It looked as if they were getting ready for some festivity.

"Here's Mr. Pan, just the man we want," cried one. "You write beautifully in the Yan style. This is just the job for you."

"Yes, indeed, Mr. Pan is the only one who can do calligraphy of this size well," chimed in the rest.

"Write what? I'm completely at sea about what's going on."

"We are getting ready to welcome the triumphant return of Commander Du. Four festooned archways are to be erected at the railway station to welcome Commander Du's train. We need to write inscriptions for the four archways."

"Who am I to write for such an important event?"

"We all agree you're the best man!" "You mustn't be modest," came the cry from all sides as a writing brush was thrust into Mr. Pan's hands.

Mr. Pan was quite overwhelmed. He took the writing brush and dipped it in the ink. After a pensive silence, he wrote, "His Deeds Surpass All Others" and on the second strip of paper, "His Might Sweeps the Southeast." On the third piece of paper he wrote, "Virtue and Benevolence So Bountiful." But as his brush formed the word "bountiful", he had a vision of press-gangs, exploding shells, houses in flame, raped women, pale-faced refugees and rotting corpses.

"This epithet shows the people's heartfelt gratitude!" cried one of the men watching, with a sigh of admiration. "The writing is more beautiful too."

"I wonder what he'll find to match this epithet," commented another man.

November 27, 1924
Translated by Tang Sheng

About the Author

YE SHENGTAO (or Ye Shaojun) is one of the better-known Chinese writers of the period following the May Fourth Movement.

Ye Shengtao was born in 1894 in Suzhou in the southern part of Jiangsu Province. Before he was six his father sent him to a private "family-school" to study; when he was twelve he changed over to a modern-style school which had just been set up locally.

In 1911 he completed his studies at middle school but because of financial hardship at home, he could not afford to continue his education further. In 1912 he began to work as a primary-school teacher, work he continued for almost ten years. While in middle school, Ye Shengtao began to write novels in the classical language which was still current at that time. His works appeared in the short story magazine *Saturday* which at that time was popular in Shanghai.

In 1919, at the time of the May Fourth Movement, Ye Shengtao began to write entirely in the colloquial language and to write for *New Tide*, one of the most progressive periodicals produced by the students of Peking University. In 1921, together with the well-known writer Mao Dun and the literary critic Zheng Zhenduo, he organized the Society for Literary Research.

After 1921 his literary reputation led him to be invited to lecture to middle schools and universities, but his most important work was as an editor in publishing houses, and over a period of more than ten years he worked in turn for two Shanghai publishers, the Commercial Press and the Kaiming Press.

The 1920s were an important period in Ye Shengtao's creative literary work. These years saw the publication of not a few collections of his shorter works, such as *Misunderstanding* (1922), *Conflagration* (1923), *Below the Horizon* (1925), *In the City* (1926), *Unwearied* (1928), and others. *Schoolmaster Ni Huanzhi* is one of the author's full-length novels; it was begun in 1928 and serialized in *The Educational Review* in Shanghai. It was published as a book in 1930. Shortly afterwards, the author published two well-known collections of children's stories, *The Man of Straw* (1932) and *Statues of Ancient Heroes* (1933).

After the outbreak o the War of Resistance Against Japanese Aggression in 1936, Ye Shengtao left Suzhou for Sichuan, which was well behind the Chinese front-line, where he continued with his educational and editorial work. He wrote a number of patriotic works encouraging resistance against the Japanese. These were collected in *Xichuan* (1944). After the victory over Japanese in 1945, he returned to Shanghai to work for the Kaiming Press and remained there until 1948.

After the founding of the People's Republic of China in 1949, Ye Shengtao was elected a member of the National Committee of the People's Political Consultative Conference and was at one time Deputy Director of the Publications Administration and Vice-Minister of Education. At present he is a member of the Standing Committee of the Fifth People's Political Consultative Conference as well as a member of the Standing Committee of the National People's Congress.

"How Mr. Pan Weathered the Storm" is one of his best short stories. It vividly depicts a cowardly and selfish intellectual, who is easily contented. Living in the chaotic period of warlords fighting each other, Mr. Pan does his best to avoid the war disaster and unemployment. Whenever there are any difficulties he gets into a panic; but as soon as there is an interval of peace he losses his head to eulogize the reactionaries. He is for ever living in a vulgar atmosphere, without any principles except to drag out an ignoble existence to protect himself. Mr. Pan is sharply exposed as the model of some intellectuals in the old society.

The Separation

Bing Xin

I uttered my first cry when the hand of a giant snatched me from a stifling net of pain.

Opening my eyes I saw the giant holding one of my heels so that I hung dangling upside down, my pink fists waving about over my head in the air.

Then another giant gently supported my back with her huge hand. Turning to a woman lying in a white bed, she said with a smile: "Congratulations! A big baby boy," and at the same time she laid me in a small basket lined with a white sheet.

I jerked my head trying to look out of the basket. Nurses in white smocks and hats swarmed round the pale, sweating woman who sighed as if she had just woken up from a nightmare, her swollen eye-lids half-closed. On hearing what the obstetrician had said, she shut her eyes with relief.

"Thank you, doctor. You must have had a hard time," she muttered.

I gave a loud cry: "No, mother. It's us who have had a hard time — we have just struggled out of death."

Mother was wheeled out of the room by the bustling white-clad nurses while I was carried out to the corridor, where a man stood at the other end looking as if he had also woken up from a nightmare. The doctor waved to him and he came over. The man stretched out his arms as if he wanted to hold me, but shrank back timidly. He bent his bemused face over me, his eyes looking concerned and surprised.

"Isn't he nice?" the doctor said.

"Er — but he has such a long head!" the man faltered.

Suddenly realizing how my head ached, I burst out crying again:

"Father, you've no idea how painfully my head was squeezed."

"Heavens! What a voice!" The doctor laughed and handed me over to a smiling nurse nearby.

Then I was put in a spacious sunny room. The walls were lined with white cot-baskets in which babies lay. Some slept quietly, their tiny fists on either side of their heads. Others cried: "I'm thirsty!" "I'm hungry!" "I'm hot!" or "I'm wet!" The nurse who was carrying me seemed not to have heard them. She walked calmly past to a bathroom at the other end of the room and laid me down on a stone table by the wash basin, with my head facing the tap. A flush of lukewarm water washed the pink mucus off my head and body.

I gave a shudder but felt fresher. Turning my head to look across the basin to the table opposite, I saw another baby, with a round head, large eyes, a dark complexion and a sturdy body, who was also being bathed by a nurse. He was awake and gazed quietly out of the window. By now I had been lifted up and dressed in a long white smock; so had he. We stared at each other across the wash basin. My nurse chatted to her companion:

"Your baby is really big and strong, but mine is fair and delicate."

On hearing this, the other fellow lifted his head and eyed me deliberately, as if with pity.

"How d'you do?" I began shyly.

"How d'you do, friend?" he answered amiably.

By this time the nurses had laid us in two baskets next to each other and left.

"Oh, I'm aching all over," I confided. "The last four hours were really tough for me as I tried to force my way out. How about you?"

"I was suffocated for half an hour or so, not too bad though. Nor did my mother suffer very much." He clenched his fists and smiled.

I didn't say any more, but sighed and felt bored. As I stared around, he said soothingly:

"You're tired, go to sleep. I think I'll do the same myself."

When I was sleeping soundly I was picked up from my basket and carried to the glass door. A group of boys and girls, their noses and palms pressed flat against the glass, looked at me admiringly in the same way as they would the toys displayed in a shop window. Pointing and gesticulating, they said that my eyebrows resembled my father's sister's, my nose was like his brother's, my eyes were like my mother's brother's and I had her sister's mouth. It was as if they were trying to divide me up among themselves.

I closed my eyes and shook my head, and then realized how my neck ached.

"I'm me. I don't resemble anyone except myself. Let me go back to sleep," I wailed loudly.

The nurse smiled. As I was being carried away I saw the youngsters leaving, pushing and laughing, and turning round to take another look. I was taken back to the big room.

My neighbour woke up at this point. "You're up. Who came to see you?"

"Don't know," I replied while I was being put back into the basket. "Probably my aunts and uncles — quite a few youngsters. It seems that they all like me."

He was silent for a moment. "How nice. It's the second day I've been here, and I haven't even seen my father."

I hadn't realized I had slept so long. By now my back and

neck didn't hurt quite so much, but I was wet. Imitating the other babies, I cried:

"I'm wet. I'm wet. I'm wet through."

As I had expected, a nurse came and picked me up. I was delighted. However, she gave me some water instead.

In the evening, three or four nurses, their starched smocks rustling, hurried into our room, picked us up and changed our nappies. My room-mates were overjoyed.

"We're going to see our mothers. Bye-bye."

My little friend was put in a big bed with the others and wheeled out, while I was carried by a nurse through the glass door into the first room on the right hand side of the corridor. Mother lay in a high bed, eagerly watching me being carried in. When I was placed in her arms she undid her top. She seemed young, her jet black hair was tucked behind her ears, and her eye-brows were curved like new moons. In the reflection of the dim bedside lamp she looked like a statue with her pale, almost bloodless face and large black eyes.

I began to suck while Mother touched my hair with her cheeks; she caressed my fingers and gazed at me with total delight and wonder.

After sucking for 20 minutes I still didn't get any milk. I was hungry and the tip of my tongue was raw, I opened my mouth and letting go of the nipple I screamed. Mother rocked me, panic-stricken, and cooed:

"Ah, my precious. Don't cry."

She rang the bell and a nurse came in.

"I'm sorry to bother you," said Mother. "I have no milk and he cries so. . . ."

"Don't worry. The milk will come eventually. He's still too little to mind." The nurse picked me up and Mother reluctantly let go of me.

When I was put back into my basket, my friend was already soundly asleep in his cot, now and then, he smiled con-

tentedly in his dreams. I glanced around. Most of my room-
mates were fast asleep: a few were half-awake, humming or
giving an occasional cry. I was famished, and wondered when
Mother's milk would come. I *did* mind, although no one seemed to realize it. Seeing all the others asleep and well-fed, I felt
both jealous and ashamed of myself; I screamed loudly hoping
that someone would see to me. I cried for half an hour before
a nurse came. She pouted sweetly, gave me a reassuring pat,
and pretended to be angry with my mother:

"Hum, really. Your Mama didn't feed you properly.
There, there. How about drinking a little water?" She thrust
the teat of the feeding bottle into my mouth. I sucked at it
greedily and gradually went back to sleep.

When we were having a bath the next day, my friend and
I chatted across the wash basin. He wagged his head and half-
closed his eyes as if he enjoyed the bath immensely.

"I had a good feed of milk yesterday," he exclaimed. "My
mother has a round dark face and is very pretty. I'm her fifth
child. She told the nurse that this was her first delivery in a
hospital. A charitable organization sponsored her here. My
father is poor. He's a butcher and slaughters pigs." At this
point drops of boric acid were squeezed into his eyes. He gave
a few cries of disgust and forcing open his eyes, he continued:

"Isn't it terrific slaughtering pigs? A gleaming knife is
thrust in and it comes out dripping with blood. I'll be a butcher
like my Dad when I grow up; not just slaughtering pigs, but
also those people who eat like pigs but who refuse to work. . . ."

I listened in silence. When he came to this part, I shut my
eyes and kept quiet.

"How about you? Did you have enough to eat yesterday?
What's your mother like?" I became excited again. "No, I
had nothing last evening — my mother has no milk. The nurse
said she will have it in a couple of days. My mother is nice

and she can read. There were piles of books on her bedside table, and the room was full of flowers."

"And your father?"

"He wasn't there; she was by herself and didn't talk to anyone. I know nothing about my father."

"Hers is the first-class ward," my friend declared. "There's only one bed in the room. My mother's ward was noisy, with a dozen or so beds. Many of the babies in this room also have mothers there, and they were all well-fed like me."

The next day I saw my father when I was taken to be fed. He was leaning against my mother's pillow. My parents' faces were tense and they looked at me thoughtfully. My father had a thin, shallow face with long eye-lashes and kindly eyes. He usually wore a slight frown as if he was thinking all the time.

"Now I've had a good look at him — he's good-looking like you," my father remarked.

"He has your big eyes," mother smiled, gently touching my face.

My father stood up and sat by the bed. He held my mother's hand and patted it gently. "We won't be lonely any more. I'll help you look after him and play with him after my classes. And we can take him with us on holiday to the mountains and to the seaside. We must pay attention to his health so that he doesn't become like me. Although there's nothing wrong with me I'm not particularly strong."

My mother nodded, "Yes, he must also learn to play a musical instrument and to paint. I can't do either of these things and feel that life isn't quite complete."

"What do you want him to be — a writer? A musician?"

"Whatever he cares to be. However, since he is a boy and China needs science, perhaps it would be better for him to be a scientist."

I was so cross at not getting any milk; that it was only their interesting conversation that stopped me from crying.

"We should begin to save for his education. The earlier we start the better."

My mother said, "I forgot to tell you my brother promised yesterday to give him a bike when he's six."

"This child has everything. Didn't my sister buy him a cradle?" My father was proud of all this.

Kissing my head, Mother muttered: "Isn't it nice, baby, that so many people love you. Be a good boy when you grow up. . . ."

I returned to my basket in a happy mood, forgetting that I was hungry. However, I found my friend deep in thought.

"Hello, I saw my father today. He's a school teacher and was discussing my future education with my mother. He promised he'll do his best for me. Mother said that it doesn't matter if she has no milk, because when I go home I can have cow's milk and later on fruit juice and lots and lots of other things. . . ." I blurted all this out in a single breath.

"How lucky you are," he smiled with what seemed like pity or perhaps contempt. "Once I'm home, I won't get any more milk because my mother'll be a wet-nurse away from home. I heard this from my father. I'll be leaving within a couple of days, then I'll be taken care of by my grandma who's over sixty. She'll feed me boiled rice-porridge and ground rice and soybean powder. However, I don't mind."

I was silenced, my feeling of contentment vanished and I felt ashamed.

He continued, his eyes shining bright with pride and courage: "You'll always be like a potted plant in a greenhouse untouched by wind or rain in a constant temperature. I'll be a blade of grass by the roadside, trodden on by men and beasts alike, and buffeted by wind and rain. You'll probably see me from your greenhouse window and pity me. But there's no need. I'll have over my head the vast sky, the fresh air, and crickets and butterflies will sing and dance for me. I'll also have many humble and brave companions who can't be destroyed by either mowing or burning and who dot by dot will embellish the whole world with green."

I was embarrassed to the point of tears, "I didn't choose to be so delicate. . . ." I stuttered.

Realizing my unhappiness, he softened and reassured me: "True, none of us want to be different from other people, but every single thing tears us apart. We'll see what'll happen to us later on."

Outside the windows snow fell like balls of cotton wool, piling over the green-glazed roof-tiles. Mother and I were to go home for the New Year, as were my friend and his mother, for she had to start work before the New Year. We only had half a day to ourselves. Then we would be submerged in the vast sea of human life. Will there be a time when we will sleep side by side under the same roof again?

We looked at each other fondly. His determined face, with its tight lips, knitted brows, far-away eyes, and slightly tilted chin, became blurred in the evening light.

"He'll slaughter pigs — and men too. . . ." I thought, closing my hands under the sheets and feeling humbled by my own worthlessness.

Coming back from our mothers in the evening we exchanged news. We would both go home on New Year's Day instead of New Year's Eve. My father thought it would be too busy and noisy on New Year's Eve and it would tire Mother out; while my friend's father had to leave home to hide from creditors, who usually come to settle up at the end of the year, and he didn't want his wife to be bothered. So we had another day together.

Since midnight there was an endless succession of firecrackers being let off everywhere. The occasional bark of a dog in the heavy snow seemed to tell us that another year of life's loves and hatreds was coming to its petty end. Before the masks of modesty and happiness were put on again tomorrow people wanted to devour, complain, curse or weep tonight for all they were worth. In this city's gloomy streets and lanes there palpitated many emotions which were drowned by the popping of firecrackers.

I shuddered and turned to find my friend biting his lower lip in silence. The night trickled away. Just before dawn I thought I heard him sighing.

In the morning two nurses beaming with New Year smiles came to bath us. One of them dressed me in flannel underwear, a pea-green sweater with a cap and socks to match, which she took out from a small suitcase. Holding me with both hands and inspecting me, she remarked:

"Hum, pretty. Your mother knows how to fit you out."

The clothes were soft and cozy, but they made me feel hot and irritable and I wanted to cry.

Meanwhile my friend was also in the hands of a nurse. I was stunned, I could hardly recognize him. Below his waist he was wrapped in a faded blue cloth. He wore a blue cotton-padded jacket, the sleeves of which were too long for him and they were so stiff that his arms stuck out awkwardly like a big kite. Glancing at the same white smocks we had just taken off on the ground, I winced, knowing that we were permanently separated, both materially and mentally.

My friend caught my eye, he gave me a smile that was both proud and a little ashamed and said:

"You look pretty in your smart clothes. I'm wearing my armour so that I can struggle for a living in the battlefield of life."

Throwing the used smocks into a laundry basket, the nurses hurried out, carrying us in their arms. I couldn't help crying loudly when we both reached the glass door, my friend couldn't control his tears either. We waved our arms wildly at each other, shouting:

"Bye-bye, dear friend."

As we went our separate ways, our cries faded away at either end of the corridor.

Mother was ready, standing in the room by my father who carried a small suitcase. Holding me in her arms, mother wiped my tears, and said soothingly:

"Don't cry, my darling. We're going home, Mummy loves you and Daddy loves you."

A wheel-chair was wheeled over. Mother sat in it, wrapped in a pea-green blanket, with me in her arms and father followed behind. After thanking the doctor and nurses who came to say good-bye, we went down by the elevator.

A car was parked in front of the half-glass door. As father opened the door a puff of snow flew in, and mother quickly covered my face with the blanket. We were soon out of the wheel-chair, into the car, and the car door slammed shut. Mother uncovered my face and I saw flowers all round us in the car and my parents' loving faces.

The road was jammed with rickshaws at the hospital gate. While waiting for the road to clear, I glanced out of the car window and saw my friend of ten days in his father's arms, followed by his mother carrying a small bundle wrapped in blue cloth. His father was wearing a black felt-hat and a cotton-padded coat, his little son's head rested on his strong shoulder under the broad rim of the hat and I saw my friend's face — fluffs of snow had drifted onto his brows and cheeks, his eyes were tightly shut and there was a wan proud smile on his lips. He had begun his battle the moment he left the hospital.

Our car sped off amid flying snow and the muffled beats of New Year gongs and cymbals. Mother holding me closer to her whispered:

"Darling! Look! What a smooth and clean world we have!"

I burst out crying.

August 5, 1931, Beijing
Translated by Cheng Wen

About the Author

BING XIN, a contemporary Chinese woman writer whose real name is Xie Wanying, was born in 1900 in Changle County, Fujian Province. In 1918 she enrolled first in the preparatory department of the Xiehe Women's University of Beijing and then in the art department of the Yanjing University. The next year she took part in the May fourth patriotic students' movement and started her literary writing. She joined the progressive Literary Study Society in 1921. After graduating in 1923, she studied in the United States until 1926 when she returned to China to teach at Yanjing University and the Women's Art College of Qinghua University. During the War of Resistance Against Japan from 1937 to 1945, she did literary work in Kunming and Chongqing. She went to Japan in 1946, teaching "New Chinese Literature" at Tokyo University. She returned to China in 1951 to continue writing children's literature and prose. She has been elected a deputy to the National People's Congress, member of the Standing Committee of the Chinese People's Consultative Conference, vice-chairman of the All-China Federation of Literature and Art Circles and council member of the Union of Chinese Writers.

Bing Xin's writings include short stories and poems, but she is best known for her prose. Her early writings include the short stories, "Two Families" and "A Wan and Sallow Person"; poem collections, *Stars* and *Water in Spring*; and the prose collections, *For Young Readers* and *The Past*. These works expose the dark rule of the feudal warlords, reflect the concerns and grievances of some young intellectuals, put forward social problems and show sympathy for oppressed working women. In the 1930s, she published "Separation", "The Girl Dong'er" and other short stories and a collection of prose *About Women*, which appeared during the anti-Japanese war. After the founding of the People's Republic, she mainly wrote prose, which include *In Praise of Flowering Cherry* and *We Have Waked Up the Spring*, and stories for children such as "Taoqi's Diary in Summer Vacation", "Again for Young Readers" and "A Small Orange Lamp". Her *Collection of Prose,* published by the Beijing People's Literature Publishing House in 1954, describes life in the new society. Bing Xin's works, her prose in particular, are popular for their unique style, which express deep feeling through natural and graceful language.

"Separation" is one of Bing Xin's early writings. Through the life of two new-born babies — "I", son of an intellectual, and "friend", son of a worker, the story demonstrates that people become separated from one another not through their own will but through social pressures and family background.

The Child at the Lakeside

Wang Tongzhao

I seldom cared to visit the famous lake although I lived in a city along its shore. Filled with reeds and large craft, it seemed exceptionally narrow and cramped and noisy. Sometimes I went rowing with a few friends in the evening, but every night it was the same bedlam. The clash of cymbals, the high-pitched squeal of fiddles, the unpleasant singing, the men's raucous shouts, the seductive laughter of painted women with sleekly oiled hair, the cries of the vendors on the little pedlar boats . . . swept the placid surface of the lake like a huge wave.

And so, whenever I went to the lake, I would close my eyes and ears to my surroundings and withdraw into my own thoughts. Occasionally, when the sunset colours were reflected on the water, I would stroll along a quiet sector of the lakeside to enjoy the breeze. I would listen to the frogs singing in the green grass after the rain and watch the twittering birds flit among the branches of the trees. I would feel rather stimulated, moved by a profound consciousness of nature and excited by innumerable far-reaching thoughts.

One day at sunset, violet and purple rays illuminated the emerald trailers of the weeping willows on the dyke. In a little pond beside a temple huge lotus leaves grew higher than a man. Although the lotus flowers, pure as carved white jade, had slowly closed their petals after noon, one or two bees, lured by their scent, still hovered, reluctant to depart. On the dark green water, scarlet clouds shimmered golden; the rapidly lowering rays in their midst were a remarkable variety of hues. Layer upon layer of colour, interweaving and interplaying, shone with a dazzling brilliance.

It had rained heavily for six or seven hours the night before. Today the sky was clear, and I walked alone along the west bank of the lake, enjoying the fresh-washed scene. My leather shoes left sharp prints on the moss-covered flagstones of the inclined path.

In the centre of the lake people were shouting, quarrelling violently. I walked slowly towards the far end of the stone-flagged path. Rustling willow trailers and the water-pepper shrubs that had just come into flower beside the trembling reeds danced in the west breeze at the edge of the water. This was perhaps the coolest and most secluded spot on the entire lake. Except for the steps of an infrequent passer-by or two, the only sound was the twittering of the little birds in the trees greeting the eventide. Frogs in the tangled grass croaked a rhythmic accompaniment.

Although this made me feel somewhat more cheerful than usual, I had no desire to retain the rapidly fading scene. For it reminded me of the words, "the dusk of the dying sun" — a phrase I found rather depressing.

My head lowered in thought, I walked with heavy weary tread. The violet and purple sunset rays were growing dimmer, the light of the sun having already more than half sunk in the reflecting water. Although I knew it was getting late. I did not wish to return home. I sat down on a large white rock by the lake's edge. Listening to the last of the cicadas droning in the late summer night, I was conscious of an air of autumn in the golden haze drifting on the water's surface. I sat alone beneath the willows and watched the dusk light fading in the distance and observed far off the tiny glow of the first lamps of evening. The weather was no longer very hot during the day; with evening came a certain soft coolness. At the same time, probably because of this coolness, I was vaguely stirred by an indefinable excitement.

As I sat wrapped in idle thought, suddenly I heard a rustling behind the willows. It came so unexpectedly in the quiet darkness, I was a bit startled. A moment later, I heard light footsteps threshing through a cove of reeds. I leaped up, circled the willows and emerged on the other side of the cove. It was quite dark by then. I couldn't see clearly. On a mud bank beside the reeds I seemed to perceive a small figure.

"Who's there?" I shouted.

But the shadow made no reply.

Ordinarily, this was a very quiet spot. At night, it was even more deserted. Now, it was growing darker and darker, and the reeds and the willows were rustling faintly. I felt a bit afraid. "Who's there?" I cried again. Just as I was turning to leave, the little dark figure on the mud bank replied in a small weak voice:

"It's me, Little Shun ... I'm here ... fishing."

He practically swallowed the last word and his voice trembled slightly. He sounded like an eleven- or twelve-year-old little boy. I was very suspicious.

"How can you fish after dark?" I asked him. "How can you see?"

Again the small shadow did not reply.

"Where do you live?"

"In Horse Head Lane...."

There was something about that weak voice that sounded familiar. I took a step closer and asked, "Have you always lived there?"

"No," the little boy replied quickly. "I used to live on Peace Street...."

Suddenly I remembered. "Oh! You're the Chens' little boy.... Isn't your father a blacksmith?"

The child pulled in his bamboo fishing pole and ran to me,

barefoot, down the mud bank. "Yes.... Papa is a black-smith. But who are you?"

I drew nearer and peered at the child's face. I could barely recognize him. What had happened to the darling Little Shun of five or six! His face was blackened — either by mud or soot. He wore a short homespun blue robe that was well up above his knees, and he reeked of mud and sweat. When he heard me call his name, he stared at me in astonishment. He didn't know who I was.

I remembered him when he was four or five — I was very fond of playing with children then. Whenever I passed his door I saw him sitting on his mother's lap beneath the big shady old elm tree. He always sang me his song about the little rooster.

More than six years had passed, and I was often away from home. People in my family told me that Little Shun had moved, no one knew exactly where. When I passed his house and saw someone else's name on the door I felt sorry, as if I had lost a constant companion!

Meeting him today again in the cool dusk by the lakeside, how could I help but be surprised? Strangest of all, how could the rosy-cheeked Little Shun with the clean white hands have become virtually the same as the dirty little beggar boys on the street? His father had been a respectable blacksmith, quite able to look after his child financially.

I led Little Shun over to the rock and made him sit down beside me. I told him how I often saw him when he was very young, and how I had played with him and made him laugh. He looked at me, bewildered. I began to question him.

"Where is your papa now?"

"At home, you might say...." Little Shun replied hesitant-ly. From his expression I could see that he thought this old friend was rather peculiar.

"Is he still working?"

"What?... He goes out every day, but he never... brings home any money.... Working?... I don't know."

"What about your mother?"

"Dead," the boy retorted briefly.

I was shocked. But of course it had to be. Little Shun's mother had been a frail little woman. People said she had borne seven children in thirteen years. Little Shun was the only one that remained alive. But I hadn't thought her time would come so quickly!

"Who else do you have at home now?"

"I've got a ma, a new one. . . ."

"Oh, is your family poorer than before? You look. . . ."

Little Shun had always been an intelligent child. At my blunt question, he stared off into the misty distance. Then he dropped his head. After a long time he said in a low voice:

"Sometimes we have nothing to eat. My papa is often away from home. . . ."

"Where does he go?"

"I don't know. . . . He doesn't come home till after breakfast. . . . I hear that he works in an opium den. . . . I don't know where."

His low voice spoke very slowly. I was beginning to understand. I felt compelled to go on.

"How . . . how old is your new ma? Is she good to you?"

"I hear she's only thirty. She comes from a family inside the East Gate. . . ." An uneasy expression stole over his face. I asked him:

"Does she beat you?"

"She? No, she has no time." He said this decisively.

If the young woman was the sole support of a family like his, she obviously couldn't have much time to spare!

"And what sort of work does she do?"

"Work? She doesn't work. But she gets very busy late every afternoon. That's why I can't stay home. . . . Every evening I come out to this cove of reeds; only here . . . just here. . . ."

"What? . . ."

Little Shun had learned to take a grown-up attitude. He wrinkled his small nose and snorted: "There are always guests in our house! Sometimes two or three in one night. Sometimes not a single one shows up. . . ."

I was rather shaken. But he continued:

". . . My ma can earn money to buy us food. . . . When they come, she chases me out. She never lets me go back till very late. My papa knows. He doesn't come home at night either. . . ."

By now I knew quite well what kind of environment Little Shun came from. It was like something in a novel: A tousle-headed child, sallow, thin, with sunken eyes, every night had to wander among the reeds, barefoot. When he grew hungry, he could talk to his friends — the birds and the frogs, or listen to the music of the wind blowing through the reeds.

His father was a waiter in an opium den. His mother — rather his stepmother — in order to keep alive did the bitterest of all things — she sold her flesh.

Only the stars kept Little Shun company when he returned home in the still, deserted night. But the following day, it was the same all over again. It was too much like a piece of fiction. I couldn't believe it. I remembered him so well as a clean, lovable child. How could he have come to this?

"What kind of people are they," I asked him, "these men who come to your house every night?"

"I don't see them very often," said Little Shun, "and then only for a moment. Some wear grey military tunics, with army caps cocked over one eye. Some smell of kerosene oil and wear thick silver watch chains on their vests. A few are dressed in long scholars' gowns. Usually we have three or four visitors a night. But sometimes not even one comes to our door."

"Why is that?"

I felt my persistent questioning was very unkind to the child. But I couldn't stop.

Little Shun laughed. "Don't you know? All the houses in Horse Head Lane are open to visitors every night! . . ." He laughed again, as if amused that I, an educated person, should understand so little.

There didn't seem to be anything else to ask him. I couldn't bring myself to make this innocent child tell any more of his tragic history. He appeared to have something on his mind; he gazed abstractedly at the stars shining palely through the dusk.

If his own mother were still alive, perhaps things would be different. I mused. The life this poor woman who is his present mother leads is no better than hell!

Ah, the family! The family organization and the pressure of the times, the urgent need to make a living! I had come for an idle stroll along the lakeside after the rain. But instead of finding relaxation, I ended with many troublesome problems knotted in my breast.

Just think of it. Suffering hunger and discomfort, a child must come to a cove of reeds at dusk and remain half the night. His mother, because the burden of supporting the whole family rests on her, must endure endlessly the worst of all humiliations. Such a life is less than human! The poor in our present society can take only this hopeless, dead-end road!

I was consumed with doubts. I felt agitated, unable to sit still. And the lakeside scene which had given me such fresh, soothing impression had long since been swallowed up by the darkness.

Knowing that Little Shun did not dare to return home yet, I didn't have the heart to leave him to watching the starlight alone by the shore. I sat down beside him beneath the willows. Though I wanted to question him further, I felt that it would be too cruel. In silence, I reflected on the fact that a child is mould-ed by his environment . . . and I trembled for Little Shun and all other children like him!

Suddenly an agitated call drifted over from the opposite bank. "Little Shun. . . . Where are you? . . ." I jumped to my feet. The child was so frightened that he dropped his fishing

pole into the water and began hurrying along a small path. I
was completely bewildered; I didn't know what had happened.
Just then a middle-aged man burst through the reeds, took Little
Shun by the hand, and rushed off with him. I heard the man
say:

"Your father was arrested by the police tonight.... They
raided the opium den.... We couldn't tell your mother. Master
Wu is calling on her. Who would dare to disturb him!...
Child, you were the only one we neighbours could notify...."

Their shadows gradually disappeared into the night, and
the man's voice faded away.

Slowly, I trudged home. Few people walked abroad in
the dense night mists. There was a weight on my chest, as if
the atmospheric pressure that evening was exceptionally heavy.
The stars that guided me were very pale, not nearly so bright as
usual.

August 1922
Translated by Sidney Shapiro

About the Author

WANG TONGZHAO (1897-1957), an important novelist and
poet of contemporary China, was born in Zhucheng County,
Shandong Province. He enrolled in the Yuying Middle School
of Jinan, Shandong Province in 1913. He entered the China
University in Beijing in 1918 and worked as university lecturer
and school teacher after graduation, while doing literary writings.
He took an active part in the New Literature Movement in 1919.
His early writings include stories "After Snow" and "Pondering".
He founded in 1921 the Literary Study Society together with Mao
Dun, Zheng Zhenduo and Ye Shengtao and other progressive
writers, and started in 1922 to have contact with Lu Xun. He

went to Japan in 1927. His works during this period include collections of poems *Snowy Morning* and *Childishness*; short stories "A Rainy Night in Spring", "The Bugle Call" and "The Trace of Frost"; and a short novel *A Blade of Leaf*. He published a reportage collection *Spring in North China* after a tour of the Northeast in 1930. Later he took part in the progressive literary activities in Shanghai and wrote *Mountain Rain*, one of his best known novels. It describes how the peasants of Shandong in spite of their strong attachment to the land fled to the cities to escape heavy taxes in a year of natural disaster and fighting, joining the ranks of the workers whose life is just as precarious. The same year he was forced to leave Shanghai because of a ban against his novel and went at his own cost to Europe to study ancient literature and art. He returned to China in 1935 and joined the Shanghai Cultural Circles' Salvation Association. In 1936 he published *Spring Flower*, a novel which reflects the ideological trend of young intellectuals after the May Fourth Movement and the different roads they choose. He moved his family to Shanghai in 1937 and taught at the Shanghai Fine Arts College. After the outbreak of the War of Resistance Against Japan, he went to teach in Jinan University. He returned to Qingdao in 1945 to become a professor in the Chinese Department of the Shandong University. After the founding of the People's Republic, he was elected deputy to the National People's Congress, member of the Shandong Provincial People's Committee, member of the China Federation of Literature and Art Circles, member of the board of the Union of Chinese Writers, chairman of the Federation of Literature and Art of Shandong Province and member of the China Democratic League. In 1957 and 1958, the Beijing People's Literature Publishing House published his *Selected Stories* and *Selected Poems*.

"The Child at the Lakeside", a short story written in 1922, depicts the life of a poor family through a child.

Big Sister Liu

Xu Dishan

Summer was unusually hot in Beijing that year. Although the street lamps were already lit, the man who sold cool crab-apple cider on the corner of the lane was still announcing his wares with a rhythmic clanging of two small brass bowls, like the accompaniment women ballad reciters use to punctuate their stories. A woman with a large basket of scrap paper on her back passed before the cider vendor. A large battered straw hat obscured her face, but when she hailed him, you caught a flash of even white teeth. Her burden weighed her down heavily. She walked placing one foot solemnly in front of the other, like a camel, until she entered her own gate.

Beyond was a small compound lined with one-storey buildings built in a hollow square. The woman lived in two dilapidated rooms on one side of the compound. Most of the yard was strewn with rubble, but before her door was an arbor of cucumbers and a few stalks of tall corn. Tuberoses grew beneath her window. A few rotting timbers beneath the arbor evidently served as seats. As she neared her door, a man came out and helped her lower the heavy basket.

"You're late today, wife."

The woman looked at him in surprise. "What do you mean? Have you gone out of your mind, wanting a wife? Don't call me that, I tell you." Entering the room, she took off her battered straw hat and hung it behind the door. Then

113

she scooped water from a large earthen vat several times in succession with half a segment of bamboo, drinking so rapidly she couldn't catch her breath. After standing a moment, gasping, she walked out to the arbor, pulled the big basket to one side and sat down on a rotting timber.

The man's name was Liu Xianggao. He was approximately the same age as she — about thirty. The woman's surname was also Liu. But, except for Xianggao, no one knew that her given name was Chuntao, or Spring Peach. The neighbours all referred to her as Big Sister Liu the scrap paper collector. That was because of her occupation — poking through rubbish heaps on street corners and lanes' ends to earn a living, buying old written matter for which she gave boxes of matches in exchange. From morning till night, beneath the blazing sun or in the icy gale, she tramped the streets, eating her full share of dust. But she had always loved cleanliness. Winter or summer, each day when she returned home she washed her face and bathed her body. Xianggao never failed to have a bucket of water waiting for her.

Xianggao had graduated from a rural elementary school. Four years ago, soldiers were marauding through his native region, and his whole family was forced to flee and scatter. On the road he met Chuntao, another refugee. They travelled together several hundred miles, then separated.

She went with a group of people to Beijing and found a job as nurse-maid in a family of foreigners whose mistress was looking for an inexperienced country girl. Because she was clean and pretty, her mistress became very fond of her. But country people don't make good servants; they can't get used to being scolded. In less than two months, Chuntao quit. Her finances at a low ebb, she decided to try collecting scrap paper. In this trade she was able to earn enough to live on.

Xianggao's story, after he parted from Chuntao, was quite simple. He went to Zhuozhou to look up a relative, but the man was gone. Family friends, hearing that he had come as a pen-

niless refugee, were not very cordial. He drifted to Beijing where someone introduced him to Old Wu, who sold crab-apple cider on the street corner. Old Wu loaned him his present quarters in the run-down courtyard, on the understanding that if anybody wanted to rent them, he would move out. Xianggao had no job, so he helped the old man sell cider and kept his accounts for him. He paid no rent and Old Wu gave him nothing for his work, but supplied him with two meals a day. Chuntao wasn't doing too badly at her paper collecting, but the people with whom she was staying wouldn't allow her to store her merchandise. She went looking for a place along the north city wall and the first time she rapped on a gate, Xianggao came out. Saving herself a lot of formalities, she rented the rooms from Old Wu and kept Xianggao on as her helper.

That was three years before. Since Xianggao could read a bit, he was able to sort through the paper that Chuntao collected and pick out the relatively valuable pieces, such as inscribed paintings or letters or scrolls written by some famous figure. With the two co-operating, business improved. Occasionally, Xianggao tried to teach Chuntao to read and write, but without much success. He couldn't read very well himself and had even greater difficulty in explaining the words to others.

Their life together, while perhaps not as idyllic as that of the mandarin duck and drake, famed symbols of connubial bliss, was in any event as cheerful as the union of a pair of common sparrows.

But to get back to the present. As Chuntao came into the room, Xianggao followed behind her with a bucket of water.

"Wash up, wife," he said happily. "I'm starving. Let's have something good tonight — onion griddle cake, alright? If you agree, I'll go out and buy the fixings."

"Wife, wife! Why can't you stop calling me that?" Chuntao demanded impatiently.

"If you'll only answer to it — just once — tomorrow I'll buy you a good straw hat in the second-hand market. Haven't you been saying you need one?" Xianggao pleaded.

"I don't like to hear it."

Seeing that she was a little annoyed, he changed the subject. "Well, what do you want to eat?"

"Whatever you like. You buy it and I'll make it for you."

After a while Xianggao returned with some onions and a bowl of sesame seed sauce, and placed them on the table. Chuntao had finished washing. She came in holding a large red card.

"This must be some big official's wedding certificate. Don't sell it in the Small Market this time. Better have someone take it to the Peking Hotel. We'll get more for it there."

"That's ours. Otherwise what right would I have to call you wife?" replied Xianggao playfully. "I've been teaching you to read for nearly two years and you still can't recognize your own name!"

"Who can read so many words? And cut out this wife business. I don't like to hear it. Seriously now, who wrote this thing?"

"I did. This morning a policeman came around to check up on the tenants. He says the martial law has been stricter the last two days. Every family has to report exactly who's staying with them and their relationship. Old Wu said that if I said we were husband and wife it would save a lot of trouble. The policeman, too, said it wouldn't look good if he wrote down that a man and a woman, unmarried, were living together. So I took that blank wedding certificate we couldn't sell last time and filled in that we were married in 1919."

"What? 1919? I didn't even know you in 1919. You'll get us into an awful mess. We never worshipped Heaven and Earth together, we never drank from each other's wine cups. How can anyone say we're husband and wife?"

Although opposed to the idea, Chuntao spoke calmly. She had changed to blue cloth trousers and she wore a white tunic. Even without make-up, her face had a fresh natural beauty. Had she been willing to marry, the local matchmaker could easily have passed her off as a young widow of twenty-three or four. Chuntao could have commanded at least a hundred and eighty dollars under prevailing market conditions.

Laughing, she folded the card down the middle. "Don't fool around. A fine wedding certificate. Let's make our griddle cakes and eat." She lifted the stove lid and thrust the card into the flames. Then she walked to the table and began to knead some dough.

"You can burn it if you like," said Xianggao with a grin. "The policeman has already registered us as husband and wife. If they make an official check, I'll say we lost it when we were refugees on the road. From now on, I'm going to call you wife. Old Wu recognizes our marriage; so does the policeman. I'm going to call you wife whether you like it or not. Wife, wife. Tomorrow I'll buy you a new hat. I'm afraid I can't afford a ring."

"Keep that up or you'll make me mad."

"Looks like you're still thinking of that Li Mao." Xianggao was not quite so high-spirited as he had been a moment before. He said it under his breath, but Chuntao heard him.

"Think of him? Husband and wife for one night, then separated for nearly five years, with no news all that time. What's the good of thinking?"

She had told Xianggao what had happened on her marriage day. When the flowery sedan-chair brought her to the groom's home, before the guests even had a chance to take their seats at the wedding feast, a man came rushing in to announce that an army of many soldiers had arrived in the two neighbouring villages. They were grabbing men to dig trenches and everybody was running away. The new couple hastily bundled their belongings together and fled towards the west with the rest of the villagers. Their second night on the road, they suddenly heard people ahead shouting, "The bandits are coming. Hide, quickly, hide!" There was a wild scramble to get out of sight. No one had time to think of anyone but himself. When the sun rose the next morning, a dozen people had disappeared, Chuntao's husband Li Mao among them.

"I think he must have been taken by the bandits," she now said. "Maybe they killed him long ago. Forget it. Let's not talk about him."

She finished making a griddle cake and put it on the table. Xianggao scooped a bowl of cucumber soup from the crockery pot. The two sat down and ate in silence.

When the meal was over, they sat beneath the arbor and chatted. A cool breeze brought tiny fireflies descending on the arbor like a myriad of falling stars, while countless real stars flashed and twinkled among the leaves of the cucumber vine. The night-blooming tuberoses slowly opened their petals and filled the garden with their perfume.

"How lovely they smell," said Xianggao. He plucked one of the flowers and put it in Chuntao's hair.

"Don't spoil my tuberoses. Wearing flowers in the hair at night — I'm no prostitute." She took the flower out, inhaled its delicate scent then placed it on the timber seat beside her.

"Why were you so late today?"

"Huh! Today I did a good piece of business. As I was coming home this afternoon, passing the Houmen Arch I saw some street cleaners pushing a big cartful of scrap paper. I asked them where they got it. They said it came from the Shenwu Gate of the old Imperial Palace.* I saw that it was full of official-looking red and yellow documents. I asked them whether they'd sell it to me. They were very polite. If you want it, they said, we'll give you a special price, and you can take it away." Chuntao pointed at the big basket resting beneath the window of the house. "I only spent a dollar for all that! Maybe it's money thrown away, I don't know. We can go through it tomorrow and see."

---

* The paper was sold by museum employees to pay their salary, which was months in arrears.

"You can't go wrong on things from the Palace. It's only stuff from the schools and the foreign business firms that I'm afraid of. Their paper is heavy and it smells bad. You never know what you're getting."

"All the shopkeepers have been using foreign paper for wrapping paper the last few years. I can't imagine where it all comes from. None of the collectors like to handle it. We have to pay more for it because it's heavy, but when we sell it we get very little."

"More and more people are studying foreign languages. Everybody wants to be able to read the foreign newspaper so that they can learn how to do business with the foreigners."

"Let them. We'll stick to picking foreign paper."

"Looks like everything will have to have a foreign label from now on. We've got 'foreign' clothes and 'foreign' hats and 'foreign' cloth. The next thing you know we'll be using 'foreign' camels!"

Chuntao laughed. "You shouldn't talk about others. If you had money you'd probably want to study foreign books too, and get yourself a foreignized wife."

"The Lord of the Heavens knows, I'll never get rich, and even if I did, I wouldn't want a foreignized wife. If I had a little money I'd go to the countryside and buy some good farm land, and we two could till it together."

Ever since Chuntao had been forced to flee from her home and lost her husband, the word "countryside" had unpleasant associations for her. "Is that what you want?" she demanded. "Before you'd even have bought your land, both you and your money would be gobbled up. The countryside's a hell. I wouldn't go back even if I were starving here."

"I'd like to see our Jinxian County again."

"The countryside's the same wherever you go. If it's not marauding soldiers then it's bandits on a raid. If it's not the bandits, it's the Japanese. Who dares go back? We're much better off right here, picking scrap paper. What we need is another person to help us. If we had someone to take your place at home going through the pickings, you could set up a stall during the day and sell direct to the customers. Besides cutting out the middleman, we'd be less likely to pass over any good items."

"Another three years at this trade and I'll be alright. If we pass over any good items, it's nobody's fault but my own. I've learned plenty the last few months. Used postage stamps — which ones are worth money, which ones aren't — I pretty near know them all. I'm beginning to get the hang of spotting the writing of famous men. A couple of days ago I found something by Kang Youwei.* Guess how much I sold it for today." Xianggao happily held up a thumb and an index finger. "Eighty cents!"

"You see! If we could pick eighty cents out of our heap of scrap paper every day, that wouldn't be so bad. Why go back to the countryside? Wouldn't that just be looking for trouble?" Chuntao's cheerful tones were like the throaty warble of an oriole in late spring. "I guarantee you'll find plenty of good stuff in the paper I brought home today. I hear there'll be even more coming out of the Palace tomorrow. That street cleaner told me to wait for him at the back door first thing in the morning. He says all the things in the Palace are being crated and sent south, but nobody wants the old paper. I saw a lot outside the Donghua Gate of the Palace too. They're practically giving it away — whole sacks of it. You go down there tomorrow and ask about it."

Before they knew it, it was almost midnight. Chuntao stood up and stretched. "I'm tired. Let's get some rest."

Xianggao followed her into the house. There was a brick oven-bed against the window wide enough to sleep three. In the tiny light of an oil lamp, the two pictures on the wall were dimly visible. One was "Eight Fairies Playing Mahjong," the other was a cigarette advertisement with a beautiful girl. It

---

* Qing Dynasty scholar and statesman.

seemed to Xianggao that if Chuntao took off her battered straw hat and put on a decent gown — not necessarily from a smart dress shop, even a second-hand one from the Heavenly Bridge Market would do — and sat on a grassy knoll, she wouldn't look much different from the fashionable young lady in the cigarette ad. That was why he liked to tease Chuntao and say that the advertisement was her photograph.

Chuntao undressed, draped herself in a thin coverlet and lay face downwards on the bed. According to their nightly habit, Xianggao massaged her back and legs. As usual, she gradually relaxed, a faint smile on her lips, as Xianggao kneaded her weary muscles in the light of the oil lamp's flickering little flame.

Already half asleep, she murmured, "You come to bed too. Don't work tonight. You have to get up early tomorrow."

Soon the woman was snoring faintly. Xianggao put out the lamp.

At dawn they rose promptly, and set off on their respective missions like a pair of ravens leaving their nest in search of food.

Just as the noon cannon sounded, and the drums and cymbals of the fair grounds on the shores of the Ten Monasteries Lake were at their noisiest, Chuntao came through the back door of the Palace, bearing a basket of paper on her back, and headed west towards the Shiya Bridge. As she neared the fair grounds, a man by the side of the road hailed her:

"Chuntao, Chuntao!"

Even Xianggao seldom addressed her by her given name. In the four or five years since she left the countryside, certainly no one had ever shouted it out like that in public.

"Chuntao, don't you remember me?"

She turned to see a beggar sitting by the roadside. The piteous cry had come from him. His face was heavily bearded. He was unable to stand because he had no legs. The white metal buttons of his tattered grey uniform were already rusting and his skin showed through the splits in his shoulder seams.

A nondescript army cap devoid of any insignia perched askew on his head.

Chuntao stared at him wordlessly.

"Chuntao, I'm Li Mao!"

She took two steps forward. Grimy tears were running down the man's cheeks into his tangled beard. Her heart beat wildly. For several minutes she was unable to speak.

"Mao, you're a beggar?" she said finally. "How did you lose your legs?"

He sighed. "It's a long story. How long have you been in Beijing? What are you selling?"

"Selling? I collect scrap paper. We can talk after we get home."

Chuntao called a rickshaw, raised Li Mao in and put her basket on the vehicle's floorboard. While the rickshaw man pulled, she trotted along behind and pushed. Old Wu, standing at the head of her lane near the north wall clanging his little brass bowls, hailed her as they went by:

"You're home early today, Big Sister. Business must be good!"

"A relative's come from the country," she shouted back in reply.

At the compound gate, the rickshaw man helped Li Mao down. Chuntao opened the gate with her key, then led Li Mao in. He crawled forward on his hands, like a performing bear, his amputated legs dragging behind him.

She brought out a suit of Xianggao's clothing and drew two buckets of water from the well, just as Xianggao did for her every day. She poured the water into a wooden tub and told Li Mao to bathe. After he finished, she filled another basin so that he could wash his face. Finally she helped him to a seat on the oven-bed, then went into the next room to bathe herself.

"Your place is nice and clean, Chuntao. Do you live here alone?"

"My partner stays here too," she answered without any hesitation.

"Are you in business?"

"Didn't I tell you I collect scrap paper?"

"Collect scrap paper? How much can you earn in a day doing that?"

"Never mind questioning me. Let me hear about you first." Chuntao spilled out the bath water and came into the room, combing her hair. She sat down opposite Li Mao.

Li Mao began his story:

"Chuntao — ah, it's too long. I'll just tell you the main things. — After the bandits captured me that night, I hated them because they had made me lose you. I watched for my chance, grabbed one of their rifles, killed two of them and ran for my life. I managed to get to Shenyang just when they were recruiting for the army, and I joined up. All during the next three years I kept trying to get news from home. People said our village had been razed to the ground; no one knew what had happened to the title-deed to our bit of land. I had forgotten to take it with me when we ran away. And so I never asked for leave to go home for a look around. I was afraid if I did, I'd lose the few dollars' pay I was drawing every month.

"So I settled down to being a soldier, just living for pay day. As for becoming an officer, I had no hope of that. Then, last year, something happened — I must be fated to a life of bad luck. The colonel of our regiment issued an order saying that any man who could hit the bull's-eye nine shots out of ten would get double pay and be promoted. In the whole regiment, not one soldier was able to hit the target more than four times in ten, and even those shots weren't in the middle. But I sent nine bullets right into the red ball, one after another. Then to show how good I really was, I turned my back to the target, bent down and fired the tenth shot from between my legs. It hit the bull's-eye exactly in the centre.

"When the colonel sent for me, I was very happy. I was

sure he was going to praise me. Instead the pig became very
angry. He swore I must be a bandit, and wanted to have me
shot. He said nobody but a bandit could shoot so well. My
sergeant and my lieutenant both pleaded for me; they guaranteed I wasn't a bad man. Although they convinced him not to
shoot me, I lost my private's rank; I wasn't even a private second class. The colonel said an officer is bound to hurt the feelings of his men sometimes, and with a sharpshooter in the ranks,
during battle he'd run the same risk of being shot from behind
as in front; that although he'd be killed in either event, he'd
rather not lose his life for the sake of someone's revenge.
Nobody had any answer to that one. People could only urge me
to quit the army and find some other trade.

"Not long after I left, I heard that the Japanese had occupied Shenyang and that dog of a·colonel had led all his troops
over in surrender. I was boiling mad. I swore I'd get the
bastard. I joined the Volunteers and fought outside of Haicheng
for the next few months. We gave ground slowly, retreating
south towards the Great Wall. Two months ago we were
northeast of Pinggu and I was on patrol duty. I ran into the
enemy and was hit in both legs. I was still able to walk then and
took cover behind a boulder and killed a couple of them. When
I finally couldn't hold out any longer, I threw my rifle away and
crawled into the fields. There I hid one day, two days — with
still no sign of our stretcher-bearers. My legs were swelling
badly. I couldn't move. I had nothing to eat and nothing to
drink. I just lay there and waited to die. Luckily a man came
by with a big cart. He picked me up and brought me to a first-
aid tent. They took one look at me and rushed me to a field
hospital in Beijing. But it was already the third day. My legs
were too far gone. The doctor had to amputate.

"I was in the hospital for more than a month. I pulled
through alright, but my legs are gone. I thought to myself — in
this town I haven't a single relative or friend and I can't go
home; even if I could, how can I till the land without any legs?

I begged the hospital to keep me on and give me a small job — any kind. The doctor said the hospital cures people but it doesn't support them and it's not its duty to find work for them. This city has no soldiers' sanatorium so all I could do was beg on the streets. Today is exactly the third day. Lately I've been thinking I can't stand this much longer; it would be better to hang myself and get it over with."

Chuntao listened intently. Her eyes were moist but she said nothing. Li Mao paused to wipe the sweat from his brow.

"And what about you?" he asked. "Though this place is kind of cramped compared with our broad, open countryside, from the looks of things you're doing all right."

"Who's doing all right? No matter how bad things are, a person still has to live. You can see people with smiles on their faces even at the gates of hell. I've been collecting scrap paper for a living the past few years. A fellow by the name of Xianggao is my partner. He and I share everything, you might say. We can get by in a pinch."

"You and he live here together?"

"Yes, we both sleep on this oven-bed." Chuntao replied without the least hesitation, as if she had definite views on the subject for a long time.

"Oh, then you're married to him."

"No, we just live together."

"In that case, are you still my wife or aren't you?"

"No, I'm not anybody's wife."

Li Mao's pride as a husband was hurt, but he couldn't think of what to say. His eyes were fixed on the ground, not that he was looking at anything of course, but because he was rather ashamed to face his wife.

"Everyone must be laughing at me for a cuckold," he said at last in a low voice.

"Cuckold?" The woman's face hardened a bit at the word, but she spoke without rancor. "Only people with money and position are afraid of being cuckolds. A man like you — who knows that you're even alive? Besides, cuckold or not, what's the difference? I'm independent now. Whatever I do can't have any effect on you."

"But we're still married, after all. As the old saying goes: 'One night of marriage, hundred days of bliss —' "

"I don't know anything about any hundred days of bliss," Chuntao interrupted. "Several hundred days of bliss have passed since then. Nearly five years without a word. I'm sure you never dreamed we'd meet again either. I was here alone. I had to live. I needed someone to help me. After living together with him all these years, of course I don't feel the same about you any more. I brought you home today because our fathers were friends, because we came from the same village. You may claim I'm your wife, but I deny you. Even if you take the case to court, I'm not so sure you'll win."

Li Mao fumbled at the pouch in his belt as if searching for something. But then he stopped and stared at Chuntao, and his hand dropped back and rested on the mat covering of the oven-bed.

Li Mao was silent. Chuntao wept. The shadows on the floor softly lengthened.

"Alright, Chuntao, if that's how you want it. I'm a cripple. Even if you came back to me, I couldn't support you," Li Mao said sensibly.

"I can't throw you over because you're crippled. But I can't give him up either. Why don't we all just live here, and no one think about who's supporting whom, what do you say?" Chuntao, too, spoke the words that were in her heart.

Li Mao's stomach rumbled faintly.

"Oh, here we've been talking all this time and I haven't even asked you what you'd like to eat. You must be terribly hungry."

"Anything at all. I haven't eaten since last night. I only had some water."

"I'll buy something." As Chuntao hurried from the house,

Xianggao gaily entered the courtyard. They collided under the arbor.

"What are you so happy about?" she asked him. "Why are you home so early?"

"I did some good business today. This morning I went through that load of paper you brought home last night, and what did I find but some Ming Dynasty petitions sent to the Emperor of China by the King of Korea — ten of them, worth at least fifty dollars apiece! I just brought a few down to the exchange to see what they'll bring from the customers: I'll take some more down later. I also found two stamped sheets of paper that the experts say are Song Dynasty. I've been offered sixty dollars for them already, but I was afraid to sell. Maybe that's too cheap. I brought them back to let you take a look. See. . . ."

He undid the cloth wrapper of his bundle and took out the documents and the stamped paper. "This is the imperial seal." He pointed at the stamped imprint.

"Except for that mark, I don't see anything special about this paper. Fine foreign paper is much whiter," said Chuntao. "Those Palace officials must be as blind as I am."

Xianggao laughed. "If they weren't a little blind how could people like us earn a couple of dollars now and again?"

He retied the bundle. "I say, wife —"

Chuntao glanced at him sharply. "I told you not to call me that."

Xianggao ignored her tone. "You've come home early too. Business must be not bad."

"I bought another basketful, the same as yesterday's."

"Didn't you say there was a lot more?"

They sent it all to the Morning Market to use for peanut bags!"

"Never mind. We've done very well today. It's the first time we've done more than thirty dollars' worth of business in a day. Say, it isn't often that we're both home together in the afternoon. Why don't we take a stroll around the fair grounds at Ten Monasteries Lake? It's nice and cool there."

He went into the house and put his bundle on the table. Chuntao followed him in. "We can't," she said. "We have a visitor today." Raising the door curtain of the inner room, she nodded to Xianggao, "Go on in."

He walked into the next room with Chuntao right behind him. "This is my former husband," she said to Xianggao, and to Li Mao she said, "this is my partner."

The eyes of the two men met. If the pupils of each man's eyes were spaced equally far apart, the lines of vision would have been exactly parallel. Neither man spoke. Even the two flies resting on the window-sill were silent. The room remained hushed for several moments.

"Your name, sir?" asked Xianggao courteously. Of course, he knew very well.

They began to chat.

"I must go out and buy a couple of things," said Chuntao. "You probably haven't eaten either," she said to Xianggao. "Will griddle cakes be alright?"

"I've eaten. You stay here. I'll do the buying."

Chuntao pushed him to a seat on the bed. "You stay here and entertain the guest," she insisted with a smile. She went out.

The two men were left alone in the room. In a situation like that, if they hadn't liked one another on sight, they might have fought to the death. Fortunately, they had formed a mutual liking. We needn't think because Li Mao had lost his legs that he couldn't fight. We must remember that Xianggao's only exercise the past four or five years had been wielding a pen. Li Mao was strong enough to have killed him. If he had a gun, it would have been even easier. One crook of the trigger finger and Xianggao would have crossed the Bridge to the Outer World.

Li Mao told Xianggao that his father used to help Chuntao's father on the farm during the busy seasons, and that the two were good friends. Because Li Mao was a crack shot, Chuntao's father was afraid he would go off and join the army. To make sure he would stay and protect the local peasants, the old man gave his daughter to Li Mao in marriage. This was something Chuntao had never mentioned to Xianggao before. Li Mao then told him of the conversation he had just had with Chuntao, and the talk came around to the question that affected them both so vitally.

"Now that you husband and wife are reunited again, I'll leave, of course," said Xianggao reluctantly.

"No. I've been away from her so long. And now I'm a cripple. I couldn't support her. It wouldn't be any use. You've lived together all these years. Why break up? I can go to a home for the disabled. I hear there's one here. I can get in if I can make the right connections."

Xianggao was surprised. He hadn't expected such magnanimous conduct from a man he had considered a rough soldier. But though his heart agreed, his mouth continued to refuse. This is the courteous hypocrisy known so well by all who have had some book-learning.

"That's not right," replied Xianggao. "I don't want to be known as a wife-stealer. And, thinking of it from your angle, you shouldn't let your wife live with another man."

"I'll write a paper disowning her, or I'll give you a bill of sale. Either way will do," Li Mao said with a smile. But his tone was quite earnest.

"How can you disown her? She hasn't done anything wrong. I don't want her to lose face. As for buying her — where would I get the money? Whatever money I have is hers."

"I don't want any money."

"What do you want?"

"I don't want anything."

"Then why write a bill of sale?"

"Because if we just agree verbally you won't have any proof. I might be sorry later and change my mind; that would make things awkward. Excuse me for talking so frankly, but that's the best way to get this thing settled. We can save the polite chatter for later."

Chuntao returned with the sesame seed buns she had bought. Seeing the two men talking together so freely, she was very happy.

"I've been thinking a lot lately about finding another person to help us," she said to Xianggao. "Now, by a lucky coincidence, Mao has shown up. He can't walk, but he'll be fine at home, sorting through the paper. You can be our outside salesman. I'll still do the collecting. The three of us will be a business company."

Li Mao made no reply, but picked up a sesame seed bun and began wolfing it down. It was as if he had just come back from the world of the starving and had no time for talk.

"Two men and a woman form a company? And you put up the capital?" Xianggao asked needlessly.

"What's the matter? Don't you agree?"

"Of course, of course. I haven't any objections." Xianggao couldn't bring himself to say what he was thinking.

"What can I do? What use will I be, sitting around the house all day?" Li Mao was rather hesitant too. He understood Xianggao's meaning.

"Now both of you just take it easy. I've got it all figured out."

Xianggao uneasily moistened his lips. Li Mao continued eating, but his eyes were fixed on Chuntao. He waited to hear what she had to say.

Collecting scrap paper is probably an occupation in which women play the leading role. Chuntao had already evolved a plan. Li Mao would stay home and pick out the used postage stamps and the picture cards in the empty cigarette packs. The job required only eyes and hands, and he could do it. She calculated that if he could find a hundred and some odd cigarette pack pictures every day, that would cover the cost of his food.

If, each day, he could also find even two or three good, relatively rare, stamps, that would be even better. About ten thousand packs of foreign cigarettes were sold in Beijing daily (the foreign cigarette packs were the ones containing the premium picture cards). Chuntao thought that she could collect, say, one per cent of these without much difficulty. Xianggao would concentrate on looking for letters of famous people and other comparatively valuable items. Needless to say, he was already an expert, and needed no further guidance. Chuntao herself would do the heavy work. Unless there was a big rain storm, she would go out every day, regardless of the wind or cold. In fact she would make a special point of working in the bad weather, because on such days some of her competitors were likely to stay home.

Glancing at the sun through the window, she estimated it was not yet two o'clock. She went out into the courtyard, put on her battered straw hat, then called through the door to Xianggao:

"I must inquire whether there's anything else being thrown out of the Palace. You look after him. I'll be back tonight and we can talk some more."

Xianggao knew it was hopeless to try and detain her. He let her go.

Several days went by in silence. But two men and a woman sleeping together on a single brick oven-bed of course was very awkward. The institution of polyandrous marriage after all hasn't too many adherents in the world, one of the reasons being that the average man cannot rid himself of his primitive concepts regarding his rights as a husband and father. It is from these concepts that our customs and moral codes arise. Actually, in our society, only the parasites and exploiters observe the so-called customs; people who have to work for a living have very little respect for them in their hearts.

Take Chuntao, for instance. She was neither a well-to-do matron or a fashionable young miss. She was not likely to go dancing at some glittering ballroom, nor would she have any opportunity to play the hostess at a big society function. No one criticized or questioned her conduct. Even if they had, it wouldn't have bothered her a whit. Only the local policeman was concerned with her comings and goings, and he was quite easy to handle.

The two men? Xianggao, with a few years of schooling, had a vague idea of the precepts of the ancient feudal philosophers. But except for a mild interest in preserving appearances, he was the same as Chuntao. From the time he moved in, he was completely dependent on her. To him, her word was law. He obeyed her because it was to his benefit to do so. Chuntao told him not to be jealous, so he cast aside even the seed of jealousy.

As for Li Mao, his demands were simple. If Xianggao and Chuntao would let him live with them for a day, he would stay for a day; if they treated him as a relative, he would be quite satisfied. Travelling around so much, a soldier always loses a wife or two. Li Mao's problem was also one of appearances.

Nevertheless, although Xianggao was not jealous, a number of other disturbing things kept coming between the two men.

The summer days were still stifling hot, but Chuntao and Xianggao were not the sort of people to go to exclusive vacation resorts. They had to get on with their work. At home, Li Mao was beginning to learn the trade. He could already distinguish between which paper should be sent to the toilet paper makers and which he should keep for a final appraisal by Xianggao.

Coming home one day, Chuntao found Xianggao waiting for her as usual. It was already late, and as she entered the house she could smell incense burning.

"When did we take to burning mosquito-repellent incense?" she called to Xianggao, who was sitting beneath the arbor. "You're liable to burn the house down too, if you're not careful."

Xianggao made no reply, but Li Mao said, "We're not trying to drive away the mosquitoes, we're just purifying the air. I asked Brother Xianggao to light it for me. I'm figuring on sleeping outside tonight. It's too hot inside. With three people sleeping together, it's really uncomfortable."

"Who does this red card on the table belong to?" Chuntao asked, picking it up.

"We talked it over today," said Li Mao from the brick bed. "You go to Xianggao. That's the contract of sale."

"Oh, so you've got it all settled among yourselves! Well, and I say it's not up to you two to dispose of me!" She walked over to Li Mao with the red card. "Was this your idea, or his?"

"It's what we both want. The way we've been living, I'm not happy and neither is he."

"You talk and talk and it's still the same question. Why must you two always think about this husband and wife business?" Angrily, she tore the card to bits. "How much did you sell me for?"

"We put down a figure just for the looks of things. No real man gives his wife away for nothing."

"But if he sells her, that makes everything alright, does it?" She walked out to Xianggao. "You've got money now. You can afford to buy a wife. Why not spend a little more and —"

"Don't talk like that, don't talk like that," Xianggao pleaded. "You don't understand, Chuntao. The last few days, the people in the trade have all been laughing at me —"

"Laughing?"

"Yes. . . ." Xianggao's voice trailed off. As a matter of fact, he didn't feel very strongly about the matter. Nine cases out of ten, he did whatever Chuntao wanted. He didn't know why she had such power over him. At times he thought a certain thing should be done this way or that, yet when he came face to face with her, she was like a queen whose every command he had to obey.

"So you can't forget you're a scholar — just because you've read a couple of books. Scared to death that someone will scold you, laugh at you."

From the earliest days, real control over the people has

been exercised not through the teachings of the sages but by
cursing tongues and blows of the whip. Curses and blows are
what have maintained our customs. But in Chuntao's state of
mind she was ready to return "A curse for a curse, a blow for a
blow." No weakling, while she didn't pick on anyone, she
wouldn't take abuse from others either. Just hear how she instructed Xianggao, and you'll see:

"If anyone laughs at you, why don't you hit him? What are
you afraid of? What we do is nobody else's business."

Xianggao was silent.

"Let's not talk about this any more. Why can't the three
of us go on living as we are?"

The room was still. After the evening meal Xianggao and
Chuntao sat beneath the arbor as usual, but both were unusually
quiet. They didn't even recite any passages from the scriptures
of the day's business.

Li Mao called Chuntao into the house. He urged her to
become Xianggao's wife officially. He said she didn't understand a man's psychology. No one wanted to be a cuckold; nor
did anyone want to become known as a wife-stealer. Taking
out a red card which was already turning brown, he handed it
to Chuntao.

"This is our marriage certificate. That night we fled, I
took it from the shrine and put it in my shirt. I'm giving it back
to you, so now we can be considered no longer married."

Chuntao accepted the card from him without a word, her
eyes fixed on the torn mat covering the brick bed. She sank to
a seat beside her crippled husband.

"Take it back, Mao dear, I don't want it. I'm still your
wife. 'One night of marriage, a hundred days of bliss' — I can't
wrong you like this. What kind of a person would I be if I
threw you over because you can't walk or work?"

She placed the red card on the brick bed.

Li Mao was deeply moved. "I can see that you like him
a lot." he said in a low voice. "You'd better live with him.

When we get a little money scraped together, you can send me back to the country, or to a home for disabled soldiers."

"It's true these last few years we've been living together, we've been getting along fine," Chuntao replied softly. "If he were to go, I'd miss him terribly. Let's ask him in and see what he thinks."

"Xianggao, Xianggao," she called from the window. No response. She went outside. Xianggao was not there. This was the first time he had ever gone out at night alone. Chuntao was stunned. She called towards the house:

"I'll go look for him."

She was sure Xianggao had only gone up to the corner. But when she asked Old Wu, the old man said he had seen him going towards the main street. She went to all of his usual haunts, but Xianggao was nowhere to be seen. It's very easy to lose a person. Once they get out of sight, they disappear without a trace.

It was nearly one in the morning when Chuntao, heavy-hearted, returned home.

The oil lamp in the room was already extinguished.

"Are you asleep? Has Xianggao come back yet?" she asked. Striking a match, she lit the lamp and peered at the brick bed. A chill of terror ran through her veins. Li Mao had hanged himself with his belt from the top of the window lattice. She managed to control herself sufficiently to climb up and lower him to the bed. Fortunately, the time had been short and it wasn't necessary to call for help. By kneading his chest, she gradually was able to revive him.

Taking one's own life for the sake of another is the deed of a knight-errant. If Li Mao hadn't lost his legs he would not have had to resort to such a measure; but for the past few days he had been thinking there was little hope in store for him, that it would be best to do away with himself and let Chuntao live in peace.

Although Chuntao didn't love him, she had a strong sense

of duty to him. She comforted and reassured him, talking to him until the sky turned light. At last he slept and Chuntao got down off the bed. On the floor she saw the charred remains of a red card — their marriage certificate. Transfixed, she stared at it for a long time.

All that day she didn't go out of the door. In the evening, she sat beside Li Mao on the brick bed.

"Why are you crying?" she asked him. Tears were rolling down his cheeks.

"I've wronged you. What did I come here for?"

"Nobody's blaming you."

"Now he's gone, and I haven't any legs —"

"You mustn't think like that. He'll come back."

"I hope so."

Thus another day passed. When Chuntao arose the next morning, she picked a couple of cucumbers from the vine and peeled and sliced them. Carelessly mixing a few ingredients, she grilled a big griddle cake, and brought it with the cucumbers to a small table on the brick bed. She and Li Mao ate together.

Then Chuntao donned her battered straw hat and fastened her basket on her back.

"You're in low spirits today, don't go out," Li Mao said to her through the window.

"I feel worse sitting around the house."

Slowly, she walked through the gate. Work was part of her very being. Even though she was depressed and unhappy, she still wanted to work. Work is the only thing Chinese women seem to understand. They don't seem to understand love. All their attention is concentrated on the routine problems of life. Love's flowering is only a blind, stifled stirring in their hearts.

Of course love is merely an emotion, while life is tangible and real. The art of talking learnedly of love while reclining behind a silken curtain or sitting in a secluded forest glade is an importation brought on ocean-going steamers — the "Empress" of this. the "President" that. Chuntao had never been abroad.

nor had she ever studied in a school run by blue-eyed foreigners. She didn't understand fashionable love. All she knew was a dull, unaccountable pain.

She wandered from one lane to the next. Endless dust, endless streets engulfed the downcast young woman. "Matches for scrap paper!" she called occasionally. Yet at times she walked by a pile of discarded paper without giving it a glance. Once or twice, when she was supposed to give two boxes of matches in payment, Chuntao gave five. After muddling through the day, she returned home with the black-cloaked ravens, those rascals who are good for nothing but cawing raucously and stealing food. At the gate she saw the new residents' identification card which the police had posted, stating that Xianggao and she, his wife, were the residents-in-charge. The pressure on her heart grew heavier.

As she entered the courtyard, Xianggao came running out of the house.

Chuntao's eyes went wide. "You've come back! . . ." she cried, and then she couldn't speak for the choking tears.

"I can't leave you. Everything I have I owe to you. I know you want me to help you with your work. I can't be so callous. . . ."

He had been drifting about aimlessly for two days. His feet seemed to be dragging heavy iron fetters, fastened at one end to Chuntao's wrist. To make matters worse, wherever he went he saw the cigarette ad with the girl who looked just like Chuntao. He was so miserable, he didn't even know he was hungry.

"Brother Xianggao and I have talked it over," said Li Mao. "He's the resident-in-charge, I'm the sub-tenant."

Xianggao helped her take off the basket, as in the old days, at the same time wiping the tears from her face. "If we all go back to the country," he said, "Li Mao will be the resident-in-charge and I'll be the sub-tenant. You're our wife."

She made no reply but went into the house, hung up her hat, and took her daily bath.

Once again Chuntao and Xianggao began reciting passages from the scriptures of the day's business under the cucumber arbor. They agreed that after they sold that paper from the Imperial Palace, they would use some of the money to set up a stall for Xianggao in the public market; perhaps they could also find a somewhat roomier place to live, too.

A moth, flying into the house from the arbor, snuffed out the oil lamp's tiny flame. Li Mao was fast asleep, for the Milky Way was already low in the sky.

"We ought to sleep too," the woman said.

"You get into bed first. I'll come and massage you in a minute."

"You don't have to. I didn't walk very far today. We have to be up early tomorrow. Don't forget to take care of that business. We haven't shown a profit for days."

"Say, I forgot to give it to you. On the way home today, I made a special trip to the second-hand market and bought you a hat that's practically new. What do you think of it?" Groping, Xianggao found the hat and handed it to her.

"How can I see anything in the dark? I'll wear it tomorrow anyhow."

A hush fell on the courtyard. The scent of tuberoses wafted lazily on the night's gentle breeze. In the room soft voices could be faintly heard.

"Wife. . . ."

"I don't want to hear it. I'm not your wife. . . ."

Translated by Sidney Shapiro

About the Author

XU DISHAN (1893-1941), whose pen name was Luo Huasheng was a renowned contemporary writer. Born in Longxi County

Fujian Province, he received his early education in Guangdong and started teaching in 1912, first in the Fujian Second Normal School and then in the Rangoon Overseas Chinese School of Burma. He returned to teach in the Second Normal School in 1915. While studying in the Yanjing University of Beijing after 1917, he was active in the May Fourth Movement. He became a tutor in the university after graduation and formed the Literary Study Society together with Mao Dun, Zheng Zhenduo, Ye Shengtao and others. He published his first short story "Love-birds" in the monthly *Fiction,* followed by others such as "The Merchant's Wife", "The Busy Spider's Web" and "Light Drizzle in Lonely Hills", and thus became an important writer of the New Literature Movement in its early period. Xu Dishan received a bachelor's degree in theology from the Religion College of the Yanjing University. The same year he went to study religious history and philosophy at Columbia University in New York. In 1924 he transferred to study religious history, Indian philosophy, Sanskrit and folklore at Oxford University in London. On his way back to China, he had a short stay in India to study Sanskrit and Buddhism. He became a professor in 1926 at the Religion College of Yanjing University. He also taught Indian philosophy and anthropology at Beijing and Qinghua universities. In this period, he compiled the *Index to the Buddhist Scriptures* and *Chinese Taoist History.* Religious philosophy and fatalist ideology can be clearly seen in his early writings such as the collection of stories *The Busy Spider's Web* and the collection of prose *Light Drizzle in Lonely Hills.*

"Big Sister Liu", first published in 1934, vividly depicts the deep affection the suffering working people show for each other and their other fine qualities by presenting a working woman who is kind and straightforward with a strong will.

Intoxicating Spring Nights

Yu Dafu

I

For six months I lived without a job in Shanghai and, because I was unemployed, changed my lodgings three times. At first I lived in a pigeon-hole on Bubbling Well Road, a prison without guards where the sun never shone. With the exception of a few ferocious gangster-like tailors, the inmates of this unguarded prison were mostly pitiable unknown scholars. That was why I named the place Yellow Grub Street. After a month or so in this Grub Street, the rent suddenly went up and I, with my few dog-eared books, was forced to move into a small hotel I knew somewhere near the race-course. Here too I met with certain kinds of pressure until I had to move again. This time I found and moved into a tiny room in the slums opposite Rixinli on Dent Road at the north end of the Garden Bridge.

The houses on this side of Dent Road stood no higher than 20 feet. The loft I lived in was extremely small and low. If, standing upright, I had wished to stretch my arms and yawn, my hands would have gone through the dusty grey roof.

Coming in from the lane through the front door, one entered first the landlord's room. Here, edging one's way through heaps of rags, old tins and bottles and other junk, one came to a rickety ladder leaning against the wall. This was the only way one could get up to the dark opening — two square feet —

which led to the second storey. This storey was really only a small, dark loft, but it was partitioned into two tiny rooms. I had the one where the trap door was; the other one was let to a woman who worked in the N Cigarette Co. As she had to go through my "room", to get to hers, my monthly rent was a few dimes cheaper.

Our landlord was an oldish man, round about the fifties, with a bent back. There was a dark oily gleam in his sallow face. His eyes were unequal in size, and his cheek bones were sharp and protruding. The lines on his forehead and face were filled with coal dust which seemed indelible despite his daily morning wash. He got up between eight and nine every day and after a fit of coughing left the house with a carrying pole and two bamboo baskets. Usually, he returned at three or four in the afternoon with the same baskets empty. Occasionally he came back with a load, the same kind of stuff as he had all over his room: rags, broken bottles and miscellaneous pieces of junk. On these days he would usually buy himself a few ounces of wine, and, sitting on the edge of the bed, would drink by himself and curse roundly in an incomprehensible language.

I met my neighbour on the other side of the partition on the afternoon I moved in. At about five o'clock, when the fast-falling spring dusk had already descended, I had lit a candle and began to arrange the books I had brought with me from the hotel, setting them up into two stacks, one big and one small. On the bigger stack I placed two 24-inch picture frames. I had sold all the furniture I ever possessed, so my arrangement of books and picture frames had to serve as a desk during the day and a bed at night. I then sat myself down on the smaller stack of books, facing the "desk", and lit a cigarette. As I sat staring at the candle and smoking I heard a slight noise under the trap door, behind my back. I looked round but could only see the shadow of my own head. But my ears told me plainly that someone was coming up. I stared intently into the darkness and then saw a pale white oval face and the upper part of a slim woman's figure emerge before my eyes. I knew immediately that she was my housemate on the other side of the partition. When I first came to get a room, the old landlord told me that besides himself there was a woman worker who lived in this house and had one of the rooms. I had taken the room without a moment's hesitation because first of all I liked the low rent and secondly, I was glad there was no real housewife and children in the house. As my neighbour came up into my room, I stood up and bowed politely. "Good evening," I said. "I moved in today. I hope we'll get along all right."

She made no answer but her big dark eyes looked at me searchingly. Then she went to her door, unlocked it and went in. That was all I saw at my first encounter with her, but for some reason I felt that she was a defenceless young thing. Something about her pale features, and her small slim figure all seemed to indicate that she was a desolate and pitiful soul. However, at that time, I myself had enough worries of my own to spare much pity for someone who at least was not yet out of work and I turned back to sit motionless on the smaller stack of books, staring at the candle light.

A week went by since my move into the slums. Every day when my neighbour went to work — she went before seven in the morning and returned after six — she would find me sitting dully on my stack of books watching the candle flame or the oil lamp. Perhaps her curiosity was stirred by my constantly keeping to myself in a sullen manner. Finally, one day when she came up the ladder after work and I stood up as usual to let her pass, she stopped and looked directly at me.

"What is it you are always reading so hard every day?" she asked in a faltering, timid voice. She spoke a soft pure Suzhou dialect but the feeling this charming tongue produced in me is impossible to describe so I'll just translate her words into ordinary speech.

What she said made me quite red in the face. The fact was that though I placed a number of foreign books before me,

as I sat woodenly thus day in and day out, my mind was actually in complete confusion and I wasn't reading a single word. Sometimes I let my imagination fill the space between the lines with strange shapes and forms; at other times I merely glanced at the illustrations and my fancy promptly conjured up fantastic images from them. Actually, at that time, I was suffering from insomnia and malnutrition and was not in a normal state at all. Furthermore, since my only possession in the world, the padded gown on my back, was too shabby for words, I hadn't been able to go out in the daytime, and in my dark little room which let in no daylight whatever, had to use a candle or the oil lamp all the time, so that my eyes, and legs too, were weak from disuse.

"I wasn't really reading," I said confusedly. "But you see, if I just sat there woodenly without doing anything, it would have looked so silly. That is why I have these books open in front of me."

She gave me a quizzical look and went back to her room, still wearing a puzzled expression.

It would be untrue to say that I had completely neglected the idea of a job or that I had done nothing whatsoever. There were moments when I felt somewhat clearer in my mind and altogether I had translated a few short English and French poems and several German short stories around 4,000 words each since I had been there. The results of my efforts I had posted off to some new publishing firms. I always did the posting in the dark of night, when no one else was stirring. I felt that I had no hope of getting a real job and that the only thing I could do was to try and make use of my dried-up brains. If I were lucky and my translation met with the approval of the publishers and were used, it would bring in a few dollars.

2

Living anywhere in the dreary foreign concessions in Shanghai one hardly noticed the passing of the days or the changing

of the seasons, and in the Dent Road slums I only noticed that
my shabby padded gown felt heavier and heavier day by day
and realized one day that spring must have grown quite old,
as the saying is.

But I, with my lean purse, was in no position to go anywhere. All I could do was to sit fixedly by the lamp in my dark
room day and night. One day — it must have been late afternoon, I suppose — I was sitting there as usual when my neighbour returned, carrying two small parcels. When I stood up to
let her pass, she put one of them down on my desk, and said,
"Here's a bit of raisin bread for you; eat it tomorrow. I've
bought some bananas, too. Will you come into my room and
eat them with me?"

I held the little parcel for her while she unlocked the door
and led me into her room. We had been neighbours for a fortnight or so and it seemed she had come to trust me as an honest
respectable man. The fear and suspicion on her face the first
time I spoke to her were no longer there. Entering her room,
I realized that it was not yet dark outside. Slanting rays of
sunlight came in through a window which faced the south and
I saw she had a bed made of two planks, a small black lacquer
table against the wall, a wooden trunk and a round stool. She
had no mosquito-net but there were two clean cotton quilts on
bed. A small tin case on the table probably held her toilet
things; it was bespattered with greasy spots. She picked up
some odd pieces of clothing which were on the stool, put them
on the bed and invited me to sit down. I felt a little embarrassed by the warm, hospitable fuss she made over me. "We are
such close neighbours! Please don't stand on ceremony with
me," I told her.

"I'm not standing on ceremony. But you always stand up
when I come through to let me pass. I really feel very much
obliged."

She undid the parcel as she spoke, offered me a banana
and peeled one for herself. As we ate, she sat down on the bed

and began to talk. "Why do you sit at home all the time instead
of going out to get some work?"

"I want to get work, but though I've looked round I
haven't been able to find a job."

"Haven't you got any friends?"

"I did have friends, but at a time like this they're not inclined to see me any more."

"Have you had any schooling?"

"Yes. I've had some years in a foreign school."

"Where is your family? Why don't you go home?"

By then, her questioning suddenly made me aware of what
was really happening to me. In the last six months or so I had
simply been fading away day by day and had practically forgotten such things even as "Who am I? What am I doing?" or "Am
I sad or happy?" My mind was full of the difficulties I had been
in during these months and I could only stare at her dully, unable
to say a word. My expression must have made her think that
I was a waif with no home. A look of sadness and loneliness
was reflected on her face too.

"You're like me, then!" she said with a sigh, and like me
lapsed into silence. I saw that her eyes were getting a little moist
so I tried to change the subject. "What do you do in the
factory?"

"Cigarette wrapping."

"How many hours do you work?"

"We start at seven and finish at six, with an hour's break
for food — ten hours a day. We're paid by the hour, and we've
got to do the lot, or we're fined."

"What's the pay, then?"

"Nine dollars a month. Three dollars for ten days, that
is — three cents an hour."

"How much do you pay for food?"

"Four dollars a month."

"If you don't lose any time in the month, then you're left

with five dollars to take home, eh? Is that enough for rent and clothes?"

"Of course it's not enough! And the foreman there is so. . . ." She shuddered. "I hate that factory. Do you smoke?"

"Yes."

"I wish you wouldn't! If you must, please don't smoke my factory's cigarettes. I do hate it so, everything about it."

I saw how fed up she was and did not know what to say. I finished my banana and looked round. It was getting dark in here too. I got up, made my thanks and went back to my own room.

Usually, because she was always exhausted from the day's work, she went to bed not long after her return; that night I could hear her pottering around in her room for a long time: She did not go to bed until after midnight. Ever since that evening, she always said a few words to me on her return, and I learned all about her.

Her name was Chen Ermei, and her family came from Suzhou, though she herself grew up in one of the villages outside Shanghai. Her father had also worked in the cigarette factory, but he had died last autumn. When he was alive they had shared this same tiny room, and went to work together every day. Now, she was all by herself. For the first month after her father's death she used to weep all the way to the factory and in the evenings come back with tears trickling down her cheeks. She was only seventeen, and had no sisters or brothers or any near kin. Our old landlord downstairs had taken full charge of the father's funeral and burial, for which task he had been entrusted with fifteen dollars by the father before his death.

"He is a good old man," she told me. "He has never had any bad intentions towards me, so I have been able to continue to work the way I did when father was living. But one of the foremen in the factory by the name of Li is wicked. He knows that my father is dead and he's been trying to get at me."

3

The weather seemed to have changed. During the past few days, the stuffy dim little room which was my lone world had become as close and hot as a damp steam oven. It was so oppressive that it made me dizzy and nauseated. At certain times of the year, particularly the season of late spring, my nerves usually drove me half crazy. I now began to go out for long walks by myself at night, when the streets were quiet. Strolling, solitary, under the narrow strip of dark blue sky I gazed at the stars and let my thoughts soar in fantasy. This was beneficial to my health. On such intoxicating spring nights, when I felt carried away, I often roamed round until it was nearly dawn before I returned to bed. After these exhausting strolls, I found I could sleep till noon the next day, sometimes even later, in fact, till it was nearly time for Ermei to return from work. After these hours of good sleep every day, I began to feel like a new person. Ordinarily, I could not make myself eat more than half a pound of bread but since I began my midnight exercises, my appetite improved until I found myself eating nearly double. Though this was a severe blow to my budget, my brain, nourished by the increased rations, was able to concentrate much better. After those night wanderings and before I went to bed, I managed to write a couple of short stories in the style of Edgar Allan Poe. Reading them over, I thought they weren't so bad. After numerous corrections and re-copying, I sent them out. I could not resist a slight hope about them, though I told myself that there had been no news whatever of the translations I sent out some time back. A few days after I had sent them I forgot about them too.

As for my neighbour, Ermei, I now saw her only occasionally when she returned in the afternoon since I was usually sound asleep when she left her room in the morning. For some reason her attitude towards me had reverted to the old one of fear and suspicion. Sometimes she used to give me a searching look, her dark limpid eyes seeming to be half-reproaching and half-advising.

About three weeks had passed since I moved into the slums. One evening, when I had just lit the candle and was reading a novel I had got from a second-hand bookstore, Ermei rushed up the stairs and confronted me. "There's a postman downstairs, who wants you! He's got a letter for you to sign for."

The look of suspicion and fear on her face was more evident than ever. She seemed to be saying, "Ah, you've been found out." I was very much annoyed at this attitude of hers, and said sharply, "A letter? Who would write to me? It can't be mine."

My indignant reply seemed to make her feel triumphant, and she said coldly, "Go and have a look yourself. You alone know what you have done."

As she spoke I heard the voice of the postman downstairs calling impatiently, "Registered letter!"

When I got the letter my heart began to thump. One of my translations of German short stories had been accepted by a magazine, and I had got a money order for five dollars. My purse was actually getting very empty and this five dollars meant that I would be able to pay the rent that was due at the end of the month and have some money left to keep me alive for several days. The need I had for this five dollars was greater than anyone could imagine.

The next afternoon I went to the post-office and cashed the money order. A short time on the streets under bright sunlight and I was dripping with perspiration. I looked at the people round me, then looked down at myself and felt self-conscious. Trickles of sweat rained down my head and neck. When I had been roaming about at night, there had been no sun and the cool air of the spring nights as I strolled through deserted lanes in the small hours was not so incompatible with the shabby padded gown that was my only wear. But now it was mid-afternoon on a warm sunny spring day and I, like a fool, did not have the sense to realize it but had walked down the street still in the same old attire. Naturally I felt abashed when I compared myself with my fellow creatures on the street, who had adapted themselves to the changes of the season. At that moment I forgot all about the rent that was due in a few days and the fast-emptying contents of my purse and turned slowly towards the clothiers on Zha Road.

I, who had not been out in broad daylight for a fairly long time, now felt for a moment that I had entered paradise when I saw the busy traffic and rickshaws rushing down the street with beautifully clothed young men and women in them, the luxurious and dazzling windows of the silk shops and jewellers', and heard the buzz of human voices, footsteps and bells and horns. I forgot my own mean existence and felt like singing and skipping as merrily as my fellow men. Inadvertently, I began to hum a long-forgotten tune from some Peking Opera. But this momentary nirvana was quickly shattered by the sharp notes of a bell when I tried to cross the street and turn into Zha Road. I looked up and saw that a trolley-bus was rushing towards me and the fat driver, leaning out, was glaring at me angrily. "Swine, have you no eyes? Serve you right if you get killed. Your life's worth no more than a yellow dog, anyway."

I pulled myself up as the trolley-bus rumbled past in a cloud of dust. I did not know why, but I found myself bursting into peals of ironical laughter. All too soon I realized that passers-by were staring at me in astonishment and I went off with a very red face.

I went into a number of clothiers, asked the prices of a couple of lined gowns and offered a price I could afford. No matter which shop I was in, all the attendants behaved as if they were trained by one master. Frowning down on me, one after the other they said mockingly, "You're not kidding, are you? If you can't afford to buy anything, don't bother us."

I went on from shop to shop until I got to a tiny place a long way down the road. I had come to realize that it was impossible to get a lined gown for what I could afford to pay, so I bought a plain blue cotton gown and changed into it then and there. Carrying my old padded gown, wrapped up in a parcel, I walked silently homewards.

"The money won't be enough for anything now, whatever happens, so I might as well have a spree," I told myself. I remembered the bread and bananas Ermei had asked me to share with her, and I turned into a confectioner's and bought a dollar's worth of chocolates, cakes and various eatables. As I stood waiting for the counter-hand to wrap it up I remembered that I hadn't had a bath for more than a month and decided I must have one.

By the time I had had my bath and returned to Dent Road with my two parcels, the food and my old gown, the lights were on in the shop windows and there were few people on the street. A cold evening breeze swept in from the bund and I shivered in my thin gown. I went back to my room, lit the candle and looked towards Ermei's door, only to find that she hadn't yet returned. I felt very hungry by now myself but I didn't want to open the parcel on the table; I wanted to share the delicacies with her. Picking up a book at random, I tried to read, but found myself having to swallow hard to curb my hunger all the time. I felt as though I had waited for ages, but there was still no Ermei. In the end my fatigue overcame me and I dozed off against the books.

4

The sound of Ermei's footsteps on the ladder roused me. I noticed that the candle had burned down two inches. When I asked her what time it was she answered, "The ten o'clock siren's just gone."

"Why are you back so late today?"

"They made us do night work because the sales have gone up. Though we get extra pay I get too tired."

"Can't you refuse to do overtime then?"

"No. There aren't enough workers, so I can't refuse."

Suddenly a tear trickled down her cheek. I thought she was crying from exhaustion and felt not only a deep sympathy but a certain thrill to discover she was still such a child. I opened the parcel and offered her my delicacies. While she ate, I said consolingly, "You're not used to night work; that's why you feel so tired. When you get used to it, it's really nothing."

She sat mutely on my makeshift desk and nibbled at a chocolate but her eyes turned on me several times as if she wanted to speak. "There's something on your mind, isn't there?" I said. "Come on, say what it is."

There was an awkward pause and then she started, falteringly, "I've been . . . er . . . wanting to ask you something for a long time. Recently you've been going out every night. Have you been mixing with bad men?"

I was very surprised at this idea of hers. She had been suspecting me of mixing with thieves and gangsters since I had been going out at night, it seemed. When she saw that her words had startled me she thought her suspicion was right and that she had found me out. She went on talking to me, her voice friendly but pleading. "Do you have to eat such rich food and wear new clothes? Don't you know what you are doing is very risky? What if you are caught? How would you be able to face people? Let's not bother about what has already happened, though. I just want you to reform from now on. . . ."

I couldn't say a word, but stared at her with my mouth agape. Her thoughts were so strange and unexpected that I didn't know how to explain. She was silent for only a few seconds and then went on, "Now take your smoking, for instance. If you cut that you'd be able to save a few coppers. I've already told you you shouldn't smoke, and particularly not the cigarettes made in my factory. But you won't listen."

Again a few tears rolled down her cheeks. I knew really that her tears were at the thought of her hated factory, but my heart would not let me think that way: I preferred to think that they were for me. I kept quiet for a minute, thinking, while she gradually calmed down. Then I explained where I had got the money, and the source of the registered letter yesterday, and told her about my going out to cash the money order and the things I bought, and about my insomnia and why I had to go out for walks at night. She accepted what I had said with no more doubts, and her cheeks were pink when I finished. With her eyes on the desk she said in a little voice:

"Ah, I was wrong to blame you. Please don't mind what I said. I didn't mean any harm. But your behaviour was so strange that my thoughts went to the worst. If you really get down to work it would be fine. That thing you mentioned — whatever it was that you sold for five dollars — couldn't you do one of that every day?"

Her simplicity touched me but at the same time an unthinkable notion swept over me. I longed to stretch out my arms and embrace her but reason checked me severely, saying, "That would be a sin. Don't you know your own situation? Do you want to poison this pure simple girl? Devil, devil, you have no right at present to love."

I closed my eyes for a few seconds while my emotions struggled with my reason, and reason won. When I opened my eyes again, the place suddenly looked brighter. I smiled gently at her and said, "It's getting late. Hadn't you better go to bed? You've got to go to work tomorrow. I promise you, starting from today, I'll cut out my smoking."

She stood up obediently and went back to her room with a happy smile.

When she was gone I lit another candle and sat down quietly to think things over.

"The fruits of my labour brought me this five dollars for the first time today but already I've spent three dollars. Added to the dollar I still had it'll only leave 20 or 30 cents after the rent's paid. What shall I do?"

"I could pawn my old padded gown, perhaps, but I don't think any pawnshop will take it."

"She's a poor little girl, but what about me? I'm in an even worse situation. She doesn't want to work, but she has to do overtime. I want to find work but I couldn't get any."

"Perhaps I could get a manual job. Oh, oh, but my useless muscles couldn't even cope with a rickshaw."

"I could kill myself, I suppose — I would have done long ago if I had had the courage. However, the fact that this word entered my head at this juncture shows that I haven't lost all my courage to do so."

"Ho, ho, what was it the trolley-bus driver called me today?"

"Yellow dog! Now that's a pretty term."

".............."

My mind went over a great number of scattered unconnected thoughts, but I could think of no really good way to get out of my present poverty. A siren from a nearby factory sounded; it must have been midnight. I stood up and changed into my shabby old gown, blew the candle out and went out for my walk.

It was quiet. All the other inhabitants of the slums were slumbering. Opposite me, in the modern blocks of Rixinli a few windows were still bright with coloured lights. The strains of the balalaika and snatches of a soft melancholy song drifted across the chilly night, probably from a young White Russian émigré girl, singing for her living. Overhead, greyish-white clouds covered the sky, piling up heavily like decaying corpses. Here and there where there was a gap in clouds, an occasional star blinked, but even the scraps of dark sky round them seemed sad and gloomy.

July 15, 1923
Translated by Tang Sheng

About the Author

YU DAFU (1896-1945) was born in Fuyang County, Zhejiang Province. He went to Japan during his early years where he studied literature at the Imperial University in Tokyo. In 1921, he set up the Creation Society, together with the poet Guo Moruo and literary critic Cheng Fangwu, who were then also studying in Japan. Yu Dafu edited the books and journals published by the Society.

The Creation Society played an important role in the development of China's new literature. It advocated enthusiastic and dauntless romanticism based upon real life. In 1925 Guo Moruo formally raised the slogan of revolutionary literature. He wrote in *Flood*, a fortnightly published by the Society, that what was demanded of revolutionary writers was "to point out the ideals of the proletariat and to present their sufferings". This slogan had a deep influence upon the new literary movement at that time. In 1926, in the first issue of the monthly *Creation*, Yu Dafu stated on behalf of the Society and its members that the purpose of this journal was to lend their yet weak voice to aid in the reformation of the surrounding irrational social conditions. During the period of the First Revolutionary War (1925-27), most of the writers belonging to the Creation Society took part in the revolutionary movement.

During the Sino-Japanese war, when the coastal areas of China were occupied by the Japanese, Yu Dafu went to Singapore where he took part in the activities against Japan and engaged in journalistic work among overseas Chinese. After the outbreak of the Pacific War, he went to Sumatra where the Japanese imperialists killed him in 1945, after the surrender.

Among his novels are *The Lost Sheep* and *Mirage*. His short stories were published under the titles of *Chicken Ribs*, *Cold Ashes*, *The Past* and *Wild Herbs*. He has also written feature stories, including *Nine Diaries*.

Yu Dafu's ideology as reflected in his works is mainly a sort of revolutionary romanticism, but heavily tinged with disillusionment so that, in the 1930s, he became divorced from reality. Only after the war against Japan did he recover.

"Intoxicating Spring Nights" is one of his earliest stories depicting the life of industrial workers in China. The author presents the miserable life shared by an intellectual and a woman worker in a cigarette factory who live as neighbours in a slum house. From the story, we can see the kind-heartedness and fighting spirit of the woman worker in her persistence under stress.

A Selection of Yu Dafu was published soon after liberation.

The Shop of the Lin Family

Mao Dun

I

Miss Lin's small mouth was pouting when she returned home from school that day. She flung down her books, and instead of combing her hair and powdering her nose before the mirror as usual, she stretched out on the bed. Her eyes staring at the top of the bed canopy, Miss Lin lay lost in thought. Her little cat leaped up beside her, snuggled against her waist and miaowed twice. Automatically, she patted his head, then rolled over and buried her face in the pillow.

"Ma!" called Miss Lin.

No answer. Ma, whose room was right next door, ordinarily doted on this only daughter of hers. On hearing her return, Ma would come swaying in to ask whether she was hungry. Ma would be keeping something good for her. Or she might send the maid out to buy a bowl of hot soup with meat dumplings from a street vendor. . . . But today was odd. There obviously were people talking in Ma's room — Miss Lin could hear Ma hiccuping too — yet Ma didn't even reply.

Again Miss Lin rolled over on the bed, and raised her head. She would eavesdrop on this conversation. Whom could Ma be talking to, that voices had to be kept so low?

But she couldn't make out what they were saying. Only Ma's continuous hiccups wafted intermittently to Miss Lin's ears. Suddenly, Ma's voice rose, as if she were angry, and a few words came through quite clearly:

"— These are Japanese goods, those are Japanese goods, hic! . . ."

Miss Lin started. She prickled all over, like when she was having a hair-cut and the tiny shorn hairs stuck to her neck. She had come home annoyed just because they had laughed at her and scolded her at school over Japanese goods. She swept aside the little cat nestled against her, jumped up and stripped off her new azure rayon dress lined with camel's wool. She shook it out a couple of times, and sighed. Miss Lin had heard that this charming frock was made of Japanese material. She tossed it aside and pulled that cute cowhide case out from under the bed. Almost spitefully, she flipped the cover open, and turning the case upside down, dumped its contents on the bed. A rainbow of brightly coloured dresses and knick-knacks rolled and spread. The little cat leaped to the floor, whirled and jumped up on a chair, where he crouched and looked at his mistress in astonishment.

Miss Lin sorted through the pile of clothes, then stood, abstracted, beside the bed. The more she examined her belongings, the more she adored them — and the more they looked like Japanese goods! Couldn't she wear any of them? She hated to part with them — besides, her father wouldn't necessarily be willing to have new ones made for her! Miss Lin's eyes began to smart. She loved these Japanese things, while she hated the Japanese aggressors who invaded the Northeast provinces. If not for that, she could wear Japanese merchandise and no one would say a word.

"Hic —"

The sound came through the door, followed by the thin swaying body of Mrs. Lin. The sight of the heap of clothing on the bed, and her daughter, bemused, standing in only her brief woollen underwear, was more than a little shock. As her excitement increased, the tempo of Mrs. Lin's hiccups grew in proportion. For the moment, she was unable to speak. Miss Lin, grief written all over her face, flew to her mother. "Ma! They're all Japanese goods. What am I going to wear tomorrow?"

Hiccuping, Mrs. Lin shook her head. With one hand she supported herself on her daughter's shoulder, with the other she kneaded her own chest. After a while, she managed to force out a few sentences.

"Child — hic — why have you taken off — hic — all your clothes? The weather's cold — hic — This trouble of mine — hic — began the year you were born. Hic — lately it's getting worse! Hic —"

"Ma, tell me what am I going to wear tomorrow? I'll just hide in the house and not go out! They'll laugh at me, swear at me!"

Mrs. Lin didn't answer. Hiccuping steadily, she walked over to the bed, picked the new azure dress out of the pile, and draped it over her daughter. Then she patted the bed in invitation for Miss Lin to sit down. The little cat returned to beside the girl's legs. Cocking his head, with narrowed eyes he looked first at Mrs. Lin, then at her daughter. Lazily, he rolled over and rubbed his belly against the soles of the girl's shoes. Miss Lin kicked him away and reclined sideways on the bed, with her head hidden behind her mother's back.

Neither of them spoke for a while. Mrs. Lin was busy hiccuping; her daughter was busy calculating "how to go out tomorrow." The problem of Japanese goods not only affected everything Miss Lin wore — it influenced everything she used. Even the powder compact which her fellow students so admired and her automatic pencil were probably made in Japan. And she was crazy about those little gadgets!

"Child — hic — are you hungry?"

After sitting quietly for some time, Mrs. Lin gradually controlled her hiccups, and began her usual doting routine.

"No. Ma, why do you always ask me if I'm hungry? The most important thing is that I have no clothes. How can I go to school tomorrow?" the girl demanded petulantly. She was still curled up on the bed, her face still buried behind her mother.

From the start, Mrs. Lin hadn't understood why her daughter kept complaining that she had no clothes to wear. This was the third time and she couldn't ignore the remark any longer, but those damned hiccups most irritatingly started up again. Just then, Mr. Lin came in. He was holding a sheet of paper in his hand; his face was ashen. He saw his wife struggling with continuous agitated hiccups, his daughter lying on the clothing-strewn bed, and he could guess pretty well what was wrong. His brows drew together in a frown.

"Do you have an Anti-Japanese-Invasion Society in your school, Xiu?" he asked. "This letter just came. It says that if you wear clothes made of Japanese material again tomorrow, they're going to burn them! Of all the wild lawless things to say!"

"Hic — hic!"

"What nonsense! Everyone has something made in Japan on him. But they have to pick on our family to make trouble! There isn't a shop carrying foreign goods that isn't full of Japanese stuff. But they have to make our shop the culprit. They insist on locking up our stocks! Huh!"

"Hic — hic — Goddess Guanyin protect and preserve us! Hic —"

"Papa, I've got an old style padded jacket. It's probably not made of Japanese material, but if I wear it they'll all laugh at me, it's so out of date," said Miss Lin, sitting up on the bed. She had been thinking of going a step farther and asking Mr. Lin to have a dress made for her out of non-Japanese cloth, but his expression decided her against such a rash move. Still, picturing the jeers her old padded jacket would evoke, she couldn't restrain her tears.

"Hic — hic — child! — hic — don't cry — no one will laugh at you — hic — child. . . ."

"Xiu, you don't have to go to school tomorrow! We soon

won't have anything to eat; how can we spend money on schools!" Mr. Lin was exasperated. He ripped up the letter and strode, sighing, from the room. Before long, he came hurrying back.

"Where's the key to the cabinet? Give it to me!" he demanded of his wife.

Mrs. Lin turned pale and stared at him. Her eternal hiccups were momentarily stilled.

"There's no help for it. We'll have to make an offering to those straying demons —" Mr. Lin paused to heave a sigh. "It'll cost me four hundred at most. If the Kuomintang local branch thinks it's not enough, I'll quit doing business. Let them lock up the stocks! That shop opposite has more Japanese goods than I. They've made an investment of over ten thousand dollars. They paid out only five hundred, and they're going along without a bit of trouble. Five hundred dollars! Just mark it off as a couple of bad debts! — The key! That gold necklace ought to bring about three hundred. . . ."

"Hic — hic — really, like a gang of robbers!" Mrs. Lin produced the key with a trembling hand. Tears streamed down her face. Miss Lin, however, did not cry. She was looking into space with misty eyes, recalling that Kuomintang committeeman who had made a speech at her school, a hateful swarthy pockmarked fellow who stared at her like a hungry dog. She could picture him grasping the gold necklace and jumping for joy, his big mouth open in a laugh. Then she visualized the ugly bandit quarrelling with her father, hitting him. . . .

"Aiya!" Miss Lin gave a frightened scream and threw herself on her mother's bosom. Mrs. Lin was so startled she had no time for hiccups.

"Child, hic — don't cry," Mrs. Lin made a desperate effort to speak. "After New Year your Papa will have money. We'll make a new dress for you, hic — Those black-hearted crooks! They all insist we have money. Hic — we lose more every year. Your Papa was in the fertilizer business, and he lost money, hic — Every penny invested in the shop belongs to other people. Child, hic, hic — this sickness of mine; it makes life hell — hic — In another two years when you're nineteen, we'll find you a good husband. Hic — then I can die in peace! Save us from our adversity, Goddess Guanyin! Hic —"

2

The following day, Mr. Lin's shop underwent a transformation. All the Japanese goods he hadn't dared to show for the past week, now were the most prominently displayed. In imitation of the big Shanghai stores, Mr. Lin inscribed many slips of coloured paper with the words "Big Sale 10% Discount!" and pasted them on his windows. Just seven days before New Year, this was the "rush season" of the shops selling imported goods in the towns and villages. Not only was there hope of earning back Mr. Lin's special expenditure of four hundred dollars; Miss Lin's new dress depended on the amount of business done in the next few days.

A little past ten in the morning, groups of peasants who had come into town to sell their produce in the market began drifting along the street. Carrying baskets on their arms, leading small children, they chatted loud and vigorously as they strolled. They stopped to look at the red and green blurbs pasted on Mr. Lin's windows and called attention to them, women shouting to their husbands, children yelling to their parents, clucking their tongues in admiration over the goods on display in the shop windows. It would soon be New Year. Children were wishing for a pair of new socks. Women remembered that the family wash-basin had been broken for some time. The single wash-cloth used by the entire family had been bought half a year ago, and now was an old rag. They had run out of soap more than a month before. They ought to take advantage of this "Sale" and buy a few things.

Mr. Lin sat in the cashier's cage, marshalling all his energies, a broad smile plastered on his face. He watched the peasants, while keeping an eye on his two salesmen and two apprentices. With all his heart he hoped to see his merchandise start moving out and the silver dollars begin rolling in.

But these peasants, after looking a while, after pointing and gesticulating appreciatively a while, ambled over to the store across the street to stand and look some more. Craning his neck, Mr. Lin glared at the backs of the group of peasants, and sparks shot from his eyes. He wanted to go over and drag them back!

"Hic — hic —"

Behind the cashier's cage were swinging doors which separated the shop itself from the "inner sanctum". Beside these doors sat Mrs. Lin releasing hiccups that she had long been suppressing with difficulty. Miss Lin was seated beside her. Entranced, the girl watched the street silently, her heart pounding. At least half of her new dress had just walked away.

Mr. Lin strode quickly to the front of the counter. He glared jealously at the shop opposite. Its five salesmen were waiting expectantly behind the counter. But not one peasant entered the store. They looked for a while, then continued on their way. Mr. Lin relaxed; he couldn't help grinning at the salesmen across the street. Another group of seven or eight peasants stopped before Mr. Lin's shop. A youngster among them actually came a step forward. With his head cocked to one side, he examined the imported umbrellas. Mr. Lin whirled around, his face breaking into a happy smile. He went to work personally on this prospective customer.

"Would you like a foreign umbrella, Brother? They're cheap. You only pay ninety cents on the dollar. Come and take a look."

A salesman had already taken down two or three imported umbrellas. He promptly opened one and shoved it earnestly

into the young peasant's hand. Summoning all his zeal, the
salesman launched into a high powered patter:

"Just look at this, young master! Foreign satin cloth, solid
ribs. It's durable and handsome for rainy days or clear. Ninety
cents each. They don't come any cheaper.... Across the street,
they're a dollar apiece, but they're not as good as these. You
can compare them and see why."

The young peasant held the umbrella and stood undecided,
with his mouth open. He turned towards a man in his fifties
and weighed the umbrella in his hand as if to ask "Shall I buy
it?" The older man became very upset and began to shout at
him.

"You're crazy! Buying an umbrella! We only got three
dollars for the whole boatload of firewood, and your mother's
waiting at home for us to bring back some rice. How can you
spend money on an umbrella!"

"It's cheap, but we can't afford it!" sighed the peasants
standing around watching. They walked slowly away. The
young peasant, his face brick red, shook his head. He put down
the umbrella and started to leave. Mr. Lin was frantic. He
quickly gave ground.

"How much do you say, Brother? Take another look. It's
fine merchandise!"

"It is cheap. But we don't have enough money," the older
peasant replied, pulling his son. They practically ran away.

Bitterly, Mr. Lin returned to the cashier's cage, feeling weak
all over. He knew it wasn't that he was an inept businessman.
The peasants simply were too poor. They couldn't even spend
ninety cents on an umbrella. He stole a glance at the shop across
the way. There too people were looking, but no one was going
in. In front of the neighbouring grocery store and the cookie
shop, no one was even looking. Group after group of the
country folk walked by carrying baskets. But the baskets all
were empty. Occasionally, someone appeared with a homespun
flowered blue cloth sack, filled with rice, from the look of it.

The late rice which the peasants had harvested more than a month before had long since been squeezed out as rent for the landlords and interest for the usurers. Now in order to have rice to eat, the peasants were forced to buy a measure or two at a time, at steep prices.

All this Mr. Lin knew. He felt that at least part of his business was being indirectly eaten away by the usurers and landlords.

The hour gradually neared noon. There were very few peasants on the street now. Mr. Lin's shop had done a little over one dollar's worth of business, just enough to cover the cost of the "Big Sale 10 % Discount" strips of red and green paper. Despondently, Mr. Lin entered the "inner sanctum." He barely had the courage to face his wife and daughter. Miss Lin's eyes were filled with tears. She sat in the corner with her head down. Mrs. Lin was in the middle of a string of hiccups. Struggling for control, she addressed her husband.

"We laid out four hundred dollars — and spent all night getting things ready in the shop — hic! We got permission to sell the Japanese goods, but business is dead — hic — my blessed ancestors! ... The maid wants her wages —"

"It's only half a day. Don't worry." Mr. Lin forced a comforting note into his voice, but he felt worse than if a knife were cutting through his heart. Gloomily, he paced back and forth. He thought of all the business promotion tricks he knew, but none of them seemed any good. Business was bad. It had been bad in all lines for some time; his shop wasn't the only one having difficulty. People were poor, and there wasn't anything that could be done about it. Still, he hoped business would be better in the afternoon. The local townspeople usually did their buying then. Surely they would buy things for New Year! If only they wanted to buy, Mr. Lin's shop was certain of trade. After all, his merchandise was cheaper than other shops!

It was this hope that enabled Mr. Lin to bolster his sagging spirits as he sat in the cashier's cage awaiting the customers he pictured coming in the afternoon.

And the afternoon proved to be different indeed from the morning. There weren't many people on the street, but Mr. Lin knew nearly every one of them. He knew their names, or the names of their fathers or grandfathers. These were local townspeople, and as they chatted and walked slowly past his shop, Mr. Lin's eyes, glowing with cordiality, welcomed them, and sent them on their way. At times, with a broad smile he greeted an old customer.

"Ah, Brother, going out to the tea-house? Our little shop has slashed its prices. Favour us with a small purchase!"

Sometimes, the man would actually stop and come into the shop. Then Mr. Lin and his assistants would plunge into a frenzy of activity. With acute sensitiveness, they would watch the eyes of the unpredictable customer. The moment his eyes rested on a piece of merchandise, the salesmen would swiftly produce one just like it and invite the customer to examine it. Miss Lin watched from beside the swinging doors, and her father frequently called her out to respectfully greet the unpredictable customer as "Uncle." An apprentice would serve him a glass of tea and offer him a good cigarette.

On the question of price, Mr. Lin was exceptionally flexible. When a customer was firm about knocking off a few odd cents from the round figure of his purchase price, Mr. Lin would take the abacus from the hands of his salesman and calculate personally. Then, with the air of a man who has been driven to the wall, he would deduct the few odd cents from the total bill.

"We'll take a loss on this sale," he would say with a wry smile. "But you're an old customer. We have to please you. Come and buy some more things soon!"

The entire afternoon was spent in this manner. Including cash and credit, big purchases and small, the shop made a total of over ten sales. Mr. Lin was drenched with perspiration, and although he was worn out, he was very happy. He had been sneaking looks at the shop across the street. They didn't seem to be nearly so busy. There was a pleased expression on the face of Miss Lin, who had been constantly watching from beside the swinging doors. Mrs. Lin even jerked out a few less hiccups.

Shortly before dark, Mr. Lin finished adding up his accounts for the day. The morning amounted to zero; in the afternoon they had sold sixteen dollars and eighty-five cents worth of merchandise, eight dollars of it being on credit. Mr. Lin smiled slightly, then he frowned. He had been selling all his goods at their original cost. He hadn't even covered his expenses for the day, to say nothing of making any profit. His mind was blank for a moment. Then he took out his account books and calculated in them for a long time. On the "credit" side there was a total of over thirteen hundred dollars of uncollected debts — more than six hundred in town and over seven hundred in the countryside. But the "debit" ledger showed a figure of eight hundred dollars owed to the big Shanghai wholesale house alone. He owed a total of not less than two thousand dollars!

Mr. Lin sighed softly. If business continued to be so bad, it was going to be a little difficult for him to get through New Year. He looked at the red and green paper slips on the window announcing "Big Sale 10% Discount". If we really cut prices like we did today, business ought to pick up, he thought to himself. We're not making any profit, but if we don't do any business I still have to pay expenses anyway. The main thing is to get the customers to come in, then I can gradually raise my prices.... If we can do some wholesale business in the countryside, that will be even better!...

Suddenly, someone broke in on Mr. Lin's sweet dream. A shaky old lady entered the shop carrying a little bundle wrapped in blue cloth. Mr. Lin yanked up his head to find her confronting him. He wanted to escape, but there was no time. He could only go forward and greet her.

"Ah, Mrs. Zhu, out buying things for the New Year? Please come into the back room and sit down. — Xiu, give Mrs. Zhu your arm."

But Miss Lin didn't hear. She had left the swinging doors some time ago. Mrs. Zhu waved her hand in refusal and sat down on a chair in the store. Solemnly, she unwrapped the blue cloth and brought out a small account book. With two trembling hands she presented the book under Mr. Lin's nose. Twisting her withered lips, she was about to speak, but Mr. Lin had already taken the book and was hastening to say:

"I understand. I'll send it to your house tomorrow."

"Mm, mm, the tenth month, the eleventh month, the twelfth month; altogether three months. Three threes are nine; that's nine dollars, isn't it? — you'll send the money tomorrow? Mm, mm, you don't have to send it. I'll take it back with me! Eh!"

The words seemed to come with difficulty from Mrs. Zhu's withered mouth. She had three hundred dollars loaned to Mr. Lin's shop, and was entitled to three dollars interest every month. Mr. Lin had delayed payment for three months, promising to pay in full at the end of the year. Now, she needed some money to buy gifts for tomorrow's Kitchen God Festival, and so she had come seeking Mr. Lin. From the forcefulness with which she moved her puckered mouth, Mr. Lin could tell that she was determined not to leave without the money.

Mr. Lin scratched his head in silence. He hadn't been deliberately refusing to pay the interest. It was just that for the past three months business had been poor. Their daily sales had been barely enough to cover their food and taxes. He had delayed paying her unconsciously. But if he didn't pay her today, the old lady might raise a row in the shop. That would be too shameful and would seriously influence the shop's future.

"All right, all right. Take it back with you!" Mr. Lin finally said in exasperation. His voice shook a little. He rushed to the cashier's cage and gathered together all the cash

that had been taken in that morning and afternoon. To that
he added twenty cents from his own pocket, and presented the
whole collection of dollars, pennies and dimes to the old lady.
She carefully counted the lot over and over again, then with
trembling hands wrapped the money in the blue cloth. Mr.
Lin couldn't repress a sigh. He had a wild desire to snatch
back a part of the cash.

"That blue handkerchief is too worn, Mrs. Zhu," he said
with a forced laugh. "Why not buy a good white linen one?
We've also got top quality wash-cloths and soap. Take some to
use over the New Year. Prices are reasonable!"

"No. I don't want any. An old lady like me doesn't need
that kind of thing." She waved her hand in refusal. She put
her account book in her pocket and departed, firmly grasping
the blue cloth bundle.

Looking sour, Mr. Lin walked into the "inner sanctum."
Mrs. Zhu's visit reminded him that he had two other creditors.
Old Chen and Widow Zhang had put up two hundred and one
hundred and fifty dollars respectively. He would have to pay
them a total of ten dollars interest. He couldn't very well delay
their money; in fact, he would have to pay them ahead of time.
He counted on his fingers — twenty-fourth, twenty-fifth, twenty-sixth. By the twenty-sixth, he ought to be able to collect all
the outstanding debts in the countryside. His clerk Shousheng
had gone off on a collection trip the day before yesterday. He
should be back by the twenty-sixth at the latest. The unpaid
bills in town couldn't be collected till the twenty-eighth or twen-
ty-ninth. But the collector from the Shanghai wholesale house
to which Mr. Lin owed money would probably come tomorrow
or the day after. Lin's only alternative was to borrow more
from the local bank. And how would business be tomorrow?. . .

His head down, Mr. Lin paced back and forth, thinking.
The voice of his daughter spoke into his ear:

"Papa, what do you think of this piece of silk? Four dollars and twenty cents for seven feet.   That's not expensive, is it?"

Mr. Lin's heart gave a leap. He stood stock-still and glared, speechless.   Miss Lin held the piece of silk in her hand and giggled.   Four dollars and twenty cents!   It wasn't a big sum, but the shop only did sixteen dollars worth of business all day, and really at cost price! Mr. Lin stood frozen, then asked weakly:

"Where did you get the money?"

"I put it on the books."

Another debit. Mr. Lin scowled. But he had spoiled his daughter himself, and Mrs. Lin would take the girl's side no matter what the case might be.   He smiled a helpless bitter smile.   Then he sighed.

"You're always in such a rush," he said, slightly reproving. "Why couldn't you wait till after New Year!"

3

Another two days went by.   Business was indeed very brisk in Mr. Lin's shop, with its "Big Sale." They did over thirty dollars in sales every day.   The hiccups of Mrs. Lin diminished considerably; she hiccuped on the average of only once every five minutes. Miss Lin skipped up and back between the shop and the "inner sanctum", her face flushed and smiling. At times she even helped with the selling. Only after her mother called her repeatedly, did she return to the back room. Mopping her brow, she protested excitedly.

"Ma, why have you called me back again? It's not hard work! Ma, Papa's so tired he's soaking wet; his voice is gone! — A customer just made a five-dollar purchase! Ma, you don't have to be afraid it's too tiring for me! Don't worry! Papa told me to rest a while, then come out again!"

Mrs. Lin only nodded her head and hiccuped, followed by

a murmur that "Buddha is merciful and kind." A porcelain image of the Goddess Guanyin was enshrined in the "inner sanctum", with a stick of incense burning before it. Mrs. Lin swayed over to the shrine and kowtowed. She thanked the Goddess for Her Protection and prayed for Her Blessing on a number of matters — that Mr. Lin's business should always be good, that Miss Lin should grow nicely, that next year the girl should get a good husband.

But out in the shop, although Mr. Lin was devoting his whole being to business, though a smile never left his face, he felt as if his heart were bound with strings. Watching the satisfied customer going out with a package under his arm, Mr. Lin suffered a pang with every dollar he took in, as the abacus in his mind clicked a five per cent loss off the cost price he had raised through sweat and blood. Several times he tried to estimate the loss as being three per cent, but no matter how he figured it, he still was losing five cents on the dollar. Although business was good, the more he sold the worse he felt. As he waited on the customers, the conflict raging within his breast at times made him nearly faint. When he stole glances at the shop across the street, he had the impression that the owner and salesmen were sneering at him from behind their counters. Look at that fool Lin! they seemed to be saying. He really is selling below cost! Wait and see! The more business he does, the more he loses! The sooner he'll have to close down!

Mr. Lin gnawed his lips. He vowed he would raise his prices the next day. He would charge first-grade prices for second-rate merchandise.

The head of the Merchants Guild came by. It was he who had interceded with the Kuomintang chieftains for Mr. Lin on the question of selling Japanese goods. Now he smiled and congratulated Mr. Lin, and clapped him on the shoulder.

"How goes it? That four hundred dollars was well spent!" he said softly. "But you'd better give a small token to Kuomintang Party Commissioner Bu too. Otherwise, he may become annoyed and try to squeeze you. When business is good, plenty of people are jealous. Even if Commissioner Bu doesn't have any 'ideas', they'll try to stir him up!"

Mr. Lin thanked the head of the Merchants Guild for his concern. Inwardly, he was very alarmed. He almost lost his zest for doing business.

What made him most uneasy was that his assistant Shousheng still hadn't returned from the bill collecting trip. He needed the money to pay off his account with the big Shanghai wholesale house. The collector had arrived from Shanghai two days before, and was pressing Mr. Lin hard. If Shousheng didn't come soon, Mr. Lin would have to borrow from the local bank. This would mean an additional burden of fifty or sixty dollars in interest payments. To Mr. Lin, losing money every day, this prospect was more painful than being flayed alive.

At about four p.m., Mr. Lin suddenly heard a noisy uproar on the street. People looked very frightened, as though some serious calamity had happened. Mr. Lin, who could think only of whether Shousheng would safely return, was sure that the river boat on which Shousheng would come back had been set upon by pirates. His heart pounding, he hailed a passer-by and asked worriedly:

"What's wrong? Did pirates get the boat from Lishi?"

"Oh! So it's pirates again? Travelling is really too dangerous! Robbing is nothing. Men are even kidnapped right off the boat!" babbled the passer-by, a well-known loafer named Lu. He eyed the brightly coloured goods in the shop.

Mr. Lin could make no sense out of this at all. His worry increased and he dropped Lu to accost Wang, the next person who came along.

"Is it true that the boat from Lishi was robbed?"

"It must be Ah Shu's gang that did it. Ah Shu has been shot, but his gang is still a tough bunch!" Wang replied without slackening his pace.

Cold sweat bedewed Mr. Lin's forehead. He was frantic.

He was sure that Shousheng was coming back today, and from Lishi. That was the last place on the account book list. Now it was already four o'clock, but there was no sign of Shousheng. After what Wang had said, how could Mr. Lin have any doubts? He forgot that he himself had invented the story of the boat being robbed. His whole face beaded with perspiration, he rushed into the "inner sanctum". Going through the swinging doors, he tripped over the threshold and nearly fell.

"Papa, they're fighting in Shanghai! The Japanese bombed the Zhabei section!" cried Miss Lin, running up to him.

Mr. Lin stopped short. What was all this about fighting in Shanghai? His first reaction was that it had nothing to do with him. But since it involved the "Japanese", he thought he had better inquire a little further. Looking at his daughter's agitated face, he asked:

"The Japanese bombed it? Who told you that?"

"Everyone on the street is talking about it. The Japanese soldiers fired heavy artillery and they bombed. Zhabei is burned to the ground!"

"Oh, well, did anyone say that the boat from Lishi was robbed?"

Miss Lin shook her head, then fluttered from the room like a moth. Mr. Lin hesitated beside the swinging doors, scratching his head. Mrs. Lin was hiccuping and mumbling prayers.

"Buddha protect us! Don't let any bombs fall on our heads!"

Mr. Lin turned and went out to the shop. He saw his daughter engaged in excited conversation with the two salesmen. The owner of the shop across the street had come out from behind his counter and was talking, gesticulating wildly. There was fighting in Shanghai; Japanese planes had bombed Zhabei and burned it; the merchants in Shanghai had closed down — it all was true. What about the pirates robbing the boat? No one had heard anything about that! And the boat from Lishi? It had come in safely. The shopowner across the street had just seen stevedores from the boat going by with two big crates. Mr. Lin was relieved. Shousheng hadn't come back today, but he hadn't been robbed by pirates either!

Now the whole town was talking about the catastrophe in Shanghai. Young clerks were cursing the Japanese aggressors. People were even shouting, "Anyone who buys Japanese goods is a son of a bitch!" These words brought a scarlet blush to Miss Lin's cheeks, but Mr. Lin showed no change of expression. All the shops were selling Japanese merchandise. Moreover, after spending a few hundred dollars, the merchants had received special authorizations from the Kuomintang chieftains, saying, "The goods may be sold after removing the Japanese markings." All the merchandise in Mr. Lin's shop had been transformed into "native goods". His customers, too, would call them "native goods", then take up their packages and leave.

Because of the war in Shanghai, the whole town had lost all interest in business, but Mr. Lin was busy pondering his affairs. Unwilling to borrow from the local bank at exorbitant interest, he sought out the collector from the Shanghai wholesale house, to plead with him as a friend for a delay of another day or two. Shousheng would be back tomorrow before dark at the latest, said Mr. Lin. Then he would pay in full.

"My dear Mr. Lin, you're an intelligent man. How can you talk like that? They're fighting in Shanghai. Train service may be cut off tomorrow or the day after. I only wish I could start back tonight! How can I wait a day or two? Please, settle your account today so that I can leave the first thing tomorrow morning. I'm not my own boss. Please have some consideration for me!"

The Shanghai collector was uncompromisingly firm in his refusal. Mr. Lin saw that it was hopeless; he had no choice but to bear the pain and seek a loan from the local banker. He was worried that "Old Miser" knew of his sore need and would take advantage of the situation to boost the interest rate. From the minute he started speaking to the bank manager, Mr. Lin

could feel that the atmosphere was all wrong. The tubercular
old man said nothing when Mr. Lin finished his plea, but continued puffing on his antique water-pipe. After the whole
packet of tobacco was consumed, the manager finally spoke.

"I can't do it," he said slowly. "The Japanese have begun
fighting, business in Shanghai is at a standstill, the banks have
all closed down — who knows when things will be set right
again! Cut off from Shanghai, my bank is like a crab without
legs. With exchange of remittances stopped, I couldn't do business even with a better client than you. I'm sorry. I'd love to
help you but my hands are tied!"

Mr. Lin lingered. He thought the tubercular manager was
putting on an act in preparation for demanding higher interest.
Just as Mr. Lin was about to play along by renewing his pleas,
he was surprised to hear the manager press him a step farther.

"Our employer has given us instructions. He has heard
that the situation will probably get worse. He wants us to
tighten up. Your shop originally owed us five hundred; on the
twenty-second, you borrowed another hundred — altogether six
hundred, due to be settled before New Year. We've been doing
business together a long time, so I'm tipping you off. We want
to avoid a lot of talk and embarrassment at the last minute."

"Oh — but our little shop is having a hard time," blurted
the dumbfounded Mr. Lin. "I'll have to see how we do with
our collections."

"Ho! Why be so modest! The last few days your business
hasn't been like the others! What's so difficult about paying a
mere six hundred dollars? I'm letting you know today, old
brother. I'm looking forward to your settling your debt so
that I can clear myself with my employer."

The tubercular manager spoke coldly. He stood up.
Chilled, Mr. Lin could see that the situation was beyond repair.
All he could do was to take a grip on himself and walk out of
the bank. At last he understood that the fighting in distant
Shanghai would influence his little shop too. It certainly was

going to be hard to get through this New Year: The Shanghai collector was pressing him for money; the bank wouldn't wait until after the New Year; Shousheng still hadn't come back and there was no telling how he was getting on. So far as Mr. Lin's outstanding accounts in town were concerned, last year he had only collected eighty per cent. From the looks of things, this year there was no guarantee of even that much. Only one road seemed open to Mr. Lin: "Business Temporarily Closed — Balancing Books!" And this was equivalent to bankruptcy. There hadn't been any of his own money invested in the shop for a long time. The day the books were balanced and the creditors paid off, what would be left for him probably wouldn't be enough to stand between his family and nakedness!

The more he thought, the worse Mr. Lin felt. Crossing the bridge, he looked at the turbid water below. He was almost tempted to jump and end it all. Then a man hailed him from behind.

"Mr. Lin, is it true there's a war on in Shanghai? I hear that a bunch of soldiers just set up outside the town's east gate and asked the Merchants Guild for a 'loan'. They wanted twenty thousand right off the bat. The Merchants Guild is holding a meeting about it now!"

Mr. Lin hurriedly turned around. The speaker was Old Chen who had two hundred dollars loaned to the shop — another of Mr. Lin's creditors.

"Oh —" retorted Mr. Lin with a shiver. Quickly he crossed the bridge and ran home.

4

For dinner that evening, besides the usual one meat dish and two vegetable dishes, Mrs. Lin had bought a favourite of Mr. Lin's — a platter of stewed pork. In addition, there was a pint of yellow wine. A smile never left Miss Lin's face, for business in the shop was good, her new silk dress was finished, and because they were fighting back against the Japanese in Shanghai. Mrs. Lin's hiccups were especially sparse — about one every ten minutes.

Only Mr. Lin was sunk in gloom. Moodily drinking his wine, he looked at his daughter, and looked at his wife. Several times he considered dropping the bad news in their midst like a bombshell, but he didn't have that kind of courage. Moreover, he still hadn't given up hope, he still wanted to struggle; at least he wanted to conceal his failure to make ends meet.

And so when the Merchants Guild passed a resolution to pay the soldiers five thousand dollars and asked Mr. Lin to contribute twenty, he consented without a moment's hesitation. He decided not to tell his wife and daughter the true state of affairs until the last possible minute. The way he calculated it was this: He would collect eight per cent of the debts due him, he would pay eighty per cent of the money he owed. Anyhow, he had the excuse that there was fighting in Shanghai, that remittances couldn't be sent. The difficulty was that there was a difference of about six hundred dollars between what people owed him and what he had to pay to others. He would have to take drastic measures and cut prices heavily. The idea was to scrape together some money to meet the present problem, then he would see. Who could think of the future in times like these? If he could get by now, that would be enough.

That was how he made his plans. With the added potency of the pint of yellow wine, Mr. Lin slept soundly all night, without even the suggestion of a bad dream.

It was already six thirty when Mr. Lin awoke the next morning. The sky was overcast and he was rather dizzy. He gulped down two bowls of rice gruel and hurried to the shop. The first thing to greet his eye was the Shanghai collector, sitting with a stern face, waiting for his "answer". But what shocked Mr. Lin particularly was the shop across the street. They too had pasted red and green strips all over their windows; they too were having a "Big Sale 10 % Discount"! Mr. Lin's perfect plan of the night before was completely snowed under by those red and green streamers of his competitor.

"What kind of a joke is this, Mr. Lin? Last night you didn't give a reply. That boat leaves here at eight o'clock and I have to make connections with the train. I simply must catch that eight o'clock boat! Please hurry —" said the Shanghai collector impatiently. He brought his clenched fist down on the table.

Mr. Lin apologized and begged his forgiveness. Truly, it was all because of the fighting in Shanghai and not being able to send remittances. After all, they had been doing business for many years. Mr. Lin pleaded for a little special consideration.

"Then am I to go back empty-handed?"

"Why, why, certainly not. When Shousheng returns, I'll give you as much as he brings. I'm not a man if I keep so much as half a dollar!" Mr. Lin's voice trembled. With an effort he held back the tears that brimmed to his eyes.

There was no more to be said; the Shanghai collector stopped his grumbling. But he remained firmly seated where he was. Mr. Lin was nearly out of his wits with anxiety. His heart thumped erratically. Although he had been having a hard time the past few years, he had been able to keep up a front. Now there was a collector sitting in his shop for all the world to see. If word of this thing spread, Mr. Lin's credit would be ruined. He had plenty of creditors. Suppose they all decided to follow suit? His shop might just as well close down immediately. In desperation, several times he invited the Shanghai gentleman to wait in the back room where it was more comfortable, but the latter refused.

An icy rain began to fall. The street was cold and deserted. Never had it appeared so mournful at New Year's time. Signboards creaked and clattered in the grip of a north wind. The icy rain seemed like to turn into snow. In the shops that lined the street, salesmen leaning on the counters looked up blankly.

Occasionally, Mr. Lin and the collector from Shanghai exchanged a few desultory words. Miss Lin suddenly emerged through the swinging doors and stood at the front window watching the cold hissing rain. From the back room, the sound of Mrs. Lin's hiccups steadily gathered intensity. While trying to be pleasant to their visitor, Mr. Lin looked at his daughter and listened to his wife's hiccups, and a wave of depression rose in his breast. He thought how all his life he had never known any prosperity, nor could he imagine who was responsible for his being reduced to such dire straits today.

The Shanghai collector seemed to have calmed down somewhat. "Mr. Lin," he said abruptly, in a sincere tone, "you're a good man. You don't go in for loose living, you're obliging and honest in your business practices. Twenty years ago, you would have got rich. But things are different today. Taxes are high, expenses are heavy, business is slow — it's an accomplishment just to get along."

Mr. Lin sighed and smiled in wry modesty.

After a pause, the Shanghai collector continued, "This year the market in this town was a little worse than last, wasn't it? Places in the interior like this depend on the people from the countryside for business, but the peasants are too poor. There's really no solution. ... Oh, it's nine o'clock! Why hasn't your collection clerk come back yet? Is he reliable?"

Mr. Lin's heart gave a leap. For the moment, he couldn't answer. Although Shousheng had been his salesman for seven or eight years and had never made a slip, still, there was no absolute guarantee! And besides he was overdue. The Shanghai collector laughed to see Mr. Lin's doubtful expression, but his laugh had an odd ring to it.

At the window, Miss Lin whirled and cried urgently, "Papa, Shousheng is back! He's covered with mud!"

Her voice had a peculiar sound too. Mr. Lin jumped up

both alarmed and happy. He wanted to run out and look, but he was so excited that his legs were weak. By then Shousheng had already entered, truly covered with mud. The clerk sat down, panting for breath, unable to say a word. The situation looked bad. Frightened out of his wits, Mr. Lin was speechless too. The Shanghai collector frowned. After a while, Shousheng managed to gasp:

"Very dangerous! They nearly got me!"

"Then the boat was robbed?" the agitated Mr. Lin took a grip on himself and blurted.

"There wasn't any robbing. They were grabbing coolies for the army. I couldn't make the boat yesterday afternoon; I got a sampan this morning. After we sailed, we heard they were waiting at this end to grab the boat, so we came to port further down the river. When we got ashore, before we had come half a li, we bumped into an army pressgang. They grabbed the clerk from the clothing shop, but I ran fast and came back by a short cut. Damn it! It was a close call!"

Shousheng lifted his jacket as he talked and pulled from his money belt a cloth-bound packet which he handed to Mr. Lin.

"It's all here," he said. "That Huang Shop in Lishi is rotten. We have to be careful of customers like that next year. . . . I'll come back after I have a wash and change my clothes."

Mr. Lin's face lit up as he squeezed the packet. He carried it over to the cashier's cage and unbound the cloth wrapping. First he added up the money due on the list of debtors, then he counted what had been collected. There were eleven silver dollars, two hundred dimes, four hundred and twenty dollars in banknotes, and two bank demand drafts — for the equivalent of fifty and sixty-five taels of silver respectively, at the official rate. If he turned the whole lot over to the Shanghai collector, it would still be more than a hundred dollars short of what he owed the wholesale house.

Deep in contemplation, Mr. Lin glanced several times out

of the corner of his eye at the Shanghai collector who was silently smoking a cigarette. At last he sighed, and as though cutting
off a piece of his living flesh, placed the two bank drafts and
four hundred dollars in cash before the man from Shanghai.
Then Mr. Lin spoke for a long time until he managed to extract
a nod from the latter and the words "all right."

But when the collector looked twice at the bank drafts, he
said with a smile, "Sorry to trouble you, Mr. Lin. Please get
them cashed for me first."

"Certainly, certainly," Mr. Lin hastened to reply. He
quickly affixed his shop's seal to the back of the drafts and dispatched one of his salesmen to cash them at the local bank. In
a little while, the salesman came back empty-handed. The bank
had accepted the drafts but refused to pay for them, saying they
would be credited against Mr. Lin's debt. Though it was snow-
ing heavily now, Mr. Lin rushed over to the bank without an
umbrella to plead in person. But his efforts were in vain.

"Well, what about it?" demanded the Shanghai collector
impatiently as Mr. Lin returned to the shop, his face anguished.

Mr. Lin seemed ready to weep. There was nothing he could
say; he could only sigh. Except to beg the collector for more
leniency, what else could he do? Shousheng came out and added
his pleas to Mr. Lin's. He vowed that they would send the remaining two hundred dollars to Shanghai by the tenth of the
new year. Mr. Lin was an old customer who had always paid
his debts promptly without a word, said Shousheng. This thing
today was really unexpected. But that was the situation; they
couldn't help themselves. It wasn't that they were stalling.

The Shanghai collector was adamant. Painfully, Mr. Lin
brought out the fifty dollars he had taken in during the past
few days and handed it over to make up a total payment of four
hundred and fifty dollars. Only then did that headache of a
Shanghai collector depart.

By that time, it was eleven in the morning. Snowflakes
were still drifting down from the sky. Not even half a customer

was in sight. Mr. Lin brooded a while, then discussed with Shousheng means to be used in collecting outstanding bills in town. Both men were frowning; neither of them had any particular confidence that much of the six hundred dollars due from town customers could be collected. Shousheng bent close to Mr. Lin's ear and whispered:

"I hear that the big shop at the south gate and the one at the west gate are both shaky. Both of them owe us money — about three hundred dollars altogether. We better take precautions with these two accounts. If they fold up before we can collect, it won't be so funny!"

Mr. Lin paled; his lips trembled a little. Then, Shousheng pitched his voice lower still, and mumbled a bit of even more shocking news.

"There's another nasty rumour — about us. They're sure to have heard it at the bank. That's why they're pressing us so hard. The Shanghai collector probably got wind of it too. Who can be trying to make trouble for us? The shop across the street?"

Shousheng pointed with his pursed lips in the direction of the suspect, and Mr. Lin's eyes swung to follow the indicator. His heart skipping unevenly, his face mournful, Mr. Lin was unable to speak for some time. He had the numb and aching feeling that this time he was definitely finished! If he weren't ruined it would be a miracle: The Kuomintang chieftains were putting the squeeze on him; the bank was pressing him; his fellow shopkeepers were stabbing him in the back; a couple of his biggest debtors were going to default. Nobody could stand up under this kind of buffeting. But why was he fated to get such a dirty deal? Ever since he inherited the little shop from his father, he had never dared to be wasteful. He had been so obliging; he never hurt a soul, never schemed against anyone. His father and grandfather had been the same, yet all he was reaping was bitterness!

"Never mind. Let them spread their rumours. You don't

have to worry," Shousheng tried to comfort Mr. Lin, though he couldn't help sighing himself. "There are always rumours in lean years. They say in this town nine out of ten shops won't be able to pay up their debts before the year is out. Times are bad, the market is dead as a doornail. Usually strong shops are hard up this year. We're not the only one having rough going! When the sky tumbles everyone gets crushed. The Merchants Guild has to think of a way out. All the shops can't be collapsing; that would make the market even less like a market."

The snowfall was becoming heavier; it was sticking to the ground now. Occasionally, a dog would slink by, shivering, its tail between its legs. It might stop and shake itself violently to dislodge the snow thickly matting its fur. Then, with tail drooping again, the dog would go on its way. Never in its history had this street witnessed so frigid and desolate a New Year season! And just at this time, in distant Shanghai, Japanese heavy artillery was savagely pounding that prosperous metropolis of trade.

5

It was a gloomy New Year, but finally it was passed. In town, twenty-eight big and little shops folded up, including a "credit A-1" silk shop. The two stores that owed Mr. Lin three hundred dollars closed down too. The last day of the year, Shousheng had gone to them and plagued them for hours, but all he could extract was a total of twenty dollars. He heard that afterwards no other collector got so much as a penny out of them; the owners of the two shops hid themselves and couldn't be found. Thanks to the intervention of the head of the Merchants Guild, it wasn't necessary for Mr. Lin to hide. But he had to guarantee to wipe off his debt of four hundred dollars to the bank before the fifteenth of the first month, and he had to consent to very harsh terms: The bank would send a representative to "guard" all cash taken in starting from resumption of business on the fifth; eighty per cent of all money collected would go to the bank until Mr. Lin's debt to them was paid.

During the New Year holidays, Mr. Lin's house was like an ice box. Mr. Lin heaved sigh after sigh. Mrs. Lin's hiccups were like a string of firecrackers. Miss Lin, although she neither hiccuped nor sighed, moped around in the dazed condition of one who has suffered from years of jaundice. Her new silk dress had already gone to the only pawnshop in town to raise money for the maid's wages. An apprentice had taken it there at seven in the morning; it was after nine when he finally squeezed his way out of the crowd with two dollars in his hand. Afterwards, the pawnshop refused to do any more business that day. Two dollars! That was the highest price they would give for any article, no matter how much you had paid for it originally! This was called "two dollar ceiling". When a peasant, steeling himself against the cold, would peel off a cotton-padded jacket and hand it across the counter, the pawnshop clerk would raise it up, give it a shake, then fling it back with an angry "We don't want it!"

Since New Year's Day, the weather had been beautiful and clear. The big temple courtyard, as was the custom, was crowded with the stalls of itinerant pedlars and the paraphernalia of acrobats and jugglers. People lingered before the stalls, patted their empty money belts, and reluctantly walked on. Children dragged at their mothers' clothing, refusing to leave the stall where fireworks were on sale, until Mama was forced to give the little offender a hard slap. The pedlars, who had come specially to cash in on the usual New Year's bazaar trade, didn't even make enough to pay for their food. They couldn't pay their rent at the local inn and quarrelled with the innkeeper every day.

Only the acrobatic troupe earned the large sum of eight dollars. It had been hired by the Kuomintang chieftains to add to the atmosphere of "peace and normalcy."

On the evening of the fourth, Mr. Lin, who had with some difficulty managed to raise three dollars, gave the usual spread for his employees at which they all discussed the strategy for the morrow's re-opening of business. The prospects were already terribly clear to Mr. Lin: If they re-opened, they were sure to operate at a loss; if they didn't re-open, he and his family would be entirely without resources. Moreover, people still owed him four hundred dollars, the collection of which would be even more difficult, if he closed down. The only way out was to cut expenses. But taxes and levies for the soldiers were inescapable; there was even less chance of his avoiding being "squeezed". Fire a couple of salesmen? He only had three. Shousheng was his righthand man; the other two were poor devils; besides he really needed them to wait on the customers. He couldn't save any more at home. They had already let the maid go. He felt the only thing to do was to plunge on. Perhaps, when the peasants, with Buddha's blessing, earned money from their spring raw silk sales, he still might make up his loss.

But the greatest problem in resuming business was that he was short of merchandise. Without money to remit to Shanghai, he couldn't replenish his stock. The fighting in Shanghai was getting worse. There was no use in hoping for getting anything on credit. Sell his reserve? The shop was long since actually cleaned out. The underwear boxes on the shelves were empty; they were used only for show. All that was left were things like wash-basins and towels. But he had plenty of those.

Gloomily, the feasters sipped their wine. For all their perplexed reflection, no one could offer any solution to the problem. They talked of generalities for a while. Then suddenly Asi, one of the salesmen, said:

"The world is going to hell. People live worse than dogs! They say Zhabei was completely burned out. A couple of hundred thousand people had to flee, leaving all their belongings behind. There wasn't any fire in the Hongkou section, but everybody ran away. The Japanese are very cruel. They wouldn't let them take any of their things with them. House rent in safe quarters in Shanghai has skyrocketed. All the refugees are running to the countryside. A bunch came to our town yesterday. They all look like decent people, and now they're homeless!"

Mr. Lin shook his head and sighed, but Shousheng, on hearing these words, was suddenly struck with a bright idea. He put down his chopsticks, then raised his wine cup and drained it in one swallow. He turned to Mr. Lin with a grin.

"Did you hear what Asi just said? That means our wash-basins, wash-cloths, soap, socks, tooth powder, tooth brushes, will sell fast. We can get rid of as many as we've got."

Mr. Lin stared. He didn't know what Shousheng was driving at.

"Look, this is a heaven-sent chance. The Shanghai refugees should have a little money, and they need the usual daily ne-cessities, don't they? We ought to set up right away to handle this business!"

Shousheng poured himself another cup of wine, and drank, his face beaming. The two salesmen caught on, and they began to laugh. Only Mr. Lin was not entirely clear. He had been rather dulled by his recent adversity.

"Are you sure?" he asked, irresolutely. "Other shops have wash-cloths and wash-basins too —"

"But we're the only ones with any real reserve of that sort of stuff. They don't have even ten wash-basins across the street, and those are all seconds. We've got this piece of busi-ness right in the palm of our hand! Let's write a lot of ads and paste them up at the town's four gateways, any place in town where the refugees are staying — say, Asi, where *are* they living? We'll go put up our stickers there!"

"The ones with relatives here are living with their relatives. The rest have borrowed that empty building in the silk factory outside the west gate." Asi's face shone with satisfaction over the excellent result he had unwittingly produced.

At last, Mr. Lin had the whole picture. Happy, his spirits revived. He immediately drafted the wording of the advertisements, listing all the daily necessities which the shop had available for sale. There were over a dozen different commodities. In imitation of the big Shanghai stores, he adopted the "One Dollar Package" technique. For a dollar the customer would get a wash-basin, a wash-cloth, a tooth brush and a box of tooth powder. "Big Dollar Sale!" screamed the ad in huge letters. Shousheng brought out the shop's remaining sheets of red and green paper and cut them into large strips. Then he took up his brush and started writing. The salesmen and the apprentices noisily collected the wash-basins, wash-cloths, tooth brushes and boxes of tooth powder, and arranged them into sets. There weren't enough hands for all the work. Mr. Lin called his daughter out to help with writing the ads and tying the packages. He also made up other kinds of combination packages — all of daily necessities.

That night, they were busy in the shop late and long. At dawn they had things pretty much in order. When the popping of firecrackers heralded the opening of business the next morning, the shop of the Lin family again had a new look. Their advertisements had already been pasted up all over town. Shousheng had personally attended to the silk factory outside the west gate. The ad with which he plastered the factory walls struck the eyes of the refugees, and they all crowded around to read it as if it were a news bulletin.

In the "inner sanctum" Mrs. Lin, too, rose very early. She lit incense before the porcelain image of the Goddess Guanyin and kowtowed for a considerable time, knocking her head resoundingly against the floor. She prayed for practically everything. About the only thing she omitted was a plea for more refugees to come to the town.

It all worked out fine, just as Shousheng had predicted. Mr. Lin's shop was the only one whose trade was brisk on the first business day after the New Year's holidays. By four in the afternoon, he had sold over one hundred dollars' worth of merchandise — the highest figure for a day ever reached in that town in the past ten years. His biggest seller was the "One Dollar Package", and it served as a leader to such items as umbrellas and rubber overshoes. Business, moreover, went smoothly, pleasantly. The refugees came from Shanghai, after all; they were used to the ways of the big city; they weren't as petty as the townspeople or the peasants from the out-lying districts. When they bought something, they made up their minds quickly. They'd pick up a thing, look at it, then produce their money. There was none of this pawing through all the merchandise, no haggling over a few pennies.

When her daughter, all flushed and excited, rushed into the back room for a moment to report the good business, Mrs. Lin went to kowtow before the porcelain Guanyin again. If Shousheng weren't twice the girl's age, Mrs. Lin was thinking, wouldn't he make a good son-in-law! And it wasn't at all un-likely that Shousheng had half an eye on his employer's seven-teen-year-old daughter, this girl whom he knew so well.

There was just one thing that spoiled Mr. Lin's happiness — completely disregarding his dignity, the local bank had sent its man to collect eighty per cent of the sales proceeds. And he didn't know who egged them on, but the three creditors of the shop, on the excuse that they "needed a little money to buy rice", all showed up to draw out some advance interest. Not only interest; they even wanted repayment of part of their loans too! But Mr. Lin also heard some good news — another batch of refugees had arrived in town.

For dinner that evening, Mr. Lin served two additional meat dishes, by way of reward to his employees. Everyone com-plimented Shousheng on his shrewdness. Although Mr. Lin was happy, he couldn't help thinking of how his three creditors had talked about being repaid their loans. It was unlucky to have such a thing happen at the beginning of the new year.

"What do they know!" said Shousheng angrily. "Somebody

must have put them up to it!" He pointed with his lips at the shop across the street.

Mr. Lin nodded. But whether the three creditors knew anything or not, it was going to be difficult to handle them. An old man and two widows. You couldn't be soft with them, but getting tough wouldn't do either. Mr. Lin pondered for some time, and finally decided the best thing to do would be to ask the head of the Merchants Guild to speak to his three precious creditors. He asked Shousheng for his opinion. Shousheng heartily agreed.

When dinner was over, and Mr. Lin had added up his receipts for the day, he went to pay his respects to the head of the Merchants Guild. The latter expressed complete approval of Mr. Lin's idea. What's more, he commended Mr. Lin on the intelligent way in which he conducted his business. He said the shop was sure to stand firm, in fact it would improve. Stroking his chin, the head of the Merchants Guild smiled and leaned towards Mr. Lin.

"There's something I've been wanting to talk to you about for a long time, but I never had the opportunity. I don't know where Kuomintang Commissioner Bu saw your daughter, but he's very interested in her. Commissioner Bu is forty and he has no sons. Though he has two women at home, neither of them has been able to give birth. If your daughter should join his household and present him with a child, he's sure to make her his wife, Madam Commissioner. Ah, if that should happen, even I could share in the reflected glory!"

Never in his wildest dreams had Mr. Lin ever imagined he would run into trouble like this. He was speechless. The head of the Merchants Guild continued solemnly:

"We're old friends. There's nothing we can't speak freely about to each other. This kind of thing, according to the old standards, would make you lose face. But it isn't altogether like that any more; it's quite common nowadays. Your daughter's going over could be considered proper marriage.

Anyhow, since that is what Commissioner Bu has in mind, there might be some inconvenience if you refuse him. If you agree, you can have real hope for the future. I wouldn't be telling you this if I didn't have your interests at heart."

"Of course in advising me to be careful, your intentions are the best! But I'm an unimportant person, my daughter knows nothing of high society. We don't dare aspire so high as a commissioner!" Mr. Lin had to brace himself up to speak. His heart was thumping fast.

"Ha ha! It isn't a question of your aspirations, but the fact that he finds her suitable.... Let's leave it at that. You go home and talk it over with your wife. I'll put the matter aside. When I see Commissioner Bu I'll say I haven't had a chance to speak to you about it, alright? But you must give me an answer soon!"

There was a long pause. Then, "I will," Mr. Lin forced himself to say. His face was ghastly.

When he got home, he sent his daughter out of the room and reported to his wife in detail. Even before he finished, Mrs. Lin's hiccups rose in a powerful barrage that was probably audible to all the neighbours. With an effort she stemmed the tide and said, panting:

"How can we consent? — hic — Even if it wasn't a concubine he wanted hic — hic — even if he were looking for a wife, I still couldn't bear to part with her!"

"That's the way I feel, but —"

"Hic — we run our business all legal and proper. Do you mean to say if we don't agree he could get away with taking her by force? Hic —"

"But he's sure to find an excuse to make some kind of trouble. That kind of man is crueler than a bandit!" Mr. Lin whispered. He was nearly crying.

"He'll get her only over my dead body! Hic! Goddess Guanyin preserve us!" cried Mrs. Lin in a voice that trembled.

She rose and started to sway out of the room. Mr. Lin hastily barred her way.

"Where are you going? Where are you going?" he babbled.

Just then, Miss Lin came in. Obviously she had overheard quite a bit, for her complexion was the colour of chalk and her eyes were staring fixedly. Mrs. Lin flung her arms around her daughter and wept and hiccuped while she struggled to say in gasps:

"Hic — child — hic — anybody who tries to snatch you — hic — will have to do it over my dead body! Hic! The year I gave birth to you I got this — sickness — hic — It was hard, but I brought you up till now you're seventeen — hic — hic — Dead or alive, we'll stick together! Hic! We should have promised you to Shousheng long ago! Hic! That Bu is a dirty crook! He isn't afraid the gods will strike him down!"

Miss Lin wept too, crying "Ma!" Mr. Lin wrung his hands and sighed. The women were wailing at an alarming rate, and he was afraid their laments would be heard through the thin walls and startle the neighbours. This sort of row was also an unlucky way to commence the new year. Holding his own emotions in check, he did his best to soothe wife and daughter.

That night, all three members of the Lin family slept badly. Although Mr. Lin had to get up early the next morning to go to business, he wrestled with his gloomy thoughts all night. A sudden sound on the roof sent his heart leaping with fear that Commissioner Bu had come to trump up charges against him. Then he calmed himself and considered the matter carefully. His was a family of proper business people who had never committed any crimes. As long as he did a good business and didn't owe people money, surely Bu couldn't make trouble without any reason at all. And now Lin's business was beginning to show some vitality. Just because he had raised a good-looking daughter, he had invited disaster! He should have engaged her years ago, then maybe this problem would never have arisen. . . . Was the head of the Merchants Guild sincerely willing to help?

The only way out was to beg for his aid — Mrs. Lin started hic-cuping again. Ai! That ailment of hers!

Mr. Lin rose as soon as the sky began to turn light. His eyes were somewhat bloodshot and swollen, and he felt dizzy. But he had to pull himself together and attend to business. He couldn't leave the entire management of the shop to Shousheng; the young fellow had put in an exhausting few days.

He was still uneasy after he seated himself in the cashier's cage. Although business was good, from time to time his whole body was shaken by violent shivers. Whenever a big man came in, if Mr. Lin didn't know him, he would suspect that the man had been sent by Commissioner Bu to spy, to stir up a fuss, and his heart would thump painfully.

And it was strange. Business that day was active beyond all expectations. By noon they had sold nearly sixty dollars' worth of merchandise. There were local townspeople among the customers too. They weren't just buying; they were practi-cally grabbing. The only thing like it would be a bankrupt shop selling its stock out at auction cheap. While Mr. Lin was fairly pleased, he was also rather alarmed. This kind of busi-ness didn't look healthy to him. Sure enough, Shousheng ap-proached him during the lunch hour and said softly:

"There's a rumour outside that you've cut prices to clear out your left-overs. That when you've collected a little money, you're going to take it and run!"

Mr. Lin was both angry and frightened. He couldn't speak. Suddenly two men in uniform entered and barged forward to demand:

"Which one is Mr. Lin, the proprietor?"

Mr. Lin rose in flurried haste. Before he had a chance to reply, the uniformed men began to lead him away. Shousheng came over to stop them and to question them. They barked at him savagely:

"Who are you? Stand aside! He's wanted for questioning at the Kuomintang office!"

6

That afternoon, Mr. Lin did not return. They were busy at the shop, and Shousheng could not get away to inquire personally. He had managed to conceal the truth from Mrs. Lin, but one of the apprentices let it leak out, and the lady became frantic almost to the point of distraction. She absolutely refused to let Miss Lin go out of the swinging doors.

"They've already taken your father. They'll be coming back for you next! Hic —"

She called in Shousheng and questioned him closely. He didn't think it advisable to tell her too much.

"Don't worry, Mrs. Lin," he comforted. "There's nothing wrong! He only went down to the Kuomintang office to straighten out the question of our creditors. Business is good. What have we got to be afraid of!"

Behind Mrs. Lin's back, he told Miss Lin quietly, "We still don't really know what this is all about." He urged her to look after her mother; he would attend to the shop. Miss Lin didn't have the faintest idea what to do. She agreed to everything Shousheng said.

Between waiting on the customers and thinking up answers to Mrs. Lin's constant questions, it was impossible for Shousheng to find time to inquire about the fate of Mr. Lin. Finally, at twilight, word was brought by the head of the Merchants Guild: Mr. Lin was being held by the Kuomintang chieftains because of the rumour that he was planning to abscond with the shop's money. Besides what Mr. Lin owed the bank and the wholesale house, there were also his three poor creditors to be considered. The total of six hundred and fifty dollars which they had put up was in jeopardy. The Kuomintang was especially concerned over the welfare of these poor people. So it was detaining him until he settled with them.

Shousheng's face was drained of colour. Dazed, he finally managed to ask:

"Can we put up a guarantee and have him released first? Unless we get him out, how are we going to raise the money?"

"Huh! Release him on a guarantee! You can't become his guarantor if you go there without money in your hands!"

"Mr. Guild Leader, think of something, I beg you. Do a good deed. You and Mr. Lin are old friends. I beg you to help him!"

The head of the Merchants Guild frowned thoughtfully. He looked at Shousheng for a minute, then led him to a corner of the room and said in a low voice:

"I can't stand by with folded arms and watch Mr. Lin remain in difficulty. But the situation is very strained now! To tell you the truth, I've already pleaded with Commissioner Bu to intervene. Commissioner Bu only wanted Mr. Lin to agree to one thing, and would be willing to help him. I've just seen Mr. Lin at the Kuomintang office where I urged him to consent, and he did so. Shouldn't that be the end of the matter? Who would have thought that dark pock-marked fellow in the Kuomintang would be so nasty? He still insists —"

"Surely he wouldn't go against Commissioner Bu?"

"That's what I thought! But the pock-marked fellow kept mumbling and grumbling till Commissioner Bu was very embarrassed. They had a terrible row! Now you see how awkward things are?"

Shousheng sighed. He had no idea. There was a pause, then he sighed again and said:

"But Mr. Lin hasn't committed any crime."

"Those people don't talk reason! With them, might makes right! Tell Mrs. Lin not to worry; Mr. Lin hasn't been mistreated yet. But to get him out she'll have to spend a little money!"

The head of the Merchants Guild held up two fingers, then quickly departed.

Though he racked his brains, Shousheng could see no other alternative. The two salesmen plagued him with questions, but he ignored them. He was wondering whether he should report the words of the head of the Merchants Guild to Mrs. Lin. Again they had to spend money! While he didn't know whether Mrs. Lin had any private resources of her own, he was quite clear as to the financial condition of the shop: After the local bank got through deducting its eighty per cent from the cash earned during the past two days, all that was left for the shop was about fifty dollars. A lot of good that would do! The head of the Merchants Guild had indicated a bribe of two hundred dollars. Who knew whether that would be enough! The way things were, even if business should improve even more, it still wouldn't be any use. Shousheng felt discouraged.

From the back room, someone was calling him. He decided to go in and size up the situation, and then determined what should be done. He found Mrs. Lin leaning on her daughter's arm.

"Hic — just now — hic — the head of the Merchants Guild came — hic —" she panted. "What did he say?"

"He wasn't here," lied Shousheng.

"You can't fool me — hic — I — hic — know everything. Hic — your face is scared yellow! Xiu saw him — hic!"

"Be calm, Mrs. Lin. He says it's all right. Commissioner Bu is willing to help —"

"What? Hic — hic — What? Commissioner Bu is willing to help! — hic, hic — Merciful goddess — hic — I don't want his help! Hic, hic — I know — Mr. Lin — hic, hic — is finished! Hic — I want to die too! There's only Xiu — hic — that I'm worried about! Hic, hic — take her with you! — hic! You two go and get married! Hic — hic — Shousheng — hic — you take good care of Xiu and I won't worry about anything! Hic! Go! They want to grab her! — hic — the savage beasts! Goddess Guanyin, why don't you display your divine power!"

Shousheng stared. He didn't know what to say. He thought Mrs. Lin had gone mad, yet she didn't look the least abnormal. His heart beating hard, he stole a glance at Miss

Lin. She was blushing scarlet; she kept her head down and made no comment.

"Shousheng, Shousheng, somebody wants to see you!" an apprentice came running in and announced.

Thinking it was the head of the Merchants Guild or some such personage, Shousheng rushed out. To his surprise, he found Mr. Wu, proprietor of the shop across the street, waiting for him. What does he want? wondered Shousheng. He fixed his eyes on Mr. Wu's face.

Mr. Wu inquired about Mr. Lin, and then, all smiles, said he was sure it was "not serious". Shousheng felt there was something fishy about his smile.

"I've come to buy a little of your merchandise —" The smile had disappeared from Mr. Wu's face and the tone of his voice changed. He produced a sheet of paper from his sleeve. It was a list of over a dozen items — the very things Mr. Lin was featuring in his "One Dollar Package". One look and Shousheng understood. So that was the game!

"Mr. Lin isn't here," he said promptly. "I haven't the right to decide."

"Why not talk to Mrs. Lin? That'll be just as good!"

Shousheng hesitated to reply. He was beginning to have an inkling of why Mr. Lin had been detained. First there was the rumour that Mr. Lin was planning to run away, then Mr. Lin was arrested, and now the competitor's shop had come to gouge merchandise. There was an obvious connection between these events. Shousheng became rather angry, and a bit frightened. He knew that if he agreed to Mr. Wu's request, Mr. Lin's business would be finished, and the heart's blood that he himself had expended would be in vain. But if he refused, what other tricks would be forthcoming? He simply didn't dare to think.

"I'll go and talk to Mrs. Lin, then," he offered tentatively. "But she only operates on a cash basis."

"Cash? Ha, Shousheng, of course you're joking?"

"That's the kind of person Mrs. Lin is. I can't do anything

with her. The best thing would be for you to come again tomorrow.   The head of the Merchants Guild just told me that Commissioner Bu is willing to take a hand in the matte. Mr. Lin
probably will be back tonight," said Shousheng with cold delib-
erateness. He shoved the list back in Mr. Wu's hand.

His face twitching, the latter hastily forced the list on
Shousheng again.

"All right, all right, if it has to be cash then it's cash. I'll
take the goods tonight.   Cash on delivery."

Scowling, Shousheng walked into the back room and told
Mrs. Lin about the shop across the street wanting to gouge
merchandise.

"When the head of the Merchants Guild was here, he really
said Mr. Lin was fine; he hasn't been through any hardships.
But we'll have to spend some money to get him out.   There's
only fifty dollars in the shop.   Now this fellow across the street
wants goods — from the looks of his list, about a hundred and
fifty dollars' worth.   Why not let him have them?   The important thing is to get Mr. Lin back as soon as possible!"

Upon hearing that they had to spend money again, tears
gushed from Mrs. Lin's eyes, and her hiccups truly shook the
heavens with their intensity.   Beyond words, she could only
wave her hand, while her head, which she rested on the table,
resounded alarmingly against the wooden top.   Shousheng could
see that he was getting nowhere, and he quietly withdrew. Miss
Lin caught up with him outside the swinging doors.   Her face
was deathly white, her voice trembling and hoarse.

"Ma is so angry she can't think straight," Miss Lin whispered urgently.   "She keeps saying they've already killed Papa!
You, you hurry up and agree to what Mr. Wu wants.   Save
Papa, quick! Shousheng, Brother, you —" At this point, her face
suddenly flamed scarlet, and she flew back into the room.

In a daze, Shousheng stared after her for a full half minute, then he turned away, determined to take the responsibility

for selling the merchandise to their competitor. At least Miss Lin agreed with him on what should be done.

The table had already been laid for dinner in the shop, but Shousheng had no appetite. As soon as Mr. Wu arrived with the money, Shousheng took one hundred dollars in his hand and concealed another eighty dollars on his person, and rushed off to find the head of the Merchants Guild.

Half an hour later Shousheng returned with Mr. Lin. Bursting into the "inner sanctum", they nearly startled Mrs. Lin out of her wits. When she saw that it was really Mr. Lin in the flesh, she agitatedly prostrated herself before the porcelain Guanyin and kowtowed vigorously, pounding her head so loudly that it drowned out the sound of her hiccups. Miss Lin stood to one side, her eyes staring. She looked as if she wanted to laugh and cry at the same time. Shousheng took out a paper-wrapped packet and set it on the table.

"This is eighty dollars we didn't have to use."

Mr. Lin sighed. When he finally spoke, his voice was dull.

"You should have let me die there and be done with it. Spending more money to get me out! Now we've got no money, we're all going to die anyhow!"

Mrs. Lin jumped up from the ground, excited and wanting to speak. But a string of hiccups blocked the words in her throat. Miss Lin wept quietly, with suppressed sobs. Mr. Lin did not cry. He sighed again and said in a choked voice:

"Our merchandise has been cleaned out! We can't do any business, they're pressing us hard for debts —"

"Mr. Lin!"

It was Shousheng who shouted. He dipped his finger in the tea, then wrote on the table the one word — "Go."

Mr. Lin shook his head. Tears flowed from his eyes. He looked at his wife, he looked at his daughter, and again he sighed.

"That's the only way out, Mr. Lin! We can still scrape together a hundred dollars in the shop. Take it with you; it'll be enough for a month or two.   I'll take care of what has to be done here."

Although Shousheng spoke quietly, Mrs. Lin overheard him. She curbed her hiccups and interjected:

"You go too, Shousheng!   You and Xiu.   Leave me here alone.   I'll fight to the death!   Hic!"

Mrs. Lin suddenly appeared remarkably young and healthy; she whirled and ran up the stairs.   "Ma!" called Miss Lin, and dashed after her mother. Mr. Lin stared at the stairway, bewildered.   He felt he had something important to say, but he was too numb to recall what it was.

"You and Xiu go together," Shousheng urged softly. "Mrs. Lin will worry if Xiu stays here!   She says they want to snatch —"

Tears in his eyes, Mr. Lin nodded.   He couldn't make up his mind.

Shousheng felt his own eyes smarting.   He sighed and walked around the table.

Just then, they heard Miss Lin crying.   Startled, Mr. Lin and Shousheng rushed up the stairs.   Mrs. Lin was coming out of her room with a paper packet in her hand.   She went back into the room when she saw them, and said:

"Please come in, both of you.   Listen to what I've decided." She pointed at the packet.   "In here is my private property — hic — about two hundred dollars.   I'm giving you two half. Hic! Xiu, I give you in marriage to Shousheng! Hic — tomorrow, Xiu and her father will leave together.   Hic — I'm not going! Shousheng will stay with me a few days, and then we'll see. Who knows how many days I have left to live — hic — So if you both kowtow in my presence, I can set my mind at ease! Hic —"

Mrs. Lin took her daughter by one hand and Shousheng by the other, and ordered them to "kowtow".   Both did so, their cheeks flaming red; they kept their heads down. Shousheng stole a glance at Miss Lin. There was a faint smile on her tear-stained face. His heart thumped wildly, and two tears rolled down from his eyes.

"Good. That's the way it'll be." Mr. Lin heaved a sigh. "But Shousheng, when you stay here and deal with those people, be very, very careful!"

7

The shop of the Lin family had to close down at last. The news that Mr. Lin had run away soon spread all over town. Of the creditors, the local bank was the first to send people to put the stock into custody. They also searched for the account books. Not one was to be found. They asked for Shousheng. He was sick in bed. They grilled Mrs. Lin. Her reply was a string of explosive hiccups and a stream of tears. Since she after all enjoyed the social position of "Madam Lin", there was nothing they could do with her.

By about eleven a.m., the horde of creditors in the Lin shop were quarrelling with a tremendous din. The local bank and the other creditors were wrangling as to how to divide the remaining property. Although the stock was nearly gone, the remainder and the furniture and fixtures were enough to repay the creditors about seventy per cent; but each was fighting for a ninety, or even one hundred, per cent for himself. The head of the Merchants Guild had talked until his tongue was a little paralysed, to no avail.

Two policemen arrived and took their stand outside the shop door. Clubs in hand, they barked at the crowd that had gathered to see the excitement.

"Why can't I go in? I've got a three hundred dollar loan in this shop! My savings!" Mrs. Zhu argued with a policeman, twisting her withered lips. Tottering, she was elbowing her way through the mass. The blue veins on her forehead stood out as thick as little fingers. She kept pushing. Then sudden-

ly she saw Widow Zhang, with her five-year-old baby in her
arms, pleading with the other policeman to let her enter. He
looked at the widow out of the corners of his eyes, and while
feigning to tease the child, furtively rubbed the back of his hand
against the widow's breasts.

"Sister Zhang —" Mrs. Zhu gasped loudly. She sat down
on the edge of the stone steps, forcibly moving her puckered
mouth.

Tears in her eyes, Widow Zhang took an aimless step,
which brought into her line of vision Mrs. Zhu panting on the
edge of the stone stairs. She practically stumbled over to Mrs.
Zhu and sat down beside her. Then, Widow Zhang began to
cry and lament:

"Oh, my husband, you've left me alone! You don't know
how I'm suffering! The wicked soldiers killed you — it was
three years ago the day before yesterday.... That cursed Mr.
Lin — may he die without sons or grandsons! — has closed his
shop! The hundred and fifty dollars that I earned by the toil of
my two hands has fallen into the sea and is gone without a
sound! Aiya! The lot of the poor is hard, and the rich have no
hearts —"

Hearing his mother cry, the child also began to wail.
Widow Zhang hugged him to her bosom and wept even more
bitterly.

Mrs. Zhu did not cry. Her sunken red-rimmed eyes glared,
and she kept saying frantically:

"The poor have only one life, and the rich have only one
life. If they don't give me back my money, I'll fight them to
the death!"

Just then, a man pushed his way out of the shop. It was
Old Chen. His face was purple. He was cursing as he jostled
through the crowd.

"You gang of crooks! You'll pay for this! One day I'll see
you all burning in the fires of Hell! If we have to take a loss,

everybody should take it together. Even if I got only a small share of what's left, at least that would be fair —"

Still swearing vigorously, he spotted the two women.

"Mrs. Zhang, Mrs. Zhu, what are you sitting there crying for!" he shouted to them. "They've finished dividing up the property. My one mouth couldn't out-argue their dozen. That pack of jackals doesn't give a damn about what's reasonable. They insist that our money doesn't count —"

His words made Widow Zhang weep more bitterly than ever. The playful policeman abruptly walked over to her. He poked her shoulder with his club.

"Hey, what are you crying about? Your man died a long time ago. Which one are you crying for now!"

"Dog farts!" roared Old Chen furiously. "While those people are stealing our money, all a turd like you can do is get gay with women!" He gave the policeman a strong push.

The policeman's nasty eyes went wide. He raised his club to strike, but the crowd yelled and cursed at him. The other policeman ran over and pulled Old Chen to one side.

"It's no use your raising a fuss. We've got nothing against you. The Merchants Guild has ordered us to guard the door. We've got to eat. We can't help it."

"Old Chen, go make a complaint at the Kuomintang office!" a man shouted from the crowd. From the sound of it, it was the voice of Lu, the well-known loafer.

"Go on, go on!" yelled several others. "See what they say to that!"

The policeman who had mediated laughed coldly. He grasped Old Chen by the shoulder. "I advise you not to go looking for trouble. Going there won't do you any good! You wait till Mr. Lin comes back and settle things with him. He can't deny the debt."

Old Chen fumed. He couldn't make up his mind. The idlers were still shouting for him to "go". He looked at Mrs. Zhu and Widow Zhang.

"What do you say? They're always screaming down there how they protect the poor!"

"That's right," called one of the crowd. "Yesterday they arrested Mr. Lin because they said they didn't want him to run away with poor people's money!"

Almost involuntarily, Old Chen and the two women were swept along by the crowd down the street to the Kuomintang office. Widow Zhang was crying as she walked, and cursing the wicked soldiers who had killed her husband, and praying that Mr. Lin should die without sons or grandsons, and reviling that dirty dog of a policeman!

As they neared the office, they saw four policemen standing outside the gate with clubs in their hands. The policemen yelled to them from a distance:

"Go home! You can't go in!"

"We've come to make a complaint!" shouted Old Chen, who was in the first rank of the crowd. "The shop of the Lin family has closed down, and we can't get hold of the money we put up —"

A swarthy pock-marked man jumped out from behind the policemen and howled for them to attack. But the policemen stood their ground, restricting themselves to threats. The crowd in back of Old Chen began to clamour.

"You cheap mongrels don't know what's good for you!" screamed the pock-marked man. "Do you think we have nothing better to do than bother about your business? If you don't get out of here, we're going to fire!"

He stamped and yelled at the policemen to use their clubs. In the front ranks, Old Chen was struck several times. The crowd milled in confusion. Mrs. Zhu was old and weak, and she toppled to the ground. In her panicky haste, Widow Zhang lost her slippers. Pushed and buffeted, she also fell down. Rolling and crawling, she avoided many leaping and stamping feet. She scrambled up and ran for all she was worth. It was then she realized that her child was gone.   There were drops of blood on the upper part of her jacket.

"Aiya! My precious! My heart! The bandits are killing people! Jade Emperor God save us!"

Wailing, her hair tumbled in disorder, she ran quickly. By the time she fled past the closed door of the shop of the Lin family, she was completely out of her mind.

June 18, 1932
Translated by Sidney Shapiro

About the Author

SHEN YANBING (1896-1981), who writes under the pen name Mao Dun, is one of the most outstanding exponents of revolutionary realism to appear in China since the New Literature Movement of 1919. He was born in Tongxian County, Zhejiang Province. Together with Zheng Zhenduo, Ye Shengtao and other writers, in November 1920 he founded the Literary Research Society, one of the first organizations to be formed in China to advocate a new outlook in literature. In 1921 he became editor of *Fiction*, a literary monthly published by the Commercial Press in Shanghai. He completely overhauled this periodical and through it launched a fierce attack on feudal and comprador influences in current Chinese literature.

From 1926 to 1927 he edited the *Minguo Ribao*, a revolutionary daily in Hankou. When Chiang Kai-shek betrayed the revolution, and the Kuomintang became firmly anti-Communist, he left Hankou and returned to Shanghai.

From then on he used the pseudonym Mao Dun in his novel-writing, which served to expose the evils of the reactionary Kuomintang regime and to reflect the revolutionary struggle of the people. He wrote the novels *The Canker*, a trilogy, in 1927; *Rainbow* in 1930;

Three Companions in 1931; and *Midnight* in 1933 as well as a number of short stories, essays and articles.

During the War of Resistance Against Japan (1937-45), Mao Dun kept up his literary activities by editing the periodical *The Literary Front* and writing the novels *Corrosion* (1941) and *Frosted Leaves as Red as Flowers in Spring* (1942), the play *Before and After the Qingming Festival* (1944), besides various short stories, essays and articles.

In 1949, after the founding of the People's Republic of China, Mao Dun was made Minister of Culture and continued to hold this portfolio until 1964.   In 1954, he was elected a deputy to the First National People's Congress, and later re-elected to the successive National People's Congresses.   Then he was concurrently vice-chairman of the China Federation of Literary and Art, chairman of the Union of Chinese Writers and vice-chairman of the Fifth National Committee of the Chinese People's Political Consultative Conference.

Since its publication in 1933, *Midnight* has enjoyed immense popularity in China.   It is generally agreed by contemporary critics that *Midnight* has played a vital pioneering part in the development of revolutionary realism in China.   The Foreign Languages Press has published *Midnight* in English and French and a collection of short stories *Silk Worms* in English, French, Spanish, Arabian and Hindi.

The Shop of the Lin Family is one of the author's masterpieces. The story describes how a shop in a small town is forced to shut down under the double oppression of Kuomintang reactionary and imperialist economic intrusion.   The story reflects the fate commerce and industry suffered under the rule of semi-feudal and semi-colonial China.

A Hired Wife

Rou Shi

He was a dealer in animal skins which he bought from hunters in the countryside and sold in town. Sometimes he also worked in the fields; early each summer he turned farm-hand, transplanting rice for other people. As he had learned to transplant the seedlings in wonderfully straight rows, the peasants always asked him to help them. But he never made enough money to support his family and his debts mounted with each passing year. The wretchedness of his life and the hopeless situation he was in caused him to take to drinking and gambling, and he became vicious and bad-tempered. As he grew poorer and poorer, people stopped lending him money, even in small sums.

With poverty came sickness. He grew sallow: his face took on the sickly colour of a brass drum and even the whites of his eyes became yellow. People said that he had jaundice and urchins nicknamed him "Yellow Fellow." One day, he said to his wife:

"There's no way out. It looks as if we'll even have to sell our cooking pot. I'm afraid we have to part. It's no use both of us going hungry together."

"We have to part? . . ." muttered his wife, who was sitting behind the stove with their three-year-old boy on her lap.

"Yes, we have to part," he answered feebly. "There's somebody willing to hire you as a temporary wife. . . ."

"What?" she almost lost her senses.

There followed a brief silence. Then the husband continued, falteringly:

"Three days ago, Wang Lang came here and spent a long time pressing me to pay my debt to him. After he had left, I went out. I sat under a tree on the shore of Jiumu Lake and thought of committing suicide. I wanted to climb the tree and dive into the water and drown myself, but, after thinking about it, I lost courage. The hooting of an owl frightened me and I walked away. On my way home, I came across Mrs. Shen, the matchmaker, who asked me why I was out at night. I told her what had happened and asked her if she could borrow some money for me, or some lady's dresses and ornaments that I could pawn to pay Wang Lang so that he'd no longer be prowling after me like a wolf. But Mrs. Shen only smiled and said:

" 'What do you keep your wife at home for? And you're so sick and yellow!'

"I hung my head and said nothing. She continued:

" 'Since you've got only one son you might find it hard to part with him. But as for your wife. . . .'

"I thought she meant that I should sell you, but she added:

" 'Of course she is your lawful wife, but you're poor and you can't do anything about it. What do you keep her at home for? You want to starve her to death?'

"Then she said straight out, 'There's a fifty-year-old scholar who wants a concubine to bear him a son since his wife is barren. But his wife objects and will only allow him to hire somebody else's wife for a few years. I've been asked to find them a woman. She has to be about thirty years old and the mother of two or three children. She must be honest and hard-working, and obey the scholar's wife. The scholar's wife has told me that they are willing to pay from eighty to hundred dollars for the right sort of woman. I've looked around for one for several days, but without any luck. But your wife is just right.'

"She asked me what I thought about it. It made me cry

to think of it, but she comforted me and convinced me that it was all for the best."

At this point, his voice trailed off, he hung his head and stopped. His wife looked dazed and remained speechless. There was another moment of silence before he continued:

"Yesterday, Mrs. Shen went to see the scholar again. She came back and told me that both the scholar and his wife were very happy about the idea of having you and had promised to pay me a hundred dollars. If you bear them a child they will keep you for three years, if not — for five. Mrs. Shen has fixed the date for you to go — the eighteenth of this month, that is, five days from now. She is going to have the contract drawn up today."

Trembling all over, the wife faltered:

"Why didn't you tell me this earlier?"

"Yesterday I went up to you three times, but each time I was afraid to begin. But after thinking it over I've come to realize that there's really nothing to be done but hire you out."

"Has it all been decided?" asked the wife, her teeth clattering.

"There's just the contract to be signed."

"Oh, what is to become of me? Can't we really do anything else?"

"It's terrible, I know. But we're poor and we don't want to die. What else can we do? I'm afraid this year I won't even be asked to do any transplanting."

"Have you thought about Chun Bao? He's only three. What will become of him without me?"

"I'll take care of him. You're not nursing him any longer, you know."

He became more and more angry with himself and went out.

"Oh, what a miserable life!" she sighed faintly yet tearlessly. Chun Bao stared at her, whimpering, "Mummy, Mummy!"

On the eve of her departure, she was sitting in the darkest corner of the house. In front of the stove stood an oil lamp, its light flickering like that of a fire-fly. Holding Chun Bao close to her bosom, she pressed her head against his hair. Lost in deep thought, she seemed absolutely dead to the reality surrounding her. Later, she gradually came to, and found herself face to face with the present and her child. Softly she called him:

"Chun Bao, Chun Bao!"

"Yes, Mummy!" the child replied.

"I'm going to leave you tomorrow. . . ."

"What?" the child did not quite understand what she meant and instinctively cuddled closer to her.

"I'm not coming back, not for three years!"

She wiped away her tears. The little boy became inquisitive.

"Mummy, where are you going? To the temple?"

"No. I'm going to live with the Li family, about thirty li away."

"I want to go with you."

"No, you can't, precious!"

"Why?" he countered.

"You'll stay home with daddy, he'll take good care of you. He'll sleep with you and play with you. You just listen to daddy. In three years. . . ."

Before she had finished talking the child sadly interrupted her:

"Daddy will beat me!"

"Daddy will never beat you again." Her left hand was stroking the scar on the right side of the boy's forehead — a reminder of the blow dealt by her husband with the handle of a hoe.

She was about to speak to the boy again when her husband came in. He walked up to her, and fumbling in his pocket, he said:

"I've got seventy dollars from them. They'll give me the other thirty dollars ten days after you get there."

After a short pause, he added, "They've promised to take you there in a sedan-chair."

After another short pause, he continued: "The chair carriers will come to take you early in the morning as soon as they've had breakfast."

With this he walked out again.

That evening, neither he nor she felt like having supper.

The next day there was a spring drizzle.

The chair carriers arrived at the crack of dawn. The young woman had not slept a wink during the night. She had spent the time mending Chun Bao's tattered clothes. Although it was late spring and summer was near, she took out the boy's shabby cotton-padded winter jacket and wanted to give it to her husband, but he was fast asleep. Then she sat down beside her husband, wishing to have a chat with him. But he slept on and she sat there silently, waiting for the night to pass. She plucked up enough courage to mutter a few words into his ear, but even this failed to wake him up. So she lay down too.

As she was about to doze off, Chun Bao woke up. He wanted to get up and pushed his mother. Dressing the child, she said:

"My precious, you mustn't cry while I'm away or daddy will beat you. I'll buy sweets for you to eat. But you mustn't cry any more."

The boy was too young to know what sorrow was, so in a minute he began to sing. She kissed his cheek and said:

"Stop singing now, you'll wake daddy up."

The chair carriers were sitting on the benches in front of the gate, smoking their pipes and chatting. Soon afterwards, Mrs. Shen arrived from the nearby village where she was living. She was an old and experienced matchmaker. As soon as she crossed the threshold, she brushed the raindrops off her clothes, saying to the husband and wife:

"It's raining, it's raining. That's a good omen, it means you will thrive from now on."

The matchmaker bustled about the house and whispered and hinted to the husband that she should be rewarded for having so successfully brought about the deal.

"To tell you the truth, for another fifty dollars, the old man could have bought himself a concubine," she said.

Then Mrs. Shen turned to the young woman who was sitting still with the child in her arms, and said loudly:

"The chair carriers have to get there in time for lunch, so you'd better hurry up and get ready to go."

The young woman glanced at her and her look seemed to say, "I don't want to leave! I'd rather starve here!"

The matchmaker understood and, walking up to her, said smiling:

"You're just a silly girl. What can the 'Yellow Fellow' give you? But over there, the scholar has plenty of everything. He has more than two hundred mu of land, his own houses and cattle. His wife is good-tempered and she's very kind. She never turns anybody from her door without giving him something to eat. And the scholar is not really old. He has a white face and no beard. He stoops a little as well-educated men generally do, and he is quite gentlemanly. There's no need for me to tell you more about him. You'll see him with your own eyes as soon as you get out of the sedan-chair. You know, as a matchmaker, I've never told a lie."

The young woman wiped away her tears and said softly:

"Chun Bao. . . . How can I part from him?"

"Chun Bao will be all right," said the matchmaker, patting the young woman on the shoulder and bending over her and the child. "He is already three. There's a saying, 'A child of three can move about free.' So he can be left alone. It all depends on you. If you can have one or two children over there, everything will be quite all right."

The chair bearers outside the gate now started urging the young woman to set out, murmuring:

"It's not as if you're being married off to him. So why are you crying?"*

The matchmaker snatched away Chun Bao from his mother's arms, saying:

"Let me take care of Chun Bao!"

The little boy began to scream and kick. The matchmaker took him outside. When the young woman was in the sedan-chair, she said:

"You'd better take the boy in, it's raining outside."

Inside the house, resting his head on the palm of his hand, sat the little boy's father, motionless and wordless.

The two villages were thirty li apart, but the chair carriers reached their destination without making a single stop on the way. The young woman's clothes were wet from the spring raindrops which had been blown in through the sedan-chair screens. An elderly woman of about fifty-five, with a plump face and shrewd eyes, came out to greet her. Realizing immediately that this was the scholar's wife, the young woman looked at her bashfully and remained silent. As the scholar's wife was amiably helping the young woman to the door, there came out from the house a tall and thin elderly man with a smooth, round face. Measuring the young woman from head to foot, he smiled and said:

"You have come early. Did you get wet in the rain?"

His wife, completely ignoring what he was saying, asked the young woman:

"Have you left anything in the sedan-chair?"

"No, nothing," answered the young woman.

---

* In old China, a bride usually cried before leaving her family.

Soon they were inside the house. Outside the gate, a number of women from the neighbourhood had gathered and were peeping in to see what was happening.

Somehow or other, the young woman could not help thinking about her old home and Chun Bao. As a matter of fact, she might have congratulated herself on the prospects of spending the next three years here, since both her new home and her temporary husband seemed pleasant. The scholar was really kind and soft-spoken. His wife appeared hospitable and talkative. She talked about her thirty years of happy married life with the scholar. She had given birth to a boy some fifteen years before — a really handsome and lively child, she said — but he died of smallpox less than ten months after his birth. Since then, she had never had another child. The elderly woman hinted she had long been urging her husband to get a concubine but he had always put it off — either because he was too attached to his wedded wife or because he couldn't find a suitable woman for a concubine. This chatter made the young woman feel sad, delighted and depressed by turns. Finally, the young woman was told what was expected of her. She blushed when the scholar's wife said:

"You've had three or four children. Of course you know what to do. You know much more than I do."

After this, the elderly woman went away.

That evening, the scholar told the young woman a great many things about his family in an effort to ingratiate himself with her. She was sitting beside a red-lacquered wooden wardrobe — something she had never had in her old home. Her dull eyes were focused upon it when the scholar came over and sat in front of it, asking:

"What's your name?"

She remained silent and did not smile. Then, rising to her feet, she went towards the bed. He followed her, his face beaming.

"Don't be shy. Still thinking about your husband? Ha, ha,

I'm your husband now!" he said softly, touching her arm. "Don't worry! You're thinking about your child, aren't you? Well. . . ."

He burst out laughing and took off his long gown.

The young woman then heard the scholar's wife scolding somebody outside the room. Though she could not make out just who was being scolded, it seemed to be either the kitchen-maid or herself. In her sorrow, the young woman began to suspect that it must be herself, but the scholar, now lying in bed, said loudly:

"Don't worry. She always grumbles like that. She likes our farm-hand very much, and often scolds the kitchen-maid for chatting with him too much."

Time passed quickly. The young woman's thoughts of her old home gradually faded as she became better and better acquainted with what went on in her new one. Sometimes it seemed to her she heard Chun Bao's muffled cries, and she dreamed of him several times. But these dreams became more and more blurred as she became occupied with her new life. Outwardly, the scholar's wife was kind to her, but she felt that, deep inside, the elderly woman was jealous and suspicious and that, like a detective, she was always spying to see what was going on between the scholar and her. Sometimes, if the wife caught her husband talking to the young woman on his return home, she would suspect that he had bought her something special. She would call him to her bedroom at night to give him a good scolding. "So you've been seduced by the witch!" she would cry. "You should take good care of your old carcass." These abusive remarks the young woman overheard time and again. After that, whenever she saw the scholar return home, she always tried to avoid him if his wife was not present. But even in the presence of his wife, the young woman considered it necessary to keep herself in the background. She had to do all this naturally so that it would not be noticed by outsiders, for otherwise the wife would get angry and blame her for purposely discrediting her in public. As time went on, the scholar's wife even made the young woman do the work of a maid-servant. Once the young woman decided to wash the elderly woman's clothes.

"You're not supposed to wash my clothes," the scholar's wife said. "In fact you can have the kitchen-maid wash your own laundry." Yet the next moment she said:

"Sister dear, you'd better go to the pigsty and have a look at the two pigs which have been grunting all the time. They're probably hungry because the kitchen-maid never gives them enough to eat."

Eight months had passed and winter came. The young woman became fussy about her food. She had little appetite for regular meals and always felt like eating something different —noodles, potatoes and so on. But she soon got tired of noodles and potatoes, and asked for meat dumplings. When she ate a little too much she got sick. Then she felt a desire for pumpkins and plums — things that could only be had in summer. The scholar knew what all this meant. He kept smiling all day and gave her whatever was available. He went to town himself to get her tangerines and asked someone to buy her some oranges. He often paced up and down the veranda, muttering to himself. One day, he saw the young woman and the kitchen-maid grinding rice for the New Year festival. They had hardly started grinding when he said to the young woman, "You'd better have a rest now. We can let the farm-hand do it, since everybody is going to eat the cakes."

Sometimes in the evening, when the rest of the household were chatting, he would sit alone near an oil lamp, reading the *Book of Songs*:

> "Fair, fair," cry the ospreys
> On the island in the river.
> Lovely is this noble lady,
> Fit bride for our lord.

The farm-hand once asked him:

"Please, sir, what are you reading this book for? You're not going to sit for a higher civil service examination, are you?"

The scholar stroked his beardless chin and grinned:

"Well, you know the joys of life, don't you? There's a saying that the greatest joy of life is either to spend the first night in the nuptial chamber or to pass a civil service examination. As for me, I've already experienced both. But now there's still greater blessing in store for me."

His remark set the whole household laughing — except for his wife and the young woman.

To the scholar's wife all this was very annoying. When she first heard of the young woman's pregnancy, she was pleased. Later, when she saw her husband lavishing attention on the young woman, she began to blame herself for being barren. Once, the following spring, it happened that the young woman fell ill and was laid up for three days with a headache. The scholar was anxious that she take a rest and frequently asked what she needed. This made his wife angry. She grumbled for three whole days and said that the young woman was malingering.

"She has been spoiled here and become stuck-up like a real concubine," she said, sneering maliciously, "always complaining about headaches or backaches. She must have been quite different before — like a bitch that has to go searching for food even when she is about to bear a litter of puppies! Now, with the old man fawning on her, she puts on airs!"

"Why so much fuss about having a baby?" said the scholar's wife one night to the kitchen-maid. "I myself was once with child for ten months, I just can't believe she's really feeling so bad. Who knows what she's going to have? It may just be a little toad! She'd better not try to bluff me, throwing her weight around before the thing is born. It's still nothing but a clot of blood! It's really a bit too early for her to make such a fuss!"

The young woman who had gone to bed without supper

was awakened by this torrent of malicious abuse and burst into convulsive sobs. The scholar was also shocked by what he heard — so much so that he broke into a cold sweat and shook with anger. He wanted to go to his wife's room, grab her by the hair and give her a good beating so as to work off his feelings. But, somehow or other, he felt powerless to do so; his fingers trembled and his arms ached with weariness. Sighing deeply, he said softly, "I've been too good to her. In thirty years of married life, I've never slapped her face or given her a scratch. That's why she is so cocky."

Then, crawling across the bed, he whispered to the young woman beside him:

"Now, stop crying, stop crying, let her cackle! A barren hen is always jealous! If you manage to have a baby boy this time, I'll give you two precious gifts — a blue jade ring and a white jade. . . ." Leaving the last sentence unfinished, he turned to listen to his wife's jeering voice outside the room. He hastily took off his clothes, and, covering his head with the quilt and nestling closer to the young woman, he said:

"I've a white jade. . . ."

The young woman grew bigger and bigger around the waist. The scholar's wife made arrangements with a midwife, and, when other people were around, she would busy herself making baby's clothes out of floral prints.

The hot summer had ended and the cool autumn breeze was blowing over the village. The day finally came when the expectations of the whole household reached their climax and everybody was agog. His heart beating faster than ever, the scholar was pacing the courtyard, reading about horoscopes from an almanac in his hand as intently as if he wanted to commit the whole book to memory. One moment he would look anxiously at the room with its windows closely shut whence came the muffled groans of the expectant mother. The next, he

would look at the cloudy sky, and walk up to the kitchen-maid
at the door to ask:

"How is everything now?"

Nodding, the maid would reply after a moment's pause:
"It won't be long now, it won't be long."

He would resume pacing the courtyard and reading the
almanac.

The suspense lasted until sunset. Then, as wisps of kitchen
smoke were curling up from the roofs and lamps were gleaming in the country houses like so many wild flowers in spring, a
baby boy was born. The new-born child cried at the top of his
voice while the scholar sat in a corner of the house, with tears of
joy in his eyes. The household was so excited that no one cared
about supper.

A month later, the bright and tender-faced baby made his
début in the open. While the young woman was breast-feeding
him, womenfolk from the neighbourhood gathered around to
feast their eyes upon the boy. Some liked his nose; others, his
mouth; still others, his ears. Some praised his mother, saying
that she had become whiter and healthier. The scholar's wife,
now acting like a granny, said:

"That's enough! You'll make the baby cry!"

As to the baby's name, the scholar racked his brains, but
just could not hit upon a suitable one. His wife suggested that
the Chinese character *shou,* meaning longevity, or one of its
synonyms, should be included in his name. But the scholar did
not like it — it was too commonplace. He spent several weeks
looking through Chinese classics like the *Book of Changes* and
the *Book of History* in search of suitable characters to be used
as the baby's name. But all his efforts proved fruitless. It was
a difficult problem to solve because he wanted a name which
should be auspicious for the baby and would imply at the same
time that he was born to him in old age. One evening, while
holding the three-month-old baby in his arms, the scholar, with

spectacles on, sat down near a lamp and again looked into some book in an effort to find a name for the boy. The baby's mother, sitting quietly in a corner of the room, appeared to be musing. Suddenly she said:

"I suppose you could call him 'Qiu Bao.' " Those in the room turned to look at the young woman and listened intently as she continued, "*Qiu* means autumn and *Bao* means treasure. So since he was born in autumn, you'd better call him 'Qiu Bao.' "

The scholar was silent for a brief moment and then exclaimed:

"A wonderful idea! I've wasted a lot of time looking for a name for the baby! As a man of over fifty, I've reached the *autumn* of my life. The boy too was born in *autumn*. Besides, *autumn* is the time when everything is ripe and the time for harvesting, as the *Book of History* says. 'Qiu Bao' is really a good name for the child."

Then he began to praise the young woman, saying that she was born clever and that it was quite useless to be a bookworm like himself. His remarks made the young woman feel ill at ease. Lowering her head and forcing a smile, she thought to herself with tears in her eyes:

"I suggested 'Qiu Bao' simply because I was thinking of my elder son Chun Bao."*

Qiu Bao daily grew handsomer and more attached to his mother. His unusually big eyes which stared tirelessly at strangers would light up joyfully when he saw his mother, even when she was a long distance away. He always clung to her. Although the scholar loved him even more than his mother did, Qiu Bao did not take to him. As to the scholar's wife, although outwardly she showed as much affection for Qiu Bao as if he were her own baby, he would stare at her with the same inde-

_____

* Meaning "Spring Treasure."

fatigable curiosity as he did at strangers. But the more the child grew attached to his mother, the closer drew the time for their separation. Once more it was summer. To everybody in the house, the advent of this season was a reminder of the approaching end of the young woman's three-year stay.

The scholar, out of his love for Qiu Bao, suggested to his wife one day that he was willing to offer another hundred dollars to buy the young woman so that she could stay with them permanently. The wife, however, replied curtly:

"No, you'll have to poison me before you do that!"

This made the scholar angry. He remained silent for quite a while. Then, forcing himself to smile, he said:

"It's a pity that our child will be motherless. . . ." His wife smiled wryly and said in an icy and cutting tone:

"Don't you think that I might be a mother to him?"

As to the young woman, there were two conflicting ideas in her mind. On the one hand, she always remembered that she would have to leave after the three years were up. Three years seemed a short time and she had become more of a servant than a temporary wife. Besides, in her mind her elder son Chun Bao had become as sweet and lovely a child as Qiu Bao. She could not bear to remain away from either Qiu Bao or Chun Bao. On the other hand, she was willing to stay on permanently in the scholar's house because she thought her own husband would not live long and might even die in four or five years. So she longed to have the scholar bring Chun Bao into his home so that she could also live with her elder son.

One day, as she was sitting wearily on the veranda with Qiu Bao sleeping at her breast, the hypnotic rays of the early summer sun sent her into a daydream and she thought she saw Chun Bao standing beside her; but when she stretched out her hand to him and was about to speak to her two sons, she saw that her elder boy was not there.

At the door at the other end of the veranda the scholar's wife, with her seemingly kind face but fierce eyes, stood staring at the young woman. The latter came to and said to herself:

"I'd better leave here as soon as I can. She's always spying on me!"

Later, the scholar changed his plan a little; he decided he would send Mrs. Shen on another mission: to find out whether the young woman's husband was willing to take another thirty dollars — or fifty dollars at most — to let him keep the young woman for another three years. He said to his wife:

"I suppose Qiu Bao's mother could stay on until he is five."

Chanting "Buddha preserve me" with a rosary in her hand, the scholar's wife replied:

"She has got her elder son at home. Besides, you ought to let her go back to her lawful husband."

The scholar hung his head and said brokenly:

"Just imagine, Qiu Bao will be motherless at two. . . ."

Putting away the rosary, his wife snapped:

"I can take care of him, I can manage him. Are you afraid I'm going to murder him?"

Upon hearing the last sentence, the scholar walked away hurriedly. His wife went on grumbling:

"The child has been born for me. Qiu Bao is mine. If the male line of your family came to an end, it would affect me too. You've been bewitched by her. You're old and pigheaded. You don't know what's what. Just think how many more years you may live, and yet you're trying to do everything to keep her with you. I certainly don't want another woman's tablet put side by side with mine in the family shrine!"

It seemed as if she would never stop pouring out the stream of venomous and biting words, but the scholar was too far away to hear them.

Every time Qiu Bao had a pimple on his head or a slight fever, the scholar's wife would go around praying to Buddha and bring back Buddha's medicine in the form of incense ash which she applied to the baby's pimple or dissolved in water for him to drink. He would cry and perspire profusely. The young woman did not like the idea of the scholar's wife making so much fuss when the baby fell slightly ill, and always threw the ash away when she was not there. Sighing deeply, the scholar's wife once said to her husband:

"You see, she really doesn't care a bit about our baby and won't admit he's getting thinner. Real love needs no flourishes; she is only pretending that she loves our baby."

The young woman wept when alone, and the scholar kept silent.

On Qiu Bao's first birthday, the celebration lasted the whole day. About forty guests attended the party. The birthday presents they brought included baby's clothes, noodles, a silver pendant in the shape of a lion's head to be worn on the baby's chest and a gold-plated image of the God of Longevity to be sewn onto the baby's bonnet. The guests wished the baby good fortune and a long life. The host's face flushed with joy as though it were reflecting the reddening glow of the setting sun.

Late in the afternoon, just before the banquet, there came into the courtyard from the deepening twilight outside an uninvited guest, who attracted the attention of all the others. He was an emaciated-looking peasant, dressed in patched clothes and with unkempt hair, carrying under his arm a paper-parcel. Greatly astonished and puzzled, the host went up to inquire where he hailed from. While the newcomer was stammering, it suddenly occurred to the host that this was none other than the skin-dealer — the young woman's husband. Thereupon, the host said in a low voice:

"There was really no need for you to bring a gift."

The newcomer looked timidly about, saying:

"I . . . I had to come . . . I've come to wish the baby a long life. . . ."

Before he had finished speaking, he began to open the package he had brought. Tearing off three paper wrappings with his quivering fingers, he took out four bronze-cast and silver-plated Chinese characters, about one square inch in size, which said that the baby would live as long as the South Mountain.

The scholar's wife appeared on the scene, and looked displeased when she saw the skin-dealer. The scholar, however, invited the skin-dealer to the table, where the guests sat whispering about him.

The guests wined and dined for two hours and everybody was feeling happy and excited. They indulged in noisy drinking games and plied one another with big bowls of wine. The deafening uproar rocked the house. Nobody paid any attention to the skin-dealer who sat silently after drinking two cups of wine. Having enjoyed their wine, the guests each hurriedly took a bowl of rice; and, bidding one another farewell, they dispersed in twos and threes, carrying lighted lanterns in their hands.

The skin-dealer sat there eating until the servants came to clear the table. Then he walked to a dark corner of the veranda where he found his wife.

"What did you come for?" asked the young woman with a note of deep sadness in her voice.

"I didn't want to come, but I just had to."

"Then why did you come so late?"

"I couldn't get any money to buy a birthday gift. I spent the whole morning begging for a loan and then I had to go to town to buy the gift. I was tired and hungry. That's why I came late."

The young woman asked, "How's Chun Bao?"

Her husband reflected for a moment and then answered: "It's for Chun Bao's sake that I've come. . . ."

"For Chun Bao's sake!" she echoed in surprise. He went on slowly:

"Since this summer Chun Bao has grown very skinny. In the autumn, he fell sick. I haven't been able to do anything for him because I haven't had any money. So his illness is getting more serious. I'm afraid he won't live unless we try to

save him!" He continued after a short pause, "I've come to borrow some money from you. . . ."

Deep inside her, the young woman had the feeling that wild cats were scratching and biting her, gnawing at her very heart. She was on the verge of bursting into tears, but on such an occasion when everybody was celebrating Qiu Bao's birthday she knew she had to keep her emotions under control. She made a brave effort to keep back her tears and said to her husband:

"How can I get hold of any money? They give me twenty cents a month as pocket money here, but I spend every cent of it on my baby. What can we do now?"

Both were speechless for a while, then the young woman asked again:

"Who is taking care of Chun Bao while you're here?"

"One of the neighbours. I've got to go back home tonight. In fact I ought to be going now," he answered, wiping away his tears.

"Wait a moment," she told him tearfully, "let me go and try to borrow some money from him."

And with this she left her husband.

Three days later, in the evening, the scholar suddenly asked the young woman:

"Where's the blue jade ring I gave you?"

"I gave it to him the other night. He pawned it."

"Didn't I lend you five dollars?" countered the scholar irritably.

The young woman, handing her head, answered after a moment's pause:

"Five dollars wasn't enough!"

The scholar sighed deeply at this and said, "No matter how good I try to be to you, you still love your husband and your elder son more. I wanted to keep you for another couple of years, but now I think you'd better leave here next spring!"

The young woman stood there silent and tearless.

Several days later, the scholar again reproached her, "That blue jade ring is a treasure. I gave it to you because I wanted Qiu Bao to inherit it from you. I didn't think you would have it pawned! It's lucky my wife doesn't know about it, otherwise she would make scenes for another three months."

After this the young woman became thinner and paler. Her eyes lost their lustre; she was often subjected to sneers and curses. She was forever worrying about Chun Bao's illness. She was always on the look-out for some acquaintance from her home village or some traveller going there. She hoped she could hear about Chun Bao's recovery, but there was no news. She wished she could borrow a couple of dollars or buy sweets for some traveller to take to Chun Bao, but she could find no one going to her home village. She would often walk outside the gate with Qiu Bao in her arms, and there, standing by the roadside, she would gaze with melancholy eyes at the country paths. This greatly annoyed the scholar's wife who said to her husband:

"She really doesn't want to stay here any longer. She's anxious to get back home as soon as she can."

Sometimes at night, sleeping with Qiu Bao at her bosom, she would suddenly wake up from her dreams and scream until the child too would awake and start crying. Once, the scholar asked her:

"What's happened? What's happened?"

She patted the child without answering. The scholar continued:

"Did you dream your elder son had died? How you screamed! You woke me up!"

She hurriedly answered, "No, no . . . I thought I saw a new grave in front of me!"

He said nothing, but the morbid hallucination continued to loom before her — she saw herself approaching the grave.

Winter was drawing to a close and the birds began twittering at her window, as if urging her to leave quickly. The child was weaned, and her separation from her son — permanent separation — was already a foregone conclusion.

On the day of her departure, the kitchen-maid quietly asked the scholar's wife:

"Shall we hire a sedan-chair to take her home?"

Fingering the rosary in her hands, the scholar's wife said, "Better let her walk. Otherwise she will have to pay the fare herself. And where will she get the money? I understand her husband can't even afford to have three meals a day. She shouldn't try to be showy. It's not very far from here, and I myself have walked some forty li a day. She's more used to walking than I am, so she ought to be able to get there in half a day."

In the morning, as the young woman was dressing Qiu Bao, tears kept streaming down her cheeks. The child called, "Auntie, auntie" (the scholar's wife had made him call her "mummy," and his real mother, "auntie.") The young woman could not answer for weeping. She wanted so much to say to the child:

"Good-bye, my precious! Your 'mummy' has been good to you, so you should be good to her in the future. Forget about me forever!" But these words she never uttered. The child was only one and a half years old, and she knew that he would never understand what she wanted to say.

The scholar walked up quietly behind her, and put ten twenty-cent silver coins into her palm, saying softly:

"Here are two dollars for you."

Buttoning up the child's clothes, she put the ten silver coins into her pocket.

The scholar's wife also came in, and, staring hard at the back of the retreating scholar, she turned to the young woman, saying:

"Give me Qiu Bao, so that he won't cry when you leave."

The young woman remained silent, but the child was

unwilling to leave his mother and kept striking the scholar's wife's face with his little hands. The scholar's wife was piqued and said:

"You can keep him with you until you've had breakfast."

The kitchen-maid urged the young woman to eat as much as possible, saying:

"You've been eating very little for a fortnight. You are thinner than when you first came here. Have you looked at yourself in the mirror? You have to walk thirty li today, so finish this bowl of rice!"

The young woman said listlessly, "You're really kind to me!"

It was a fine day and the sun was high in the sky. Qiu Bao continued to cling to his mother. When the scholar's wife angrily snatched him away from her, he yelled at the top of his voice, kicking the elderly woman in the belly and pulling at her hair. The young woman, standing behind, pleaded:

"Let me stay here until after lunch."

The scholar's wife replied fiercely over her shoulder:

"Hurry up with your packing. You've got to leave sooner or later!"

While she was packing, she kept listening to his crying. The kitchen-maid stood beside her, comforting her and watching what she was putting into her parcel. When the young woman left she carried the same old parcel she had brought.

She heard Qiu Bao crying as she walked out of the gate, and his cries rang in her ears even after she had plodded a distance of three li.

Stretching before her lay the sun-bathed country road which seemed to be as long as the sky was boundless. As she was walking along the bank of a river, whose clear water reflected her like a mirror, she thought of stopping there and putting an end to her life by drowning herself. But, after sitting for a while on the bank, she resumed her journey.

It was already afternoon, and an elderly villager told her

that she still had fifteen li to go before she would reach her own village. She said to him:

"Grandpa, please hire a litter for me. I'm too tired to walk."

"Are you sick?" asked the old man.

"Yes, I am." She was sitting in a pavilion outside a village.

"Where have you walked from?"

She answered after a moment's hesitation:

"I'm on my way home; this morning I thought I would be able to walk the whole way."

The old man lapsed into sympathetic silence and finally hired a litter for her.

It was about four o'clock in the afternoon when the litter carriers entered a narrow and filthy village street. The young woman, her pale face shrunken and yellowed like an old vegetable leaf, lay with her eyes closed. She was breathing weakly. The villagers eyed her with astonishment and compassion. A group of village urchins noisily followed the litter, the appearance of which stirred the quiet village.

One of the children chasing after the litter was Chun Bao. The children were shouting and squealing like little pigs when the litter carriers suddenly turned into the lane leading to Chun Bao's home. Chun Bao stopped in surprise. As the litter stopped in front of his home, he leaned dazed against a post and looked at it from a distance. The other children gathered around and craned their necks timidly. When the young woman descended from the litter, she felt giddy and at first did not realize that the shabbily dressed child with dishevelled hair standing before her was Chun Bao. He was hardly any taller than when she had left three years before and just as skinny. Then, she blurted out in tears:

"Chun Bao!"

Startled, the children dispersed. Chun Bao, also frightened, ran inside the house to look for his father.

Inside the dingy room, the young woman sat for a long,

long while. Both she and her husband were speechless. As
night fell, he raised his head and said:

"You'd better prepare supper!"

She rose reluctantly, and, after searching around the house,
said in a weak voice:

"There's no rice left in the big jar...."

Her husband looked at her with a sickly smile.

"You've got used to living in a rich man's house all right.
We keep our rice in a cardboard box."

That night, the skin-dealer said to his son:

"Chun Bao, you go to bed with your mother!"

Chun Bao, standing beside the stove, started crying. His
mother walked up to him and called:

"Chun Bao, Chun Bao!" But when she tried to caress him,
the boy shunned her. His father hissed:

"You've forgotten your own mother. You ought to get a
good beating for that!"

The young woman lay awake on the narrow, dirty plank-
bed with Chun Bao lying, like a stranger, beside her. Her mind
in a daze, she seemed to see her younger son Qiu Bao — plump,
white and lovely — curled up beside her, but as she stretched
out her arms to embrace him, she saw it was Chun Bao, who had
just fallen asleep. The boy was breathing faintly, his face pressed against his mother's breast. She hugged him tightly.

The still and chilly night seemed to drag on endlessly....

Translated by Zhang Peiji

About the Author

ROU SHI (1902-31) is the pen name of Zhao Pingfu who was
born in Ninghai County, Zhejiang Province. He entered

the First Normal School of Hangzhou, Zhejiang, in 1918 and started writing in 1923. After leaving school, he then taught in a primary school before going to Shanghai in 1928 where he took part in the New Literature Movement. With the support of the great writer Lu Xun, he formed the Dawn Blossom Society. Besides creative writing, he also introduced to the Chinese people literature and graphic arts from foreign countries, especially from eastern and northern Europe. He joined the League of Left-wing Writers in 1930 and was admitted into the Chinese Communist Party in the same year. He was arrested on January 17, 1931 by the Kuomintang reactionaries and killed soon after.

Rou Shi's early writings included the collection of short stories *The Madman*; a short novel *Three Sisters* and the full-length novel *Death of the Old Age*. The novel *Threshold of Spring* written in 1929 was one of his important works, and Lu Xun wrote a preface for it.

"*A Hired Wife*", the best of his stories, appeared in 1930. It depicts a young woman whose husband hires her off to a landlord in the neighbouring village to support their family. For three years she lives an unbearable life, having left her own child to become a tool for producing a child for another man. Under the author's pen, the hired wife, both mother and slave, appears vividly before the reader's eyes.

Mr. Hua Wei

Zhang Tianyi

Tracing back our genealogies, I found he was a kinsman of mine. I called him "Mr. Hua Wei". He felt this form of address was not too good.

"Now, now, brother Tianyi!" he said. "Why don't you drop the 'Mr.'? Just call me brother Wei. Or call me Ah Wei."

After making these remarks, he put on his hat and said:

"Brother Tianyi, let's have a talk another day. I've always wanted to have a good long talk with you, but I never have the time! Today Chairman Liu drafted a spare-time work plan for county magistrates, he wants me to give an opinion on it and make some revisions for him. At three o'clock I have another meeting."

Here he shook his head and forced a bitter smile. He explained that he was not at all afraid of hardship: everybody had to suffer a little during the Anti-Japanese War. It was just that he had to have enough time at his disposal.

"Commissioner Wang telegraphed me for the third time, requesting me to go to Hankou. How can I manage to that, for heaven's sake!"

So saying, he shook hands with me hastily and climbed into his private rickshaw.

He always carried leather briefcase under his arm, and a knobby, gleaming black walking-stick in his hand. On the fourth finger of his left hand he wore a wedding-ring. When he took a cigar, he bent his ring finger slightly and cocked high little finger, forming the shape of an orchid.

The ordinary rickshaw pullers of this city were not brisk runners, but walked deliberately along as if taking an after-meal stroll. But the private rickshaw pullers were an exception. With a ding-ding, ding-ding, ding-ding, they forced their way forward. The other rickshaws immediately pulled over to the left, the wheel-barrows swerved quickly. The carrying-poles hastily fell back to the roadside. Pedestrians hurriedly sought refuge in the stores on either side of the street.

The private rickshaw bells rang endlessly, their steel wires shone brightly. There was hardly time to see them clearly — in an instant they were far, far away, as fast as lightning.

And — according to statistics compiled by several high-level workers in the Anti-Japanese Resistance, the quickest of them was Mr. Hua Wei's rickshaw.

Time was of the greatest importance to him. He once said:

"If only the system of sleeping at night could be abolished. I wish there were more than 24 hours in a day. There is too much national salvation work to be done."

He drew out his watch and looked at it, and the muscles on his plump face at once became tense. He frowned and strenuously pursed his lips, as if he were collecting all his energy on his face. He left right away: he had to go to the Refugees Relief Association to attend a meeting.

As usual — everyone had assembled in the meeting hall, sitting there waiting for him. When he got off the rickshaw at the entrance, he happened to step on the foot bell, which went "Ding. . . ."

The comrades looked at one another, saying, "Ah, here comes Mr. Hua Wei." Some of them drew a deep breath. Some pulled a long face as they glanced at the doorway. One even clenched his fists and glared as if getting ready for a fight.

Looking very dignified, Mr. Hua Wei walked in with

unhurried gait, and his dignified air seemed to dispel the bustle of a few minutes before. He stopped at the entrance for a second to let everyone get a good glimpse of him, as if to inspire confidence in the comrades and assure them that they might feel at ease before any difficulty which might confront them. He also nodded his head. Instead of looking at anyone in particular he fixed his gaze on the ceiling. This was a kind of salutation to the whole assembly.

The hall was quiet. The meeting began. Someone was turning over papers, making a rustling noise.

Mr. Hua Wei sat modestly at a neglected corner of the room, far away from the chairman's seat. He showed reluctance to act as chairman.

"I can't act as chairman." He made a gesture with his cigar. "The Board of Directors of the Workers' National Salvation Association is holding a meeting of the standing committee today. The Society for Research on Popular Literature and Art is also meeting today. I also have to attend a meeting sponsored by the Wounded Soldiers' Relief League in a little while. As you know I don't have sufficient time at my disposal: I'm only permitted to stay here for ten minutes. I would like to propose Comrade Liu as chairman."

As saying, he clapped his hands gently, a slight smile playing at the corners of his mouth.

While the chairman was making his report, Mr. Hua Wei kept on striking matches to light his cigar. He put his watch in front of him and frequently looked at it in a way that suggested he was making calculations.

"I have a proposal to make," he spoke in a loud voice. "Our time is very precious. I hope the chairman will make his report as simply as possible. I hope he will finish it in two minutes."

After striking matches for two minutes, he suddenly stood up. He waved his hand at the chairman who was still chattering away.

"All right! All right! Though the chairman hasn't finished his report, I understood everything. Because I have other meetings to attend, let me make a few suggestions first."

He stopped for a moment, puffed twice on his cigar and glanced around at the audience.

"I have two simple suggestions to make." He moistened his lips. "First, each member must avoid slackening. On the contrary, you must increase your efforts. This needs not to be emphasized, for you are all hard-working young people who are enthusiastic in your work. I'm very grateful to you. But there is another matter you must always keep in mind, and that is my second point."

He puffed twice on his cigar again but only hot air issued from his mouth. He struck another match.

"The second point is that the young members should recognize one leading centre only. Only under the leadership of a leading centre can you close ranks and become united. And only under the leadership of one leading centre can national salvation work be developed. Young people are enthusiatic and hard-working but because they lack knowledge and experience, it is easy for them to make mistakes. If there is no leading centre from above, they may commit irretrievable errors."

As he watched the expression on the faces around him, the muscles on his face contracted and were forced into a smile. He continued, "You are our young comrades, so I will speak very frankly and without reserve. You want to take part in national salvation work, so there is no need for polite compliments. I should think that each and every one of you young comrades will accept my suggestions. I am very grateful. Well, I must apologize, but I have to leave now."

He put on his hat, tucked his briefcase under his arm, nodded towards the ceiling, stuck his belly out and walked out.

When he reached the entrance, however, something else occurred to him. He pulled the chairman aside and said to him in a low whisper:

"Your work — do you have any difficulties?" he asked.

"In the report I gave just now, I mentioned one thing, we. . . ."

Mr. Hua Wei pointed his forefinger at the chairman's breast:

"Uh, uh, uh . . . I know, I know, I don't have sufficient time to discuss this matter. Later — you may come to my home to consult me about any work plan you have in mind."

The long-haired young man sitting by the side of the chairman had been watching them intently, and now broke in impatiently:

"Last Wednesday we went to see Mr. Hua three times, but you weren't at home."

Mr. Hua stared at him coldly and snorted as he said, "Oh yes, but I had other business," and then resumed his talk with the chairman in a low voice:

"In case I'm not at home you may consult Miss Huang. She knows my views and she can advise you."

Miss Huang was his wife. He always called her by this name before a third person.

After this communication he left in earnest. Soon he arrived at the meeting of the Society for Research on Popular Literature and Art. He found that the meeting was underway and someone was stating his opinions. He sat down, lit his cigar and clapped his hands rather gloomily.

"Mr. Chairman!" he called, "since I have to attend another meeting today, I cannot wait till this meeting is over. I have some suggestions that I want to raise now."

Thereupon he stated two suggestions: first, he told them that all of those present were from local cultural circles, that cultural work was very important and had to be executed with increased efforts. Second, cultural workers must recognize a leading centre and under the leadership of the local leadership centre they must close ranks and become united.

At quarter to six he arrived at the conference room of the

Board of Directors of the Workers' National Salvation Association.

On this occasion his face assumed a smile and he nodded to everybody.

"I'm terribly sorry, I'm three-quarters of an hour late."

The chairman smiled at him and still smiling he put out his tongue, looking as if he had done something wrong and was afraid of being scolded. He looked around and chose a seat by the side of a man with a small moustache.

"Did you get drunk last night?" He whispered to him with a serious and confidential expression.

"I was all right, only my head was a little dizzy. How about you?"

"Me? I shouldn't have had three glasses of hard liquor," said he solemnly. "Especially Shansi spirits, I can't drink too much of that. Director Liu insisted on me finishing them off. As soon as I got home, I fell asleep. My wife said she would tackle Director Liu about this, and interrogate him about why he made me drunk. See how much trouble he has caused!"

After this exchange he opened his briefcase hurriedly and took out a slip of paper. He wrote a few words on it and passed it over to the chairman.

"Please wait a minute," the chairman interrupted the man who was giving a speech. "Mr. Hua Wei has to leave on other business. He has a few suggestions which he would like to raise right away."

"Mr. Chairman!" He made a bow. "Gentlemen!" He made another bow. "I must first apologize for having come rather late and because I am obliged to leave rather early...."

Then he stated his suggestions. He declared that the Board of Directors was the leading organ and that it must function as the leading centre at all times.

"The masses of people are complex. Especially in the present masses there are extremely complex elements. It would be very, very dangerous if we should fail to exercise our leading function. In fact, work in every field here calls for a leading centre. We have a heavy responsibility to bear, but no matter how difficult it is, we must bear this responsibility."

After he had repeatedly emphasized the importance of the leading centre, he put on his hat and went off to a banquet. He was thus kept busy every day. He would go to Director Liu's office to arrange various matters. He would attend meetings of various organizations. And every day he would either be invited to dinner or invite people himself.

Each time his wife saw me, she would complain to me of Mr. Hua's sufferings.

"Oh, he suffers such a lot! There's so much work to do that he doesn't even have time to eat!"

"Why doesn't he take on fewer responsibilities and concentrate on one job?" I asked.

"How could he, he has to exercise leadership everywhere."

But there was one time when Mr. Hua got a great fright. Some people from women's circles organized a War-time Nursery Association without summoning him.

He started to make inquiries and investigations. He tried in various ways to find out who was responsible.

"I know your committee has already been elected. I think you can still add more members."

When he saw the other falter at this, his face fell.

"The point is whether it is possible for your committee to exercise leadership. Can you give me a guarantee that there'll be no harmful elements in your committee? Can you give me a guarantee that in your future work there'll be no mistakes, no slackening? Can you give me a guarantee? Can you? If you can, please give me a written note and if later . . . if there's any trouble, you will be responsible."

He also declared: This was not his own idea. He was only seeing it was put into effect. So saying he pointed at the other's breast with his forefinger.

"If you can't guarantee what I've mentioned to you, isn't your organization going to become an illegal one?"

After two rounds of such negotiations Mr. Hua Wei became a committee member of the War-time Nursery Association. Thereafter, whenever the committee held a meeting, Mr. Hua would stop by for five minutes with his briefcase under his arm, and after raising one or two suggestions, he would climb onto his rickshaw.

One day he invited me to dinner. He said that someone had brought him some cured meat from his hometown.

When I arrived at his place, he was losing his temper at two young men who looked like students.

"Why didn't you go yesterday?" he roared. "I asked you to send several people there. But when I stood on the platform to give a speech, you weren't even there. I really don't understand what you were up to?"

"Yesterday I went to a newly organized Refugees' Study Group."

Mr. Hua Wei leaped up violently.

"What! What! A newly organized Refugees' Study Group? Why don't I know about it, why haven't you told me about it before?"

"We decided upon it ourselves the other day. I called on you several times but you were never home. . . ."

"So, you have secret activities!" he glared at one of them. "Tell me honestly what is the background of this study group. Be honest!"

The other seemed to flare up:

"What background! We are all Chinese! It was a decision of the Ministerial Conference. There are no secret activities. . . . You didn't attend our meeting, or if you did, you didn't stay till the end. When we looked for you, you weren't home. . . . We couldn't just keep holding up the work!"

Mr. Hua Wei threw down his cigar and struck the table with his fist in fury, *dong*!

"Damned fool!" He ground his teeth and his lips quivered. "Just be careful! You, ... you...." He fell on the sofa, his mouth contorted in pain. "Damn them! . . . young fools! ..."

Five minutes later, he raised his head and looked around as if in fear. His two guests were gone. He drew a long breath.

"You see, you see! brother Tianyi! How can one deal with the young people of today!"

That evening he drank heavily, abandoning all restraint, muttering curses at those young fellows. He broke a teacup. When his wife helped him to bed, he suddenly gave a shudder and said:

"There's a meeting at ten tomorrow."

Translated by Zhang Mingzhu

About the Author

ZHANG TIANYI was born in Nanjing in 1906. In 1924 he graduated from high school and started to study painting, but after one year in the university he was forced to give up his studies for financial reasons. He led a precarious existence between spells of unemployment as a clerk in government offices, a newspaper man and a teacher. He started writing in 1928. Since 1949 he has been a member of the editorial board of the monthly *People's Literature*. Now he devotes most of his time to children's books.

He has written a number of novels including: *A Year, The Cog-Wheel* and *In the City*. The best known of his collections of short stories are *Pursuit, Counter-Attack, United, Spring Breeze* and *Fellow Countrymen*. His most popular children's tales are *Great King Tu Tu, The Big Wolf, The Story of Luo Wenying* and *The Secret of the Magic Gourd*. *Big Lin and Little Lin* was written in 1931.

Some of his short stories such as *The Secret of the Magic Gourd*, *Big Lin and Little Lin* and *The Big Wolf* have been translated and published into English and other foreign languages.

Mr. Hua Wei is a satirical short story published in 1938. It meticulously depicts a sophisticated and mean person, Mr. Hua Wei who, without any learning, is only a claw riveted in the cultural field by the Kuomintang reactionaries. Through this story, Zhang Tianyi exposes the Kuomintang for their real hostility towards the Communist Party while shamming an anti-Japanese stand.

The Diary of Miss Sophia

Ding Ling

Dec. 24 — It blows again today! The wind awoke me before daybreak. And now the servant comes in to make the fire. I know I'm not going to be able to sleep any more. I also know if I don't get up I'll soon be dizzy. I'm too fond of mulling over many strange things when I lie under my quilt. The doctor told me the best thing is to sleep a lot, eat a lot, and not to read or think, but this is precisely what I can't manage to do. I can't ever get to sleep before two or three in the morning, and I'm always awake before it's light. It's impossible not to think of the many irritating things that come to one's head during weather like this. You can't go out to amuse yourself in all this wind, and shut up indoors you find nothing to read. What else are you going to do? Can one sit there like an idiot waiting for time to go by? Day by day I wait, dragging on, wishing this winter would end soon. With the warm weather my cough is bound to improve; then I can go back south if I like, return to school if I like. This winter is too long!

I'm heating milk for the third time as the sunlight hits the paper window-panes. Yesterday I heated milk four times, not always because I wanted to drink it but to ease my vexation on a windy day. Of course this kind of thing can while away an hour or so, but sometimes it actually adds to my annoyance. I stopped doing it all last week. But yesterday, out of desperation I had to rely on it again, patiently, like an old man, to pass away some time.

The newspaper comes. I begin and systematically read first the big-character headings in domestic news, then the important foreign news, and finally the local miscellaneous news. I finish reading about education, political information, economic conditions, and the price of bonds. . . . After all this I go back and review the all too familiar advertisements of positions for men and women, calls for registration of men and women students, lawsuits over family division of property, and even items like ads for cosmetic remedies, the latest shows at the theatre and movies. After I know all this backward and forward I finally put aside the newspaper. Occasionally, I do find a new ad or two, nothing more than an announcement of an anniversary sale in some fabric shop or some obituaries.

Emptiness after the paper, I sit sullenly in front of the stove. What annoys me is nothing new. Everyday, I listen to the other tenants shout for the servant in the corridor outside my window and I get a headache. The voices are loud, coarse, and monotonous: "Waiter, bring boiling water!" or "washing water, waiter!" As everyone knows, this kind of voice can grate on your nerves. Then all day there are people speaking into the telephone downstairs. But if there's no sound at all the silence is fearfully gloomy. Especially the four whitewashed walls. Wherever you sit, they seem to stop your eyes. If you escape into bed the white ceiling weighs down on you. I can't find anything which doesn't disgust me: there is the pockmarked servant with the food that smells just like the dishcloth, the window frame which is impossible to keep clean, and the mirror over the wash-basin. . . .

That mirror can make your face look a foot long, and if you turn just a little slantwise it will flatten enough to scare you. I'm annoyed again and again by all these things. Maybe I'm the only one feeling this way, but in that case I would rather find something new to be displeased or dissatisfied with, although anything new, good or bad, seems miles away from me here.

Wei arrives after my midday meal. His characteristically quick steps reach me from the other end of the corridor and comfort me, as if releasing me from a suffocating room. But I don't know how to express it. When Wei comes in I receive him in silence. He thinks I'm annoyed again, so holding my hands tightly in his he says over and over again, "Sister, sister!" And I, I smile, of course. I know what I'm smiling about. I know what's hidden behind those eyes, those lively eyes. How long is it, now, Wei, that you've been in love with me? But am I captivated by him? Naturally, I cannot take any responsibility for this. This is how a woman should behave. Actually I'm faithful enough. I don't think there can be another woman who would refrain from playing with him the way I do. Furthermore, I truly feel sorry for him. I can hardly keep from pointing out to him: "Wei, is it possible for you to change your ways? You only displease me this way!" If Wei were a little cleverer, I could get to like him more. But he only knows how to express his sincerity in this honest way!

He is satisfied when he sees me smile and skips over to the bed and takes off his coat and his big fur cap. If he turned to look at me now, he'd surely feel a little unhappy from what he could see in my eyes. Why is it he is unable to understand me better? I always wish for someone who can understand me thoroughly. Without understanding, what use have I for love and sympathy? My father and my sisters and my friends all love me with such a blind love. I really don't see what is it that they love in me: my arrogance, my bad temper, or my consumption? Sometimes I feel both angry and sad at this, yet they all give way before me, love me all the more, murmuring words of comfort that are so wrong I want to strike them. At such times I truly wish for someone who can understand me. Even a scolding from such a person would bring me happiness and pride.

When people don't come to visit me, pay attention to me,

I long for them or feel angry at them. When they do come, I can unintentionally embarrass them. I can't help this. Recently, just to see if I could discipline myself, I've tried to hold my tongue, to suppress remarks which leap to my lips and lacerate the feelings of my friends, though I say these things in jest. Because of this, one can imagine in what mood I sit with Wei. But if he should get up and talk about leaving, out of my loneliness and depression I would hate him. Wei has known this for a long time, so he sits here right on through the afternoon and evening. It's ten o'clock before he leaves. I'm not deceiving anyone including myself. I know that Wei's remaining here doesn't profit him any. It only makes me take him for granted and even pity him more for his deficiency in the art of love.

Dec. 28 — Today I invite Yufang and Yunlin to come to the movies with me. Yufang brings Jianru along. I feel almost like crying with rage. Instead I let out a laugh. Jianru! She is so capable of destroying my self-respect. Because her face and bearing are so much like that of my childhood best friend, I found myself pursuing her. And she, she deliberately encouraged me to be close to her. But I met with unbearable treatment from her. Whenever I think about this, I hate my past and my irretrievably shameful behaviour. I wrote her eight long letters in a single week and never had a reply. What on earth was Yufang thinking, deliberately inviting her to come when she knows perfectly well I'm unwilling to dig up my past, as if purposely to provoke my hatred? I am so peeved! As to my laughter, neither Yufang nor Yunlin would notice that there's anything strange in it, but Jianru would. She could assume an air of innocence and chat with me as though there were nothing between us. I am about to say something sharp to her but I curb my words, remembering my own resolution. Besides, if I were so much in earnest, this would only give her satisfaction. I bear with this and go out with them.

It is early when we get to the Zheng Guang Cinema and we meet a number of girls who come from my native place. I pay them no courtesy at all, for I detest these automatically smiling faces and the sight of all these people going into the theatre. While Yufang is busily chatting, I slip away, abandoning my guests, and quietly return home. Nobody will forgive me but myself. Everybody is criticizing me but none of them knows what people arouse in me and what I have to endure. People say I'm eccentric, but none of them sees how I accommodate them and try to please them. But people are entirely too unwilling to encourage me to say what goes against the grain. They often give me opportunities to reflect upon my behaviour, leaving me to drift farther and farther away from people.

The hostel is utterly quiet this midnight. I've stretched out in bed for many hours straightening my mind of a lot of things. What have I really to be sad about?

Dec. 29 — Yufang telephoned me early this morning. She's honest and wouldn't tell any lies. She says Jianru is sick, and probably this is so. Yufang also says I'm the cause of it and wants me to go so that Jianru can explain. But both Yufang and Jianru are wrong. Sophia doesn't like to listen to explanations. I don't believe there is anything in the universe which needs any explanation. If friends get along together, that's well and good. If not, and one of them causes the other suffering, that too is natural and aboveboard. I think I'm big-hearted enough never to revenge myself on others. Still, now that Jianru is sick on my account, I feel oddly happy. The news that anyone is sick because of me will never be unwelcome to me. Moreover, Jianru's illness can even lessen a little of my own feeling of self-condemnation.

I am at a loss to know how to analyze my feelings. Sometimes I can feel a vague and indefinable sorrow for a patch of white cloud being dissolved by the wind. But when a man over twenty — (Wei is four years older than I) — sheds tears, drop after drop, onto my hand, I laugh with satisfaction like a savage. Wei comes to see me with a gift of stationery he has just bought from East City. And because he smiles and looks happy, I perversely provoke him, not to be satisfied till he cries. "Spare your tears," I then tell him. "Don't think I'm like other women who are so fragile they can't bear to see a teardrop. . . . Go home if you have to keep on crying. I detest tears. . . ." He naturally doesn't leave, neither does he defend himself or get angry. He merely sits there, crouched in a corner of the chair, shedding those silent, simple, endless tears which come from nowhere. And I, naturally I am satisfied now, and actually begin to feel remorseful. So I stroke his hair and use a sister- ly voice to tell him to wash his face. He is smiling before his eyes are dry. I've made a good man miserable purely to satisfy my heartless nature. Yet after he's gone I truly wish I could call him back. I want to tell him one thing: "I know my own weakness. Please stop loving the kind of woman who doesn't deserve to receive such pure love!"

Jan. 1 — I don't know how the New Year merrymakers are celebrating this day. I only add an egg to my milk. The egg was brought to me by Wei yesterday. I received twenty eggs from him, and after cooking seven of them with tea leaves and sauce I still have thirteen, which will probably last me two weeks. If Wei comes in at noontime I can look for at least two cans of delicacies. I hope so much he will come. Because of this I went to the market and bought four boxes of candy, two packages of pastries, and a basket of oranges and apples. All this is for him to eat when he comes. I'm certain that today he alone will come.

But the noon meal is past and he isn't here. I've written five letters, all with the fine paper and pen he bought me the other day. I wish I could receive some beautiful cards, but I didn't. Even some of my sisters, who like to do this sort of

thing, have forgotten to give me my due. It is nothing not to
have the cards, but it vexes me to think that they've forgotten
me. But I've never sent anyone a New Year's greeting, so I
suppose this is only what I deserve.

Supper too I eat alone. I'm filled with ennui.

In the evening Yufang and Yunlin come in, bringing with
them a tall young man. They're lucky, those two. Yufang has
Yunlin to love her. She is satisfied and so is he. Happiness is
not in having someone to love, but in two people avoiding
stronger ambitions, sharing thoughts with each other and passing the days contentedly. Of course there are some who think
this life too commonplace to be worthwhile. That might be true
of somebody else but not of my Yufang. She is a good person.
She has her Yunlin, so she wants to see "all lovers united".
Last year she tried to make a love match for Mary, and hopes
that I will grow to love Wei. That's why she asks about
him every time she comes. She and Yunlin and the tall one are
eating up all the good things I bought for Wei.

That tall one is handsome! This is the first time I've ever
been struck by any man's good looks. In the past I've never
paid any attention to such things, but always thought it a man's
job to talk, to show good judgement, and to be cautious. But not
so when I look at this tall friend of theirs. I'm beginning to see
that man can be cast into a nobler mould. Next to him Yunlin
looks so insignificant and clumsy that I pity him. If he were
conscious of this misfortune, of how he appears next to this big
man, he would be so grief-stricken over his own vulgar bearing
and manners. I wonder even more how Yufang would feel if
she were aware of the contrast between the two men, the one
so tall and the other so puny!

How shall I describe him, this stranger. Obvious to anyone is his stature, his fair face, thin lips, and soft hair. All this
is pleasing enough to the eye. But there is something else, a
certain elusive, indefinable grace in his carriage which sways
your heart. When I ask his name, he has a way of handing over

his card with an unexpectedly smooth and unhurried gesture. I raise my eyes and ah, I see those bright red, finely drawn lips. How could I tell anyone that I'm looking at those tempting lips like a child longing for candy? Even though what I want won't injure anyone else, I know that in this society I will not be permitted to take what I want to satisfy my stirrings, my desires. So I bend my head and patiently, silently read the words on the card:

"Ling Jishi, Singapore. . . ."

He is talking freely and without restraint, as though he were among old friends. Can it be that he is deliberately mocking my shyness? It is because I must force myself to resist temptation that I dare not raise my eyes to look at that disturbingly exciting figure. Even my poor, shabby slippers, of which I was never ashamed before, keep me from going into the lamplight in front of the desk. Furthermore, I'm angry with myself. Why am I so restrained and artless in my speech? I've always despised the way people make acquaintances, but I'm discovering now how dull, foolish, and stupid I must appear to other people. Aiya! He must think me a silly country girl newly come to the city!

Yunlin and Yufang sense that I'm acting unnaturally, and they think I'm displeased about their friend. They keep interrupting him, and soon they take him away. Am I supposed to be grateful for a kindness like this? I watch the three figures, one tall and two short, disappear in the courtyard below, and while I watch I know I hate to return to this room with the imprint of that man's foot on the floor, the sound of his voice, and the crumbs of the cake he was eating only a few moments ago.

Jan. 3 — I've coughed without stopping for two nights now. I would never have any confidence in medicine. How can there be any relationship between medicine and my illness? I'm clearly tired of that bitter liquid but I still take it as prescribed. If I cut it out altogether what would I have to rest my hopes upon? Threat of suffering before death is evidently God's way of imposing patience on people, keeping people from embracing death. As for me, it's because my life is so short and limited that I crave more living. I'm not afraid of death but I feel I haven't enjoyed all there is to life. I want to make myself happy. Night and day I dream of a way to experience no regret at the time of my death. I imagine myself lying on a bed in a beautiful room with my sisters kneeling on the bear rug next to my bed praying for me and my father turning towards the window softly sighing. And I would be reading many long letters from people who love me, from friends who would shed honest tears in remembrance of me. I desperately need this kind of love, and I crave all these things in impossible dreams. But what have people given me? For two more days now I've been imprisoned in this hostel and not a single friend has been to visit me. Nor have I received a single letter. I cough in bed. I cough when I sit next to the stove or at the table. I still think of these hateful people. . . . Yes, I have one letter, but it only adds to my annoyance, and nothing more than mere annoyance. This is from a coarse and vulgar man from Anhui who used to irritate me. The pages are filled to overflowing with declarations of love, "this love" and "that love". This only disgusts me. I tear them into tiny pieces without finishing it.

I . . . can I tell what I really want? . . .

Jan. 4 — Things go wrong more and more. Why should I think of moving, and why in my confusion should I have lied to Yunlin? Lied so effortlessly, as though lying were part of my nature. How sad Yunlin would be if he knew Sophia can lie to him too. She's always been such a loving little sister to both of them. Of course I didn't do it purposely and I'm sorry for it now. Still, can I make up my mind? Shall I move or not?

I can't help telling myself — "You're thinking of the shadow of that tall man!" Yes, and for days and nights I've been falling into that temptation. Why hasn't he come alone to see me these last few days? He ought to know that he has no

right to make me think of him so much. He should come up
here and tell me how he has thought of me too. If he comes, I
wouldn't refuse to listen to his words of affection for me.
Moreover, I'd tell him about the desire in my heart. But he
hasn't come and I guess all my fantasies can only dissolve into
thin air. Do you mean to say that I should go see him? No
good would come from a woman with such lack of restraint, let
alone trying to win other people's respect. I can't think of a
good way out, so I leave here after the noon meal in all this
wind to search out Yunlin over in East City.

Yunlin studies at the Jing Du University and lives in Youth
Street, which runs between the first and second colleges. I'm
lucky to find him in, even Yufang isn't there. He is surprised
that I've come on so rough a day but I tell him I've dropped in
on my way back from the German Hospital. He believes this
to be the truth. When he asks me how I feel I easily turn the
conversation back to the other night and before long I learn that
my tall man is living in the fourth dormitory next to the second
college. Soon I'm sighing and saying in many different words
how lonely and dull my life is over in the West City. I lie again
and tell Yunlin that my one wish is to be near Yufang, knowing
that she will soon move into his place. I ask Yunlin to look
for a room nearby, and he is of course pleased and agrees with
alacrity to help me.

While we're hunting a room we run into Ling Jishi and
he goes around with us. I feel happy, so happy that my timidity
flees and I fix my eyes directly upon him several times, but he
doesn't notice it. He asks after my health and when I tell him
I'm fully recovered he smiles unbelievingly.

I've selected a small, mouldy room with a low ceiling in
a hostel next to Yunlin's. Both my companions disapprove
of it, saying it is too damp, but I insist that I want to move
tomorrow. Why so quickly? I'm bored with the old place, and
besides I'm impatient now to be near Yufang. Yunlin can't do

anything but yield and promises to come to me tomorrow morning with Yufang to help me.

How can I tell anyone? The only reason I've selected this room is that it's just about midway between the fourth dormitory and Yunlin's place.

He has not said goodbye to me, so I go back with them to Yunlin's. I'm laughing and talking freely now and I've scrutinized every bit of him. I feel there isn't any of him that does not need the imprint of my lips. Does he know I'm looking at him and thinking about him? Later I deliberately say I'm thinking of asking him to teach me English. Yunlin laughs, but he seems to be embarrassed and mumbles his reply. I say to myself that he is not a bad sort if, tall and big as he is, he can still blush. This makes my fires blaze all the more warmly. Yet I don't want people to see through me, to figure me out too easily. So I force myself to return early.

As I think it over, I can't imagine my wilfulness driving me into any worse position. Let me stay in this room with its stove. Is it possible to say that I've fallen in love with that man from Nangyang* when I don't know him at all? What nonsense is all this, about his brow, his lips, the corners of his eyes and his fingertips . . . ! I must be bewitched. This isn't anything anyone should want, should think about. I'm not going to move; I'm going to stay here and concentrate on resting. I'm determined now. I'm sorry, sorry for all I've done wrong today. No decent woman would ever have done it.

Jan. 6 — Everybody is surprised to find that I've moved. Jin and Ying from the South City, Jiang and Zhou from the West City have all come to this low and damp room. I laugh and roll over in my bed, and they think I've grown more childish. This makes me laugh all the more and makes me want to tell them what is really in my heart. Wei comes in the after-

---

* South Seas, applied to Southeast Asia and the islands of Oceania.

noon. He is most displeased of all because I didn't discuss the matter with him, and I'm now farther away from him. When Yunlin comes in he won't even talk to him, and his face is dark with anger as Yunlin looks at him amazed and puzzled. I think it is all so funny. "He's got the wrong end of it," I say to myself, "what a pity!" Yufang stops talking about Jianru. Since I have seemed so anxious to live next to her, she's decided to move in with Yunlin in about three days, for she doesn't want me to be lonely here. Both she and Yunlin are even kinder to me than before.

Jan. 10 — I see Ling Jishi almost every day now, but I never say much to him and am determined not to be the first to mention English lessons. It amuses me to find him going to Yunlin's one or twice each day now for I'm sure they weren't so intimate before. Although he's asked me how things are after moving, I've replied only with a smile, as if I didn't understand what he's driving at. I have not once asked him to visit me because I'm still unwilling to take for myself the thing I desire. I must seek every conceivable means of having it offered to me voluntarily. I'm using all my ingenuity on this now, as though I'm engaged in a fierce struggle. Yes, I'm perfectly aware I'm a woman with all the woman's ways. A woman likes nothing better than concentrating on the man she is to conquer. I want to possess him so that he offers up his heart unconditionally and kneels before me pleading for a kiss. I'm insane, mad. I'm scheming and turning over and over in my mind every step I'm to take. I'm utterly insane.

My excitement is going completely over the heads of Yunlin and Yufang who think I'm getting better. I don't want them to know anything, and I look pleased every time they tell me how much improved I seem to be.

Jan. 12 — Yufang moves in but immediately Yunlin moves out. Is there such a pair as this in all the world — afraid to live together for fear of having children! I think they themselves cannot be certain that embracing each other in bed will have other consequences, so they're avoiding the chance by not letting their bodies even come into contact with each other! As to kissing and embracing otherwise, this is guaranteed against danger. All it needs is privacy and there's no risk at all! So they do this from time to time, gently, because it is not forbidden. I can't help laughing at them. These puritans! How is it that they don't feel the urge to embrace each other's naked bodies? Why suppress this expression of love? How can two people plague themselves with things not worth worrying about even before they get under a single quilt together? I don't believe love can be rational and scientific! Instead of being annoyed at my mocking them, they're proud of their purity and accuse me of childishness. I can understand the feelings of their hearts but I can't explain all the strange things in this world.

We're telling ghost stories at Yunlin's — or Yufang's it now is — and not leaving until late. When I was still a child I always used to sit on my aunt's lap and listen to ghost stories from the *Liaozhai* told by my uncle. I loved to hear them, especially at night. My fear I kept secretly to myself for otherwise uncle would have gone away to his study and the children wouldn't have been allowed to come down from bed, and that would have meant no more ghost stories. Then in school I learned some of the common sense of science, and the confidence with which my teacher inspired me soon led me to disdain fear of ghosts. Now that I'm grown up I always deny that any ghosts exist. Yet the mere mention of the word never fails to give me goose pimples and make my pores open. People never know that I try to divert the conversation into other channels when ghosts are mentioned because I know such talk will lead me to sad thoughts of my dead aunt and uncle once I'm alone under my covers.

The black little lane is filled with shivery shadows. I won't be entirely surprised if some monstrous yellow face or a hairy hand should rise from some frozen corner. Yet with my tall bodyguard by my side I've really no need to fear. Therefore to Yufang's anxiety I reply, "Never mind, I'm not afraid." Yunlin leaves with us and turns away southward to his new room. His rubber-padded steps fade away into the night. My companion passes his arm around my waist.

"You must be afraid, Sophia!"

I try in vain to free myself. My head is under his arm. How ridiculous I must look here encircled in the arm of a man a whole head taller than I! Crouching, I slip from under, and he also releases me and stands there while I knock at my door. Although the lane is pitch dark, I can feel his eyes, and my heart beats more quickly while waiting for the door to open.

"You are afraid, Sophia!"

The wooden latch rasps back of the door and the servant is asking, "Who's there?" I turn —

"Good —" He grasps my hand in his, and I stop speaking. The servant is obviously surprised to see me followed in by such a giant of a man. My boldness is of no use, now that we're alone in this room. I can't bring a single polite phrase to my lips. Bidding him sit down, I turn to wash my face. Ghosts are entirely forgotten.

"Do you still want to learn English, Sophia?" he asks suddenly.

He is the one to bring up the matter of English! Of course he doesn't want to waste his time teaching. Does he think he can fool a woman of twenty with talk like this? I'm amused.

"Too dull," I reply. "I'm afraid I am unequal to it. I might disgrace myself."

He doesn't answer but fingers a picture of a baby standing on my desk. It is my sister's one-year-old daughter. I have finished washing my face now and I'm sitting across the desk

from him. He looks from me to the picture and back to me.
Yes, the baby girl is much like me.

"Doesn't it look like me?" I ask.

"Who is it?" His voice is really in earnest.

"Isn't it lovable?"

He persists in his question. I realize what's in his mind.
Once again it's my impulse to lie.

"Mine!" and I grasp the picture from him and kiss it.

He believes me, I see, and I'm pleased with the deception.
His charm and attractiveness seem reduced now. Otherwise how
can I remain so indifferent to his eyes and his lips, showing
surprise at my answer? But now this triumph has cooled my
fervour. After he's gone I'm sorry. Didn't I throw away every
possible opportunity? It only needed some kind of response to
the pressure of his hand to let him know he wouldn't be refused.
He would surely then have grown bolder. I'm sure that if I
don't find such a person repulsive, such boldness between the
sexes could produce ineffable happiness, a feeling as though the
flesh were melting away. Why should I have treated him with
such sharp aloofness? For what, anyway, did I move to this
broken-down little room?

Jan. 15 — I'm not at all lonely now, passing the days at my
friends' homes and the evenings talking with my new friend.
Yet I am more ill than ever and still more disheartened. What
can I desire, seeing that nothing helps me? Could it be that I'm
in love? I laugh at almost everything, yet the thought of death
makes me sad. I understand the expression on Dr. K's face.
I know, say it. Is it hopeless now? Who can guess, among all
who see me laugh, how much I cry in the middle of the night?

Ling Jishi has been coming to me for several evenings
running now, announcing to others that he is teaching me English.
He really begins to do so in earnest, but I take the book away
from him. "Don't tell people you're teaching me English," I
say. "Nobody will believe you. I'm sick."

"Will I be able to teach you when you're well, Sophia? If only you'll let me —" he replies quickly.

My new friend is so attractive, yet I hardly pay any attention to this.   Still, I'm sorry to see him go away unsatisfied every evening. So, as he's putting on his coat, I tell him:

"Please excuse me for my illness." He thinks I'm standing on ceremony with him.

"Never mind," he replies, "I'm not afraid of infection."

After he's gone I think there might be some other construction to be placed on his answer. I can't be sure people are as simple and innocent as I think.

Jan. 16 — I have a letter from Sister Yun in Shanghai which is horribly depressing. "There's no use either in life or in love for me any more," she writes. Neither the comfort I give her nor my tears help any. I can guess what her married life is like although she doesn't speak of it explicitly in her letter. Why does God play tricks on those who love? Sister Yun was always of a nervous and sentimental temperament. She could not bear the obvious cooling off and the false front of affection in her life. I want her to come to Beijing. But can she? I doubt.

I show it to Wei, and he is deeply concerned, for the man who is the cause of my sister's mood is his own brother. I tell him what my philosophy of life has grown to be, and as usual all he can do is weep. I watch unmoved while his eyes turn red and he lifts the back of his hand to wipe the tears away. I make things worse by making cruel comments on everything he does. It doesn't occur to me that he is one of the most honest people on earth. Then leaving him there without a word I slip out the door. Not until nearly midnight do I return from the deserted park where I've fled to avoid all friends. All I can think is that life is meaningless. Better to die quickly and get done with it.

Jan. 17 — I may have been mad. If I am really insane I won't mind it so much. I won't be conscious of life's problems and complexities then. Today I'm drinking a lot of wine which has been put away for six months because of my illness. Even though the blood in my sputum is redder than the wine itself, I have to drink it since I am no longer in control of myself. I feel as though my heart is under the control of something else. And this wine, it seems that it could poison me tonight. I'm tired of thinking about all those complicated things now. . . .

Jan. 18 — I'm still lying on this bed here, but soon I'll leave this place, maybe forever. Can I say that I'll ever enjoy things again — this pillow, this quilt? Yufang, Yunlin, Wei, Jin, and Xia are all sitting around me dejectedly waiting for daybreak to get me to the hospital. Their whispering has awakened me and I lie silently thinking about yesterday morning, not interested in talk. Only the lingering odour of blood and wine in my room brings me back to reality and makes my heart ache and tears stream from my eyes. They are so silent, so sorrowful and gloomy. They make me feel as though death were coming close. Suppose I should just sleep on without ever awaking, would they sit around my stiffening corpse in just this same way?

They see that I'm awake and come over to speak to me. Now I really fear the parting of death. I grasp their hands and look closely into each of their faces, as if this could fix them indelibly in my memory. Their teardrops fall on my hand, as if I were leaving them for a long journey to the kingdom of death. Wei especially cries till his face is swollen and ugly. Ai! I say to myself, "Dear friends, please give me a little happiness." And I'm smiling now. I ask them to help me pack a few things, so they drag out the big wicker chest under the bed and bring me some small packages tied up in flowered handkerchiefs. "I want them," I say. "I want to have them with me when I go to the hospital." I show them that these packages are full of letters, and I add, laughing, "including yours." This seems to lighten their mood a little. Wei quickly takes out a photograph album from the drawer, as if wanting me to take it. I smile, because in it are seven or eight pictures of him alone. I also let him kiss my hand and rub it against his face. Now this room no longer looks as if it really contains a corpse. Day is breaking and the sky is now milky white. They are busy looking for a rickshaw and getting my things together. I'm going to the hospital.

Mar. 4 — Twenty days have passed since the telegram announcing the death of Sister Yun arrived. I myself have been improving steadily and I've been brought back to this same room by the same friends who took me to the hospital. The room has been swept clean, and a small foreign-style stove has been put in to keep me warm. I don't know how to express my gratitude to them, especially Wei and Yufang. Jin and Zhou have remained two nights to look after me and, lying in bed the whole day long, I feel as comfortable here as if I were not in a hostel but at home. Yufang is going to stay with me a little longer, and when the days get warmer she's going to look for a place in the Western Hills where I can go for a long rest. I'm anxious to leave Beijing. But the weather is still very cold even though it is already March! Yufang insists on staying here. I cannot absolutely refuse her, so the small bed put in only a few days ago now remains for her use.

My days in the hospital have changed my outlook too. This is truly due to the care of my friends, which has warmed my heart. The world seems to be full of love. I was especially proud when Ling Jishi came to see me at the hospital. It seems to me that only a man with his grace should go and visit a sick girl-friend in the hospital. I was keenly aware that the nurses envied me. One day pretty Miss Yang asked about him.

"Who is that tall man?"

"A friend," said I, ignoring the impolite implications in her query.

"Someone from your home district?"

"No, from the South Seas."

"Schoolmate, then?"

"No."

Then she smiled knowingly. "Only a friend?"

I had no cause to blush. But I was too shy and embarrassed to disabuse her and the way I lay there distressed, with eyes tightly shut, made her walk off, still smiling. After that I continued to be annoyed at her. And to avoid trouble, I lied to those who asked me about Wei, saying he was my own brother. A good friend of Zhou's I either said was a relative or someone from my home district.

When Yufang is at class and I'm alone in my room, I look over the letters I've received in the past month. This makes me happy and contented, thinking of all the people who remember me. I need people's good wishes and remembrance, the more the better. As for father, needless to say he sends me another picture of himself, his hair whiter than before. My sisters are well, but too busy taking care of their children to write me often.

Before I finish reading my letters Ling Jishi comes. I'm about to stand up, but he stops me. He holds my hand, and I'm so happy I could cry. I say to him:

"Did you think that I would come back to this house?"

He gazes through the window at a shop on the other side, looking displeased. So I tell him the other two guests have left, the bed is for Yufang. When he hears this he tells me he wouldn't come here tonight for fear Yufang might be annoyed at him. I'm secretly satisfied. "So you're not afraid I might be annoyed?"

He sits on the bed and slowly tells me what's happened to him this month, how he crossed swords with Yunlin. He was in favour of my leaving the hospital early, but Yunlin insisted I shouldn't. Yufang was on Yunlin's side. Ling Jishi realized that he'd known me only recently and his opinion didn't carry weight, so he washed his hands of the whole matter, and when he met Yunlin in the hospital he simply left first.

I know what bothers him but I deliberately say: "Why do you talk about Yunlin like this? Without him I would still be in the hospital — it's so comfortable there." He silently turns his head without answering me.

He leaves just before he thinks Yufang will arrive, softly saying that he will come back tomorrow. Soon Yufang does return, but she doesn't ask and I tell her nothing. Out of concern for my illness, she doesn't want to tire me out by too much talking, and I'm glad enough to turn my thoughts to other idle topics.

Mar. 6 — Yufang has gone off to her classes, and I'm alone here thinking about the strange relations between man and woman. I'm not boasting, but I think I've had more experience along this line than most of my friends put together. Still, I don't understand these relationships, especially now. My heart jumps whenever that tall man is with me, and I feel shy and afraid while he sits there at his ease, telling me of his past life, sometimes with my hand in his, always calm and simple and natural. But soon my hand cannot remain placidly in his; it grows more and more feverish. When he gets up to leave, I feel unaccountably anxious, a sense of disquiet taking command of me. As I fix my gaze on him, I'm not sure whether I'm looking for his pity and sympathy or whether I hate him. But whatever my eyes do say, he does not make it out. Even if he does understand, all he says is: "Yufang is coming." He's afraid of Yufang. What should I say to that?

There was a time when I would much rather keep my chaotic and unreasonable thoughts to myself. But now I begin to feel the need of somebody to understand what is going on inside of me. I've sometimes tried to talk in a vague way with Yufang, but she just carefully tucks my quilt around me and busies herself with my medicine. I'm a little overtaken with sadness.

Mar. 8 — Yufang has moved back, but Wei wants to take over the nursing duty. I know if Wei comes he would be better than Yufang. If I want some tea at night, I wouldn't have to lis-

ten to that deep snoring and have my head ducked under the
covers. Of course I couldn't accept his offer, and when he insists I tell him: "Your presence would be inconvenient for me.
Besides, I'm feeling better now." He still wants to show me the
empty room next to mine which he can occupy. Just as I wonder
what to do with him Ling Jishi comes. I thought they didn't
know each other, but Ling Jishi is already shaking Wei's hand,
saying they had seen each other twice at the hospital. Wei is cool
to him so I smile and say to Ling Jishi:

"This is my younger brother. He's young and inexperienced
in company. Come and see him often."

Wei, acting like a child, dejectedly gets up and leaves. I
hide my unhappiness in front of these two and feel a little apologetic towards Ling. But he doesn't mind and asks:

"Isn't his family name Bai? How can he be your brother?"

I say laughing: "Then do you only allow Lings to call you
their brother?" And he laughs too.

When young men get together they always want to talk
about "love". Although I seem to understand some of it, I can't
express it. I know the little things that take place between man
and woman — perhaps I see them too clearly. This may even be
the reason why I feel confused about "love" itself and lack the
courage to nourish love. For the same reason, I sometimes doubt
if I am a girl simple and innocent enough to be loved. I therefore suspect the "love" I hear on people's tongues and the "love"
I receive. I have always been troubled by this ever since I began
to have a glimmer of understanding. When I was in school people slandered me and humiliated me so that even my friends deserted me. Later, out of fear of the oppression of this love, I
finally left school. As I was growing up, I've always felt this
kind of entanglement to be meaningless and rather disdained
the intimacy it inferred. Wei has always proclaimed his love for
me. Then why does he bring me sorrow instead of joy? Take tonight, for example.

He comes in and the sight of me seems to start him weep-

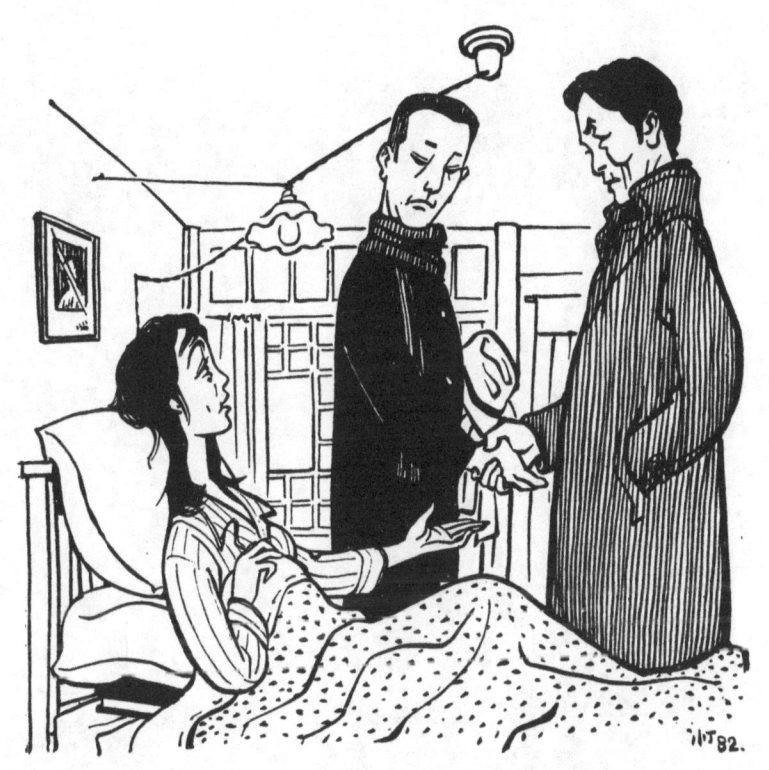

ing and sobbing without restraint. I ask him again and again, "What is it, Wei? Tell me what troubles you. I beg of you, say something!" But he just weeps on without reply. This had never happened quite this way before. I can't imagine what his trouble is, so how can I begin to figure it out? When he's finally exhausted with weeping, he bursts out: "I hate him! I hate him! I don't like that tall man who's now your friend!" Oh! So now he's venting his anger on me. I can't help laughing. Is this love, this meaningless jealousy and selfish desire to possess? I laugh, and it is not very comforting to my poor ambitious Wei. Indeed, my disregard rouses his great anger, and his glistening eyes glare as though he could bite into human flesh. "Come, now!" I say. But he hangs his head, shakes with sobbing, and walks out, his hands rubbing his eyes.

This may be a true expression of so-called violent love. Yet to express it spontaneously leads naturally to failure. I don't want falsehood or artificiality in love. But neither does childish behaviour like this move me. Maybe I was born with a hard heart. If so, I deserve the sorrows and vexations which my disagreeable nature brings down upon me.

But this has roused my own feelings and makes me think of the kind of tenderness that is open, straightforward, and yet sensitive. This attitude is so intoxicatingly enjoyable that it stirs feelings of melting intimacy. I scribble on a card and call a servant to take it at once to the fourth dormitory.

Mar. 9 — The sight of Ling casually sitting here in my room makes me pity Wei. I hope no one else like me ignores or despises the priceless sincerity which ends up by plunging myself into such bottomless despair. I hope some pure-hearted girl accepts his love and fills the great emptiness he must feel.

Mar. 13 — I haven't written anything for several days. Whether it's due to my bad mood or the lack of so-called emotion, I don't know. Since yesterday I've wanted to cry. People imagine I am dreaming of my home and lamenting my continued illness. If they find me gay, they think me happy and congratulate me on these signs of returning health. They're all the same. To whom can I open my foolish heart, which disdains tears yet cannot summon up laughter? Since I understand perfectly my own lingering desires in this world and the distress that results from every effort to attain them, I can no longer feel sorry for myself for the pain which comes on so inexplicably. How can I then express all my regrets and self-hatred with my pen?

Yes, I'm complaining again. But since all this is revolving in my own mind, there's no harm in it. I've never had the ability to display before others my worries and miseries, although many indiscriminately call me lonesome, proud, and queer. I don't want to complain. I want to cry. I want somebody to hold me close, to weep on. I want to say, "I'm wasting myself again." But who will understand me and caress away my tears? I can only swallow my tears in laughter.

It's hard to say why I feel this way. I haven't fully agreed with myself that I'm in love with that tall man. Yet what a special place he occupies in my scheme of things! His stature, his good looks and soft eyes and sensitive mouth can of course attract girls who like this sort of thing, and his proud manners will win the affection of some. Yet am I to be attracted by this Nanyang Apollo just because of his senseless beauty? I'm fully aware from what he's told me of his outlook and pathetic desires. What does he want? Money. A young wife who'll receive his business friends in the drawing room. A few fat sons dressed in fine linens. What is love to him? Something he can buy with his money in brothels where he can enjoy the pleasures of the flesh on a soft sofa with a slender, perfumed body on his lap and smoke cigarettes like a young gallant and, crossing his knees, talk leisurely with his friends. And if he happens not to enjoy it, he can return to his wife. He would be an enthusiastic speechmaker, a tennis player. He would go to Harvard and become a diplomat, an ambassador. Or perhaps he would go into his father's business, be a rubber merchant in Singapore, a capitalist! These are his dreams and the boundaries of his existence. Except for concern over the unsatisfactorily small dimensions of amounts of money he has been getting from his father, he has nothing to lose sleep over. Or perhaps the scarcity of beautiful women in Beijing, a defect which makes the parks and theatres less attractive. What can I say now? When I realize that in that noble figure of a man resides so cheap and mean a soul, and that I've accepted from him intimacies that measure up to less than half of what he squanders away at the brothels! When I think of the time he brushed my hair with his lips, I could cry for shame. Don't I offer myself to him for his amusement like the girls who sell their smiles? But the blame can only be on me, and this adds to my suffering. If I were harder, I'd check his boldness and then I'd think his timidity was because he has never experienced passion. Ai! How I should damn myself!

Mar. 14 — Is this love? Perhaps only love has the power to work such rapid changes in one's thoughts. I detested that handsome man when I lay down to sleep, but upon waking from my dreams it is the image of that cheap trader which first comes to my mind! Is he coming today? This morning? Afternoon? Then I pick up the large volume of Wilson's speeches Ling left here last night and fondle the bound edge of it with my fingers.

Mar. 14, evening — I can act out such beautiful dreams with Ling playing the principal role, the hero and the villain at the same time. With thoughts of him I can spend my morning in the ambience of love drinking the sweet wine of youth. And with thoughts of him too I realize what this business of life really is, and, disheartened, I begin to think of death again. I even hate my willing downfall. Actually what I'm getting is the lightest of punishments! Truly, sometimes for the sake of my beloved I ask myself, "Do I have the strength to kill somebody?" To better preserve my beautiful dreams and avoid diminishing my life I

had better leave immediately for the Western Hills. But Yufang
tells me she hasn't heard from her friend who's looking for a
place for me. How can I rush her? Nevertheless, I've decided
to let the tall fellow have a taste of arrogance, insult, and un-
reasonableness from me.

Mar. 17 — Wei went home displeased the other night. Today he comes back carefully and voluntarily to make peace. He
makes me laugh, but at the same time appears lovable to me. If
a woman only wants a loyal man to be her lifelong companion,
she would find no one more dependable than Wei. I asked him
laughing: "Does Wei still hate his sister?" He shyly replied: "I
don't dare. But please understand me, sister, I only ask that you
don't abandon me. I have no other designs. I'll do anything for
you to make you happy!" Isn't this sincere and moving? How
does he compare with that fair face and red lips? But later I said:
"Wei, you are a good man, the future will surely bring you many
satisfactions." He replied with a sad smile: "Not in this world!
But I wish for what you said. . . ." What is this, to add to my
suffering? If I only could kneel down in front of him and beg
him to give me only the love of a brother or a friend. For selfish
reasons only, I could wish for fewer complications and more happiness. Wei loves me and knows how to say nice things. But
he neglects something: first, he should scale down his hopes, secondly, he must hide his love. I feel unbearably apologetic about
being unable to do anything for that honest man.

Mar. 18 — I'm again asking Xia to look for a place for me
in the Western Hills.

Mar. 19 — Ling has not been here for several days. Of
course I can't deck myself out prettily, nor receive guests properly, nor manage household affairs. I suffer from consumption and
I have no money. Why should he come to me? I don't have to
have him come. Yet that he should have stopped coming pains

me and proves his frivolity. But is it possible that he is honest, like Wei, and that when I wrote, "I'm sick. Please don't come to trouble me," he took me seriously and hesitates to disobey? This makes me want to see him again, if only to make sure just how this monster thinks of me in his heart.

Mar. 20 — I've been to Yunlin's three times today without meeting the one I want to see. Yunlin seems to suspect my purpose for he asks me whether I've been seeing Ling lately. I'm back here disheartened. I'm impatient with myself and with everything, for can I deny that I've been thinking of him almost constantly?

At seven o'clock Yufang and Yunlin come to ask me to join them at the English debate in the Third College. Ling is captain of the B team. My heart jumps at this last news but I refuse to go, pleading my illness. I was hoping to avoid him. I'm a useless weakling, and I can't stand excitement. But as they rise to leave, I ask them to convey my greetings to Ling. Ai — How stupid and meaningless!

Mar. 21 — I've just had my milk and eggs and there's a familiar knock on the door and a familiar tall shadow against the paper windowpane. I want to jump to the door but something keeps me silent in my chair.

"Are you up, Sophia?" The voice is so soft and tender it makes me want to cry. Can he know that I'm already sitting in a chair? Can he know that I'm refusing him because I have no way to vent my anger? He gently opens the door and comes in but I don't dare raise my eyes for him to see the tears in them.

"Are you better, Sophia? Have you just got out of bed?"

I can't speak.

"You are really angry with me, then, Sophia. All I can do now is leave."

Of course it should suit me to have him go, but I suddenly raise my head and with my eyes stop his hand from opening the door. He understands, the rascal, and boldly grasps both my hands.

"You've been playing with me, Sophia. Every day I've passed here without daring to come in. If Yunlin hadn't told me you couldn't possibly be angry with me I wouldn't have dared come today. Tell me, Sophia, are you annoyed with me?"

Anyone can see that if he takes me in his arms and showers kisses on me now I'll cling to him weeping and say, "I love you! I love you!" But he is cool. So cool that I hate him. Yet I'm thinking, "Come, embrace me, I want to kiss your face!" Of course, his hands still hold mine, and his eyes are fixed upon me. I study his face looking vainly for signs that he will grant what I am waiting for. Why is it that he only knows that I'm useless and contemptuous, that he cannot understand the special place he occupies in my heart? I wish I could just kick him out. But I am held by other emotions, so I only shake my head and indicate I'm not irritated about his coming. I yield again to his shallow emotions and sit and listen to more of his self-satisfied talk about his vile enjoyments and the philosophy of "making money and spending money". I even let him give me many hints as to how to be a woman. These things now make me despise him, silently curse him and mock him, and inwardly hit my heart with my fist. Yet when he haughtily walks out of my room I can't help but want to cry. And because I'm suppressing my hot desires, I have not pleaded with him to stay a while. Ai! he's gone!

Mar. 21, evening — What was my life a year ago? Under the unwavering love of Sister Yun I pretended to be sick and lay in bed reluctant to get up. Because I wanted to bask in her unfailing concern for me, and because of those tears of desperation she shed over her inability to comfort me, I would bury my face in my arms and cry over trivialities. Sometimes I end up with a sweet sadness from a day of solitary contemplation, but even that kind of loneliness is a sentiment I'm reluctant to let go, as if within it I can taste a hint of sweetness.   At night I would stretch out on the grass in the French Park and listen to Sister Yun sing a song about *The Peony Pavilion*. This is something I would rather not think about, because had she not fallen in love with the palefaced man, as if tricked into it by some god, she would surely still be living and I wouldn't have drifted to Beijing alone, to struggle with my illness without anyone to care for me. I have some friends here, and they are quite concerned about me, but can I weigh in the balance what I can sense about our relationship against Sister Yun's love? When I think about her I ought to cry hard as I used to do like a spoilt child.   In the past year, because I've grown up a little, I often suppress my crying for fear people will be annoyed at me.   Recently, I can't understand why I feel so anxious.   I can't even find the time to weigh the good and the bad in what I've done, what I've been thinking, my health, my reputation, and my future.   The whole day long my confused mind revolves around something I don't want to think about, because this is what I want to escape from. And that makes me suffer from an unbearable irritability. But aside from saying "death is what I deserve", I have no other hope. Dare I ask for sympathy and comfort? Yet it seems that I'm begging for it now.

Yufang and Yunlin come here after supper. It is already nine and I still don't want them to go. I know Yufang stays so as not to hurt my feelings, but Yunlin insists on going on the pretext of preparing for tomorrow's lesson. So I carefully reveal to Yufang some of my recent distress. I only hope she can understand me and accomplish for me what I have failed to do: force me to change my way of living. But, putting the wrong interpretation on my words, she gives me this friendly advice: "Sophia, you are not honest enough. You are too careless with your eyes, though you don't do it intentionally. You should know that people like Ling, unlike those fellows who went around with us in Shanghai, don't have many opportunities to be with women, and are not used to getting their attention. Take care that he doesn't suffer from disappointments later. It's clear to me. How can you end up loving him?" Doesn't it seem that the blame is now on me? If instead of asking for help I were complaining, would I have avoided hearing these words which make me even angrier, sadder than before? Restraining my anger, I laughed and said: "Sister Fang, don't make me out to be that bad!" Yufang is willing to stay the night but I insist that she go.

There are talented girls who on the provocation of the slightest suffering can write poetry, in the new style or the old — "Oh, I am sensitive and so full of sorrow..." or "Oh how sad my heart" — but I am unpromising and untalented. I am oppressed by a poetic situation yet even in tears I fail to express the conflict of my emotions. For this inferiority of mine, I should have compensated by behaving satisfactorily, even taking a thousand steps backward to win glory in praise in the mouths of the shallow and the eyes of the backward. I should have held either pen or gun. Shall I actually bury myself in this pain, far more insufferable than death, all for the soft hair and red lips — of a man?

I'm dreaming about the medieval knights of Europe — not a bad comparison if you have seen Ling. If he can even preserve that special Eastern quality of gentleness. God has given him all the advantages, but why did he not add a little intelligence? Ling doesn't even understand real love, truly not, though he already has a wife (Yufang said so tonight), though once in Singapore he rode a bicycle in pursuit of a lady in a rickshaw, and was in love with her for a while, and though he used to visit houses of pleasure. Still, has he really been loved by a woman? Has he loved a woman? I can't be sure.

A strange idea flickers in my mind. I've decided to teach that university student a lesson. Things are not as simple as he thinks in this world!

Mar. 22 — I have written these daily records in a state of confusion. They were begun at the persistent request of Sister

Yun. Although she's been dead for a long time, it still goes on as a sort of tribute to her memory and all her loving guidance. No matter how little I desire to take up the pen, even if I'm already in bed, the sight of her picture on the wall is sufficient to pull me up to write a page or two if only to avoid the accusation of my memories. Of course I'm unwilling to show it to anybody but her. First, because it was written specially for her and, second, I fear the pain of being shown up by people of intelligence, as if I might really feel guilty of some crime because other people worship their moral conventions. So this black-covered book has always been hidden beneath my pillow. But today I acted against my better judgement though out of need. Wei has for so long misunderstood me and in doing so has caused himself much unhappiness and me much discomfort. I believe that in my behaviour I have always made my attitude perfectly clear. Why doesn't he understand? How can I be blunt and forbid him to love me? I've often thought that if it weren't Wei but another man I'd know how to handle him better. But he is almost unbearably good. I can only show him my diary to let him know just how hopeless his love is and how shallow and inconsistent a woman I am. If he had ever understood me truly, I would have regarded him as the only friend to whom I could have ever opened up my heart and I would have hugged him close. I would have wished for him the love of the most beautiful woman in the world.

Now he's read the diary through several times and he's shed tears over it, although he is remarkably composed. I hadn't expected it.

"Do you understand me now?"

He nods.

"Do you believe in me now?"

"In what way do you mean?"

So I understand his nod. Who could understand me? Even if he understood this diary, it would express only one part in ten thousand of my thoughts. This too pains me — the inadequacy of this diary. That I should show anyone this attempt at an explanation of myself in words is itself painful enough. And now Wei, fearing lest I do not get his point, adds at last, "You love him! You love him! I'm not worthy of you!"

I want to take this diary and rip it into shreds. Have I not wasted it? But to him, I can only say, "I want to sleep. Please come tomorrow."

Don't ever ask anything of this world. Can anything be worse than that? If Sister Yun had lived to read these pages, I'm sure she would have clasped me to her and shed tears. Now that she is gone. How should I weep over this diary of mine?

Mar. 23 — Ling says to me: "Sophia, you're a strange girl." I know he doesn't mean to praise me out of any real understanding of me. What surprises him are the things he finds unfamiliar. The torn gloves. The dresser drawer over there without perfume in it. The new, but strangely torn, cotton gown, and the little old toys that have been saved for so long. What more? Queer laughter. He sees nothing beyond these and I've told him nothing about myself. When he exclaims, "Hereafter, I've got to devote all my efforts to making money!" I only laugh. When he talks of how he and some friends chased after girl students in the park, he concludes, "interesting indeed, Sophia," I only laugh the more. Of course, I'm sorry I've been unable to make myself clearly understood and respected by him. Now I want nothing but to go off to the Western Hills.

Mar. 24 — When he is alone with me, the sight of his face and the sound of his voice make my feelings rise. Why shouldn't I rush over to kiss his lips, his shoulder, all of him? Sometimes words like these are on my lips! "My Ling, let me caress you!" Yet reason — no, I've never been reasonable — say, self-respect — has always checked me. Ai! No matter how cheap or small his ideas, he has unquestionably turned my heart inside out. Why then do I refuse to acknowledge my love for him? And I'm sure, should he hold me firmly in his arms, should he surrender his body to my kisses and then throw me into the ocean or the fire, I'd wait for death contentedly — for it would forever preserve my love. Ai! I *do* love him! Only death at his hands would satisfy me!

Mar. 24, midnight — I have made up my mind. To save myself from temptation of the flesh and a fall into decadence, I'm going to Xia's tomorrow in order to avoid Ling. This pain has had me in its grip long enough!

Mar. 26 — In order to avoid one involvement, I run into another which makes me rush back to my own place. On the second day of my visit to Xia, Mengru also comes. Although she comes to see someone else, I feel very displeased. At night, she begins to hold forth on some recently acquired theory on emotions, directing its hidden sarcasm towards me. I remain silent, but unwilling to grant her any satisfaction, I lie awake on Xia's bed and wait till daybreak before returning with anger in my heart.

Yufang tells me a room has been found far out in the Western Hills. She even found a companion for me, a very good friend of Yufang's who's also recuperating from illness. I should be glad at this news, but barely does a hint of gladness cross my face when a shadow of sadness creeps across it. Although I left home quite young, drifting around, I've been close to relatives and friends. The Western Hills are only a score or so li away, yet for someone like me who's already twenty, this is the first time that I'm going to a strange place alone. If I should quietly die in these hills, who's going to be the first to discover my corpse? Can I be sure I won't die there? Maybe others would laugh at me for worrying over these little things, but they've actually made me weep. I ask Yufang if she could bear the thought but she only laughs, saying it's a childish question. What is there to think about in moving such a short distance? I wipe away my tears sheepishly only when Yufang promises to come up to the Hills to see me once a week.

In the afternoon I go to see Wei. He too says he will come up to see me every week, on a day Yufang can't go.

I'm back here this evening alone to arrange my things. I weep over leaving all my friends in Beijing. But the thought that none of them is shedding tears drives away mine. I'm going to leave this old city alone, quite alone. And in my loneliness I think again of Ling. No, actually, thoughts of him can't be said to be here, or coming again. They're in my mind all the time. I can only say: "Let me talk of my Ling again." The gap between us these days is of my own making, but to me it is an incalculable loss. Yet while I mean to loosen his hold on me, I've only helped tighten it. Since I can't pluck him from my heart by the roots, why should I not see him? This annoys me greatly. I can't leave him like this. I can't go to the Western Hills all alone. ...

Mar. 27 — Yufang went to the Western Hills early this morning to arrange my rooms for my arrival. I'm going out tomorrow. I can't be grateful enough to her. I want to stay over another day here — but I can't very well say so. And just now comes Ling! I grasp both his hands.

"I've not seen you for days, Sophia!"

I want to cry, to hold him and cry. Instead I laugh and can't help shedding tears at the same time. He is surprised that I am moving to the hills. Then he sighs. He turns to comfort me, and I smile. He squeezes my hands so tightly they hurt. As if resenting something, he says:

"You're smiling! You're smiling!"

The pain in my fingers fills me with a glowing sense of comfort and well-being, as if my heart were at the same time being struck by something. I want to fall into his arms. There is a knock at the door and Wei comes in. He is perfectly aware I don't want him here, so he stays. "Don't you have a class now?" I nod meaningfully to Ling, and we walk out together. He asks when I'm due to leave. I tell him and ask him if he'll return. He promises to do so quickly. And I look upon him now joyfully. All his smallness is forgotten. To me now he is a fairy-tale lover of romance. Yes, Sophia now has a lover!

Mar. 27, evening — It's five hours since I drove Wei out. How can I describe this lapse of time? Like an ant on a burning pot, I'm sitting, standing, and walking to the door to peek through the crack. He's not coming! I'm sure he's not coming. I want to cry because I'm going to leave here in lonely sorrow after all.   Isn't there a single person in all Beijing who will feel with me when I go? Yes, I'm leaving tomorrow. Nobody in Beijing will have to be bored any more by the ill Sophia. If only for her friends' comfort, it's good for Sophia to go out to the hills to die. Yet that they should all be content to see her leave alone without getting any affection! It probably won't harm anyone or move anyone even if she doesn't die. Stop it! Stop it! Stop thinking! What is there to think about? If Sophia hadn't been so greedy for affection, wouldn't she be satisfied with the apparent sympathy of her friends? I'll stop talking about friends. I'm sure Sophia will never be content with human friendship. But what will satisfy me? Ling promised to come and it's already nine o'clock.   And would I be happy if he came? Would he give me what I desire?

He hasn't come and I hate myself unto death. A long, long time ago I knew at least how to conduct myself towards certain types of men.   Now I'm just a silly fool.   When I asked if he was coming, how could I reveal my begging eyes? One should not be too honest to a handsome man, he will only despise you. Yet I love him. Why should I employ indirect tricks? Shouldn't I express love openly and directly? And if it injures no one, why shouldn't one kiss a hundred times over?

He promised, but he isn't keeping his promise. It is obvious he is just playing with me. It wouldn't have been a loss to you, my friend, to preserve some show of kindness before Sophia leaves!

I'm mad, without sense or coherence tonight. How useless words are at a time like this! Tiny mice seem to be gnawing at my heart. Or is a fire smouldering there? I want to break something or run out into the night air. I cannot control the stirring of my emotions. My passion is like a bed of needles, piercing me whether I lie this way or that, or like a cauldron of boiling oil, and I'm listening to the gasp of the flames inside me and feeling the great heat on my body. Why don't I run out? I'm waiting here for the birth of some vague and meaningless hope. It is red lips I'm mad about! If it were still possible to hope — I can't keep myself from laughing as I put the question to myself — "Love *him*?" Ha! Ha! Ha! Sophia wouldn't be such damned fool as to love that South Seas Islander! Is it possible that I can't do something which leaves everyone else unhurt — simply because I won't acknowledge my love for him? If he really doesn't come tonight, how can I willingly and indifferently go up to the hills?

Twenty minutes to ten!

Mr. 28 — Three o'clock in the morning. In this world Sophia yearns too deeply and too earnestly after sympathy and understanding. That's why she's forever drowning in the distress of disappointment. Only she knows how many tears she sheds. Let's call this record a collection of Sophia's tears, drop by drop upon her heart, rather than a diary of her life. That would be truer. Yet now this diary is approaching its end. Sophia no longer needs it. Tears comfort her or release her anger because she is aware of the senselessness of life. Tears only express that absence of meaning. On its last page Sophia should celebrate happily. From the infinite depths of disappointment she suddenly emerges to feel a satisfaction that should mean final happiness. But from that satisfaction I only find victory, and from that victory, loneliness, and a deeper understanding of my pitiful, ludicrous self. Before this, the little patch of "beauty" which has haunted me vanishes. This beauty was the elegance of that tall fellow.

How to explain the psychology of a woman driven to the brink of insanity by the figure of a man? Obviously I cannot love him, for locked within his noble proportions is a lowly, ugly soul. Nonetheless I admire him and think of him. I even feel all life would lose significance without him. How often have I thought that if only my lips could meet his one day I'd be glad to see my body dissolve in the laughter of my heart. More — for a gentle caress by this knightly person, for the lightest touch of his fingers upon any part of my body, I have been prepared for any sacrifice.

I should go mad. All the traces in my fantasy have at last become real, effortlessly and like a dream. But from it, did I experience what I imagined would be a soul-intoxicating happiness?

No.

When Ling came at ten o'clock last night and began telling me haltingly how he'd been thinking of me, my heart leaped, but I soon became afraid when I caught his burning eyes, feverish with desire. And when I heard those hideous vows coming out of his vile mind, my self-respect was rekindled. The stream of trite and creepy love-talk would have swayed other women and won him someone's heart, but when it was turned upon me, the power of those words drove me ineffable distances from him. Poor fool! You were endowed with a beautiful body but God has his joke by cheapening your spirit! Do you think my hope is a family, my joy, money, my pride, social position? What a pitiful man you are before me!

I almost want to cry over the tragedy of him. But with his eyes still riveted on me, full of passion, how fearsome he becomes! More, if all he wants is satisfaction of the flesh, he could have destroyed my heart with his lust. But half-weeping, he says:

"Sophia, believe me. I will not fail you!"

Poor simple fool. He doesn't know yet that all he arouses with his blubber is my contemptuous pity. I even laugh and say how funny it is when he says he understands love and loves me. Don't those hot eyes which hold his desires tell me he knows only his shallow, despicable desires, and nothing more?

"Be smarter, my friend, and go away. Off to a house of pleasure. That's the place for the joys you're looking for!" That is what I ought to be saying. It's what I'm thinking since I now clearly see his measurements. I ought to tell this beast of creatures to get out. I mock him. Yet when he boldly wraps me in his arms, all my pride and my self-respect flee and I am completely possessed by all he has: his elegant appearance. In my heart I'm saying, "Tighter! Hold me close and don't let me go, for I'm leaving tomorrow!" If I had any self-control left, I would have thought of something besides his good looks and thrown him from the room like a stone. Oh dear! What kind of words or emotions should I repent with? He, Ling Jishi, a despicable creature, has kissed me, and I received it in silence. What did I feel in my heart with his soft warm lips on my face? I can't swoon into the arms of a lover like other women are supposed to do. I looked at him with wide eyes. "I've won! I've won!" I thought. The power he had to haunt me was revealed to me in his kiss. I now know the taste of it. And with it I despised myself. I thrust him from me and wept.

He ignored my tears, perhaps thinking how tender and smooth his lips were on mine, satisfied in the certainty that my heart must have dissolved in the intoxication of his love. He sat close to me and poured forth a new stream of nauseating things all in language I abhorred.

"Stop this babbling," I said. "Maybe tomorrow I will die."

I don't know what he thought when I said this. He tried to kiss me again. My face avoided his and his kiss fell on my hand. I made up my mind. I was in full possession of my faculties and I wanted him to go, to get out. He lingered with a wondering, complaining expression on his face. "Why are you so stubborn and stupid?" I said to myself. It was half past twelve when, finally, he left.

After he was gone, I went over what had happened. I would like to tear my heart out from me and beat it with all my strength. Why could I stand the kisses of a man I despise? I do not love him, I mock him, yet I let him embrace me. Has this shell of a knight the power to pull me down so low? I've defiled myself. Man is his own fiercest enemy. My heaven, how shall I begin to revenge and retrieve all I've lost? Life has been my own toy. I've wasted enough of it away, so it is of no material importance that this new experience has plunged me into a new abyss. I don't want to stay in Beijing and I don't want to go to the Western Hills. I'm going to take the train southward where no one knows me and waste away what's left of my life. Out of the pain, my heart revives. And now I look on myself with pity and I laugh.

"Live and die your own way, unnoticed. Oh, how I pity you, Sophia!"

Translated by A. L. Chin, first appeared in *Straw Sandals*, Harold Isaacs ed., the MIT Press, pp. 129-69.

About the Author

DING LING, a well-known contemporary woman writer, was born in 1904 in Hunan Province. Her father died while she was still a child. Her mother, influenced by the revolutionary ideas stirring the country at the end of the Qing Dynasty, broke with the feudal clan and took her daughter away with her to live an independent life in town. Having hated the reactionary feudal ruling class from childhood, Ding Ling in her teens gave up her formal education and went to Shanghai to find the road to revolution.

In Shanghai she studied in a girls' school set up by the Communist Party, where most of the teachers were Party members or progressives.

In 1927, she started writing novels. Her first works, *Meng Ke* and *The Diary of Miss Sophia*, excited considerable attention when they were published in the *Xiao Shuo Yue Bao* (Fiction Monthly), the only literary journal of that time. She followed them with a number of stories, including *Flood* and *Mother, When I Was in the Xia Village* and several other stories.

In 1930, Ding Ling joined the League of Left-Wing Writers, and the following years she became editor of its magazine *North Star*. In 1932, she joined the Communist Party. In 1933 she was thrown into jail in Shanghai by the reactionary Kuomintang authorities, to be released only in 1936, thanks to the efforts made by the Party. She then went to Yan'an. After the outbreak of the War of Resistance Against Japan in 1937, she headed the Northwest War Service Corps, and edited the literary supplement of the Party paper *Liberation Daily*.

In 1946-47, Ding Ling spent many months as an active member of land reform work teams in North China. *The Sun Shines over the Sanggan River* is the work not merely of a writer who went to the villages to observe land reform, but of one who took part in the struggle. The novel, which in 1951 won a Stalin Prize, has been translated into thirteen languages.

After the liberation of new China, Ding Ling was chief of the Art and Literature Section of the Ministry of Propaganda and at the same time served as vice-chairman and Party secretary of Union of Chinese Writers and chief editor of *People's Literature*.

In 1957 she was wrongly taken as a Rightist and was sent to do forced labour in a farm in the Northeast for as long as twelve years. At the time of "cultural revolution" she was again wrongly imprisoned for five years. After the fall of the gang of four she was rehabilitated at long last. In 1979 she was elected as member of the fourth session of All China Federation of Literature and Art, vice-chairman of the Union of Chinese Writers. Now she is going on with her novel writing.

"The Diary of Miss Sophia" is one of her best works. It tells about a petty-bourgeois young woman, her complex emotions when she is in love, her betrayal of conventional ideas and her longing for liberation of the individual character.

Mrs. Shi Qing

Ai Wu

Just as on any other day, the morning sun spread its fine light over the wooded valley, until the dewy leaves and grass glistened with a dazzling brightness. But fine as the day was, Mrs. Shi Qing felt thoroughly dejected. Her face, crumpled in misery, looked like an overcast sky which threatened to rain at any moment.

Everything was topsyturvy. In the house, stools had been overturned and lamps broken. Footprints crisscrossed before the door and the spinach had been trampled in her vegetable garden. The tomatoes crushed into pools of red juice got on her nerves particularly. They looked so like the blood her husband had shed in his struggle with the *bao zhang** the previous night.

After a bus had rumbled past, an unusual, ominous silence fell upon the highway on the hillside. In the sunlight the jagged rocks scattered over the hill looked as ugly as bald scabby heads. Viewed from a distance, the road was lost among the rocks. A strong atmosphere of primitive savageness hung over the place.

Mrs. Shi and her children lived in the only cottage in the valley; but she had never had such a fearful sense of loneliness

---

* Shortly after the War of Resistance Against Japanese Aggression Chiang Kai-shek started a civil war against the Chinese people. The peasants, then unwilling to serve in the army, were always taken away by force, generally at night, by the *bao zhang*, head of a hundred households under the Kuomintang regime.

when her husband was at home. The slope between the stream and the hill kept her busy day and night. With a blue kerchief round her head, she went there every day to dig, weed or pick vegetables. Even after the stars had come out, a light evening mist had swallowed up the woods and cottage, and the baby left by the door had begun to cry, she could still be found working in the fields, gathering melons, beans, egg-plants or peppers. Next morning she would sell them at the market five li away and buy some rice with the proceeds.

Now Shi Qing the master of the house had gone, perhaps never to return. She had cried and cried the previous night at his departure, beating her breast and tearing her hair. And this morning found her standing on the bank of the stream, gazing disconsolately into the distance. In her despair, she had stretched out her hand for a rope to hang herself. But then a vision of her five children flashed across her mind, and their prattle seemed to be ringing in her ears. She took a fresh grip on herself.

Mrs. Shi knew she must live on for her children's sake, if not for her own. The *bao zhang* had struck her in the arm the day before when she rushed to her husband's defence; but medicinal herbs could easily cure that. So long as she had the use of her hands, she was sure she could keep the slope in cultivation and bring up her children. The past nine years had shown that Shi Qing, as a school servant, could never earn enough to feed the whole family; and it had only been thanks to the vegetable plots into which she had put so much work that the family pot had been kept boiling.

So Mrs. Shi made up her mind to live on and open up more of the waste land. "Heaven bless my man and send him back safe and sound!" she prayed.

She spent her days hoping and toiling. As time passed her sun-tanned face grew thin and her eyes sad and dim. She seldom smiled, but when selling vegetables at the market often quarrelled with people over trifles.

When their family first came here nine years ago, it had been a barren place. Overgrown with brambles, twisted shrubs and weeds, it was rarely visited even by sheep or cattle. Few woodcutters or herdsmen cared to show up in this remote valley. All the year round, the only sign of life was the birds that flew above the woods. Hunters, it is true, came over once or twice; but they soon lost interest in the place because the brambles tore their trousers and made it hard to find the quarry.

However, to escape bombing during the War of Resistance Against Japanese Aggression, a state college from another province had been evacuated to the open ground on the other side of the valley; and Shi Qing, a school servant, had built a simple thatched cottage on this side for his mother and wife. The school grounds, including the valley where their cottage stood, had been requisitioned by the government and made over to the college. In the evenings, groups of students would stroll and sing beside the stream, until the whole valley echoed to their songs. In summer they went rowing, the white of their uniforms flashing among the green reeds. Nobody could have called the valley lonely then.

The Shis were not emigrants from some other province, who had moved here with the college. Their home, where Shi Qing had been a peasant working on rented land, was only a few days' journey from this valley. But, thinking that if he worked for a state organization the *bao zhang* would be unable to plague him any more, Shi Qing had put down his hoe and moved over to the college. Since then his horny hands, accustomed to tending young wheat and rice, had learned to serve the teachers and students.

Since farming was his second nature, he itched to plough the fertile dark slope the moment he set eyes on it. Besides, prices were rocketing, and he could not hope to support his family on his meagre wages and rice allowance. So he devoted his free time in the evenings and on Sundays to clearing away the shrubs, brambles and weeds on the slope.

His wife joined him with even greater enthusiasm. As soon as she had finished preparing the two meals of the day, you could see her sturdy figure in faded blue working away on the land, her patched sleeves rolled up over her elbows. Often she got her hands scratched and her clothes muddied, but she kept hard at it even when she was big with child. It was she, in fact, who did most of the work there; and her competence won her endless praise from the professors' wives who strolled that way.

The soil for its part did not disappoint them. It yielded them vegetables in spring and winter, wheat and rape in summer, and beans and gourds in autumn, all of which could be exchanged for rice. They raised chickens and pigs too. And a new baby arrived every other year, until the little cottage was teeming with life.

When Shi Qing's mother fell ill and died, they buried her at one end of the slope where her spirit could easily watch over the place to protect the family from evil. And at the spring and winter festivals each year, the whole family went solemnly to sweep her grave and offer sacrifice.

Since settling down in the valley, they had lived undisturbed. So far nobody had come to investigate them or to collect rents or taxes, and they were apparently in undisputed possession of the valley. The *bao zhang* did indeed come once to look at the place; but even he dared not stir up any trouble after he learned that Shi Qing was working for the college.

With a little money on hand, the Shis started improving and enlarging the cottage to make of it a solid, permanent home. They planted orange and loquat trees around the house, and peach and plum trees on the bank of the stream. In spring the trees were bright with blossom, in autumn the branches were loaded with golden fruits — there was always something to delight the eyes of travellers looking out of the bus as it passed on the other side of the valley.

In those days Mrs. Shi was well content. Sometimes when a bus rumbled by, shaking the valley, she would raise her head to look at the passengers packed inside and the luggage piled on top. "What keeps folk always on the move?" she wondered. "Why don't they stay peacefully at home like us?"

As soon as the War of Resistance Against Japanese Aggression ended in victory, the college moved back to its original location. A native of Sichuan and head of a big family, Shi Qing could not afford to go so far with it. Nor did he like the idea of leaving the land he had cultivated with his own hands for almost a decade. So he and his family stayed on alone in the valley.

The land requisitioned for the college was now given back to its original owner, Landlord Wu. And the school buildings were turned over to him as compensation for the use of his land. There was one big stone building, and into this the landlord moved. Bird cages were hung in the veranda outside the principal's office, while fowl ran in and out of the office door. The classrooms and dormitories, being flimsy, dilapidated structures, were left empty, soon to be filled with cobwebs.

Shi Qing lost both his job and the protection the college had given him. First of all the *bao zhang* came to make trouble. Then he brought some thugs to Shi's cottage one night, to force him to join the Kuomintang army. They threatened him and shook their fists in his face. After a vain struggle, Shi Qing was taken away.

The place was deserted. No more songs echoed in the woods, and nobody strolled by the stream at dusk. A sombre silence settled upon the valley, broken only occasionally by the buses that rolled by. Mrs. Shi kept a stiff upper lip, and fought against her loneliness. All the company she had was the steep cliffs, the gently flowing stream, and the trees that whispered in the wind. Even her mother-in-law's grass-covered grave mound became a source of comfort. Above all there were the children, grown bigger now, who filled the place with their shouts and laughter. Gradually she grew accustomed to her loneliness, though sometimes, looking at the passing bus, she would murmur wistfully: "When will he come back to us?"

One day, four months after Shi Qing had left, three men swaggered up to the vegetable garden. Two of them, who were wearing jackets, started measuring it with a tape. Putting down the child at her breast, Mrs. Shi called out to them:

"Don't tread on the seeds I've just sown!"

But the men with the measuring lines went on tramping up and down, paying no attention to her at all.

"Are you deaf?" she sang out furiously. "Why don't you do as you're asked? Do you think seeds will grow after you've trampled them like that?"

The measurers threw her a casual glance, then went on as if this had nothing to do with them.

"What are you shouting about?" retorted the third man, dressed in a long gown, who was standing on the slope looking on contemptuously as he puffed slowly at a cigarette.

"This is my land!" she snapped, breathless with anger. "Haven't I the right to protest?"

"Your land, eh?" said the smoker with a sinister laugh.

"It's time she woke up," put in one of the measurers.

"Your land? When did you buy it?" went on the smoker huffily.

For a moment, the question put her out. But, being an intelligent woman, she found the answer a minute later.

"Of course it's mine! The school gave it me."

"Gave it you?" sneered the smoker. "The school'll get a lawsuit out of it."

By this time the two other men were measuring the plot of land surrounding the cottage. As they approached the house, Mrs. Shi's two dogs, which had been barking at them from a distance, closed in on them furiously. And she was so enraged that she wouldn't lift a finger to wave the dogs back. Bitterly angry, she went to inspect the damage they had done. In some places, cabbage which had just begun to sprout had been crushed out of existence; and her heart bled at the sight as if it were her own children that had been trampled upon. Loosening the soil around them to uncover the dead seedlings, she cursed:

"Damn you! The way you destroy things, you'll come to a bad end yourselves!"

When the intruders had left, the valley became quiet again. Leaves rustled lightly in the wind and woodpeckers tapped at tree trunks. Mrs. Shi sat down in the doorway to suckle her youngest again.

"Ma, who were those men?" the eldest child asked uneasily.

"That's none of your business," Mother snapped. "They're a gang of bandits."

She was appalled at the damage done. Of course, the seeds themselves hadn't cost much; but how many of them would come up now after all this trampling? Wasn't it as bad as open theft? However, she could do nothing but pray quietly:

"Heaven help us! Don't let people like that come again."

But Heaven proved as irresponsive as wood or stone. A day or two later the men turned up again. This time only the two men in short jackets had come. They marched right up to the cottage, shouting at the dogs that were barking at them. When Mrs. Shi saw them her face clouded.

"What do you want now?" she asked uneasily.

"Come to tell you something!" one of them yelled. "You've to pay Landlord Wu three hundred thousand yuan deposit for the four mu of land you've rented from him. The money'll be returned to you when you stop using the land." Producing a sheet of paper from his pocket, he continued, "It's time you got wise. This is Landlord Wu's land, not yours, you're tilling. He has the deed. You can't beat him in a lawsuit even if you have the county magistrate on your side."

Knowing that all this was put down in black and white, Mrs. Shi thought it would be useless to argue, and her face was a picture of despair. But bracing herself, she cried furiously, "I couldn't raise such a sum, even if I sold my children!"

"What are you shouting about?" was the scathing reply. "That's only the deposit. You'll have to give the landlord another five *dou* of rice per year as rent."

"It just can't be done!" cried Mrs. Shi. "Look at this land — what rice can it grow? You must want to kill us, demanding all that rice!"

"Why are you bawling at me? Just to show you've a loud voice?" The man suddenly lashed himself into a fury. "If you don't want to pay, you can clear out. Nobody will stop you."

"That's right — better clear out," growled the other man, who all this time had been brandishing a stick at the dogs. "I've never seen such a place — a vixen of a woman, and regular savage dogs."

Thrusting the agreement at her, the two men made off without a glance behind. Too angry to speak, Mrs. Shi tore the paper to pieces and threw it after them. Then, looking at the slope behind the cottage, she said bitterly, "I'm not to be turned out of the valley that easy! For ten years we've toiled to get this place into shape. Our sweat during all those years would fill hundreds of buckets. Even if they come to drive me out, I'm not going."

Mrs. Shi was no longer haunted by a sense of loneliness and isolation. Her only fear now was that Landlord Wu might make more trouble. She was determined not to move from the valley, no matter what dirty tricks he might play. She couldn't afford to leave the place. During her ten years' stay here, she had come to know the hills, the woods and the little stream so well that she always thought of them as her own. Her heart warmed at the sight of the slope over which she walked barefooted from dawn to dusk, the green vegetables, ruddy oranges and yellow melons. Looking for firewood in the hills, she would pick only withered branches, but never had the heart to hack at the living wood;

for these trees were her neighbours, and she loved to watch them grow.

The little stream was another of her favourites. Without its water, she knew she would have had difficulty in growing anything. Every New Year's Eve she would go to its bank, and in heartfelt gratitude burn incense and paper money there. When astonishment was expressed at the unusual size of the beans and tomatoes she took to market, she would say cheerfully, "It's good land over there. The soil is rich, and there's a stream nearby."

But then, afraid such a glowing picture of the valley might tempt other people to move in, she would frown and add with a sigh, "The only trouble is the weeds. If you leave them for three days, they choke the place up. We have to work twice as hard there as anywhere else, drat it! It's back-breaking work."

It is easy to understand Mrs. Shi's consternation when they threatened to drive her away. She felt she must hold on to this valley at all costs. Landlord Wu must have eyed this land greedily for some time; but it was only now that her husband had gone that he dared bully her.

"All right! They think they can get away with it because I'm a woman. Well, I'll show them what a woman can do," she promised herself, nodding emphatically.

She put her hoe, scythe and axe right beside the door. If anyone came to throw her out, she would seize one of these implements to show him that a woman like herself was not to be bullied. When working in the field, she would straighten up from time to time to see whether anybody was coming up the small path on the left side of the valley. Sometimes she even sent her children to play on the hill from which they could keep an eye on the entrance to the valley. She didn't want to be caught napping.

A few days later, an old man showed up. Armed with a club, Mrs. Shi stood guard at the cottage door, her eyes fixed on the approaching figure. Her face was grimly set. The dogs barked furiously. The atmosphere was so tense that the youngest child was frightened and started crying.

The old man halted before the door, his face flushed. He was thoroughly annoyed with Mrs. Shi for not calling off the dogs, greeting him or offering him a seat.

"Why stare at me like that? Think I'm a bandit?" he asked ironically. With nothing but a pipe in his hand, it did seem unlikely that he had come to use violence.

Mrs. Shi relaxed a little, but still asked uneasily, "Who are you?"

"I'm *jia zhang*,*" he answered irritably, as if offended that she did not know who he was. "I've come about this land of Landlord Wu's. I know the rent's a little high. But just think — you've used his land a good ten years without paying him a single cent. Any other landlord would have come to collect rent long ago. He's really been very good to you. After I put in a word for you he agreed to reduce the deposit to 290,000 yuan and the annual rent to ten *dou* according to the new system of weights. Damn that dog!" He gave a shout, and shook his pipe at one of the dogs which had run up.

This time Mrs. Shi drove the dog away. But she had missed the end of the man's speech.

"Ten *tou*!" she sang out. "That's a strange reduction! He's raised it from five to ten."

"Can't you listen properly?" He glared at her. "I said ten *tou* according to the new system of weights. No wonder people call you unreasonable. You jump on a man without even hearing him through."

"I can't pay ten *dou*!" she retorted. "Just look at these children. Their Dad has been taken away by force, and I've the five of them to feed single-handed. What money have I for rent?"

"It can't be helped." Looking at the grimy, ragged children,

---

* Head of ten households under the Kuomintang regime.

the old man sighed and shook his head. "But as long as you're on his land you must pay Landlord Wu the deposit and rent. Who ever heard of getting land for nothing?"

"Won't you talk to him, please? Beg him to have a heart. I'll pay him somehow when my husband comes home."

"What if he never comes back?"

"Mercy! How can you say such a thing?" Mrs. Shi groaned. "What'll become of us if he never comes back?"

"There's no telling what'll happen to a soldier on the battlefield," he said coldly, turning his face away. Then, feeling he had spoken too harshly, he struck a different note. "Maybe Heaven will preserve him and send him back to you some day."

"How I hope so!" the woman responded gratefully.

By now the old man had lost patience with Mrs. Shi. Shaking his pipe at her, he said, "To get back to the rent — I advise you to agree to Landlord Wu's terms. He won't press you right now; you can pay him at the end of the year. But that 290,000 yuan deposit has got to be paid right away." He took a look round, then suggested, "Why don't you sell your pig and chickens?"

"The pig is too small," replied Mrs. Shi in despair. "Even if I sold it, I couldn't raise enough."

"Don't you have any savings?" the *jia zhang* asked, affecting surprise. "Didn't the school pay you something when it moved away?"

"Yes, it did," she confirmed angrily. "But since then my husband has had no job, and prices have been going up every day. It didn't take two months for that little sum to melt away. If I had any money left, my children wouldn't be so thin and ragged."

Again the old man sighed and shook his head.

Suddenly Mrs. Shi looked up, her eyes gleaming with hope. Pulling at his sleeve, she implored, "Please put in a good word for me. Ask Landlord Wu to have pity on us and cancel the

deposit. As for rent, I'll give him whatever the land yields —
pumpkins or potatoes, or whatever's in season."

"What an idea!" The man broke into a laugh. "Do you
think with a great stock of fish and meat in his house he wants
pumpkins and potatoes? He wouldn't even feed his pigs with
them. His pigs get rice mixed with chaff. It's no use hoping for
that. I wouldn't dare suggest it."

"He's asking for the impossible!" Mrs. Shi sighed in distress.

"He *is* too grasping," the old man agreed, experiencing a
wave of righteous indignation. "His son's an officer in the army
and sends him plenty of money every year. It wouldn't hurt
him in the least to cancel the deposit."

"If he could only see it that way!" she exclaimed.

Disconcerted, the *jia zhang* began to move off, sighing,
"What am I to say to the landlord? I've really got a hard nut
to crack."

"Just tell him you can't squeeze oil out of a bamboo," Mrs.
Shi shouted after him.

"Why don't you go and tell him yourself? I don't care two
straws about it!" the man yelled back angrily without a glance
behind.

It was clear now that Landlord Wu had sent the *jia zhang*
as a messenger. So he wouldn't resort to force after all! This
set her mind at ease, and she determined to tell any future messengers that she couldn't pay Landlord Wu the deposit but
would let him have for rent whatever her fields yielded. Of
course, she reflected, she must be more polite to future
messengers and plead with them as best she could, so that when
they went back they would put in a word for her. She should
ask them in and give them a seat and a cup of tea, then open
the rice bin to show them how short her family was running of
food. After that, she would lead them to her fields and point
out that the garlic wouldn't sprout for another month and the
cabbages wouldn't be ready to eat until winter. At present all

she had was potatoes, and she would gladly give the landlord a bushel of them if he wanted. It wouldn't be her fault if he turned down the offer. She must try to be reasonable, so that she would have nothing to fear even if the county magistrate took up the case himself.

For some time no one else turned up, and Mrs. Shi felt calmer. On the slope which she watered every day the green shoots of garlic and the emerald onions were ready for marketing. Her cabbages, which she carefully kept free from slugs, were growing daily greener. She would send some to Landlord Wu together with several crates of golden oranges and tangerines. If he were generous enough to stop pestering her for the rent and deposit, she knew how to show herself grateful.

Mrs. Shi knew that the rich cared little for pumpkins or potatoes. But they did like oranges and tangerines and fresh vegetables. Didn't they often send people to buy such things from the market? In addition, she meant to give the landlord a pair of fat hens as a New Year gift. While feeding her fowl, she made a careful study of them, comparing their merits and defects. The white ones were no good because they would bring bad luck,* while the black ones looked unclean. After much deliberation she chose a yellow pair with black spots, and resolved to send these to the landlord even if they turned out champion layers.

One night, woken by her dogs' furious barking, Mrs. Shi heard something crackling nearby and saw that the room was brightly lit and smoke was pouring in. Realizing with a shock that the kitchen must have caught fire, she rose and ran out barefooted. Her first thought was to fetch water from the stream; but the fire was spreading so fast that she must first rescue her children who were still sleeping soundly. One by one, she dragged them out, together with their bedding and clothes. Then the hens, let out of their coop, flapped away.

---

* White used to be worn for mourning in China.

In and out she ran to salvage her things until her hair caught fire.

Flames raged and roared over the thatched roof, leaping and cackling in an orgy of destruction. In less time than it takes for a meal, the whole cottage was burned to the ground. Even the branches of the orange trees beside it were badly scorched. Nothing was left but heaps of smouldering ashes.

Mrs. Shi broke down completely when she thought of the cottage she had built with her husband and repaired from year to year, the furniture she had slowly accumulated, and the pig now burned to death. She cried and cried, as if to give vent to all the bitterness she had ever known.

Having put the children to sleep under an orange tree, she sat down beside them. She fixed her eyes dazedly on the smouldering ashes. "How did the fire start?" she wondered. The kitchen fire had gone out while she was washing up after supper, and as she was sweeping the ground she recalled putting the firewood a safe distance from the stove before she went to bed. How could the fire have started? The more she thought, the more suspicious it seemed. Finally she was convinced that somebody must have set fire to the house. Was this part of Landlord Wu's wicked plot to drive her out of the valley?

For a little while she dozed off beside her children. Then day broke. She burst into tears again at the sight of the dead pig and cracked pickle pots, the rice reduced to ashes and the furniture burned to the semblance of charcoal. With her hoe, scythe and axe badly damaged, and the wooden water bucket gone, what had she left to work with? The loss of the building was not so serious — they could sleep under the trees. But what would become of them if she couldn't dig, scythe and water the vegetables? If the pig hadn't been burned, she could have sold it to buy new tools. But the pig was dead and the chickens were too small to sell. Even a laying hen wouldn't fetch much. As for the vegetables, they wouldn't be marketable for two or three months. The potatoes which could have lasted the family half a year had been turned into cinders. The immediate problem was food. She shuddered from head to foot at the thought of the difficulties confronting her. She felt worse than when her husband had been taken away. For then she had still had the means to till the land and bring up the children. But now starvation stared her in the face.

Putting her eldest son on guard over the bedding she had salvaged the previous evening, Mrs. Shi went to the market, carrying her baby on her back. There, tears streaming down her sallow cheeks, she told people the terrible thing that had happened to her. A number of folk were sympathetic and gave her money, clothes or rice. One old woman, who knew her, even helped her to carry the things home.

On their way back, Mrs. Shi told her friend how Landlord Wu had sent the men to intimidate her and how she suspected him of being responsible for the fire. Looking round fearfully, the old woman tugged at her sleeve and whispered:

"You take my advice, and go away. You're the only family in this lonely spot. What if Wu...."

Mrs. Shi turned pale. It was some minutes before she managed to say, "What can we live on if we go away?"

"Yes, but think — do you want to be killed? A rich, powerful man like that — he wouldn't stop at anything!"

Anger and bitterness welled up in Mrs. Shi's breast. "I'll have it out with him even if it kills me," she said desperately.

"That would never do!" Her companion put out a restraining hand. "What chance has an egg against a rock? What'll happen to your children if you get killed?"

For a moment the old woman was deep in thought. Then, pulling at Mrs. Shi's jacket, she suggested, "Why don't you go back to your own parts? It's always easier to eke out a living in the place where you were born and bred."

"We've got no land there. It was because we couldn't make a living that we left. Otherwise we'd have gone back long ago."

"But you've still some of your folk there, haven't you?"

"We've been away more than ten years. Who knows whether they're still alive? Even if they are, a fat lot they'd care for beggars like us."

"At least they wouldn't bully you or do you in."

"But what would we live on? I wouldn't earn enough to feed my five children even if I could bring myself to leave them and go out to work."

The old woman fell silent. Sighing repeatedly she went away.

Once more Mrs. Shi made up her mind not to leave the valley under any circumstances. The strip of soft green along the slope somehow gave her consolation and strength. "Before long the vegetables will save us," she mused. But at the back of her mind lurked the fear — suppose he really means to do us in? "All right," she told herself. "I'll fight it out with him. This plot of land has given us so much all these years, I'd gladly lay my bones here."

Every day, a half-broken crock in hand, Mrs. Shi went to fetch water from the stream to the vegetable garden. At night she slept with her children under the orange trees. Exposed to the night air, all her children caught cold and developed coughs; and the baby's fever was so high that he refused her milk. The hens, left unprotected in the night, were carried off one after another by wild cats and weasels. Only the dogs were left.

The unhappy mother was beset by terrible anxiety. She prayed to Buddha to make her vegetables ripen overnight, so that she could sell them the next day and buy an axe, a saw and a scythe. Then she could saw bamboos and cut reeds to set up a shack for the family.

One night she was wakened again by her dogs' furious barking. Springing up, she gripped a stone which she kept by her, preparing to fight back if she was attacked. But no one came. The dogs were barking in the direction of the slope, and it occurred to her that somebody might be stealing her vegetables. But they were still too small to be worth stealing. Perhaps some wild animals had come down from the hills. So instead of going over to the slope, clutching the stone tightly she stood bravely on guard over her five sleeping children.

Then the dogs stopped barking, and once more a sombre silence descended on the valley. Countless dim stars flickered in the black sky. Mrs. Shi lay down, but could not sleep. She was still afraid that wild animals might pounce out of the darkness to carry off her children. "If only my husband were here!" she thought. "I wouldn't mind going to the end of the earth to join him, if only I knew where he is. This place gives me the creeps."

The next morning Mrs. Shi hurried towards the slope, to see whether the tracks left on her vegetable plot were those of animals or men. But before she was near enough to make out any tracks, she saw that all her vegetables had been pulled up and scattered in all directions. Her heart bled at the sight. Gone now were her hopes that the vegetables might save them. She was speechless with anger. Realizing that Landlord Wu must be at the bottom of this, she threw caution to the winds and made straight for his house, beginning to curse as she ran.

But when she came to the end of the valley, the path between the cliff and the stream was blocked — a palisade had been built across it, and the gate in the palisade was firmly closed. Hard as she pushed, it would not budge. And it was so high that any attempt to climb over it was out of the question. She could do nothing but hammer on it with a stone.

Presently a man came up to the gate.

"What are you doing, pounding on the gate like this?" he shouted furiously.

"Open it, quick! I want to see Landlord Wu!" She stopped knocking.

"What for?" The man cocked his head on one side and planted his hands on his hips.

His haughty air infuriated Mrs. Shi.

"As if you didn't know! He's pulled up my vegetables and burned down my cottage. I'm going to have it out with him!"

She hammered on the door again, screaming, "Open up! Open up!"

"You crazy bitch," the man thundered. Drawing a pistol from his belt, he threatened to fire if she didn't stop knocking.

"How do you know it was the landlord? Did you see him?"

The sight of the pistol frightened Mrs. Shi. She stopped pounding on the gate. But when he did not fire, she took courage again and said, "Who else could it be? He's the only man round here who'd do such a vile thing."

"Hold your tongue!" Then, lowering his voice: "He'll send you to jail if he hears you!"

"I'm not afraid even if he tries to kill me!" She started beating on the door again. "Open the door, or I'll smash it to pieces!"

"See if I don't kill you!" the man yelled, pointing his pistol at her breast.

"Go on! Shoot!" Mrs. Shi urged, leaning forward.

But the man lowered his pistol.

"Shooting's too good for you," he sneered. And with that he turned and made off.

"Why don't you open the door, you son of a bitch?"

She struck and struck until her hand began aching; but the door stood firm. Then she sat down beside it, panting in exhaustion.

After a good rest she realized that there was nothing she could do about the door. Besides, as the man had said, a quarrel with Wu would get her nowhere since she had no evidence against him. And it would be no use taking the case to court. She had come to fight the landlord in a fit of fury, but she hadn't been able to get at him; and now her good sense reasserted itself.

Her thoughts turned again to her children, and passionate mother love filled her whole being. She must never abandon them. She must find a way to bring them up.

She got up and went slowly home.

The slope looked lonelier now that the cottage had been burned down and the vegetables torn up. They had no shelter from wind and rain nor hope of a living from the land; and the wicked landlord might be plotting further mischief. There was no alternative but to leave.

Mrs. Shi had no idea where to go. She knew only that if they stayed here her children would starve to death.

Having put together the things they must take with them, she went to have a last look at the orange, peach and plum trees, and was seized with a desire to hack them all down. She didn't want that accursed landlord to enjoy the fruit. But the fire had destroyed her axe and saw. She could only hope that eating her fruit would make him ill.

Last of all, she took her children to their grandmother's grave to bid her farewell. "Ma!" Mrs. Shi burst out crying. "We can't stay here with you. We've no choice but to go begging. May your spirit protect the children wherever we go!"

Then, their bedding on her back and the baby in her arms, she led them away. The two older girls carried a pot for boiling rice, while the little boys trudged along empty-handed — there was nothing else to carry. With the dogs at their heels, they made their way along the bank of the stream to the market.

The kindly folk who had already helped them out once found it difficult to give more; but she managed to get a bite of food for the children. They passed a miserable night in the open near the bus station. And the next morning, knowing no further help could be looked for here, they set out for the nearest town.

For the last time, their valley came into view. It was veiled in a light white mist. The golden rays of the morning sun had reached the pinewoods on the hill, but the fruit trees by the stream and the cultivated plot on the slope were still wrapped in the shadows of night.

The children saw it first, and shouted happily, "There's our home, Ma! Look! Down there!"

Mrs. Shi stole a glance at the valley, then lowered her head, fighting to keep back her tears.

"When shall we come back, Ma?" the children were asking.

"When the oranges are ripe," Mother said, swallowing her tears.

The children were satisfied. But presently one of them asked:

"Ma! Where are we going?"

The question staggered her. There was a long pause before she thought up an answer.

"To find Dad," she told them.

That made the children happier than ever. With shouts of laughter they started calling excitedly for their father.

Mrs. Shi broke down, big tears rolling down her cheeks.

After a good cry she felt better. The children's peals of laughter cheered her up. She took heart. Biting her lips, she reaffirmed her determination to defy all difficulties and bring her children up.

August, 1947
From *Chinese Literature*

About the Author

AI WU was born in 1904 in Fanxian County, Sichuan Province. His grandfather was a peasant and his father was a country schoolteacher. He studied in the Provincial Normal College in Chengdu.

In 1925 he went to Yunnan Province and worked as a shop assistant for more than a year. In 1927 he wandered to Burma where he became an assistant in a stable for five months. Afterwards he went to Rangoon and Singapore. For some time he worked in a newspaper office as a proof-reader, then became a primary school-teacher and editor of a newspaper supplement.

In 1931 Ai Wu returned to Shanghai. In the same year he joined the China League of Left-Wing Writers and began publishing his short stories in the *Literature Monthly*.

Before liberation he wrote many novels and short stories, mostly about labouring people and oppressed men and women, whose spirit of resistance he praised. Since liberation he has published short stories, novels and *Homeward Journey and Other Stories*.

In 1957 Ai Wu created the novel *Steeled and Tempered* which took the life of iron and steel workers as its main theme. He stopped writing for several years in the period of "cultural revolution".

Sister Shi Qing, written in 1947, is a short story in which Ai Wu depicts a peasant woman living in a deserted village whose husband has been conscripted. After ten years' oppression by the landlord, she is forced to leave her home and fields she had cultivated with painstaking efforts and wander with her children. This moving story shows us the miserable life of the labouring people in the old society.

Ai Wu today is a full-time writer.

Harvest

Ye Zi

I

It was nearly Qing Ming Festival.* Rain had been pouring down for days, and the sky remained overcast without the slightest sign of clearing up.

Uncle Yunpu, still in the shabby padded gown that had seen him through the winter, sat near the entrance of the Cao Ancestral Temple. He was shivering slightly, as if his body found it hard to withstand the chill that penetrated his bones. Looking up to survey the sky, he muttered something under his breath and then looked down again.

"Heavens! Is it going to be like last year?" he whispered.

Then turning to his wife, who was sitting at the foot of the stage** in front of the temple, he said hesitatingly, "They say at the beginning of March one should be able to take off his padded clothes. But it's nearly Qing Ming and still too cold to go without them. Could it be that this year will be as bad as last?"

She made no reply. She was busy nursing little Sixi at her breast.

---

* A solar period which usually falls on April 5 or 6.

** A stage is often attached to the Chinese temple where in the old days theatrical performances were given on festival occasions.

The weather was really dreadful, enough to worry anyone to death. The rain had not let up for more than a month, ever since the lunar calendar marked the beginning of spring. People felt terribly afraid. In the past, a bitter cold spell around the beginning of spring meant that it would be a flood year.

"Heaven above, if it's going to be the same...." Uncle Yunpu once more gazed up at the sky, while tapping the pipe in his hand on the stone steps.

"It couldn't be!" said Mrs. Yunpu after a pause, in a rather offhand manner, her face still turning towards the child in her arms.

"Why couldn't it be? Didn't we have a cold spell like this at the beginning of spring in 1924 and 1926? Besides, this year Heaven is going to make people really suffer."

Uncle Yunpu was irritated by his wife's casual answer. He felt sure this year's fate was already sealed. Had not the oracle in the Guan Di* Temple stated clearly that it was going to be a bad year and that death would take a toll of sixty to seventy per cent of the population?

These fears were inspired by memories of past suffering, deeply engraved in the mind of Uncle Yunpu. He remembered the year 1924 when he had just managed to scrape together one meal a day, and this of yams and wild herbs which he had gathered here and there. The year after was slightly better, but the following year they were again reduced to tree bark and roots. But last year — Heavens! Uncle Yunpu hardly dared think about it.

Last year there had been eight mouths to feed in his household. This year there were only six left. Besides Uncle Yunpu and his wife, there was their eldest son, twenty-year-old Liqiu, who was his father's right-hand man. The second son, Shaopu,

---

* God of Chivalry. Originally called Guan Yu, he was a famous general during the period of the Three Kingdoms in the third century. Later he was deified by the feudal ruling class.

who was fourteen, had started to help with work in the fields too. Yingying, the ten-year-old daughter, helped her mother make rain hats, and the youngest was Sixi, the baby, still breast-fed. Uncle Yunpu's father and the six-year-old boy, Tiger, had died last September from eating Mercy Powder.*

What a jolly family he had had, and not a single member who ate without working! Who would say Uncle Yunpu wasn't destined to become rich? Yes, Uncle Yunpu would have become prosperous if not for tough luck that had brought a succession of wars, droughts and floods year after year, crushing him so that he could hardly raise his head.

Last year, that dreadful year, had been worse than a night-mare. Because of wars and natural calamities, he had been compelled, in desperation, to rent seven mu** of Mr. He's land in the hope that his fortune might take a turn for the better. After all, there were many hands in his family; each extra mu of land cultivated would mean just so much more at harvest time. He had hoped that after deducting the rent to be paid to He there would be some grain left for themselves. If they could manage to get enough to eat for a year or two, there would be no question but that they would become prosperous. Uncle Yunpu had made up his mind to sell his entire property, which consisted of the little hut they lived in, and become a tenant of Mr. He's.

He had moved his whole family into the ancestral temple in March and had become caretaker of the ancestral tablets, for which duty he was given a string of cash at the oblation in spring and autumn. Mr. He had taken over his hut and had allowed him to cultivate his seven mu of land at the customary rate of seventy per cent of the harvest. Had Uncle Yunpu actually been

---

* Fine white clay, believed to be sent by Guanyin, the Goddess of Mercy, and used by people as food during famine.

** A mu is equivalent to 1/15 hectare or 1/6 acre.

able to keep the thirty per cent of the harvest in his own hands, he would have considered himself quite lucky.

At first, he had really felt extremely happy. He and his sons had laboured unstintingly, and he felt doubly reassured by the fact that the rice seedlings were growing well in the nursery and the rain was just right. If he was careful in his cultivation and they managed a good harvest, everything would be all right, he had thought.

Pretty soon the seedlings were transplanted to the fields; they took root and started to shoot. It was not long till ears of grain appeared; with a few more days of mild south wind he could count on the appearance of a golden field of rice. Uncle Yunpu had been filled with joy. Was this not ample reward for his unceasing hard labour?

He had felt like jumping up and down for joy. But it happened that one day, Heaven changed its mind. Huge drops of rain started pelting down from the southwest, and soon the shower spread to the village. In barely half a day, the water in the ponds had begun to rise. Uncle Yunpu was suddenly seized with uneasiness; he was afraid that the precious rice flowers would be destroyed by the heavy downpour, and his harvest ruined. But by afternoon the rain had stopped. Uncle Yunpu felt light-hearted, as if a heavy burden had been lifted from his shoulders.

In the middle of the night, however, the sky had suddenly turned so dark that it was impossible to see even two feet ahead. The clanging of gongs sounded from all sides; racing feet and shouting voices clamoured against the whirling of the wind. Uncle Yunpu knew that some accident had taken place. In great haste, he woke his son Liqiu, and in the dark they raced towards the sound of the gongs.

They ran into a neighbour, Little Second Scar, on the way and learned that both the West and South Streams had risen thirty feet. Caojialong was threatened by breaches in the dykes protecting the village. The gongs were sounded to call the people together to reinforce the dykes.

Uncle Yunpu was stunned. For the water suddenly to rise ten yards in a night was a rare phenomenon. It had not occurred in forty or fifty years. He was in a panic. The faster the gongs beat, the more unsteady his steps became. The night was dark and the path slippery. He fell time and again, and picked himself up with great difficulty. Finally his son took his arm and they ran on together. But they had gone only a few paces when they heard a loud crash, as if heaven itself had burst open. Uncle Yunpu's legs shook like leaves in the wind. Instantly waves of turbulent water rushed at them. Liqiu quickly lifted his father onto his back, turned around and raced home. Just as they entered their door, the water reached the stone steps.

The water had broken through a corner of the dyke at Xindukou, forcing an opening about three hundred feet wide, and Caojialong's fields of gold had disappeared in the water.

Uncle Yunpu was half crazed. His proceeds from half a year's hard work and the subsistence of his whole family were in that one instant washed away. All day he went about moaning, "Heavens, oh my Heavens! My kernels of gold have dissolved in the water!"

And so now once again Uncle Yunpu saw fateful signs of disaster appear. He could not help but feel desperately worried. From June the year before up until that moment he had not had one solid meal of rice. The water had receded in July, and the famine-stricken peasants had gone out of the village together to beg for food. But when they had reached Ningxiang, they had been taken for rebels and driven away. After this incident no one had been allowed to go far from his front door. It was said that the county government had received thirty thousand dollars for famine relief; actually not a single grain of rice ever reached the peasants in the countryside. Mr. He bought seventy piculs*

---

* A picul is equivalent to 50 kilogrammes or 110 pounds.

of soya beans from the provincial capital for the relief of the
famine in the village. Uncle Yunpu managed to borrow fifty
catties* at the unheard-of price of six and a half dollars, to
which was added an interest rate of four and a half per cent per
month. But there were eight in Uncle Yunpu's house, and eventually even the grass was all eaten and they simply could not carry on any longer. Uncle Yunpu went down on his knees to Mr. He
and obtained on loan another thirty catties of beans. In September, Mercy Powder was discovered at Huajia Dyke and the
villagers went down in crowds to dig it up for food. Uncle
Yunpu and Liqiu managed to get about three piculs. The
family filled their stomachs with that for a day or so, and as a
result, the grandfather departed this world, taking with him
the six-year-old little Tiger.

When the famine-stricken villagers were on the very brink
of starvation, Mr. He had talked to the county magistrate,
guaranteeing on their behalf that they would not riot. After
innumerable entreaties, a few exit permits had been issued, and
thus the peasants had been able to leave their village homes.
Uncle Yunpu and his family had been sent to a busy town where
they had wandered for four hungry months. They had not returned until the end of the year. All this had happened last
year.

Now the villagers were making rain hats of bamboo as a
temporary measure to keep alive. In the rainy season if a person
made ten rain hats a day he could earn two meals of thin gruel.
Uncle Yunpu and Liqiu split the bamboo while Mrs. Yunpu,
with Shaopu and Yingying helping, worked day and night weaving the hats. Work, work, work, they must keep at the weaving.
What else was there for them but weaving? If only they could
keep alive until the autumn harvest!

But for over a month now the spring rains had been un-

---

* A catty is equivalent to 1/2 kilogramme or 1.1 pounds.

relenting and it was bitterly cold. Everyone in the village was
seized with the same fear.

"Merciful Heaven, is it going to be like last year again?"

2

The sky eventually cleared up. People ventured out of the
gloomy houses in which they had been hibernating for over a
month, and looked about. Hopeful smiles hovered on pale,
sallow faces. Children pranced around in groups under the
sun, their bare legs sporting over the soft muddy ground.

The water was still high — in the ponds, the fields and the
lakes. Young grass was springing up everywhere and sparkling
raindrops hung from the rushes like little silvery pearls. The
willows too had begun to sprout. Spring sunshine after a long
period of rain lent an atmosphere of vitality and freshness to
everything in the village.

People started to chatter among themselves and bustle with
activity. On the paths near the fields, small groups of people
walked about barefooted, loitering here and there, now pointing at the ponds, now examining the ditches and talking of this
and that problem. All of them were making plans and preparations for the work of the coming season.

There was a sudden slump in the market for rain hats since
the weather had cleared up in that vicinity. The men could no
longer stay at home all day to cut the strips, and as a result
work slackened for the women and children. The tight screws
of livelihood were immediately felt within the whole village.
The only thing to do was to work hard in the fields and yet one
must eat when working.

Uncle Yunpu, who had prayed day in and day out for the
rain to stop, now had his wish fulfilled. But a smile only flickered fleetingly over his face; it disappeared immediately to be
followed by tightly knitted brows. It was still too cold to dis-

pense with his padded gown. The sun imparted only a faint
tinge of warmth to Uncle Yunpu's body, but he did not bother
about that. He was worried only as to how he could get over
the present crisis — how to get a few good meals of rice so as to
have strength enough to go to work in the fields.

The drop in the market for rain hats meant cutting out
their daily meals of thin gruel. Uncle Yunpu was therefore more
worried than ever. He was convinced that it was his fate to
suffer; he had not known an hour of comfort since the day he
was born. By the time he was fifty, he had undergone any number of hardships, but he had yet to see one happy day. The
fortune-tellers said that his old age would be spent in comfort,
but that was something which would come about only after he
had turned fifty-five. It was hard for him to believe in something so far in the future. Neither of his sons was at all worldly-
wise, and he found it most difficult to maintain a household of
six during those years of hard luck.

"I must find a way out somehow!" He would repeat this
sentence over and over again in his mind whenever a tough
problem confronted him and sometimes he would be able to
think of a good solution. Uncle Yunpu had never completely
given up hope. The present crisis, he knew, was an extremely
difficult one, so again he was turning the words over in his
mind.

"There's Mr. He, Mr. Li, Mr. Chen. . . ." As he paced back
and forth at the foot of the stage, one by one the figures of these
men floated before his eyes. But how harsh and unrelenting
were their faces! They inspired him with uneasiness and dread.
He shook his head and sighed, casting the thought of these people aside, and turning his mind in another direction. Suddenly
he remembered a person who was of a different sort.

"Liqiu, will you go right away to see Uncle Yuwu?"

"What for, Dad?" asked Liqiu nonchalantly from the
doorstep where he sat splitting bamboo.

"Tomorrow the weather will be really fine and warm;

everyone is planning to go to the fields. We have to start too. And the first day we should at least have a full meal. It will be a sign of better things to come and will give us strength to do our work. But there's no more rice in the house."

"I don't think Uncle Yuwu can do anything about it."

"Still, it won't do any harm to go and see, will it?"

"Why bother to go there for nothing? I don't think they're any better off than we are."

"You're always talking back to your father. How do you know whether they are like us or not? I told you to go and see."

"But Dad, it's true. They are probably harder up than we are."

"Nonsense!"

Recently, Uncle Yunpu had often felt that his son was not as obedient as before. He seemed to want to argue over everything. Liqiu had quarrelled many times with his father over ordinary household affairs. He was often quite indolent and unwilling to work, and sometimes behaved like an utterly rebellious, unfilial creature.

Uncle Yuwu was not necessarily in such drastic straits as he, because there was only Yuwu and his wife in the family, no one else. The year before, when all the peasants in the village had left and become refugees, Yuwu had stayed at home. All by himself, he had managed to eke out a living for his family of two. Furthermore, he never borrowed from anyone. Three days ago, he had been seen with a basket in front of the butcher shop near the ferry. He had bought a piece of meat and some wine, and had sauntered on, quite pleased with himself. How could anyone say he was so hard up?

Uncle Yunpu suspected that his son was again behaving like a lazy beggar, refusing to obey orders. He was unable to suppress his anger.

"You wretch, are you going, or aren't you? You're always opposing me in one way or another!"

"It's no use going."

"You'll go if I tell you to go, and I forbid you to talk back to me like that!"

Raising his head, Liqiu gently put down the knife with which he had been cutting bamboo. His young heart was heavy with hidden pain. Unable to stand the worried look on his father's face, he turned and went off without another word.

"Just say: My father sent me to ask Uncle Yuwu to please help us just a little. Once we tide over this difficult time, we'll promptly return you what we owe!"

"Uh. . . ."

The moon had just peeped out from behind the tree branches, only to be swallowed up again by dark clouds. Not a single star was in sight. The darkness was like an all-encompassing black lacquer screen.

"What did Uncle Yuwu say?"

"He didn't say much. He only said: Please give my regards to your Dad. I am very sorry, but yesterday we were eating pumpkin and today there's just this bit of thin gruel left."

"Didn't you say I'd pay him back right away?"

"I did, and he even showed me their rice jar. It was empty."

"And what about his wife?"

"She smiled at me but didn't say anything."

"They're lying!" Uncle Yunpu said indignantly, pounding his fist on the small table. "Only three days ago I saw him buying meat, and bless him, he says he has no rice today. Who the devil believes that!"

Nobody made a sound. Mrs. Yunpu came over, and the children strained their ears to hear the conversation. In the huge ancestral temple there was not a single light. The darkness was oppressive and weighed down their spirits.

"Then what are we to do tomorrow when work in the fields must begin?" Mrs. Yunpu asked anxiously.

"There's nothing but starvation for all of us. This good-for-nothing has been dashing about for Heaven knows how long, and hasn't brought back even a single grain of rice!"

"But Dad, what could I do?"

"Oh, go off and die, you worthless fool, and leave me alone!"

Having scolded his son so severely, Uncle Yunpu was immediately sorry. Die! Ah, what was the good of wishing his son dead? His heart contracted, and in spite of himself two big tears rolled down his shrivelled old cheeks. He groped for his pipe, and turning around, went out.

"Where are you going, old man?" asked his wife.

"Are we to eat sand tomorrow or what, if I don't go out to see what I can do?"

With sorrow in their eyes the family watched the retreating back of Uncle Yunpu until it was swallowed up by the darkness. One by one the children went in to sleep. Like little puppies, they tumbled about, finally settling down here and there in the back room, and lay quiet. Only Mrs. Yunpu and Liqiu remained in the front room, their lustreless eyes wide open in the tense atmosphere while they waited for Uncle Yunpu to return. A tightness had already started to clutch at their hearts.

Late that night Uncle Yunpu came back with a mournful look on his face. He swung a little sack down from his back onto the earthen floor.

"Damn it! Here is three dollars and sixty cents' worth of horse beans."

Three pairs of hungry eyes were fixed on the little sack. Uncle Yunpu's eyes were still wet with tears.

3

Standing beside the mouth of the ditch in one corner of their field, Liqiu swung his hoe lazily. Responding to the movement of his hoe, the excess water in the field gradually flowed out of the ditch into the pond. But Liqiu felt extremely tired, and his arms were devoid of strength. Somehow his usual vitality was missing.

Everything was so uncertain. Moodily he gazed out over the fields spreading towards the distant horizon. It seemed to him that it was just no use in working hard; one could never feel sure that hard work would achieve anything. He was quite disheartened by the years of natural and man-made disasters, and everything at present made him feel lost and bewildered. Yet he could think of no way out of the distressing situation.

Dragging his hoe behind him, he stepped over to another opening in the ditch. The past rushed to his mind like an incoming tide. Every swing of his hoe seemed to cut into his heart. His father was getting old and his brother and sisters were so young. All that had happened during the past four or five years indicated that their family was heading for disaster. The way out was still so unclear. He knew not how he could find a way out for them.

Suddenly he remembered what his neighbour, Big Lai, had whispered to him in secret some time ago. Turning it over carefully in his mind, he found that there was irrefutable logic and reason behind it. True enough, in years like these, unless a person depended on himself, he had no one to depend on. The whole world was against the poor; unless the poor stood up for themselves and did something, there would be no hope for them all their lives. Moreover, Big Lai had stated with great certainty that the world would belong to the poor in the near future.

Thus, Liqiu recalled the extraordinary events which had taken place four years before, when the Peasants' Association* was in power.

---

* In 1926-27 when the Chinese Communist Party co-operated with the Kuomintang against feudal warlords, Peasants' Associations were formed in many provinces to oppose the landlord system and demand land. These associations were suppressed after the Kuomintang betrayed the revolution.

"Oh, if only that world would come again!"

He smiled. Suddenly a figure passed by him. Startled, he turned and saw Big Lai, the very person he had been thinking about.

"Hey! Where're you going, Cousin?"

"Ah, Liqiu. So you folks have also started work in the fields."

"Yes, Cousin. Come, let's talk." Liqiu stopped swinging his hoe.

"Where's your Dad?"

"Over there carrying peat. Shaopu is with him."

"How are you people getting along these days?"

"Miserably, of course! How else? Today, there is no one home making rain hats. All three of us are working in the field. Last night my Dad went to Mr. He and borrowed ten catties of beans which gave us a meal of a sort before we came to work. Otherwise. . . ."

"You're not doing so badly. You still manage to borrow beans from Mr. He."

"Who wants to borrow from him? Never again! My Dad had to beg and beg. He kowtowed too, and promised to pay an exorbitant price. And how about you people, Cousin?"

"We too find it hard to manage from one day to the next."

A minute's silence and then the customary smile returned to Big Lai's face. He nodded to Liqiu and said, "Let's continue our talk this evening, Liqiu."

"All right."

After Big Lai had hurried off, Liqiu continued his work. His hoe swung up and down in the field, from one end of the ditch to the other. The sun hung high in the sky as if to notify people that it was already noon. The sound of people singing, so long absent from the village, was again in the air. Quite tired, the peasants made their way home, but smoke — the sign of food cooking — curled from very few huts.

Uncle Yunpu's body ached all over although he had made

only twenty or thirty trips carrying peat the day before. His legs and shoulders pained as if pierced by hundreds of sharp needles. The pain and discomfort kept him awake practically all night and when he got up at dawn he felt worn and limp. However, he composed himself and pretended there was nothing unusual for fear that if he betrayed signs of weakness it would discourage his sons.

"After all, I'm getting old," he pondered sorrowfully.

From the kitchen, Liqiu brought out two bowls of what remained of the beans, and placed them on the table. The smell of the cooked beans made Uncle Yunpu's mouth water. The three who were working the fields shared the food equally, getting over half a bowl each. The beans tasted much more delicious than usual, but half a bowl was, after all, so little that when tucked away in the stomach, filled ever so small a corner.

The men went to the fields and struggled for a while, exerting great efforts of will, as if to make up for their waning physical powers. They felt as if they had shouldered a heavy yoke which was weighing them down. They could barely manage to lift even a hoe or a small wooden plough. From time to time stars flashed before their eyes and the world would start to reel. After a few rounds, the men were forced to return home.

"How can we go on like this?"

The family gathered together, children as well as grownups. Six pairs of eyes red from the gnawing pangs of hunger, stared at one another sorrowfully. All felt that there was nothing to say.

"Oh, Heaven!"

Gritting his teeth and summoning the remainder of his fading courage, Uncle Yunpu again turned to go to Mr. He's. On the way he figured out how he was going to approach Mr. He and what he was going to say, mentally going over the whole scene step by step. Presently he found himself at the gate of Mr. He's estate.

"Well, what is it you want, Yunpu?" Mr. He asked, as he sat enthroned in his massive arm-chair.

"I — I —"

"What?"

"I would like again to ask Mr. He. . . ."

"Beans? I can't lend you any more. There're many people in this village, you know. Do you think I want to feed your family alone?"

"I'll return the debt with added interest."

"Who cares for your interest? You think other people don't pay interest? It's no use."

"Please, Mr. He, you must save us. Neither old nor young have eaten in my family."

"Go away, how can I bother so much about the likes of you! Go away!"

"Mr. He, oh, save us!"

Uncle Yunpu burst into tears of desperation. Then one of Mr. He's hired hands came and pushed him out of the gate.

"How dare you come here and cry, and bring us bad luck, you old devil!" said the hired hand fiercely, banging the door in his face.

Dragging one foot along after the other, Uncle Yunpu made his way home. He muttered recriminations against himself, reproaching himself for not saying the things he had planned to say and for not broaching the subject gradually step by step. Now he had bungled the whole thing and got nothing out of his visit. What could he do to get over the present difficulties?

At the edge of Square Pond he suddenly stopped in his tracks. Gazing at this dark green pond, he was seized with a strong impulse to take a simple little jump into the water and thus end the remaining sad bit of his life. But the thought of his family, the old and the young, kept him from taking the plunge.

Mrs. Yunpu and the children stood by the entrance of the ancestral temple, anxiously waiting for the appearance of Uncle

Yunpu, who, they trusted, would bring them good news. Pangs of hunger burned within them like a consuming flame. Their eyes were red and they felt dizzy.

Jingqing, otherwise known as Baldy, came into the room, accompanied by a man with a thick beard. Immediately, Uncle Yunpu felt as if a thousand sharp daggers had been thrust into his heart. His legs and hands shook nervously, and tears streamed down his face. Having ushered the guests into the front room and seated them on a bench, he took himself into a corner and stood there. Mrs. Yunpu was still hiding inside. Her eyes had long since become red and swollen from weeping. The two younger children, too weak to get up, were still in bed. Their thin faces were as yellow as wilted cabbage leaves.

Liqiu stood near the door with Shaopu behind him. The eyes of both were wet. They looked at the bearded man dully and quickly turned their heads away.

After a few minutes of silence the bearded man said impatiently, "Baldy, where is the child?"

"She's still inside. A ten-year-old called Yingying." The bald-headed man nodded as if to tell him not to be impatient.

Mrs. Yunpu emerged from the back room, walking as if each foot was dragging a half-ton weight, and holding in her hands a little suit of clothes, newly patched. She was trembling so much she was hardly able to make her way across the room. Catching sight of the bald-headed man, she somehow managed to address him. Then hot tears welled out of her eyes and she was unable to go on. Uncle Yunpu quietly hid his face in his sleeves and both Liqiu and Shaopu hung their heads and wept silently.

The bald-headed man became worried. Glancing quickly at his companion, he turned to Mrs. Yunpu and said comfortingly:

"Why should you feel so heart-broken, Mrs. Yunpu? Won't Yingying be better off to go along with Mr. Xia than she would be at home? She'll have plenty of food and clothing, and if she happens to get a good master, she'll live a comfortable life. Didn't all go well with Guisheng's daughter, Chu-er, and another girl Taoxiu? Besides, Mr. Xia —"

"Cousin Jingqing, now I feel I just simply cannot sell her. Last year when we were so hard up, we went begging as far as Hubei Province, but we still refused to sell her. There's more reason why I can't sell her this year. She, my baby Ying, my flesh and blood, oh . . . !"

"Ah!" said Xia, the bearded man, shooting a quick glance at Baldy.

"What, Yunpu?" cut in Baldy hurriedly. "Changed your mind? Last night it was all decided —" But before he had finished the sentence Mrs. Yunpu rushed at her husband crying and cursing at the same time:

"It's all your fault, you old devil! You can't even support your children and you call yourself a man! Now that you have nothing to put into your stomach, you go ahead and sell my daughter! You good-for-nothing, you're fit only to die. Oh, you wretch! We might as well all die together and be done with it. Sell my daughter, will you? No, a thousand times no!"

"Didn't you agree to it last night? I didn't make the decision alone. Baldy, isn't she a shrew!" Uncle Yunpu backed away from his wife, his face stained with tears.

"Let's go," said the bearded man impatiently. He stood up.

But Baldy quickly stopped him. "Wait a little. She'll think better of it in a moment. Come, Yunpu, let's talk outside."

Baldy dragged Uncle Yunpu away, but Mrs. Yunpu continued to cry and rave. Liqiu went up to her and helped her to a bench. He knew that the factors leading to this tragedy were not simple. The family had had nothing to eat for three days. No one wanted to buy rain hats any more, yet the work in the field could not be left undone. Therefore when Baldy had come last night and made the proposition, Liqiu had not opposed it very strongly. Although he was heart-broken about

his sister and hated to have her sold, there was no other way to
help them out of the present predicament outside of this last
resort. He had lain awake the whole night, torn by the sorrow
and conflict in his heart. He had felt that he couldn't bear to
even look at his poor little sister who was soon to be sold, and
had got up before daybreak. Now that his mother was crying so
bitterly, he had not the heart to tell her that it was all necessary
and unavoidable.

"Come, Mama, just let them go!"

Mrs. Yunpu made no reply. Baldy and Uncle Yunpu returned; once again everyone was silent.

"Well, Mrs. Yunpu, what is your final decision?" asked
Baldy.

"Cousin, will my Yingying be able to come home sometimes once she is gone?"

"She will if she finds a master nearby. Besides, you people
can go to see her often."

"But if she has to go far?"

"That will not happen."

"It's all the old devil's fault. Why didn't he die an early
death?"

Yingying came out from the back room carrying baby Sixi
in her arms. With surprise and suspicion she glanced at the
strange scene around her. She handed the baby to her mother
and then stared at everyone in the room with big round eyes.

With the exception of the two outsiders, all present were
again seized with heart-ache and remorse.

"Is she the one?" asked Xia, the bearded man, who, having been nudged by Baldy, now began to stare at Yingying.

After much negotiation, Xia agreed to pay only two dollars
for each year of the child's life. Yingying was ten, so the price
was set at twenty dollars. Both parties had to pay one dollar
each to Baldy as commission.

"Alas! What kind of a world is this?"

Uncle Yunpu held the nineteen pieces of silver in his hand,

but he was so stunned by what had happened that he turned numb as a block of wood. With one sleeve he kept wiping the tears that welled up in his eyes, and at the same time he stared unbelievingly at the money. "Oh, Heaven! Is this the money for my precious, my Yingying!"

Mrs. Yunpu changed Yingying into the clean patched suit and told her that she was going to Uncle Xia's house to have a few good meals and that she'd be coming back. But still Yingying could not hold back the rapidly flowing tears.

"Mama, can I come home tomorrow? I don't want to go away and have things to eat alone."

The family followed Yingying with tearful eyes. They couldn't take their eyes off her. It was, after all, their last look at their little girl.

After Baldy had taken Yingying away, Mrs. Yunpu behaved as one completely possessed. Several times she started out as if to chase after them. They heard Yingying turn back and call to them from a distance, "Oh, Mama, I don't want to have a full stomach all by myself! I want to come home tomorrow."

Thus, for the time being, the family was able to keep alive. With the nineteen dollars they bought a little over two piculs of unhusked rice. It was enough to feed the five members of the family for sixty days or more. The father and sons had to work hard on the farm to find new sources of income.

It was three days before Qing Ming that the sowing was to begin, but there was not a single household in the village that had the seeds to sow. For the solution of this problem, Mr. He went to the county seat to seek out the county magistrate. Unless the sowing was done in time there would be no harvest in the autumn.

Everyone was expecting good news from Mr. He. In this, the people knew they would not be disappointed, because every year they had been able to get seeds on loan. The county magistrate himself was clearly aware that "the magistrates depend on the

people, and the people depend on the land". If nothing was
done about seeds for sowing, in the end no one would benefit.
Therefore Mr. He was readily able to get the magistrate's
promise whereby one thousand piculs of grain were to be issued
to Caojialong to be handled by Mr. He.

"What! The seed grain costs us eleven dollars per picul, on
top of which the money must be repaid at four per cent interest?
This must be the work of that scoundrel He."

All the villagers were cursing He, but all of them, nevertheless, quietly carried off seed grain from his house.

Life and work soon engulfed the village in an ever increasing whirl of activity. The people were all struggling desperately. All their hopes lay in the great coming harvest.

4

The seedlings were transplanted, then the fields were weed-
ed twice. But Heaven again made sport of the hardships of
the poor. For more than ten days there was not even the slightest
drizzle. The sun hung in the air like a ball of fire. The water
in the fields had dried up; only a trace of moisture remained in
the soil.

Having sold his daughter and obtained seed grain on loan,
Uncle Yunpu worked hard to get his seedlings transplanted.
By now he was so busy he could hardly find time to breathe.
He still had no notion as to where to get fertilizer, and nature
had not been generous with rain. Really, it was worrisome.
If it was going to be a drought year, they must make prepara-
tions early.

He told Liqiu to go up to the stage and bring the water-
wheel down so that they could mend it. If in three more days
there was no rain, it would be impossible to get along without
using the water-wheel.

Everyone was praying in his heart: Oh, Heaven, please take pity on us and send us just a wee bit of rain.

One day, two days ... how hard-hearted Heaven was! It purposely pretended not to hear the people's prayers. The horizon was still cloudless and the burning sun seemed to challenge the very existence of the universe. Scorched by the sun, everything had begun to wilt. The fields dried up; now and again one would come across a great crack which looked like the gaping mouth of some ferocious animal panting and emitting a burning hot breath.

The fields could wait no longer. The splashing of water-wheels could be heard in both Zhangjiacha and at Xindukou. The seedlings hung their heads as if complaining of thirst. Their blades had become dry and curled up. People had not forgotten the sufferings left by the flood the last year. Who would stand by and watch the crops dry up and die? They would give their lives to make the final struggle.

After breakfast, Uncle Yunpu walked to Square Pond in silence, carrying the frame of the water-wheel, his two sons beside him with the other parts of the water-wheel. The sun beating on their backs made their flesh burn and itch. Even the ground underfoot was scorching hot.

The sound of water-wheels' turning came from all directions. The water in the ponds was being hauled up to the fields by manpower. Uncle Yunpu fixed his water-wheel and father and sons mounted it. The wheel started to move, water went up the pipe and flowed into the fields.

The peasants were bathed in sweat from head to foot. The sun gradually moved directly overhead and blazed upon the earth like a fierce fire. Little wisps of blue smoke seemed to curl from the people's mouths. Their feet felt heavier and heavier. Eventually the water-wheel seemed like a half-ton rock requiring ever so much effort to press the foot pedals down. Starting upwards from the ankles, the aching of the muscles spread over the whole body, finally reaching the neck. At times, it felt as if a little knife were cutting and scraping the ankles and the legs. It was especially hard for Shaopu, whose tender young body suffered agonies. Uncle Yunpu too — was he not feeling just as tired? His feeble old legs were fatigued through and through before the work had proceeded more than a few minutes. But he refused to show any signs of weakness. If Heaven wanted him to suffer, he had to bear it even if it meant giving up his old life. The morale of his sons depended on his courage. Besides, it was their first day working the water-wheels, and he couldn't afford to set them a bad example by groaning and complaining. He had to bear up no matter how much he was suffering. "Step down hard, Shaopu!" He kept on reminding his younger son, while he himself gritted his teeth and pushed the wheel around. When the pain in his legs was too much for him to bear, he would let his long restrained tears flow, and they would roll down his cheeks mingled with the sweat of his brow.

At long last Mrs. Yunpu arrived with their lunch. The father and sons got off the water-wheel.

"Oh, Heaven, why must you always work against us poor people?" Uncle Yunpu queried, as he lightly massaged his aching legs.

"Mama," Shaopu said to his mother with a woeful face, "my two legs are already useless."

"Never mind, have a good meal now and come back home early this afternoon. With a little rest you'll be all right again."

Shaopu said nothing more. He took up a bowl and filled it full of rice.

Uncle Yunpu and Shaopu were practically cripples after the hard labour of those few days. But Heaven remained as hard-hearted as ever! The water pedalled up each day was only enough to keep the seedlings from dying on that particular day. Liqiu was the strongest of them all. He was not tormented by the aches and sores that bothered his father and brother. But he continued to be indolent and unwilling to exert his strength, as if such labour as the turning of the water-wheels and the working of the fields was not the kind of thing he preferred doing. He was often away from home. When his father wanted him for something, he would have to look all around for him. Uncle Yunpu was therefore doubly vexed with him. "He is a lazy-bones, a rebellious, unfilial good-for-nothing!"

The moon emerged from behind the leafy trees and scattered its sheaves of silvery light. It was no longer as hot as during the day; a gentle breeze whispered through the fields. Besides some women and children, there were very few people sitting leisurely around to get a breath of air.

Taking advantage of the cool moonlit night, people were doing a double amount of work. The splashing of water-wheels mixed with melodious singing could be distinctly heard. To the peasants, summer nights were ideal for field work — no heat or hubbub as during the day.

Uncle Yunpu, again unable to find Liqiu, was as mad as a bull seeing red. At mealtime he had told Liqiu that since it was a fine evening they must plan to put in some night work. He had hoped Liqiu would not go gadding about again. But who would have thought that the lad would again disappear in the twinkling of an eye, leaving Uncle Yunpu fit to burst! Recently several people had come to Uncle Yunpu to tell him that his son, Liqiu, had gone wild, and that they didn't know what he was doing every night running around with Big Lai and his kind. They all advised Yunpu to use a strong hand with his son before something serious happened. Uncle Yunpu had listened. Several times he had become so enraged he could have bit his tongue off. The more he thought about it now, the angrier he got. He went up and down the village calling Liqiu but there was no answer. There wasn't the slightest trace of the boy. Then he told Shaopu to go along ahead, and wait for them at the water-wheel. Even if he couldn't find Liqiu, the two of them would have to get to work and pump some water into the fields. Grinding his teeth with rage he went out again to look for that unfilial son of his.

He made a few more rounds, but there was still no trace of Liqiu. He turned back in disgust. Then suddenly, from the distance he heard their water-wheel turning. Rushing back, he saw that Liqiu and Shaopu were already busily working the wheels. Choking with rage, he was at first unable to utter a word. But after a pause he shouted furiously, "You worthless wretch, where have you been keeping yourself!"

"What? Am I not here working the water-wheel as I should be?" Liqiu replied gravely.

Uncle Yunpu gave him a fierce look and with an oath climbed up on the wheel himself to join in the work.

The moon crept further up over the tree tops and gradually moved towards the west. Slowly, silence took over the fields.

In the east, pearl-white clouds had already made their appearance. A few stars were still lingering in the sky, blinking and twinkling away. The cock had crowed twice. Uncle Yunpu sat up in bed in the dark and sighed deeply after surveying the pale sky. Hard work both day and night had left him feeling as if he simply could not keep it up any longer. His bones and muscles all seemed to ache even in his dreams, but nevertheless he would not relax for a minute nor would he complain about fatigue for fear such weakness would affect his sons.

The demands of livelihood lashed him to toil on night and day. He could blame no one for it. Now at least he had within his grasp a shred of new hope. He could now look forward to the autumn. Perhaps then, he would be able to realize his dreams.

But just now he would have to get up very early. It was still summer, a long time before autumn and that world of his dreams.

His children slept as soundly as piglets. How deep is the

sleep of the young! How he envied them their sweet dreams!
However, for the harvest in autumn, for that dream world of
his, he had to harden his heart and wake his sons even though
the new day had scarcely begun.

"Hey, get up, Liqiu!"

"Shaopu, Shaopu, it's time to get up."

"What is it, Dad? It's not even light yet," muttered
Shaopu stirring in his sleep.

"It's long since daybreak. We must go and work the
water-wheels."

"But we've just fallen asleep. I haven't even had time to
turn over. How can it be daybreak so soon?"

"Liqiu, Liqiu!"

"Get up!"

"Uh, huh. . . ."

"Hey, get up, you laggard!"

Finally Uncle Yunpu had to tweak their ears sharply before
he could get them out of bed.

"What's the matter with you, it's still pitch dark outside!"
said Liqiu, rubbing his eyes and extremely annoyed.

"You lazy-bones, it took me all this time to wake you, and
now you complain about its being too early!"

" 'Get up, get up!' I don't know what we get up in the dark
for. We can toil our lives away, but we'll only be slaving for
others."

"You're just lazy. Who's slaving for others?"

"We are. Isn't it so? Once the rice is threshed, see how
much of it you get."

"Nonsense. I suppose you think a bunch of robbers will
come and take everything? You're a fool, and you're just talking rubbish. You've been doing nothing but gad about outside
lately. You're so irresponsible you neglect everything at home.
You've changed for the worse. People all say you are mixing
with Big Lai and the likes of him all the time. You've probably become what they call a . . . Communist!"

Uncle Yunpu was really angry. He wanted to grab his son by the nape of the neck and give him a good beating to release the pent-up anger within him. His voice grew louder and louder as he fumed and cursed. Mrs. Yunpu was also awakened.

"What are you fussing about in the middle of the night? The children have worked hard all day. You should at least let them sleep a while. Look, it's not even daylight yet."

"It's all your fault, you old witch, produce these good-for-nothing devils."

"Who are you swearing at?"

"It's you I'm cursing. You do nothing but spoil them."

"All right! So you hate them, do you? Then take them out and kill them one by one! Why torture them with slow death? Or else you can sell them all so that they won't be eyesores to you any longer. But why fuss and fume like this in the middle of the night?"

Uncle Yunpu was now in a towering rage. He felt that recently his wife had been unreasonably lenient with the children, to the detriment of their family interests.

"You're crazy. Don't you want to eat? You —"

"What if I am crazy? But you, you sell your own daughter so you can eat. Now perhaps you'll want to sell your sons! Give me back my Yingying. Oh, I simply can't bear to live any longer! Ah — ah —"

Crying and screaming she rushed at Uncle Yunpu. The thought of her daughter Yingying made her hate Yunpu so much that she wanted to scratch his eyes out.

"Why bring up the subject of Yingying? After all we didn't sell Yingying for my sake alone." Uncle Yunpu turned away from her and left the room. For the thought of Yingying brought tears to his eyes no matter how hard he tried to hold them back.

"Give me back my Yingying!"

Dawn was lighting up the east. The sons stood there rooted to the floor listening to the quarrel between their parents.

Mention of their sister also brought tears of pain to their eyes.

The day was again extremely fine. Liqiu nudged Shaopu, and together they trudged out carrying their tools. Uncle Yunpu, looking extremely sorrowful, followed them out of the door.

"Ah — ah —!" The mother's woeful voice trailed out of the inner room after them.

The morning breeze swept across the fields and the luscious green rice seedlings rippled like waves. There was the special coolness of morning in the air.

"Where shall we work today?"

"Let's go in the direction of Huajia Dyke."

5

"Liqiu, you are not pious enough. You'd better not carry it."

"Uncle Yunpu, you carry the canopy, and you, Little Second Scar, beat the gong."

"There is no one to play the flute! Old Wang, where is your instrument?"

"Damn it! Nobody's willing to help! We still need three more sedan-bearers."

"Count me as one, Uncle Big Nose!"

"I'll be one."

"Me too."

"All right, you three be the sedan-bearers. Everyone must wash his face. Little Second Scar, be sure you wash yourself clean. Otherwise the god will feel offended."

"Now sound the gong and start playing the flute."

"Sound the gong, Little Second Scar, don't you hear? What's the matter with you, are you deaf?"

Dong, dong, dong!

A group of people carrying the image of Guan Di made for the fields.

For over twenty days there had not been a single patch of cloud. The ponds and streams near by had all gone dry. The fields lay yawning, criss-crossed with inch-thick cracks. Most of the rice plants were dry and curled up. If this continued for another three or four days everything would be finished.

Guan Di's image had been brought to the village three days before. The villagers had sacrificed an ox and burned a catty and a half of incense for the occasion. But there was still no sign of rain, while more rice plants wilted.

That was why everyone felt there must be a reason for the god's reluctance to send them rain. After a great deal of consultation by those in charge of the prayer for rain, many more libations and entreaties were sent up accompanied by kneeling and koutouing, yet none of this produced any result whatsoever.

"Does this mean everything is finished this year?"

"Don't worry, Uncle Big Nose! Let's carry the god out and let his lordship take a look around. See whether he can bear the heart-rending sight of the fields."

"All right, perhaps the god has not seen the condition of the fields. Three years ago when there was a drought, it started to rain only after we had taken the god out to survey the scene. Yunpu, you go and get a few young people; we also need a gong, a drum and a flute."

"Ah!"

Very soon the provisional troupe was organized; and following the banners, gong, drum and canopy, the green sedan-chair carrying the image of Guan Di was borne aloft on the shoulders of four stalwart men.

Starting from Xindukou and Huajia Dyke, they went as far as Hongmiao and made several rounds of the temple before returning. But the sun was still as hot as fire and the people felt as if they were being roasted. The ground was so hot that one could hardly bear to put his foot down. There seemed to be fire everywhere and the people seemed to be struggling in flames that were enveloping them.

Not a drop of rain rewarded their efforts. Then Guan Di was taken over by the people to the next village. Everywhere people were busy praying for rain.

"Merciful Heaven, we've had a year of flood and a year of drought. Now what exactly do you want of us?"

Suddenly the wind shifted and blew from the northeast, whistling and whining in the tree tops. The stars and moon were gone. Many people stood outside looking at the sky.

"There's lightning over in that direction."

"As the saying goes, 'Lightning in the east; no break in the west.' I doubt if we'll have rain!"

"But that is in the north."

"Good! 'Lightning in the south, opens the fire door; lightning in the north, and the rain will pour!' Tonight there should be some rain. Oh, Heaven!"

"We'll have to depend on the mercy of Heaven."

"Yes. After all, none of us has committed any sins. Why should Heaven wish to see us starve?"

"It's not likely that we will."

Then suddenly came the pattering of rain on the roof amidst the clamour of human voices. There was a coolness in the air and it seemed as if the drops of rain were falling on the happy hopeful hearts.

"This is surely the mercy of Heaven!"

The oppressive weight on the hearts of the people was gradually melted to nothingness by the raindrops. Then a storm broke. Rumbling thunder and blinding flashes of lightning lashed out at the world.

The rain lasted only about twenty-four hours, but it was enough to save the crops. The fields were again replete with water, and the shrivelled blades of rice straightened out once more. They swayed and danced in the wind like young maidens in fluttering gowns. The plants were going through their period of most rapid growth. On every lip was a silent prayer for at least twenty more days of good luck. Then the golden grain would appear and only then could it be considered wealth in hand.

The rain had been heaviest in the southwest; there the sky remained dark and overcast. Again dread welled up in the people's hearts. Too much rain in the southwest made people again apprehensive, this time of flood. The peasants had no peace of mind whatsoever.

The West Stream was gradually swelling as it flowed, and the Dyke Administration sent only a few people to patrol its dykes. There was no need to worry about the West Stream, however, as long as there was no added trouble from the South Stream. It could just go ahead and rise. One day, two days passed and the water continued to rise. Slowly it became nearly level with the dykes. Uncle Yunpu began to worry like everyone else.

"What! How could the West Stream alone rise to such a height!"

The people demanded unanimously, "Hurry, we had better do something about it! What happened last year must not happen again."

The bitter experience of the previous year had taught them that they must take precautionary measures against flood early. Again the strident gongs sounded. Crowds of people carrying hoes and cotton-wadded quilts ran towards the dykes.

"Anyone who doesn't come out to work on the dyke deserves to be dragged out and given a good beating," fumed Uncle Yunpu, so busy that he was sweating all over.

"Even the women must come out. If it turns out like last year, none of us will survive."

"Come, everybody must come and reinforce the dykes!"

Gongs sounded in every village.

In the night, torches and lanterns lit up the dyke, making it look like a long coiling illumined snake. During the day, noisy groups of people gathered here and there in great confusion. The officers from the Local Defence Bureau and their deputies rode around on their horses patrolling the locality. They were, after all, charged with the heavy responsibility of maintaining order. They were afraid that there might be rebels mixed up in the crowd — something they must guard against.

"Those low-down dogs! Acting like lords and bullying people! They live on our grain and do nothing but think of ways to harm us. Every single one of them. . . ."

"I feel like tearing them to pieces. One of these days I'm just going to —"

Most of the people who had suffered at the hands of the Local Defence Bureau men cursed secretly after letting them by. Even after they had gone quite a distance, Liqiu was still making faces at them behind their backs.

The water was still rising, and at places it had already spilt over the dyke. The muddy water, which more than once had robbed the peasants of their lives, was regarded by them with great fear and awe. They watched the water overflowing with the deepest of hatred and dread.

"As long as the South Stream doesn't rush down, it'll be all right," people tried to comfort each other, as they continued to work with hoes and shovels.

The water stopped spilling over.

Suddenly the stream seemed to flow backwards in a few places. As soon as this was noticed a great commotion spread among the people.

"Where does it start flowing the other way?"

"At the mouth of the Lanxi rivulet!"

"Oh, dear! None of us will live through this."

"Oh, Heaven! Is this to be the end of us all?"

"Lord Guan Di, if this year is going to be like last year. . . ."

The water in the South Stream was swelling. The West Stream, encountering a heavier flow from the South Stream, was unable to accommodate it, and the result was a continuous rise in both streams.

The beating of the gong became more frantic. Peal upon peal, it rent the air, awakening again in people's minds the terror and misery of previous disasters. Even the women and children went to the dyke and helped by piling up earth with their hands. Most of the older people like Uncle Yunpu were already on their knees. "Heaven and the all-forgiving Goddess of Mercy! Please, please, let us not have a flood this year."

"Buddha, if you protect us against this flood, we'll act ten plays in your honour."

"Heaven is punishing us!"

After two days and nights of desperate struggle, everybody's eyes were bloodshot and their bodies like cotton wool, they were so tired. The West Stream, however, was no longer at the peak of its turbulence, and with the influx of water from the South Stream, it flowed backwards and retreated a long distance. The South Stream flowed down without resistance.

The water level dropped.

Thousands of hearts which had been pounding with foreboding for days were at last set at ease. The people opened their mouths and breathed a sigh of relief. Shouldering their hoes and quilts, the peasants dragged their limp bodies home. Smiles of victory lit up their faces.

"Hey, Cousin Big Lai, come over for a visit this evening," Liqiu said to Big Lai before they parted at the cross-roads.

6

The burden of life and work weighed down upon the whole village like a heavy yoke. When the rice started to ear up, the peasants worked desperately. The people would be saved if they could only last through the next twenty critical days.

Although there was not a single grain of rice at home, Uncle Yunpu was still all smiles. His heart was at ease. After the two false alarms there was ninety per cent certainty of a good harvest. The rice plants were strong and thick, and the heads seemed sturdy — better than any in the past ten years. To Uncle Yunpu, the world was filled with joy and great expectations.

But he did not indulge in excessive day-dreaming. He simply seized upon the present and estimated what it would be like in twenty days or so. Gazing at the green fields, the big sturdy rice plants and the heads of rice about to turn golden, he could scarcely believe his own eyes, and he wondered whether or not he was dreaming. But there they were, actually standing before his eyes! Real, not imaginary. He was practically in toxi-cated with happiness.

"Ha ha, can life this year really be so wonderful?"

Now he would get some results from the fatigue and hard work of the past. From the time they started sowing up until then, Uncle Yunpu actually had not had a moment's rest. Immediately after the seedlings were planted, there was the drought. Just when they had some rain, there was the threat of flood. Like a pail that went ceaselessly up and down in the well, his heart had thumped and had not known any peace or quiet. He was as flattened out as a dead snake. He had not had one decent, satisfying meal in all that time. Even after Yingying was sold the family still ate thin gruel, to say nothing of the days before that when they had had nothing to eat. He could hardly lift his legs when working in the fields and his body had wasted away to practically nothing but skin and bones. Only after all that fear and privation was Uncle Yunpu privi-leged to see those long ears of rice. How could he feel anything but delighted? The crop could now be considered wealth in hand. He must think over carefully what to do with it.

First they must have a few good meals. The children really were too dreadfully starved, poor things. He must arrange to see that they have a few substantial meals to restore their energy. Then a few piculs of rice could be sold so that they could get a few new clothes. The children were hardly clothed like human beings. They would have a jolly, cheerful Mid-Autumn Festival, pay back all their debts, and save the remainder for the New Year. Of course preparations must be made for the few deficient months next year, and then the new.

He must arrange to have both Liqiu and Shaopu betrothed. Indeed, Liqiu showed every sign of being in need of a wife. Let it be the latter part of next year then. He would get both of them married. The year after that there would be grandsons. He'd be a grandfather!

Everything was all right except that Yingying was missing. Uncle Yunpu's heart ached with sorrow. If he had known that the harvest this year was going to be so good, he would not have sold Yingying for anything. Of all his children, Yingying was his favourite, the one who was always so filial and obedient. Now, he himself had sold dear little Yingying to that old man, Xia, whose face was all covered with beard. She had been taken away in a little boat, but where, Uncle Yunpu had not yet been able to find out.

Yingying's fate was indeed pitiful, poor little thing! They had heard nothing about her since she left. The better the year, the more food they had, the more sorrowfully would Uncle Yunpu think of Yingying. It was all because Yingying had been destined by fate never to have even one decent meal at home. If Yingying had suddenly appeared in front of Uncle Yunpu, he would have taken the poor child to his breast and wept away his sorrow. But it was no longer possible to find Yingying and bring her back. She could never be found again. Only her tiny thin image would remain in Uncle Yunpu's heart, a wound which would never heal.

Except for this one thing, there was nothing but happiness

and joy for Uncle Yunpu. Everything was fine. He told his sons repeatedly that they must not mention Yingying's name. They must not prick his heart and reopen the old wound.

There was no more rice in the house, but Uncle Yunpu was not worried in the least, because he already had a way out. In a fortnight they would be able to really eat. With what he had to show in the field, he was not afraid that people would refuse to lend him a little grain.

Mr. He tried desperately to get people to borrow his grain. He was ready to send eight or ten piculs to anyone and at not such a high price either — only six dollars per picul. Mr. Li also had grain for loan at six dollars per picul and without interest. It was pretty good grain, too.

The people in the village had to eat. They had to try to tide over the next fortnight or so somehow. But no one wanted to borrow grain from Mr. He or Mr. Li. It would be a great pity to do so, because one picul borrowed now would mean three piculs to be returned in less than a fortnight.

It was better to tighten one's belt and get over this fortnight or so without borrowing.

"It's all the doing of landlords! They live by exploiting us. When we were practically starving, they wouldn't lend us an ounce of grain even though we koutoued to them. Now, when the crops in the fields are a certainty, they look all over the place for people to lend their stuff to. For something over ten days they want three piculs for every picul borrowed. If these dogs don't die a premature, painful death, Heaven has no eyes."

"Uncle Big Nose, didn't you borrow grain from him too? Yes, Heaven has no eyes. The more wicked the people, the more prosperous they become."

"You're right! Heaven will not punish them. If we wish to get them punished, we must depend on ourselves to do it."

"How do we depend on ourselves? When you say that, Liqiu, you must have something up your sleeve. Come, tell us what's on your mind."

"I've nothing up my sleeve. But to my way of thinking the grain we reap is ours to eat ourselves; we shouldn't let these parasites have one grain of it. No rent, nor will we pay back what we borrowed. Really, what right do they have to demand things of us?"

"That's child's talk. After all, the land belongs to them," Second Lai said grandiosely, as if lecturing him.

"Belongs to them? Why don't they cultivate their own land then? What sort of land would it be if other people didn't cultivate it for them? Second Lai, you are so dumb! Do you really think the land is theirs?"

"Then whose land is it?"

"Yours and mine. The land belongs to whoever tills it."

"Ha ha, Liqiu, this is the kind of thing they said when there was the Peasants' Association in 1926-27. You fool, ha ha!"

"What are you laughing at, Uncle Big Nose? Are you saying the Peasants' Association was no good?"

"It was good, but they'll chop your head off for saying so. Aren't you scared?"

"What is there to be scared of? As long as we are united and work together, we are stronger than they. Don't you know how it is in Jiangxi Province?"*

" 'Unite and work together' — what you say is right. But — ha!"

After chatting a while, Uncle Big Nose, Second Lai, Shellhead and all the others agreed that what Liqiu said was correct. The Peasants' Association formed in 1927 had been really good, except that it had not lasted long and consequently many

---

* Referring to the revolutionary base in Jiangxi Province, where, under the Workers' and Peasants' Government, the peasants rose against the landlords and distributed the land.

people had suffered. If there was to be another such association, it ought to be formed to last.

"Well, Liqiu, and what about the guns in the Local Defence Bureau?"

"Pooh, when the time comes, couldn't we disarm them?"

Since his eldest son was away from home all day, Uncle Yunpu had to attend to everything himself. There was no more rice in the house, and he had to go over to Mr. Li's to borrow a picul. "You have five or six to feed in your family! Will one picul be enough? Why not take a couple of piculs more?"

"Thank you very much, Mr. Li."

In the end Uncle Yunpu took only one picul. When they needed oil and salt, they could now get them from the store on credit. Tian, the butcher, his face wreathed in smiles, often asked with hypocritical concern, "Brother Yunpu, wouldn't you like some meat for your table?"

"Oh, no! We are still a long way from eating meat."

"Never mind, you just come and get some any time!"

From then on Uncle Yunpu began to feel that he was getting to be quite a somebody. Whoever he met in the street would nod and greet him with a smile. At home things had also begun to improve. There was one thing, however, which marred his happiness; his eldest son had turned out to be such a disappointment. He was never around when there was any work to be done, and Uncle Yunpu had to take care of everything himself. Dashed were all his hopes of enjoying a leisurely old age.

The heads of rice turned more golden by the day, and as they did the smile on Uncle Yunpu's face broadened. He was always busy. He mended the winnow and also the mats for sunning the grain. Then he asked one neighbour to help with the threshing, and another to help bind the straw. He was running around from morning till night, but always smiling. This year his life was really three times better than usual. He could expect to reap at least thirty-four to thirty-five piculs of unhusked rice per picul of seed. This certainly was a good year for the poor.

The year before there had been a flood because the dyke had not been maintained in good repair. This year it was very important to repair the dyke, and make it one foot thicker. Then there would be no need to worry about flood. This was of course the responsibility of the peasants. Men from the Dyke Administration had already long ago come and reminded them of it.

"Cao Yunpu," they had demanded, "you must pay eight dollars fifty-eight cents for dyke repair."

"Of course we must pay up. Only a little more than the price of a picul of rice. I'll bring it to the Administration myself after the harvest. Thanks for coming. It's our duty to pay." Uncle Yunpu replied, smiling. Unless the dykes were repaired, it would not be possible to prevent a flood next year.

The *chia* chief* also came to contact Uncle Yunpu in the name of the director of the Local Defence Bureau. "Uncle Yunpu, you're to pay eight dollars forty cents defence tax this year. The Bureau has already sent down a notice."

"Why so much, Chief?"

"We're collecting for two years' taxes. Did you pay last year?"

"Oh! Last year! All right, I'll send it over by and by."

"There's also a patriotic tax of five dollars seventy-two cents, and an anti-Communist tax of three dollars and seven cents."

"Oh! And what are those taxes for, Chief?"

"Bah, old fossil, you're just an old muddlehead. Are you still in the dark when the Japanese have already reached Beijing? The money will be used to buy arms to save the country and fight the Communist bandits, stupid!"

---

* Head of ten households under the Kuomintang regime.

"I know, I know. I — I'll send it over."

Uncle Yunpu refused to worry, however, he was not one
to let petty sums of money bother him. He would reap a boun-
teous harvest and in four or five days his pockets would be
lined with gold. What was there for him to worry about?

7

Uncle Yunpu now felt more than ever that his disobedient
eldest son was the one great disappointment in his life. Whenever work reached a critical stage, Liqiu could be counted on
to be absent from home. This irritated Uncle Yunpu so that
he would pace the room in fury. He could never find out what
his son was up to outside. The lad would go out early in the
morning and would not come back till after midnight. Their
neighbours had already begun threshing all around them and
their own grain was so ripe and golden that it would fall off by
itself unless it was reaped soon. "That cur, away from home
all day. He doesn't care how urgent the work around here is."

Now he was forced to go out and hire a team of harvesters.
He cursed roundly as he walked towards the main dyke. The
sun was just right. It would indeed be a pity not to get the
grain reaped and threshed. If Liqiu had been home, the father
and sons could have managed as a three-man harvesting team.
But with Liqiu away, Uncle Yunpu had to go to the dyke and
hire harvesters from outside the locality.

Most of these harvesters came from Xiangxiang County
and that vicinity. Carrying their bedding rolls, they would
usually come around in teams of four at the beginning of autumn. They would roam the counties bordering the lake, spe-
cializing in reaping and threshing rice for the local people. Their
wages were not excessive, but it was customary to feed them
fairly well.

Uncle Yunpu soon hired a team, and the four strong men

with their shabby bedding on their shoulders followed him back. By the time they had started to work the sun was already quite high. Uncle Yunpu told Shaopu to stay in the field and supervise the hired men while he himself went around to look for Liqiu.

By dark the grain from an area planted to twenty catties of rice seed had been harvested. He had to pay four strings of cash as wages for the work. And still Liqiu was nowhere to be found. Uncle Yunpu was quite beside himself with rage. The harvest, though, was unprecedentedly bountiful — twelve piculs of unhusked grain from twenty catties of seed. His happiness was marred only by his irritation with his son, who was such a disappointment.

It really was not worthwhile hiring a team of harvesters. Besides the wages, the men devoured bowl after bowl of luscious white rice, the thought of which made Uncle Yunpu's heart sink. When he remembered how in the past they themselves had faced starvation he felt ready to grab Liqiu by the neck and choke him to death. They certainly must not hire harvesters again. Even if he were to depend only on Shaopu's help, he could still manage to get the grain harvested from an area planted with some ten catties of seed at least.

It was quite late but Uncle Yunpu was still wide awake when he heard Liqiu outside whispering softly to someone. Anger again took possession of him. Opening his eyes wide he shouted, "You wastrel! You night-hawk! So you still dare to come back! You neglect everything at home, leaving me, an old man, to struggle along alone. I won't live another day! Today it's either your life or mine! See what you can do against an old grey head!" So saying, he snatched up a stick and rushed at his son in fury. Behind the thrust of the stick lay the force of his resentment at the loss of four strings of cash and all the precious white rice consumed by the harvesters.

"Uncle Yunpu, please don't hold it against him," put in

another voice. "This time it's really because we asked him to help us with some business."

"What sort of business? And what business have you taking him away from his work? You, who are you . . . Cousin Big Lai, don't you know how heavy our work is these days? And he, the scoundrel, just went off like that!" He was furious, that the stick shook violently in his hand.

"You're right of course, Uncle Yunpu, but this time he was really helping us in some very important matter," put in yet another in an attempt to placate the old man.

"So you people connive with him to make me suffer! The chicken knows nothing of the troubles of the duck; do you people understand our affairs?"

"Yes, Uncle, but he is back now, and tomorrow he'll help you in the fields."

"Work in the fields!" Liqiu repeated indignantly. "We'll work ourselves into the grave but we won't even get a square meal for it, while those parasites get everything ready-made. Just you wait and see. We work our fingers to the bone, but will we get anything for it? I made up my mind long ago."

"Who's going to rob you of it, you swine?"

"There are plenty of people who'll rob us. Our bit of grain won't even be enough to go round. We can go on working like this for eight years, ten years but still we won't have anything to show for it."

"You swine, you're just plain lazy and can only talk rubbish. Since you don't want to work for a living, do you think food will drop from heaven for you to eat? How dare you argue with me!"

Once again Uncle Yunpu swung his stick as if to whack the head of his unfilial son.

"Now, now, Liqiu, you mustn't argue any more," put in one of the men. "Uncle, why don't you go and get some rest? But it's true, the world is no longer what it used to be. The peasants simply can't hold up their heads. They know nothing but work from one end of the year to the next, but whatever they reap is sent off to others picul by picul. Taxes, levies, payment for this and payment for that — what is left for themselves? To make matters worse, the market price of grain has been dropping steadily. Unless we think of a way out, we'll be up against it again. That's why we. . . ."

"Nonsense! All my life, I've thought of only one thing — work. All I know is, we must work. Otherwise there will be nothing to eat."

"Yes, Liqiu, listen to what your Dad says. We'll see you later."

After the young people had gone, Liqiu went to sleep with his clothes on. But Uncle Yunpu's mind was uneasy, with an entirely new and strange burden on it.

The day after Liqiu's return, the grain was carried in from the fields in baskets. Fat and yellow, it really resembled gold.

There was not a single person in the village who did not rejoice. This year's harvest was at least thrice better than ordinary. No wonder people smiled and laughed. After all, this rich harvest was the reward for struggling on empty stomachs, for toiling day and night under great stress and worry over a series of calamities.

When people met one another, they smiled and nodded. They commented on the fact that Heaven, after all, was not blind, and would not let the poor people starve. They talked about their past sufferings: flood, drought, bitter work, fear and the pangs of an empty stomach, but now everything was going to be all right.

Trade gradually became brisk in the market. Commodity prices doubled within two or three days while the bottom dropped out of the rice market. Six dollars, four dollars, three dollars . . . the price dropped until it was only a dollar and a half for the best quality, late-crop rice.

"How can it drop like that?"

With the slump in the price of grain, the hopes and joys of

but a few days before were dampened. People's hearts tightened with each drop in price. Furthermore, the rise in commodity prices made life for the peasants no less hard in this year of bumper harvest than in ordinary years, if not more so. This grain, the fruit of their hard struggle, gained at the cost of their sweat and blood — who would be willing to sell it at such a low price?

When Uncle Yunpu first heard the news, he was not very much alarmed. He was dazed by the golden grain so that he could not believe that such wonderful life-saving treasure would not sell for a good price. Even when Liqiu told him that the price of rice continued to drop rapidly, he remained undaunted. His eyes fixed in anger, he shouted, "It's only you bunch of ne'er-do-wells creating alarm by spreading rumours. Only a drop in the price of rice! What is there to get excited about? If nobody wants to pay a good price for rice, can't we keep it and eat it ourselves? If they don't want it, let them all starve."

However, it was one thing to give vent to one's feelings, and quite another to stop the drop in the price of rice. Uncle Yunpu could do nothing about the latter. The news that the late crop was priced at a dollar twenty per picul spread throughout the vast countryside.

"One dollar twenty cents! Only a fool would sell at that price."

Even though the price of rice had dropped so, even if the grain would not bring in a cent, Uncle Yunpu still pushed his sons to work with might and main. After the crop was threshed, the straw had to be dried and the grain spread out to sun. It then went through the winnow and was stored in the barn. By ceaseless toil all day under the fierce rays of the sun, they eventually turned the moist, dirty, rough grains into sturdy, clean, golden grains. He kept assuring himself that he would keep this precious life-saving treasure as food in the house for the next three years rather than sell it at such a low price. The

grain was, after all, everything he had sweated and laboured for
for the past six months.

After the autumn harvest the fields were as devastated as
after a battle. The disordered countryside seemed to have
settled down to take a breath — one uneasy breath before
catastrophe was to destroy it.

8

Liqiu, the eldest son, unalterably opposed to inviting the
landlords to dinner to discuss the rent, stamped out of the house
in disgust. Although Uncle Yunpu felt upset about it, he continued to make preparations for the dinner with the greatest of
care. He believed that at the dinner he would surely earn a
little pity and sympathy from them. Furthermore, he was old,
and in the eyes of his creditors, his age would perhaps merit
some consideration.

A chicken, a duck and two steaming bowls of fat pork!
The dinner was so good that Uncle Yunpu found his own mouth
watering. He changed into a neatly patched suit of clothes and
made Shaopu sweep the front room clean. The sun was not yet
high.

Earlier in the morning, Uncle Yunpu had been to Mr. He's
and Mr. Li's estates. After he had tendered his verbal invitation with as great ceremony as he could master, both Mr. Li and
Mr. He promised to come. Director Chen of the Dyke Administration was also invited, and Mr. He promised to bring along
enough people to fill out the table.

The table was already laid, but the guests had not yet arrived. Uncle Yunpu was standing by the door peering out expectantly when in the distance he saw two lines of dark shadows
moving in his direction. He rushed inside and told Shaopu and
Sixi to stay in the back room. They must not be around to irritate the guests. Once more he wiped the four benches and made

sure that everything was tidy. Then he stood by the door and awaited the arrival of his guests.

There were seven altogether. Besides Messrs. He and Li and Director Chen, each of the landlords brought his book-keeper. There were also two strangers, one with a beard, and the other, a handsome young gentleman.

"Yunpu, you really shouldn't have gone to so much trouble!" said Mr. Li squinting through small beady mouse eyes, his sparse whiskers straggling.

"Not at all, not at all. This is not half good enough. I hope you will excuse such an ordinary meal. I'm too old now, really, to do very much," Uncle Yunpu replied with utmost humility, huddling himself into a small knot and stressing the word "old". His face was fixed in a forced smile.

"We told you not to go to any trouble, but you insisted! Ha ha!" Mr. He laughed, revealing uneven, yellow teeth framed with bloodless lips.

"Oh, Mr. He, this is nothing! It's just to show a tenant's gratitude. Mr. He must pardon any slips."

"Ha ha!"

Director Chen followed with a few added formalities. Then Shaopu started to bring out the food.

"Please help yourselves!"

Chopsticks and spoons were sunk into the food and it was swooped up as in a whirlwind. Uncle Yunpu and Shaopu, who acted as waiters, stood by respectfully on either side, their eyes fixed on the delicacies spread before their guests. Their mouths watered, and they had to swallow hard as they watched the guests chew up great pieces of the fat pork with obvious gusto. Shaopu almost broke down in tears, he was so overcome by his craving for just one little taste. If Uncle Yunpu had not been around, he would have rushed to the table and snatched up a piece of the meat for himself.

For half an hour they stood thus, watching excitedly as if observing a battle. Then all was over. The guests had finished their meal. Shaopu cleared the table and went off to make tea. The guests strolled about a bit, and then gathered around the table again.

His head bowed, Uncle Yunpu stood by the door, waiting respectfully for the guests to begin the conversation.

"Well, Yunpu, now the meal is over, what is it you want to say? You can tell us now."

"Mr. He, Mr. Li and Mr. Chen, I'm sure you know about all my difficulties. I can only beg of you. . . ."

"But this year's harvest is good."

"That's true, Mr. He, it is."

"Then what is it you want to say?"

"I — I want to beg of you. . . ."

"Well, go ahead and say it."

"Honestly, last year was very hard for us, and for the time being we still suffer from it. My family, both old and young, must eat every day. I have no way of making money, but must depend on what I get from the land. I would like to ask Mr. He and Mr. Li. . . ."

"And what is your wish?"

"I can only ask Mr. He to be lenient and cut down on the rent just a little. And I beseech Mr. He to be kind and merciful in regard to the seed rice and beans I borrowed this year and last . . . and Mr. Li, I beg you. . . ."

"Oh, I see. Now I fully understand what you mean. You only want us to collect less grain from you, is that it? But Yunpu, you should also realize that last year everybody suffered from the flood. Perhaps it was harder for us than for you, and therefore harder for us to get over it. Our expenses are at least thirty times greater than yours, but who will earn extra money for us? We have to depend on the rice we collect as rent. As for the beans I loaned you last year, it's hardly right for you to ask me to be merciful now, because those beans actually saved your lives. Wasn't I merciful to have made you

the loan in the first place? How can you have the face to say
you're not willing to pay back the debt?"

"It isn't that I don't want to pay back the debt. But I beg
Mr. He to please be lenient on the interest."

"I know, I know. I certainly can't permit you to suffer in
anyway. But you were not the only person who borrowed
beans. If I let you pay less, other people would also want
to pay less, and that would never do. As for the seed rice,
that certainly is not my business. I was only handling it. It
belonged to the county granary, so how can I make a decision
about that?"

"Yes, of course, I know how it is, Mr. He. But I am getting old. This time I only ask Mr. He and Mr. Li to be specially
charitable. If the harvest is good next year, I certainly will
not hold back anything. Only this time everything depends on
your mercy."

Uncle Yunpu's face wore an extremely pathetic expression,
and a sob rattled in his throat as he talked. Whatever happened, he had to plead and beg and get all he could then and there.
At the very least, he had to beg to be left with enough to feed
and clothe his family for the rest of the year.

"No, nothing doing. In ordinary years I might be a little
lenient, but this year I simply can't. If everyone was going to
be as troublesome as you, what would happen? Besides, I
haven't the time to bother with them all. Still, I am sorry for
you. I cannot let you suffer. How much will you have left in
your hands after paying your debts and taxes? Why not give
me the figures and let me see."

"It couldn't be that Mr. He doesn't already know the figures. The rice I reaped came to one hundred and fifty piculs
in the husk, from which Mr. Li will demand payment, Mr.
Chen must be paid, and from which must also be deducted the
money for the Local Defence Bureau, the taxes. . . ."

"How did it happen you reaped so little?"

"That's all. I swear it."

"Then let me do some calculations for you."

Mr. He then turned and called to his bookkeeper who was wearing a blue gown, "Dixin, please calculate the amount of rent and money Yunpu owes me."

"Master, the figures are at hand. The money he owes for rent, the seed rice and the beans borrowed, plus interest, come to one hundred and three piculs five pecks and six pints of grain altogether. We price Yunpu's grain at a dollar thirty-six a picul."

"Well, Mr. Li, how about you?"

"Not more than thirty piculs I should think."

"About ten piculs to the Dyke Administration," added Director Chen.

"Then Yunpu, you are still not in the red. What are you being so troublesome about?"

"Please, Mr. He, what's to be left for my family to eat! There're also the taxes to pay. Please, Mr. He, I must beg of you to be merciful."

Tears were streaming down Uncle Yunpu's face. As a last resort he would try to arouse the pity of his creditors by begging until the bitter end. He finally went down on his knees before them and kowtowed several times, knocking his head on the ground as if he were worshipping Buddha.

"Please, Mr. He and Mr. Li, you must save this old skin of mine."

"Uh! Uh . . . all right, Yunpu, I promise you. But you must not keep back a single kernel of the grain you owe me for the rent and debt. When you find it really hard to manage in the future, I'll again lend you some grain to feed your family. Furthermore, you must send in your grain by tomorrow. One day's delay and I shall have to charge one day's interest, four and a half per cent; don't forget, four and a half per cent!"

"Oh, Mr. He!"

Early the next morning, Uncle Yunpu, his eyes full of tears,

woke Shaopu, and together they opened the door of the barn. Mr. Li's and Mr. He's hired hands were waiting outside. This showed how considerate they were. They were afraid that Uncle Yunpu could not manage to transport so much grain in one day by himself and had sent their own hired hands over to help carry it.

Golden, sturdy grain was measured picul by picul and taken from the barn. Uncle Yunpu felt a thousand sharp knives stabbing his heart. Tears rolled down his cheeks and his whole body shook. Yingying's tear-stained face, his aching muscles, the burning sun, the storming flood, Mercy Powder, tree bark — memories of all these miseries crowded into his mind.

The hired hands had already slung their carrying poles, which balanced two baskets of rice each, onto their shoulders. Turning back, they said to Uncle Yunpu, "Let's go."

It took all Uncle Yunpu's strength to heave a pole up onto his shoulder. The grain seemed to weigh a thousand catties, and sweat poured down his face. He glared with hatred towards the estate of Mr. He as he stepped out of his own door. He had taken only a few steps before he felt as if he were treading on nails. He wanted to put down his load and rest a moment. His head was swimming, and the ache in his heart was too much to bear.

"Oh, Heaven!" he shrieked as he fell to the ground, spilling all his grain.

"Shaopu, Shaopu, your Dad has fainted."

"Dad, Dad, oh, Dad!"

"Yunpu, Yunpu!"

"Mama, Mama, come quick, something's happened to Dad."

Mrs. Yunpu flew out of the house and they carried Uncle Yunpu to the foot of the stage. She massaged his limbs gently.

"Where does it hurt?"

"Huh. . . ."

Uncle Yunpu didn't open his eyes. Nonetheless the hired

hands carried off the grain basket by basket. As they tramped
past the place where Uncle Yunpu lay, their footsteps pounded
upon Yunpu's heart. Blood oozed from his mouth.

Just then, the *chia* chief burst in with a committeeman and
two armed soldiers. They were followed by five or six men
with baskets and carrying poles.

"What's happened? Is Yunpu ill?"

Shaopu walked over to greet them, "No, he just did a bit
of work and had a stroke!"

"Oh!"

"Yunpu, Yunpu!"

"What is it, Chief?" Shaopu asked in his father's stead.

"We're collecting the taxes. The anti-Communist tax, the
patriotic tax and the defence tax. Altogether your Dad owes
seventeen dollars and nineteen cents, which, computed in grain,
is 14.303 piculs priced at a dollar twenty per picul."

"Oh! When must you have it?"

"We'll take it right away."

"Oh! Oh!"

Shaopu looked at his Dad lying prostrate there, then he
turned to the soldiers and the *chia* chief, at a complete loss. Mr.
He's and Mr. Li's hired hands had jumped into the barn and
were measuring out the grain themselves and taking it away.
The *chia* chief quickly pushed in also.

"Come!"

The men with the baskets swarmed in, ready to share in
the loot.

"Are they all robbers then?" Shaopu's head cleared, and
a great indignation filled his heart. Blood rushed to his eyes
as he stared at them, and rage swept over him. He simply could
not understand why the grain they had reaped by hard labour
was given to other people to be carried away by the picul. And
such beastly, unreasonable people at that! He grated his teeth.
So intense was his desire to grab one of these robbers and give

him a good beating that he was restrained only by the threatening glares of the armed soldiers standing by.

"Oh, oh. . . ."

"Dad, are you feeling better?"

"Oh!"

Within half an hour the hired hands were all gone. Then the *chia* chief slowly stepped out of the barn and, with his eyes on the committeeman, said, "It's all gone. He and Li took the rent and the dues for the Dyke Administration and that left us short 3.35 piculs for the taxes."

"Then give him three days to have the shortage brought to town. You notify him."

"Shaopu, remember to tell your Dad that he's short 3.35 piculs for taxes. He must send it to the Bureau himself within three days, otherwise soldiers will come to arrest him," the *chia* chief said fiercely.

"Uh!"

Shaopu watched them disappear through hazy eyes, then turned towards the barn. There was nothing left but the thin bare boards of the floor. He felt dizzy, the whole world was going in circles.

"Oh, oh!"

"Dad, oh, Dad!"

9

Liqiu came back very late that night.

"So there really are robbers who pilfer grain, just as I said." Uncle Yunpu had been conscious only part of the time. He took Liqiu's wrist in a tight grip and said tremulously, "Liqiu, where is our grain? This year, this year, we've had an unusually rich harvest."

Liqiu's heart was heavy. He set his teeth, and in an effort to comfort his father, said, "Never mind, Dad, why feel so bad? Didn't I tell you it would happen like this? Sooner or later there's going to be a day of reckoning, but we mustn't allow ourselves to be fooled again. Most of the people in the village have already decided not to pay any rent or taxes. There's no doubt but that it will lead to a real struggle. Tonight I must go to a meeting."

"Ah!"

Uncle Yunpu felt as if he had been through a horrible nightmare. It was beginning to dawn on him why his son Liqiu had been away from home so much. The thought of the Peasants' Association formed in 1926-27 suddenly came to him. With great effort he opened his eyes and with a wan smile said haltingly, "Well, good, good! You go then. And I hope Heaven will bless you."

May 1933
From *Chinese Literature*

About the Author

YE ZI (1912-39), one of the young Chinese writers of the 1930s whose real name was Yu Hecun, was born into a revolutionary family in Yiyang County, Hunan Province. His father was the secretary of the county's peasant association and his sister was a leader of the women's movement. Under their influence, Ye Zi also did revolutionary propaganda work while still at middle school. After the Northern Expeditionary Army captured Wuhan in 1926, he went to Wuhan and entered the Third Branch College of the Wuhan Military Academy run by the Northern Expeditionary Army. After Chiang Kai-shek's betrayal of the revolution on April 12, 1927, Ye Zi's father and sister were both arrested and killed by the Kuomintang reactionaries. Ye Zi fled his hometown and went to Nanjing, Shanghai and other places, where he earned his living as an army soldier, a primary school teacher and an editor in a newspaper office. He started literary writing by taking part in the New Literature Movement in 1933 in Shanghai. The same year he joined the Chinese Communist Party and published his short stories "Harvest" and "Outside the Barbed Wire Entanglement". His short novel *Stars* appeared in 1936. He died of illness in 1939.

"Harvest" was Ye Zi's first short story. With the nationwide anti-rent movement of the peasants that swept the country following the failure of the First Revolutionary Civil War in 1927 as its theme, the story describes how the tenant peasants of Hunan are aroused to revolt and resist the landlords' cruel exploitation and oppression. This story reveals that only under the leadership of the Communist Party could the poor peasants win their struggles against the landlord class.

A Moonlit Night

Ba Jin

Li's boat was waiting to set sail for the city.

A round moon rose slowly above the mountains and cast its beams on the shore of the river. It was a small river in the darkness at the foot of a mountain. Shimmering in the moonlight, the water flowed gently. The moonlight floated along its surface as if wanting to meander with it into the Yangtze. Second by second the darkness faded, but it still was a net that covered everything. The mountains, the trees, the river, the fields, the houses — all were enmeshed in it. Though soft and pliant, the moonlight could not seep through its holes.

Extending into the river was a stone jetty, and beside it Li's boat was moored. The boat was surrounded by thickly growing water-lilies. Many purple flowers were in blossom. The leaves pressed against the prow.

An oil lamp gleamed feebly inside the boat. From the shore it looked like a sleeping craft hidden in the dark shadows. No voices could be heard; it was like a deserted isle. But there were indeed people on board.

Two passengers were lying in the canopied cabin. A small boy sat dozing in the prow. Li, the boatman, sat in the stern, peacefully smoking. No one spoke; it was as if too much had been said already and nothing new could be added. They all knew the schedule well. The passengers were regular customers. Every evening at dusk the boat sailed to the city, and returned the following morning. This fixed routine seldom varied. Regular passengers took the boat several times a week, always arriving at the same hour. Without saying much they would lie down in the cabin and sleep, awakening just as the boat was reaching the city. Sometimes they would go ashore there, sometimes a few would take the small steamer to the provincial capital. The younger passenger tonight was the village schoolteacher. His home was in the city. He returned there every Saturday night. The older man, a salesclerk in a shop in the city, lived in the village. His boss often sent him to the provincial capital on business.

Moonlight on the prow combed the tousled hair of the little boy. He seemed unaware of this. He only slowly moved his head from side to side. His eyes were closed wearily. But once in a while he would open them suddenly and stare at the path along the shore, or look at the water. When he saw that nothing was stirring, he would mutter something to himself and again doze off.

"Strange. Why isn't Gensheng here yet?" the schoolteacher asked in a low voice, as he rolled over in the cabin. He looked towards the prow then, opening the small port-hole beside him, put his head out.

All was exceedingly still. No lamps shone. The clan temple on the shore was also asleep. The path lay flat and extended in the moonlight. No feet walked upon it. Just outside the port-hole and very close to the teacher's head many purple lilies were blooming.

He drew back into the cabin and closed the port-hole. Wang Sheng, the salesclerk, shouted to the boatman:

"Do you know what time it is, Li? Why don't we sail?"

"Gensheng isn't here yet. It's still early. What are you worried about?" Li replied from the stern.

"He always comes at seven. But tonight —" the schoolteacher inserted. He felt for his watch, then pushed open the port-hole to look at it. "— Tonight it's already seven-forty. He's not coming."

"Yes, he is. He's sure to come. He's got some things to take into the city." The boatman was positive. "Mr. Jun, don't worry. Mr. Wang, you're an old passenger. I meet the small steamer every day and I've never missed it yet — you know that."

Mr. Jun, the teacher, said: "Gensheng has never been late before. He always comes very early. Now he's making us wait."

"Maybe something's delaying him," suggested Wang Sheng, the salesclerk, crossing his right ankle over his left.

"There couldn't be. I know him. He doesn't smoke opium and he doesn't drink. Nothing's delaying him. He'll be here soon." The boatman walked slowly along the edge of the boat to the prow. "Lin," he called. The little boy who had been dozing immediately rose to his feet.

Li glanced at him, then stepped on to the stone jetty. Taking a few steps along the shore, he returned. The full moon hung directly in front of him. Its silvery beams, like cool water, bathed his head refreshingly.

Near the banian tree beside the clan temple, a dark shadow emerged.

"Gensheng is coming," Li said to himself. "Get ready," he instructed the child. "We're going to sail the moment Gensheng gets here."

The child murmured an assent. Putting one end of a long bamboo pole into the water, he leaned on it, bringing the boat around flush with the shore.

Li stood on the stone jetty. The dark figure came closer. He saw that the man, who was carrying a small wicker hamper, was quite short. He wasn't Gensheng. His name was Zhang. The proprietor of a little village general store, Zhang was also going to the city tonight.

"So you haven't sailed yet?" Zhang hastened on to the jetty and smiled at Li.

"You're just in time. We're waiting for Gensheng." There was a note of anxiety in Li's voice.

"Eight o'clock. He's certainly not coming," the teacher shouted from the cabin.

"It's odd that he's still not here. He usually comes on board very early." Zhang stepped into the boat. Placing his hamper to one side, he sat down on the deck and lit a cigarette. He smoked slowly, facing the moonlight.

"Hey, Li, is Gensheng there?" A bob-haired woman in a black muslin tunic and trousers approached barefoot along the shore. She hailed Li from the jetty.

"Everyone's waiting for Gensheng tonight. He must be hiding. You ought to know where he is," Li said reproachfully.

"You mean he hasn't come?" the woman demanded anxiously.

"Not even his shadow!"

"You're not kidding, are you? I'm worried." The woman sounded quite upset.

"Who's kidding? I haven't the time. What I want to know is — Is your husband taking this boat tonight or not?" Li's expression was serious.

Uttering an anguished cry, the woman turned and ran.

"Wait, sister, wait!" called Li. What was wrong with her?

The woman ran, heedless, along the shore, weeping and calling Gensheng's name.

The sound of her shouts made Li very uncomfortable. He stood on the jetty woodenly.

"What's the matter?" asked the three passengers, startled. Zhang could see fairly clearly. The salesclerk crawled to the end of the cabin for a look. The teacher again opened the porthole and poked his head out.

"The devil only knows," Li grumbled, turning away.

"Husband and wife probably had a spat, and Gensheng

left her in a huff. It must have been like that," Zhang surmised. "And people say a husband's lot is a happy one. Ha-ha!" He flicked his cigarette butt into the water and spat. Then he laughed again.

"Gensheng never quarrels with his wife. It must be something else. I'm sure," Li said gravely. He was puzzled. What could it be?

"Gensheng, Gensheng!" The woman's piercing calls flew through the night, flew far into the distance, one pursuing the other, each more tragic than the next, all trembling with despair.

"Well, Li, how about it?" the teacher rolled over and shouted. He shut the port-hole. No one answered him.

"Let's sail," the salesclerk urged impatiently. He was afraid he'd miss the small steamer to the provincial capital.

Still listening to the woman's cries, Li was growing more disturbed by the minute. Instead of answering his passenger, he stood motionless on the jetty, listening to the woman calling for her husband. "This won't do," he suddenly said to himself. "She's out of her mind." He quickly jumped ashore and ran along the path.

The child who had been dozing in the prow, leaped up and raced after him. "Papa, where are you going?"

Li kept running. He didn't reply. The child's voice at once faded, without leaving even a small scar in the air. The air was occupied by the woman's unhappy shouts. One strip, another, new, old. The moonlight seemed composed of them. They trembled unceasingly, those heart-breaking cries. It was as if a vibrant life was being destroyed — torn to shreds, strip by strip, bit by bit.

Three people ran upon the muddy path. The woman, the boatman, the child, each chasing the other. Then the child stopped and turned back.

The boat still lay by the jetty. The three passengers came out and sat in the prow. They discussed Gensheng curiously.

But it was all guesswork. Each used his imagination to the utmost. The conversation became lively.

The tragic cries of the woman grew softer, then stopped. Li caught up with her beneath a tree. She sat leaning against it exhaustedly, her hair awry, her face streaked with tears, her eyes staring at the grove of trees on the opposite shore. Weeping softly, she looked like a ghost.

"What's the matter with you, sister, are you crazy? Whatever's troubling you — tell me!" Li shouted, seizing her by the arms and shaking her.

Raising her head, Gensheng's wife stopped weeping. She stared at him with large black eyes as if she didn't recognize him. After a long time, she finally said mournfully, "Gensheng, Gensheng. . . ."

"What about Gensheng? Speak up," Li pressed.

"I don't know," the woman said vaguely.

"Pei!" Li spat disgustedly. "You don't know. Then why are you crying? You're mad!"

"They must have arrested him. They've arrested him for sure!" she shouted wildly, a look of terror coming into her face.

"Arrested him? Who? You say someone's arrested Gensheng?" Li asked, frightened. His heart pounded. Gensheng was his friend. He's an honest man, Li thought. Why should anyone want to arrest him?

"It's Tang Xifan's work. It must be!" the woman said, weeping. "Yesterday Gensheng told me that Tang had gone to the county magistrate and accused him of being in league with bandits. I didn't believe it. But when Gensheng went out this afternoon, someone saw some of Tang's men following him. There were a lot of them, and a detective. Gensheng hasn't been home since. I'm sure they've arrested him."

"That Tang is a money gouging old bastard. But what has he got against Gensheng? You must be wrong, sister. Did you see anybody grab him with your own eyes?" Li roughly consoled her. His tone was not so harsh as it had been a moment before.

"Wrong? Just because you don't believe it! Tang lost his job as township chief and he's in a terrible rage. He sent a man to kill Mr. Ping. But not only did he fail to kill Mr. Yi, his job as township chief was taken away! A few day ago Gensheng and Mr. Ping's brother organized some kind of peasants' union to fight him. I pleaded with Gensheng not to set himself against that old bastard, but he wouldn't listen. All day long he's been ranting about overthrowing the bad landlords and wicked gentry. Now he's finished. Even if they don't cut off his head, they'll never let him come home alive. In league with the bandits — that's a capital crime!"

"I don't believe Tang's all that tough," muttered Li.

"He's got money. The county magistrate is his good friend. He listens to Tang!" Gensheng's wife gradually recovered. Her voice grew louder and her eyes shot sparks. Anger overrode her distress. "Even a good man like Mr. Ping, he wants to murder. . . . Have you forgotten Aliu? His case and Gensheng's are exactly the same." Again a look of fear came to her face.

Li was silent. Yes, he remembered what happened to Aliu well. Aliu was an honest fellow. During the busy farming seasons, he worked as a hired hand. At other times, he earned his living as a porter. Once he didn't want to pay an extra tax on his carrying-pole and, with a few other porters, marched down to Tang's place and raised a row. Tang was in charge of collecting this tax. Two days later the county police arrested Aliu. He was given fifteen years on suspicion of being in league with the bandits. When Aliu was arrested, he was carrying a load to Li's boat. Li saw it all clearly. An honest fellow who had never done any wrong, yet the county magistrate said he was in league with the bandits. What was the world coming to! Li believed Gensheng's wife now.

His face fell. A heavy stone seemed to be pressing on his heart. Clasping his hands, he pondered. But he couldn't think of any solution. His head began to ache. Many things flashed through his mind. He was very confused. Seizing the woman's arm, he commanded: "Get up, quick. If Gensheng's been nabbed we have to think of how to save him. What's the good of you sitting there, crying?" He pulled her to her feet. They walked quickly down the path along the river.

Before they had gone very far, they saw the little boy running towards them. He was running very fast, crying, "Papa," an awful expression on his face. "Gensheng. . . ." Grasping his father's arm, he could say no more.

"Where is he?" the woman demanded in a trembling voice. She rushed up to the child and shook him.

"Speak, Lin, what is it?" Li was also very agitated. He had a frightful premonition.

The boy's head was drenched with sweat. His small face was terrified. "Gensheng . . ." he stammered. "He's. . . ." Pulling them both by the hand, he ran.

In a grassy hollow near the shore, the three passengers were squatting. The hollow was much lower than the path. The child was the first to reach it. "Papa, look! . . ." he shouted, badly scared.

Gensheng's wife uttered a wild scream and ran forward. Li followed.

Purple water-lilies bloomed in profusion along the shore. Kneeling in the grass, the teacher separated the water plants with his hands. A swollen body lay quietly in the water. The black muslin clothes were hooked on a tree root. There was a hole in the back of the tunic, slightly to the left.

"Gensheng," the woman wailed, throwing herself down and embracing the body. She wept as though her heart would break.

"He's finished." The teacher turned his head and spoke sadly to Li in a low voice.

"They must have shot him first," said the salesclerk. "Look at the blood."

"Let's haul him out of there," the small proprietor proposed.

Li sighed heavily. Tightly gripping his son's shivering arms, he stared at the water.

The cries of Gensheng's wife smote the air without cease, like the shreds and pieces of a shattered heart. They permeated the moonlit night. The air, the ground, the water — all seemed to be crying — every tree, every blade of grass, every flower, every water-lily.

Quietly, the village, the small river, lay in the moonlight. The whole countryside seemed to be weeping in this tragic atmosphere, with no exception. In everyone's eyes were tears.

It was a beautiful moonlit night. There was no wind or rain. But Li's boat, which never missed the steamer before, missed it for the first time that night.

1933
Translated by Sidney Shapiro

About the Author

BA JIN is the pen name of Li Feigan, who was born in Chengdu, Sichuan Province, in 1904. His father served for some time as a county prefect. In his childhood, Ba Jin studied at home with a private tutor. As he grew older, he was deeply influenced by the socialist concepts then spreading in China, especially those of the utopian socialists.

In 1920 he entered the Sichuan Provincial Foreign Languages School and studied English. At the same time he served as editor on a number of magazines, such as *Fortnightly*, which were propagating the new ideas. In 1923, he went to study in Shanghai where he wrote *Fog, Rain,* and *Lightning* — three parts of a novel entitled *Love* — and *The Family* and *Spring* — the first two parts of another trilogy novel called *Turbulent Currents*.

In the autumn of 1933 in Beijing, he became a member of the editorial board of *Literature*, a quarterly magazine. In November of the following year, he went to Japan. He returned to Shanghai

in 1935 and took up the duties of editor-in-chief of the Cultural Life Press.

When the war with Japan broke out in 1937, Ba Jin, together with Mao Dun and other progressive writers, published in Shanghai such magazines as *Outcry* and *Beacon*. Later, he was active in literary affairs in many places in southwest China and continued writing. He completed *Autumn* — the last part of his *Turbulent Currents* trilogy, and a long novel called *Fire*. In addition, he translated Turgenev's *Father and Son* and *Virgin Soil*. After victory, in 1946, he again went to Shanghai to resume his work as editor of the Cultural Life Press.

Shanghai was liberated from the Kuomintang in 1949 and Ba Jin was elected to the People's Political Consultative Conference. In 1950 he was sent to Warsaw as a delegate to the Second World Peace Conference. He went to Korea both in 1952 and 1953, where he lived with the troops and wrote many pieces about the Korean war. In 1954 Ba Jin was elected as a deputy to the first session of the National People's Congress.

From 1958 to 1962, Beijing People's Literature Press published *Works of Ba Jin* in instalments, fourteen volumes altogether, including his complete works written from 1927 to 1946. He stopped writing during the "cultural revolution" due to persecution by Lin Biao and the gang of four. After the fall of the gang of four, he was elected as a deputy to the fifth session of the National People's Congress. Now he is vice-chairman of the All-China Federation of Literature and Art and chairman of the Shanghai branch of the Union of Chinese Writers.

A Moonlit Night is a story about a peasant, who resolutely takes part in the struggle against the local tyrants and evil gentry with other members from the peasants' association. Finally he is murdered by the enemy.

Crescent Moon

Lao She

Yes, I've seen the crescent moon again — a chill sickle of pale gold. How many times have I seen crescent moons just like this one, how many times. . . . It stirred many different emotions, brought back many different scenes. As I sat and stared at it, I recalled each time I had seen it hanging in the blue firmament. It awakened my memories like an evening breeze blowing open the petals of a flower that is craving for sleep.

*   *   *

The first time, the chill crescent moon really brought a chill. My first recollection of it is a bitter one. I remember its feeble pale gold beams shining through my tears. I was only seven then — a little girl in a red padded jacket. I wore a blue cloth hat Mama had made for me. There were small flowers printed on it. I remember. I stood leaning against the doorway of our small room, gazing at the crescent moon. The room was filled with the smell of medicine and smoke, with Mama's tears, with Papa's illness. I stood alone on the steps looking at the moon. No one bothered about me, no one cooked my supper. I knew there was tragedy in that room, for everyone said Papa's illness was. . . . But I felt much more sorry for myself. I was cold, hungry, neglected.

I stood there until the moon had set. I had nothing; I couldn't restrain my tears. But the sound of Mama's weeping

drowned out my own. Papa was silent; a white cloth covered
his face. I wanted to raise the cloth and look at him, but I didn't
dare. There was so little space in our room, and Papa occupied
it all.

Mama put on white mourning clothes. A white robe without stitched hems was placed over my red jacket. I remember
because I kept breaking off the loose white threads along the
edges. There was a lot of noise and grief-stricken crying,
everyone was very busy; but actually there wasn't much to be
done. It hardly seemed worth so much fuss. Papa was placed
in a coffin made of four thin boards; the coffin was full of
cracks. Then five or six men carried him out. Mama and I
followed behind, weeping. I remember Papa; I remember his
wooden box. That box meant the end of him. I knew unless I
could break it open I'd never see him again. But they buried
it deep in the ground in a cemetery outside the city wall. Although I knew exactly where it was, I was afraid it would be
hard to find that box again. The earth seemed to swallow it like
a drop of rain.

*   *   *

Mama and I were both wearing white gowns again the next
time I saw the crescent moon. It was a cold day, and Mama
was taking me to visit Papa's grave. She had bought some gold
and silver "ingots" made of paper to burn and send to Papa in
the next world. Mama was especially good to me that day.
When I was tired, she carried me piggy-back; at the city gate
she bought me some roasted chestnuts. Everything was cold,
only the chestnuts were hot. Instead of eating them, I used them
to warm my hands.

I don't remember how far we walked, but it was very, very
far. It hadn't seemed nearly so far the day we buried Papa,
perhaps because a lot of people had gone with us. This time there
was only Mama and me. She didn't speak. I didn't feel like
saying anything either. It was very quiet out there. On that
yellow dirt road there wasn't a breath of sound.

It was winter, and the days were short. I remember the grave — a small mound of earth. There were some brown hills in the distance, with the sunlight slanting on them. Mama seemed to have no time for me. She set me down on the side and embraced the head of the grave and wept. I sat holding the hot chestnuts. After crying a while, Mama burned the paper ingots. The ashes swirled before us in little spirals, then lazily settled back on the ground. There wasn't much wind, but it was very cold.

Mama began to cry again. I thought of Papa too, but I didn't cry for him. It was Mama's pitiful weeping that brought tears to my eyes. I pulled her by the hand and said, "Don't cry, Mama, don't cry." But she sobbed all the harder and hugged me to her bosom.

The sun was nearly set and there wasn't another person in sight. Only Mama and me. That seemed to scare Mama a little. With tears in her eyes she led me away. After we had walked a while, she turned and looked back. I did too. I couldn't tell Papa's grave from the others any more. There were nothing but graves on the hillside. Hundreds of small mounds, right to the foot of the hill. Mama sighed.

We walked and walked, sometimes fast, sometimes slow. We still hadn't reached the city gate when I saw the crescent moon again. All around us was darkness and silence. Only the crescent moon gave off a cold glow. I was worn out. Mama carried me. How we got back to the city I don't know. I only remember hazily that there was a crescent moon in the sky.

*　　　*　　　*

By the time I was eight, I had learned how to take things to the pawnshop. I knew that if I didn't come back with some money, Mama and I would have nothing to eat that night — Mama would never send me except as a last resort. Whenever she handed me a small package it meant there wasn't even thin gruel in the bottom of our pot.   Our pot was often cleaner than a neat young widow.

One day I was sent to the pawnshop with a mirror. This seemed to be the only thing we could spare, though Mama used it every day. It was spring, and our padded clothes had just been placed in hock. I knew how to be careful. Carrying the mirror, I walked carefully but quickly to the pawnshop. It was already open.

I was afraid of that pawnshop's big red door, afraid of its high counter.   Whenever I saw that door, my heart beat fast. But I'd go in just the same, even if I had to crawl over the high door-sill. Taking a grip on myself, I would hand up my package and say loudly, "I want to pawn this." After getting my money and the pawn ticket, I would hold them carefully and hurry home.   I knew Mama would be worried.

But this time they didn't want the mirror. They said I should add another item to it. I knew what that meant. Putting the mirror in my shirt, I ran home as fast as my legs could carry me. Mama cried; she couldn't find anything else to pawn. I had always thought there were a lot of things in our little room. But now, helping Mama look for a piece of clothing to raise some money on, I saw that we didn't have much at all.

Mama decided not to send me to the pawnshop again, but when I asked her, "Mama, what are we going to eat?" she cried and gave me her silver hairpin. It was the last bit of silver she had left. She had taken it out of her hair several times before, but she had never been able to part with it. Grandma had given it to her when she got married. Now Mama gave it to me — her last bit of silver — to pawn together with the mirror.

I ran with all my might to the pawnshop, but the big door was already shut tight. Clutching the silver hairpin, I sat down on the steps and cried softly, not daring to make too much noise. I looked up at the sky. Ah, there was the crescent moon shining through my tears again.

I wept for a long time. Then Mama came out of the shadows and took me by the hand. Oh, what a nice warm hand. I forgot all my troubles, even my hunger and disappointment. As long as Mama's warm hand was holding mine, everything was all right.

"Ma," I sobbed, "let's go home and sleep. I'll come again early tomorrow morning."

Mama didn't say anything. After we had walked a while I said, "Ma, you see that crescent moon? It hung crooked just like that the day Pa died. Why is it always so slant?"

Mama remained silent. But her hand trembled a little.

*   *   *

All day long, Mama washed clothes for people. I wanted to help her, but there wasn't any way I could do it. I would wait for her; I wouldn't go to sleep until she finished. Sometimes, even after the crescent moon had already risen, she would still be scrubbing away. Those smelly socks, hard as cowhide, were brought in by salesmen and clerks from the shops. By the time Mama finished washing the "cowhide" she never had any appetite.

I would sit beside her, looking at the moon, watching the bats flit through its rays, like big triangular water-chestnuts flashing across beams of silver then quickly dropping into the darkness again.

The more I pitied Mama, the more I loved the crescent moon. Gazing at it always eased my heart. I loved it in the summer most of all. It was always so cool, so icy. I loved the faint shadows it cast upon the ground, though they never lasted very long. Soft and hazy, they soon vanished, leaving the earth especially dark and the stars especially bright and the flowers especially fragrant. Our neighbours had many flower bushes. Blossoms from a tall locust tree used to drift into our courtyard and cover the ground like a layer of snow.

*   *   *

Mama's hands became hard and scaly. They felt wonderful when she rubbed my back. But I hated to trouble her, because her hands were all swollen from the water. She was thin too; often she couldn't eat a thing after washing those stinking socks. I knew she was trying to think of a way out. I knew. She used to push the pile of dirty clothes to one side and become lost in thought. Sometimes she would talk to herself. What was she planning? I couldn't guess.

*   *   *

Mama told me to be good and call him "Pa" — she had found me another father. Mama didn't look at me when she told me this. There were tears in her eyes, and she said, "I can't let you starve!"

Oh, so it was to keep me from starving that she found me another Pa? I didn't understand much, and I was a little afraid. But I was kind of hopeful too — maybe we really wouldn't go hungry any more.

What a coincidence! As we were leaving our tiny flat, a crescent moon again hung in the sky. It was brighter and more frightening than I had ever seen it before. I was going to leave the small room I had grown so accustomed to. Ma sat in a red bridal sedan-chair. Ahead of her marched a few tootling musicians who played very badly. The man and I followed behind. He held me by the hand. The crescent moon gave off faint rays that seemed to tremble in the cool breeze.

The streets were deserted except for stray dogs that barked at the musicians. The sedan-chair moved very quickly. Where was it going? Was it taking Mama outside the city, to the cemetery? The man pulled me along so fast I could hardly catch my breath. I couldn't even cry. His sweating palm was cold, like a fish. I wanted to call "Ma!" but I didn't dare. The crescent moon looked like a large half-closed eye. In a little while, the sedan-chair entered a small lane.

*   *   *

During the next three or four years I somehow never saw the crescent moon.

My new Pa was very good to me. He had two rooms. He and Ma lived in the inner room; I slept on a pallet in the outside one. At first I still wanted to sleep with Mama, but after a few days I began to love "my" little room. It had clean whitewashed walls, a table and a chair. They all seemed to belong to me. My bedding was thicker and warmer, too.

Mama gradually put on some weight. Colour came back to her cheeks, and the scales left her hands. I hadn't been to the pawnshop in a long time. My new father let me go to school. Sometimes he even played with me. I don't know why I couldn't bring myself to call him "Pa" — I liked him a lot.

He seemed to understand. He used to just grin at me. His eyes looked very nice then. Mama would privately urge me to call him "Pa". I didn't really want to be stubborn. I knew it was because of him that Mama and I had food to eat and clothes to wear. I understood all that.

Yes, for three or four years I don't recall seeing the crescent moon; maybe I saw it and don't remember.

But I can never forget the crescent moon I saw when Pa died, or the one that rode before Ma's bridal sedan-chair. That pale chill light will always remain in my heart, shiny and cool as a piece of jade. Sometimes when I think of it, it seems as if I can almost reach out my hand and touch it.

*   *   *

I loved going to school. I had the feeling that the schoolyard was full of flowers, though, actually, this wasn't so. Yet whenever I think of school I think of flowers. Just as whenever I think of Papa's grave I think of a crescent moon outside the city — hanging crooked in the wind blowing across the fields.

Mama loved flowers too. She couldn't afford them, but if anyone ever sent her any, she pinned them in her hair. Once I had the chance to pick a couple for her. With the fresh flowers in her hair, she looked very young from the back. She was happy, and so was I.

Going to school also made me very glad. Perhaps this is the reason whenever I think of school I think of flowers.

*   *   *

The year I was to graduate from primary school, Mama sent me to the pawnshop again. I don't know why my new father suddenly left us. Mama didn't seem to know where he went either. She told me to continue going to school; she thought he'd probably come back soon.

Many days passed and there was still no sign of him. He didn't even write. I was afraid Mama would have to start washing dirty socks again, and I felt very badly about it.

But Mama had other plans. She still dressed prettily and wore flowers in her hair. How strange! She didn't cry; in fact she was always smiling. Why? I didn't understand. For several days whenever I came home from school, I'd find her standing in the doorway. Not long after, men began to hail me on the street:

"Hey, tell your Ma I'll be calling on her soon!"

"Young and tender, are you selling today?"

My face burning like fire, I hung my head till it couldn't go any lower. I knew now, but there wasn't anything I could do about it. I couldn't question Mama, no, I couldn't do that. She was so good to me, always urging, "Read your books, study hard."

But she was illiterate herself. Why was she so anxious for me to study? I grew suspicious. But then I would think — she's doing this because she has no way out. When I felt suspicious, I wanted to curse her. At other times, I would want to hug her and beg her not to do that kind of thing any more.

I hated myself for not being able to help Mama. I was worried. Even when I graduated from primary school, what use would I be? I heard from the girls in my class that several of the students who graduated last year became concubines; a few, they said, were working "in dark doorways". I didn't quite understand these things, but from the way my classmates spoke, I guessed it was something bad. The girls in my class seemed to know everything; they loved to whisper about things which they knew perfectly well were not nice. It made them blush, yet, at the same time, look quite self-satisfied.

My suspicion of Mama increased. Was she waiting for me to graduate, so that she could make me —? When I thought like this, I didn't dare go home. I was afraid to face Mama. I used to save the pennies she gave me to buy afternoon snacks, and go to physical training class on an empty stomach. I was often faint. How I envied the other kids, munching their pastries. But I had to save money. With a little money I could run away if Mama insisted that I —

At my richest, I never managed to save more than ten or fifteen cents. Even during the day, I used to gaze up at the sky, looking for my crescent moon. If the misery in my heart could be compared to anything physical, it should be that crescent moon — hanging helpless and unsupported in the grey-blue sky, its feeble rays soon swallowed up by the darkness.

*   *   *

What made me feel worst of all was that I was slowly learning to hate Mama. But whenever I hated her, I couldn't help remembering how she carried me piggy-back to visit Papa's grave — and then I couldn't hate her any more. Yet I had to. My heart . . . my heart was like that crescent moon — only able to shine a little while, surrounded by a darkness that was black and limitless.

Men constantly came to Mama's room now; she no longer tried to hide it from me. They looked at me like dogs — drooling, their tongues hanging out. In their eyes I was an even tastier morsel than Mama. I could see it.

In a short time, I suddenly came to understand a lot. I

knew I had to protect myself. I could feel that my body had something precious; I was aware of my own fragrance. I felt ashamed; I was torn by one emotion after another. There was a force within me that I could use to protect myself — or destroy myself. At times I was firm and strong. At times I was weak, defenceless, confused.

I wanted to love Mama. There were so many things I wanted to ask her. I needed her comforting. But it was just at that time that I had to shun her, hate her — or lose my own existence.

Lying sleepless on my bed and considering the matter calmly, I could see that Mama deserved to be pitied. She had to feed the two of us. But then I would think — how could I eat the food she earned that way?

That was how my mood kept changing. Like a winter wind — halting a moment, then blowing fiercer than ever. I would quietly watch my fury rising within me, and be powerless to stop it.

*   *   *

Before I could think of a solution, things became worse. Mama asked me, "What about it?" If I really loved her, she said, I ought to help her. Otherwise, she couldn't continue taking care of me. These didn't seem like words that Mama could speak, yet she said them. To make it even clearer, she added:

"I'm getting old. In another year or two, men won't want me even if I offer myself for nothing."

It was true. Lately you could see the wrinkles on Mama's face no matter how much powder she used. She no longer had the energy to entertain a lot of men; she was thinking of giving herself to only one. There was a man who ran a steamed bread shop who wanted her. She could go to him right away. But I was a big girl now. I couldn't trail after her bridal sedan-chair like I did when I was a child. I would have to look after myself. If I would agree to "help" Mama, she wouldn't have to go to him. I could earn money for us both.

I was quite willing to earn money, but when I thought of the way she wanted me to do it, it made me shiver. I knew next to nothing; how could I peddle myself like some middle-aged woman? Mama's heart was hard, and the need for money was harder still. She didn't force me to take this road or that. She left the choice to me. Either help her, or we two would go our separate ways. Mama didn't cry. Her eyes had long since gone dry.

What was I to do?

* * *

I spoke to the principal of my school. She was a stout woman of about forty, not very bright, but a warm-hearted generous person. I was really at my wit's end, otherwise how could I have said anything about Mama.... Actually, I didn't know the principal very well, and every word I spoke seared my throat like a ball of fire. I stammered and took a long time to get out what I had to say.

The principal said she was willing to help me. She couldn't give me any money, but she could give me two meals a day and a place to live — I could move in with an old woman servant who lived at the school. She said I could help the scribe with his writing — but not right away, because I still needed more practice with my handwriting.

Two meals a day and a place to live — that settled the biggest problem. I didn't have to be a burden to Mama any more.

Mama didn't ride in a bride's sedan-chair when she left this time. She simply took a rickshaw and went off into the night. She let me keep my bedding.

Mama tried not to cry as she was leaving, but the tears in her heart gushed out after all. She knew I couldn't come to see her — her own daughter. As for me, I had forgotten even how to weep properly — I sobbed open-mouthed, the tears smothering my face. I was her daughter, her friend, her solace. But

I couldn't help her. Not unless I agreed to something I just couldn't do.

After she had gone, I sat and thought. We two, mother and daughter, were like a couple of stray dogs. For the sake of our mouths, we had to accept all kinds of suffering, as if no other parts of our bodies mattered, only our mouths. We had to sell all the rest of us to feed our mouths.

I didn't hate Mama. I understood. It wasn't her fault; it wasn't wrong of her to have a mouth. The fault lay with food. By what right were we deprived of food?

Recollections of past troubles flooded back on me. But the crescent moon that was most familiar with my tears didn't appear this time. It was pitch dark, without even the glow of fireflies. Mama had disappeared into the darkness like a ghost, silent, shadowless. If she were to die tomorrow, she probably couldn't be buried beside Papa. I wouldn't even be able to find her grave. She was my only Mama, my only friend. And now I was left alone in the world.

*   *   *

I could never see Mama again. Love died in my heart, like a spring flower nipped by frost. I practised hard with my writing so that I could help the scribe copy minor documents for the principal. I had to become useful — I was eating other people's food. I couldn't be like the other girls in my class, who did nothing but watch others all day long — observing what other people ate, what they wore, what they said. I concentrated on myself. My shadow was my only friend. "I" was always in my mind, because no one loved me. I loved myself, pitied, encouraged, scolded myself. I knew myself, as if I were another person.

My body changed in a way that frightened and pleased me, yet left me puzzled. When I touched it with my hand it was like cupping a delicate, tender flower.

I was concerned only with the present. There was no

future; I didn't dare to think too far ahead. Because I was eating other people's food, I had to know when it was noon and when it was evening. Otherwise I wouldn't have thought of time at all. Without hope there isn't any time. I seemed nailed down to a place that had no days or months. When I thought of my life with Mama, I knew I had existed for fifteen or sixteen years. My schoolmates were always looking forward to vacations, festivals, the New Year holiday. What had these things to do with me?

But my body was continuing to mature. I could feel it. It confused me. I couldn't trust myself. I knew I was growing prettier. Beauty raised my social status. That was a consolation — until I remembered that I never had any social status to begin with; then the consolation turned sour. Still, in the end, I was proud of my good looks. Poor but pretty! Suddenly, a frightening thought came to me — Mama wasn't bad looking either.

*   *   *

I hadn't seen the crescent moon for a long time. Even though I wanted to see it, I didn't dare look. I had already graduated and was still living at the school. In the evenings I was alone with two old servants — a man and a woman. They didn't quite know how to treat me. I was no longer a student, yet I wasn't a teacher; nor was I a servant, though in some ways I resembled one.

At night I walked alone in the courtyard. Often I was driven into my room by the crescent moon. I hadn't the courage to face it. But in my room I would picture it, especially when there was a slight breeze. The breeze seemed able to blow those pale beams directly to my heart, making me recall the past, intensifying my forebodings of tragedy. My heart was like a bat in the moonlight — a dark thing in spite of the light; black — even though it could fly, still black. I had no hope. But I didn't cry. I only frowned.

*   *   *

I earned a little money, knitting for some of the girl students. The principal let me. But I couldn't make much because they knew how to knit too. The girls only came to me when they were too busy to do it themselves. Still, my heart felt lighter. I even thought — if Mama could come back, I could support her.

When I counted my money, I knew this was just an idle dream. But it made me feel better anyhow. I wished I could find her. If she would see me, she'd surely come away with me. We could get along, I thought. But I didn't altogether believe this myself. I was always thinking of Mama. Often, I saw her in my dreams.

One day I went with the students on an outing in the country. On the way back, because it was getting late, we took a shortcut through a small lane. There I saw Mama! Outside this steamed bread shop was a big basket with a large wooden object in it painted white to look like a steamed bread. Mama sat by the wall, pulling and pushing a lever that blew up the fire in the oven. While we were still quite a distance away I saw Mama and that white wooden steamed bread. I recognized her from the back. I wanted to rush over and embrace her. But I didn't dare. I was afraid the students would laugh at me. They wouldn't let me have such a Mama.

We came closer and closer. I lowered my head and looked at her through my tears. She didn't see me. The whole group of us brushed by her. Intent on pulling the bellows' lever, evidently she didn't see a thing.

When we were far beyond her, I turned around and looked back. She was still plying that lever. I couldn't see her features clearly; I had only the impression of a few stray locks hanging down over her forehead. I made a mental note of the name of the lane.

*　　　　*　　　　*

It was as if a little bug was gnawing at my heart. I had to see Mama or I'd have no peace.

Just at this time, a new principal was appointed to the school. The stout lady who was leaving told me I'd better start making other plans. As long as she remained she could give me food and lodgings, but she couldn't guarantee that the new principal would do the same.

I counted my money. Altogether I had two dollars and seventy some odd cents. This would keep me from starving for the next few days. But where was I to go?

There was no point in sitting around worrying. I had to think of something.

Go see Mama — that was my first idea. But could she let me stay with her? If she couldn't, it might provoke a quarrel between her and the steamed bread seller; at least it would make her feel very badly. I had to think of things from her viewpoint. She was my Mama, and yet she wasn't. We were separated by a wall of poverty.

After mulling it over, I decided not to go to her. I had to bear my own burdens. But how? I didn't know. The world seemed very small — there was no place for me and my little roll of bedding. Even a dog was better off. He could lie down anywhere and sleep. I wouldn't be permitted to sleep on the street. Yes, I was a person, but a person was less than a dog.

What if I should refuse to leave? Would the new principal drive me out? I couldn't wait for that. It was spring. I saw the flowers and the green leaves, but I felt no breath of warmth. The red of the flowers and the green of the leaves were only colours to me; they had no special significance. Spring, in my heart, was something cold and dead. I didn't want to cry, but the tears flowed from my eyes.

*   *   *

I went job-hunting. I wouldn't go to Mama. I wouldn't depend on anyone. I would earn my own food.

Hopefully, I searched for two whole days. But I brought back a harvest of only dust and tears. There was no work for me to do. It was then that I truly understood Mama, really forgave her. At least she had washed smelly socks. I wasn't even able to do that. Mama took the only road that was left. The learning and morality the school had given me were just jokes, playthings for people with full stomachs and time to spare. The students wouldn't permit me to have a Mama like mine; they sneered at women who sold themselves. That was all right for them; they got their meals regularly.

I practically made up my mind — I would do anything, if only someone would feed me. Mama was admirable. I wouldn't kill myself — although I had thought of it. No, I wanted to live. I was young, pretty, I wanted to live. Any shame would be none of my doing.

                    *   *   *

Thinking like that, it was as if I had already found a job. I dared to walk in the courtyard in the moonlight. A spring crescent moon hung in the sky. I saw it and it was beautiful. The sky was dark blue, without a speck of cloud. Bright and warm, the crescent moon bathed the willow branches with its soft beams. A breeze, laden with the fragrance of flowers, blew the shadow of the willow branches back and forth from the bright corner of the courtyard wall to the darkened section. The light was not strong; the shadows were not deep. The breeze blew tenderly. Everything was warm, drowsy, yet gently in motion. Below the moon and above the willows a pair of stars like the smiling eyes of a fairy maiden winked mischievously at that slanting crescent moon and those trailing branches. A tree by the wall was a galaxy of white blossoms. In the moonlight, half the tree was snowy white, half was dappled with soft grey shadows. A picture of incredible purity.

That crescent moon is the beginning of my hope, I said to myself.

                    *   *   *

I went to see the stout lady principal again, but she wasn't home. A young man let me in. He was very handsome, and very friendly. Usually, I'm afraid of men, but this young man didn't frighten me a bit. I couldn't very well refuse to answer his questions — he had such a winning smile. I told him why I wanted to see the principal. He was very concerned. He promised to help me.

That same night, he came and gave me two dollars. When I tried to refuse, he said the money was from his aunt — the stout principal. She had already found me a place to live, he added; I could move in the next day. I was a little suspicious at first, but his smiles went right to my heart. I felt it was wrong to doubt a person who was so considerate, so charming.

*　　　　*　　　　*

His smiling lips were on my cheek, and I could see the crescent moon smiling too, upon his hair. The intoxicated spring breeze had blown open the spring clouds to reveal the crescent moon and a pair of spring stars. Trailing willow branches stirred along the river bank, frogs throbbed their love songs, the fragrance of young rushes filled the spring night. I could hear water flowing, bringing nourishment to the tender rushes so that they might quickly grow tall and strong. Young shoots were growing on the moist warm earth; every living thing was absorbing spring's vitality and giving off a lovely perfume.

I forgot myself; I had no self. I seemed to dissolve into that gentle spring breeze, those faint moon beams. Suddenly, a cloud covered the moon. I had lost the crescent moon, and myself as well. I was the same as Mama!

*　　　　*　　　　*

I was regretful, yet eased. I wanted to cry, but was very happy. I didn't know how I felt. I wanted to go away and never see him again. But he was always on my mind, and I was lonesome without him.

I lived alone in a small room. He came to me every night — always handsome, always tender. He provided me with food, he bought me clothing. When I put on a new gown, I could see that I was beautiful. I hated the clothes, but I couldn't bear to part with them.

I didn't dare to think; I was too indolent to think. I drifted about in a daze, rouge on my cheeks. I didn't feel like dressing up, yet I had to. There was no other way to kill time. While putting my finery on, I adored my image in the mirror; then, when I finished, I hated myself.

Tears came easily to my eyes now, though I managed not to weep. My eyes — always moist and glistening — looked lovely.

Sometimes I would kiss him madly, then push him away, even curse him. He never stopped smiling.

*   *   *

I knew there was no hope from the start. Any wisp of cloud could cover a crescent moon. My future was dark.

Sure enough, not long after, as spring was changing to summer, my spring dream ended.

One day, just about noon, a young woman came to see me. She was very pretty, in a vapid, doll-like way. The moment she entered the room she began to weep. There was no need for her to say anything; I knew already.

She hadn't come to raise a row, nor did I want to quarrel with her. She was a simple, honest sort. Crying, she took my hand. "He deceived us both!" she said.

I had thought she was also a "sweetheart". But no, she was his wife. She didn't berate me. She just kept repeating, "Please let him go!"

I didn't know what to do. I felt very sorry for the young woman. Finally, I consented and, at once, she was all smiles. She appeared to be completely guileless, and quite naive. All she knew was that she wanted her husband.

*   *   *

I walked the streets for hours. It had been easy enough to

agree to what that young woman had asked, but what was I to do now? I didn't want the things he had given me. Since we were parting, I ought to make the break complete. But they were all I had to my name. Where was I to go? Would I be able to get food that day? His gifts at least were worth a little money. Very well, I'd keep them. I had no choice.

Quietly, I moved away. Though I had no regrets, there was an emptiness in my heart. I was like a lone and drifting cloud.

I rented a small room. Then I went to bed and slept right around the clock.

*   *   *

I was good at economizing. Since childhood I had known how precious money was. I still had a couple of dollars, but I decided to go out and look for a job immediately. Though I had no great hopes, it seemed like the safest course.

But job-hunting hadn't become any easier just because I was a year or two older than last time. I kept trying, not that I thought it would do any good, but because I felt it was the proper thing to do.

Why was it so hard for a woman to earn a living? Mama was right. She took the only road open to a woman. Though I knew it was waiting for me, not far off, I didn't want to take that road yet.

The more I struggled, the more frightened I became. My hope was like the light of a new moon; in a little while it would be gone.

Two weeks later, just as I was about to give up, I stood in a line of girls in a cheap restaurant. The restaurant was very small; the boss, who was looking us over, was very big. We were a rather attractive bunch — all primary school graduates, but we waited for that great broken-down tub of a boss to pick one of us as if he were an emperor.

He chose me. Though I wasn't the least grateful, at the

moment I couldn't help feeling good. The girls all seemed to envy me. As they left, some had tears in their eyes. A few cursed under their breath — "How can women be worth so little!"

*   *   *

I became the small restaurant's Second Hostess. I didn't know anything about waiting on tables and I was rather scared. The First Hostess told me not to worry — she didn't either. She said the waiter took care of that. All the hostess had to do was serve tea, hand out damp face cloths and present the bill at the end of the meal.

Strange. First Hostess wore her sleeves rolled up to her elbow, but the white linings were quite spotless. Tied to her wrist was a fancy handkerchief embroidered with the words "Little Sister, I love you". She was always powdering her face, and the lipstick on her big mouth made it look like bloody ladle. When lighting a cigarette for a customer, she would press her knee against his leg. She also poured the drinks; sometimes she took a sip herself. To some customers she was very attentive; others she would completely ignore. She had a way of batting her eyes and pretending she didn't see them. It was up to me to look after the ones she neglected.

I was afraid of men. I had learned from that little experience of mine — love or no love, men were monsters. The customers at our restaurant were particularly repulsive. They put on a great show of grabbing for the bill. They played noisy drinking games and ate like pigs. They picked fault over the smallest trifles, and cursed and raged.

While serving them tea or handing out face cloths, I kept my head down and blushed. They talked to me and tried to make me laugh. But I wanted nothing to do with them. At nine o'clock, when my first day's work was over, I was worn out. I went to my little room and lay down, without even taking my clothes off, and slept until the next day. When I awoke, I felt better. I was self-supporting, earning my own keep. I reported for work very early.

*   *   *

When First Hostess showed up, after nine, I had already been on the job two hours. Contemptuously, but not altogether unkindly, she explained, "You don't have to come so early. Who eats here at eight o'clock in the morning? And another thing, droopy puss, don't always be pulling such a long face. You're supposed to be a hostess, not a pallbearer. Keep your head down like that all the time and nobody'll give extra tips. What do you think you're here for? You're dressed all wrong, too. Your gown should have a high collar — and where's your chiffon handkerchief? You don't even look like a hostess!"

I knew she meant well. If I didn't smile at the customers, I'd lose out and so would she, for we all split the tips equally. I didn't look down on her; in one sense, I even admired her — she knew how to earn money. Playing up to men — that was the only way a woman could get along.

But I didn't want to imitate her, though I could see clearly enough that the day might be coming when I would have to be even more free and easy than she to earn my food. But that would be only when all other means failed. The "last resort" was always lying in wait for us women. I was just trying to make it wait a little longer.

Angrily, I gritted my teeth and struggled on. But a woman's fate is never in her own hands. Three days later the boss warned me — he'd give me two more days; if I wanted to keep the job, I'd have to act like First Hostess. Half in jest, First Hostess also dropped me a hint:

"One of the customers has been asking about you. Why don't you quit holding back and playing so dumb? We all know the score. Hostesses have married bank managers — there've

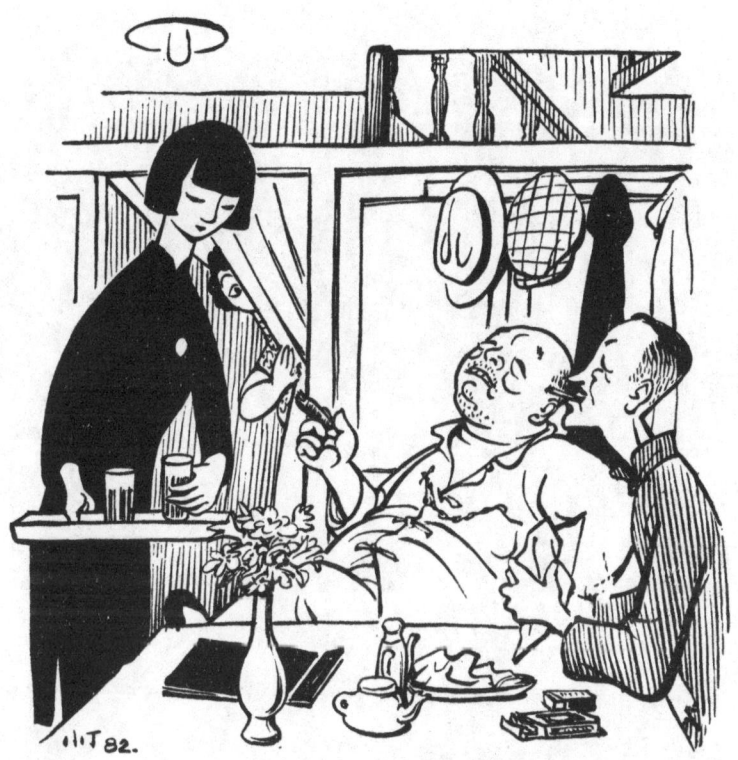

been cases. We're not so cheap. If we're not too prissy, we can ride around in a goddam limousine with the best of 'em!"

That burned me up. "When did you ever ride in a limousine?" I queried.

Her big red mouth opened so wide with surprise, I thought her jaw was going to drop off. Then she snapped, "None of your nasty lip. You're no lily-arsed lady. You wouldn't be here if you were!"

I quit. I took my pay — a dollar and five cents — and went home.

*   *   *

The final shadow had taken another big step towards me. To avoid it, I first had to come closer to it. I didn't care about losing the job, but I was really afraid of that shadow. I knew how to sell myself. Ever since that affair, I understood quite a bit about relations between men and women. A girl had only to relax her hold on herself a little, and the men would sense it and come running. What they wanted was flesh; when they had satisfied their lust, they would feed you and clothe you for a time. Afterwards, they might curse and beat you, and cut off your income.

That's the way it is when a girl sells herself. At times she's very content. I've known that feeling myself. It's all sweet love talk for a while; later you become depressed and ache all over. When you sell yourself to one man, at least you get words of love and bliss. But when you're on sale to the general public, you don't even get that. Then you hear lots of words Mama never used.

The degree of fear was different too. Though I just couldn't accept the advice of First Hostess, I wasn't quite as afraid of a private affair with one man. Not that I was thinking of selling myself. I had no need of a man — I was less than twenty. I only thought that it might be fun to go around with one. How was I to know that as soon as I went out a few times with a new friend he would demand what I feared the most!

It was true I had once abandoned myself to the spring breeze, and let a young man have his will.   But later I knew he had taken advantage of my innocence, hypnotized me with his honeyed words.   When I awoke, I realized it was all an empty dream, with nothing to show for it but a few meals and some new clothes.   I didn't want to earn my food that way again. Food was a proper practical object that should be earned in a proper practical way.   But if that proved impossible, a woman had to admit she was a woman, and sell her flesh.

More than a month passed.   I still was unable to find a new job.

*   *   *

I ran into some of my old classmates.   A few had gone on to middle school; some were just living at home.   I wasn't much interested in them.   Talking with them, I could see that I was cleverer than they.   In school, they used to be the smart ones. Now the tables were reversed.   They seemed to be living in a world of dreams.   All very smartly turned out, they were like merchandise in a store.   Their eyes shone when they met a young man and their hearts seemed to melt in a poetic reverie.

Those girls made me laugh, but I had to forgive them. Food was no problem to them; it's easy to think of love when your belly is full. Men and women weave nets to ensnare one another.   The ones with the most money have the biggest nets. After bagging a few prospects, they leisurely take their pick. I had no money.   I couldn't even find a quiet corner to weave my net. But I had to catch someone, or be caught myself.   I was clearer on such matters than my ex classmates, more practical.

*   *   *

One day I ran into the doll-faced young wife again.   She greeted me as if I were one of her dearest friends, but there was some confusion in her manner.

"You're a good person," she stammered, very earnest. "I was sorry later I asked you to let him go. I would have been better off if he stayed with you. Now he's found himself another. He's gone away with her and I haven't seen him since!"

Questioning her, I discovered that she and he had married for love. Apparently she still loved him, but he had run off again. I was sorry for the little wife. She was still dreaming; she still believed that love was sacred.

I asked her what she was going to do now. She said she had to find him, that they were mated for life. But suppose you can't find him? I asked. She bit her lips. She had parents and in-laws; she was under their control. She envied me my freedom.

So someone actually envied me. I wanted to laugh. My freedom — what a joke! She had food, I had freedom. She had no freedom, I had nothing to eat. We both were women, both were frustrated.

*   *   *

After meeting the little doll-face, I gave up the idea of selling myself to one man. I decided to play around; in other words, I was going to use "romance" to earn my meals. I couldn't be bothered about moral responsibility any more when I was hungry.

Romance would cure hunger, just as a full stomach was necessary before you could concentrate on romance. It was a perfect circle, no matter where you started from.

There wasn't much difference between me and my class-mates and the little doll-face. They had a few more illusions; I was a bit more straightforward. There is no truth more vital than the empty stomach.

I sold my meagre possessions and bought myself a complete new outfit. I didn't look bad at all. Then I entered upon the market.

*   *   *

I had imagined I could play at romance, but I was wrong.

I didn't know as much about the world as I had thought. Men weren't trapped quite that easily. I was after the more cultured types, men I could satisfy with a kiss or two. Ha-ha, they didn't go for that line, not one bit. They wanted to take advantage the very first time we met. What's more, they only invited me to see a movie, or go out for a walk, or have some ice-cream. I still went home hungry.

The so-called cultured men never failed to ask what school I graduated from, what business my family was in. It was plain enough — they didn't want you unless you had something to offer. If you couldn't bring them any real gain, the best they were willing to give was ten cents worth of ice-cream in exchange for a kiss.

It was strictly a cash on delivery proposition. The doll-faces didn't understand this, but I did. Mama and I both understood. I thought of Mama a lot.

*   *   *

They say some girls can earn a living playing at romance. But I just didn't have the capital; I had to drop the idea. For me it had to be straight business. My landlord ordered me to get out. He was a respectable man, he said. I didn't even give him a second glance. I moved back to the small flat where Mama and my first new Papa used to live. This landlord didn't say anything about being respectable. He was much nicer and more honest.

Business was very good. The cultured types came too. As soon as they found out I was for sale, they were willing to buy. With this kind of arrangement they got their money's worth, with no reflection on their social status.

When I first started I was very scared. I wasn't yet twenty. But after a couple of days I wasn't afraid any more. I could turn them limp as sacks of wet sand. They were pleased and satisfied; they advertised me to their friends.

By the end of several months, I knew a lot. I learned to

size a man up the first time we met. The rich customer would always inquire about my background, and make it plain that he could afford me. Very jealous, he would always want me all to himself. Even in brothels he wanted to monopolize — because he had money.

To that type of man I wasn't very courteous. If he raged I didn't care. I could quiet him down by threatening to go to his wife. Those years at school weren't spent in vain. I didn't scare easily. Education has its advantages. I was convinced of that.

Some men would show up with only a dollar in their hands, terrified of being cheated. To this sort, I would explain the terms of our transaction in careful detail. They would then meekly go home and get some more money. It was really a scream.

The worst of the lot were the small-time punks. Not only didn't they want to spend any money, but they were always trying to make something on the deal — stealing half a pack of cigarettes, or a small jar of cold cream. It was bad policy to offend these boys — they had connections. Get tough with them, and they put the cops on you.

I didn't offend them. I played them along until I got to know an official on the police force, then I finished them off one by one. It's a dog-eat-dog world; the worse you are the better you make out.

Most pitiful of all were the young student types, with only a dollar and a handful of small change clinking in their pockets, nervous perspiration standing out on their noses. I pitied them, but I took their money just the same. What else could I do?

Then there were the elderly men — all quite respectable, some of them grandfathers. I didn't really know how to treat them. But I knew they had money; they wanted to buy a little happiness before they died. So I gave them what they were after.

These experiences taught me to recognize the true nature

of money and man.   Money is the more powerful of the two.
If man is an animal, then money is his gall.

*   *   *

I discovered I had caught a disease. It made me so
miserable I wanted to die. I rested, I strolled about the streets.
I longed for Mama. She could give me some comfort. I thought
of myself as someone who hadn't long to live.

I went to the little lane where I had last seen her plying
the bellows' lever. But the steamed bread shop had closed
down. No one knew where they had moved to.   But I persisted.
I simply had to find her. For days I roved the streets like a
ghost. It was no use. I wondered whether she was dead, or
whether the shop had moved to somewhere outside the city,
maybe hundreds of miles away.

In this gloomy frame of mind, I broke down and cried. I
put on my best clothes, made up my face, and lay down on my
bed and waited for death. I was sure I wouldn't last long.

But I didn't die. There was a knock at the door. Someone
had come looking for me. All right, show him in. With all my
strength, I gave him a full charge of my infection. I didn't
think I was wrong. The fault wasn't mine to begin with.

I began to feel a little better. I smoked, I drank, I behaved
like an old hand of thirty or forty. There were dark circles under
my eyes, my hands were feverish. I didn't care. Money was
everything. The idea was to eat your fill first; then you could
talk about other things.

And I ate not badly at all. Why not have the best! I had
to have good food and nice clothing. That was the only way I
could do a little justice to myself.

*   *   *

One morning as I sat draped in a long gown — it must have
been about ten o'clock — I heard some footsteps out in the
courtyard. I had just got out of bed. Sometimes I didn't get
dressed until noon. I had become very lazy lately. I could sit

around like this for an hour, sometimes two, thinking of nothing, not wanting to think of anything either.

The footsteps approached my door, softly, slowly. I saw a pair of eyes peering in through the door's small glass panel. After a moment, they vanished. I sat listless, too lazy to move. A few minutes later, the eyes came back again. This time I recognized them. I got up and quietly opened the door. "Ma!"

          *   *   *

What happened next I can't exactly say. Nor do I remember how long we cried together. Mama had aged terribly. Her husband had gone back to his native village, sneaking away without a word. He didn't leave her a cent. She sold the shop's few implements, gave the store back to the landlord and moved into a cheap room.

She had already been searching for me over half a month. Finally, she thought of coming to her old flat, just on the off chance that she might run into me. Sure enough, there I was. She hadn't dared speak to me. If I hadn't called her, perhaps she would have gone away again.

When we stopped crying at last, I began to laugh hysterically. What a farce! Mother finds daughter, but daughter is a whore. In order to bring me up, Mama had been forced to become one. Now it was my turn to look after her, so I would have to remain one.

This oldest profession is hereditary — a woman's speciality!

          *   *   *

Though I knew that words of comfort were just empty talk, I was hoping to hear them from Mama's mouth. Mama was always good at fooling people, and I used to take her cajolery as consolation.

But now she had forgotten how to do even that. She was scared stiff by hunger, and I didn't blame her.

She began checking through my things, questioning me about income and expenses, apparently not the least troubled by the nature of my work. I told her I was sick, hoping she would urge me to rest a few days. Nothing of the sort. She said she'd buy me some medicine.

"Are we always going to remain in this business?" I asked her. She didn't answer.

Yet, in a way, she really loved me and wanted to protect me. She fed me, looked after my health. She was always stealing glances at me, the way a mother watches a sleeping child.

The only thing she wouldn't do for me was tell me to quit my profession.

I knew well enough — though I wasn't too pleased about it — that aside from this, there was nothing else I could do. Mama and I had to have food and clothing — that decided everything. Mother and daughter or no, respectable or no, the need for money was merciless.

*   *   *

Mama wanted to look after me, but she had to stand by and watch me be ruined. Though I wanted to be good to her, sometimes she was very annoying. She tried to run the whole show — especially where money was concerned. Her eyes had lost their youthful shine, but the sight of money could make them gleam again. She acted like a servant when there were customers around, yet if any man should pay less than the agreed price, she'd curse him and call him every name under the sun.

It made things awkward for me. Of course, I was in business for money, but that didn't mean we had to curse people. I knew how to be rude to a customer, but I had my own methods. I brought him around easy. Mama's way was too crude; she offended people. From the point of view of money, that was something we shouldn't do.

Maybe I was young and naive. Mama only cared about money, but she had to be that way; she was so much older.

Probably in another couple of years I'd be the same. A person's heart ages with the years. Gradually, you get to be hard and stiff — like silver dollars.

No, Mama didn't stand on ceremony. If a customer didn't pay in full, she'd keep his brief-case, or his hat, or anything worth a little money like a pair of gloves or a cane. I hated rows, but Mama was right. "We have to make every dollar we can," she said. "In this racket, you age ten years in one. Do you think anybody will want you when you look seventy or eighty?"

Sometimes, when a customer got drunk, she'd drag him out to a lonely spot and strip him of everything, right down to his shoes. The funny thing was the man never made a fuss about it afterwards. Maybe he didn't know how it happened, or maybe he caught pneumonia from the exposure. Or maybe, remembering how he got into that state, he was too embarrassed to complain. We didn't care, but some people had a sense of shame.

*   *   *

Mama said we age ten years in one, and she was right. After two or three years I could feel that I had changed a lot. My skin grew coarse, my lips were always chapped, my eyes bloodshot. I would get up very late, but I always felt tired.

I was aware of these things, and my customers were even less blind to them. Old customers gradually stopped coming around. As to new customers, though I worked still harder to please them, they got on my nerves. Sometimes I couldn't control my temper; I'd rant and rave so, I didn't recognize myself. Talking nonsense became a habit with me.

My more cultured customers lost interest because my "charming little love-bird" quality — their favourite poetic phrase — was gone. I had to learn to behave like a streetwalker. Only by painting my face like a clown could I attract the uneducated customers. I spread my lipstick on thick, I bit them — then they were happy.

I could almost see myself dying. With every dollar I took

in, I seemed to come closer to death. Money is supposed to preserve life, but the way I earned it, it had the opposite effect. I could see myself dying; I waited for death.

In this state of mind, I didn't want to think of anything. There was no need. I only wanted to live from day to day — that was enough.

Mama was the mirror of my coming self. After peddling her flesh for years, all that was left of her was a mass of white hair and a dark wrinkled skin. Such is life.

*   *   *

I forced myself to laugh, to act wild. Weeping a few tears would never have washed away my bitterness anyhow. My way of living had no attraction, but it was life after all, and I didn't want to part with it. Besides, what I was doing was not my fault. If death seemed frightening, it was only because I loved life so dearly. I wasn't afraid of the pain of dying — my life was more painful than any death. I loved life, but not the way I was living in.

I used to picture an ideal life, and it would be like a dream. But then, as cruel reality again closed in on me, the dream would quickly pass, and I would feel worse than ever. This world is no dream — it's a living hell.

Mama could see that I was feeling low, and she would urge me to get married. A husband would give me food, and she could get a cash payment for her old age. I was her only hope. But who would marry me?

*   *   *

Because I had known so many men, I forgot completely the meaning of love. I loved myself — no, I didn't even love myself any longer. Why should I love anyone else? Still, if I were to marry, I would have to pretend, to say that I loved him, that I was willing to spend the rest of my life with him.

And that is what I did say — to several men. I swore it, but none of them wanted to marry me. The rule of money makes men sharp. They were quite willing to have an affair with me. That was much cheaper than going to a brothel.

If it didn't cost anything, I guarantee all the men would say they loved me.

*   *   *

Just about this time, I was arrested. Our city's new chief of police is a stickler on morals; he wants to clean out all the unregistered brothels. The licensed women can go on doing business, because they pay tax.

After my arrest, I was sent to a reformatory where I was taught to work — washing clothes, cooking, knitting. But I already knew how to do all that. If I could have earned a living by any of those methods, I would have quit my own bitter profession long ago.

I told that to the people at the reformatory, but they didn't believe me. They said I was a loafer, immoral. They said that if I not only learned to work, but also loved to work, I could become self-supporting, or find a husband.

They were very optimistic. I didn't share their confidence. They were very proud of the fact that they had "reformed" about a dozen women and found them husbands. For a two-dollar licence fee and a guarantee from a responsible shopkeeper, any man could come to the reformatory and pick a wife. It was a real bargain — for the man.

To me it was a joke. I flatly refused to be "reformed". When some big official came down to investigate us, I spat in his face. But they wouldn't let me go. I was a dangerous character. Since they couldn't reform me, they sent me to another place. I went to jail.

*   *   *

Jail is a fine place. It convinces you that there's no hope for mankind. Never in my dreams did I imagine any hole could be so disgusting.

But once I got here, I gave up any idea of ever leaving

again. From my own experience, I know that the outside world isn't much of an improvement.

I wouldn't want to die here, if I had any better place to go. But I know what it's like outside. Wherever you die, it's all the same.

Here, in here, I saw my old friend again — the crescent moon. I hadn't seen it for a long time.

I wonder what Mama is doing.

That crescent moon brings everything back.

Translated by Sidney Shapiro

About the Author

LAO SHE (1899-1966) is the pen name of the writer Shu Sheyu, who was born in Beijing. In 1924 he went to England, where he was a lecturer in Chinese at the School of Oriental Studies, London University. It was in London that he wrote his first three novels. After his return to China in 1930 he taught at Qilu (Cheeloo) University in Jinan and Shandong University in Qingdao. He continued to write during the War of Resistance Against Japan (1937-45). When he was in Chongqing, he took an active part in organizing the National Writers' and Artists' Resistance Association. Later he left China for the United States, where he gave lectures and continued to write until his return in 1949. He threw himself into the work of new China as a member of the Cultural and Educational Committee in the Government Administration Council, a deputy to the National People's Congress, a member of the Standing Committee of the Chinese People's Political Consultative Conference, vice-chairman of the All-China Federation of Literature and Art and vice-chairman of the Union of Chinese Writers as well as chairman of the Beijing Federation of Literature and Art.

Before liberation he wrote many works of literature, including his best novel *Camel Xiangzi* (or *Rickshaw Boy*), to expose and denounce the old society. After the founding of new China he wrote the plays *Dragon Beard Ditch*, *Spring Flowers and Autumn Fruit*, *Fang Zhenzhu*, *Teahouse* and many other works which are loved by the people. He enjoys great prestige in China and was named a "People's Artist" and a "Great Master of Language".

Lao She was persecuted to death by Lin Biao and the gang of four in 1966 at the beginning of "cultural revolution".

Crescent Moon is one of the short stories written in the early stage of Lao She's creative life. The story portrays the miserable life of a mother and her daughter before liberation and how the two generations, driven by destitution, deteriorate into prostitution.

The Husband

Shen Congwen

That spring, after a whole week's rain, the river rose.

Whenever this happened, the opium boats and boat brothels moored by the bank came so close to the shore that they were tied to the pillars of the stilt buildings.

Idlers drinking tea in Four Seas Teahouse, if they leaned out of a window over the river, had a fine view of "misty rain and red blossom" by the pagoda on the other shore. They could also watch the women on the boats lighting opium pipes for their customers. This convenient proximity enabled people on shore or on the river to hail their acquaintances, and then to meet, chat, flirt or shout abuse. The customers in the teahouse, having paid up, left by a musty corridor and sloshed through the mire to the boats.

Once aboard, by paying from fifty cents to five dollars, they could smoke opium and sleep or have it off with the women, just as they pleased. The buxom young country women with big buttocks would gladly wait on a man all night, and could make him feel at home.

On the boats, as elsewhere, they called this doing "business". They had all come here to do business. Put like this, it was no different from other work, neither immoral nor injurious to health. Each came from the country, from a peasant household, and had left her mill and calf, her sturdy young husband, to follow some other villager she knew to do business on this

398

boat. Little by little, in the course of business, she would become citified and cut off from the country; little by little, she would pick up certain bad habits required only in a town. She would have degenerated. But because this was a slow process, taking time, it passed unnoticed. Besides, many of them always retained their countrified simplicity. So there was never any lack of young women for these boat brothels on the river in town.

The reason was very simple. A woman in no hurry to have children, if every month she sent home two evenings' earnings, could keep her honest, hard-working farmer husband in comfort in the country. He had an extra income this way, while the woman remained his wife. Thus many young husbands sent their wives to town while they stayed quietly at home tilling the land. This was a common practice.

If a husband missed his wife doing business on a boat, or wanted to see her during a festival, since she could not go home, he would change into freshly laundered clothes, hang at his waist the tobacco pouch he always wore at work and make his way to town with, on his back, a whole crate of sweet potatoes, cakes of sticky rice and the like. He would ask at the wharf, starting with the first boat, till he discovered his wife's whereabouts. Then he would go aboard, careful to leave his cloth shoes on the deck outside the cabin. As he gave his wife the things he had brought, he would eye her from head to foot with stupefaction. For by now naturally, to him, she had changed out of all recognition.

Hair in a big, glossy chignon, fine plucked eyebrows, white powdered face, rouged lips, and that citified air, those citified clothes — all these staggered and flustered her husband from the country. It was easy for her to sense his stupefaction. She might break the silence to ask, "Did you get that five dollars?" or "Has our sow had a new litter?" The way she spoke, too, had naturally changed out of all recognition. It was free and easy like a matron in town, quite unlike the shy, timid speech of a daughter-in-law in the country.

When she asked about money or the pig at home, her husband could see that even on this boat he still had his status as husband, that this lady in town had not completely forgotten the countryside. This emboldened him, slowly, to get out his pipe and flint. Then came his second surprise: she snatched them away and thrust into his big, horny hand a machine-made cigarette. Again his surprise was short-lived. Soon he was puffing the cigarette and chatting. . . .

After the evening meal, he was still smoking one of these strange-tasting cigarettes when a visitor arrived. He looked like a boat-owner or shopkeeper, in cowhide jackboots. From one corner of his pocket protruded a thick, bright silver chain. He reeled on board, tipsily shouting that he wanted a good fuck. His raucous voice and swagger reminded the husband of their village head and the more powerful of the local gentry. So, without needing to be told, he ducked out to skulk in the back cabin, holding his breath. Not smoking now, he gazed blankly through the gloaming at the river. Darkness had changed it. Lamps gleamed in boats and on the bank. Then his thoughts were bound to turn to his chickens and piglets at home, as if these were his sole friends, his family. Now he was close to his wife, but far from home. A feeling of loneliness came over him. He wished he could go back.

Did he go? No. It was thirty li away, and on the road he might meet wolves, wild cats or a night patrol, all best avoided. No, he couldn't go back. The madam on the boat was bound to keep him to see an opera and go to Four Seas Teahouse. Besides, now that he was here, he must have a look at the brightly lit streets and the townsfolk. So he stayed sitting in the back cabin, enjoying the river scene till she was free. When finally he went ashore, he walked to the bow along a narrow passage on the edge of the boat, holding on to frame of the awning. After seeing the sights he came back the same way, making sure to keep his voice down so as not to disturb the customer still lying in the cabin smoking opium.

When it was time for bed, a watchman's drum sounded in town and he heard a rub-a-dub too on Xiliang Hill. He peeped through a crack in the cabin. The man was still there. The husband could raise no objection. He lay down to sleep alone in a new quilt in the back cabin. At midnight, when he was sleeping or letting his thoughts wander, his wife found time to slip in to offer him some crystal-sugar. She remembered what a sweet tooth he had, so although he had been asleep, had already eaten, she stuffed a small lump of sugar into his mouth. She then left, looking rather ashamed of herself. As her husband sucked the sugar, it seemed as if just because of this he ought to condone her behaviour. While she went on waiting on the guest, he quietly went back to sleep.

There were many, many husbands like this in Huangzhuang. The place bred healthy girls and honest fellows. But the soil was really poor, and more than half of their small yield was exacted from them by the authorities. So no matter how hard the villagers worked on the land, for three months out of twelve they had nothing to eat but sweet potato leaves or chaff. It was hard to make ends meet. Though they were up in the hills, it was only twenty li to the wharf where the women went to make a living. The man could see all the advantages of this. In name the woman still belonged to him; the sons she bore belonged to him; and when she made money he invariably got his share.

The boats were drawn up all along the river, too many for anyone new to the place to count. The man who knew their number and their order, who remembered each boat and what the oarsman looked like was the old river warden of the fifth district.

This warden had only one eye. The other had been gouged out in a fight on the river in his youth with a ruffian whom he had killed. But he seemed to see better with one eye than with two. He was in sole charge of that river, having as much power over the little boats as the Emperor or President of China had over the land.

With the river in spate, the Warden was extra busy. It was his job to check up to see if the parents on any of the boats had gone ashore, and babies were crying for milk. Were there any rows in which he should intervene? Were any boats in danger of cutting adrift because there was no one in charge? Today, this gentleman also had to investigate some trouble which had started on shore but which now involved the river. There had been three robberies in town in the last few days. According to the Public Security Bureau, every nook and cranny in town had been searched, but there was no trace of the loot. Once this search had been conducted by those reputable functionaries in town, the responsibility had shifted to the Warden. He had been notified, by those lying security officers, that at midnight tonight he and the armed river police were to search all the boats for bad characters.

This news reached him in the morning. That kept him busy all day. First he had to do his duty by some people who often treated him to good meals and drinks; then, going from boat to boat by the bank, he talked with the occupants of each. He had to find out whether they had any suspicious strangers on board.

A river warden, on the water, has absolute power and knows all that goes on there. This one had long been influential among the boatmen and because he had fallen foul of the law, the authorities, as their custom was, used him to exercise control over the river. But he was older now, and times were changing — changing to his advantage. He was well-off, had married and liked a drink now and then. He had children, lived in comfort and little by little had become a peaceable, honest man. Whereas his job was to help the authorities, at heart he sympathized with the boat people. That being the case, he had become an exemplary character, no less respected than the magistrate, yet neither hated nor feared. He was godfather to many of the prostitutes. Because of these social connections, he always sided with the boat people.

Now he crossed a plank to a newly painted "flower boat" at the foot of a relatively quiet shop on stilts where lotus seeds were sold. He knew to whom it belonged. Stepping aboard he called, "Seven!"

No answer. No young woman appeared. Neither did the proprietress. The Warden was experienced. Thinking that perhaps some young fellow was fooling about in the cabin in broad daylight, he stood in the bow looking round and waited a while.

Presently he called out again. Called Madam and Wuduo too. Wuduo was a girl of twelve, skinny, with a shrill voice, who was usually left in charge when the grown-ups went ashore. She did the cooking and shopping and was often beaten and cried, but before long she would start singing again. However, Wuduo made no appearance either. He thought he could hear someone breathing in the cabin, and knew they would hardly have left the boat unattended, nor could they all be asleep. So he peered into the dark cabin and called, "Who's there?"

Still there was no answer.

Rather exasperated, the Warden asked loudly, "Who is it?"

A male voice which was strange to him faltered, "It's me." He added, "They've all gone ashore."

"All of them?"

"Yes. They. . . ."

As if afraid that this answer had given offence, for which he must make amends, the man scrambled out of the darkness to stand in the doorway. Holding gingerly on to the frame of the awning, he stared awkwardly at the visitor.

His eyes travelled upwards from the pigskin boots, as smart as if polished with wild persimmon juice, to the soft, russet deerskin pouch, to the folded arms and the pair of muscular, hairy hands, one finger of which sported an enormous gold ring. Last of all he eyed the square-jawed face, which looked as if pieced together out of countless bits of orange peel.

He realized that this was a man of substance, so in imitation of the townsfolk he said, "Please take a seat inside, sir. They'll soon be back."

Judging by his accent and starched clothes, he seemed to be a peasant fresh from the country. Finding the women out, the Warden had meant to leave; but now, intrigued, he stayed.

"Where are you from?" he asked in a fatherly way, to put the young fellow at ease. "I don't know you."

The youngster appeared to be thinking: I don't know you either. "I came yesterday," he answered.

"Is the wheat in the country in ear yet?"

"The wheat? The wheat in front of our waterwheel, ha! That pig of ours, ha, those. . . ."

Suddenly recollecting that he hadn't answered the question and that he was speaking to a respectable townsman, to whom he shouldn't have mentioned "our waterwheel" or "pig", the young fellow broke off, tongue-tied.

He looked timidly at the Warden with a faint smile. He wanted to be understood and excused — he was an honest fellow, and hadn't meant to talk rashly.

The Warden realized this. From their brief exchange he had gathered that this was a relative of someone on the boat. "Where has Seven gone?" he asked. "When will she be back?"

Now the young man answered more carefully, but he gave the same reply: "I came yesterday. . . . Yesterday evening." Then he explained that Seven had gone ashore with the proprietress and Wuduo to burn incense, leaving him to mind the boat. To make clear his status he added that he was Seven's husband.

Since Seven called the Warden "Godfather", he felt no need to stand on ceremony with this "godson" he had met for the first time. After a few more remarks, the two of them presently went into the cabin.

There was a small bed in there. On it were neatly folded quilts of silk and red printed calico. The visitor sat, as the custom was, on the edge of the bed. Light came through the cabin door, so that though it looked dark from outside one could see all right.

The young man found a cigarette and matches for the visitor, clumsily upsetting the little pot containing dried chestnuts beside him. Round, glossy brown chestnuts scattered all over the floor. The young man retrieved them to put them back in the pot, not realizing that he ought to offer the visitor some. But the visitor made himself at home. He picked up some chestnuts, cracked them open and ate them, remarking how good they were, dried in the wind.

"They're fine chestnuts, don't you like them?" The Warden saw that his host had eaten none.

"I like them. These grew on the tree behind my house. It bore a whole lot last year. You should've seen the way they popped out of their prickly jackets!" He laughed, almost as if he were speaking of his children.

"Chestnuts this size are hard to come by."

"I picked out the biggest."

"Did you?"

"Yes, because Seven fancies them. That's why I kept them."

"Do you have monkey-chestnuts there?"

"What are monkey-chestnuts?"

The Warden told him a story. "Some monkeys lived high up in the hills. Anyone who swore at them was pelted with chestnuts as big as your fist. So when people wanted those chestnuts, they'd go to the foot of the hill and curse the monkeys, then wait to pick up the chestnuts."

Talk of chestnuts loosened the tongue of this inarticulate young man. Finding this stranger congenial, he volunteered all sorts of information about the countryside. First he explained the place-name Chestnut Hollow, then described how strong and handy a plough handle made of chestnut wood was. He had been hankering for talk about home, because after his arrival the previous day there'd been clients the whole night there. drinking and smoking, so that he'd had to stay cooped up in the back cabin, with no one but Wuduo as company. And Wuduo slept like the dead. First thing today, he'd had no chance to chat with his wife, who said she must go to Seven Li Bridge to burn incense, and left him all alone in charge of the boat. He'd sat waiting for hours, and still she wasn't back. Though he went aft to stare at the river, everything on which was novel to him, he felt bored. Earlier on, lying in the cabin, it had occurred to him that if the river near his village rose like this one, carp would swarm inside the palisade across it! Once caught, they could be dried in the sun and hung up by a willow twig through the gills. He had been thinking over the size of the catch when, at this visitor's sudden arrival, all the fish seemed to have plunged back into the water.

The visitor appeared not averse to such conversation. So here was a good chance for the young man to tell him everything he'd been planning to tell his wife.

He told the Warden how things were in the village, and what a little rascal his piglet was. Describing how his mill had just been repaired, he threw in a joke about the stone-mason. Then he talked about a small sickle, a sickle of which the Warden could have no idea.

"Now was that strange, or wasn't it?" he said. "I swear I hunted high and low for it. Under the bed, on the lintel, in the barn — everywhere. But no sign of it. It had vanished. I put the blame on Seven, so that she cried. But still it couldn't be found. And all the time — drat it! — it was hiding in a rice crate on the beam. For half a year. Eating rice! Covered with rust it was, the wretched thing! Do you get what I'm saying? How could it have been in that rice crate all the time? It had always hung on the window. Then I remembered. I'd bloodied my finger one day whittling wedges, and in a rage I'd hurled the sickle away. . . . Now I've whetted it well in the brook, it isn't too bad. Still has a good bite. If you aren't careful, it draws blood. I've not told Seven yet. She can't have forgotten how she cried that day. It's found now." He chuckled. "Yes, it's found at last."

"All's well that ends well," said the Warden casually.

"Yes, I'm glad to have got it back. Because I'd suspected Seven of dropping it into the brook and not liking to tell me. Now I know she didn't lie to me. I understand. I wasn't fair to her. I swore, 'If you don't find it, I'll beat you up!' Mind, I didn't lay hands on her. But she was so frightened, she cried half the night."

"Do you use it for mowing?"

"Oh, it has many uses. Not mowing, no. That small sickle is so handy, I use it to peel sweet potatoes or carve a flute. It's tiny, so well forged it cost three hundred cash. We all carry one like that on us — understand?"

"I understand," said the Warden. "Everyone needs one."

Thinking he really understood, the young man went on, touching on many subjects. Even his hopes of a baby next year, which he should have discussed with his wife when they shared one pillow. He did not scruple to talk crudely either. At long last, when the Warden rose to go, he remembered that he hadn't asked his name.

"What's your name, sir? If you'll leave a card, I can tell them. . . ."

"No need. Just tell them a tall man in boots like these came aboard. Tell her not to take any customers this evening. I shall be coming on business."

"No customers, and you'll be coming?"

"That's right. I'll come for sure. And I'm going to ask you to a meal, as we are friends."

"Friends, yes, friends."

The Warden clapped his big hand on the young man's shoulder, then jumped ashore and went on to another boat.

After the Warden had gone, the young man tried to guess who he could be. It was the first time he had ever talked to such a personage, who had made an excellent and unforgettable impression on him. Not only had the gentleman talked to him, he had called him a friend and promised him a meal. He must be one of Seven's best customers. Must have paid her plenty of money. In his elation he suddenly felt like singing. He softly sang a folksong:

> Our fishery fills with carp
> As the river rises;
> Big carp and small,
> Like sandals of all sizes.

He waited and waited, but still Seven did not come back. Not a soul came. He thought of the tall man's poise and fluent way of talking. He recalled his boots, polished till they shone, as if with the best wild persimmon juice. He recalled that massive gold ring, worth goodness knows how much money. What made it so attractive? He recalled the gentleman's nods and speech, so like those of a governor — this was Seven's God of Wealth!

Towards noon, the people on other boats started cooking. Smoke rose everywhere from the damp fuel, making everyone's eyes water, then drifted across the river like flimsy silk. In the eating-houses on the bank, cooks could be heard clinking the sides of pans with their slices; in nearby boats cabbage sizzled in the pans. Still Seven was not back. But her husband hadn't learned how to light damp firewood, so the stove remained cold and mute. Finally he gave up his attempts to light the fire.

As he sat, hungry, on a little stool, going without his meal and drumming the deck, he had to think of something. A reprehensible notion came into his head. Another mental picture of that pouch, so proudly bulging with money, destroyed his peace of mind. He felt disgusted by that square-jawed face, which now seemed to him made up of distillers' grain and blood. Memories could be maddening! Take that instruction given to

him, her husband! "Tell her not to take customers this evening.
I'll be coming." To hell with it! The rudeness of that big blab-
mouth! Why should he say that? What reason could he
have? . . .

These speculations added to his anger, which was aggravat-
ed by hunger; and this simple young fellow's hurt feelings en-
gendered a more primitive emotion.

He was unable to sing now. His throat was too constricted
with jealousy. No more happiness for him. He decided to go
home the next day — back to the land.

In this black mood he tried once more to light the fire,
with, of course, no success. Thereupon he chucked all the firewood into the river.

"Damn you! Go and get lost in the sea!"

But before the wood had floated ten yards, it was salvaged
by someone on another boat, who seemed to have been waiting
for drift-wood. She promptly lit it with a piece of old rope,
so that in a jiffy the boat was filled with smoke as the fire
crackled and sputtered. The sight made the young man angry
and ashamed. He decided to leave before his wife came back.

At the end of the street he met his wife with Wuduo. They
were hand in hand, laughing and talking. Wuduo was carrying
a fiddle, brand-new by the look of it, a finer one than he had
ever dreamed of.

"Where are you going?"

"Home."

"I told you to mind the boat, but you're going home! Who's
annoyed you? Why be so small-minded?"

"I'm off. Let go of me."

"Come back to the boat."

His wife looked adamant. And as he could see she had
bought the fiddle for him, he could not insist on leaving. He
rubbed his burning temples, muttered, "Oh, all right then," and
followed her to the boat.

The proprietress came panting up, red in the face, carrying the lights of a pig. She was scuttling along like a thief, afraid to be caught and hauled off to the yamen. As she came aboard, Seven called out from the cabin, "Imagine, ma! My man is talking of leaving!"

"What an idea! Before even seeing an opera."

"We met him up the street, glowering. Must be because we're so late."

"Well, he should blame me or blame Buddha. Blame the butcher. I shouldn't have haggled with the fellow so long, and he shouldn't have pumped so much water into these lights."

"No, I'm the one to blame," said Seven, sitting down in the cabin. As her husband was just opposite, she slipped off her tunic to let him see her flimsy red silk bodice embroidered with mandarin ducks. She had made it only last month.

He eyed her in silence, feeling a stir of excitement.

At the stern, Madam and Wuduo were talking.

"Who's taken our firewood?"

"Who washed the rice?"

"He can't have got the fire to light. . . . He's from the country where they only burn pine-branches."

"We opened a fresh bundle yesterday, didn't we?"

"None left."

"Go and fetch another. Don't say anything."

"All he can do is wash rice!" Wuduo giggled.

The young man listened to this without a word, sitting quietly in the cabin, his eyes on the new fiddle.

"It's been tuned," his wife told him. "Try it."

First he said nothing, then he put the fiddle on his knee to inspect the pine resin on it. When he plucked the strings, strange sounds flowed from his fingers. A smile dawned on his face.

Soon the cabin was full of smoke. Called out by his wife, he took the fiddle to play standing in the bow.

During the midday meal Wuduo said, "Brother, if presently you play *Widow Meng Jiang Weeps at the Great Wall*, I'll sing it."

"I don't know it."

"Don't try to fool me. I've heard you play very well."

"I'm not fooling you. I can only play *The Mother Sees Off Her Daughter*."

"Seven tells me you're a good fiddler," said Madam. "So when we saw this fiddle at the temple fair, I thought of you and said we must buy it for you. We were lucky to get it cheap. In your village you couldn't get one for a dollar, could you?"

"No. How much did it cost?"

"A hundred and six cash. A bargain, everyone said!"

Wuduo chuckled. "Who said?"

"Who said it wasn't, brat?" Madam sounded angry. "What do *you* know? None of your lip!"

Wuduo stuck out her tongue in dismay at her gaffe.

In fact they had got the fiddle, free of charge, from a friend who sold them. That was why Wuduo was scolded for butting in. Seven only laughed. Thinking this was because of the old woman's tactlessness, her husband just smiled.

After bolting his food he started to play the new fiddle. It had a lovely clear timbre. Wuduo, beside herself with delight, laid down her bowl and chopsticks to sing. When Madam rapped her over the head with her chopsticks, she gulped down her rice, then washed the bowls and pan.

That evening, the awning fixed over the front cabin, he fiddled while Wuduo and Seven sang. The kerosene lamp had a red paper cover which flooded the cabin with a rosy light as if for some wedding or festival. His spirits rose, it was so lively. But before long two soldiers, roaring drunk on shore, heard this singing.

The two drunks staggered to the side of the boat. Gripping its gunwale with their muddy hands, slurring their words they bellowed, "Who's that singing? Let's have your names. For a

good song you'll get five hundred cash. Hear that? We'll give
you five hundred."

At once the fiddling stopped. All became quiet.

Thud, thud! The drunks kicked the boat, then tried to take
off the awning, but couldn't find where it was fastened. "Don't
you want money, you bitches?" one of them yelled. "Playing
deaf and dumb, are you? Who dares whoop it up here? I'm
not afraid. Not even of the Emperor. If I'm afraid, strike me
dead! Our top brass, rotten, stinking turtle-eggs the whole lot —
I'm not afraid of them!"

The other cried hoarsely, "Come on, you whores. Help us
gentlemen aboard!"

They started hammering with a stone and let loose such a
flood of abuse that all on the boat were frantic. Madam hastily
turned down the lamp and went out to raise the awning.
Seven's husband, when he heard the soldiers' shouts, had tucked
the fiddle under one arm and dashed into the back cabin. Soon
the drunks with their dirty talk were in the front one. They
grabbed hold of Seven and kissed her, then kissed Madam and
Wuduo too.

"Who was that fiddling here?" asked the gruff-voiced soldier. "Get the fiddler here and sing us another song."

Madam was too scared to speak, and Seven didn't know
what to do. The drunkards cursed them again. "Stinking
bitches, fetch that cuckold to play for us. We'll give him a
thousand. What could be more handsome? A thousand cocks.
If you don't get a move on, I'll burn this boat! Hear that, old
witch? Quick! If you make me lose my temper, you'll be sorry!"

"There are just the few of us having fun here, sir. There's
no one else. . . ."

"Come off it, old hag! Stinking, wizened old cow! Get that
fiddler here. The bastard! I want to sing." He lurched to his
feet, meaning to search the back cabin. The proprietress
panicked, gaping in consternation. Seven in her desperation
caught hold of the drunkard's hand and laid it on her breast.

Taking the hint, he sat down again. "All right. Fine. I can afford it. I'll sleep here tonight! . . ." He sang two lines from an opera.

After he had flopped down on Seven's left, his crony without a word lay down on her right.

When things seemed to have quieted down in the front cabin, her husband next door called softly to Madam, who tiptoed over, the soldiers' insults rankling in her mind.

"What's up?" he asked, at a loss.

"They're harmless, those officers, when they're drunk. They won't be staying long."

"Better get rid of them. I forgot to tell you: today a big square-jawed fellow came. Looked like a high official. He told me you weren't to entertain any guests, as he's coming this evening."

"Did he have leather boots and a booming voice?"

"That's right. And a big gold ring on his finger."

"He's Seven's godfather. So he came this morning, did he?"

"Yes. He chatted quite a while and ate some chestnuts."

"What did he say?"

"Said he'd be coming for sure, and you weren't to take any customers. . . . And he promised to invite me to a meal."

Madam wondered why the Warden was coming. Surely he didn't want to spend the night there? They were the same age — could *she* have taken his fancy? . . . She couldn't make it out. Although an old procuress is so used to scandalous goings-on of every kind that nothing can make her blush, being called all those dirty names had wounded her pride. She tiptoed to the front cabin, pursed her lips at the sight of the disgraceful scene there, and swearing "Swine!" returned to the back cabin.

"What's up?"

"Nothing."

"Have they gone?"

"They're sleeping."

"Sleeping?"

Though she couldn't see his face clearly, his voice conveyed what he felt. She said, "Brother, it's rarely you come to town. Let's go ashore and have some fun. I'll invite you to an opera. Tonight they're playing *Qiu Hu Plays Three Tricks on His Wife.*"

He shook his head but said nothing.

After the soldiers had fooled about and left, under the lamp in the front cabin Wuduo, Madam and Seven made fun of their drunken behaviour. Seven's husband stayed in the back. Madam went to call him a couple of times, but for some reason unknown to her he ignored her. So she turned to examine the banknotes, as she could tell genuine ones from counterfeit. These four were genuine. She showed Seven the serial numbers and the designs, then sniffed at the notes, remarking that they surely came from the Muslim eating-house. They reeked of beef.

Wuduo went back a second time to say, "Brother, they've gone. Let's finish our singsong. Then. . . ."

Seven pulled her away, as if she had something on her mind.

All was quiet. In the back cabin, Seven's husband had been softly plucking at the strings of the fiddle. But now he left them alone.

From the shore they heard gonging and the blare of a *suona*. Some shopkeeper was having a wedding and guests had come to offer congratulations. There would be an opera. Things would be lively all night.

Presently Seven went softly to the back cabin. But she returned in no time. Obviously her attempt at conciliation had failed.

"What's wrong?" asked Madam.

Seven shook her head and sighed. "He's so bull-headed. Let him be."

Thinking that the Warden wouldn't be coming now, they

all turned in, the proprietress, Seven and Wuduo in the front cabin, the man in the back.

The search party came at midnight, led by the Warden. The river was utterly quiet as four police, fully armed, stood guard in the bow while the Warden and the patrol leader, flashing a torch, stepped into the front cabin. By now Madam had trimmed the lamp. Being experienced, she knew this was nothing serious. Seven sat up in bed, her jacket over her shoulders, and having greeted both men told Wuduo to pour tea. Wuduo, still half asleep, was thinking of the strawberries she dreamed she had picked.

Madam woke Seven's husband and pulled him out. At the sight of the Warden and a black-uniformed officer, he was too frightened to speak. Were they in serious trouble?

The patrol leader, with a show of sternness, demanded, "Who is this?"

"Seven's husband," the Warden told him. "Just come from the country to see her."

Seven added, "He just arrived yesterday, officer."

The officer looked at husband and wife in turn, then said no more, taking the Warden's word for it. While making a desultory search, he noticed the pot of chestnuts. The Warden promptly grabbed a handful to stuff into the pocket of his smart uniform. The officer simply smiled.

Presently the patrol moved on to another boat. But before Madam could refasten the awning, a policeman came back to announce, "Tell Seven, madam, that our officer will be coming back to investigate her carefully. Understand?"

"Is he coming now?"

"After finishing this patrol."

"Is that true?"

"When have I ever lied to you, you old bitch?"

Madam beamed, to the surprise of Seven's husband, who had no idea why she should be investigated. But as he saw Seven lying in bed, he got over his earlier bad temper. He wanted to patch things up, to go to bed with her and talk over certain family affairs. So he sat himself down on the edge of the bed. Madam, guessing what he had in mind and knowing that he was still in the dark, told Seven, "The officer's coming presently."

Seven bit her lip in silence, her thoughts wandering.

He got up early to leave. Not saying a word, he fastened his straw sandals and found his tobacco pouch. When all was ready, he sat on the edge of the bed, as if he had something to say but could not get it out.

Seven asked, "Didn't you agree, last night, to have lunch today with godfather?"

He shook his head by way of answer.

"He's preparing a feast just for you! Four main dishes, four side ones and a chafing dish. How can you back out when he's doing you such an honour?"

"...."

"Don't you want to see an opera?"

"...."

"Rosy Heaven Restaurant serves pork dumplings at noon. You know you like those dumplings!"

"...."

He was set on going. Seven was in a quandary. She went out, coming back to take out of her purse the notes given her by the soldiers the night before. She counted them. There were four. Folding them up, she thrust them into her husband's left hand. He said nothing. As if guessing his thoughts, she asked Madam, "Let me have the other three." These were handed over and Seven, after counting them, thrust them into her husband's right hand.

He shook his head and threw the notes on the floor. Then covering his face with his horny hands, he started sobbing — unaccountably — like a child.

This looked bad. Wuduo and Madam disappeared into

the back cabin.   To Wuduo it seemed strange, ridiculous, for such a big fellow to cry! But she didn't laugh.   Standing in the back cabin she spotted the fiddle hanging from the beam, and wished she could sing a song, but somehow or other she couldn't get a note out.

When the Warden came to invite the visitor from far away to a meal, he found only Madam and Wuduo on the boat. From them he learned that both husband and wife had gone back to the country.

Written on April 13, 1930 in Wusong
Translated by Gladys Yang

About the Author

SHEN CONGWEN, a celebrated contemporary writer, was born in 1903 in Fenghuang County, Hunan Province. He began his career by publishing short pieces in Beijing's newspapers and magazines. Having taught "exercises in composition" in universities since 1928, he has written many stories of different themes in varied styles. He published more than twenty collections of stories, mostly short stories, such as "After Rain", "Eight Steeds", "Big and Little Ruan", "The Man Crossing the Mountain", "Live", "Advisor" and "Unemployed".   A greater part of these stories are love stories about young people with complicated plots and minute descriptions. The short novel *Border Town* is his representative work, which describes the love between an old ferryman's granddaughter and the two sons of an army commander at the ferry. In such a complicated plot, it portrays the peaceful life and customs of the local people in a remote minority region in western Hunan.

His short story "The Husband" depicts the miserable life of the poor peasants in old China.   A peasant sends his young wife on a boat near a small town to do the "business" of actually selling her own body, while he himself is a husband in name only.

Hands

Xiao Hong

None of our form had ever seen hands like hers: blue, black, yet purple too, discoloured from the finger-tips to the wrist.

For the first few days we called her "The Monster". In the break, racing round our class-room, we gave her a wide berth. But as for her hands, no one asked her one word about them.

At roll-call, hard as we tried to control ourselves, she sent us into fits of laughter.

"Li Jie!"

"Here."

"Zhang Chufang!"

"Here."

"Xu Guizhen!"

"Here."

In swift and orderly succession, one stood up as another sat down. But things slowed up each time Wang Yaming's name was called.

"Wang Yaming, Wang Yaming.... Speak up!" One of the other girls might prod her. Then she would stand up, her dark discoloured hands hanging by her sides, her shoulders sagging; and staring at the ceiling she would answer:

"*Hei-erh.... Hei-erh.*"

No amount of laughter disconcerted her, and not till several

minutes had gone by — or so it seemed — would she sit down solemnly, making her chair creak.

In one English lesson, the mistress took off her glasses to rub her eyes with a smile.

"Don't say *hei-erh* next time. Just say 'here'."

The rest of us started giggling, scuffing our feet on the floor.

But in our English class the next day when Wang Yaming was called, we heard the same old: "*Hei-erh.   Hei-erh.*"

The English mistress fumbled with her glasses. "Did you learn any English before you came here?" she asked.

"You mean the English language? Yes. My teacher was pock-marked. . . . He taught me *pen-ssu-erh* and *pen*. But I never learned this *hei-erh*."

"It's 'here', not *hei-erh*.   Say: here, here."

"*Hsi-erh. Hsi-erh.*" Her extraordinary accent made the whole class hysterical. But Yaming sat calmly down to turn the pages of a book with her dark, discoloured hands. In fact she started chanting softly to herself:

"*Hua-ti . . . tsei-ssu . . . ah-erh. . . .*"*

In the maths class, she read out problems as if she were declaiming an oration.

"$2x + y = ... x^2 = ...$"

At the lunch table, grasping a steamed roll in one black hand, she would ruminate over the last geography lesson. "Mexico produces silver. . . . Yunnan . . . wait a minute, Yunnan has marble!"

At night she would hide herself in the cloak-room to study; at the crack of dawn she would sit on the landing with a book. I kept coming across her wherever there was the least light. One morning during a snowstorm, when the branches outside the window seemed draped with white cotton wool, I saw someone

---

* "What . . . these . . . are. . . ."

apparently asleep on the windowsill at the far end of the long
corridor in our dormitory.

"Who's that? It must be cold there!" In my leather shoes
I clumped across the floor — as it was a Sunday the school was
unusually still.   Some of the girls were dressing up to go out,
some were asleep in bed.

While some distance away, I noticed the pages of a book
on her knees flapping this way and that in the wind.

"Who can it be? Working so hard on a Sunday!" On the
point of calling out, I caught sight of those black hands.

"Wang Yaming, Wang Yaming... wake up!" This was
the first time I had called her name and I felt rather awkward.

"Ha.... I was asleep!" She interspersed all her remarks
with this abrupt laugh.

"*Hua-ti...tsei-ssu...yu...ai....*" She started chanting
again before even finding the place in the book.

"*Hua-ti...tsei-ssu....* How difficult English is!... Not
like Chinese which has proper radicals for every character....
These words twist and turn like snakes squirming through my
head, till I'm so muddled I can't remember a thing. The English
mistress says it's not hard, and none of you seem to find it
hard either.   I must be slow in the uptake: country folk's brains
don't work as fast as yours.   My father's even worse.   He says
the only character he knew as a boy was our surname Wang, and
learning that took him a good half hour. *Yu...ai...yu...ah-
erh....*" She started reading out different words at random.

The wind from the small opening on the wall was whirring,
while from time to time snowflakes flew in to congeal in pearly
drops against the window.

Her eyes were bloodshot.   Insatiably greedy to learn, she
was stretching out her black hands for a prize beyond her grasp.

I saw her in corners, in spots with merely the faintest glimmer of light, poring over her books like a rat gnawing at something.

The first time her father came to see her, he said she had put on weight.

"I say, you've grown fat! So the grub's better here than at home, eh? Work hard! After three years' hard work, even if you aren't a sage at least some sense will have been drilled into you."

For a week afterwards in our form we did nothing but mimic her father.

The second time her father came to see her, she asked him for a pair of gloves.

"You can have mine. Study, if you study hard, what's a pair of gloves? Hold on, there's no hurry.... Take these first, they'll keep you snug! I don't go out much anyway, Yaming. I'll buy myself another pair next winter, Yaming." He was talking so loudly at the reception-room door that quite a crowd had gathered. It was "Yaming this" and "Yaming that" as he told her the news from home.

"Third sister's paying a visit to your second aunt: she's been away two or three days. Our pig gets an extra two handfuls of beans everyday: you should see the size of it now and the way its ears stick up.... Your elder sister came home and salted us two vats of scallions...."

He was talking away, hot and flushed, when the headmistress picked her way through the crowd to confront him.

"Won't you sit down in the reception-room...."

"There's no need, no need! That would take time and I can't stop. I've a train to catch.... I must get back to make sure the children are all right...." He took off his leather cap and bobbed his steaming head. Then he pushed open the door and started out, as if the headmistress had driven him away. He turned back, though, to peel off his gloves.

"You keep them, dad. I don't really need gloves."

Her father's hands were dark and discoloured too, bigger and blacker than hers.

In the newspaper-room, Yaming asked me:

"Tell me, is it true? Do you have to pay if you sit and talk in the reception-room?"

"Pay? What an idea! Of course not."

"Don't shout! If the others hear, they'll make fun of me again." She tapped the paper I was reading. "My father saw the teapot and bowls in the reception-room and said if we went in and the porter served tea we'd have to pay. I told him we wouldn't, but he didn't believe me. He says even in the smallest inns you have to pay for just a bowl of water. So you must pay more in a big place like our school."

Before this the headmistress had lectured her several times:

"Those hands of yours — can't you wash them clean? Try using more soap! Give them a thorough scrubbing and soaking in hot water. At morning drill on the playground, when hundreds of white hands go up, you're the only freak. A real freak!" With transparent fingers, like some bloodless fossil, the headmistress tapped Yaming's black hands, holding her breath rather fearfully as if forced to pick up a dead crow. "The colour's worn off a good deal — you can see the skin now on the palm. That's much better than when you came, when your hands looked like iron. . . . Are you keeping up with your class? You must work harder. In future you needn't attend morning exercises. Our school wall is low, and in spring you know how many foreigners stroll past and how often they stop to look over the wall. You may join in the drill again when your hands are white."

"I asked my father for a pair of gloves. If I wear gloves, no one will see my hands." She opened her satchel and took out her father's gloves.

The headmistress smiled and coughed. Her pale face flushed. "That's no use! If you're dirty, wearing gloves won't make you clean."

When the snow on the artificial mountain in the garden melted, the porter rang the bell with unusual vigour, the willows in front of the windows put out green shoots, and the playing

field seemed to smoke as it steamed in the sun. The sports
teacher's whistle in the distance echoed through the crowd of
girls among the trees.

We ran and jumped, we twittered like a flock of birds. We
were drugged by the honey-sweet air, by the breeze from the
tree tops fragrant with fresh leaves. Spirits cabined and confined by winter expanded like matted cotton wadding fluffed
out again.

As we left the sports ground we heard a voice from upstairs, which sounded as if it were floating up to the sky:

"What a lovely warm sun! Are you hot? . . ." Yaming
was standing at the window, looking out across the willows in
tender leaf.

By the time the willows were in full leaf, shading the yard,
Yaming had gradually wilted. Dark shadows lay under her
eyes, her ears seemed thinner, even her shoulders had lost their
old aggressive sturdiness. On the rare occasions when she came
out to enjoy the shade of the trees, her hollow chest reminded
me of a consumptive.

"The head says I'm behind the rest of the form. It's true:
I am behind. If I can't catch up by the end of the year —
ha! — will I really have to stay down?" Though she still laughed
when she spoke, her hands were trembling. She thrust her left
hand behind her back while her right made a bulge under the
lapel of her jacket.

We never knew her to cry till that day when a high wind
lashed the willows outside the window and, turning her back on
the class-room and on us, she wept to the blustering wind. That
was after a party of visitors had left, and she hid her eyes with
her black hands, now starting to fade.

"Still crying! What good will that do? What you should
have done was keep out of the visitors' way. Look at you —
a regular scarecrow! I'm not just talking about your two black
hands: look at that jacket — I declare it's nearly grey. All the
other girls have blue jackets, you're the only exception. When

clothes are too old and shabby they don't look clean. . . . We can't break the regulations about uniform just for you. . . ." The head clamped her lips together, and clutched Yaming's collar with one pale white hand. "I told you to wait downstairs till the visitors had gone. Who told you to stand in the corridor? Did you imagine you were invisible there? Wearing those enormous gloves, too. . . ."

With the glossy tip of one black patent leather shoe, the head kicked a glove which had fallen on the floor.

"Did you think it was perfectly all right to stand here in those gloves? Disgusting objects!" She stamped on the glove and laughed sarcastically — it was big enough for a carter.

How Yaming cried! Even after the wind had dropped she was still crying.

She came back after the summer holiday. The late summer was as cool as autumn, and the setting sun stained the paving stones vermilion. We had clustered under a crab-apple tree and were nibbling its fruit when Yaming's cart rumbled up from Lama Mount. In the absolute silence which followed the cart's arrival, her father unloaded the luggage while she carried in her basin and small bundles. We didn't make way at once as she came up the steps. Some said: "You're back!" "So it's you!" Others just gaped.

Not till her father had stumped up the steps with a white towel flapping at his belt did someone exclaim:

"Well! See how black her hands are again after a summer at home? As black as iron."

I didn't pay much attention to those iron-black hands at the time, not till autumn came and we moved to a different dormitory. Half asleep that evening, I heard a commotion next door.

"I don't want her! I refuse to sleep next to her!"

"So do I!"

Though I pricked up my ears I couldn't hear anything clearly, only a buzz of laughter and noisy argument. But going to the corridor that night for a drink of water, I saw someone sleeping there on a deck-chair and recognized Yaming instantly. Her black hands were over her face, her quilt was half on the floor, half over her legs. My first thought was that she must have been reading by the corridor light; but there were no books beside her. Instead, all around her were scattered her odds and ends of belongings.

The next night the headmistress walked up to Yaming, sniffing. Then she inspected the beds in one room, patting the smooth white sheets with one slender hand.

"Here in this row there are seven beds to only eight girls, while over there nine girls are sleeping on six beds." She tugged at one quilt and moved it a little to one side, then told Yaming to put her bedding there.

Yaming was so pleased that she whistled as she made her bed — the first whistling I ever heard in a girl's school.

When the bed was made she sat down on it, open-mouthed, tilting her chin up a little, as if it had shown a tendency to droop. The head had gone downstairs: she may have left the dormitory and gone home. But now the old matron with lack-lustre hair shuffled in to pad to and fro.

"Upon my word, this won't do. . . . Such an unhygienic girl! Crawling with bugs! Of course nobody wants to sleep next to her." She took a few steps towards my corner and rolled her eyes at me: "See that quilt! Smell it! It has an unpleasant odour two feet away. . . . The idea of anyone sleeping next to her! First thing you knew, bugs would be all over you. Take a look and see how filthy that wadding is!"

Matron liked to talk about herself: since her husband had studied in Japan and she had gone there with him, she counted herself a "foreign-returned student" too.

"What did you study?" some of the girls once asked her.

"You don't have to study any special subject! In Japan you speak Japanese, you learn Japanese customs — that's studying abroad, isn't it?" Her conversation was larded with such expressions as "unhygienic," "the idea!" "filthy." She referred to lice as bugs.

"A filthy girl has filthy hands!" She hunched her massive shoulders and hurried out as if a cold blast had struck her.

"A girl like that . . . I don't know why the head keeps her." After the bell sounded for lights out, matron could still be heard talking in the corridor.

On the third night, Yaming decamped with her bundles and bedding again, and the pasty-faced head walked up to our wing again.

"We don't want her. We're full up!"

The girls called out before the head had time to lay a finger on their bedding. This happened in the next room too.

"We're full up too. There are even more of us here: nine to six beds — how can you add any more!"

"One, two, three, four. . . ." The head started counting. "No, you can take one more. There should be six girls to four beds, but there are only five of you. . . . Here, Wang Yaming."

"No, I'm keeping that for my sister who's coming tomorrow. . . ." A girl ran over and held the quilt firmly in place.

Finally the head took Yaming to a different dormitory.

"She's got lice, I won't sleep next to her. . . ."

"Nor will I!"

"Wang Yaming's quilt has no cover, she sleeps next to the cotton. If you don't believe me, just look!"

Finally they made joke of the whole business, pretending that they dared not go near Yaming for fear of her black hands.

In the end, the owner of the black hands slept on the deck-chair in the corridor. When I got up early, I used to find her rolling up her bedding and carrying it downstairs. Sometimes I met her in the cellar which served as a store-room; and as this was naturally in the evening, I could see her shadow on the wall as I talked to her, her hands the same colour as the hair they were rumpling.

"Once you're used to it, it's the same thing sleeping on a

chair. It's somewhere to sleep, that's all that matters. The main thing is study.... I wonder how many marks Miss Ma will give me for my English in the next exam? If I don't pass, will I have to stay down next year?"

"Don't worry. You don't stay down for failing in one subject," I assured her.

"My father says I must finish school in three years: he can't afford to keep me here even one term more.... I just can't twist my tongue round those English words. Ha!..."

The entire dormitory was disgusted with her, even though she slept in the corridor, because she coughed every night.... And she started dyeing her stockings and blouses there too.

"Old clothes dyed are almost as good as new. I mean to say, if you dye your summer uniform grey it'll do for the autumn.... Or you can buy white stockings and dye them black...."

"Why don't you buy black stockings?" I asked her.

"Black stockings are machine-dyed and too much alum is used.... They don't wear well, but ladder almost as soon as you put them on.... Home dyeing is better. A pair of stockings costs nearly half a dollar.... Who's going to throw money away like that?"

One Saturday evening some girls boiled a chicken in a small pan. It was our practice to cook something good on Saturdays. When the chicken was dished up — I was there when this happened — it was black! I thought it must have been poisoned. The girl dishing it up gave such a shriek that her spectacles nearly fell off.

"Who did this? Who? Who was it?"

Yaming turned towards us and lumbered into the kitchen. She pushed her way through the others with her usual laugh.

"It was me! I didn't know you'd be using this pan so I dyed two pairs of stockings in it. Ha!... I'll go...."

"Where'll you go? You...."

"I'll go and wash it."

"How can we cook in a pan that's stewed your stinking stockings? D'you think we still want it?" The pan hurtled with a clatter across the floor. And pandemonium broke out as the girl in spectacles hurled the black chicken after it.

When they had gone Yaming picked up the chicken.

"Well, now!" she said to herself. "Just because I dyed two pairs of new stockings in it, they don't want the pan! How can new stockings stink?"

On winter evenings, when the lane from the class-rooms to our dormitories was deep in snow, we used to charge ahead and make a dash for it or turn round and round in a flurry of snow if there was a high wind, walking backwards or sideways. First thing in the morning we had to set out again, and in December our feet were numb with cold even if we ran. We grumbled and complained, and some girls called the head a "horrid old cat" because the dormitory was so far from the class-rooms and we had to sally out before it was light.

Sometimes I met Yaming by herself in the lane, when the distant sky and the distant snow were sparkling and the moon cast our shadows before us as we plodded along. There was no one else in sight. The wind howled through the roadside trees, and window panes creaked and groaned as the snow drove against them. The temperature, well below freezing, made our voices crisper than usual. But when our lips were as stiff and numb as our legs, we had to stop talking. All we could do then was listen to the snow going crunch! crunch! under our feet.

By the time you pressed your finger on the bell your legs were almost ready to fall apart: your knees sagged as if they wanted to give way.

One morning some time that winter I set out from the dormitory with a novel I wanted to read under my arm. As I turned to pull the wicker gate to after me, a shiver ran down my spine. The sight of those shadowy buildings in the distance, the sound of the wind-driven snow hissing after me, did nothing to allay my fears. The stars were faint and small. The moon had set or been swallowed up by grey, leaden clouds.

With each step I took, the more endless seemed the road. I longed to meet someone on the way, yet dreaded it too; for on a moonless night you could hear footsteps before anyone appeared — till a figure sprang up without warning out of the ground.

My heart was still pounding as I climbed the school steps, and it was with a nerveless hand that I pressed the bell. Suddenly I sensed that someone was beside me.

"Who's that? Who's there?"

"Me! It's me."

"Were you walking behind me?" An even more fearful idea, for I had heard no footsteps but my own on the road!

"No, I wasn't behind you, I've been here for some time. The porter won't let me in. I've been calling for goodness knows how long."

"Didn't you ring the bell?"

"Ha, ringing the bell is no use! He turned on the light and came to the door, and looked out through the window. . . . But he wouldn't let me in."

The light inside went on and the porter, grumbling noisily, opened the door.

"Trying to get in at this time of the night! As if that could help you to pass when you're bound to fail!"

"What's that? What are you talking about?" As soon as I spoke, the porter changed his tune.

"Miss Xiao! Have you been waiting long?"

Yaming and I went together to the cellar. She was coughing, her face was peaked and pinched, and she shivered for several minutes like an old woman. The tears brought to her eyes by the wind were still on her cheeks as she opened her lesson book.

"Why didn't the porter let you in?" I asked.

"I don't know. He said I was too early, I'd better go back. That was the head's order, he said. . . ."

"How long did you wait?"

"Not too long. Anyway, what does a short wait matter? The time for a meal maybe, ha!"

She studied differently now. Her voice had lost its former resonance and she simply mumbled. Her shoulders, once so sturdy, had shrunk and narrowed. She stooped and her chest had grown hollow.

I was reading a story aloud, but kept my voice down for fear of disturbing her. This was the first time that any such scruples had troubled me — why was it the first time, I wondered?

She asked what I was reading. Did I know the *Romance of Three Kingdoms*? Sometimes she picked it up to look at the cover or turn over a few pages. "You others are so brainy. You hardly look at your books, but you aren't a bit scared of exams. I'm just plain stupid. I'd like to rest sometimes and read a story or two . . . but I can't. . . ."

One Sunday when the dormitory was empty, I was reading aloud that passage in Upton Sinclair's *The Jungle* where the working girl Maria collapses in the snow, and the snowy landscape outside brought the scene home vividly. I was quite unaware that Yaming was standing behind me.

"Will you lend me one of the books you've finished with? All this snow gets on my nerves, but I've no family here and nothing to buy. Besides, going into town means spending money on fares. . . ."

"Your father hasn't been to see you for a long time, has he?" I imagined she was homesick.

"How can he? The return fare by train comes to over two dollars. . . . Besides, there's no one at home. . . ."

I put the translation of Upton Sinclair's novel into her hands since I'd finished it already.

"Ha!" she laughed. She bumped twice into the bed as

she started examining the cover of the book. After she went out I heard her in the corridor reading the first sentence aloud as she'd heard me doing.

Some time later — it must have been a holiday for the dormitory was deserted — the whole place was utterly silent all day till moonlight started streaming through the window. I heard a rustling by my pillow as if someone were groping about, and opened my eyes to see Yaming's black hands. She laid the book she had borrowed down beside me.

"Find it interesting? Did you like it?"

At first she did not answer. Then she covered her face with her hands, and her very hair seemed to tremble as she breathed:

"Yes!"

Her voice was trembling too. I sat up in bed. But she ran away, her face still buried in hands as black as her hair.

The long corridor was empty. I could see the cracks in the floor-boards in the moonlight.

"Maria seems a real live person, and look at the way she collapses in the snow — I do hope she doesn't die! She mustn't die! But if the doctor knows she has no money, he won't treat her. . . . Ha!" Her high-pitched laugh made the tears in her eyes brim over. "I went for the doctor once when my mother was ill, but do you think he would come? First he asked me for the cab fare. I told him the money was at home and begged him to come straight away — she was very bad. But do you think he would? He stood in the yard and asked: 'What does your family do? You're dyers, eh?' I don't know why, but as soon as I told him we were dyers he went back into his room. . . . I waited for some time and then knocked again. He called from inside: 'I can't attend your mother. Go away!' I went home. . . ." She dabbed her eyes again before going on: "After that I had to take care of two younger brothers and two younger sisters. Father dyed the black and the blue things, my elder sister dyed the red. The winter that her marriage was arranged, her future mother-in-law came in from the country to stay with us. At first sight of my sister she cried: 'Mercy! She's got hands like a butcher!' After that, father wouldn't let any of us dye one colour only. My hands are black, but if you look hard you can see traces of purple. My two younger sisters are the same."

"Aren't your sisters at school?"

"No. I'm to teach them later on. Only I don't know how much I've learned myself. If I don't study hard, I'll be letting my two small sisters down.... Dyeing one bolt of cloth brings in no more than thirty cents ... and how many bolts do we get in a month? Garments are ten cents apiece, regardless of size, and most sent to us are big ones.... When you take away the cost of fuel and dyes ... see what I mean? To pay my school fees they've had to scrape up every penny, even the little spent on salt.... Don't you see, I have to work hard, I simply have to!" She reached for her book again.

I went on staring at the cracks in the floor. Her tears, to my mind, were worth far more than my sympathy.

One morning, before it was time for the holidays, Yaming tidied up her satchel and her bits and pieces — her big luggage was already firmly roped and stood by the corridor wall.

No one bid her goodbye or said any parting words. To leave the dormitory each of us had to pass the deck-chair where she slept, and she smiled at each of us, gazing far away through the window in between. We tramped and clattered along the corridor, down the stairs and across the yard; but at the wicker gate she caught up with us and called out to us, panting:

"My father hasn't come yet. Each extra hour I can study is all to the good...."

She put all she had into those last extra hours. During the English lesson, she busily copied all the new words on the blackboard into her notebook. Not only this, she read them aloud and put down quite unnecessarily the words we already knew. The second period was geography, and she laboriously copied into her notebook the map the mistress drew on the board.... Apparently she set great store by every moment of this final day: she was not going to let it slip by unrecorded.

During the break I looked at her notebook: it was full of mistakes. Some of the English words had a letter missing, some had a letter too many.... She had lost her head completely.

That night, since her father still hadn't come to fetch her, she spread her quilt over the deck-chair again. For the first time she went to bed early and slept soundly. Her quilt was drawn up nearly to her head, her shoulders were relaxed and she breathed deeply. There were no books beside her tonight.

The next morning, when the sun still hung over the trembling, snow-covered boughs and the birds had just left their nests, her father arrived. He stopped on the landing, put down the big felt boots slung over his shoulder and wiped the icicles off his beard with the white towel round his neck.

"So you failed, eh? Well...." The icicles melted on the stairs in drops of water.

"No, we haven't had the exams yet. The head told me I needn't take them — I couldn't pass...."

Standing on the landing, he turned his face to the wall and the white cloth hanging at his belt was completely still.

Yaming had dragged her luggage to the landing, and now she fetched her satchel, basin and other odds and ends. She handed the enormous gloves to her father.

"I don't want them, you wear them!" With each step he took, his boots left muddy imprints on the floor.

Since it was still very early, few girls were there to watch. With a faint chuckle, Yaming slipped on the gloves.

"Put on the boots! You've made a mess of your schooling, but don't let's have your feet frozen." Her father untied the string fastening the boots together.

The boots came up over her knees, and she fastened a white felt hood over her head like a carter.

"I shall be back." I don't know to whom she was talking. 'I'll take my books home and study hard and then I'll come back.... Ha!" She picked up her satchel again and asked her father:

"Is the cart at the door?"

"Cart? What cart? We're walking to the station.... I'll carry your things."

Yaming flip-flopped down the stairs in her felt boots. Her father led the way, a corner of the bedding roll in his discoloured hands.

Slender shadows cast by the morning sun bobbed up and down in front of them and crawled up the wicker gate. From the window, they looked as insubstantial as shadows. There they were in full sight, but not a sound did they make.

They passed through the wicker gate and headed into the distance, trudging in the direction of the hazy morning sun.

The snow on the ground was like little splinters of glass, more and more dazzling the farther away it was. I stared at the distant snow till my eyes were smarting.

March 1936
Translated by Gladys Yang

About the Author

XIAO HONG (1911-42), a celebrated woman writer whose real name was Zhang Naiying, was born in Hulan County, Heilongjiang Province. She entered the First Girls' School of Harbin in 1929, and left home to escape a family-arranged marriage two years later. In 1933 she wrote short stories "Trek" and "Tornado". She went to Shanghai in 1934 and made the acquaintance of Lu Xun. In 1935, she published a short novel, *Field of Life and Death,* which was one of the first literary works to reflect the life and struggle of the people of northeast China under the rule of Japanese imperialism. Lu Xun wrote a preface for it. Xiao Hong went to Japan in 1936 for health reasons and returned to China after the outbreak of the War of Resistance Against Japan in 1937 when she wrote short stories "Hands", "Small Town in March" and "Calls from Wilderness". Her short novel *Bole, a Good Horse-Judge* appeared in 1940. In the same year, she went to Hongkong where she wrote *National Spirit*, a pantomime commemorating Lu Xun, a biography *In Memory of Mr. Lu Xun* and a novel *The Hulan River*. She died of illness in Hongkong in 1942 at the age of thirty-two.

Her short story "Hands" describes how a dye worker's daughter is looked down on in school because of her black hands, strongly criticizing bourgeois school education.

Three Peerless Fighters

Liu Baiyu

1. How the dissension started

Some people think that we soldiers are too simple: they think that we do nothing except fight and sleep. But, in fact, it's not like that.

In our company it's like being at home — the difference is that our home might be now in a trench, and now on some peasants' haystack. We have our share of family joys, and we also have our share of family troubles.

I don't want to talk about other places, but let me tell you about our squad.

This business took place a little while ago, when we welcomed a soldier back to our squad. Shouldn't this have been a joyful event? Instead, it led to dissension.

He was a war hero who was rushing back to the front before he had completely recovered from his wound. We thought him a soldier who really deserved a welcome. In the evening the whole squad sat in a circle on the kang (a brick bed). On the way here, he was afraid that he wouldn't be able to overtake us, so he was happy beyond measure to have all of us around him now. With the help of gestures he vividly described how he had come here by train, and how he had helped newly emancipated peasants to overthrow their landlords. People kept bursting into laughter at his stories. Then we began to talk animatedly about

436

things that had been happening in our company. At the end a comrade said, "We've been thinking about you ever since you left. In the last few days the whole regiment has been buzzing with the story of your heroic feat, we're all full of admiration. The regimental commander tells us to learn from you! He says you are a valiant hero." As we were all feeling happy with each other, another soldier suddenly broke in. Although he didn't say more than a sentence, it was enough to start off the dissension.

2. Yan Chengfu

Yan Chengfu, the war hero introduced above, is the main character in this story.

No one knew then what his background was, but you could tell at a glance that he came from a humble home. He was always a young tiger in the squad, and in battle he became even more headstrong, a real tiger.

When he was wounded, he got fed up buffing his bottom on a hospital bed, so he went home. There he saw the poor entering a new life. They were well-clothed, there were horses at their mangers and land beyond their front gate. His heart filled with an immense happiness. That evening when the Peasants' Association celebrated his return, he said resolutely:

"Let me tell you so you get it straight. The war is won, there's no question of that! I came back to see if you were putting up a thorough struggle against feudalism. Now I've got it straight too. Now we only have to wait for the good news. On the battlefield I shall never disgrace the name of our Laladun."

Before daybreak he had disappeared. Yan Chengfu returned to the hospital, visited every comrade in the ward and then left for the front.

During his absence from the army, people used to talk about his heroic feat. Each person would tell the story to

several others, and they in turn would pass it on to more, so
that it circulated far and wide rather in the same way as a legend
from the past. In fact it was a story really worth telling. One
day, we were engaged with the enemy in an unexpected encounter and Yan Chengfu was right in the firing line. All of a sudden he dashed forward alone and a few minutes later he had
lost contact with us. The enemy's machineguns and 60 mm
mortars spewed smoke and fire everywhere. Hell! We thought
Yan Chengfu was finished, a martyr for the revolution. The
company commander was mad with rage, and with reddened
eyes charged forward with his men. You wouldn't guess what
happened next! Right at this critical moment the enemy ranks
were suddenly thrown into confusion, and we came upon them
just as their firing slackened off. What had happened was this.
After making a couple of false turns, Yan Chengfu somehow
managed to make his way into the enemy's temporary headquarters, and at the moment of our asssault, he threw in a hand-
grenade, of course creating confusion in the enemy ranks. Now
he led out at the point of his rifle an important-looking captive,
a regimental officer! Yan Chengfu bawled out that this fellow
had just now been directing the troops. Once we captured this
place, we immediately pushed on forward deep into the enemy's
rear. In our next action, Yan Chengfu again came to the fore,
shouting, "It's Yan Chengfu to the fore again!" .When we heard
his cry, our spirits rose. It was our squad's task then to charge
the enemy, and in this critical situation he was wounded and lost
consciousness. The company commander ordered us to carry
him behind the lines and hand him over to the stretcher-bearers
in the woods nearby.

3. Old Cruller

Old Cruller was then nickname we gave Li Fahe. We used
it so often that people seemed to have forgotten his real name.

Even the political instructor sometimes addressed him in this familiar way.

Old Cruller was an old soldier. Somebody also called him "Old Never Progress", but he didn't seem to mind.

After we had taken the Pass* some of us were promoted to the rank of platoon leader, but he still remained a soldier. Nevertheless he was satisfied with his lot, and if someone asked him about it, he would smile amiably and say:

"I'm quite content — I'm not worried!"

His problem was liberalism, never taking things seriously. He never broke any major rule, but he constantly infringed the minor ones though he had been in the army more than three years. He must have fought in more than a hundred battles but he never emerged with a hair out of place. Of course, he was cunning enough in battle, and when it was really going hammer and tongs, he was there — fast, furious, and right on the ball. However, he was politically undeveloped, and broke all the rules which governed our daily lives. No medal was ever hung around his neck. Now, to get back to our story, during our welcome to Yan Chengfu that night, he suddenly made a remark out of the blue. He had been sitting to one side rolling tobacco leaves and puffing away, but when people were praising Yan Chengfu, he suddenly pushed the others aside and stuck his head in, saying,

"Seems to me it was sheer luck that got the medal."

At this remark, Yan Chengfu exploded. Scowling ferociously he immediately came back, "What do you mean, luck?"

Old Cruller looked at him with a long, unhurried gaze.

"I've been in more than a hundred battles, big and small, but there's no bullet hole on my body. This is real skill. You may be a hero all right, but you're still just a beginner when it comes to battle action."

---

* Shanhaiguan, the mountain pass where the Great Wall meets the East China Sea.

This dash of cold water dampened everyone's spirits. The squad leader said it was late, time to put out the lamp and go to sleep, and since then Yan Chengfu and Old Cruller made a practice of ignoring each other.

4. Zhao Xiaoyi

If the quarrel between Yan Chengfu and Old Cruller had stayed just between the two of them it would still have been fairly simple, but now Zhao Xiaoyi got involved.

Zhao Xiaoyi was a young soldier, only 19 years old, who came over during the liberation of a Kuomintang area when he was liberated in our summer offensive. Because he was rather young, he hadn't been too deeply poisoned, so he was sent up as a reinforcement right away instead of being sent to the rear. Zhao Xiaoyi seemed lively and innocent on the surface but inside he still had his suspicions. He never uttered a word at our discussions, but stared around him, thinking, "When two tigers are fighting, one is bound to get the worst of it, I'll see who's getting the upper hand and take his side." So his aim in our regiment was this: don't be active but don't be backward either. He was inclined to find fault with everything and whenever he felt he wasn't being treated correctly as a former prisoner-of-war, he swore, "Where's our special treatment now? — all a lie!" The fifth squad was a model squad, and the squad leader ran it with a firm grip, but even a hard piece of stone can have a crack on it. After Zhao Xiaoyi had been with us for some time, his liberalism naturally drew him closer to Old Cruller. That evening, when Old Cruller and Yan Chengfu flew at each other, he was secretly on the side of Old Cruller, for he was rather annoyed by Yan Chengfu's stories about the peasants' new life, landlords being overthrown, heroes and so on, and the next day he tried to approach Old Cruller. Old Cruller, however, had his principles: he was willing to smoke a few pipes with young Zhao, but as for talking about their feelings, no, he wouldn't do that. He thought to himself, I came through the Pass, but you were a prisoner-of-war. Since young Zhao couldn't find any comfort here, he went looking for Yan Chengfu instead, and got his temper up by telling him that Old Cruller had said:

"What's so great about Yan Chengfu? See how he does in the next battle!"

Of course, Yan Chengfu was ready to listen to something that concerned him, and after this his relationship with Old Cruller got even worse, turning away when they saw each other.

But when young Zhao talked about his own feelings, Yan Chengfu was not interested. Why was this?

Yan Chengfu's feeling was, I am an emancipated fighter from the liberated area, but you are a captive from Chiang Kai-shek's area. His attitude of superiority disappointed young Zhao very much, and he became very depressed.

In this way, after four or five days, the model squad was no longer a model.

5. Li Zhanhu, the squad leader, is worried

As the quarrel developed, Li Zhanhu, the squad leader, was greatly worried. The model squad that he had personally built up was falling apart under his eyes, so no wonder he was worried.

Li Zhanhu was a good squad leader, always the first to act whenever there were any difficulties. You mightn't realize that it isn't easy to lead a squad. Ten people have ten minds, and a successful leader must unite the ten minds as one. Li Zhanhu never raged or glared at his men. He was an old soldier who had come through the Pass, a patient instructor who won an approving thumbs-up from everyone. The appearance of dissension within the squad made things extremely difficult when they were on the march or fighting. These three never spoke a word to one another. If you put them on sentry duty in consecutive shifts, they wouldn't hand over to each other. If you put them together to eat, Yan Chengfu would sit facing east and Li Fahe would face west, always back to back. If you made them sleep on the same kang, when Li Fahe went to sleep, Yan Chengfu would bundle up his bedding with a snort and sleep on the floor. One day, Li Zhanhu sought each of them for a face-to-face talk. First, he talked to Yan Chengfu. After he had talked for some time, Yan Chengfu said:

"I'll serve the people, but won't put up with insults. You'll see whether I'm a coward or not on the front line." And then he stood up and walked off.

Then he went to Li Fahe. Li Fahe continued to smoke while listening to him, and when the squad leader came to the end, he said,

"I'll no matter what always serve the people. There's no question about that."

The squad leader then talked to Zhao Xiaoyi, who finally said,

"Ah, squad leader, before I didn't understand anything, but now I have been liberated, I have received an education. I serve the people, what else can I say?"

After all this trouble, the three still stuck to their "serve the people". The squad leader's enthusiasm turned into irritation, and he muttered: "You'd think these three had come to some agreement!" He was really stuck for a way out, and neither tears nor laughing could help in the least.

It was right at this point that the regiment issued a call for unity and solidarity. Since the fifth squad had been a model squad before, the political instructor intended to give it special training, and spent a few days with it to get acquainted. It was quite a surprise for him to find how things were under the surface, and he shook his head in disapproval. This made Li Zhanhu so upset that tears came to his eyes. Grabbing the political director he said: "Instructor, there is still hope for the fifth, give us three more days!" The request was granted, and the leader thought, "What should I do!" He decided on a "surround and annihilate" tactic, and straightaway called the three men together. In a few sentences he laid bare the problem of their dissension. Unexpectedly, the three came back at him with one voice, "There's nothing wrong, squad leader!" He was pleased to hear this and he told them about winning for the fifth squad the title of model squad. But the next day none of them had budged an inch, and they all continued to ignore each other. This greatly upset the squad leader, who burst into tears of rage when he was alone. As they were to engage in battle the following day, they were fully occupied with preparations for combat, and no progress was made in the matter of unity.

6. A piece of bone

The following day the battle took place under an overcast sky and some rain. After it was over, Li Zhanhu led his men off the field. As they were passing through a stretch of desolate grave-mounds, he noticed a piece of bone on the ground. He stopped, bent over to pick up the bone and looked at it. The men in the squad looked at him with curiosity, and he put a question to them:

"Do you know whose bone is this?"

Standing in the rain they began to discuss it. Some said it came from a poor man while others said it was from a rich man. Finally, Li Zhanhu had his say:

"I think it is a poor man's bone. When landlords, rich peasants or people who are well-off die, they are buried in coffins and proper tombs. Their bones wouldn't be scattered around here. The poor have nothing to eat while they are living and they have nowhere to rest in peace after they die.

The wind and rain scatter their bones far and wide. Who bothers about the poor!"

After returning to camp, the soldiers busied themselves spreading hay and watering the ground. Looking around, Li Zhanhu noticed that Yan Chengfu, Li Fahe and Zhao Xiaoyi were missing, and there was still no sign of them when it was time to eat. He rushed towards the barracks. Young Zhao had thrown himself on the kang as soon as they came back and was still there. The squad leader thought he might have had another row with Old Cruller or Yan Chengfu, and tried to console him:

"Ah, young Zhao, that's the way people are. When they're together, they grumble but when they're apart they long to be together again."

He clambered up on the kang to take Zhao's arm, but Zhao suddenly turned around and with a loud groan threw himself into the squad leader's arms and burst into tears.

After he had cried for a spell, he told the squad leader a story, and both the listener and the teller were in tears.

The squad leader went to the company headquarters at once and gave the political instructor a blow-by-blow report. The political instructor was also very moved by this story, and told him to return to his squad and look after young Zhao. On his way back Li Zhanhu drew on his allowance to buy a few eggs, which he brought back and boiled for young Zhao. When Zhao picked up the bowl, he burst out sobbing. Now what young Zhao said and what the squad leader heard will have to wait for a while, because now we'll turn to something else.

7. Now for Yan Chengfu and Old Cruller

Yan Chengfu was very depressed, and thought of looking for a quiet place to stay in for a while, so he walked over to the grain bins in the back yard. Old Cruller was also on his way there, his head bent. If they hadn't heard the other's footsteps, they would have bumped into each other. Yan Chengfu lifted his head and saw Old Cruller, and at the same time Old Cruller also lifted his head and saw Yan Chengfu, and as if someone gave the order, "About turn!" they both snapped their heads around and stalked off.

After walking backwards and forwards for a while, Yan Chengfu left the village.

Old Cruller rolled a cigarette and smoked it as he went looking for a deserted spot, walking beside the wall with his head bent low.

As Yan Chengfu passed into the forest from one direction Old Cruller went into the forest from the other direction, and as Yan Chengfu came to the river bank, Old Cruller also came to the river bank. Once again they met.

Yan Chengfu flew into a rage, cursing to himself. If it hadn't been that he refused to be the first to speak, he would certainly have given Old Cruller a good cursing.

Just at this moment the squad leader came looking for them. Taking each by the hand he led them back at once.

Back at the camp, neither of them felt like eating and went straight to bed.

8. A lamp is lit at night

In the evening a lamp was lit. The squad leader examined the shoes lined up under the side of the kang and selected two worn-out pairs. After rolling a hemp thread on his knees, he started to mend the shoes. As he was working, young Zhao got up and offered to do the job for him, but the squad leader refused to let him take them. He tried to console him with a smile, "Go back to sleep! You don't look well, and there might be some fighting at daybreak.'' After a while, Yan Chengfu abruptly sat up, startling the squad leader. He stretched out his hand to grab the shoes, but the squad leader again refused, saying, "You look pale, you're not well. Don't you think you'll have enough to do later? Go to sleep!" Yan Chengfu sat there stunned for a moment and then lay down again. Suddenly there was a rustling noise, and Old Cruller got up and said in a low voice, "You go to sleep. I'll do the mending." The squad leader said smilingly, "Ordinarily, I would ask your help even you didn't volunteer. But today you're not well, you should rest!" But then the whole squad got up. None of them had been asleep, and they were all looking around at one another. Young Zhao at once burst into tears, and between sobs retold the story he had related to the squad leader that day.

"My dad was a pigman, he lost a pig, the landlord beat him up, he had a fit and died, before he was buried I was pressganged by the Kuomintang.

"I wept and struggled, they soaked a leather whip in cold water and beat me till I was more dead than alive. I said that I had to see dad once more even if I had to die for it, and the KMT said: 'If your dad's dead, all he'll do is stink up the ground, what's there to see?' That was two years ago! There was no one to bury my father, and nowhere to bury him. The wind and rain will scatter his limbs in all directions...." Unable to finish he burst into loud weeping again.

At this, Yan Chengfu rushed forward and enfolded young Zhao in his arms:

"I'm sorry, young Zhao! I used to despise people from Chiang Kai-shek's area. I didn't know that you were also one of the poor, one of the sufferers."

Once he started to speak, Yan Chengfu couldn't hold back the tears as he told the story of his own sufferings.

"Your dad was killed by a landlord, and my ma met the same fate. When I was eighteen, dad was arrested and made to do hard labour, ma was poisoned to death by the landlord and my brother was beaten to death with a rake by the landlord, I watched it in secret, but I didn't wait to be found, I ran away as fast as I could to the Liao River. I stared at the river, and I was really thinking of jumping in and putting an end to it all. Then I thought: I don't know if my dad's dead or alive, and I'm the only one left of the Yans. If I stay around, sooner or later I might be able to get my revenge. If I'm dead, the landlord would be even more content. After that I lived a beggar's life for a whole year! At summer time, I carried corn in the fields. In winter, after everyone had extinguished their fires for the night, I used to creep to a pigsty to sleep. . . ."

At this, except for Old Cruller, the whole squad wept. Ordinarily, people used to talk about unity and solidarity, but they had never become as close as they were now, seeing their own sufferings in the sufferings of others. Young Zhao gazed across at Yan Chengfu, and Yan gazed back at him. Then Yan said,

"When I heard your story, I realized that poor people suffer in the same way everywhere."

Young Zhao said: "You're right, when I heard your story I realized that in the Communist Party and the Eighth Route Army the poor help the poor. In the last few days I was too stupid to understand this, I feel unworthy of the revolution and also of myself."

The squad leader Li Zhanhu said, "Everyone should speak up! If we don't tell our own people about our sufferings, who should we tell them to?"

As the sun set the night grew dark. How many people in this world can sleep safe and sound? How many people ponder over their sufferings, the tears falling mixed with blood! As one finished his tale of grievance another began, and in the fifth squad that night the bitter tears flowed without stop, and the lamp stayed lit until the dawn of a new day.

9. What about Li Fahe?

Only Li Fahe, a great weight pressing on his heart, failed
to open his mouth. He sat there that night without a murmur.
As he thought of the past and of the future, his self-disgust kept
increasing; the others felt their sufferings very painfully but a
thick callus seemed to have formed around his heart. He asked
himself savagely: "All of them belong to the poor, am I then the
rich?" He thought how when he was a young man in his home
village he was fond of dancing the *yangge* and singing in the
operas. Taking advantage of the fact that he was well-known
as a loafer, the landlord in one swift move proceeded to clean
him out of house and home. When he was driven out of the
village he didn't even have a pair of trousers to hide his nakedness. He left his wife behind in the village. If she didn't hitch
up again during those years, she must have suffered very badly.
Dissipation and degradation were all that were left to Li Fahe,
and he even lost his thirst for revenge. If he hadn't met up
with the Communist Party and the Eighth Route Army, his
whole life would have been worthless. But he had been a soldier for four or five years, first inside the Pass and then outside,
and recalling this he really felt unworthy of the revolution, of
his commanders and of himself. After that night, though he
didn't say a word to anyone he secretly came to a decision.
"Goldthread root is bitter but my fate is bitterer still. It's time
to come to a decision!" He thought of the political director, his
senior officer, who had never spoken wrongly of him; he thought
of the squad leader, his old comrade-in-arms who humoured
him in everything; he thought of young Zhao, the child of a
bitter fate; he thought of Yan Chengfu — he really intended to
shake hands with him and patch up their quarrel, but, just as
the words came to his mouth, he thought again: "Hasty judge-
ments come to grief, we shall see!"

10. A common destiny brings unity
on the firing-line

A few days later, our troops went into battle again. When the fighting heated up our company joined in. Originally the fourth squad was supposed to be the shock brigade but within the first fifteen minutes it disintegrated and the order was given for the fifth squad to rush to the fore. With eyes glaring and fists clenched, Li Zhanhu said: "Comrades! Don't forget the sufferings we spoke of the other night. Don't forget the sufferings of young Zhao and of Yan Chengfu. The time has come to revenge your fathers, mothers, brothers and sisters!" They burst on to the battlefield like ten rockets. The political director crawled up to inspect the fifth squad personally, and Li Zhanhu said,

"Give us our duties, the wrongs of fifth squad must be avenged!" Yan Chengfu took on the task of blowing up a hole so they could break through. He ran forward with a package of explosives, the whole squad flat on the ground watching him. They saw him running forward, he had only another dozen steps to go, and then he stumbled and fell. Not waiting for Li Zhanhu's word, young Zhao sped like an arrow to his side. Two steps away from Yan Chengfu he also tumbled over, but he still tried hard to crawl forward, but he was hemmed in by the enemy's intense fire and couldn't move a step further. All this time, Li Fahe had been watching closely what was happening. In front of them, bullets rained down in a burst of firing. He suddenly said to the squad leader, "Leave this to me. Give me a sub-machinegun, I'm going after both of them, and I won't come back until the job's done." Under this heavily concentrated enemy fire, it was hardly reasonable to send anyone out to risk his life, and the eyes of the whole squad were on Li Fahe as by turn he raced forward and crouched on the ground. As they watched with bated breath. Li Fahe finally reached Yan

Chengfu's side where he lay prone. Wiping the sweat from his
brow, Li Zhanhu continued to watch them. Now, the three men
could neither move forward nor turn back, just like a spent
bullet. Yan Chengfu had been hit on the shoulder and blood was
oozing from the wound but he still kept a tight hold on the explosives. The two looked at each other in silence, a look which
spoke volumes. Li Fahe carried Yan Chengfu over to a low-
lying spot and asked, "How is it?" Yan Chengfu gritted his
teeth:

"It doesn't matter, we must go, we can't retreat."

Then Li Fahe crept over to young Zhao, who was wounded
in the leg, and bleeding over the ground. He carried young
Zhao to the side and asked, "How is it?"

"My leg's hurt."

"Can you still fire a gun?"

"Yes!"

"OK. You cover him from here and I'll cover him from
over there. Even if it means our own lives we'll see that Yan
Chengfu carries out his task. Right?"

Young Zhao nodded, and Li Fahe crawled back, the blood
staining his body as he picked his way through the corpses.
Cannon and machineguns blazed fiercely from both sides, and
every inch of ground was covered in flames. Young Zhao's hair
caught fire and smoke came from Li Fahe's trousers. The squad
saw that they weren't moving, and Li Zhanhu, burdened by
the thought of their heroic sacrifice, was getting ready to organize another explosion. Suddenly the sound of firing came
from in front. Li Fahe's sub-machinegun roared, and young
Zhao, gritting his teeth, also started firing. Covered in blood,
Yan Chengfu at once clambered to his feet and dashed forward.
A second later, there was a sudden flash closely followed by a
great roll of thunder, and the enemy's stronghold collapsed. A
column of black smoke ascended to the sky. Then suddenly a
burst of applause rose from our side. The breach was made,
and our troops plunged through with shouts of "Kill!"

11. The medals sum up our story

The battle was won, an enemy division was completely annihilated, and the fifth squad alone captured 58 prisoners. Not long after, a victory celebration was held. The political director told us to organize a band, so we invited three peasants to join four of our comrades, and the sound of trumpets, waist-drums, fiddles and gongs filled the air.

And now let's get back to Yan Chengfu, Li Fahe and Zhao Xiaoyi, who were standing shoulder to shoulder in front of the squad. Introducing them as "the three peerless fighters", the political director stepped up to them and pinned a medal on each breast. The red medals sparkled and shone.

Yan Chengfu looked at Li Fahe, and Li Fahe looked at Zhao Xiaoyi, then they all clapped vigorously. When they were asked to make their reports, the three said in one voice:

"It is all due to our squad leader."

Li Zhanhu stood up and said, "We are poor people, and we have suffered a lot. Let's turn our sorrow into strength and unite, and then, we'll be peerless the world over."

Translated by Zhang Mingzhu

About the Author

LIU BAIYU, a well-known contemporary writer, was born in 1916 in Beijing. His first short story "Icy Sky" was followed by others such as "On Pastures", "Illness" and "Red Snow". His first collection of short stories *On Pastures* was published in 1937. In 1938, he went to Yan'an to join the Yan'an Literary and Art Work Troupe and toured the anti-Japanese base areas in north China. During this time, he wrote another collection of stories, *At the Foot of Mount Wutai*. While in the Taihangshan Anti-Japanese Democratic Base Area, he wrote many works reflecting the struggle and life of the soldiers and people.   They include a collection of reportage, *Guerrilla War*, and collections of stories, *Story of Longyan Village* and *Happiness*. In 1944 he went to Chongqing to work for *Xinhua Daily* of Chongqing, editing its supplement. He was sent to the Northeast China Liberated Area in 1946 and during the War of Liberation he became an army correspondent. During this period, he wrote a full-length book of reportage *Touring the Northeast* and other works such as the short novel "Flame in Advance", and short stories "Political Commissar", "Three Peerless Fighters" and "Blood Relationship".

He continued his literary writing after the founding of the People's Republic.   From 1951 to 1954, he published works of nonfiction, *Korea Is Advancing in Battles* and *A Pledge of Peace*, and a collection of stories, *Happiness in War*, which exposed the crimes of the aggressors and eulogized the heroic struggles and militant friendship between the Chinese and Korean peoples. His works appearing between 1956 and 1959 reflected the socialist revolution and construction and people's new ideas and habits in China.   They include collections of prose — *Torch and the Sun*, *Sunrise*, *Red Agate*, *Three Days on the Yangtze* — and collections of short stories, *Bright Youth*, and *People Who Advance with the Dawn*. After 1976, he wrote more prose — such as "Song of the Red Sun", "Great Creators", "The Towering Taihang Mountain" and "Song of the Oilfield" — which praised the old proletarian revolutionaries and people who participated in the development of socialist economy.

Since the founding of the People's Republic, Liu Baiyu has headed many organizations of literature and art. He has been the vice-chairman of the Union of Chinese Writers, secretary of the secretariate of the Union of Chinese Writers, vice-minister of the Ministry of Culture and director of the Cultural Department of the General Political Department of the People's Liberation Army. He was elected deputy to the Fifth National People's Congress in 1978.

His short story "Three Peerless Fighters", written in a flowing and vivid traditional style, reflects the political work and fine quality of the people's army through a description of different types of soldiers.

Land Mines

Liu Qing

"Left, right, left! Left, right, left! Down with Japan!"

"Down with Japan."

"Left, right, left. Left, right, left. . . ."

It was April, and the sun was setting behind the grey hills to the west as the militia squad was drilling on a square in Lidao Village in the Taihang Mountains. The militiamen were running round in a circle. The drill-master inside the circle appeared rather impatient as he moved by the side of the front man calling "left, right, left" in the hope of getting them to run in step like real soldiers. Though they chorused, "Down with Japan," in thundering unison, their footsteps still sounded ragged.

The sight was too much for Li Shuyuan, the old man with a red-tasselled spear on sentry duty at the crossroads outside the temple, who could not help laughing so loud that his grey beard bristled. As the militiamen were all a generation or two younger than him and included his own two sons he did not pull his punches.

"You're a disgrace to your parents! You. . . ." He started coughing, then added in earnest, "Fighting the Japs needs real swords and guns, or even the Eighth Route Army. Hillbillies' legs are too stiff: they can't march in time."

"Left, right, left. Left, right, left. . . ."

The militia were drilling so hard in the square, kicking up dust as they ran, that they probably did not hear him. Then the old man, feeling left out, put his arms round his spear, lean-ed against the mud wall and started smoking.

The boom of another explosion came from far away to the west.

The old man's heart missed a beat and he could not but feel rather depressed. There had been several of them every day for a long time. It could not be thunder on so clear a day in April. Was it artillery? The sound was not sharp enough. The day before yesterday many troops had marched west through Lidao Village and some of them had spent the night there. The story began to spread that the explosions came from the Japanese blasting tunnels for a railway heading south that they were building very fast, and that as soon as the work was completed they would start mopping up the villages by the line. What would happen here then?

He sighed.

During last summer's mopping up his two rooms facing north together with the front gate of his compound had been burned down by the Japanese. Of the two caves that had surviv-ed the fire, he shared one with his two sons, Jinbao and Yin-bao, while his wife, his two daughters-in-law and Jinbao's baby were in the other. They had been making do like this for al-most a year.

"Make do," he said to his family and other villagers. "We've got no choice. You must never forget how the enemy drove us into the mountains and had us running about from morning to night like ants."

Talk of the mopping up reminded him of it all, and now a new terror was threatening him. Then he reflected that thousands and thousands of their own soldiers had headed to-wards where the enemy was building the railway. What was up?

Glancing down at the murmuring brook, he said to him-self,

"When the Japs have been kicked out, I'll not have to

stand on sentry duty at the crossroad and the lads can go back
to work in the mountains. They won't have to drill here every
few days." He took another look at the square.

"Left, right, left! Left, right, left." They were still running
and shouting.

He could pick out his boys Jinbao and Yinbao at a glance.
They were his. They blinked the way he did and they both had
their mother's forehead. Nobody had sons as fine as his. "The
Japs can burn down my houses, kill and eat up my oxen, but
if I've got my sons happy and carefree, I've got everything."
When feeling low he often sighed like this. It made him seem
rather stubborn, but he knew what he meant.

"Look!" Yinbao picked up a date-wood dummy hand-
grenade and threw it whistling hundreds of feet through the air.
Almost everyone smiled. Most of them congratulated him, or
made jokes about it except for his elder brother who stood there
looking quite cross.

The sight made the old man even angrier with Yinbao.
"Idiot," he grumbled, quite disheartened. "He's barely twenty
and he's only just learned how to write his own name. He's
been a guard in the village office for a few days. What does he
want to show off for? Those village boys, electing him a squad
leader in the militia!"

He felt that in times like this by far the best thing for a
family was to stick together. Deeply upset about Yinbao, he
turned away and squatted down on the ground. He found that
his pipe had gone out.

He slowly filled his pipe as if deep in thought, tucked it
behind his knee, took the flint out from his breast pocket, struck
a light at the second attempt, put the lighted artemisia leaves
into the pipe, clamped the pipe in his bewhiskered mouth, and
started smoking angrily.

As he smoked one pipeful after another the sun sank in the
direction where the Japanese were said to be tunnelling to build
the railroad. The glory of the sunset which had crowned the

mountain tops soon faded away, leaving the earth covered with boundless night. Columns of smoke rose from the chimneys and joined in a cloud over the village.

A soldier was coming from the east along the road by the creek. Li Shuyuan knocked the ashes out from his pipe and stood up with the help of his spear. When the man came nearer, he asked as usual:

"Travel pass, fellow countryman?"

"Haven't got one. My unit is behind me." He breathed hard as he spoke, probably because he had been walking too fast.

"Our Eighth Route Army?"

"Yes. Where's the village office?" he asked hastily.

He seemed to be on urgent business, so the old man pointed with his two-foot-long pipe at the temple which had been badly damaged by fire by the Japanese and said trustingly, "Over there! It's in the two rooms that survived the fire."

The soldier turned away without waiting for him to finish. The old man suddenly shuddered like a child. He had a foreboding that something unusual was going to happen. But what? If the troops behind him camped here that would be nothing strange. But so many troops had marched through the day before yesterday.

A moment later a crowd of people appeared on the road the soldier had taken, carrying things in pairs, walking fast with their carrying-poles bent and swaying as if with heavy burdens. They came round the bend in the road with their military escort in an endless stream. When the front carriers had almost reached him more pairs were still coming round the corner. Someone asked him the way to the village office. He pointed it out to his inquirer absent-mindedly, keeping his gaze fixed on the road as if he were counting the numbers, but in fact his eyes were swimming and his head was in a whirl. In an instant he saw the things they had brought laid one after the other in rows

on the open ground outside the temple. The soldier was gesticulating and busily giving them directions.

The civilian and the soldiers milled around as if in a noisy
market, unfastening their carrying-poles, wiping off their sweat,
or taking off their shoes and socks to examine their feet. The
sounds of talking and coughing were mixed up with the noise
of carrying-poles being thrown down.

The militia had finished their drill and run over. Ignoring
the soldiers' yells of "Get out! Keep away!" they pushed inside
the crowd and soon were mixed up with the civilian porters. Li
Shuyuan left his sentry post and was drawn in too.

The porters were standing in clusters, talking:

"They look small, but they're heavy!"

"It's too far."

"If it's any farther I'm done for."

The militiamen looked at them and then at their loads with
suspicious eyes. Suddenly, Li Shuyuan called out with desperate
urgency and all his might from among the crowds:

"Yinbao! Yinbao!"

Yinbao straightened up and walked away. It was he who
had dared like a young explorer to touch that mysterious round
thing laid on the wooden frame. He was soon lost in the crowds.
When people asked with curiosity where they had been brought
from and where they were being taken to, the porters shook
their heads slyly. Only on repeated inquiries would they whisper
into the villagers' ears, "Mines!"

2

Yinbao laid down his bowl and chopsticks after supper,
wiped his mouth with his hands, and opened the door, ready to
go, as if on urgent business. His father, who was sitting on the
brick bed-platform, looked at him closely and asked:

"Where are you going, Yinbao?"

Yinbao already had one leg out of the door.

"Wait a moment, I want to talk to you."

"What about?" Yinbao turned back unwillingly and stood there, evidently anxious to leave immediately.

But his father stopped him, refusing let him go out on a night when so much was happening in the village. The usual routine after supper was for the oil lamp to be put out, when Li Shuyuan would sit on the bed-platform smoking his long pipe, Jinbao would pace the floor with his baby in his arms, and the daughters-in-law would wash the dishes then sit in the corner of the platform with their mother-in-law. Then the whole family would start talking in the darkness, not lighting their lamp, not only because the war made oil so expensive but also because they economized this way in peacetime too. Their conversation had no set topic: it wandered from how the hens were laying to the oxen not eating maize stalks and to rats in the granary. They chatted till they became sleepy and then each went to bed, fumbling in the dark. Yinbao would often not join them, but put down his bowl and chopsticks after supper and go from house to house to fool around with his pals. Since the beginning of the war against Japan everyone had been organized to some extent, but he was more involved than anyone, always going to meetings or classes. A large room in the village had been cleared out and hung with portraits of famous personages and slogans in red and green, and here the youngsters swarmed and chatted till late at night. But tonight his old father made him stay at home and gave him a dressing-down.

"You're so damned stupid!" The old man sat there with one leg bent and the other stretched out. Pulling his pipe that looked like a black pole from his bewhiskered mouth he roared angrily:

"Mines are terrible things. They're for killing the Japs. You're just a country boy: why did you want to touch them? Did you think you'd get rich that way? Suppose it had blown up? Then what?" He glared at Yinbao in silence for a moment.

Then, he bit on his pipe again and sucked it so that it sounded like a mouse squeaking. It glowed in front of him in the darkness.

"How awful!" The old woman tutted and hunched her shoulders in fear.

The room was filled with the suffocating odours of the old man's tobacco, sour pickles and coal smoke. After the dishes were washed the fire in the stove was covered with a layer of muddy coal dust, in the centre of which a hole was made with the poker, letting out an arrow-like blue flame that flickered and danced. Yinbao stood there with one foot on the ground and the other on the stove, gazing at the blue flame. He would not admit he had been wrong.

"They don't go off that easily."

"How do you know?" asked the old man, sticking to his line of argument. "Only old soldiers know how to handle them. How could you be so sure that it wouldn't explode?"

"Tut, tut." The old woman looked at Yinbao, her shoulders hunched. Although she had never seen a mine, she realized that it was something terrible.

Jinbao walked slowly up and down with his baby in his arms. The daughters-in-law glanced at Yinbao expecting him to say something, but he held his tongue. The old man began to lecture him, saying that he was not to go out after supper.

Meanwhile, the village was filled with tension and chaos. Dogs could be heard barking everywhere in the villagers' yards, showing that there was constant coming and going. There were soldiers, porters, cadres from the village, and people looking after food, firewood and drinking water. A sentinel was posted on every road. If so much as a shadow was seen in the distance the sentries would yell, "Hey there," at which you had to stand there trembling in fear before being cross-questioned.

"What will you be doing? Carrying onions or selling garlic?" The old man stretched out his arm to knock the ashes from his pipe, and then re-filled it before it went out. "What's the world coming to?" he continued, sucking at his pipe. "All this talk of capturing and wiping out spies. Mind you, there really are some traitors. But you don't have to be involved in anything — just one wrong word and you can be in trouble." He sucked at his pipe again.

He drew in a mouthful of smoke and then puffed it out. There was a dead silence. He thought how times had changed. In the old days he would have hit the lad with his shoe. Now, he couldn't bully a man who was fighting the Japanese. So he had to bring his lecture to a mild end:

"You'd better think my advice over carefully and decide whether I'm trying to help you or harm you."

Silence reigned in the dark room.

Fifteen or so miles west of Lidao Village, across hills, ditches, rivers, villages and woods, a motor road ran from north to south. This was where the Japanese soldiers who had wrecked the village twice were building a railway. The explosions made by blasting tunnels could be heard in the village every day. Tonight, large piles of mine were stacked up by the temple. From all around came the noise of barking, yelling and talking.

Li Shuyuan's family kept listening in tense silence to what was going on outside. They were not talking naturally as before but were murmuring from time to time, "Oh! Listen!" Then, they all held their breath, cocking their heads to one side. After a little while, someone called twice from outside:

"Li Shuyuan! Li Shuyuan. . . ."

Everyone in the room froze.

The old man kept on listening with his head to one side and then he said to Jinbao: "Put the baby down. Go and see what's happening!"

"I'll go. I think it's the village policeman's voice," said Yinbao, who was just about to leave.

"Let your brother go!" The old man stopped him in anger and disgust.

"Tut, tut, tut. . . . How did you dare?" said the old woman, glaring at Yinbao.

Jinbao handed the baby to his wife and went slowly out. "Who's there?" he shouted in the desolate and gateless yard that had been burned out by the Japanese troops. His heavy footsteps gradually died away.

It was a long time before he returned, opening the door and shouting roughly without waiting for them to ask what had happened:

"Go to bed early!"

"Why?"

"We've got to carry the mines away at dawn tomorrow."

"Why?"

"We've got to carry the mines away at dawn tomorrow," he repeated emphatically, then slowly told them of the village policeman's instructions. "All the militiamen have to go. We take over from the other porters here, and we'll probably have to take them right to the spot."

Li Shuyuan gazed dumbfounded at Jinbao.

"The spot?" asked the old man in bewilderment. "What spot?"

"No need to ask. I'm sure we'll be taking them straight to the front," interrupted Yinbao without thinking. "It's obvious, when so many of our troops have gone where the Japanese are building their railway. The next few days are going to be busy ones." He was evidently very pleased at the prospect.

"Listen to your elder brother!" said the old man, eyeing him furiously as he turned to Jinbao.

"Yinbao must be about right," said Jinbao in his usual slow way. "The village policeman said it's about 15 or 20 miles away. I don't think he knows exactly where any more than the rest of us."

Jinbao did not pass on most of what he had been told. The village policeman had grabbed his sleeve in the dark and talked to him expressively for quite a long time, trying like a mobilizing officer to convince him that the Japanese would definitely be defeated. The policeman had described the Eighth Route Army's preparations as if he had seen them himself: all they were waiting for was the mines. Jinbao was not in the least impressed. It was as if he had forgotten it all: he was not even frightened. He was indeed one of the most unimaginative of peasants.

But although the old man had not been told all this it did not take him long to understand, and he started to be upset by this unexpected development. What could he do? The militia had previously carried rations, wounded soldiers and ammunition, but not these infernal mines, and right up to the firing line too. He wondered whether there was any way of getting his sons off this duty, but there wasn't. It was hopeless. High up on the wall of the temple army propagandists had painted in big red characters that he could not read himself but had asked the primary school teacher to read to him, "Soldiers and civilians co-operate to fight Japan." The teacher had explained the meaning of them for quite a while, and he had nodded his head with approval: "Yes, we've really got to fight the Japanese. It's vital. Although I'm only a peasant, I understand." It looked as though the pressure was on and the boys had to go. It was their duty.

"I suppose they'll have to take them," he muttered after reflecting for a while.

"Oh! My God! My heart goes with them!" said the old woman in a trembling voice.

"Don't be afraid." He turned to console his wife. "See how many people in the village are going. If all the militiamen are going. . . ." He turned to his sons and told them, "Be careful when you carry those things. Look after yourselves. Whatever you do don't handle them recklessly when you get there. Will you be taking food with you?"

"We've been told to take dry rations, not grain that needs cooking," said Jinbao.

"Fetch some baked flour," ordered the old man. "Bring some good, finely ground flour with chaff." Then he muttered as if he had just remembered something, "We don't have much left. When the Japanese drove us into the mountains, we each carried a bag of baked flour to eat. Well, you take it all. It won't cause us any hardship at home: we won't need it. In a few days we'll grind more flour. Who knows when the damned Japs will come again?" He seemed to be going to mumble on for ever.

The old woman broke in, still staring coldly at him:

"Don't chant your scriptures!" She was disgusted with his miserliness. "Why should they take flour baked with chaff? We have several pounds of wheat flour in the store-room. We can make them pancakes. They don't go on jobs like this every day, so why don't we give them pancakes instead of flour cooked with chaff? There might not be any water in the fields where they're going."

The old man said nothing for a while. Finally he gave his orders: "Go to bed. Your wives will get your food prepared!"

In the middle of that night most of the families in Lidao Village lit their oil-lamps, which looked from a distance like countless stars in the sky as they shone on the window paper. Wherever the lights gleamed, columns of black smoke rose from the stoves above from the roofs of the houses. The peasant women were busy cooking for their sons, husbands or brothers who were sleeping off the fatigue of spring ploughing up in the hills during the previous day. The next day at dawn they would set forth to they knew not where. A large pile of mines lay in front of the temple and on the village streets the soldiers stood guard with guns on their shoulders to protect them.

3

In the morning twilight, the whole village was full of noise and activity. The streets were full of people rushing around.

There was a hubbub of voice calling people's names, talking in loud voices, and asking for ropes and carrying-poles. When the sun rose the village fell into deep silence as if it had lost its soul. Soon Jinbao and Yinbao disappeared with the noisy crowd carrying the mines along the road to the west, one pair after another.

Li Shuyuan seemed to have lost all his spirit. He felt as if he had suddenly become a poor, lonely and helpless old man. It had been painful enough when he had come back to find his own house burned down after the enemy's retreat. Now he felt almost the same pain seeing his own sons go to help fight the Japanese. After grieving over the loss of his house he had suddenly woken up from a dream in which he had indulged for decades. Land and property was worth nothing compared with human life, which was far more precious than anything else in the world. He even found great consolation in seeing how bitterly his neighbours grieved over their murdered kinsmen. "Let it be," he said. "There will be peace after the Japanese are driven out by the Eighth Route Army, and then Jinbao and Yinbao can build a new house." The world he knew, cared about and had confined himself to all his life was very small, being limited to his own family. In the chaos and destruction of wartime he put all his hopes in his sons. Naturally he felt depressed now that they had gone to the front.

He suddenly brightened up. The battlefield was dangerous and mines were terrible, but when so many young people had gone from the village, why should anything happen to his sons rather than anyone else's? Anyway, in times like this you could only accept your fate and trust to luck. The Japanese had killed several people in the village last time but his family had come through unscathed. He felt that fate must be on his side.

Now that he had cheered himself up he felt much better.

After breakfast, the old man opened the ox shed and led the ox to the brook to drink. On his way back he saw Wei Peigui, another old man who lived at the east end of the village, taking his ox to the brook. As each pulled his ox to one side of the village street to let the other pass Li Shuyuan happened to ask:

"Has your boy gone?"

"Yes," answered the other, "I saw Yinbao and my son carrying the same mine. . . ."

"No!"

"I thought so. But my eyes are weak, so I might not have seen properly," answered Wei Peigui with indifference, driving his ox down the slope.

Li Shuyuan was in an agony of worry. After he tied his ox by the open ground outside his house, he strolled around the village, inquiring everyone he met:

"Did you notice who was Jinbao's partner this morning?"

"No, I didn't. . . ."

Nobody had noticed it. Li Shuyuan thought they were much too self-centred, not paying any attention to other people's interests. Before his sons left, he had repeatedly told them that they should stay together to look after each other and he had emphatically told Jinbao that wherever he went he should keep a good eye on Yinbao, who was so rash and reckless. In the moment of their departure the great turmoil and uproar had made the old man giddy, and his eyes had been swimming as he saw the men being counted, picking the mines up in pairs, and setting off.

Finally, he went to the village office. The village leader was so disgusted at him that he kept on working without paying him the least attention. Without the assistance of the village policeman he would have been too embarrassed to speak up.

"What are you inquiring about?" the village policeman asked with a smile.

"Nothing important! I simply want to know . . ." the old man stammered.

"Don't worry, Uncle Shuyuan!" The village policeman clapped him on the shoulder and said gently, "You can rest as-

sured that nothing will go wrong. It doesn't matter who the
partner is. Just think, Jinbao is already a father! He wouldn't
be the right partner for someone as energetic and lively as Yinbao. I saw Yinbao paired up with Wei Peigui's son. Don't
worry! . . ."

This news made the old man feel better.

He went home and fetched a handful of incense-paper that
he took straight to the main hall of the temple. After the yellow
incense-paper was lit and reduced to ashes, he looked at the
God of War's statue hopefully and mumbled through his
whiskers:

"If you protect my sons and keep them safe I'll offer you
a five-foot-long silk banner at your festival this year." He repeated this many times. Had the statue been alive it would have
shouted, "Stop bothering me."

He then returned home and was not seen again on the
village streets.

The sound of the tunnels being blasted to the west could
be heard even indoors. The explosions came at quite short in-
tervals, sometimes shaking the window paper. The sound evoked
thoughts and recollections of battlefields, enemies and fighting.
Now Li Shuyuan's sons were marching in the direction from
which the explosions were coming. "The mines," the old man
muttered to himself dreamily all day long, "the mines. Terrible!"
He intended to say more but he could not.

At midnight, people were awakened violently from their
deep sleep. Huge explosions like earthquakes came from far
away to the west of Lidao Village. Sometimes they rolled over
the western sky like spring thunder, and sometimes the urgent
bark of machine-guns sounded like drums beating in the village
temple.

"The whole world's being turned upside down," Li Shuyuan murmured to himself in his blind terror.

He threw his clothes on hastily, without buttoning them
up, but holding the lapels of his jacket together with his sturdy

hands as he rushed out into the yard from his room where he was left alone in his sons' absence. He glanced towards the western sky, which was as gloomy as usual, but the explosions were continuing.

"The battle's started . . . the mines . . . my boys. . . ."

His mind darted from thought to thought. In many places lamps were being lit. He saw some coming on and others going out, so that they seemed to dance around like a will-o'-the-wisp, that made him so frightened his hair stood on end. Somewhere a baby was bawling. He felt thoroughly impatient and restless.

He sighed as shooting stars flashed across the sky. Then, walking into the thatched shed, the old man took out a sifter of millet straw and dumped it into the ox's manger. Once woken up at night he could never shut his eyes again. He was tormented by contradictions: the mines would do heavy damage to the cruel enemy but he was also worried about his sons who had gone to deliver them. He only remembered to feed his ox when the explosions had stopped for a very long time.

After feeding the ox he went into the room where the women were staying to find them already dressed and sitting huddled together on the brick bed-platform. The moment he stepped inside there were several more distant explosions, the familiar boom of artillery that in recent years they had rarely been free of for ten days on end.

It was now daybreak, and the booms continued.

"Listen! They're firing again," muttered the old woman, glancing at her husband. She was as pale as a sheet of paper. "Are the boys on their way back yet?"

"Yes, I'm sure they are." The old man tried to sound as definite as he could, hoping to cheer them up. "They'll turn back the moment the mines have been delivered. They'll be marching back through the night. Civilians are no use at the front." He was not only saying this to comfort himself, but also because he hoped in his heart it was true.

"Who can tell what will happen on the battlefield?" said his elder daughter-in-law, rocking her baby in her arm.

"You're right," agreed the second daughter-in-law, who was sitting opposite him.

"Go and get breakfast ready!" The old man cut short their unpleasant remarks. "You're both black crows and neither of you is a cheerful magpie! Why don't you say something to bring good luck? You. . . ."

They went to cook breakfast without another word. They fetched water from the vat, poured it into the pan, and then used a poker to revive the fire that had been covered with coal-dust. Then they filled a grain measure with millet and stood it on the sill of the stove. The old man sat on the bed-platform, mumbling away to himself with his pipe between his teeth:

"I told them over and over again when they set out that the resistance war depends on the whole people, not on our family alone. That's what the army says. Anyway, the right way these days is to look after yourself first. But they don't understand that, the fools."

He propagated his absurdities with such eloquence that the women, who were kept busy all day with sewing and cooking, could not produce a counter-argument.

"That's so," said the old woman, tutting and staring at the ceiling in fear.

They all froze where they were, sitting, standing, or carrying a basin. They turned their heads to one side, their eyes filled with worry and anxiety. Only when the explosions started dying out did they begin to move again.

"I made a pledge before the God of War," the old man nattered on, "that if he protected my sons and brought them back safely I would offer him a five-foot-long silk banner. Our temple really gets results, it's much better than any of the other temples round here. Just think how many banners of all different sizes are hanging there to show that favours asked for have been granted."

The crack of gunfire came again from afar, sounding as if someone were hammering nails in the next room. The more he talked, the more he showed how worried he was. The heavier the gunfire became the more he talked, till he ended up sounding like a madman talking deliriously.

Not much breakfast was eaten. The old man did not even finish one bowl of porridge. Probably the fighting would not come as far as Lidao Village. He drew a package of land deeds from the chest, stuffed them inside his jacket and then tightened his belt. He went out with his belly protruding like a pregnant woman and his pipe in his hand.

He squatted under the cliff at the western end of the village, keeping his pipe in his mouth and watching the road along which the porters had taken the mines. From time to time, some other old man would see him and squat beside him, smoking and chatting for a while. When all the others left, he remained there as if on sentry duty. He waited until the sun sank in the west and he had no more tobacco leaves left in his bag, but nobody appeared on that road.

He sighed and returned home, his pipe in his hand.

4

In the evening, Li Shuyuan saw a crowd of people on the open ground by the temple where the mines had been piled.

Wondering what they were doing, he strolled over.

The village head, deputy head, ward head and the leaders of the Peasant's Salvation Association were all there, talking noisily with a group of ordinary peasants. They did not change the subject when he appeared. He took a look at their faces in silence — every dirty, wrinkled or young face was beaming with joy.

"We'll send twenty men if you want. .. ."

"Yes, we can send twenty, thirty or even forty men below the age of 45 from our Lidao Village."

The village head walked slowly to and fro with his hands in his sleeves and then he stood still suddenly:

"We have plenty of hands. The trouble is that a lot of these people don't go when sent. They may all complain it's unfair if we have to discuss it in the village office."

"Then you had better issue orders."

"I think that everyone will be glad to do this duty," cut in the village policeman with warmth. "Nobody will mind going to carry back the booty won by our soldiers in battle. They've been longing to do this every day."

"The messengers said a while ago that some people may have to go 70 or 100 miles away."

"You go and discuss it, and whoever you send will have to go."

"You're absolutely right!"

The old man, his eyelids quivering and his glance sweeping from one speaker's face to another, began to get a vague idea of what they were discussing. With a kind of happiness in his heart he did not quite understand, he slightly parted his lips behind his bushy whiskers, showing a row of yellow teeth. He asked quietly:

"Did we win?"

"Yes, we won!" The village policeman stepped forward before him and smiled as he ribbed him: "You don't have to worry any more about who Yinbao was carrying the mine with. Don't you understand yet? The army wants civilian porters again, but this time to carry back what they won in battle." He chuckled, and the old man could not help joining in, laughing like a child.

His two days of terror, his fear of the artillery from the battlefield and his anxieties for his sons all were swept away by this triumphant news. For a moment he seemed to be as stimulated as if he had taken some drug. In his imagination he could see the victory — the dead bodies of the enemy were strewn around on the ground just as the dead villagers had been in the enemy's raid on the village. Now, it was the turn of the soldiers and the civilians to take back what the enemy had stolen from them. He rested his hopes on Yinbao because he was more quick-witted than his elder brother. He would probably be able to get something good. He deserved some compensation from the Japanese for having his house burned down.

"So that's why the mine-carriers aren't back yet," he exclaimed dreamily as if he had just woken up from sleep.

"Back? You daydreamer! They're recruiting more porters from several counties all around. The porters who've gone already won't be back," said someone with a laugh.

He grunted in assent and nodded. "As I said before, we need the Eighth Route Army to fight the Japanese!" At the thought of mass meetings, he laughed: "The masses can do nothing but waving paper banners! . . ."

The village head paced along with his hands in his sleeves, then stood still.

"Grandad! What a thing to say!" The village head pressed his argument home relentlessly. "Without the masses could the mines fly there by themselves?"

"Of course they have to be carried," answered the old man shamefacedly.

"Well," continued the village head, "they say several big towns were taken last night and over thirty miles of enemy railway was destroyed. Lots and lots of civilians from within several miles of the line took part in the fighting. They outnumbered the soldiers, and they did very well."

"Then my Jinbao and Yinbao did their bit too." He tried to cover up his embarrassment by saying this with an air of pride.

"Of course," someone answered with indifference.

Then he started boasting:

"Indeed! Whatever my sons do they do well."

"Well, you cadres had better go to the village office to discuss it." The village head did not wait for him to finish before urging them to go.

They all dispersed, some with the village head to the office, some to the river to fetch water, and some back home.

That evening every family talked about what had happened on the western front. In front of their ox-sheds, in the doorways of their thatched cottages, beside the closets, on the brick bed-platforms, by their stoves, or sitting on stools, people talked with admiration about the terrible power of the land mines. All sorts of strange stories about the fighting were passed by word of mouth from one peasant to another — that thousands of the Japanese had been killed by the mines, and none survived; that the railway they had built had been completely destroyed, and the tunnels too; they could build very fast, but we could destroy even faster; that three whole cavefuls of gold, silver, jade and treasures stolen by the Japanese had been recovered intact. . . .

When Li Shuyuan went home, he told his wife to stop frowning and his daughters-in-law to stop worrying.

"We won," he said slowly, fingering his beard and ignoring everyone's impatience. "The Japanese were wiped out! Their railway has had it. We've seized any amount of things from them! The boys are safe and sound. Someone saw them."

The batch of villagers sent with the mines had not returned when another group was sent for the war trophies. Lidao Village appeared even more quiet than a couple of days before. Nothing stirred except the cocks crowing on the hillsides, on roofs or in people's yards. It looked as if everyone had gone to work in the mountains. But this year there had been hardly any spring rain, so it was impossible to plant seeds on the stone-hard clods. People had gone to the battlefront as that was where they were needed.

"What's the world coming to?" Li Shuyuan sighed.

He sank into a state somewhere between gloom and optimism. He had never experienced such times in all his life. As a peasant all his life he didn't understand the psychological changes in the peasants, not even his own sons. Why had Yinbao changed so much? As for himself. . . .

"I'm old," he said to himself. "My father left me a couple of acres when he died which I've worked with my own hands all my life. Now I've got two sons and still the same two acres. I've never met with disaster or had any lucky windfalls. I've never lost my temper with people, quarrelled, or had a noisy slanging match with anyone."

With his sons away nothing was being done in his fields. Besides feeding his ox, he would wander around the village streets or the grassy slopes by the roadside after his meal with an old basket of mulberry-tree branches in one hand and an iron spade in the other, looking for animals' dung as carefully as if for something he had lost. As soon as he discovered a pile of cow's or dog's dung, he would shovel it into his basket and then go on searching.

There were more booms.

He did not know why the artillery had been firing continuously for a couple of days now that our side had won. This was the reason why he was not completely optimistic. Having gathered his dung, he usually put his spade and basket outside the temple and went into the village office. After making two dry coughs, he opened the door and went in:

"May I smoke here?"

"Please," someone answered. People were busy writing, reading newspapers, checking the accounts of rations and fodder, or calculating with the abacus. Nobody had time to chat with him. He would squat on the ground, watching them work and smoking his long-stemmed pipe till the room was filled with the dense smoke. He stood up and asked:

"Any news from the militia?"

"Not yet," someone said. He opened the door and slipped quietly out. He stuck his pipe in his belt and went mournfully back home with his muck-gathering gear.

When he entered the room, his wife asked:

"Any news of when they'll be back?"

"Yes, people in the village office said they'll be back soon." So saying, he took off his shoes and sat at his usual place at the end of the bed-platform that had been left vacant by the death of his father. He smoked hard, sucking noisily, and soon the room was filled with the dense smoke of the strong tobacco he prepared himself. The women started coughing. His wife glared at him with irritation:

"That smoke will turn your insides black."

"I can't help it! What else can I do but smoke?" He put down his pipe with a mournful face. "I've never known such times." All the sorrow and pain of his life was concentrated in this moment.

In one night bitter sorrow had shaken Li Shuyuan. Things had become so complicated.

5

When Li Shuyuan's family was taking supper that evening, there was a sudden hubbub of footsteps, yelling, talking and general commotion from the village street. It sounded as though the porters had returned from their mission. They must have done, to judge from such remarks as, "This pole's yours, take it!" or "Hey, I've got the wrong rope."

"I'll go and take a look," said Li Shuyuan, putting his bowl down.

Just then there were heavy footsteps in the yard, after which the door opened and in came Jinbao, pale, exhausted, and with his shoulders stooped. He threw the ropes on the floor, propped the pole up by the door, and said nothing. The old man, looked and looked at him, then suddenly gasped in desperation as if in a fit of asthma:

"Where's Yinbao? . . . Yinbao?"

Everyone stared anxiously at Jinbao, but he replied slowly and calmly:

"Him? He's not coming back! He joined the Eighth Route Army at the front!"

The old man sighed deeply and hung his head.

Laughter and talking could be overheard from their neighbours' houses all around. Everyone was smiling now that the men were back, and the children were shouting. But in this silent room the oil lamp shone with a dim and gloomy light while a tongue of bluish fire flickered in the stove.

Yinbao's wife lowered her head for a while and then looked up again, a young and beautiful smile still playing about her lips. She saw her father-in-law's head bent so low that it looked as if it would fall off his shoulders.

"Dad," said Yinbao's wife gently, "why do you look so sad? He's safe and sound and still alive, not. . . ."

The old man jerked his head up suddenly pointing his finger at Jinbao said through his teeth:

"You're a zombie."

Jinbao told them all about Yinbao, but he was too clumsy to express himself well. That night nearly every family in Lidao Village talked about scenes and stories the like of which had never been heard of for hundreds of years but which they had witnessed with their own eyes. Yinbao's story, though no more than an interlude in the whole, was the most intimate, the most moving and the most widely and deeply spread. Even young children barely able to talk and old people were struck speechless.

The mine carried by Yinbao and Wei Peigui's son had destroyed an iron bridge. They had followed the soldiers to the foot of the bridge, buried their mine there and then taken cover behind a rock with the fuse. They were told by the soldiers that when the mine exploded they should go back to the village where they had eaten. When the mine went off and blew up the bridge, and the Eighth Route Army soldiers charged the enemy guarding it, Wei Peigui's son had run back, but Yinbao had been drawn into the attack and dashed forward without realizing what he was doing. Seeing a soldier fall dead in the assault, he took up his rifle and pressed forward with them like one possessed. After the firing ceased, he still followed them without realizing what he was doing, crossing mountain after mountain without making a noise. Probably he had forgotten fear, but he dared not leave the soldiers either. At daybreak, the soldiers discovered among their number of young peasant with a rifle on his back but no grenades, bullets or ammunition belt. They asked if he had joined up with them because he had lost his guerrilla unit. He told them that he was a civilian porter sent to deliver land mines and that as it had been too dark for them to see who he was he had tagged along with them. Then the soldiers remembered him, breaking into roaring laughter that resounded in the mountains. Someone asked: "So are you a porter or a soldier?" He said that he didn't mind as long as he was fighting the Japanese. Then the soldiers burst into thunderous applause, yelling: "Welcome! You're in." And he had gone with them.

The story was told everywhere with great effect by all the other peasants but was summarized too simply by Jinbao. The old man stared at him:

"What was the matter with him? Was he pressed or did he volunteer? You zombie!"

"They welcomed him and he volunteered."

The old man spat on Jinbao then turned away to yell: "He may have volunteered but I didn't. I'm his Dad." Spraying spittle with the last word, he continued, "If they do this nobody will be prepared to be a porter! I'm going to see the village head."

He wanted to go to the village office immediately but his family would not let him go as it was dark, and besides he ought to watch what he said. So many people had joined the army during the anti-Japanese war. Since they were not going to get him to come back again, it would be a shame to make people gossip or laugh at them. The old man grumbled because he was not convinced.

Next morning he just swallowed a few mouthfuls as he had no appetite, then went to the village office. While walking along the village street with his head down, he thought how arrogant the village head was and decided to pick a quarrel with him. If the village head ignored him he would force him to draft a petition to get his Yinbao back. He'd make a row if that were necessary, and in his imagination it had already started. His Yinbao had been born in the tenth month of his mother's pregnancy and they had brought him up day by day, cleaning up when he wetted himself or moved his bowels. The resistance war involved everybody, so was it right that his Yinbao had to go?

Wang San came along with his ox. Li Shuyuan thought he would make some remarks by the roadside, waving his long-stemmed pipe, to see what Wang had to say.

"You're getting covered with glory in your old age." Wang San congratulated him with admiration before Li Shuyuan could open his mouth. "Your Yinbao was the king of the mine-carriers. If everyone acted like him we'd have no worries about driving out the Japanese."

The old man was tongue-tied. It would be useless to reason things out with him. So, before he moved away, he asked casually:

"Going to water your ox?"

"Yes," answered Wang San, adding, "oh! Yinbao is wonderful!"

He felt a little puzzled! Why was Wang San talking to him with such earnest and sincere politeness. Everybody used to dislike him and to say behind his back that he was a cold-blooded man. On seeing him, they would greet him with a cold smile or turn away, pretending not to have noticed him.

He wondered what the world was coming to as he walked along.

"Grandad!" Another youngster addressed him in this very friendly way. "Everyone at the front says your Yinbao is a war hero. So now you're a hero's father."

He saw a broad smile on the young man's face that he could not but return. As he walked on, he met another man.

"Lidao Village has produced a hero, and he's from your family. . . ." The man had seemed to be joking, but when he came nearer, he asked with real concern, "Where are you going?"

He answered by pointing along the road with his pipe.

These wonderful words he'd never heard before and the attitude to him he'd never seen before made him puzzled. Instead of storming into the office in a fury, he opened the door hesitantly as he went in.

"Oh! Here comes Grandad," said everyone in chorus. Those who were on chairs stood up, those who were lying on bed-rolls sat up, and those who were writing put down their pens and looked up. He opened his bleary eyes wide with astonishment, not knowing what to do. He had never been treated like this before. Usually he would sit at the edge of the brick-platform, or squat on the floor, smoking his pipe silently and being ignored by everyone. But now. . . .

"Take a seat, please." The village head brought a chair over to him hospitably and said with admiration, "How lucky you are! You have such a wonderful son." He picked up a mimeographed newspaper someone had brought from the county the previous night.

"We've just read his story in the paper."

"Was it in the newspaper?" The old man's face was twisted into a grimace.

"All the details — even the village, the district and the county."

The old man took the paper with trembling hands and looked as if he were going to read it. But apart from the words Li Shuyuan which seemed familiar he could read nothing.

After holding it numbly in his hands for a while he gave it back to the village head who read it out to him.

The village head laid it on the table, opened a cupboard, and took out a package pasted with red paper on which words were printed in gold. He put it into the old man's hands and said:

"This is a packet of cigarettes from Quwo I was given. You have probably smoked your home-grown tobacco all your life. I give you this with the congratulations of the village office. Last night a messenger was sent here from the county to tell us that the government is discussing what sort of award to give your family."

The old man tried to hold back his tears.

"My goodness! In the newspaper," he murmured to himself. He took his leave hastily and went out of the temple, holding his gift with one hand and his sleeve with the other to wipe his tears away like a child.

Casting a glance at the open ground where the mines had been piled the other night, he thought:

"I'm old and I've got one foot in the grave, but the world is changing me. I never imagined in all my days that something like this would happen to me. I don't understand the present world. Oh! Yinbao! You've become a dragon or a tiger. You. . . ."

Wei Peigui was standing on sentry duty on the road to the temple.

"Hey! What's that you're holding?"

"Cigarettes from Quwo! I don't know the make." Li Shuyuan held it up for Wei Peigui to see and said calmly: "This is a gift from the village head, who said that I'll be highly rewarded by the county authorities. I'm old, my sight is failing, but in the village office just now I could barely hold back my tears."

Translated by Zhang Mingzhu

About the Author

LIU QING (1916-78) was born in Shaanxi Province. While still in middle school, he joined the Communist Youth League of China and began reading revolutionary literary works. In 1934 he started writing and translating short pieces. Some of his early efforts were published in Xi'an periodicals. In 1935 at the time of the "December 9th" Student Movement, he worked as an editor on the student publication *Salvation Front*. In 1936, when the "Xi'an Incident" occurred, he helped edit the magazine *The Students' Voice*. He joined the Chinese Communist Party the same year. After graduation from middle school in 1937 he became an editor on the *Northwest Cultural Daily*. He went to Yan'an in 1938. From then on he worked in the anti-Japanese army and took part in many political activities, which brought him into direct contact with the people.

During the War of Resistance Against Japan he wrote a number of short stories, most of which have been collected in a volume entitled *Land Mines*. After victory he went to the Northeast where, in 1947, he wrote his first novel *The Planting of the Grain*. He returned to northern Shaanxi the same year to join the war of liberation.

In 1949, after the People's Republic of China was established, he went to Beijing. His novel *Wall of Bronze*, a story of how the peasants in northern Shaanxi supported the war of liberation, was published in 1951.

In 1952, he settled down in a small village not far from Xi'an and was appointed secretary of the Communist Party Committee of Chang'an County. Taking a direct part in countryside activities in the years that followed, he became thoroughly familiar with the peasants and rural life. As a result, he produced a number of excellent articles (compiled in the book *Three Years in Huangfu Village*) and a short story *Iron-Piercing Hatred*.

He completed a novel — *Builders of a New Life* part I in 1959 which describes the life in the countryside after the land was distributed among the tillers. In the "cultural revolution", Liu

Qing was persecuted cruelly by Lin Biao and the gang of four. Before he died in 1978 in Beijing he managed to finish the second part of *Builders of a New Life*.

"Land Mines" is a short story written by Liu Qing in the period of resistance against Japan. It tells the story of the head of a self-defence corps, Yinbao, son of a poor peasant. As Yinbao helps the Eighth Route Army transport land mines, he also takes part in the fighting to help defeat the Japanese aggressors. Later he renders outstanding service and joins the Army.

Liu Qing was a council member of the Union of Chinese Writers; and was a vice-chairman of its Xi'an chapter.

A Native of Yan'an

Cao Ming

Granny Wu would never forget the morning of November 16, 1937.

Her home was at the Main North Gate in Yan'an. To her right were four or five mud houses, where various goods were bought and sold. At each doorway was a meagre display of goods, salt, dried dates, wooden combs, nails and cotton. There was a larger house, on the walls of which were hung a few halters, two pairs of pink cotton stockings and some white towels.

Granny Wu's family tilled the land, and their doorway was particularly dilapidated. The season's harvest had been gathered and the threshing was over, so her two sons, the younger only fourteen, led their donkey to another county to trade, while she and her daughter-in-law worked at home.

Since there was a touch of cold in the air, she was wearing her shabby cotton-padded jacket. That day, while the sun was shining on her doorway, she carried a low stool out and sat down there to sew cloth soles.

Her home faced a main road which led down to a level embankment and a broad river bank. The Yan River flowed noisily towards the east. On the hill across the river was Wangjiaping — the Headquarters of the Eighth Route Army. To the left of Wangjiaping was the main road leading to Chuankou and to the right was Yangjialing, where Chairman Mao lived.

The bells of the draught animals mingled delightfully with the sound of the rushing torrents of the Yan River. This music made the local people love life even more. Even the drivers yelling at their beasts became talented poets of their daily life, putting their experience, their desires and their emotions into countless ballads. The wave-like cadence of those songs, now high and strident, now low-pitched, and the waves of feeling in them expressed the singers' determination to climb every mountain, overcome backwardness and poverty and break through the enemy's blockade.

Granny Wu loved these folk songs. After the arrival of the Communist Party in North Shaanxi and she was allocated land she had composed quite a few folk songs herself praising the Red Army,* and Chairman Mao. Now, while she sat there stitching cloth soles she sang in a low voice:

> Don't mind his ragged clothes
> Don't mind his clapped-out gun
> The enemy can't get near him
> And in battle none can rival him.
>
> Chairman Mao is like our own loving mother,
> He is stronger than mother in every way.
> What official hasn't been corrupt?
> But he is one who doesn't covet wealth.
>
> The land belonged to the landlords,
> And the peasants toiled in vain.
> It was Mao Zedong's bright idea,
> First divide the land, then overthrow
>   the local despots.

---

* Before the "July Seventh Incident" in 1937 when war was declared against Japan the people in North Shaanxi called the Eighth Route Army the Red Army.

Her hoarse voice was suddenly interrupted by a large shadow. A tall Red Army soldier was standing before her, and some distance away were several men with pistols at their waists. He wore an old grey uniform, the sleeves of which had several holes made by cigarette burns. He stood with his back to the sun. She felt a kind of unusual brightness shining over him which dazzled her blurred eyes so that she couldn't see his face clearly. He was about fifty. As she was sizing him up slowly, he broke out first:

"Granny, how are you?"

"Fine!" The word "fine" was used by the poor only after the Red Army came to North Shaanxi.

"Have you got enough to eat?" asked the Red Army soldier amiably and with deep concern.

"We've got enough grain. We were given two acres of land and a donkey." Then holding her ragged sleeve up between her fingers, she continued: "The shortage is here."

Glancing at the old woman's badly worn clothes, he thought hard for a while then stretching both hands out he said resolutely:

"We've got these! We've got these! With hands to work with, we'll never starve or freeze to death. All the problems will be solved gradually. If we unite to drive out the Japanese, and China has independence then everything will be fine."

Hearing the words "fight the Japanese", she got more excited; exposing her decaying front teeth she said with force:

"We are determined to get rid of the Japs. That's the opinion of the people. You can't rely on Chiang Kai-shek. Eh, he should re-educate himself a bit. If he continues to fight against his own people, he will fall into the deepest pit of hell. Let's see what kind of bad end he'll come to."

"We rely on ourselves, Granny. We must mainly rely on the people to wipe out the enemy. We must also unite with those who are willing to fight Japanese imperialism. We can't win unless we have firm faith. You are quite right. The oppressed people have got brains." He bent forward to say the last few words.

Granny Wu gave an embarrassed smile at this praise and hurriedly said politely:

"I'm too old to be of any use! If my mind hadn't been enlightened by the Communist Party I would still be a die-hard reactionary! I can't read or write. Unlike the others, I haven't seen Chairman Mao, nor have I heard him speak. But, I have eyes and I can see clearly what they have done. I can tell right from wrong and I am very grateful for what they have done for the poor!..."

Granny Wu was about to carry on talking, with the intention of pouring out all her joy and gratitude to this stranger whom she already thought of as an old acquaintance.

A messenger, holding a big brown horse, went up to the tall Red Army soldier and said something to him. He turned round and bid her farewell in a simple, profound and moving tone of voice:

"Well, good-bye, Granny! Take care of yourself and you'll be able to see the final victory of the people!"

The simple courtesy of the Red Army was familiar to her. She raised herself a little and said: "Good-bye!"

Instead of getting on to his horse the tall, powerful man walked to the river bank with his usual stride, followed by the four Red Army soldiers with pistols hanging from their waists who Granny Wu had not noticed before.

"Ma, who have you been talking to for such a long time?" asked her daughter-in-law, when she came out of the house, putting down the winnower and shaking the flour off her body.

"I expect he's a cadre, I've been talking to him." She pointed to the group of people who had just left.

The younger woman shaded the sun from her eyes with her hands and looked carefully in the direction indicated by her mother-in-law. She exclaimed in surprise:

"Ma, that's him. Ma, that's him!"

Granny Wu was alarmed; she stood up slowly:

"Who is he?"

"He is Chairman Mao, Ma, that's him. I heard him speak at the May Day celebration; I've also heard him speak at the mobilization meeting."

"Is that him? Ay, that's him," muttered the old woman. The young woman started running with her newly released bound-feet towards the distant crowd. The old woman staggered up, trembling with excitement. Waving her right arm about, it wasn't clear whether she was seeing Chairman Mao off or was feeling sorry for herself for missing such a giant of the age.

"That's Chairman Mao!"

"That's Chairman Mao!"

"There's no mistake, it's really him!"

The shopkeepers all ran out of the houses, trying hard to identify the tall shape as that of their beloved leader. A few intellectuals who had just come here from the south, eagerly joined the masses, and confirmed what the people were saying. One of them even said that once he had seen Chairman Mao have a long chat with the peasants in the fields. By now there were about ten people all watching with rapt attention the group that was getting further and further away. Chairman Mao had crossed the Yan River on horse back and had slowly made his way to Yangjialing. His mighty figure grew as he went further away and his genius and solemn appearance seemed to become a tangible brilliance which shone with the sun. The shadow disappeared when it got to the slope of Yangjialing but people seemed to be still able to see the giant walk steadily up the hill into a newly white-washed old cave.

The old woman who had never been taken seriously before, now unexpectedly became the centre of attention. Previously, she had thought that a woman's place was at home doing the house work, so she had been unwilling to attend mass meetings and even when propaganda teams arrived at her home, she received them coolly. However, after chatting with Chairman Mao and then being shown so much respect, she suddenly changed. Her conservative thinking became more enlightened, she began to display her hidden wisdom. She talked eloquently about the ordinary things she had heard in the past and they became part of her experience. Moreover, she felt that from now on she had enough courage to take on anything, however difficult. She sat placidly among the people, proudly enjoying their admiration and answering their questions.

"Immediately I felt that his eyes were different from other people's, they were grey, really exceptional! Ay, without such eyes, how could he see so clearly the suffering of the poor!"

The old woman straightened her back and continued with her description. It seemed as if she had become over ten years younger. "Moreover, I noticed that his forehead was rather broad, what an intelligent head! He can solve problems which have baffled hundreds and thousands of people. The bridge of his nose was so straight that. . . ."

"How is it that you could see his eyes were grey when you said that he had his back to the sun?"

"Don't interrupt! Listen to her."

"Judging from his straight nose, you can tell that he has an upright conscience. Can you name a ruler from the past who hasn't oppressed the common people? After China became a Republic, it was ruled by Chiang Kai-shek. He made things even worse!

"Only the Communist Party works for us wholeheartedly. For generations we didn't have any land. Now, we've got land, cows and sheep. Everybody can see that they don't have any privileges, they eat the same food as their soldiers, five cents a day for food, and they wear shabby clothes. It's said that their parents and children living in the Kuomintang areas are being tortured every day by Chiang Kai-shek.

"Did you hear that during the 8,000 mile Long March, Chairman Mao met an old woman who was about to freeze to death? He immediately took off his goat-fur-lined waist coat and put it on her. Have you ever seen anyone serving the people so wholeheartedly? I've lived fifty-three years and it's the first time I've seen such a great man...."

Now, the old woman's emotions swelled up like mountain torrents during the monsoon season, or as if thousands of galloping horses were charging inside her head and shaking her soul. While she talked she wiped away her tears of emotion.

"You are quite right!" Wang Xianggui, the blacksmith cut in. "I was told that on the 8,000 mile Long March several cadres were so exhausted that they wanted to rest for three days and three nights. Chairman Mao said to them, 'Have a good rest! I'm going to tell you a story about victory.' After he finished his story, everyone was inspired with enthusiasm and didn't even want to rest for three hours, because they all wanted to march forward towards the final victory. I've also heard that when they were crossing the grass-lands, they ate wild vegetables and leather soles. Some subordinates prepared some unripen wheat flour for him but he gave the flour to the comrades who were sick."

"Who isn't afraid when the word 'landlords' is mentioned. But the Communist Party has suppressed them. Without Chairman Mao and the Communist Party, we don't know how long we would still have to suffer!" sighed the primary school teacher, stroking his long beard.

"How the ruling class harmed us! My bound-feet were only unbound after the Red Army arrived. If it wasn't for feudal oppression wouldn't we women be the same as men?" Her daughter-in-law began talking but before she could finish, the man from the south butted in:

"Things were plentiful in the south, but under the oppression of Chiang Kai-shek we were forbidden to fight against the Japanese so we came to the liberated area. Here we found freedom. Although the millet here is somewhat coarse, it is more delicious than the fish and meat over there. No wonder the French say: 'Without freedom one might as well die.'

"Among the ordinary people, even an illiterate old granny knows the common truth but people over there are not allowed this kind of education. When we were in school, we taught ourselves a little about the theory of class struggle but we had to keep it to ourselves. We would be put to death if we mentioned it publicly."

Another student from Nanjing described Chiang Kai-shek with scorn:

"Chiang Kai-shek doesn't dare to go out without his armoured car. In fact he has three armoured cars, just as a wily hare has three burrows. Quite unlike Chairman Mao who can walk and chat to people in the streets. . . ."

"Chairman Mao is on our side," Old Wang cut in. "We hope he will live for two hundred years!"

"Ah, when the whole country is liberated, may the people of the whole country be able to see Chairman Mao," remarked another peasant sympathetically.

The students laughed naively: "What the Communist Party stands for has been well known to people for a long time. Peasants in the countryside, workers and students in the cities are all longing for an early liberation."

They chatted with enthusiasm the whole morning and didn't disperse until they had poured out their innermost thoughts.

From that day on, Granny Wu responded enthusiastically to every call of the local government. She frequently set a good example for the men and young people in their work.

Ten years has passed. The Shaanxi-Gansu-Ningxia Border Region has had its Mass Production Movement, its Cotton Planting and Spinning Movement, its Literacy Movement, its Public Health Movement and so on. In spite of the increasingly savage military and economic blockade by the Kuomintang, the situation in Granny Wu's home, like the homes of many people in the border region, had greatly improved through the combined efforts of the people and the army.

Her one-room mud house had turned into a new three-cave dwelling. Her old donkey had died, but she left behind a strong jackass, and Granny Wu had bought a cow. Even the family's ragged clothes and beddings had been replaced by new ones. Her eldest son had become a district official and his wife was also a spinning champion, and they had two handsome babies. Her younger son, after his marriage, had joined the Self-Defence Corps. Granny Wu herself was famous throughout the district for having learned 1,500 characters by heart at the advanced age of sixty-three.

Although her steps were not as brisk as before she was still so vigorous and cheerful that she transmitted this to anyone coming into contact with her. What pleased her most was to raise both hands and mimicking Chairman Mao's gesture say:

"We have these, we have these! With these labouring hands, we can solve any problem!"

Then, opening her mouth, revealing her last few teeth, she laughed loudly.

In March 1947, Chiang Kai-shek and Hu Zongnan's army invaded Yan'an. After destroying the enemy's main force, the people and the army voluntarily evacuated this empty town. At that time, Granny Wu had been ill in bed for two months. She refused to be persuaded by her son and daughter-in-law and was determind to stay in Yan'an.

"I want to see Hu Zongnan buried here with my own eyes."

The valleys, bridges and fields were all mined. With the exception of the local people, no one dared to move about. Half an hour after the covering force had left, Chiang Kai-shek and Hu Zongnan's army became bold enough to rush into the town of Yan'an yelling and shouting.

When the enemy soldiers caught Granny Wu, they acted as if they had captured something valuable. They laughed contemptuously:

"We thought that there must be treasure hidden in Yan'an, but there's nothing but a skinny old granny!"

While the troops were laughing obscenely, one low-ranking officer squeezed forward, and after ordering the soldiers to make room, he asked:

"Are you a native here?"

"I am a Yan'aner!" answered Granny Wu, lifting up her head.

"In what direction did the main forces of the communist army retreat? How far have they gone?"

"Who knows how far they've gone. They left three days ago."

The officer stamped his foot and roared, "Three days ago? We've been tricked by the Communists. It's a pity our senior officers are as timid as mice; they kept shelling but were afraid to come in. We can't level these mountains even if we use up all the shells in America. . . . Well, in what direction did the covering force retreat?"

Weakly, Granny Wu pointed to the narrow mountain path, "They left a few hours ago. If you hurry up, you may catch them up."

On hearing this, the low-ranking officer was about to report it to his superiors when Granny Wu stopped him:

"Officer, I see you're an honest man. To tell you the truth, they've laid a lot of mines there. If you want to chase them, it's better take this narrow path. You should go through there quickly, the faster the better. When you get on to the main road, walk carefully by sticking to one side of the road. . . ."

The officer thanked the old woman and ordered his soldiers to watch her.

They sent a company of cavalrymen to chase the Communists at lightning speed along the path pointed out by the old woman.

Granny Wu seated herself on the millstone in front of her house groaning. While the hooves of the galloping horses were running along the narrow path, a terrible deafening explosion thundered through the whole valley.   Forty to fifty dead soldiers and horses were thrown in every direction. Scarlet blood flowed down the hillside to the main road like tiny rivulets after the rain.

Granny Wu seemed to suddenly recovered from her illness. She laughed loudly and vigorously, as if another bomb had exploded inside her body. She laughed as if her sides would split. However, she was immediately seized by numerous devilish hands. One of the soldiers aimed his gun at her, but was stopped by the low-ranking officer who walked up to her and asked in a muddle-headed way:

"Did you know that this meant death for you?"

"Yes, I knew." She stopped laughing.

"What did you do it for? I don't understand. Is there anything more precious than life?"

"What for? For him!" she answered solemnly.

"Who's he?" He felt somewhat perplexed.

"The benefactor who leads us!"

"He has fled! You'll die here in his stead!"

"No, he's forever with us, we'll never die, we'll win!"

"Why did you tell us to walk through that narrow path quickly?"

"Stupid! So that more of you will be killed!"

The low-ranking officer nodded his head and finally understood the strong willpower of the people of northwest China. After he had finished his questioning, he took up his pistol and fired three shots at Granny Wu's chest.

This old woman destroyed some of the enemy's strength with her patriotic honesty and wisdom. In her dizzy semiconsciousness before death the wave-like songs, now strident, now deep, of the northwestern people who were prepared to sacrifice everything to defeat the savage onslaught of the enemy, sounded once more.

Marx's birthday, 1947
Translated by Zhang Mingzhu

About the Author

CAO MING, a contemporary woman writer whose real name is Wu Xuanwen, was born into a poor family in 1913 in Shunde County, Guangdong Province. After the Japanese aggressors invaded northeast China in 1931, she took part in the anti-Japanese patriotic propaganda activities in rural areas. She started writing in 1932. The next year she went to Shanghai and joined the League of Left-wing Writers. Her first short story "Fall" was published the same year followed by a short novel *Despair*. During the war against Japan, she went to Guangzhou, Chongqing and other places, doing anti-Japanese propaganda work. In this period, she published "Liang Wu's Annoy", "A Peasant Woman", "Bride", "A Lost Smile" and other short stories. She joined the Chinese Communist Party in 1940 and went to Yan'an the next year to participate in the Yan'an Rectification Movement and the Yan'an Forum on Literature and Art. In this period she wrote the short stories "He Is Not Dead" and "A Native of Yan'an". After the victory of the anti-Japanese war in 1945, she went to the Northeast to do mass work, mainly among workers. In 1948 she wrote *The Motive Force*, a famous novel describing the workers' life. Her second novel *Locomotive* appeared in 1950. She was the deputy Party secretary of the First Steel Plant of the Anshan Iron and Steel Company from 1954 to 1964, during which time she wrote short stories "Birth", "Song of the Spring" and "Girl's Worry", and her third novel *Riding Waves*. She went to Beijing in 1964 to concentrate on writing and became a member of the All-China Federation of Literature and Art Circles and council member of the Union of Chinese Writers.

The short story "A Native of Yan'an" depicts an old woman peasant in the Northern Shaanxi Revolutionary Base Area, who, remaining unyielding before the Kuomintang reactionary army, eulogizes the Communist Party and its revolutionary leader for emancipating the oppressed people.

The Memento

Zhou Libo

It was now autumn and the days were getting cooler. Xiao Liu had regained much of his health. By holding on to wall, he was able to move around the room slowly. We were all pleased at his recovery. That summer, quite a number of people had died in the prison. Late each night dozens of corpses, wrapped in weed-mats, were pulled through a hole in the wall beside the prison gate. The expression "corpse hole" became the most obscene swear words in the prison. Xiao Liu was not physically strong. Particularly after he fell ill in such a dangerous season, it was marvellous to see him recover and we could once more enjoy the warm peaceful autumn evenings together. But, before long he met with another mishap.

As soon as he was a little better, Xiao Liu resumed his secret contact with someone outside the prison. One night, constable No. 205, a good-natured Indian Buddhist, was taking over his night shift. He brought us a long letter about the situation outside and five packets of tobacco. Just as he was handing these things to Xiao Liu, we could see under the gloomy light the giant shadow of a man on the white-washed wall opposite the staircase. Everyone tried to guess who it was. Some said it was the Chinese policeman guarding the fourth floor; others said that it was the Indian police sergeant on night patrol. But whoever it was made no difference to the fact we were discovered receiving things from outside. The British police

would soon come and make a raid. Recently, the night shift
had been taken by the notorious British guard No. 27. My
room-mate Lao Zheng told Xiao Liu to throw the tobacco into
the slop-bucket and hide the letter. Tobacco was used as money
inside the prison. With a "white louse", in other words, a
pinch of tobacco as small as a louse, one could buy quite a lot
of medicine, rice, and other daily necessities or even a new cotton blanket in winter. Five packets of tobacco was enough to
improve the situation of many sick people among us. It was a
pity to throw it away, but, there was no alternative. The
hardest problem was where to hide the letter. We didn't want
to tear it up and throw it into the slop-bucket, since we hadn't
had time to read it yet. Moreover, white paper was strictly
forbidden among us prisoners because it was too conspicuous.
There was nowhere it could be safely hidden. All the prison
cells were identical, three walls were built of reinforced con-
crete, and the other consisted of iron gates. There were no
cracks in the walls and no dark corners. Someone suggested
passing the letter to constable No. 205 and asking him to keep
it on him for a while or perhaps hide it somewhere outside the
cell and think of a way out later. This wouldn't work either.
The Indians were often searched and there was nowhere outside the prison cell where something could be hidden. The
structure of the walls, windows, doors, corridors and railings
was very basic and of the same colour. Nothing could be hidden, because anything of a different colour would stand out.
Others suggested giving the letter immediately to No. 205 to
throw out of the window. However, it was the same inside and
out; both were lit up by electric lights which were never turned
off and guarded all night by American and British soldiers. It
was impossible not to notice a ball of white paper dropping
from the fifth floor. We were all desparately trying to think of
a way, but the more anxious we got the more our minds went
blank.

"Pass it to me! Pass it to me!" Xiao Chen broke out excitedly.

"What are you going to do with it?" Ah Jin asked, his pleasant firm voice faltering.

"I've ripped open the sleeve of my cotton-padded coat. Give me the letter. Quick!"

"What! Xiao Chen, have you forgotten what happened in the north jail last year?"

Before Ah Jin had time to finish, the demon-like giant shadow of No. 27 silently appeared outside Xiao Liu's room. He had on a pair of rubber-soled boots worn only in surprise raids of this kind. The three burly Chinese policemen and the lean interpreter who accompanied him all wore cloth-soled shoes in order not to make a noise when they walked. They opened Xiao Liu's door, and squeezed into his room. The rustling of blankets and the sound of mugs falling over could be heard. Xiao Liu was pushed out of the room by a Chinese policeman. He was barefooted, and was trying to chew and swallow something.

"Open up the mouth!" yelled No. 27 in awkward Chinese, as he dashed out of the room.

"Open your mouth!" barked the interpreter in Chinese, as he followed him out of the room.

In the still of the night, their yelling sounded loud and clear and full of menace. Xiao Liu was not intimidated by them, he was swallowing something with difficulty. The interpreter ordered the Chinese policemen to tie Xiao Liu's hands behind his back. His mouth was forced open, and a scrap of damp white paper was found inside his left cheek. It was a tiny remnant of that letter. No. 27 took it and examined it under the electric light. The few words that remained were made illegible by saliva. Throwing away the scrap of paper, and turning round, he aimed a sudden kick at Xiao Liu who turned over on the ground, his bare head knocked against the cement floor, making a nerve-shattering sound.

"Speak out, who brought in that letter?" barked the interpreter ferociously, staring at Xiao Liu. No. 205 turned pale; he moved quietly to a dim corner. Getting no reply, the interpreter bent down and said mildly: "Come on, tell the truth, and I'll help you. I promise you won't be punished for it."

Xiao Liu remained silent and rubbed his chest where he had been wounded. They dragged him up and seizing him by both arms forced him downstairs. We were so choked with anger that we could hardly breathe; we were at a loss to know what to do. No. 205 came over, wiping the tears from his eyes with a handkerchief, he promised to bring us news.

Shortly before daybreak, Xiao Liu was carried back, his chest black and swollen and vomiting blood from his mouth. His backside was torn to shreds. His room-mates wanted to put some ointment on his wounds, but it was impossible to remove his white shorts which were soaked with blood at the crotch and stuck to his flesh. He lay prostrate on the cotton blanket on the floor. His groans gradually became fainter.

No. 205 got hold of the following information: Xiao Liu passed out after the first few strokes. He was then revived with water. They wanted him to tell them who had brought the letter in. When he refused, he was given two more strokes. One of the Chinese policemen standing nearby said: "He'll kick the bucket if you flog him any more." So they stopped. Briefly, that was what had happened.

It was past midnight on September 12, 1933. I can still remember the scene vividly. It was cold. Although it was still late autumn, the night wind blowing through the window brought a wintery chill. We lay on the floor, wrapped in cotton blankets, still awake. Now and then we looked at the narrow strip of sky through the bars of the window to see if it was getting light. At daybreak, we could send for that doctor from Guangdong to have a look at Xiao Liu. He was seriously injured and had lost a lot of blood. We couldn't carry on without him, just as we couldn't bear to part with an ideal or a soul which is pure. Crickets chirped outside the windows, while the night wind wailed dismally. The sound of shackles rattling could be heard far away from the long-term prison block. This was intermingled with the long drawn-out yawns of the guards on night duty and the light snoring of some sleeping prisoners. I felt drowsy too and was just about to fall asleep when suddenly there were loud knocks on the prison wall. We sprang from our beds and ran to the door. As if in a dreamy haze I heard someone beyond the wall say: "Xiao Liu's dead." Can it be true? I rubbed my eyes and tried to listen more attentively. Very distinctly I could hear the people in the next room reporting Xiao Liu's last moments. He was mentally alert right to the end. He wanted to ask a favour from anyone who was about to leave prison to take a message through the Revolutionary Mutual-Aid League to his newly married wife, Ah Fang, to tell her not to grieve, to live on bravely, and to marry again soon.

The person telling the story finally said in a trembling voice: "Friends in distress, in his last moments Xiao Liu told us that he had nothing to leave us as a memento except one sentence. He hoped that after we get out of prison, we will continue with the struggle. And if we should remember him, we should remember his words: 'It is a wonderful thing to sacrifice oneself for the cause of communism.' "

Next morning, before breakfast, four criminal prisoners led by an Indian police sergeant came for the corpse. We stood at the door, taking a last look at him. He lay quietly and rigidly on the stretcher. A new dark grey cotton blanket covered his head and body, but his bare feet were poking out of it. In this way he left us forever! He was to be wrapped in weed-mats as usual, and placed in a hole in the prison to wait until nightfall. That was how he left this earthly hell.

It was now night and time to pull him out of the hole. Some prisoners in nearby cells suggested holding a memorial meeting. This idea was met with the unanimous approval of all the prisoners except a Trotskyite, who thought it meaningless. No one took any notice of him. Everyone started discussing and making plans. The man living in one of the middle cells was appointed chairman of the meeting, and the men living in the end cells, namely, cells No. 1 and No. 46 acted as lookouts. If the British guards should come, they would give the alarm by knocking on the wall. There was a "telephone station" in every other cell ready to pass on any reports or speeches to the whole building. After the chairman's memorial speech, Ah Jin first gave an account of the martyr's life. Xiao Liu's surname was originally Yang; his first name was Ah Er. His home town was Lanxi in Zhejiang Province. His brother Ah Gui had been killed in Chiang Kai-shek's massacre at Zhabei, Shanghai, on April 12, 1927. Xiao Liu felt that this event influenced him deeply; it made him realize what he should do with his life. In 1928, he was arrested for joining the "Workers' Security Group", when he was an unskilled labourer in the Ri Hua Cotton Mill in western Shanghai. He was quite young then, just 16 years old. The "Emergency Law Against Endangering the Republic" had not been invented then. He was charged with causing a disturbance in the concession area and got two months' imprisonment. Later he was arrested twice more. First he was sentenced to one year in prison and the last time for five years. Then Ah Jin continued with a sigh: "This then is the story of his youth. Not long before he was last imprisoned, he lived with a woman mill worker, Ah Fang. It was only eight days before he was arrested again. They loved each other very much. Up till now Ah Fang would come to see him every three months, sobbing and weeping all the time, saying she would wait for him forever. Now, she'll never see him again. The Anglo-American imperialists and their Chinese running dogs imprisoned him time after time, and finally they flogged him to death! Comrades!" Ah Jin was so excited that his voice trembled with agitation. "We shall never forget this atrocity! We

shall never forget our comrade and fellow-fighter, our dear
Xiao Liu!"

After Ah Jin, a few more people spoke. Finally, Lao
Zheng began his talk. All the criminal prisoners below the
fourth floor knew that we were holding a memorial meeting.
Partly out of curiosity and partly out of common sympathy,
they asked people to speak louder so that they could hear too.
So, Lao Zheng unbuttoned his padded coat, and held on to the
iron bars of the prison doors with both hands. He pressed his
lips tightly together, in an effort to make himself completely
calm. He spoke loudly in simple Chinese, pausing after every
few words: "Fellow sufferers, sufferers upstairs and downstairs!
The person who has just died was flogged to death by No. 27.
He was flogged until he died! As we all know, the strongest
man can only stand four strokes of this rubber whip. Although
he was ill he still got four strokes!"

He shouted so loudly that his voice became hoarse, but after
a pause, he continued:

"Today, they flog him to death, tomorrow, it could be
anyone of us!"

These words struck the hearts of the people downstairs.
They listened even more attentively and kept very quiet while
he continued:

"However, as long as we stick together, we've nothing to
fear! There are more than eight thousand of us, while there are
less than forty foreign crooks. The two thousand and more Chinese and Indian policemen are all on our side. As you all know,
during the hunger strike in the winter of 1930 the policemen also
went on strike!"

When No. 205 heard this he seemed to remember what had
happened. He was deeply moved and tears welled up in his
eyes. He quickly turned his head, and pretended to look at the
night outside the window. Lao Zheng continued:

"Fellow sufferers! Let me say it again, as long as we stick
together, we have nothing to fear! Moreover, the most detestable

thing there is are running-dogs. There are running-dogs every-where. They come in all shapes and sizes. Our Xiao Liu died because of them! We still all remember the black shadow on the wall that night. Besides, practically all of us in the jail have been done by those detectives."

His speech aroused the common hatred felt for spies and enemy agents. People roared with fury: "Down with spies!" "Down with traitors!" The uproar filled the whole building. Amidst the tumult, two incidents took place: on the fifth floor, the Trotskyite, who had opposed our memorial meeting, was slapped on the face by his room-mate. On the fourth floor, an enemy agent, who was imprisoned for smuggling opium, was sworn at and beaten. His groans could be heard on the fifth floor.

When the tumult had calmed down a little, Lao Zheng continued: "Fellow sufferers! In conclusion, I have one more thing to say: Those of us in jail should remember our hatred. Not only should we fight the running-dogs, but we should also carry on the revolution as soon as we get out of here and drive out the British and U.S. imperialists. We have a lot of things to do and we will also encounter many difficulties. We should keep well in mind. . . ."

"The screws are coming!" someone shouted from below, and Lao Zheng's speech was interrupted. Someone in the next cell knocked on the wall, softly giving the alarm, but Lao Zheng continued calmly:

"We should never forget," he repeated, "Xiao Liu's dying words."

No. 27 and his gang rushed to the door of our room. They opened the door and dragged Lao Zheng out of the room. No. 27 pulled out his truncheon from his breeches, but quite unexpectedly, before he could raise his truncheon, his massive body fell to the ground in the corridor. Lao Zheng had struck the first blow. He had learned boxing; and instinctively aimed at the vulnerable spot below his enemy's waist. A Chinese policeman was about to come to his superior's assistance, but was stopped by the meaningful glances of his two colleagues. The interpreter's face turned pale, he immediately dashed to the stairs, yelling: "Riot! The communist bandits have rioted!" No. 205 barred his way at the end of the corridor and, grabbing his bony shoulders, shook them fiercely, and told him not to be so noisy! No. 27 picked himself up from the ground, and throwing away his truncheon, pulled out a pistol from his waist. The black muzzle was aimed at us. We all closed our eyes and waited for the explosion of the shot. But there was silence. No. 27 had forgotten the bullets. This carelessness was caused by the fact that they were used to controlling the eight thousand prisoners just with truncheon, also they felt that No. 27's physical prowess made it unnecessary to use fire arms. This time he was taken off-guard, but he made a mad dash at Lao Zheng. Just then five or six mugs flew out from the adjoining cells, one of which hit him on his left eye. More mugs came plus a few tin-coated slop-bucket lids. From several hundred prison cells, upstairs and downstairs, people were all yelling furiously, shaking the iron bars and pounding on the walls. No. 27, covering his head with both hands, made a hasty retreat to the staircase. The fanatic cheers lasted a long time. It was mingled with subdued sobs. The struggle had started. This was a desperate struggle to avenge new and old hatreds. It was a clash of iron wills against the iron bars of the jail. It extinguished the depression and grief felt over many years. It cheered the people up and brought tears to their eyes. The policemen on night shift all remained neutral, while the British and American soldiers withdrew into their sentry boxes to evade trouble, holding their rifles at the ready but not daring to fire. No. 205 was so excited that he ran back and forth along the corridor with tears streaming down his face. Sticking his right thumb up, he kept on telling us:

"Madras! Madras! There was this kind of commotion in India too."

"Silence! Let's be silent!" Ah Jin shouted hoarsely, trying to quieten down the tumult. He tried a few times but without success. Eventually taking advantage of a natural break in the uproar, and imitating Lao Zheng, he said, pausing after every few words:

"Please pay attention, everybody! The foreign crooks will come back again! They'll come to pick on some of us. We must unite, and be prepared. If they should come and beat us up again, let's go on hunger-strike."

"Good! Let's go on hunger-strike!" everyone from upstairs and downstairs roared together. They were extremely excited to be reminded of this final method of struggle. After the uproar there was wild clapping. Some of them hit the iron rails with wooden slippers, others beat their folded blankets against the cement floor which sounded like the boom of far-off cannons.

No one knew whether it was because of the lack of staff or because of a pretence at "civilized behaviour" that the authorities were unwilling to make the situation worse. That night, the foreigners didn't show their faces, and nothing happened in the office. When he returned to his room, Lao Zheng seemed rather tired. He sat on a blanket by the iron gate with his elbows on his knees and his head propped up in both hands. He was gloomy and downcast, which was in contrast to his robust appearance. When the criminals downstairs roared "Long Live the Communist Party!" and the solemn strains of the *Internationale* filled the air, he wept. This strong resolute man wasn't usually moved when others wept. Now, he was sitting inside the iron gates, with his head in his hands, his gleaming tear-drops falling onto the patch of light on the floor. To avoid them being noticed, he promptly hid them under his feet. We were well aware that these tears were tears of sorrow and gratitude. He felt sad because he had just lost a good comrade and the Communist Party of China had lost a good fighter. He felt gratitude because the common criminals downstairs were on our side in the struggle. Moreover, every failure and every death might bear more fruit. Just as more people were joining in the singing, Ah Jin told me to put out my hand to take something, and he passed me a half-worn shoe. I recognized the shoe as belonging to Xiao Liu. Wearing this shoe, he had spent countless days of hunger and sadness with us! With this shoe on his foot, he had paced up and down with us in the hot summer days. Suddenly a picture of him lying on a stretcher with his bare feet sticking out of the cotton blanket flashed across our minds. Was it really him? He was standing up! We were talking, talking about the dawn, about a time when we can neither weep, nor have anything to weep about. He turned round. There was a smile on his bluish pale face. I stared into space for I don't know how long before I took another look at that shoe and discovered a piece of cloth torn from the sleeve of a prisoner's suit on which was written a row of large characters. It was written with fresh blood. Xiao Liu had bitten the forefinger of his right hand to make it bleed. The words written in blood appeared to be shining bright, but our eyes were blurred by tears and only after much efforts could we make it out that it was Xiao Liu's last words:

"It is a wonderful thing to sacrifice oneself for the cause of communism."

At the end of the memorial meeting, amid the singing of the *Internationale*, we passed Xiao Liu's shoe with the words in it, slowly and solemnly from one cell to another, from person to person and to all the innocent surviving souls in this five-storeyed building.

Translated by Zhang Mingzhu

About the Author

ZHOU LIBO (1908-79) was one of China's well-known contemporary writers.

After finishing junior secondary school in 1927, Zhou Libo
went to Shanghai after being forced by poverty to leave school. In
1929, he passed the entrance examination at the free University for
Workers. Eight months later, however, he was expelled by the
reactionary university authorities for his Leftist ideology and revolutionary activities.

In the winter of 1931, on the recommendation of a schoolmate,
he got a job as proof-reader in a Shanghai printing-house. In 1932
he was arrested by the Kuomintang reactionaries for taking part in
a strike at the press and was sentenced to two and a half years in
prison. Released in 1934, he joined the China Federation of Left-
Wing Writers and was admitted to the Communist Party of China.
From that time on, he held a number of posts, serving as editor of
magazines and newspapers, war correspondent, translator of
English, and teacher and head of the Editing and Translation
Department at Lu Xun Arts' Institute in Yan'an.

After the country's liberation in 1949, Zhou Libo helped to
write the scenarios of the films *Victory of the Chinese People* and
Liberated China. In 1955, he was made chairman of the Hunan
Provincial Federation of Literary and Art Circles. He was also
deputy to the National People's Congress and member of the Chinese
People's Political Consultative Conference.

Zhou Libo began creative writing as a member of the China
Federation of Left-Wing Writers in the mid-30s. He wrote a
number of sketches and articles on literature while working as an
editor for the magazine *Literature of the Week*.

Written after he had participated in the land reform in
northeast China in 1946, Zhou Libo's *Hurricane* has been widely
acclaimed by the reading public and made into a film of the same
title. In 1954 he published his novel *The Flowing Molten Iron*
based on the life of steel workers. *Great Changes in a Mountain
Village*, another novel by Zhou portraying China's agricultural co-
operation movement, came out in 1957. His other works include
My Impressions of the Shanxi-Qahar-Hebei Border Region,
Southward Journey and the prose collection *Diary at the Front*. His
writings are distinguished by keen insight, tight structure, forceful

characterization and wit. He was good at using dialects which also add to the local colour of his works.

In addition to writing, Zhou Libo translated into Chinese a number of literary classics including Sholokhov's *Virgin Soil Upturned* and Pushkin's *Dubrovsky*.

The short story "The Memento" describes how a group of Chinese workers and other revolutionaries jailed by the British colonial authorities in Shanghai organize a protest against the British police's beating to death a Chinese worker, Xiao Liu. They dedicate their victory in the struggle to the young worker as a memorial.

The Marriage of
Young Blacky

Zhao Shuli

I

In the village of Liujia Valley were two oracles, a man and a woman. Everyone in the neighbouring towns and hamlets knew about them. The man was called Liu the Sage. The woman was called Third Fairy.

Liu, who had been a small merchant, never made a move without first consulting the stars. Third Fairy was the wife of a fellow named Yu Fu. On the first and the fifteenth of each month she draped a red cloth over her head and strutted about, claiming to be a heavenly spirit.

Each of these oracles hated a particular phrase. Liu the Sage abhored "Not right for sowing". Third Fairy abominated "The rice is overdone". Both had their reasons.

A number of years before, there had been a spring drought. Not until the third day of the fifth month did they finally get a little rain. The following morning everybody rushed out to sow millet. Liu the Sage checked the farmers' almanac and calculated on his fingers. Then he announced: "Today is not right for sowing." The fifth was Dragon-Boat Festival Day, and he had never worked on that day. The sixth according to

his calculations was a lucky day, and he sowed his seed. But
by then the soil had gone dry again. Less than half the millet
came up.

There was no more rain until the fifteenth. While others
were out hoeing around their sprouts, Liu and his two sons had
to re-sow their empty patches. A young neighbour, meeting
him on the street that evening after supper, asked innocently,
"Would you say today is right for sowing or not, uncle?" Liu
the Sage glared at him and walked away. Everyone laughed,
and the story rapidly spread.

One day a man came to ask Third Fairy's divine aid in
curing an ailment. Seated behind an incense table, she pretended
to go into a trance and sang incantations. The man knelt before
her. Third Fairy's daughter Qin, who was then only nine, had
put the rice on to boil for the noonday meal. Attracted by her
mother's singing, she forgot about it, and slipped into the room
to listen. When the man went out a moment to relieve
himself, Third Fairy hissed at her daughter: "Take that pot
off, quick. The rice is overdone." The man overheard her. After
he left he told everyone of these prosaic words he heard from a
medium who was supposed to be communing with the gods.
People who liked a joke often asked one another in her presence:
"How's the rice? Is it overdone?"

2

Third Fairy had been divinely gifted for a full thirty years.
It began when she was fifteen. The prettiest girl in village, she
had just married Yu Fu, a quiet, hard-working honest young
man. Yu Fu's mother had died when he was a child, and when
he and his father went out to work in the fields, his bride was
left alone at home. Fearing that she might be lonely, other
young men of the village drifted in to keep her company. Soon

there was a whole crowd of them, and the house rang with their laughter.

Yu Fu's father thought these goings-on disgraceful. He blew up and berated the young men so roundly that they didn't dare show themselves again. But the bride went into hysterics. She wept all day and the following night. In the morning she neither combed her hair nor washed her face. She wouldn't even eat. She just lay in bed and refused to get up.

Father and son were helpless. An old woman neighbour invited a medium for them. The medium consulted the gods and said the bride had been possessed of a supernatural being called Third Fairy. The girl herself moaned and muttered a lot of mystic nonsense. Thereafter, on the first and the fifteenth of each month a divine spirit was said to enter her body. People burned incense before her and begged for instructions on how to get rich or cure illnesses. That was when her incense table was first set up.

Young men again started calling. Although they claimed they wanted to consult the heavenly oracle, what they really wanted was to view the heavenly image. Third Fairy guessed what was on their minds. She dressed in her best clothes and made herself up alluringly. It wasn't long before she had all the young men wrapped around her little finger.

That was thirty years before. Most of the young men of that day now wore beards, and the majority had grown children and daughters-in-law of their own. Except for one or two bachelors, few had time to idle with Third Fairy. But, although she was forty-five, Third Fairy still liked to play the coquette. She continued to wear embroidered shoes and trousers with fancy cuffs. The front of her head was bald, but she covered this with a black kerchief. Unfortunately powder couldn't smooth over her wrinkled face. It only made it look like a frosted donkey turd.

Not satisfied with her few old bachelors, Third Fairy gathered round herself another troupe of youngsters, even more numerous and more mischievous than her admirers of former days.

What was it about Third Fairy that attracted so many young men? The answer lay in her daughter Qin.

3

Third Fairy gave birth to six children, but five of them died. Only Qin, a daughter, survived. At two or three, she was very cute. Third Fairy's admirers loved to hold the child in their arms. "She's mine," one would say, picking her up. "No, she's mine," another would insist, taking her over. By the time the girl was five or six, she realized there was something improper in these claims.

"If anyone says that again," her mother advised, "you just reply: 'I'm your aunt. Be more respectful to your elders.'" Qin did so, and this put a stop to the insulting remarks.

Now she was eighteen. Idle gossips said she had it all over her mother at the same age. Young men sought every excuse to talk with her. When she went to wash clothes by the stream, the young men immediately found that their own clothes were dirty. When she gathered wild herbs, they discovered that wild herbs were exactly what they needed most.

At mealtime, neighbours liked to bring their food over and chat with Third Fairy while they ate. Some lived at the other end of the village and the round trip was a full li, but they didn't mind. This had been going on for thirty years. But the present generation of young men began manifesting their enthusiasm only two or three years before. Third Fairy at first thought her own charm was the cause. But gradually she saw it was Qin the young men were really interested in.

Qin was quite different from her mother, however. Although she too laughed and chatted, she was a prudent girl. The only boy with whom she was fairly friendly was Young Blacky. One day two summers before, she was home alone when Wang, another boy, dropped in.

"Here's my chance at last," he leered.

The girl's face stiffened. "You shouldn't talk like that. You're a big boy now."

"You don't have to put on an act with me," the boy sneered. "You'd soften up soon enough if I were Blacky. Why don't you give us all a little taste? The pot has no right to call the kettle black." Seizing her arms, he whispered: "Come on. Quit pretending."

To his surprise, she let out a scream: "Wang, what are you doing?"

Hastily, he let go and slipped away. "Just wait," he muttered. "I'll get you yet."

4

Everyone in Liujia Valley hated Wang. Only his cousin Xing could get along with him. Wang's father had been a petty tyrant. For years his favourite sport had been to tie people up and beat them. By the time Wang was seventeen, he was his father's worthy assistant. Xing, too, learned to play jackal to the tiger. Any time the old man wanted a dirty job done, he had only to give the order to Wang and Xing.

In the early years of the War Against Japanese Aggression, the countryside was overrun with traitors, enemy spies, deserters and bandits. Wang's father was dead by then and the two cousins did the inside work for a gang of deserters. They told them whom to kidnap, then acted as intermediaries to arrange the ransom, giving each side the impression that they were their friends. Later, the Communist-led Eighth Route Army came and smashed the deserter and bandit gangs, and the two cousins returned to Liujia Valley.

The peasants living in this remote mountain region were

then rather timid. After months of chaos during which many
people were killed, the Liujia Valley residents were even less
inclined to stick their necks out. Other villages formed new
administrations and set up societies to help the war effort, but
no one in Liujia was willing to hold any post. Even the mayor
had to be appointed by the county government.

Not long after, the county authorities sent people to supervise elections for village officers. Wang and Xing thought this
was their chance to seize power. The villagers were only too
glad to get someone to serve. Xing was chosen chairman of the
military committee, Wang was elected political committeeman,
Wang's wife became head of the women's association. A few
old men were pressured into accepting the remaining offices.
But of course an old man couldn't be the leader of the Anti-
Japanese Youth Vanguard. Xing nominated Young Blacky for
no other reason except that he was a nice-looking boy. Although
Blacky's father, Liu the Sage, didn't like the idea, he didn't dare
oppose Xing, and the boy was elected.

The mayor was not a native, and knew little about village
affairs. Wang and Xing were able to ride roughshod over everyone even more easily than they had before. They had only to
deceive the mayor and no one could refuse to do their bidding.

In the next few years, a'though some of the other officers
were changed, the cousins remained in their positions. The
people hated them to the marrow of their bones, but no one
dared say a word against them. They were afraid of the consequences if they tried to overthrow the cousins and failed.

5

Young Blacky was the second son of Liu the Sage. Once
in a counter-assault he killed two of the enemy and was award-
ed the title of Sharpshooter. During the Spring Festival he and
a group of amateurs toured the local villages and staged

theatricals. He was so handsome the women couldn't take their eyes off him.

He never went to school, but he learned to read and write a little from his father. Instead of the classics or the standard texts, they used the old man's prognosticating books. Though only six, Young Blacky was very bright, and he quickly memorized all the professional fortune-teller phrases. His father liked to show him off. The child was so cute, visitors asked him to predict their fortunes just to hear his responses.

Later, Liu the Sage pulled his famous "not right for sowing" boner, and was berated by his wife and his older son Big Blacky and laughed at by the villagers. Young Blacky also came in for his share of ridicule. Although he was already thirteen, people still teased him like a child. To chaff Liu they would ask Young Blacky in his father's presence: "Give us a prediction. Is today right for sowing?"

Children his own age, if they rowed with Young Blacky about something, would get back at him by chanting: "Not right for sowing, not right for sowing."

The boy felt so humiliated he kept away from people for months. Then he talked the whole thing over with his mother. They decided they'd never have any faith in the Sage's prognostications again.

Young Blacky and Qin had been friends for two or three years. It started when he was seventeen and joined other young people merrily whiling away the long winter evenings at the home of Third Fairy. Soon he and Qin grew very attached. They couldn't seem to let a day go by without seeing each other.

Someone offered to be a matchmaker, but Liu the Sage wouldn't hear of it. He had three reasons. First, their horoscopes didn't match. Young Blacky was "metal", while Qin was "fire", and fire could consume metal. Second, Qin was born in the tenth month, which was unlucky. Third, the girl's mother had a bad reputation.

By coincidence, famine refugees were passing through the village, and one of them offered to give his nine-year-old daughter to any family that would feed and raise her. Liu thought this was a good bargain. After casting her horoscope he declared that she and his son were a heaven ordained pair. He took her into his home as Young Blacky's future wife.

Although to Liu the Sage this seemed entirely fitting and proper, the boy was dead against it. Father and son quarrelled for several days. Liu insisted.

"If you want to raise her, that's up to you," exclaimed Young Blacky. "Anyhow, I don't want her."

The result was that the little girl remained, but it wasn't clear what exactly her relationship to the family was.

6

Ever since Qin rebuffed him, Wang longed for revenge. One day Blacky was ill and didn't show up for militia practice.

"He's shamming," Wang said to Xing. "He spends all his time playing around with that Qin girl. We ought to bring him up for criticism."

Xing had been spurned by Qin himself. Naturally he completely approved Wang's idea. He told Wang to get his wife to arouse the women's association, so that they would censure Qin also. Wang's wife was now the head of the women's association, and she hated Qin because her husband had often gone to her house. She was delighted with the censure proposal. It was a chance too good to miss. Dropping her housework, she at once swung into action.

The following day two criticism meetings were called. The military committee censured Blacky. The women's association censured Qin.

Since he was innocent, Blacky refused to admit that he was wrong. Xing ordered that he be tied up and turned over to the village authorities. Fortunately, the mayor had a clear head.

"Young Blacky was ill with malaria, he wasn't faking," he told Xing. "So far as being in love is concerned, that's not against the law. You can't arrest him for that."

"But he's engaged to another girl."

"Everyone knows that he doesn't agree to the match, and he's quite right, too. The little girl is only twelve. When she grows up she won't agree either. There's no reason why Blacky shouldn't fall in love with someone else. Nobody should interfere."

Xing fell silent. Blacky was still angry.

"What about tying a person up without cause?" he asked the mayor. "Is that against the law or not?"

The mayor had just managed to soothe them down when Qin burst in, with the head of the women's association in tow. "Mayor," she cried. " 'Show the loot to prove a theft, catch both lovers to prove a tryst.' Is the head of the women's association allowed to accuse people without a shred of evidence?"

Xing, afraid Wang's wife might spill the beans and reveal his connection with the plot, hastily exited. On learning the circumstances, the mayor, after nearly talking himself dry, at last restored peace.

7

Since the censure meetings had exposed their romance to the public eye, and since Young Black and Qin had learned that it was entirely reasonable and legal anyway, they began seeing each other openly.

Third Fairy was very upset. Although she and Qin were mother and daughter, they had been on bad terms for several years. Third Fairy loved young men, but the young men loved Qin. She had looked on Blacky as a succulent morsel. But because of Qin, he eluded her.

For some time she had been thinking of marrying Qin off and getting her out of the house. But her own reputation was so bad, no family wanted to become related to her. After the censure meetings, rumours spread that Blacky and Qin were planning to get married, with or without their parents' consent. If that were true, thought Third Fairy, she'd never even be able to joke with Young Blacky again. What a pity. She therefore asked everyone she could to find Qin a husband.

"Hoist the recruiting flag and hungry men will come." A wealthy retired brigadier named Wu, who had served under the warlord Yan Xishan, had recently lost his wife. He saw Qin at a temple fair and was quite struck by her. He sent a matchmaker with a proposal of marriage. Third Fairy was more than willing. A few days later Wu sent engagement gifts to confirm the match. Third Fairy thought everything was settled.

But Qin and Young Blacky had just about made up their minds. Naturally, the girl wouldn't listen to her mother. The day the gifts were delivered, she and Third Fairy had a big argument. Qin threw Brigadier Wu's jewels and silks on the floor. After the matchmaker hurriedly departed, the girl exclaimed:

"I won't have any part of them. If you want his things, you marry him."

Third Fairy was in a quandary. For several hours she lay upon her bed. After the evening meal, she said she could feel the "spirit" taking her. She yawned a couple of times and began to chant. First the "spirit" blamed her husband for not being able to run the household properly. Next she announced that Qin's marriage to Brigadier Wu had been ordained by heaven and that anyone who opposed heaven would die. Her husband dropped to his knees and begged for mercy. The "spirit" directed that he give Qin a beating. When the girl heard this, she knew there was no reasoning with this fake medium of a mother. She quickly departed, leaving Third Fairy to babble on without her.

Quietly, she hurried in search of Young Blacky. By chance she met him on the road, looking for her. Hand in hand they stole to a cave they knew to talk over how to deal with Third Fairy.

8

Qin told Young Blacky the whole story of how her mother had arranged the marriage, how she had feigned being taken by the "spirit", and the words she chanted.

"Don't worry," he advised. "I asked a comrade in the district government. He said any boy and girl who want to get married can go to the district office and register. No one can stop them."

Hearing footsteps, Blacky put his head out and looked. Four or five men were standing in the shadows. One of them shouted:

"Arrest them both." It was the voice of Wang.

Blacky grew angry. "Arrest who?" he cried. "Nobody's broken any law."

Xing was there too. He ordered his men: "Nab him. We'll see whether he's broken any law or not. That fellow's been giving me trouble for a long time."

"I'll go wherever you say," Blacky retorted, "even to the Border Region government. You've got nothing on me."

"Go?" sneered Xing. "We're not going to let you stroll there. That would be letting you off too easy. Tie him up."

Blacky fought valiantly, but he was outnumbered. In the end, they tied his hands behind his back.

"There's a girl in there too," said Xing. "Tie her up also. You need two culprits to prove this kind of thing. She said so herself."

Qin was seized and tied as well.

People who heard the noise hurried out from the village.

When, in the light of the torches, they saw the young couple bound with ropes, they could guess well enough what had happened.

Blacky's father, Liu the Sage, fell on his knees before Xing. "There's no bad blood between our families," he pleaded. "For the sake of my honour, let him go."

"This matter is out of our hands," Xing retorted. "We have to turn him over to the higher authorities."

"Don't interfere, pa," said Blacky. "It doesn't matter where he sends me. I didn't commit any crime. I'm not afraid of him."

"Tough, are you?" cried Xing. To the three militiamen he said: "Take them away."

"Where to?" asked one of the militiamen. "The village government office?"

"What for?" replied Xing. "The last time we sent him there, the mayor let him go. Take them to the district military committee and let them be tried according to martial law."

Blacky and Qin were hauled away.

9

None of the neighbours had dared plead for the young couple. Now they urged Liu the Sage to go home.

Liu sighed. "I knew trouble was brewing. The other morning as I was crossing the ridge on the way to my field I met a woman riding a donkey. She was dressed in mourning. I knew right then we were in for it. According to my star this year, if I see mourning I ruin my luck. I've been afraid to go anywhere, trying to avoid it, but in the end I couldn't escape. And last night Blacky's ma dreamed she heard an opera being sung in the temple. And this morning a crow lit on our roof and cawed a dozen times." He sighed again. "There's no escaping fate."

Although irritated with his loquaciousness, his neighbours offered a few words of comfort, then all returned to their homes.

But who could sleep? In Liu the Sage's house, only the little girl was able to relax in slumber. Liu took three coins and manipulated them to cast Blacky's horoscope. He blanched at the result.

"Frightful, frightful," he exclaimed. "When they elected him head of the Anti-Japanese Youth Vanguard I told him not to take the job. But the little wretch had to play the big shot. Now they're going to court-martial him. If he weren't leader of the Youth Vanguard, he couldn't have broken any military law."

His wife clapped her hands and stamped her feet in anguish. "My poor boy," she wailed, "who would have thought that you'd get yourself into such a mess?"

"Don't worry," said Big Blacky, the elder brother. "The thing has already happened. What if he goes to the district government? This isn't a murder case. I don't think it's very serious. I'll run up there and see what's going on. Now you two go to sleep."

He lit a lantern and set out.

After seeing him off, Liu the Sage returned to his divinations. A little later, he heard a woman crying in the distance. The voice kept coming nearer and nearer until it was outside his window. The next thing he knew, it had entered his door. Before Liu could see who the woman was, she grabbed him by the arms and ranted:

"Give me back my daughter. Where has your son lured her? Give her back to me."

Young Blacky's mother was infuriated by these remarks. When she saw that the intruder was Third Fairy, she leaped out of bed and seized her, shouting:

"I'm glad you've come. It saves me the trouble of looking for you. You and your daughter have seduced my boy, and you

have the gall to insult me. Come on. We'll go to the district
government and settle this."

The two women tussled. Liu the Sage tried in vain to pull
them apart, losing all interest in astrology. When Third Fairy
saw that Blacky's mother was really out for her blood, she became a bit frightened and broke away. Blacky's mother chased
her as far as the gate. She continued to hurl curses after Third
Fairy when blocked from further pursuit by Liu the Sage.

10

Liu didn't sleep all night. "Why isn't he back yet? Why
isn't he back yet?" he kept saying of Big Blacky. At dawn, he
could contain himself no longer, and set out for the district government. Before he had gone half the distance, he saw Big
Blacky and three militiamen approaching. With them were a
district government clerk and messenger. While they were still
quite far apart, Liu hailed his son:

"What about it? Is it serious?"

"Nothing to it," the young man shouted back. "Don't
worry."

After they all had met, the militiamen and the clerk continued on towards the village. Big Blacky introduced his father
to the messenger.

"The district government wants to see you and Third
Fairy, pa," he said. "Go ahead. There's nothing to worry about.
Young Blacky and Qin were released as soon as they got there.
The district has known for some time that Wang and Xing are
bad eggs. They've both been arrested. That clerk is going to
our village to hold meetings and investigate their crimes. When
I got to district, the questioning was already over. I was told
it's all right for Qin and our Young Blacky to get married."

"I'm glad he hasn't broken any law," said Liu. "But that

marriage is impossible. Their horoscopes don't match. Do you know what district wants to see me about?"

"No. Probably nothing very important. Go ahead. I'll tell ma when I get home."

"It looks like your son has notified you for me, old neighbour. Why not go along?" said the messenger. "I'll go and notify the other person." He and Big Blacky walked on together.

When Liu the Sage reached the district government office, he found Young Blacky and Qin sitting on a bench. Pointing at his son, he exclaimed: "Troublemaker. They've let you off. Why don't you go home? Are you trying to worry me to death? Shameless wretch."

"What's all this?" the district chief interjected. "Is the district government office a place to swear at people?"

Liu the Sage fell silent.

"Are you Liu Xiude?" the chief asked him.

"Yes," retorted the Sage.

"Are you raising a girl at home to be Young Blacky's wife?"

"Yes."

"How old is she?"

"Twelve."

"She's too young to be engaged. Send her back to her mother. Young Blacky is already engaged to Qin."

"She has only a father, and he's a refugee who's gone heaven knows where. There's no place to send her back to. I know the law says she's too young to be engaged, but lots of girls in our village are at her age. Be merciful and let this engagement stand."

"Any party to an illegal engagement who's not willing can break it."

"But both families agree."

The district chief asked Young Blacky: "Do you agree?"

"No, I don't," replied the boy.

Liu the Sage glared at him. "That's not for you to decide."

"You didn't ask his consent when you made the engagement," said the district chief. "He doesn't need yours to break it. Today people choose their own partners in marriage, old neighbour. You have no say in the matter. If that little girl you're raising has no other home, you can consider her as your daughter."

"I can do that, all right. But I must beg you to be merciful and not let him become engaged to Qin."

"You can't interfere in that."

"Be merciful, I beg you. Their horoscopes don't match. They'd be miserable all their lives," cried Liu. He turned to Young Blacky. "Don't be such a muddle-head. This will affect your whole life."

"Old neighbour," said the district chief, "don't you be such a muddle-head. Your son would really be miserable all his life if you forced him to marry a twelve-year-old girl. I'm telling you this for your own good. If Young Blacky and Qin want to get married, they can whether you agree or not. You can go home now. The little girl can be your daughter if she has no place else to go."

Before Liu the Sage could renew his pleas for the district chief to "be merciful", a messenger escorted him out the door.

II

Third Fairy had gone to Liu the Sage's home that night for two reasons. First, she wanted to show what a rumpus she could raise if she really tried. Second, she wanted to provide a cover for her actual feelings. As a matter of fact, she was quite happy that Qin had got into trouble, and when she returned home that night she slept well.

The next morning she continued lolling comfortably in bed. Though her husband was very anxious over the arrest of their

daughter, he had no idea what to do about it. Not daring to call Third Fairy, he cooked breakfast himself. When it was nearly ready, she leisurely rose and began combing her hair.

"Are you going to see about Qin?" he asked.

"What for?" retorted Third Fairy. "Let her get out of this scrape herself, if she's so smart."

Her husband dared say no more. He put the cooked food on the side of the stove to keep it warm until Third Fairy finished making up.

As they were starting their meal the messenger arrived from district with a summons for Third Fairy. She seemed quite pleased.

"Our daughter is grown now and we can't handle her any more," she drawled. "We hope the district chief will punish her."

After breakfast she put on her best clothes — a new kerchief, embroidered shoes, fancy-hemmed trousers. She added another layer of powder and stuck several ornaments in her hair. Then she told her husband to saddle the donkey. She mounted and, with him driving the beast from behind, rode to the district government office.

The messenger led her to the chief's room. She dropped to her knees and kowtowed.

"Please give me justice, your honour," she intoned.

The chief, who had been writing at his desk, saw a woman kneeling before him with lowered head, her hair full of silver ornaments. He thought it was a young wife who had sought his help two days before, after quarrelling with her mother-in-law.

"Doesn't your mother-in-law have a guarantor?" he asked. "Why don't you go to him?"

Bewildered, Third Fairy raised her head. When the chief saw a middle-aged woman, her face caked with powder, he realized his mistake. The messenger quickly explained:

"This is Qin's mother."

The chief looked her over. "So you're Qin's mother. Get up. No need to put on an act. I know the whole story. Get up."

Third Fairy rose to her feet. The chief asked:

"How old are you?"

"Forty-five."

"Why do you deck yourself out like that? Don't you know what you look like?"

A girl of ten or so who had been standing at the door, watching, giggled. "Go outside and play," the messenger ordered. The girl fled.

"Can you invoke the spirits?" the chief demanded.

Third Fairy dared not reply. The chief asked her:

"Did you find a suitor for your daughter?"

"Yes."

"How much did he give?"

"Three thousand five hundred."

"What else?"

"Some silks and jewelry."

"Did you talk it over with your daughter first?"

"No."

"Does she agree to the match?"

"I don't know."

"I'll call her and you can ask," said the chief. He turned to the messenger. "Bring Qin here."

The little girl who had been chased away spread the story that the chief was questioning a forty-five-year-old woman who powdered her face and wore embroidered shoes. The neighbourhood women came flocking to see, filling half the courtyard.

"Just look at that," they chattered. "Forty-five if she's a day."

"How do you like those trousers?"

"And those shoes!"

Third Fairy, who hadn't blushed in years, felt herself reddening. Perspiration rolled down her cheeks. The messenger, escorting Qin, said to the women in a voice deliberately loud so that Third Fairy could hear:

"What are you gaping at? She's human, isn't she? Haven't you ever seen anyone like that before? Make way, make way."

The women burst into laughter.

When Qin arrived, the chief said to Third Fairy: "Ask your daughter whether she's willing."

But Third Fairy had ears only for the women in the court-yard. "Forty-five," they were saying, "and she wears embroidered shoes." Sweating with embarrassment, Third Fairy kept mopping her face. She couldn't utter a word.

The ladies outside changed the subject. "That's her daughter. . . . Doesn't make up nearly so fancy as her mother. . . . They say she can invoke the spirits. . . ."

One of them who knew the story of "the rice is overdone", told it in full. By then Third Fairy was ready to die.

"If you won't ask your daughter I'll ask her for you," said the district chief. He addressed himself to Qin: "Are you willing to marry the man your mother has chosen?"

"No. I don't even know him."

"Did you hear that?" the chief asked Third Fairy. He explained about the freedom of choice provisions in the Marriage Law, and said that Qin's engagement to Young Blacky was entirely legal. He advised Third Fairy to return the money and gifts to Brigadier Wu and let Qin marry Young Blacky.

Very ashamed, Third Fairy agreed to everything.

12

When the three militiamen arrived in Liujia and said that district had arrested Xing and Wang and were sending a clerk to investigate their crimes, the villagers were delighted. After the noonday meal, a mass meeting was called in the temple yard. The mayor explained the purpose of the meeting and asked everyone to expose the evil Xing and Wang had done.

People were afraid of retaliation if the two rascals couldn't be overthrown, and at first no one spoke. A few of the more timid even whispered: "Enduring in silence brings peace."

"That's what I once thought," said a young man who had been victimized by the two scoundrels. "But the more I endured, the less peace I had. If you fellows won't speak out, I will."

He told how Wang had brought bandits to his house to extort money from him, and related four or five other crimes that Wang committed. "That's all I'll say for now. Let some of the others speak," he said. "Then I'll go on."

That broke the ice. Peasants rose one after another to expose the wickedness of Xing and Wang — blackmail, driving people to suicide, robbery, rape. They sent militiamen out to cut their firewood, they ordered villagers to hoe their fields. They confiscated grain, imposed taxes, used the militia as their private police. . . . By sunset, fifty or sixty illegal acts had been revealed.

On the basis of this evidence, the two were sent up to county for a formal trial. There, besides being ordered to pay compensation for all the damage they had caused, they were each sentenced to fifteen years in prison.

When the results of the mass meeting became known, the villagers took courage. New cadres were elected. No one dared cast a vote for any rascal. Even Wang's wife, who was voted out of office, changed her tune. "I'll be progressive from now on," she avowed.

There was a metamorphosis in our two oracles as well.

Third Fairy had been mortified by the stares of the women that day in the district chief's office. When she returned home she took a long look at herself in the mirror. She really was ridiculously over-dressed. A woman with a daughter who'd soon be married — who was she trying to fool?

She made up her mind. From head to toe she converted her appearance to one more suitable to her age. The incense table with which she had been invoking the spirits for the past thirty years, she quietly dismantled.

When Liu the Sage got back from the district office that day, he again bemoaned to his wife the fact that Qin and Young Blacky's horoscopes didn't match.

"It's time you got rid of those astrology charts," his wife said. "All your life you've never even broken wind without first consulting them. You said Blacky was in terrible trouble, but nothing happened. It seems to me Qin is a nice girl. She'll be a good wife to our son. What is this nonsense 'their horoscopes don't match'? Have you forgotten 'not right for sowing'?"

With his own wife no longer believing in his occult powers, Liu the Sage lost courage. He never tried to demonstrate them again.

Qin and Young Blacky also came home. They observed that the mood of their parents had changed and asked neighbours to put in a word for them. The two oracles, deciding to sail with the wind, consented to their marriage.

Both families joined in the preparations. After the ceremony, Qin moved in with Young Blacky. They were very happy. Neighbours said they were an ideal couple.

In the privacy of their room, the newlyweds often joked. Young Blacky mimicked Third Fairy and chanted: "Marriages are ordained in heaven." Qin, imitating Liu the Sage, cried: "District chief be merciful. Their horoscopes don't match."

Once, naughty children, listening at their window, overheard them. The result was that our oracles were given new nicknames. Third Fairy was called "Heaven-Ordained Marriage", and Liu became known as "Unmatched Horoscope".

May 1943
Translated by Sidney Shapiro

About the Author

ZHAO SHULI (1906-70) was born into a peasant family in Shanxi Province.

He turned to literature in 1926, trying his hand at stories which were later published in a small newspaper in his native province.

When the War of Resistance Against Japanese Aggression broke out in 1937, he served as district head in the local administration of the anti-Japanese government. Later, he was made editor of the literary column of several anti-Japanese newspapers.

His real literary career, however, started only in 1943. His writings since then include *The Marriage of Young Blacky, Rhymes of Li Youcai, Change in Li Village* and *Registration,* to mention only a few.

The Marriage of Young Blacky is Zhao Shuli's masterpiece in which he tells the story of a couple of youths in the communist base area. To win the right to marry, Young Blacky and his girl friend struggle against feudalism and people's old ideas. The story eulogizes democratic power and the experiences of the young generation growing up in the countryside.

Lotus Creek

Sun Li

It was a summer night in the year 1940. The moon had risen and the little courtyard was delightfully fresh and clean. The rushes split during the day were damp and supple, just waiting to be woven into mats. A woman was sitting in the yard plaiting the long soft rushes with nimble fingers. The thin, fine strands leaped and twisted in her arms.

Baiyangdian Lake lies in the middle of the province of Hebei and is known all over China for its reeds and rushes. I can't tell you the exact area grown with them nor the yearly output. All I know is that each year when the rush flowers blow in the breeze and the leaves turn yellow, the whole crop is cut and stacked in the squares round Baiyangdian Lake like a Great Wall of reeds. The women plait mats in their threshing-fields or courtyards, vast quantities of silvery, snow-white mats. And in June, when the water in the creek is high, countless boats ship them away, until soon towns and villages in all parts of the country have these finely woven mats with their lovely designs.

"Baiyangdian mats are best," is quite an axiom.

The young woman in the yard was plaiting a mat, seated on the long stretch of it already accomplished where she seemed enthroned on virgin snow or on a fleecy cloud. From time to time she strained her eyes towards the creek, another world of silver white. Light, translucent mist had risen over the water, and the breeze was laden with the scent of fresh lotus leaves.

The gate was still open — her husband wasn't home yet.

It was very late before her husband came home. He was twenty-five or twenty-six, a barefoot young fellow in a large straw hat, a spotless white shirt and black trousers rolled up over his knees. His name was Shusheng and he was chief of the anti-Japanese guerrillas in Lesser Reed Village, as well as the leader of the Communist Party branch there. Today he had taken his men to the district town for a meeting. His wife looked up with a smile as he came in.

"What kept you so long today?"

She stood up to fetch him some food. Shusheng sat on the steps.

"Never mind about that — I've eaten."

She sat down on the mat again. Her husband's face was rather flushed and he seemed out of breath.

"Where are the others?" she asked.

"Still in town. How's dad?"

"Asleep."

"And Xiaohua?"

"He was out half the day with his grandad shrimping and went to bed hours ago. Why haven't the others come back?"

Shusheng gave a forced laugh.

"What's wrong with you?"

"I'm joining the army tomorrow," he said softly.

His wife's hand twitched as if a reed had cut it, and she started sucking one finger.

"The district committee called this meeting today. Very soon now, they say, the Japs are going to try to set up more bases. If they manage to get a base at Tongkou — which is only a few dozen li away — that will alter our position here completely. The meeting decided to form a district brigade to keep the Japs out. I was the first to volunteer to go."

His wife lowered her head and muttered:

"Always a step ahead of the others, aren't you?"

"I'm chief of our village guerrillas and one of the cadres: of course I have to take the lead. The others volunteered too. They didn't dare come home, though, for fear their folk would try to hold them back. They chose me to come back and explain things for them to their families. Everyone felt you had more sense than most wives."

His wife digested this in silence.

"I won't try to stop you," she said presently. "But what about us?"

Shusheng pointed to his father's room and told her to keep her voice down.

"You'll be taken care of, naturally. But our village is small and seven fellows are joining the army this time. That doesn't leave many young men at home. We can't look to others for everything: the main burden will fall on you. Dad's old and Xiaohua's too young to do much."

His wife felt a lump in her throat but held back the tears.

"So long as you know what we're up against, that's all."

Shusheng wanted to comfort her but time was short. He still had many things to do before leaving.

"You shoulder the load while I'm away. When we've driven the Japs out and I come home, I'll make it up to you."

With this, Shusheng set off for some neighbours' houses, promising to come back and explain matters to his father.

He didn't come back till cock-crow. His wife was still sitting like a statue in the yard, waiting.

"What instructions have you got for me?" she asked.

"Nothing really. Mind you go on making progress while I'm away. Work hard and learn to read and write."

"Uh-huh."

"Don't fall behind the others."

"Uh-huh. What else?"

"Don't let the Japs or traitors take you alive. If you're caught, fight to the finish." This was the main thing he had to say, and his wife assented in tears.

When day broke she made a little bundle of a new cotton suit, a new towel, a new pair of cloth shoes. The other wives had similar bundles for Shusheng to take. The whole family saw him off. His father, holding Xiaohua's hand, said:

"You're doing the right thing, Shusheng, so I won't stop you. Go with an easy mind. I'll look after your wife and boy for you, don't worry."

The whole village, men and women, young and old, turned out to see him off. Shusheng grinned at them all, stepped into a boat and rowed off.

But there must be something of the clinging vine about women. Two days after Shusheng left, four young wives gathered in his house to talk things over.

"Apparently they're still here: they haven't gone yet. I don't want to be a drag, but there's a jacket I forgot to give him."

"I've something important to say to him."

Shusheng's wife said:

"I heard that the Japs want to set up a base at Tongkou. . . ."

"There's not a chance of our running into them, not if we pay a flying visit."

"I didn't mean to go, but my mother-in-law insists that I ought to see him. What for, I'd like to know!"

Without breathing a word to anyone, the four of them took a small boat and paddled to Ma Village across the river.

They dared not look for their husbands openly there but went to a relative's house at one end of the village.

"You've just missed them," they were told. "They were still here yesterday evening but left some time in the night. No one knows where they've gone. You've no call to worry, though. I hear Shusheng was made a vice-platoon leader straight off: they're all in tremendous spirits."

Shame-faced and blushing, the women took their leave and rowed off again. It was nearly noon, without a cloud in the sky, but on the river was a breeze from the paddy fields and rushes in the south. Theirs was the only boat afloat on this endless expanse of water like rippling quicksilver.

Disappointed and rather upset, each woman was secretly laying the blame on her heartless brute of a husband. But young people are incurably optimistic and women have a special knack of forgetting their troubles. Very soon they were laughing and chattering again.

"So they just up and left!"

"I'm sure they're having the time of their lives. This means more to them than New Year or getting married."

"They're like wild horses: they won't stay tied up in a stable."

"No, they all break away."

"Take it from me, that man of mine hasn't given one thought to his home since he joined the army."

"That's true. Some young soldiers once stayed in our house. Singing from dawn to dusk they were: we've never larked like that! I was fool enough to think that once they had nothing to do, they'd start looking glum. But what do you suppose? They painted a whole set of white circles on our courtyard wall, and squatted down one by one for target practice, still singing all the time!"

They paddled easily along while water gurgled on each side of the boat. One of them scooped up a water chestnut, still tiny and milky white. She threw it back into the river. The water chestnut floated placidly there, where it would grow.

"I wonder where they've gone."

"He can go to the end of the earth for all I care!"

"Look! A boat!"

They all raised their heads and gazed into the distance.

"Why, they're Japanese soldiers — see that uniform!"

"Quick!"

They rowed on for dear life. One started wishing they had never taken such a risk, another blaming the husbands who had deserted them. But in no time they put these thoughts out of their heads. They must row fast — the larger boat was coming after them.

The Japanese were going as swiftly as they could.

It was lucky that all these young wives had grown up by the river: their boat went like the wind. It shot forward like some flying fish, hardly skimming the water. They had been in and out of boats since they were children, and could paddle as fast as they could spin or sew.

If the enemy overtook them, they would drown themselves in the river.

The large boat was making quick headway. No doubt about it, those were Japanese. The young women clenched their teeth and fought down their panic. They did not let their hands tremble. The oars plashed loudly, steadily through the water.

"Head for Lotus Creek! It's too shallow for a boat that size."

They raced for the creek, a good many mu in extent, where as far as eye could see massed lotus leaves reached towards the genial sun like a solid wall of bronze. Their pink buds, thrust up like arrows, seemed sentinels watching over Baiyang-dian Lake.

They rowed for the creek and with one final effort drove their small craft in among the lotus. Some wild ducks flapped their wings and flew off with shrill cries, whirring low over the water. A volley of shots rang out!

Pandemonium broke loose. Sure that they had fallen into an enemy ambush with no hope of escape, they jumped all together into the water. But presently, realizing that all the shots were aimed towards the river, they caught hold of the boat's side and peered cautiously out. Not far away under a broad lotus leaf they saw a man's head — the rest of him was submerged. It was Shusheng. Looking right and left, each soon discovered her husband — so this was where they were!

But the men under the lotus leaves were too busy aiming at the enemy to so much as glance at their wives. Quick shots rang out, and after four or five volleys they threw handgrenades and rushed forward.

The grenades sank the enemy boat with everything on board, leaving nothing but smoke and fumes of saltpetre on the surface. With shouts and laughter, the men started salvaging trophies. They dived as if they were after fish. They raced to retrieve enemy rifles, cartridge belts, and sack after sack of dripping flour and rice. Shusheng swam with a great splashing after carton of biscuits bobbing on the waves.

Soaked to the skin, the wives climbed back into their boat.

Holding the biscuits high in one hand and paddling hard with the other, Shusheng shouted towards them:

"Come out of that, you!"

He sounded angry.

They rowed out — what else could they do? Without warning a man popped up from under their bows, and Shusheng's wife was the only one to recognize him. It was the captain of the district brigade. Wiping the water from his face, he demanded:

"What are you doing here?"

Shusheng's wife answered:

"We were taking them some more clothes."

The captain turned to Shusheng:

"Are they all from your village?"

"That's right. A bunch of backward elements!" He hurled the biscuits into their boat and disappeared with a splash, reappearing some distance away.

The captain laughed.

"Well, your trip wasn't wasted. If not for you, our ambush wouldn't have been so successful. But now you've completed your mission, you'd better hurry home and dry your clothes. The situation is still pretty serious."

By now the men had loaded all their trophies on their boats and were ready to move on. Each of them had plastered a large lotus leaf on his head to keep off the midday sun. The women rescued their bundles which had fallen into the water and threw them over. Then the men's three boats made off quickly towards the southeast, to be swallowed up soon in the heat haze over the river.

The women lost no time in starting back, bedraggled as drowned rats. But all the excitement they had been through soon set them laughing and chattering again. The one in the stern made a face over her shoulder.

"Did you ever see the like? Just couldn't be bothered with us!"

"As if we'd lost face for them!"

They laughed, knowing that they hadn't exactly covered themselves with glory. Still:

"We haven't got rifles. If we had, we could take on the Japs without hiding in the creek."

"Well, so at last I've seen fighting! What's so wonderful about it? As long as you don't lose your head, anybody can squat there and let off a gun."

"When a boat sinks I can dive to collect stuff too. I promise you I'm a better swimmer than they are — I can go down deeper than that."

"Let's set up a unit when we go back, or we'll never be able to leave the village again."

"Looking down on us the moment they join the army! In another two years they won't think us worth talking to; but are they all that much better?"

That autumn they learned to fire rifles. When winter came and the time to catch fish in the ice, they took it in turn to take out the sleigh and whizz back and forth over the ice, patrolling the village. When the enemy attempted to "mop up" the marshlands, they worked in coordination with the army, slipping fearlessly in and out of the sea of reeds.

Translated by Gladys Yang

About the Author

SUN LI was born in the countryside of Hebei Province in 1913. After graduation from senior middle school, he became a clerk in Beijing. He had a hard life then, though he did write a number of commentaries and an occasional poem. During the war against Japan, he took a post in the Shanxi-Qahar-Hebei base area. He was transferred to the Fuping mountain area in 1939, to work as a correspondent, editor and teacher. Meanwhile, he started writing stories. In 1943 he studied and worked in the Literature Department of the Yan'an Lu Xun Art Academy. His well-known short story, "Lotus Creek", was written at that time. It tells the story of the women of Baiyangdian Lake in central Hebei who organized themselves to fight the enemy while their husbands were away in the war against Japan.

After the surrender of Japan, Sun Li returned to the central Hebei region to take part in the work of land reform. He became the editor of the literary column of *Tianjin Daily* after the liberation of that city in 1949. Currently, he is a council member of the editorial board of the literary monthly, *New Harbour*.

His works include: a novel, *Stormy Years*; a novelette, *The Blacksmith and the Carpenter*; short stories and collection of writings including *Parting Advice, Guide* and *Reminiscences of Baiyangdian*. "Lotus Creek" and other stories have been warmly received by readers around the world.

My Two Landlords

Kang Zhuo

Tomorrow I will be moving from Xiazhuang to Shangzhuang. I went to look over my new house today. The house that had been allotted to me was near the main road in western Shangzhuang. My new landlord was an old man named Chen Yunnian. When I returned to Xiazhuang, my old landlord Shuan Zhu asked me about the new house and offered to accompany me there the next day but I refused:

"I haven't much luggage! You cadres must be very busy as the winter school has just started. Please don't bother!"

He insisted, saying:

"It's nearly two miles away! I'll do it on my way to the market tomorrow. Enrolment for the winter school is nearly finished. It's no trouble at all."

The next day, I finally gave in. After he had put my luggage on his donkey, and yelled at it to start, we walked along the river bank.

It was a fine day in early winter. The sun shone warmly. The river was covered with a thin layer of ice. Where the ice had melted, the gently flowing water gurgled softly. We were overtaken by most of the people going to the market. We walked slowly and chatted. Shuan Zhu didn't pay any attention to his donkey, which was well-behaved and walked slowly in front of us, sometimes stopping to sniff at the droppings left by other animals, or else it stretched its head and chewed a

538

stalk or two of withered grass by the roadside; sometimes it turned round to look at us as if waiting for us. When Shuan Zhu yelled at it, it speeded up for a few paces, then it would resume its slow amble.

Shuan Zhu and I mostly talked about his studies. He told me that he was unhappy about me moving away.

"After today, how can I continue with my lessons? Where can I find another teacher like you?"

"It mainly depends on oneself! In other words, you've improved a great deal. You can do it on your own."

Then he told me that he might come and see me and asked me not to forget him. He wanted me to continue teaching him and said that he still found difficulty in reading the *Shanxi-Qahar-Hebei Daily*.

"Lao Kang, don't forget to buy a pocket dictionary for me. Please don't forget."

"Of course I won't forget!"

"Ah, how nice it would be to have a dictionary!" he sighed to himself and patting me on the shoulder, he paused and looked at me. Some young men in his neighbourhood had seen a pocket dictionary some time ago at the office of the director of the District Youths' Salvation Association and as a result of what he said nearly every keen student wanted to buy one. But because of the enemy's blockade, although I asked everywhere, I couldn't get one, not even a second-hand copy from any of our offices. The comrades working in the same office as me all used to have dictionaries, but they had either given them away to cadres from the countryside or else they'd lost them in the "anti-mopping-up" campaigns. . . .

The little donkey walking in front of us met a jackass. The two animals wanted to get closer and become more intimate. So they jostled and bumped against each other. The jackass, after being led away by its master, stretched its neck and brayed loudly for a while. Shuan Zhu ran and pulled his donkey back and then we continued on our way. We were

silent for quite a long time. Suddenly Shuan Zhu burst out
laughing. With his face close to my shoulder, and his eyes
half-closed he asked:

"Lao Kang, is it true that you haven't yet got a lover?"

"I . . . I. . . . When have I ever told you lies?" I understood
what he meant and blushed involuntarily. "I believe you've
got one!" I quickly responded.

"No, no, of course not!" His face turning scarlet.

Lowering his head and smiling, he turned aside abruptly
and yelled at his donkey. It was only then I suddenly noticed
he was wearing his new cotton-padded coat and a pair of lined
trousers instead of his ragged padded ones. The puttees on
his legs were neatly bound. Round his waist was a leather
belt which he wore on the battlefield during the Hundred-Regiments Campaign. A new white towel was wrapped round his
head. If there was nothing out of the ordinary, why had he
dressed himself up? He was twenty-two, a year older than me.
According to the rural custom, he ought to be married by now!
Perhaps he really does have a girl friend and has a date with
her today. As this wild flight of fancy leaped to my mind,
I ran up to him and got hold of his shoulder.

"Shuan Zhu, you really have got a lover, haven't you?
There's no need to hide it from me!"

"No, no, of course not!" He blushed deeply, and quickly
cracked the whip which was in his hand. The donkey started
running. He stammered: "Hurry . . . hurry up! . . . We're nearly there! Let's hurry up!"

It was true that shortly we arrived at Shangzhuang Village.
I was then busy tidying up my room. When I came out of
Chen Yunnian's yard to get my luggage from the donkey's
back, I did not know why Shuan Zhu acted so coy and shy all
of a sudden. He offered to carry the luggage in for me but he
didn't move. When I picked it up myself, he rushed forward
to snatch it from me but seemed uncertain whether he wanted

to enter the yard: he looked at it surreptitiously before he carried my luggage in.

My landlady, a grey-haired old woman demanded: "Has he arrived?" Then she tottered into the room with a broom in her hand. She crawled up onto the kang (brick bed) and knelt down to sweep it. The landlord's little boy peeped timidly into the room from the door-way. The red enamel mug fastened to my satchel aroused his curiosity and after looking at me he bounced into the room. I smiled at him and this encouraged him to come nearer and to touch the mug. Shuan Zhu and I began to smoke our long-stemmed pipes. Gradually a kind of uneasiness crept over him, he seemed to have lost his composure: he put down his pipe after only a couple of puffs; then he took the towel off his head and mopped his sweat, he called my name but didn't say anything else. I happened to glance behind me and saw two young women standing by the door.

The woman standing outside the door was the one I had seen yesterday. Noticing that I was watching her, she lowered her head a little, and pulling at the corner of her dress, she said gently: "So you've moved in!" The woman standing inside the door was a little older. She smiled at me while stitching the sole of a shoe. I looked at Shuan Zhu, who put his towel on his shoulder and said:

"Well.... I'm going...."

Before I managed to say anything, the young woman standing outside asked Shuan Zhu: "Did you accompany him here?" Then, she pushed the other woman further into the room so as to make room for her inside too.

"I . . . I must go to the market, it's on the way so I helped this comrade with his luggage!"

"You know each other!" I said. They both smiled, but neither of them answered. Shuan Zhu again mopped his sweat with the towel. The boy then turned round and said:

"He's the director of the Youths' Salvation Association in Xiazhuang. Is that right, sister?"

"That's him!" The woman stitching the sole replied casually.

Having finished sweeping the kang, the old woman got off and patted the dust off her clothes. After exchanging a couple of words with me, she questioned Shuan Zhu: "Are you from Xiazhuang? From which family? Did you come here with this comrade. . . ."

"He's an important cadre in Xiazhuang, the director of the Youths' Salvation Association, and also the leader of the Anti-Japanese Youth Team!" The young woman at the door promptly answered her mother on Shuan Zhu's behalf. Lifting up her head and looking into the yard she added: "Mother, is there anything you want from the market?"

"Your father has just gone there, what else do I want?"

"He's going there too!"

"That's right, I . . . I've to go now. . . ." As he said this, Shuan Zhu turned his head, glanced quickly at the young woman and then left uncertainly. I noticed the young woman blush, her head almost touching her breast. I also noticed that when Shuan Zhu got to the courtyard he turned his head to have another look, and the young woman also glanced at him out of the corner of her eyes. The other young woman stitching the sole gave her a look and then hustled her away.

After they had all gone, I began to slowly arrange my luggage and my office stationery. There wasn't even a desk in the room. The boy brought me a low table for the kang. Presently the old woman came with a handful of dried brittle dates. Then she began chatting to me.

I learned by chance that there were five people in my landlord's family: the old man was 50; the old lady was three years older than him; their little boy was called Jin Suo and the two young women were his sisters. The younger sister's name was Jin Feng. The old woman's hair was turning grey. She was rather tall with a broad, ruddy brown face. She seemed vigorous and quick in her movements and was a smart talker. The twelve-year-old boy was interested in my stationery, my wash kit, my overcoat and so forth. He even dared to put my tooth-brush into his mouth. His mother glared at him but he didn't care. He then took a tube of my tooth-paste and ran out with it shouting:

"Sister, sister, hey, look at this!"

That afternoon when I came back from a meeting, I sat on the threshold reading the newspaper. My room was on the eastern side of the courtyard and opposite it was an animal pen. On the terrace of the room to the north, the two young women were sewing. Jin Feng, the younger sister, didn't look over twenty. She was slim, with a square face. Her dark brown eyes, although they weren't jet black and shining, were sparkly and full of life. It was a pity that people in these mountainous valleys, being poor, could seldom get foreign cloth or flowery material. Like the rest of the other women, she was dressed in black and her trousers were patched in several places. However, she had kept herself clean and tidy. She was mending a pair of boy's cotton-padded trousers, they were probably her brother's. The elder sister look about thirty. Although her round face was fair with rosy cheeks, she had quite a few wrinkles round the corners of her eyes and on her forehead. The bottoms of her cotton-padded trousers were tied with cord like a typical middle-aged woman. She was still stitching the sole of a shoe. While I was reading my newspaper, I couldn't help taking a peep at them. On several occasions, I met Jin Feng's glance. I felt somewhat uncomfortable and went into my room.

After supper, I was busy checking my colleagues' rooms and getting odds and ends of furniture. When I got back, it was already dark. I lit my lamp and was about to rest for a while. In those days people still used kerosene lamps. Probably my landlord was attracted by the light in my room. The old woman came in with Jin Suo, followed by her elder daughter who stood near the door stitching her sole. Jin Feng brought in two pieces of yellow-millet date pudding in a bowl and put it on the low table on the kang. As she invited me to eat, she flipped over what I had written which was lying under the lamp and looked at it. Just as I was getting worried the old man came in laughing loudly and nodding his head. He pointed to the date pudding with his pipe and said:

"Please eat! We've nothing better! For ten or twenty miles around, there's only our village which grows dates. Taste something special! Ha, ha...."

I declined and then I asked him:

"Are you just back from the market? What did you buy there?"

"I came back not long ago. I bought several pounds of millet and some cloth."

"Comrade! Let's treat each other as one family," the old woman said. "We haven't had new clothes for over three years. Now, we've managed to buy some cloth with which to make a quilt, some uppers for shoes, some socks, clothes to replace what's worn-out and some patches. Eh, isn't it wonderful!"

The old man, squatting near the kang, kept urging me to have some pudding. He lit his pipe with a flint and continued from where the old woman left off:

"It's not bad this year! Wasn't there a Democratic Movement last autumn? Ever since a good village head was elected the Peasants' Association has worked. My rent has really been reduced! The rent I owed has also been cancelled. It's the first time I've felt easy about things!"

"Though we reap more we get less of it!" retorted the old lady with a scowl, looking askance at her husband. "This family relies completely on the drudgery of old people! Out of the band of people who sit down and eat, we've neither farm labourers nor farm hands."

"I'm going to work on the farm next year!" Jin Feng said promptly. Jin Suo also cuddled up to his mother and said:

"Ma, I can collect manure and gather firewood too. Okey ma?"

"Okey! But I wonder whether you can actually do it!"

"If the whole family is united, life will be easier!"

After saying this, I ate a piece of the pudding. Jin Suo went to ask his father for a pencil. Jin Feng took a red one from her pocket and waved it at him.

"Jin Suo, look!"

Then brother and sister began to fight over the pencil but was scolded by the old woman. The young woman standing at the door shouted at them not to interrupt my work. The old man then stood up:

"Jin Suo! You've got one on the plate where your mother keeps her needles. You needn't wrangle about it!"

Jin Suo went to get the pencil. The others slowly left one by one, but Jin Feng was the last to leave. She took out a new exercise-book bound with white newspaper and asked me to write her name on it. She also asked me to teach her to read whenever I had the time. Finally she left. I walked to the door-way and watched the family retiring to their room to the north. I felt that I had met another good landlord and I was very happy. In fact, I had been reluctant to part with Shuan Zhu, my landlord in Xiazhuang.

My life here was the same as in Xiazhuang: during the day I was busy with my work and nobody came to bother me, but in the evenings Jin Feng and Jin Suo used to come over to ask me the meaning of a word or to practise writing by my lamp. I also taught politics in the winter school. So I gradually got to know the people in the village. Sometimes Jin Feng brought other young women with her to ask me about words they didn't know. She said:

"Comrade Lao Kang! You should do your best to teach us in the same way as you taught ... taught Shuan Zhu in Xiazhuang."

"How did you know I taught Shuan Zhu and the others in Xiazhuang?"

"Why shouldn't I?"

The other two women, whispered goodness knows what in each other's ears and giggled. Jin Feng grabbed hold of them, hitting and cursing: "You beasts...." They slunk out of the room.

Shuan Zhu also came over frequently. One day, when Shuan Zhu arrived, the old man was out and the old woman and Jin Suo had driven away with the donkey to grind the grain. He was dressed up in his belt and puttees as before. After chatting casually with me, and asking me a few new words he took out his new diary which was bound with white newspaper. It seemed as if I had seen it somewhere before. While I read, I explained and corrected things. Moreover, I praised him a great deal for his progress. Then, the landlord's two daughters appeared. Shuan Zhu acted as if ants were crawling over him, and discomfort showed in his whole body.

This time the elder sister stood by the side of the kang leaning against the red cupboard sewing a cloth-sock. As usual she was silently engrossed in her work with her head down. Jin Feng was sewing an upper for her father's shoes. With a laugh she went forward to the low table and looked at Shuan Zhu's diary.

"Shuan Zhu, did you write this?"

"Yes, of course!"

"You've used up half the pages already!"

Shuan Zhu seemed to be unwilling to let Jin Feng see his diary; and wanted to cover it up with his hand, but I insisted he let Jin Feng see it. Shuan Zhu had no choice but to move away from the kang and rubbing his face with his hand, he paced up and down the room. I said to Jin Feng:

"Shuan Zhu is better at writing than you!"

"That's because he's a big cadre!"

"Stop, stop," Shuan Zhu snatched his diary away and asked Jin Feng:

"How's your studies getting on? You ought to show me your note-book!"

"Don't worry! Recently Lao Kang has been teaching me three words everyday. I'm bound to catch you up!"

"I say, Shuan Zhu, how did you know that she's got a note-book too?"

As soon as I asked this, Shuan Zhu blushed and quickly changed the subject. He then went out of the room. Jin Feng chased after him:

"Shuan Zhu! When you get back, go and ask the Women's Salvation Committee in your village. . . ."

I couldn't hear the rest of their conversation. They seemed to chat for quite a long time in the yard. Jin Feng's sister glanced at me and then at the yard; she sighed and left without a word.

"Say, why don't you learn to read?" I asked her casually. She sighed again:

"It's no good when I'm so unhappy. I haven't the patience! . . . Besides, I'm too old!"

She smiled at me and then went away. What sadness over-whelmed her? Her smile seemed to hide some great sorrow . . . was she old? Since I moved here, I've seen her on many occasions talking and laughing merrily with her younger sister and the other young women of the village. She seemed to be about twenty-five or twenty-six, but she acted like a middle-aged woman. Was she married?

In 1940 the Shanxi-Qahar-Hebei Border Region had just held a democratic election and the Eighth Route Army had fought the battle of the Hundred-Regiments Campaign against the enemy. On August 13, the Shanxi-Qahar-Hebei branch of the Communist Party published its "Twenty Articles on the Administrative Work for the Border Region". The Double Tenth Programme had to be explained to the people in my political class in winter school. They were extremely anxious about it! After

I had explained each article of the Programme, Jin Feng would drop in the following night or the night after that, asking me to explain it once more. Each time her father came to listen too. Invariably the old woman and Jin Suo were also present. Even the elder daughter who had been so off-hand about learning to read would come occasionally. While they listened, they raised many questions. I talked late into the night but nobody seemed tired. Sometimes Jin Suo would doze off in his mother's arms, sometimes he would stand on the kang, with his arms round my neck and ask: "What is the Communist Party like? Have you seen the Communist Party? Why is it so good?" Jin Feng, sitting opposite me, would glare at him reproachfully until the old lady took him away. Then she would look at me quietly, her eyes twinkling. After listening for a while, she would lean on the table on the kang and jot down something in her notebook. . . .

This was a peaceful family. In winter, the young women sewed while the old man fed the pigs, collected dung, and the boy would go up the hillside with his father to gather firewood. The old woman did the cooking, she also ground the flour and fed the chicken. Since the border region was democratically governed, their rent had been reduced. Their life wasn't bad at all! They managed to eat two or three meals made of wheat flour a month.

But, in my opinion there was a problem in this family. I heard them quarrelling on several occasions. They never created a scene and they mostly quarrelled in their own room so I was unable to make head or tail of it. When I asked about it, they were all evasive. Only Jin Suo said something:

"It's about my sister!"

"What's the matter with your sister?"

"I don't know!"

Once I heard them quarrel for quite a long time. Suddenly, the old man ran into the yard yelling furiously. I ran out at once. He was kicking and screaming so much that his saliva flew about:

"I . . . I'm not going to bother myself with your affairs! You decide for yourselves. I don't want to concern myself for nothing."

Saying this, he left in a huff. When I asked him why he got so angry, he didn't take any notice of me. What had happened in the landlord's room? Who was sobbing desolately? I asked Jin Suo and he said that it was his elder sister who was weeping! I was too embarrassed to ask any more, so I returned to my room feeling rather depressed.

However, after a while, it seemed as if nothing had happened. Things returned to normal and I felt easy again.

One noon, I gave a lecture on the Double Tenth Programme to the women's winter school. That evening the landlord's family all came early. As I still had things to do I asked whether it would be all right to give the lectures tomorrow? The elder sister suddenly seemed different from usual and she said with a smile:

"You'd better give your lectures today! After the class we'll. . . ."

"Go on with your lecture, Lao Kang," urged Jin Feng, so I had to give in. When I noticed the old man was absent, I asked whether he wanted to listen too, but they all replied that we needn't bother about him, so, I carried on with my talk.

Today I was going to talk about Article 14 of the Double Tenth Programme. I spent about four or five days on each article so I had been teaching for quite a long time. It was now already December, according to the Chinese lunar calendar, the coldest month in the year. In this mountainous valley, it had become terribly cold. Early that morning there were snow flakes in the sky and the sun didn't shine all day. I felt rather cold. I moved away the low table on the kang and invited the family to sit round the charcoal burner. My landlord's elder daughter put her sewing down on the red cupboard. She refused to get up onto the kang, but standing beside it, she listened attentively with her head bent. The old woman kept her eyes fixed on me. After every few words she would mutter her approval. Jin Feng asked a lot of questions. The lecture that day was on the article dealing with the question of women; their social position, marriage, the practice of child-brides, getting divorce and married and so on. . . . Jin Feng kept asking: "What's a child-bride? Why is the age of marriage 20 for men and 18 for women. . . ." Her sister occasionally lifted her head and glanced surreptitiously at me.

A gust of strong wind suddenly blew open the door which had not been closed properly. The lamp flickered twice. Jin Suo who was sleeping under my overcoat moved nearer to me, moaning incoherently, "Ma, Ma!" I thought I heard an old man cough in the cold wind outside my window and I quickly asked who it was. Jin Feng too called out, "Pa!" but no one answered. Jin Feng's sister closed the door and I went on with my lecture.

On this occasion I talked for a particularly long time and Jin Feng asked a great many questions. After they had left, I felt completely exhausted but I had to stay up late in order to get my work done.

The next day, I got up very late. After a hasty breakfast, I went to attend a meeting. When I returned the landlord's family had already begun to cook lunch. The elder daughter was working the bellows under the kitchen range outside their room. The old woman seemed to be arguing with somebody inside the room. Suddenly her elder daughter pushed the handle of the bellow away, stopped what she was doing and shouted towards the room:

"Ma! Why are you so backward in your thinking? I'm suffering like hell, now you want to send Jin Feng to her death too! You . . . do take a look at the world!"

I couldn't hear what was said inside the room. I was rather busy for a few days, so I was unable to pay much attention to their affairs.

Our cadres held meetings continuously for three days in our office. After the meetings had finished I felt a bit more relaxed. After breakfast, taking advantage of the fine weather, I asked a few comrades to go and play basket-ball in the recreation ground to the south of the village. At the cross-road, I saw the old man riding towards the south on his donkey. It seemed to me that he had been unhappy for the last few days, and I had not spoken to him for several days. So, I went up to him and asked:

"Where are you going?"

"Oh, Oh. . . . To see a relative!"

Judging from his expression, I guessed that there was something on his mind. What was the matter? After the game was over, I went home. As soon as I entered the yard, my landlord's elder daughter looked at me and smiled. Jin Feng kept pulling at her sister's clothes and hitting her but her sister kept smiling. I couldn't help smiling either and asked what the matter was. Jin Feng lowered her head and ran into her room. Jin Suo asked: "What have you been eating the past few days?" "Are you going to have something nice tomorrow?" added his elder sister. "For the last few days we've just had millet," I said. What was the matter? Why did they want to know? I hadn't the least idea! The elder daughter had behaved very oddly recently; she kept smiling mysteriously at me, while Jin Feng lowered her head and slipped away whenever she saw me. She had stopped talking to me and didn't ask me about new characters any more; she had also stopped studying. Even at the winter school whenever I looked at her, she would blush. It was very puzzling!

The next day, I saw Jin Feng about to kill a hen and the family were making white steamed rolls. What was going to happen? I was completely baffled. In the afternoon the old woman suddenly dragged me home for dinner. I tried hard to resist but she was insistent. Jin Suo also helped her to persuade me.

"I'll get into trouble!"

"Get into trouble? You're coming even if it means a threshing! The dinner is in your honour. We want your advice on an important matter!"

Red in the face and feeling depressed I went to their room. Neatly arranged on the spotless low table were chopsticks and wine cups. Jin Suo brought in a pot of heated wine and the old woman poured a cupful for me. I was so embarrassed that I couldn't utter a word. Meanwhile, I heard two women arguing outside in a low voice beside the kitchen range. "You must bring in the food!" "No, I won't!" "Don't then! It's nothing to do with me!" "Ha, ha, ha...." A fit of laughter followed, which sounded like Jin Feng's sister's. Then they continued: "I beg you!" "Why beg me? Beg that man!... Ha, ha, ha." "You beast!" Jin Feng, with her head lowered almost to her breast, brought in a big plate of roast meat, vegetables and steamed rolls. She kept turning her face away from me. After putting down the food, she ran out of the room, her face flushed crimson. A burst of smothered giggles was heard from outside.

The old woman forced me to drink a cup of wine and eat a chicken leg. Then after shouting at Jin Suo to go out, she began speaking:

"The other night, you mentioned to us that nowadays women are allowed to choose husbands for themselves? And if a husband and wife don't get on they can end their marriage.... Oh! See, I've forgotten it again: Can ... can they get a divorce? Oh dear, it's because of this! Lao Kang, you don't know how much I've suffered!"

The old lady, sitting opposite me on the kang, leaned towards me. After every few words she would hastily wipe her eyes with the corner of her dress, but as soon as she did this the tears would stream down her face again. She closed her eyes in an effort to control herself, then she leaned forward even closer towards me and said:

"My elder daughter was married at sixteen. That was eight

years ago. Her husband is ten years older than her. Ever since she got married, she has been badly treated by her parents-in-law. Since the outbreak of the anti-Japanese war, they've beaten and starved her. Oh dear! Not only has she suffered intolerably, whenever I think of it my heart aches for her. She . . . she is my flesh and blood!''

The old lady was weeping so bitterly that she could hardly continue. I was astonished to hear that her elder daughter was only twenty-four! I asked:

"When did she come back?"

"She came back last autumn. She won't be returning to her husband! At the beginning of last year her husband's family came for her, but nothing has been heard since then. It's said that her husband has been secretly carrying on with an immoral woman! What does he care about her? She has sworn she will never go back! Besides, her husband lives in the area under enemy occupation!''

"In that case she should get a divorce! There are sufficient grounds!"

I was deeply moved by what she had told me and by her tears. The old woman continued:

"Lao Kang! No, let me first talk about my second daughter. My elder daughter has met a terrible fate and my second daughter has nearly fallen into the same trap! Jin Feng is now nineteen. At fourteen she was engaged to a man, seven years older than her. People say that this man is a reactionary. Last autumn during the elections he was publicly struggled against! I've seen the man. Oh! . . . Help yourself, Lao Kang!''

After she had filled my cup with wine and offered me a big piece of roast chicken, she continued:

"He's quite ugly, not keen on work, but fond of talking nonsense and of eating and drinking and fooling around with whores! Last September, he met Jin Feng somewhere and immediately pressed her to marry him. He said he wanted to marry Jin Feng this winter but she absolutely refused to. Her sister also disapproved of this marriage. So, I keep putting this matter off. Now, his family want her to marry him this spring. Lao Kang, what can we do about it? Dear me! What a lot we have to put up with. . . ."

"You can cancel the engagement!"

"What did you say?"

"It was only an engagement. Jin Feng doesn't want to marry him and he is quite a few years older than her. If he's really backward in his thinking it's legal to break off the engagement and cancel the contract."

"Is it true?"

"Of course!"

The old lady opened her eyes wide, and took a deep breath as if she had laid down a heavy burden. She then urged me to have more to drink. After drinking a couple of mouthfuls of wine, I felt a bit more relaxed. I glanced at the door and thought I saw her elder daughter sitting on the threshold. I couldn't see her clearly as she was hidden by the door. Suddenly I noticed someone's shadow on the paper window behind my back. When I turned round to look at it, it immediately disappeared. I resumed my conversation with the old woman. The shadow outside the window seemed to re-appear again. I then remembered that night when I talked about divorce and Jin Feng's sister was so engrossed by it that she kept on staring at me. But the Double Tenth Programme did not mention anything about breaking off an engagement. I also forgot to talk about it. Before Jin Feng left she seemed to have a question she wanted to ask, but in the end she didn't.

"Lao Kang! Our plan is to deal with Jin Feng's case first and then her elder sister's. About divorce, it's allowed in the Programme, isn't it? Ever since that night, her elder sister has been extremely happy. Let's wait for a while before settling her problem. Ay! That night you forgot to mention that Jin Feng could break off her engagement too! That caused us to have a big row!"

The old lady pursed her lips in resentment and then cheered up again:

"Just think: if one can divorce after getting married, why can't one break off an engagement?"

"We're all rather stubborn! Ay! They do say that I'm cleverer than my husband. We argued so furiously with him that he was forced to go and see the man's family about the marriage. Eh, let's wait till he comes back!"

"Fine! There's no problem! As long as you have sufficient cause you may go and talk to the village and to the district head and it will be dealt with."

In the yard, the two young women began arguing in a light-hearted way. Jin Suo came into the room and was lifted up onto the kang to have lunch. I took the opportunity to get off and leave. When I got to the yard, Jin Feng's sister clapped her hands and laughed merrily. I told them to go and eat. Jin Feng slid past me bashfully and quickly ran into the room, followed by her sister who smiled at me:

"Ha, ha, ... Everything's settled!"

From then on, the family looked more cheerful, except for the old man, who was silent after he got back. He didn't talk to me for many days. Every day he would hang about in the street, either squatting in a corner and talking to some old men or to the village cadres. A few days later, the village cadres spoke to me about Jin Feng's case: Jin Feng's fiancé was certainly a reactionary who might be involved in something more serious. Later I heard from them that the district government had given its approval for Jin Feng to break off her engagement. When I got back, I asked Jin Feng's sister. She told me all about it. She also told me that she was going to divorce her husband next spring.

This news made me exceptionally happy. In spite of her shyness I began to tease Jin Feng. She slowly became less shy. She started studying again and moreover she often came to my room by herself during the day; sometimes for her lessons, and at other times simply for a chat. I didn't think it was quite proper, but I didn't know what to say. I muttered some vague objections, but her sister smiled at me and said:

"Oh! Comrade Lao Kang, are you shy? You are in charge of education for the masses, are you still affected by feudal ideas?"

I couldn't help blushing. Fortunately after this Jin Feng never came again during the daytime. Whenever she came in the evenings she would ask either her mother, her brother, her sister or some other women to accompany her. So things were fine.

Time flew fast. The heavy snow was followed by strong winds, and soon it would be the Chinese New Year. One morning, while I was working at home, Shuan Zhu suddenly came over. He had not shown up for about 20 days. He was wearing his belt and puttees and on his head was a new home-made padded-cap. He had a small parcel in one hand.

"Lao Kang! It's nothing special! I've brought you 20 eggs as a New Year present!"

I wanted to tell him off. There was no need to give me a present! He handed me his diary to look at. On seeing a newly printed copy of "*Yang Ko* Dance Plays" on my low table, he quickly picked it up:

"Ha! Ha! We were just saying we hadn't any entertaining books. This is just what I want!"

As I was busy then, I told him that I didn't have time to correct his diary. He replied that he was in no hurry and that he would come for it in a couple of days. Who was outside? It was Jin Feng. Shuan Zhu went out to talk to her. What were they talking about in such hushed voices? After a while they both came in, and leaning against the red cupboard, they chatted. It was a pity that I was busy writing, I didn't hear a thing they said.

After the Chinese New Year, Shuan Zhu came over even more frequently. He came every few days. He always came

when I was taking my mid-day nap. As soon as he entered
the yard he would call out to me. When I came out to meet
him, to invite him in, he would hand me his diary or else chat
for a moment and then quickly leave. Later, I discovered that
during the day Jin Feng and her sister always sat on the terrace
sewing. Each time Shuan Zhu came Jin Feng would immediately go into her room. I was puzzled at the fact they had not
greeted or spoken to each other for a long time. What was
up? A rumour went around the village that Jin Feng and Shuan
Zhu were courting.... When I asked Jin Feng's sister about
this, she only remarked:

"They've been in love for a long time! I don't know what's
going on these days? I've asked Jin Feng but she won't tell
me. You'd better ask Shuan Zhu about it!"

Shuan Zhu wouldn't tell me anything either. He only
gave me an embarrassed smile and asked me to wait and see!

Later on, the gossip got worse, some of the village cadres
and even the comrades in my office began to ask me about them.
What did I know? I only knew that when Shuan Zhu came to
ask me questions about his lessons, he would not come into my
room, nor did he talk to Jin Feng, for as soon as she saw him
she would disappear into her room. I did notice one thing:
recently Jin Feng often went out. Once, Jin Suo ran in shouting:

"Hey!... My second sister and Shuan Zhu have gone to
the date grove!..."

"What's it you're shouting about?" The old man glared
at Jin Suo.

"I've seen them!"

"You.... You bastard!"

The old man stamped his feet, and went inside, muttering
curses. I pulled Jin Suo aside, but I didn't find out what it
was all about except that the gossip in the village got even
worse, and the old man became more and more bad tempered.
He wouldn't speak to me for many days and he frequently

swore at his family. But when he met Jin Feng he didn't swear at her, but merely went off in a huff.

Spring came and it became warmer! The blossoms of the poplar trees fluttered to the ground. The date trees were sprouting delicate green leaves and bursting into tiny green flowers. The villagers were busy carrying manure to the fields. After supper, I went with a shovel to the western part of the village to dig the vegetable patch for our unit. On my way back in the evening, a cadre came over to me to discuss something, so we sat under a Chinese scholartree. The evening twilight was shining on the gate of our house not far away on the other side of the main road! A crowd of women were sitting and chatting noisily in front of the gateway, making shoes for the army. Suddenly, I saw Shuan Zhu coming up from the main road with a shovel on his shoulder. I remembered he had half an acre of yams growing in the valley to the north of Shangzhuang Village. The women sitting at the gate also noticed him. They bustled about without anyone saying a word. Then slowly one by one they went indoors carrying the piece of wood they were sitting on. Shuan Zhu seemed uncomfortable. He walked rather slowly and awkwardly. Only Jin Feng was left outside the gate. She seemed not to have noticed anything. She turned her head abruptly to look, then she continued sewing with her head lowered, and her lips pressed together. Neglecting the comrade beside me, I looked ahead and saw that Shuan Zhu hadn't noticed me. He shuffled forward slowly and only after he was a long way off from the gate did he look back. After a couple of steps, he stopped and took another look. He did this quite a few times. I distinctly saw Jin Feng glancing at him from under her eyelids.

That night, I did not sleep well. Early the next morning, I went to Xiazhuang to see Shuan Zhu.

Shuan Zhu was still in bed. His mother, brother and sister-in-law greeted me. While they were serving me breakfast they said: "We don't know what's the matter with him!

He hardly says a word, and he's listless. We asked him if he was unwell but he said no. Everyday after breakfast he goes off to work in the field looking depressed."

"Don't worry! He'll be all right after I've talked to him."

I pulled Shuan Zhu out of bed. After breakfast we walked to work together and sat by the edge of the field. I asked him:

"What's the matter? Pour it all out!"

He remained silent. Even after I had urged him for a long time he was still brooding. I got angry. I jumped up and shouted:

"How backward can you be? You're supposed to be an important cadre!"

He then smiled at me and pulling me down beside him he said:

"I'll be frank with you! I've wanted to ask for your help long ago!"

"Of course, I'll help you. Go on!"

"I fell in love with Jin Feng a long time ago. We've been engaged for ages."

"Why don't you make it public?"

"I've been stupid! We're too shy and neither of us knew how to tell people or to whom to tell it to."

"Why did you stop talking to each other lately?"

"What? We've talked quite a lot!"

Grabbing hold of my neck, Shuan Zhu laughed. He said that every time he came to see me he would make an appointment with Jin Feng to meet in a quiet corner inside the date grove so that they could chat. Whenever he came to my yard, Jin Feng would go into her room, and signal with a needle when their next appointment would be. If she gave the window paper of the fifth pane from the east three pricks, it meant they would meet in three days' time; if she gave four pricks, it meant they would meet in four days' time. Three pricks on the seventh pane meant meeting in the morning, and five pricks on the

same pane meant meeting in the afternoon. As he was talking,
I hit him with my fist and burst out laughing. His face flushed
and then he buried his face in his hands laughing. I teased him:

"Did you misbehave?"

"I wouldn't dare! We only held hands just like you comrades do!"

I hit him again. It was no good him being shy. He had
to speak out. I promised him everything would be all right.
I went to his home. After listening to my explanation, both
his mother and his brother agreed to his marriage. Returning
to Shangzhuang I talked to my landlady and to Jin Feng's sister,
they also approved of the match. Now, the only obstacle was
the old man. In the evening, I invited him over and explain
the situation to him in detail. He remained silent until I
had finished.

"I have no objections. To tell the truth, Lao Kang, don't
think that we old folks are good-for-nothing, but we've got
these stubborn brains, which can't be easily changed. Ha!
Ha!..." He puffed at his pipe and he smiled at me. "These
stubborn brains are very different from the modern heads of
the young. We'll see about it when I've discussed it with my
old cronies. Ha! Ha!"

Before things were settled, I had to go and work in the
countryside. I handed the matter over to the village cadres
and I also wrote letters to the Youth Salvation Association and
to the County Women's Salvation Association before I left for
Yixian County.

While I was away in the countryside, I kept thinking about
this matter. Twenty days passed very quickly and I hurried
back. On the way, I unexpectedly came across a student's
pocket dictionary in the big market to the north of the village.
I snapped it up. It was a shame that there was only one copy
left! When I got back, Jin Feng snatched it away as soon as
she found that it was a small dictionary. I was upset and told
her that Shuan Zhu had asked me to get it for him over a

year ago. She refused to hand it back and kept asking me how much it cost. I was furious and ignored her.

Two days later, after I had reported to my senior officer about my work, the village cadres told me that Jin Feng's matter had been successfully settled. Both families and the district government approved of the match. The couple were formally engaged. I was overjoyed. When I got back to my room I immediately called on Jin Feng. Her sister came out and told me that she had gone with her mother to grind flour. I promptly asked:

"Are they engaged?"

"Yes, they're engaged! I got my divorce too!"

I couldn't help jumping for joy! She continued:

"They exchanged presents two days ago. Shuan Zhu gave her two towels, two pairs of socks, some note-books and pencils. She gave him that little book she snatched from you, a pair of shoes with thick soles, a pair of warm socks, and some note-books and pencils."

"What are you babbling about?" asked Jin Feng as she ran in. I laughed loudly, and bowed. She blushed. Her sister took out a new white towel from her pocket, waved it in front of her and then gave it to me, saying to her sister:

"Shouldn't you give Lao Kang one of your towels? When I saw him come back, I took one for him. Do you mind?"

"He certainly deserves it!" Her mother remarked as soon as she entered the room. Jin Feng snatched the towel from her sister, and casting a sidelong glance at me said:

"He's going to get a nice one! This evening Shuan Zhu will come with a white towel and the warm socks that I made. Those are for him! That towel is much better than mine!"

Everybody laughed cheerfully when Jin Suo came in. He kept bouncing up and down and shouting with his neck stretched out, "Yipee!" As soon as the old man Chen Yunnian entered the yard, he smiled and then stamped his feet crying, "Hey. . . .

Hey. . . ." He glanced at us and promptly returned to their room,
as if he was feeling embarrassed.

Drafted at Zhangjiakou
May 23, 1946
Translated by Zhang Mingzhu

About the Author

KANG ZHUO, a well-known contemporary Chinese writer
whose real name is Mao Jichang, was born in 1920 in Xiangyin
County, Hunan Province. He received his early education in his
hometown and Changsha. He went to Yan'an in 1938 after the
outbreak of the anti-Japanese war and studied in the Literature
Department of the Lu Xun Art College. In the same year he joined
the Chinese Communist Party. After graduation, he became a
secretary in charge of propaganda work in the Eighth Route Army.
He started publishing his writings in 1939 and wrote after 1940
"Plum Blossom", "Disastrous Tomorrow", "Withdrawing Land"
and other short stories reflecting the life and struggle of the people in the anti-Japanese base areas. After 1945, he joined in the
land reform movement in rural areas, and wrote the short stories
"Early Spring", "Zhang Feiju, a Worker" and "My Two Landlords". He became the secretary of the Preparatory Committee of the
First National Conference of Literary and Art Workers after Beijing
was liberated in 1949. Since then, he has concentrated on writing
and produced "While I Am in the Countryside", "Buying Cattle",
"The First New Year", "The First Month in the Spring" and other
short stories. His stories which appeared around 1950 reflected the
agricultural co-operative movement, such as "Sowing in Spring and
Harvesting in Autumn", "On Holidays", "Stockman" and "The
First Step". In 1954 he became a member of the editorial board
of *Literature and Art*, a national literary magazine, and secretary

of the secretariate of the Union of the Chinese Writers, member of its leading Party group and the director of its writing committee. In 1958 he was the vice-chairman of the Hebei Federation of Literature and Art and member of its leading Party group. He was transferred to Hunan in 1962 and became the vice-chairman of the provincial Federation of Literature and Art and its deputy Party Secretary.

"My Two Landlords", his representative work, describes the love between the son and daughter of two landlords in the liberated area who resist the old feudalistic customs and habits.